MW01173511

Ě

ELSEWHERE

Ę

a novel

by Roger Alan Bonner

Also by Roger Alan Bonner

Sentinel

The Vote Trader

Red Night Revenge

Milky Way Tango

Milky Way Boogie

Milky Way Gala

Thirds

Thirds Rising

Thirds Aflame

The Nebula Tales

The Belt Stories

Copyright, disclaimer, and keywords

186,334 words, 35 chapters, 129 scenes.

ISBN 978-1-948988-23-0.

My thanks to Geralt, Andrea Piacquadio, and Pixabay for the beautiful images used in the covers of this book. Book covers ©2024 Roger Alan Bonner. All rights reserved. Published by Red Frog Books Company.

Keywords: apps, artificial intelligence, dancing, downloads, drums, elderly, fantasy, rock and roll, science fiction, sex, social network, technology, touch, uploads, virtual reality.

How did th
a movie of

Table of Contents

1. Prison Guitarist

Johnny B. Goode sat on the bed in his cell, stroking his guitar, touching the strings. He played, the fingers of one hand dancing along the fingerboard, the other guiding a pick through a rippling phrase in E minor. Beyond the bars to his cell, up and down the corridor, a guy shouted; a couple of others clapped.

He stared at the fingerboard, moved his left hand, and watched the same dance in G minor. Johnny frowned - the first was easy; the second, hard - well, this sucks; let's try it again in E minor.

A moment later, he grinned - maybe I'll just play it in E minor, leave it at that. Screw G minor. Yeah, that's right, go with the flow. Don't fight the current.

From across the corridor, a bass voice rumbled, "Hey, Johnny, you're sounding good. You've come a long way since you moved in. When you get out, you could turn pro, play for money, man."

Johnny turned his head and looked at the black man standing across the corridor, his arms spread wide. "Thanks, Rafe. Yeah, that's the plan."

"When you getting out, anyway?"

"Thursday. You believe that shit? I disappear on Thursday, finally."

"Two fucking days. Two days, man. You behave yourself, you hear?" Rafael said. "The lifers hear you're getting out, they'll fuck with you."

Johnny nodded. "I got friends here. I think I'll be okay."

"Yeah, friends are good. And count me in, too, if you need a little muscle. You'll be okay. You got plans for being out?"

Johnny shrugged, glanced at Rafael, then looked down at the guitar. He hit a chord and looked up again. "Ah, you know. The usual - halfway house, flirt with the P.O., then find some kinda grunt job."

“What if the P.O.’s ugly?”

“I haven’t touched a woman in a couple years, so how ugly you thinkin’?” Johnny said.

“Coyote ugly.”

Johnny frowned at the black man. “Geez, fuck that.”

Rafael laughed. "You need to go online to find a job. That's how it happens anymore. It's easy. Find yourself a library, get a card. They'll let you use a computer."

Skepticism crossed Johnny's face, his lips a straight line. "Not my style. I want to see my employer face-to-face, get a read, look him over."

"Where you gonna go?"

"Back to Philly."

"Yeah, Philly's big. You'll find something."

Johnny nodded. "I think so." He hit a chord, hard, then looked up. "Maybe I'll cook. Get a room, be a cook, flip burgers. Then do the rounds; I want to get a gig, play guitar for somebody."

Rafael laughed. "Yeah, you're handsome, you could do it. A Marlboro man, right?"

"I don't smoke."

Rafael laughed, the strong bass voice of a large man. "Well, you look like the Marlboro Man. You gonna be buried in them dancer girls. Women love music, and they absolutely love the guy making it, especially if he's a little crazy. You need to amp up the crazy, just a bit. I don't criticize, but you're kinda quiet."

Johnny chuckled. "I say what I have to say, then I stop."

Rafael laughed. "They love crazy guys even when they're ugly. Yeah, you'll be okay."

"I don't know about that." He looked over at Rafael. "Okay, yeah... maybe. I hope."

Rafael laughed again. "You been here a couple years. I never asked, tryin’ to be polite, but what you in for, anyway?"

"Aggravated assault."

"Two years for aggravated assault? You got off light, no?"

Johnny shook his head. "I don't think so, not at all. I hit the guy once, just once. But I admit, I was aggravated." He thought back to the courtroom - a couple witnesses said I hit the guy once. I think the judge took that into account. Only once. How bad could it possibly be? Well, it could be three broken ribs. I was surprised. Luckily, the prosecutor was dumb as a post. I got off light, but it still pisses me off. If you can't take a punch, you need to mind your manners. Think first, then talk. Better yet, don't say anything.

That guy was fragile and stupid, a nasty combination. Ah, well. Fuck it. Bad luck.

Rafael grinned. "Yeah, you look like a one-punch guy."

Johnny nodded and sat quietly for a moment. "Rafael. You're here on drugs, right?" He looked across the corridor.

Rafael nodded. "Isn't everyone? But I'm special; I'm up on manslaughter too, one of the lesser flavors. Yeah, six years, three behind me, three to go."

"You want to learn guitar? After all, the guys have gotten used to having some music. Be a shame to let that end. Maybe you could take over the entertainment. You got big hands, you could do it. I got some spare strings you can have."

Rafael was quiet for a moment. "You're not taking your guitar? You serious?"

"I figure I'll get another electric when I get out."

"Wow, that's incredibly kind of you, Johnny. Yeah, I could give guitar a whirl. I love the blues."

"Okay, you got it. In a couple years, you'll be the one going pro."

Rafael chuckled. "Now you're just sweet talkin' me, sugar."

***

Rafael Evans eased into consciousness, slowly. For long minutes, he did not know what was happening, who he was, or where he was. He felt no pain; he was not afraid. He was not uncomfortable. He did not move his arms or legs, did not open his eyes. Did not swallow, or cough, or talk.

He lay there, still - I am breathing... my God, I am breathing! I remember now how that feels, how that felt. For so long, I didn't need to breathe. But how long has it been, anyway? I remember uploading. And I remember life before uploading. When your memories are solid state, you forget nothing, nothing at all, ever.

Or so I'm told. I wonder if that's really true. Forever's a long time.

But my memories of Elsewhere feel thin, like faded movies of someone else's backyard. Like an old man's memory. I remember how they looked, and what I saw, but not what they smelled like, or felt like.

He lay there and waited patiently, having forgotten the feel of moving arms, legs, hands, enduring, then experiencing, the strange sensations that accompanied the gradual ascent to wakefulness as a biological entity, a biped, a vertebrate, a human being.

He lay under a thin blanket and focused his attention on the unfamiliar sensations - the blanket touching his skin, lying down, his back to a sheet, hunger, a stomach that had had no food for days, eyes which last opened days ago, fingers which had touched nothing in days. It felt like years ago. It felt so far as to be beyond memory.

He touched a thumb with his fingers; his fingernails were long.

Memory returned, slowly at first, then flooded in. He remembered bits and pieces of the last twenty-three years, thirteen years of growing up and fighting and surviving in Cleveland's east side, the dirty, dangerous place called Hough, and four years of surviving the state penitentiary in Youngstown, home of Ohio's baddest bad asses. Half of them, anyway.

He smiled - I met two types of guys at Y-town, dangerous or not, one or the other. The dangerous guys preyed on anyone else they could. On the outside, they preyed on women; inside, on smaller, weaker men.

That was stupid. Watch out for the little guys; they have something to prove. Every so often, they find a tough guy with his throat cut at three a.m.; the guy went to sleep and didn't wake up.

He laughed, a coarse, guttural sound. He tried to clear his throat, failed. And he realized something else, something astounding, stupendous - in lending his body and mind to an experiment that might have killed him, that was expected to kill him, he had in fact survived. He was here, in life, breathing.

I'm alive? How 'bout that?

So, all was forgiven, or would be. Rather than a convict facing more time, Rafael Evans was soon to be a free man, with an income, with an apartment. He remembered making that deal with the state of Ohio and the big social network, Willow - you risk your black ass, boy, and if you survive this, we'll let you go. You'll be free, Scot-free, your debt to society hereby discharged.

We'll let you out; it's up to you to stay out, so mind your business, you hear?

He remembered thinking - freedom? Where do I sign? Putting my life on the line was a ballsy move, but not the first, far from the first. It was a good move, as it turned out. He felt another novel sensation... and he smiled again. I done good.

Nothing beats getting lucky... or winning.

He savored the memory of the agreement like a glass of fine red wine; then he put it aside and moved on. He remembered the trial and was stunned at its clarity, at the thousands of small things he had noticed as he sat in the courtroom waiting for the judge and jury to decide his fate.

He smiled weakly for a moment - they weren't wrong. They said I killed a man. Okay, yeah, granted. I did that. I would do it again, too. In fact, I might do it again.

But next time, let's not get caught, eh? When you're angry, do nothing. Except maybe run. Get even later, when you're chilly.

He remembered the legal maneuvers of the prosecutor, which he now understood, though he did not understand at the time. He remembered the pitifully inadequate, ham-handed, sloppy, ignorant tactics of his public defender.

Of greater importance, he remembered everything he had learned in his brief stay in the memory chips of that amazing computer, where time passed so slowly that a minute felt like a month, or a couple of months. It was an unbelievable experience, being granted so much time, a second life, in fact, more than one, and he did not waste it. He spent every spare moment studying cybernetics, electrical engineering, and mathematics. And law. He neither ate nor slept. He needed none of that.

The prison let him do that; they encouraged learning, especially if it kept a big black man busy and quiet rather than pissed off and seething, looking for trouble.

He consumed electronic files at the speed of bits and bytes. At the end, he understood much about what made that computer work. He also understood what that prosecutor had done to put him in prison. And what his defender could have done for him, should have done, but did not.

Rafael winced - I'm being stupid. Anyone who expects good performance at fast food wages is being stupid.

More important, he now understood much of a world that had discovered electricity, computers, software languages, all the wonderful styles of mathematics which they did not teach in high school. He laughed - well, not my high school, anyway. He understood how society had conformed itself to the orderly and useful world of computers and the marriage between computers and communications.

Time passed, and he moved beyond the remembering. When his body recovered from the inactivity, when he could finally stand up again, they sent him to a rehab facility. They gave him a basketball to play with. His own personal basketball. He laughed at that - here, you're a black man, you people all play basketball, don't you? Of course you do.

They thanked him many times for his participation. When he left rehab, they would give him an apartment and a lot of money, enough for the rest of his life. They asked that he submit to physical exams every month, for a while. ELSEWHERE. That was what they called it now - a trademarked word to help the public identify the new services, a cyber world where all entities were electrical, cybernetic, conjured from a side of the physical universe backed by mere decades of understanding. Or less.

But no, he did not want to return to the cyberworld, to ELSEWHERE. No, he had work to do, right here on earth, in the physical world, the world of meat and brain and blood, into which he had been born and from which he would someday die.

Rafael remembered his eyes - I can see some light, as if I were in a room, and the room is lit. He opened them slightly, so they were slits in his face. He looked down and saw or felt wires attached to his forehead, his chest, his left arm, his neck.

As Rafael contemplated his grimmest of intentions and plans, a blurry view of a man in a long, white coat, wearing a stethoscope, probably a doctor of some sort, entered his field of view.

The man bent towards him and looked down. "Welcome back, Rafael. How do you feel?"

Rafael tried to open his eyes wider; that worked on one eye. He looked up. "I'm okay, I guess."

"Good. I'm Doctor Rossi. I work for Willow. I care for our test subjects, including you."

"Water? Please?" Rafael said.

The doctor did not turn away. "Only a bit. I'll give you a small sippy cup. I know you'll be thirsty, but I want you to sip the water. Okay?"

"Okay."

The doctor turned away, then returned with a tiny cup, the size of a medicine cup. It was filled with clear water. He helped Rafael raise his head, then held the cup as Rafael took a precious, wonderful, fragrant sip of cool water. The feeling of water rolling down his throat was spectacular.

Rafael's eyes found the doctor's. "More."

The doctor emptied the cup into Rafael's mouth and lowered his head to the pillow. "Thanks, doc, that was wonderful. Better than wonderful."

"You can have more in a little while. How do you feel?" the doctor said.

"A bit tired. More than I expected."

"Well, we have little data, but I'm not surprised."

"How have other people handled the download?" Rafael asked.

Doctor Rossi stared at Rafael. "Other people? Actually... you're the first person to survive downloading from Elsewhere."

"You're shitting me!" Rafael said.

Rossi shook his head. "I'm not. When I first walked in here, my job was to keep you alive. But you seem to have handled the download well. Your body is weak from inactivity. So now, we'll turn to rehab. But make no mistake, you just made history, Rafael.

"So to begin, I'd like to check your moving parts, to see how well they work. We did these tests before you uploaded, so this will help us understand the effects of uploading and downloading on a human. We'll start slow, so you can remain in bed. Is it okay for us to do that?"

"Sure," Rafael said.

"Okay, good. Here we go. Lift your left foot by several inches...

"Now the right foot...

"And the left arm...

"And the right arm...

"Blink three times for me...

"Now blink the right eye...

"Now the left eye...

"Open your mouth wide...

"Stick out your tongue...

"Point it to the right...

"Now to the left...

"Now watch the tip of my finger as I move it...

"Point your right index finger up...

"Now the left index finger...

"Raise your right knee...

"Now the left knee... " The doctor straightened up. "Okay, that's good. Everything I see seems in good working order. I'll bet you're tired from all that, though."

"Actually, yeah," Rafael said. "I'm not surprised. I was in Elsewhere for a long time. Moving feels weird. I feel out of shape. I feel weak."

"Now that's interesting," Doctor Rossi said. "If you had to guess, how long would you say you were in Elsewhere?"

"Oh... let me think about that," Rafael said.

After a long pause, Doctor Rossi said, "What do you think? Maybe three, four months?"

"Oh, longer… longer than that, anyway," Rafael said. "Maybe... a couple of years." He thought some more. "Yeah, that sounds right."

"Years," the doctor nodded. "In fact, today is Monday. You uploaded last Monday, at about this time in the afternoon. You were in Elsewhere a week."

Rafael's eyes opened wide. "Bullshit. I know that's bullshit."

The doctor shook his head. "Not at all. Here on Earth, you're a biological entity, an animal. Your thoughts proceed at the speed of your nervous system, about a hundred miles an hour." The doctor waved a hand casually, as if everybody knew this. "But in Elsewhere, your nervous system runs at the speed of light. Your thinking, your living, your reflexes, everything... is about three million times faster on Elsewhere than on Earth."

"So... a day on Earth feels like, what? Twenty-five days in Elsewhere?"

The doctor smiled and nodded. "More like... a second on Elsewhere feels like a day on Earth. So, a minute on Elsewhere feels like a couple of months on Earth."

"Okay... in that case, I have a question."

"Which is?" Rossi was smiling at Rafael.

As Raphael almost asked his question, a new thought occurred. "Can I go back to Elsewhere if I want to? I mean, I remember the contract said that I could leave any time I want to. But can I return?" Rafael said. He smiled at the doctor – if I settle a few scores here in Animal World, I might need to evade prosecution. And I need to stay out of Hough. Elsewhere could help.

Doctor Rossi looked away, then back at Rafael. "Okay, let me think about that... well, first, I don't speak for Willow. I just work here. That said, if you were to tell them that you and I - or you and your scientist friends - have some scientific questions about whether people can upload repeatedly. Put your request in scientific terms, see? Make it sound like we're testing something. You'll be speaking their language. You do that, and I bet Willow would let you return to Elsewhere."

A wave of satisfaction and fatigue washed over Rafael. He tried and failed to focus his eyes on the doctor. "Listen, doc, this has all been fun, but I am suddenly too pooped to participate. How about we pick this up later?"

Rossi looked at Rafael and nodded. "Okay, you're healthy, Rafael. You've earned a good night's sleep, so we'll talk later. I'll leave a cup of water next to your bed. Take it in sips, please. And there's a buzzer on your monitor if you need a nurse or any kind of help, that red button, okay?"

Rossi watched a faint smile cross Rafael's face and his eyes close, the face of a man falling like an autumn leaf into deep sleep.

***

On the morning of just another workday, Jerrell Adri awoke and moved through his morning tasks with smooth efficiency earned from repetition - coffee, shower, clothes, teeth. He moved around the kitchen and the bathroom like a jet running through a pre-flight checklist. On completing the checklist, he slapped the velcro tabs on his shoes, grabbed a backpack containing his laptop, and left the apartment for a central hallway. The stairway was there, three floors down to the sidewalk. An elevator was down the hall; he used the stairs.

He emerged onto the sidewalk at 5th and Dickinson and looked east, past the 95 artery, out to the Delaware River. He stood for a moment and listened to the sounds of south Philly waking up and going to work. The occasional big truck passed by with a soft swish of big tires. He began walking towards Willow's headquarters, several blocks away on Passyunk Square.

In a couple of blocks, Jerrell could look over the row houses and see the upper half of Willow's headquarters. The Woody, they called it, eighty-seven stories of black reflective glass.

Jerrell saw the tower and grinned - that sucker looms over south Philly, but that's not the half of it. No one calls it Passyunk

Tower. My English is not always good, but I would recognize 'Passyunk.' No, people don't say that. When the tower was completed, some local graffiti artist painted a message - ERECTION - in florid, colorful capital letters, highlighting several shades of pink.

When CEO McLeesh learned of the graffiti, he ordered his people to preserve it under a layer of transparent epoxy. Naturally, local church officials, politicians, and citizens with time on their hands protested. McLeesh shrugged and told a reporter, "At Willow, we celebrate creation. We honor that from time to time. And... in light of the forty thousand jobs we brought to south Philadelphia, we hope the city can tolerate some of our eccentricities. It is just graffiti, but we view it as art."

Jerrell smiled at the memory - a brilliant, rapacious, genius businessman, with unexpected artistic sensibilities. He doesn't just buy art, he appreciates it. How weird is that?

So, in honor of local art, an anonymous comedian named the tower The Woody. The name stuck, and now residents use it without noticing. Jerrell chuckled at that - like a lot of English, it has the benefit of brevity; McLeesh did not complain about it. He said that people could call his tower whatever they want.

Jerrell looked at the tower - I like it; The Woody sounds better than 'Willow Corporate Headquarters.' And it's shorter. The name, that is, not the... never mind.

He walked down Dickinson, ignoring the Woody, keeping track of the little shops and stores on the first floor of three- to six-story rowhouses. There was a grocery store, selling mostly cigarettes, beer, and Lotto tickets. The next block offered a barber shop, a repair shop specializing in leather shoes, and a video game store. Naturally, there were a couple of Chinese restaurants.

The block after that had a surprise, the office of an auto rental store. Jerrell stared at that, one rowhouse in a long line of rowhouses - where can they put their cars? A sign in the window explained:

WE DELIVER AND PICK UP
SATISFACTION GUARANTEED
OR MONEY BACK

He read the sign - well, okay then, that's convenient. If they didn't deliver, they'd have to put their office in Camden; Philly wouldn't have room. Camden, yeah, good luck with that.

Closer to Passyunk Avenue, Jerrell passed his favorite local bar, *Clooney's*. He would occasionally venture to *Clooney's* for acoustic music and a chance to talk to the local lovely ladies, which in Jerrell's view included any woman under thirty, breathing, viable, with decent teeth. His affection for the place was sustained by the music, since he regularly returned to his apartment without speaking to anyone.

Jerrell passed *Clooney's* and soon arrived at and entered the *Sunshine Cafe*. The Cafe was small on the outside, spacious on the inside. He looked across the sea of tables and chairs and saw several acquaintances, co-workers at Willow. He smiled at a secretary in operations - you're young and gorgeous. Yeah, I'd love to know you better. But you're an executive secretary, so out of my league. I might have a shot if you were a staff secretary. Maybe. But not today.

Jerrell saw another acquaintance, a middle-aged man, a vice president in product development. He nodded politely and kept moving.

At the coffee station, he assembled a tall American coffee, blond and sweet, and waved his ring at the payments sensor. Turning, he carefully maneuvered the coffee to his usual table near a back wall and sat down, his back to the wall.

Like many others in the cafe, Jerrell's laptop was powerful, offering every capability money could buy. He logged into

Willow's network and ran an automated scan for internal memos, announcements, and press releases.

He stuck a microphone disk to the side of his throat and an earpiece into his left ear. In a voice only the computer could hear, he said, "Load Mary." A grid of small images appeared on the screen, each image showing a teen-age girl. He chose and expanded the base image, from the upper left corner, a teen-age girl with a blank expression under long brown hair, dressed in a blue t-shirt and shorts, atop bare feet.

Jerrell stared at the image - okay, my sweet, someday, if I do my job, you will be famous, an internet icon. You and your sisters will entertain millions, or even billions, of women on Willow. You will talk to them, listen to them, comment on their stories, their dreams, their problems. And they will then find Willow a more comfortable and inviting place to spend time, and money, let us not forget money.

Jerrell stared at the image - in your present state, you are perfect, a future beach bunny, once you fill out a bit. I see your type at Cape May all the time, and I stare every time. Left to myself, I wouldn't touch a thing, not a hair on your head, or anywhere else, not your eyes, not anything. But forget all that. I need you to appeal, not to me but to women, in particular young women, and that is a very different matter.

I know, it's disappointing, but there it is. If I were to follow my tastes, your beauty and freshness might intimidate our customers. Can't have that.

So, let us start. You need to look slightly better than average. Jerrell said, "Split and load Survey Demographics zero eight two zero nine five. Filter by location. Display performance measures." A grid appeared in a side window; each element displayed several numbers capturing the effectiveness of the avatars in raising the satisfaction of teenage, female visitors to Willow.

"Done," said the laptop.

"Map performance, USA, Canada, and Mexico."

"Done."

Damn, you're fast; he looked at the screen, where a map appeared, identifying avatar performance in each location, assuming the avatars were optimized (from those currently available) to each location.

"Okay, computer, listen carefully... tie the map to the avatars, automatically update the results for any changes in the avatars. Indicate positive changes in performance in blue; negative changes in red. Suppress vocal response."

The computer gave a quiet beep.

"Okay, continue and load Mary."

The grid of avatars reappeared on the screen.

"Display Mary One."

The laptop beeped and displayed a larger picture of the upper-left avatar.

"Okay, now... enlarge her breasts... Jesus, no, smaller... smaller still... okay, good." He mumbled, "I want to see them without having them hit me in the face. She should be attractive, normal even, without looking like a hooker or an 'after' photo for a massage parlor. Can you handle that?"

The laptop was silent; Jerrell grimaced - why do I bother asking? Artificial intelligence does a fine job imitating dumb humans.

He watched the screen, which did not react to the latest comment. He looked at the map, which showed red throughout the northeast, down as far as North Carolina, blue in the deep south, as far west as Texas, lighter blue in the midwest and plains, red across the north central plains, and dark red on the west coast.

Jerrell stared for a long moment - repeat as needed, everybody likes what they like, for their own reasons. Let me guess; in educated populations, young women want to be slender. In less educated places, they want to be buxom. So... what does that mean?

I have no idea. Maybe slender means healthy, and buxom means children. Or maybe dumb guys like women with large breasts. They remember Mother. Who knows? Anyway, it's the women who count; most men are off the network, thus irrelevant.

Except for porn, of course.

Jerrell chuckled. "Computer, vary Mary number one for the top ten qualities, correlate performance results with customer data on marriage rates, college participation, and church attendance."

"Task will require twenty-two minutes," the computer said.

"Take your time," Jerrell leaned back, looked around the cafe, and took a sip of tepid coffee. For a minute, he did not catch anyone's eye; everyone seemed to be deep into their work, eyes locked on laptops.

Jerrell stood up, stretched, and moved into a yoga pose, then another, and another, and another.

Soon, the laptop beeped, and Jerrell sat down. He looked into the screen, then hit a key, which led to another screen, and another, and another.

He stared at the results for a long time, then mumbled, "Well, these need work. But it's a start; it's a start."

A young man with blond hair and a Norwegian jaw caught Jerrell's eye. He put his laptop on standby, smiled at Jerrell, stood up, and walked over. "Can I visit?"

"Sure." Jerrell stared at the young man; let's see.. you are? "How've you been?" Ah... that's it. Lars. You are Lars.

Lars sat down across from Jerrell. "Okay, I'm good. Listen, have you seen McLeesh's latest press conference this morning?"

Jerrell shook his head. "No. I don't keep track of our PR announcements."

Lars chuckled. "Living the life of the unwrinkled brow, eh?"

"I stay busy." Jerrell stared at the young man - get to the point.

"Well, this one's worth checking out. This morning, McLeesh announced a new product. They call it ELSEWHERE."

Jerrell nodded. "Oh, that's catchy. What is it?" Right up there with 'fantasy.'

Lars looked into Jerrell's eyes for a moment. "ELSEWHERE is a service that enables you to upload yourself - your mind, your personality, your memories, your opinions, your beliefs... everything you are... everything between your ears - onto an electronic network, where you will continue to live, essentially as a very large, self-aware, self-directed, dynamic, electronic file."

Jerrell stared at Lars. "Okay, I'm certain I do not understand. How much of what you just said is actually true?"

Lars repeated what he had said. He was quiet for a moment. "It's all true. But you have questions."

His eyes and mouth wide open, Jerrell nodded. "A couple. First, when did all this happen?" A skeptical expression crossed Jerrell's face. "We haven't brought out any significant new products in over a year... no, make that two years. Every time I turn around, someone is bitching that Willow's lost its touch."

Lars nodded. "I wondered about that. It's possible... actually, now I think of it, it's likely... that Willow's been working on this a long time." Lars glanced around. "If they diverted a ton of money to it, that would explain no other new projects."

"Okay," Jerrell said. "So... let's say you upload. So now, you're on the network and no longer in your body. What happens to your body?"

"Ah, McLeesh covered that. Willow puts it in cold storage for up to five years, no charge. After that, you pay to keep it in cold storage," Lars said.

"If you try it and don't like it, can you leave ELSEWHERE and come back to your body? Return to life as a normal person?"

"Yes. Willow guarantees all of that. It's not a one-way trip," Lars said.

"And you don't age," Jerrell said.

"Correct. Neither on the network nor in cold storage. After all, electronic files don't age, at least not in solid state storage."

Jerrell sat there thinking, then he looked up. "Storing a body would cost a fortune."

Lars smiled smugly. "Yeah, but this is an opportunity for McLeesh to remind everyone how clever he can be. He loves that. So... what if you could find a place that's really, really cold?"

"Like the North Pole," Jerrell said.

"Like the North Pole, or a mountain range in a cold climate, closer to an airport, or a road, northern Russia, the Rockies, Canada, somewhere like that. Maybe he's bought land in Greenland. Or even outer space."

"Okay, does anyone know how Willow is doing it?" Jerrell said.

"No one seems to know, not within Willow anyway, but I bet many people are busting their butts to find out. Willow is spending a mountain of money to get this thing up and running."

Jerrell stared at him - yeah, like every big tech company would like to know all about this. And every big Chinese company, and everybody's big companies. "So, where's the money coming from? McLeesh does nothing without a price tag attached."

"I don't know why you say that," Lars said. "Look at Willow. That's got no direct fees attached to it."

Jerrell seemed disappointed at that answer. "You're right, it doesn't" - Willow makes its money on advertising, a lot of advertising. Jerrell paused - it can't be advertising. McLeesh is already tapping that market as hard as it can be tapped, and he's already got access to every human on the planet, though I'm sure he wouldn't concede that.

Lars stood up; the conversation was over.

"Thanks, good seeing you." Jerrell watched Lars return to his table - how will ELSEWHERE make money? It is a certainty that McLeesh has a plan. What could it possibly be?

Jerrell was just about to close his laptop and leave the cafe when a thought drifted through his mind, shouting at him all the way. What was it? What was it?

Then the thought landed - internet access is tenuous, and security procedures are a pain in the gluteus maximus. It would save me a lot of time if I could bypass all that corporate crap and just get to work.

Jerrell sat there - I need a side door, a kitchen door, into the Willow software. A door that will open only for me, so it must be encrypted, and only I will know the key.

He leaned back in his chair - now, what would make a good key? Let's see... a secret key that changes daily. How about... how about... how about the price of something physical, like... the price of oil. No, that's a number, easily cracked. Okay, a character string, like... the name of the destination of the day's first flight out of Dulles Airport. Not the schedule, of course, but the actual first flight.

Yeah. Big airport, global destinations. That'll do fine.

I will call it, kitchendoor. Easy to remember. And I'll need an app for that.

Now, I can't charge for the app, since Willow owns my output. Should I sneak it through?

No, let's play it straight.

2. Elsewhere

Sonya walked along the sidewalk, a tall young woman, slender and blond, well-dressed, in low heels, moving fast with grace. A young woman with a job, a destination, and a schedule. She arrived in front of the Sunshine Cafe, went through the front doors at speed, almost bumped into the woman in front of her, and stopped suddenly. She watched for the woman to move, then turned right and headed for Jerrell's usual table.

Jerrell sat there; when he spotted her, he smiled.

She dropped her handbag onto a chair, tossed her head, casting shimmering blond waves, and said, "Hi." She sat down.

"What's going on? You look unhappy."

"Hang on." She turned to a robotic server passing by. "Excuse me, server? Could I get a cappuccino, please?"

The robot was humanoid, a tall structure of metal and plastic with a built-in tray in front and waldos on opposite sides, designed to carry food and drink. It stopped and turned towards Sonya. "Certainly. Creamer? Sweet?"

"Sweet."

"Of course." The robot turned and rolled away.

She turned back to Jerrell.

"Hard day already?" he said.

"I hate my job."

Jerrell tried to think of something consoling, came up with 'tomorrow's another day.' He decided not to say anything.

She aimed a hangdog look at him. "When I started, I thought it was the perfect job. Willow put on a big push for the business of 'female style' companies. You know, fashion, clothes, cosmetics, hairspray, all that."

Jerrell nodded. "Makes sense. Women spend billions on their looks."

"Yeah, but I'm in customer service." Her mouth set in a straight, flat line. "So all I hear are the complaints, the problems, everything that can go wrong, or that anyone wishes would go right."

"Yeah, lipstick on a pig usually pisses off the pig."

She looked at him sharply. "You know, that kind of comment is not helpful." Sonya paused and looked away, then she looked back at him. "My entire day is negative. I used to have the occasional day like that; everybody does. But now, it's every day. It's dragging me down."

The server arrived with her coffee, put it on the table, and waited.

Sonya looked at the robot. "Don't tell me, let me guess. You're waiting for a tip?"

"Of course, Ma'am."

"Are you also programmed for poor service?" she said.

"Absolutely not."

"Then there's no point in tipping you, is there?"

For a few long seconds, the robot was silent. Then it said, "I see your point." It turned and motored away. She looked at Jerrell. "Sorry. I feel like I'm just barely staying afloat. I have a job, but not a life."

Jerrell hid a smile - Sweetie, you're a tech worker at a Big Tech, and you're barely afloat? There are a million women who would love to be you. I bet you're used to fresh ground coffee, carbonated, filtered water, fresh swordfish, and steak. "Maybe you should ask to be re-assigned."

She looked at him. "Yeah, but they love my work. At least, they say they love my work. It makes me wonder if I'm being manipulated and used, like the guy who's well paid to take out the garbage every day. It might be a respectable job, and somebody's got to do it, but other than pay the bills, it's got nothing to recommend it. My job is not about fashion; it's about complaining customers."

Jerrell shrugged. "Paying the bills is important. Giving customers a voice is also important." Jerrell held onto a wince - Gods, I sound like a damn boy scout.

Sonya nodded. "Maybe, but I don't like what I see when I look at the future. I don't see any chance for advancement. And if I'm doing exactly the same thing ten years from now? That scares me. It feels like... a waste of life."

Jerrell sat there, thinking. "You know, it's odd that Willow, and for that matter, the other tech firms, don't make better use of A.I. in customer service. I mean, it seems like a natural fit. According to you, customer service is boring and repressive. Perfect for A.I.s."

"Yeah, there's another reason to fear my future," Sonya said.

"Seriously, why doesn't Willow have A.I.s to handle the problems and the complaints?"

She looked at Jerrell, and a smile crossed her face. "Jerrell, you're a really smart guy, and I find it fascinating, and maybe slightly charming, that you could be so naive. Think about it, a woman sits down at a counter or a computer and discusses fashion with a robot? Let's say she's dissatisfied with the shade of blue in her eyeliner. Does that sound plausible to you? And what would a robot know about fashion, anyway?"

Jerrell was silent.

Sonya said, "An A.I. provides information to women who want sympathy."

Jerrell shrugged - so? You program the A.I. to fake it. You know... 'tell us what you think, your opinion is important to us.' That sort of thing. Better not to mention that. "Everyone else is doing it. People talk to A.I.s about surgery, financial planning, education, and spacecraft design." He waved his hand at each example. "I don't see why cosmetics and fashion would be off limits."

Sonya's mouth went sideways briefly. "I wouldn't discuss fashion with a robot. I mean, to take one example, can robots match color?"

"I bet A.I.s could be taught to match colors. That's not out of range, not at all."

Sonya nodded. "Yeah, coulda, shoulda." Sonya froze. "I wonder if Willow is planning to replace me someday with a bot." She sat there, thinking, her mouth slightly open. "They wouldn't tell me, would they?"

Jerrell was silent for a moment, then shook his head. He reached out for a sip of coffee. Sonya's coffee sat untouched, growing cold. She shook her head and set off blond waves again, then looked at Jerrell. "I'm sorry, you probably think I'm all 'me, me, me,' complaining about my problems."

"I don't think that at all," he said. "Everyone has problems. People talk to figure them out, to solve them. That's a good thing."

"So what creative thing are you working on right now?"

Jerrell shook himself and warmed up to his topic. "Well, I have a fascinating, creative, difficult, subtle project here. One of those questions we cannot give to A.I.s. I have to create avatars that Willow can use to populate its networks with quasi-people who are cheerful, happy, and positive by design. Upper management, which means McLeesh and his pathetic collection of showgirls and 'yes' men, has decided they are alarmed at the growth of competing networks aimed at young women, also known as teenagers and young adults."

"Sure." Sonya nodded. "It's been a decade since Willow first appealed to young people, men or women. And now there's Flower, and Raindrop, and Run Tu. And that's just off the top of my head. The vultures are gathering."

"And Digger and Dancer and Donner and Blitzen. Exactly," Jerrell said. "So I'm working on an avatar which I have named, creatively, Mary." He looked at Sonya. "Would you like to take a look?"

Sonya nodded. "Okay."

Jerrell turned his laptop to face Sonya. "Meet Mary. Actually, her name is Mary One." Sonya stared at the display. "What do you think of her?"

Sonya peered at Mary and grinned. "Oh yeah, I'd say expectations are rocketing. She's a good one."

Jerrell continued, "She is the base prototype for an avatar whose task it will be to entertain and engage young women between, say, fourteen and twenty, on Willow's network. To talk to them about their dreams, their complaints, their problems, their lives, their boyfriends, their lack of a boyfriend, their drapes, their dog, their sexuality, drugs, whatever it takes to get them to return to Willow regularly... also their hairspray, eyeliner, yoga studio, and self-defense lessons. I admit, watching Willow give dating advice creeps me out."

Sonya stared at the display. "She's supposed to be fourteen? A little on the buxom side, don't you think? Or maybe even... heavyset?"

"Really?" Jerrell turned the laptop and stared at the display. He tilted his head. "I don't see it."

Sonya rolled her eyes. "Jerrell, for heaven's sake, do you actually know any fourteen-year-old girls?"

His mouth opened, but no sound emerged. "Uh... well... no, I don't. But we have data on height and weight of girls by age. Mary's height and weight are exactly at the median for the USA."

She looked at Jerrell. "Where's your data come from, Oklahoma? Tell me something - do you think girls are attracted to homely women, or are they attracted to good looking women?"

"Well, they might be more comfortable and less intimidated looking at a homely woman, right?"

"Good heavens." Sonya shook her head. "Young girls are most engaged looking at a girl or a woman who is attractive, but not so attractive that the young girl cannot aspire to look that good."

"So average doesn't do it?"

"Jerrell, you tell me. Do women aspire to look average?"

Jerrell paused - well, the Ugly might, but the others?... probably not. He almost spoke, but stopped himself - women do not aspire to be realistic; better not to mention that. "So... we need better than average, within one standard deviation." He sat there thinking, took another look at the image, then turned the display away from Sonya. He looked at her. "Thank you. This has been very helpful."

The two of them were quiet for a moment, then Jerrell said, "Hey, have you heard about Willow's latest product? It's called 'Elsewhere.' Does that ring a bell?"

Sonya shook her head. The waves in her hair, and her scent, washed across Jerrell's senses. He took a breath, tried unsuccessfully to clear his head, and said, "Don't worry, you'll hear about it. Willow has developed a technology allowing a person to upload themselves to an electronic network, where they can live and be active without all the consequences of being an animal with a body. They will be alive... as a very large, complex, dynamic, electronic file."

"I don't understand," Sonya said.

Jerrell grinned. "Probably no one does. This is the Latest New Thing. It sounds as if Willow figured out the interface between the brain and an electronic network. They can store a person's mind - their opinions, cognition, memories, everything - in an electronic file on a network that will create an artificial environment where the person can live. The customer can interact, remember, form opinions, communicate, everything. And here's the real kicker, that file can be downloaded back into their body, with their memories intact, and they can be revived and returned to life as a normal, biological human being. They will have their original memories as well as those acquired living on the network."

"I still don't understand."

"You have questions," Jerrell said.

Sonya tilted her head. "A couple, like, what happens to their body while they're on the network?"

Jerrell smiled. "Oh, that. Willow will put the body in cold storage up to five years. That's a freebie. Longer than that, the customer pays for continued storage."

Sonya sat there for a long moment, staring off into a distance that she did not see. "Are you serious? Where did you hear all this?"

"Today, here. A friend of mine, a guy named Lars, stopped by and talked about it."

"I know Lars. Blond guy with a square jaw."

Jerrell nodded. "That's the guy."

"So Willow actually did this."

"It's been publicly announced; it'll be all over the media," Jerrell said.

Sonya pulled out her phone and her fingers flew over its face. "Yeah, here it is, on the cable news, the dominant story, big headline, WILLOW ANNOUNCES A NEW WORLD." She turned the phone to face Jerrell.

He stared and read a bit of the text, then nodded. "They're excited, as well they should be."

"Listen, I need to get going, but I'd like to talk about this," Sonya said. "Can you get together after work? We could go to my place, grab pizza, or something."

Jerrell sat there and tried not to look like a guy whose heart was racing - do I hear correctly? The Princess wants me to stop by her place for pizza and talk? Wow, a dream evening, I get to do something other than hang out at my apartment, and with the Princess, at her apartment, no less.

"Uh, yeah, sure, that sounds okay," Jerrell said.

"Okay, I have to go to the Woody. I expect to be free about five."

"Let's text when we're free and take it from there."

"Okay, see you then." Sonya stood, swung her bag over her shoulder, and left the cafe. Jerrell watched her all the way to the door, then looked around and noticed several other guys watching her.

He smiled - yeah, she's something special. Everyone thinks so.

He stood up and went to the coffee server, assembled a tall American coffee, blond and sweet, and waved his ring at the payments sensor, then returned to his table. Jerrell glanced at the clock on his laptop; he had thirty minutes to get to the office of his immediate supervisor, a man named Miles... there was time enough to finish his coffee.

He thought about Sonya - I can imagine, I like to imagine, I would like to see... Sonya in the kitchen, chatting away like she does, cooking something, or dishing out a dessert, and later turning to me and saying something like, "It's time you and I got to know each other a lot better. Follow me." And I would, into the bedroom, and ecstasy.

Obviously, I dream better than I live. Well, who doesn't?

It matters not. That will never happen.

Jerrell shook off the fantasy, capped his coffee, loaded his laptop into a backpack, and headed out the door. Minutes later, he was entering the Woody, along with a moving crowd of other Willow employees of every color, shape, and disposition. The Woody was a very international place.

A massive bureaucracy ran Willow. Some were well educated; others, less educated, were creative or expert in a critical area.

The height above ground reflected the corporate status of each office. Board members were on the eighty-seventh floor, just above the CEO, the president, the senior vice-presidents, legal, marketing, and finance. Then followed research and development, new products, and international.

Software development was far below all of these, with human resources on the second floor, and corporate ethics in the basement. Jerrell smiled at that; Willow is not subtle - yes, we are in favor of ethics, particularly in outsiders. But for insiders, and this is a proprietary secret, the corporate mantra is, the means justify the ends, and do not get caught, and if caught, you have only yourself to blame, so do not blame, or even mention, Willow.

You may admit to being, or rather, to having been, a Willow employee.

Jerrell left the elevator at the twenty-eighth floor, looking for the deputy assistant director of Software 1, Michael Bliss. Mr. Bliss reported to a layer of higher management, to the assistant director, then the associate, then the director, after that the deputy vice presidents, the vice presidents, and the senior vice presidents. Jerrell had seen these higher officers a handful of times. He routinely met with Mr. Bliss but rarely with anyone higher.

As he walked down the hall, Jerrell smiled - this is a good arrangement. They pay me well. Beyond that, notwithstanding my pursuit of a relationship, I am an introvert. I live, walk, and breathe in my head. I've never been popular anywhere, not even second grade, and I've never had many friends. So this works just fine.

He arrived at the office of Mr. Bliss, checked his watch - a minute early, no problem - and tapped on the door. The door promptly opened a few inches, and Jerrell entered the office.

Mike Bliss sat at his desk, staring into a large monitor. He looked up. "Jerrell, hello, hello. Get yourself in here; have a seat."

Jerrell sat down opposite Bliss. "Hey, Mike, how are things?"

Mike Bliss looked flustered; his movements were jerky, not the smooth movements of a man relaxed. "Funny you should ask; things are crazy at the moment, with this Elsewhere intro. Have you been reading about that?"

"Not much," Jerrell said. "I've been busy."

"Yeah, yeah, I'll bet. That's the great thing about a staff job; you get your assignments, and you do them. Life is simple. Between you and me, I miss it."

"Yes, sir. You're paying the wages of advancement."

Bliss nodded, then laughed. "Something like that." He looked at Jerrell for a moment. "But enough of that; let's talk about your Marys. But before I get into that, I just want to say, people here are impressed with your work. The first Marys have been a big hit, and they're giving us measurable improvements in interaction on Willow. That is a huge deal. It's difficult to understand how big that is, since nobody really knows how big Willow is. But trust me, it's big."

"That's good to hear, thank you."

"Okay, good," Bliss said. "So tell me in one page what you're working on now."

"Ah, yes," Jerrell said. "I've constructed the basic template for all the Marys. Broadly speaking, she's a teenage girl, somewhat attractive but no bombshell, better looking than average, more polite than average, well-spoken. A nice girl with a bit of money. Educated, but no geek.

"What remains is to develop variations on the template, regional, racial, and cultural variations. Some of that is a simple procedure with one of Willow's A.I.s; for example, it is easy to introduce variations in appearance.

"The complicated part, which remains, is introducing variations in her behavior, opinions, speech, and beliefs. Again, that is an exercise with an A.I.; I doubt it could be done effectively otherwise. I'm working on that now. I expect to be burning through a lot of A.I. time."

Bliss nodded and was quiet for a moment. "Okay, here's the big question - how long will it take you to finish?"

"That question has no single answer, since it depends on how many Marys we decide to develop. Here's what I would suggest: let me do, say, a dozen or a couple dozen Marys. Then we can deploy them and watch the results. We can keep going until the proven benefits are too low to pursue. What do you think about that?"

Bliss smiled. "I could have written that answer." He leaned back in his chair. "Jerrell, you continue to impress. I believe you have management potential."

"Really? You think so?" Jerrell grinned, looked at Bliss. "You're not just being nice to me, are you?"

Bliss slapped his hand against his desk. "Absolutely, I am, but that's not the point. You can think on a broader scale, redefine a problem in broader terms to support a more flexible, more effective solution." Bliss looked at Jerrell for a moment. "That's what management boils down to, you know. As a manager, you must influence a variety of clients - other managers, investors, lawyers, engineers - who have their own roles and concerns. Managing means you accommodate them all. And you, Jerrell, know this instinctively, though you might not be aware of it."

"Wow, thank you. Maybe I should head off to B school."

Bliss made an approving face, then said, "Not a bad idea, but first you need to finish the Marys."

Jerrell nodded. The two men talked for another fifteen minutes. Jerrell covered the preliminary performance and survey results for the current crop of Marys, and concluded by saying, "That's what the data says. In the south, they like them busty and blond, in the northeast, muscular and brunette, on the west coast, thin and blond."

"Okay, I believe all that. That's a start. Keep going. We'll talk later." Bliss thanked him and excused himself, and Jerrell left the office.

As Jerrell exited into the early afternoon, he paused for a moment - it's 1 p.m., I've got time. Let's see, half an hour to the grocery store, half an hour to shop, fifteen minutes to home and drop off the groceries, plenty of time before Sonya is free.

He sent her a text:

Finished at the W. Text me when you want some company. Jerrell.

He pocketed the phone and went on his way.

***

That evening, Sonya was exhausted when she reached her apartment. She came through the front door, shouted, "Hello, I'm home." She paused to listen, then proceeded straight to the kitchen. Her roommate, Terika, was sitting at the kitchen table eyeing a marijuana cigarette. When Sonya entered the kitchen, Terika, without looking up, said, "Hi."

"Hi, yourself," Sonya said. "Everything okay?"

She put down the cigarette. "About as okay as I expect it to be. Your boss is all over the news this evening."

"Who? McLeesh?"

"Yeah. Apparently, Willow just developed a new technology, which they'll be marketing soon. I think their public launch date is a week away."

"Oh?"

"Yeah," Terika said. "It sounds pretty wild. Willow claims they can upload people to an electronic network, just like you'd upload any electronic file."

Sonya paused with a bottle of wine in one hand, a glass in the other. "You want some?"

"Please."

Sonya reached up into a cabinet, hooked a finger around the stem of a second glass, then put both glasses on the table. She unscrewed the cap of the wine and poured some of it into the glasses.

Sonya sat down, picked up her glass and raised it in a toast. "Here's looking at you."

"You, too." The two women drank.

"Okay," Sonya said. "Back to the beginning - what happened?"

"Your creepy CEO announced a new service from Willow, which will enable anyone to upload themselves to an electronic network."

"Upload..." Sonya wore a helpless expression. "A friend mentioned this, but what does it mean? Will the person be alive after they upload?"

"Yes. The body will be inactive; Willow will store it. The person will be conscious and alive on the network."

"God. What must it be like to live on an electronic network?"

Terika smiled. "Yeah, that's a good question; I don't think anyone knows. Oh, wait... no, there's a guy who did it. A black guy named Rafer or Rafael something. He did it. He uploaded, Willow stored his body, and he returned to his body a week later, alive and with his old and new memories intact. They woke him up, and he seems none the worse for wear."

Sonya stared at her roommate. "Are you sure about all this? It sounds brand spanking new, so how much can we possibly know?"

Terika looked bored. "Hey, what do I know? I'm just telling you what I saw on the news. If you pop your laptop open, I bet the story is all over the place, everywhere... or... it's a massive hoax and someone, starting with the founder of Willow, is playing a joke on the entire world."

Sonya stood up, left the kitchen, and soon returned with her laptop. She sat down, opened the laptop, and tapped several keys. "Central Cable News ought to have something."

In seconds, her eyes were wide as she read. "Jesus, you're right. This headline is in forty-point font."

"What's it say?"

Sonya held up both arms and hands, as for a proclamation. She exclaimed, in a lecture-hall voice, "WELCOME TO ELSEWHERE."

Sonya lowered her arms and continued, "Willow is going to sell a service that lets a person upload their mind, personality, memories, everything to a digital network. You will literally leave your body, which they will preserve in cold storage until you decide to return to your body."

"So CCN thinks it's real."

"Yeah, they do."

Terika's face showed exasperation; she looked at Sonya. "This is crazy. I mean, what can it possibly be like to turn into an electronic file and store yourself on a computer network? And what can you do while you're there? And why would anyone have any interest in something like this?"

Sonya's eyes were riveted on her laptop. "Hold on, I'm reading." She sat there reading. "Okay, Willow will put you in cold storage; that part is true. And it's free." She looked at Terika. "Free, huh. That's hard to believe."

Terika laughed. "You think the part about its being free is hard to believe? Oh, wow."

"Yeah. I haven't wrapped my head around this yet." Sonya kept reading. "Okay, you'll be able to do anything an electronic file can do. You will be unable to do what that a biological entity can do. So you can process information, you can move around the network. Well, that sounds okay."

She reached for her glass, which Terika had refilled, and emptied it in one long draught. Sonya continued, "However, you will not need or be able to breathe, therefore you cannot suffocate or drown. You will be able to see, speak, and hear. There are apps for all those." She kept reading. "Oh, okay, here's the kicker - no touching, no strokes, no hugs, no sex. You won't be able to feel any of that, or anything. No sense of touch."

"Well, fuck that," Terika said. She emptied her glass.

Sonya froze, thinking. She stared out the window, then looked at Terika. "So, who would want to do this? Would anyone want to do this? I mean, Willow must think that many will want to upload. Otherwise, they wouldn't have spent the money. Isn't that so?" She fingered her wine glass.

Sonya looked at Terika. "So, who wants to do this?"

"For one, people who don't care about sex," Terika said.

"Yeah, but who's that?"

"Well, have you had sex, ever?"

"No, but that doesn't mean I don't care about it," Sonya said. "I'm just looking for the right guy."

"Let me ask you something; when you shop for shoes, you try them on, first. Right?"

Sonya sat there and frowned.

"I am not hearing an answer," Terika said.

"Yes, I try them on."

"In economics, we call that revealed preference. Your choices reflect your preferences, your opinions. In your case, you care about shoes more than you care about sex."

"That's ridiculous," Sonya said. "Trying on shoes is nothing like fucking a guy."

Terika stared at her. "And you know this... how? I thought you hadn't done it yet. I think, for what it's worth, that men and shoes provide comfort. At least, if you're lucky. Shoes, of course, also provide style, for those who care about that sort of thing." She twirled her wine glass. "Most guys? Not so much."

Sonya was silent.

Terika waved a hand. "Okay, whatever. Let's move on."

The two women sat silent for a long minute.

Terika said, "Hey, anyone who's terminally ill would be interested in uploading. The cancer patient, someone like that. You won't die on the network, unless the network shuts down, and even then they can back up your file and revive you."

"I have seen no mention of that," Sonya said.

"Well, I'm guessing, but it follows from saying you can do anything a digital file can do. You can copy a digital file, so you'll be able to copy yourself. And digital files don't grow old."

Sonya nodded - yeah, as long as you have the server capacity. She smiled - on the other hand, maybe personality is like the brain, most people get by on five percent of what's available. Or less. She smiled and returned to reading. "Oh, this is interesting. They have apps that emulate certain functions. Like reading data, reading text, looking at images or graphs. Listening to music. They have apps for all that."

"But no app for sex?"

Sonya's eyes arrowed into the screen. "No, no mention of an app for sex. Actually, why would you need an app for sex? You do it, or you don't. Of course, you would need an app for touch."

"Yeah, sex without touch? Good luck with that. That's so typical, get the trivia right, ignore the important stuff. Why am I not surprised?"

Sonya grinned and looked at Terika. "Hey, if they had a sex app, what do you think they'd call it?"

"Lightning Rod?"

"Fire Hose?"

"How 'bout Gron, the Hammer."

The two giggled.

Sonya became serious. "Listen, here's a thought - do you know... have you ever known... anyone who was not afraid of dying?"

Terika wore a contemplative expression. "No... no... I can't say I have. I know many who say they believe in Jesus and heaven and hell and all that stuff. But they don't want to die. They don't want their friends or lovers or parents or children to die, and when someone dies, their friends and family get pretty upset."

Sonya stared at Terika – maybe all that theology is just a massive pile of bullshit that people have used to cover their fears.

"What?" Terika said.

Sonya said, "Oh, my God. Lots of people will want to upload. Anyone afraid of death will want to, don't you think? Lots."

"Really?" Terika thought for a moment. "I don't know about that."

"T, we're all dying, right? Mortal man, doomed to die? All that?"

Terika nodded. "Huh. I could see someone deciding to live in the real world, the world of blood and bone, until they get old enough that they see significant decay. If they screw up and wait too long, they might die. So... waiting is risky. At some point, they'll upload and maybe live forever."

"Yeah, that sounds right," Sonya said. "After all, old people aren't getting laid, so why not upload?"

"Not so fast, Missie. My mom is in her fifties. She's on a dating site. She gets laid once in a while. So she says. Anyway, I know she's still interested in horizontal cardio."

"Yeah, but fifties isn't that old."

"I guess that's true, but even she has a hard time. She says that men first die below the waist. The legs go first," Terika said.

Sonya's eyebrows rose. "Then everything else down there?"

"I think so, yeah."

"Huh, I didn't know that." Sonya made a face. "That's a bummer."

Terika shrugged. "Get it early, girl."

***

In the afternoon, as Jerrell sat at his kitchen table, working on one of the Marys, his phone chimed, a text from Sonya:

I'm at home, 501 Sears, #C, pick up wine and stop by.

Jerrell replied: *On my way.* He attached a fantasy, a photo of a dodo bird trying to fly. He sent the text and the picture and immediately froze - is that picture stupid? Shit. It is, isn't it? It is stupid. Well, too late now.

He closed his laptop and left the apartment. His cell directed him to Sears Street. On the way, he stopped at a wine shop. Shelves lined the walls, reds on the right, whites on the left. A thin, balding man stood behind a small counter in the middle.

Jerrell turned to the right and froze; the red shelves were half full. He moved closer and scanned the bottles; the least expensive red bottle, a Chilean merlot, was $199.99. "What the hell?" Jerrell looked at the man. "What happened to your reds?"

"Elsewhere happened," the man said. "My reds buyer is uploading. Don't worry, we'll get it fixed, but it'll take time. Meanwhile, this is what's available."

"I can't believe what I'm about to do," Jerrell mumbled. He turned and moved to the white shelves. After a minute, he selected a pinot blanc and brought it to the counter.

"You don't like white wine?"

"White wine is for girls; it's too close to tap water to be worth the price. I cook with it, but I don't drink it," Jerrell said.

The owner shrugged. "To each his own." He bagged the bottle and handed it to Jerrell. "That isn't a red, so it's a lot better chilled."

Jerrell mumbled. "Lipstick on a pig." He turned and left the store. Ten minutes later, he was walking down Sears Street, which seemed to be a bit of an oasis for young urban women; there was a yoga studio, a salad bar, a clothing consignment store, a cosmetics counter, and a drugstore. Jerrell looked around - I bet they drink a lot of white wine in this neighborhood.

He found Sonya's address; she buzzed him in at the front door. He climbed a flight of stairs. At apartment C, she was standing in the doorway, looking sad and disheveled.

Jerrell walked up to her and handed her the bagged bottle of wine. "Hey, what's going on? Hard day?"

"Not especially, this is what I usually look like after a day at work. If you find it offputting, I sympathize. But I hate my job. That's why I look like this."

Jerrell made a face and tried not to evaluate that comment - I learned this lesson many times, most people, but especially women, look for sympathy before analysis. They do not need to make sense, and often they do not. And they definitely do not need to be informed of that fact.

And I know... why am I infatuated with a woman who doesn't make sense? Two reasons: first, do any of them? Second, I'm an involuntary captive of raging hormones. My hormones are yelling at me to breed, whereas the minds of women are yelling at them not to breed with a skinny Indian.

So far, the minds are winning.

He followed her into the kitchen. "Well, let's celebrate how good you look in the mornings, then."

She glanced at him. "Thank you." Sonya frowned. "Sorry. I feel like I'm just managing to stay afloat. I have a job, but not a life." Sonya sat down, then she straightened, reached into the bag, and extracted the wine. "What's this? You bought white wine?" She peered at him. "You feeling okay?"

Jerrell sat down. "Long story. Probably never happen again. If you looked for a job, what would you look for?"

She looked up from the wine. "Okay, there are two options. One is sensible, and other one might sound crazy; I'd like your thoughts, particularly on the latter."

Jerrell shrugged. "Okay."

"Alright, the sensible option is advertising and marketing."

"That sounds okay," Jerrell said. "You seem suited to it, and you could do it anywhere. What's the crazy option?"

"I could upload to Elsewhere."

Jerrell laughed. "Oh, brother. Seriously?"

Sonya said hurriedly, "I know, that sounds insane, but anything as new as Elsewhere would probably sound insane. So let's do this: while you're here, let's make a list of pros and cons, okay?"

"Sure." Jerrell nodded. "But if we're going to do this, we should drink, maybe heavily."

"Good idea." Sonya twisted the cap off the bottle while Jerrell got up and took two goblets from a cabinet. She poured the wine.

Jerrell sat, then raised his glass. "Here's to crazy career moves."

Sonya clinked her goblet against his. "Excelsior." They drank.

Jerrell put down his goblet. "Okay, let's start with the pros."

"Okay," Sonya said. "I would turn from a human female into an electronic file. Now, uploading is free; there's no charge. While I'm there, Willow will store my body at no charge for five years. That's got to be expensive, right?"

"Sure. More expensive for you, as an individual, than for Willow, as a large corporation," he said.

"Alright. I would lose all the expenses of maintaining a body and a presence as a human being, an animal," she said. "Rent, insurance, health care, food, clothing, shelter, taxes, would all disappear."

"Taxes? You're dreaming."

Sonya nodded. "Okay, maybe not taxes. Have they arranged to collect taxes on Elsewhere? Whatever. Everything else would vanish."

"So far, so good," Jerrell said.

"I would be immortal."

Jerrell shook his head. "Not immortal. All things under the sun come to an end, eventually. Let's just say your life expectancy would increase by a lot. Twenty-fold or more. I think that's fair."

She nodded. "Okay. That's a plus. On top of that, I understand that time compresses in Elsewhere. One hour in Elsewhere is equivalent to a month as a human being on Earth." Sonya looked at Jerrell. "Is that true?"

Jerrell shrugged. "I don't know about the number, but that sounds right. Electronic signals are way faster than biochemical signals." He thought for a moment. "Though the software might get in the way."

"Okay," Sonya said. "A four-year degree takes four academic years of study, with summers off, that's thirty-six months in all. So I might able to get another degree, a real degree, in less than two months."

"At thirty-to-one, one point two months; that's plausible," Jerrell said. "Agreed."

"My body would not age; I could return to it anytime I wish. Willow guarantees that."

"So you could upload for a couple months, get another degree, and return to animal life," Jerrell said. "You would miss roughly five or six weeks of animal life, in exchange for four years of academic life on Elsewhere."

"Yeah, so... this is like a money-back guarantee. If for any reason I don't like it, I can leave it and return to animal life," Sonya said.

"That's a good point."

Sonya sat there, thinking. She picked up her goblet and finished her wine. Jerrell looked at his wine and did the same. "Okay," she said. "That's all I've got."

Jerrell poured another glass for each of them. "Now, let's do the negatives," he said. He picked up his wine and took a long drink. Sonya did the same.

"As a human," Jerrell said. "We all have our time on Earth. As far as I know, it happens only once; we are granted a certain amount of time, a lifespan, which varies. It can be short or long. No one knows. We live as long as we stay healthy, usually less than a hundred years. By contrast, on Elsewhere, you are depending on an electrical network. If that network goes out, so do you. A power outage, a war, an earthquake, or a hacker could end you, even on Elsewhere."

"Yes, but would you be dead? When the power comes back on, the electronic files all fire up again. After all, corporations get hacked all the time, but they don't die. So that sounds more like an interruption, less like a death. No one returns from death."

Jerrell smiled. "You're not a Christian?"

Sonya barely stopped herself from rolling her eyes. "Many people have their own stories, which they believe, or so they claim. I think they're just stories."

"Okay. I think so, too," Jerrell said.

"Next."

"You have the major senses - sight, hearing, touch, taste, smell. Willow can probably emulate sight and hearing, but not the others. And I doubt that as an electronic file, you'll feel pain or fear."

"Okay, maybe not," she said.

"So, living on Elsewhere, you'll lose a good deal of what it means to be human. And if you return to animal life, having forgotten the warnings associated with fear, with pain, with human instincts, I'm not sure you would survive as a human being. You might learn on Elsewhere to ignore warnings that humans face, and respond to, every day."

"Who knows?" Sonya said.

Jerrell made a face and shook his head from side to side. "That sounds dicey. Some things have to be experienced. In addition, if you lost smell, taste, touch, you would never appreciate a rose, you would never appreciate wine, even white wine, you would never appreciate the touch of a friend, or a lover. And you would certainly never experience anything like the joys of sex, and having a child, and raising a child."

"All true," Sonya said. "But I do not enjoy these things now. And I don't know if I ever will, even as a human being."

Jerrell's mouth dropped open. "Wow, really? Then I feel sorry for you. I plan, and I certainly hope, to experience all of those things. I'm sorry to find that you don't share those desires."

"Some people go into old age without experiencing any of them," Sonya said. "Others die before they can experience them. Nothing is guaranteed."

"Maybe not, but the things we're discussing are common; they are common elements of being human."

Sonya was silent for a long minute. "Okay, that's fair."

"So there it is," Jerrell said. "There are many things about being human that you would give up to upload to Elsewhere. I guess it's a complicated choice."

"Let's drink the rest of the wine," Sonya said.

"Is there more?"

"I have a bottle of red, but I was saving it for a special occasion," Sonya said.

Disappointment briefly flashed across Jerrell's face. He looked at Sonya. "So, is this a special occasion?"

Sonya smiled. "It just might be."

3. Sex, Lemon and Tonic, and Rock & Roll

Johnny B. Goode hit the last power chord, blasting a harmonically united, three-octave sound out into the crowd, waited a few seconds, then put his hand over the guitar strings, muting them. At that instant, the bass line stopped, the last hit on a cymbal launched and rang and faded slowly, and the song ended.

Mac's Tavern was packed; many in the crowd were standing and applauding. In front of the bandstand, the dancers soon turned away and returned to their tables and their drinks. A few people stayed on the dance floor and waited for another number; one was a tall, slender blond with an expensive, shaggy haircut. She stared at Johnny. He made a face and winked at her. She smiled back. He spoke into the microphone, "Thanks, everyone. Time for a break. Back in twenty, so stay tuned."

Johnny stood there, tuning his guitar, gently plucking each string and listening to the quiet tone. When he was satisfied, he lifted the guitar from his body and set it into a guitar stand.

His bass player sidled over and said in a low voice. "You've got style, Johnny. A good stage presence. I think you'll fit into this band nicely."

Johnny said. "Thanks. I think so, too."

The bass player glanced at the blond, then nodded in her direction. "That tall one likes you."

Johnny glanced at the bass player. "Yeah, she's that kind of girl, melts over 'I love you forever'." He didn't look at the blond.

"Yeah, you've got that glow that turns on the ladies. And muscles, too. I bet she's turned on now," the bass player said.

"You can keep that bet. Maybe we'll never know."

"Oh, I don't know; you could take her out to the truck," the bass player said. "See if she'd like a little horizontal roll and rock."

Johnny nodded. "Tempting, but my dating radius is measured in yards, not miles." He glanced at the bass player. "Besides, I got to deal with my parole officer, so let's just finish our set, load up, and head home. I'm tired. I want to catch up on my sleep, in my own bed for a change." He smiled at the bass player. "See how I cleverly worked 'sleep' into the conversation?"

"Alright." The bass player slid the guitar strap over his head and leaned his instrument against a massive monitor. "I'm gonna grab a beer. You want anything?"

"Tonic and lime. No, make it lemon."

"Alright."

"Thanks." Minutes later, the bass player returned with a lemon and tonic. Twenty minutes came and went, and they played another set, then shut down for the night.

After the last song, Johnny stood at the microphone and thanked the crowd. He slid the guitar off his shoulders and set it aside. The blond approached him. "Hi, Johnny. I'm Grace. You play beautifully."

He smiled. "Thanks, angel. I mean, Grace. Your dancing inspires me."

She grinned. "Now you're sweet talkin' me."

He aimed a playful expression at her. "Uh, oh, you caught me. And I know, I know, you get that a lot, don't you? I don't want to be just another guy hitting on you, though I guess that's what I am."

She nodded. "You're not. I like you. I'd like to get to know you a bit. And I just want to add, I'm smarter than I look."

Johnny almost voiced agreement, but he was fast; he stopped himself - that's an odd thing to say. But what's the answer? 'No' seems wrong; 'yes' also seems wrong. Let's say nothing. He recovered and smiled. "Really? You look smart enough. Smarter than me, probably."

The smiled left her face. "Seriously, Johnny, flirting aside, would you like to hang out after the show?"

Johnny smiled at her - it took a lot of nerve to ask that question, didn't it, princess? "That's very kind, but we've been on the road for several weeks. I'm pretty tired, and I would hate to disappoint you. A gorgeous woman deserves the best, don't you think? Can I take a rain check without making you mad at me?"

She shook her head. "I'm not mad at you."

Johnny smiled. "That's a relief. I don't want to make you mad."

She nodded. "Maybe next time, then?"

Johnny nodded. "Yeah, next time. I'm sure we'll be back at Mac's."

"Yeah, you packed the place; they ought to be pleased. Alright, then. Next time." Grace smiled at him. "I'll see you later." He watched her return to a couple of female friends. In a minute, they finished their drinks and turned to leave. She looked back at Johnny, and he gave her a little wave.

Wow. Country girls. I cannot believe I just turned her down.

It's been a while... three years, more than two anyway. Prison's not a good place for recreational sex, and getting into some guy's hairy butt never appealed to me. But the truth is, as nice as she is, Grace is too far away. When I find someone to make the other half of a couple, I want them closer, so we can make it a steady routine. Maybe even move in together.

That would be different.

No more drinking, no more hit-and-run, no more one-night wonders. Been there, done that; it's a lark, a memory, a hobby but not a career.

The other three band members had rented a commercial van; Johnny helped them load their equipment. Soon, the drummer said, "Okay, we're packed, I'll drive."

The bass player shook his head. "No way. Johnnie's the designated driver. He can drive."

Johnny put an arm around the drummer. "I know, it seems unfair. You're a victim of the reputations of drummers over the years. Everyone thinks the drummer is likely the craziest guy in the band. But look at the bright side - you can drink all you want and tell your stories without being distracted with little white and yellow lines, speed limits, and all that legal stuff."

The drummer looked at Johnny. "You should run for office." That attracted a couple of snarky comments.

"Ouch," Johnny said. He moved behind the wheel as the others boarded the van. Before rolling out onto the highway, Johnny turned to the others and said, "Alright, what shall we sing?"

"Sally Round Heels," the drummer said.

" 'Sally Round Heels' it is," Johnny said. The song, sung by lonely men everywhere, burst forth, of a mythical girl who will like you and make love to you without tripping over your numerous faults and shortcomings. Who will stick with you through thick and thin, and give you that one precious chance to show you're smart enough not to let her go.

Ever.

The song ended, and Johnny grinned to himself - Sally Round Heels is out there; I know a couple of guys who have married her, the lucky sods. I know she exists. Right now, I'm busy, trying to live like a civilian. But we'll be back at Mac's, and I bet Grace will be there. If she's not, no problem, I'll take that for an answer, but if she is, then maybe we can start up something, and maybe it'll be good. And it's not all that many miles to go, is it?

I need to be flexible, tolerant.

That could happen. Lots of things could happen. Don't push; let the game come to you in its own time.

He drove the band back to south Philly, to the corner of 21st and Mercy streets. By then, the bass player was sober enough to drive. Johnny said his goodbyes, grabbed his guitar case, hopped out onto the sidewalk, and gave a sloppy salute as the van drove away.

He walked half a block down Mercy to a dilapidated rowhouse, climbed up rickety stairs to a narrow porch, and unlocked the front door. He entered the house; the foyer was dimly lit, and Johnny didn't immediately see the landlady, Ms. Rickenbacker, a round, aging woman who had mistreated her husband, lost him to prison, and promised herself that she would be respectful of ex-cons. Johnny suspected ulterior motives.

"Johnny, you're back," she said.

Johnny jumped at the sudden sound. "Holy Christ!... sorry, but you scared me. I didn't see you." He leaned his guitar case against the wall.

"You're up late," she said. "I waited up for you."

"You shouldn't wait up, Ms. Rickenbacker. I'm in a band; that's my job. It's graveyard shift; we make our money in the evenings, mostly on the weekends. Tonight, for instance, we played til past eleven, took an hour to pack up, another hour to drive back, and it is... he checked his cell phone... one twenty A.M., which could have been worse. You should be in bed."

"Have you been drinking?"

"No, Ma'am, in fact, I'm the designated driver."

"I believe you," Ms. Rickenbacker said. "But I don't understand how you ended up in prison. You're better than the guys we usually get here."

Johnny shrugged. "Well, a guy was trying to push me around... actually, he was trying to push my date around, so I belted him."

"That doesn't sound like it's worth prison," she said.

"I will admit, looking back, I wish I hadn't hit him so hard. I did more damage than I meant to."

"I couldn't work your hours."

"We played Thursday in Westchester," Johnny said. "Friday in King of Prussia, and tonight in Ephrata. So it was a good weekend. But late nights are part of the gig."

"You play in bars; do you drink?" she said.

"Lemon and tonic, Ma'am."

"Maybe tomorrow - or today, I guess - you can relax for a change."

Johnny shook his head. "No. Rehearsal at two; we're adding a couple new songs, and Monday morning I'm seeing my P.O."

"Okay," she said. "Good. I think I'll turn in. Good luck with the P.O."

"Thanks, Ms. Rickenbacker. Good night."

"G'night, Johnny." She headed towards the back of the house, and Johnny hoisted his guitar and climbed the steps to #2, up and to the left, two doors short of the bathroom.

He entered the room, gently set the guitar case against the wall, and looked out the window at south Philly. The darkness was deep and solid, broken by the lamps lining 21st Street.

Johnny took a deep breath - another day, another dollar.

He fell into bed without removing his clothes.

***

As usual, Monday morning rolled around too soon, and almost before he awoke, Johnny was up, showered, dressed, caffeinated, brushed, and on the 21 bus.

He disembarked after a dozen blocks in front of a large, square, office building marked ADMINISTRATION. Inside the bank of front doors, the building register directed him to the basement, where 'Parole Office' could be found. There were two secretaries, a man and a woman, behind plexiglass windows. Johnny approached the man. "Hi, there. My name's John Goode, here to see Wendolyn Jefferson."

The man said, "Okay, I'll buzz her." A few seconds later, he pointed with a pen. "Down that hallway, fourth door on the left."

"Thanks."

Johnny went down the corridor, knocked on a door, and entered a room with a single window, a table, and three chairs, two of which held a middle-aged black woman in business wear and a beautiful young woman with dark hair and dark eyes.

Johnny looked between them. "Ms. Jefferson?"

"That's me," the black woman said. "Ah, John, thank you for coming. It's good to meet you. Please, sit."

Johnny glanced at the young woman and sat down.

Ms. Jefferson said, "Is it John or Johnny?"

"My friends call me Johnny. John works, too."

Ms. Jefferson nodded. "Okay. This is Julia Chu. I asked her to attend because she could help you. Julia is an accountant, a financial expert. She can help you manage your money, if you wish. I invited her because our customers often have a hard time with that."

Johnny smiled at Julia. "Yeah, that might come in handy. Thank you."

Julia said, "Nice to meet you."

Ms. Jefferson questioned Johnny - are you comfortable being out of prison? He laughed at that one. Do you have plans to find a place to live once you leave the halfway house? Are you working? Do you need any help with anything, anything at all? We're here to help you be comfortable so that you stay out of prison.

Johnny answered the questions politely. Yes, I am working, as a guitarist; yes, I plan to move into a house with roommates to save on rent. At the moment, I don't need a day job; my lifestyle is quite simple. No, I am not using drugs. I have the occasional beer.

At the end of the meeting, Johnny thanked Ms. Jefferson and Julia and left the Parole Office. Out on the sidewalk, as he stood in front of the building, Julia emerged. Johnny called to her, "Hey,

Julia, are you busy? I have a couple of questions about money. Can I buy you lunch?"

"Your treat?"

"Sure."

She nodded back; they found a retro diner, took a booth away from the door, and ordered coffee from a human waitress.

The waitress left, and Johnny said, "That's a nice touch. I don't like to order from a bot. You can't ask a bot, 'so, what's good?' You won't get a straight answer."

Julia mimicked the low voice of a man, "It is all calories, which are necessary for life. So eat your calories."

Johnny laughed. "Exactly. Thank you, Mister A.I."

"What's the name of your band?" Julia asked.

"Nightshade."

"Hey, I've heard of you."

"Really? You do the club scene?" Johnny said.

She nodded. "I go to a place in south Philly, the *Wooden Spoon*. They have live music, dancing, a bar. I'm there just about every weekend. That's how I stay in shape and blow off a little steam from time to time."

He looked at her - yeah, you look like you work out. You look good, really good. I think... I think I'll keep that to myself. This one probably gets hit on, so hitting on her is like... volunteering for target practice. Been there, done that. "I'll have to check it out. Lately, we've been playing at clubs out in the suburbs, or worse."

"Let's talk about money."

"Okay," Johnny said.

"How's yours holding out?"

Johnny pursed his lips. "Okay, I guess. This weekend we had three gigs, so I'm doing okay."

"Do you have a bank account?"

"One of today's errands," Johnny said.

"How much are we talking?"

"My cut from the band was about forty-five hundred dollars," Johnny said.

"Wow. You guys must be good."

"We'll travel for a good cut of the proceeds, yeah," he said. "There's other money as well."

"How much?" Julia said.

Johnny looked up, made a face. "A couple hundred grand."

"Two hundred thousand?" Julia's mouth dropped open. "You just got out of prison and you have two hundred thousand dollars? Do I even want to know how you got that?"

Johnny held up his hands, in surrender. "I'm clean; it was legit, all of it. Look, I love playing guitar, and I love guitars, so I'm always looking at them. I collect them, the older, the better. I go to flea markets, goodwill stores, outdoor markets, estate sales. If I spot an interesting guitar, I buy it, clean it up, and later, sometimes much later, sell it."

"Yeah, but that can't be making much money," Julia said.

"You don't think so? Okay, I have a Fender guitar that's seventy-three years old. I got it before I went on my secret mission for the government."

"Secret mission...?" Julia looked puzzled, then she laughed.

"Before I went away, I got it insured. What do you suppose it might be worth?" Johnny said.

Julia made a face. "Beats me."

"Three hundred and seventy thousand dollars," Johnny said.

"What!?"

Johnny laughed, then looked around the diner. "Yeah, that's what I said when I hear it. Now, guess how much I paid for it?"

Julia shrugged and held up her hands.

"Less than a hundred dollars. It was sitting in a wooden barrel in a goodwill store, in pretty good condition, with Chuck Berry's signature on it, in red felt-tipped pen. He was a famous guitarist a long time ago. I had the signature checked; it's the real deal."

Her mouth dropped open, and her eyes were wide.

Johnny smiled. "Now, that guitar doesn't need a bank; it's in a storage unit outside Philly, with several others. But I do need banking for some cash that I've got. And there's one other concern."

Julia waved a hand. "Banking's not a problem."

"I know," Johnny said. "But here's the problem - I just joined this band. There are three other members. They're terrific musicians, but they know nothing about money, or about other adult subjects - rent, mortgages, interest rates, insurance, taxes, all that stuff."

"Sounds like you need help," Julia said.

"Yes, so... can you handle the band's money, the income, the expenses, the record-keeping, receipts, taxes, all of it? Can you do that?"

"It'll cost you," Julia said.

"An arm and a leg?"

"Five percent of gross receipts," she said.

"And I don't want to pay taxes," Johnny said.

"Again, that's simple," Julia said.

Johnny sat up straight and stared at her. "Really? How is that simple?"

Julia glanced around to see if anyone might overhear, then she looked at Johnny. "Look, Congress thinks the IRS, and civil servants, and taxes, are all evil. So IRS guys get paid like shit and treated worse. As a result, they take the job, get trained up, then leave for the private sector. Now, the IRS lives on receipts. In an audit, you need to back up your tax return with a mountain of receipts.

"So manipulating the IRS means first, you save every receipt you can, relevant or not. Hell, try to collect them. Second, you underestimate your income, overestimate your costs. You offer receipts as proof. Third, if you're audited, you delay, so that the original agent leaves before resolving your case; then you have to deal with a new guy, an untrained guy. That guy, you pick his pocket.

"The drill is simple," Julia said.

Johnny thought about that for ten seconds, then said, "Okay, five percent. Done."

She smiled at him, and Johnny smiled back - I bet you look good naked. In fact, I know it. But now you're my accountant, and I'm your client. We have an official, arms-length relationship. So I need to behave myself, because I can find another woman. Maybe not as beautiful, not as smart, but much more workable.

And I don't need to worry about paying taxes. That's a huge plus, so let's not fuck this up; don't let your dick run your career. Okay, I can behave myself... while I'm sitting here trying to be an adult. I didn't see where this might go until it was too late.

I'm not getting the Boyfriend Vibe. Should I aim one of my bandmates at her? Like the drummer? The crazy drummer?

Nah. That's stupid. She doesn't need the help. Besides, she's not a girl for the drummer. She's not the type. Some women are bored with life; it doesn't satisfy their dreams. It eats at them. Those women look for men who are slightly crazy, hopefully entertaining, even funny, and not homicidal, i.e. drummers.

"I'm glad that's settled," Johnny said. "So... what's for lunch?" He reached into a stack of menus, handed one to Julia, and opened his.

***

High in the Woody, Alistair McLeesh stood at the window and stared out at New Jersey - it's amazing, everyone thinks of our neighbor in terms of industry, pollution, horrendous industrial smells, chemical plants. And they're not entirely wrong. But from up here out to the horizon, I see nothing but green, a forest that covers everything I can see. Oh, I can see nearby too, Camden and all that urban and suburban development. But move beyond that, thirty, forty miles out, and you're in dense, dark, green forest.

You know what the difference is? Here in Philly, it's a city. You're surrounded by people; you cannot escape them. The lights never go out. So you take a vacation, go to the beach, everyone loves that, right? But at the beach, again... you are surrounded by people.

But drop yourself in the middle of that forest, and it's just you and the local four-legged residents, several of whom will have you for lunch if you're not careful. So you need to watch yourself. But it's quiet in a way city folks cannot imagine.

And at night it's dark like they've never seen dark. It's black, absolute, unrelieved black. You cannot see your hand in front of your face.

I'm tempted to buy a piece of that. I'm always tempted to buy anything that seems nice, or valuable, or precious. If you have money, use it, don't park it. Yeah, that's wise, but if the news media caught wind of that, I would end up... wait for it... surrounded by people.

My presence would raise local property values. Oh, boy.

He glanced behind, then turned back to the view - this conference starts in fifteen minutes. The guys, and the girl, will begin to arrive in ten. I'll tell them, no actually, I'll have Mitchell tell them, that a test subject survived ELSEWHERE. He moved to a computer network, and we chilled his body; he spent a week in the computer. I'm told that from his perspective, he was there for a couple of years. That came as a surprise, though it shouldn't. I guess it makes sense.

Then we warmed him up, moved him back into his body, and woke him up.

And he awoke. And he remembered who he was! And where he had been. Eureka!

So it's full speed ahead on ELSEWHERE.

That's amazing news. And I'm happy about it. Real happy.

McLeesh grinned - yeah, that's right, Alistair. You done good. It's been a long while since I could admire what this place has turned into. There's been a steady stream of unimaginative, incremental innovations - a dating service, real estate listings, half-assed news listings, entrepreneur centers, blah, blah, blah. The data say these things make us money. But Jesus, sometimes I'm amazed that we've been able to stay awake and report for work.

But now we've got ELSEWHERE, an absolute bomb we are dropping on our world.

I must admit, I'm worried. ELSEWHERE scares me a bit. McLeesh frowned - no, let me be honest, I need to be honest, it scares me a lot. But it's okay. It's okay if your creation frightens you. It shows you're serious, that you're doing actual work, with a real impact on the world.

I spent a lot of money and political capital making this happen. I drop-kicked half of the senior management out the door, paid out generous severances to get these guys out of the way. And their crime? They were too fucking agreeable.

I brought in a battalion of people who, though unqualified, are creative. A few of them are bat shit crazy; at least, I think so. Most of them are just plain weird, even by my standards. So to rely on them, I have to be tolerant, and I have to encourage others to be tolerant.

Because these people are good to have around; they have ideas. They have imagination. Okay, much, maybe most of it, is insane. But some of the insane stuff might work.

Like ELSEWHERE.

Sometimes, they still surprise me, and that's hard to do. He smiled - I like surprises. I look forward to surprises.

It hasn't been entirely smooth; my managers despise each other. Of course they do, they're all different. They speak English and have little else in common. Some of them are hard-headed, quants, business people who follow the numbers. I value them. Others are artists, or psychopaths, who occasionally let us see into that dark, dangerous jungle growing between their ears. And I value them too.

A few of them are visionaries. They see into the future. I cherish those people.

In a couple of minutes, they will walk through that door, sit down, and we'll brainstorm this technology. What can we do with it? What are the possibilities? What are the big opportunities, if any? And what are the risks? And the big question - are there any existential risks for our company, our country, our species?

I already know the answer, but what exactly are those risks?

We need to make a thousand decisions, nearly all of them complex. I don't need to tell these guys, they'll be working overtime for a while. Let's see...

... Mikkelson will yak about the legal issues, disclaimers, corporate structure. He'll want us to be judgment-proof. He always wants that, and he can never have it. We're too big to be judgment-proof, so it's a waste of time to think about that. So you might wonder, why do I keep him around? Because we need to know what he knows, even if we choose to ignore it.

... Jensen is my greediest and simplest executive. He'll want to charge an upfront fee. I doubt that will fly in this case. Most people will be reluctant to try this. Do what? Are you kidding? Upload myself to an electronic network?

So let's not stand in their way, okay?

... besides, it'll be razor dash razor blade marketing. Give away the razor, gouge 'em on the blades.

... Ngomo will want to push this project in an international direction. And eventually we will. But I think first we need to show it can work on a small scale, so we'll start with the USA. We need to prove it to ourselves.

... and then there is Beckler. Hans Beckler, my German exec and madman. Hans is handsome, witty, multi-lingual, articulate, and by far the smartest and most dangerous exec in Willow, maybe as smart as me, maybe smarter. He's also crazy. The others work for Willow, but Hans works for no one but Hans.

His Willow contract is nothing but a cover.

Hans will want to form a commercial employment center and business center, so that ELSEWHERE can handle B2B commerce, corporate procurement, and all that. He'll want to tailor the rules and the environment so that ELSEWHERE can handle not only human uploads but also A.I.s. And why not? A.I.s are already electronic, they're already on networks, but they're limited, so ELSEWHERE could become a channel allowing people to interact intimately with A.I.s and extend what they can do and what humans can do.

The humans can teach the A.I.s... they'll even do it for free. Naturally, the owners of the A.I.s will pay a small fee.

At least, that's what I expect to hear from Hans.

ELSEWHERE is already set to be an atomic bomb. I know that much already. Whether it fails or succeeds, it will be big. We've certainly spent enough, hundreds of millions to pay off the families of the people who tried it and died. How many were there? I don't recall. Dozens, multiple dozens.

So it'll be a bomb, an atomic bomb.

Beckler, my brainy psychopath, would turn it into a thermonuclear bomb. A planet killer. And if it detonated and screwed up the world beyond recognition, Hans would apologize and say something like, well, okay, jawohl, that went badly, but to make an omelet, you must break a few eggs, no?

A weak smile crossed McLeesh's face - where did that German sense of humor come from, anyway? I mean, how did the Germans, back when everyone wore the fur of something they had killed, acquire that rich, twisted sense of humor?

His eyes were pointed at the forest, and he finally noticed the trees - ultimately, Hans will learn as much as he can about this kind of network. He will share just enough to perform his duties and meet expectations, then he will quit and set up a competing network, competing but better. He's got billionaire written all over his amoral self. He's not there yet; he will leave Willow to get there.

I would bet a million dollars he's already started that project.

He won't sign a non-compete, and if he did, I couldn't enforce it. He would sidestep it. Worse, he would smirk at me. And he'd be right. I need to figure out what to do about Hans.

McLeesh heard a sound behind him. He turned and smiled at an executive, his senior VP of Legal. "Hey, good to see you. Thanks for coming. How are things going?"

4. Unemployed

Friday after work, Jerrell headed home, vaguely but deeply depressed. He stopped in front of his door - there is no reason to feel down; nothing bad has happened. It did not help.

On the way home, he had stopped by the sub shop where he purchased most of his meals. As usual, he arrived on autopilot, thinking about Sonya, about Willow, about the Marys. When he walked up to the door and grabbed the handle to open it, the door would not budge. Jerrell came to an abrupt halt, grabbed the handle again and gave it a good, hard pull, and pulled a muscle in his shoulder.

"Ow! Shit! Son of a... "

In pain, he grabbed the shoulder and leaned forward to look through the glass. The shop was locked up and empty; he saw no one. Then he noticed the small note taped to the window, facing out:

CLOSED UNTIL FURTHER NOTICE, TWO EMPLOYEES UPLOADED. APOLOGIES FOR ANY INCONVENIENCE.

"What the hell?" Jerrell backed up to the sidewalk, staring at the shop as if hoping for a reprieve. But the shop stayed closed. He stood there - alright, I need to arrange some food, I could have it delivered, and pay a ridiculous delivery fee, or I could stop by the grocery and actually buy food for a change. Otherwise, what do I have at home? God only knows. I haven't thought about it in a while.

Jerrell muttered, "I've been busy, so who knows what's in my frig. I certainly do not."

When he got home, Jerrell laid his laptop on the dining room table and went into the kitchen, opened the refrigerator, and looked in the cabinets for food. There was some. He began preparing dinner - he boiled a small portion of rice in water and opened a can of tuna. Jerrell remembered, a man at the grocery store had asked, the tuna's for your cat, right? Jerrell had not answered him. When the rice was ready, he mixed in pepper and olive oil to season it, added the tuna, and pulled a half-empty jar of pickles from the frig.

That was dinner. Jerrell was soon no longer hungry. He sat there, staring at the wall - I should get out, go somewhere with a crowd, some place I can talk to a woman, or anyone. Anyone would do, anyone at all.

Weekends were the worst, two and a half days of a long void, a nothingness. Most of the time, he would strain to hear the sounds of the city coming into his apartment through the windows and walls. The rest of the time, the only sounds would be those coming from the TV - an internet broadcast, or a movie, or a soccer match or other sporting event - or the sound of water falling in the shower, or his feet padding softly across the apartment, or his voice, talking to himself, about the news, about Willow, about women, or the occasional fantasy conversation with Sonya, or with a woman who had caught his eye, to whom he had never spoken, though he might have wanted to.

Would you like it a little harder, or perhaps softer, my dear? Does this feel good, are you tired, should we take a break? I have a wonderful oil here; can I offer you a massage?

Just tell me what and where something hurts. I'll fix it for you.

But most of the sounds played against a heavy backdrop of quiet, like the sounds of his fingers on a keyboard, rubbing his hands together, wiping a paper towel across the screen of his laptop, or scratching an itch on his ear, or scratching his chin, the only place on his body with a few whiskers.

But he did not leave the apartment. He sat at the dining room table and opened his laptop, to do a little work, just enough to kill Friday night. But before he started, the laptop beeped, a notification, a text. Jerrell looked and saw it was from Sonya. His expression brightened for a moment - hey, maybe she wants to come over, or better, she wants me to go to her apartment. Maybe she wants to spend the weekend together; we could even go to the beach, spend a few days, sleep together, and wake up, and have breakfast together.

He opened the text to read:

Jerrell,

I've decided to upload to Elsewhere. I don't know, am I crazy? I'm frightened and excited and nervous and skittish, everything all at the same time. I want to thank you for being such a good friend, though this is not really goodbye. We can still keep in touch, and I hope you want to do that.

Anyway, wish me luck. I'll see you when I see you.

Sonya

Jerrell sat there, silent, unmoving, a stone likeness of a man, his eyes riveted on the laptop. He re-read the text, then read it again.

He sat there, still and silent, for what felt like a long time. Then he finally stood up and said, "Fuck this." He headed for the front door, to go somewhere, anywhere else, and do anything except sit in his apartment thinking about Sonya.

He walked half a block, turned to the south, and walked several blocks to Mountain Street, which was lined with residential buildings reaching two to three stories, except for a single block of commercial establishments, including a refurbished warehouse, the Metals Exchange. Passing it, Jerrell heard music, a single acoustic guitar, so he wandered into the warehouse, into an open space lined with food vendors near the walls and small cafe tables everywhere else.

Inside, he moved to the side, and stood there admiring the space and the activity. There were over a hundred people occupying some of the tables, sitting together in twos, threes, and fours, drinking beer and wine, eating, and talking. The far end of the space was separated by a two-story room divider made of heavy fabric. The guitarist was on the far side of the divider.

Jerrell stared at the people - okay, everybody is drinking, so let's find something to drink. Maybe we can blend in. He walked over to one vendor and asked for a bottle of red wine, a pinot noir, but the man behind the counter shook his head. "All we have is white."

Jerrell nodded. "Thanks, anyway." He walked down the line of vendors, found one selling red wine, and bought a bottle along with a complimentary cup in thick glass with METALS on the side. Jerrell moved to a table located against a wall, sat down, opened the wine and filled the cup.

He took a sip and winced. "Geez, I think I'll let you breathe a bit." He sat there looking around. No one noticed him, and he saw no one he knew. He finished the first glass, then poured a second. For a while, Jerrell watched the other people sitting in the Exchange, but he felt so isolated, they might as well have been a thousand miles away.

The tones of an amplified acoustic guitar washed over the space and the crowd. Jerrell forget about the crowd and listened to the music. As he listened, he sipped his wine.

When the acoustic music concluded to scattered applause, Jerrell's bottle was half full. Twenty minutes later, the quiet was elbowed aside by the scream of an electric guitar, offered with skill and energy and conviction. A pounding bass and percussion line followed, and throughout the Exchange, people rose from their seats and headed to the other side. Energetic rock and roll music echoed across the building, and in minutes fewer than twenty people remained at the tables; everyone else had moved to the music.

Jerrell was briefly tempted to follow the crowd and dance, but it occurred to him that he should drink the rest of his wine - I could share my wine, but if there were no music, would I want to sit here and drink the rest of it? He smiled - of course I would. So let us do that. Hopefully, the music will last for a while, at least another hour. Meanwhile, I will finish my wine.

In minutes, Jerrell's bottle was empty. He nodded, gave the bottle a consoling pat, and stood up. Then he wavered - by the Gods, I believe the wine has affected me. So I need to be a bit more careful. First, do not fall over. Second, do not bump into other people or into any of the furniture. Move carefully, with purpose and direction. And do not fall over.

Try not to look drunk. If not, then try not to look drunker than the other drunks. Do not fall over.

If you fall over, try not to land on concrete. Yeah, okay, that's workable. That, I can manage. I can fall into a table, if I need to.

Thus encouraged, he turned and carefully crossed the vast expanse of the Exchange. When he passed the room divider, the crowd noise and the sound of the music doubled in intensity and volume. He walked up to the dance floor, watched the other dancers for several minutes, then decided that he did not know how to dance as everyone was dancing.

The dancing was individual, not in pairs. Jerrell stared at the dancers - why, this is simple and rhythmic. Some people seem to be telling a story, others are simply shuffling their feet.

Understanding crossed his face - I know how to do this. This could be a *kathak,* like back in my village. It's got rhythm, and poetry, and it tells a story. Here, they call it blues, or rock and roll. Back home, they call it kathak. So let's do that.

Jerrell walked to an open section of the floor, faced the band, and began to dance a simple *kathak,* a dance to a story of a man whose parents arranged his marriage to a woman he did not love. At first, the man and his wife were unhappy, but over time, as he came to know her, he was able to relax and talk candidly with her. With time, he liked her, then loved her, and their marriage turned from a sadness and a burden into a wondrous expression of joy, admiration, and magic.

Jerrell stepped in a rhythmic pattern to the simple pounding of the rock music, then added the sweeping arm and hand movements of the *kathak*, capturing the emotions and desires expressed in the story. After a minute, he looked around the dance floor; several people, a man and three women, had moved close to him and were imitating his movements. Soon, they formed a recognizable group of synchronized dancers. Jerrell tried to watch them as he danced.

More people joined the *kathak* until several dozen were engaged in a rhythmic, syncopated dance. Later, after an hour of dancing, Jerrell realized that he was no longer intoxicated.

Eventually, he stopped dancing, though many others continued. A young woman called to him, "Keep dancing. It's beautiful."

Jerrell smiled at her and shook his head. He moved off the dance floor but soon realized she followed him and caught up with him. She touched his shoulder. "Hey, excuse me. What do the hand gestures mean?"

Jerrell turned to her. "The first three gestures show dissatisfaction and disappointment between a man and his new arranged bride. Like this..." He stood and showed her the movements. "The next three symbolize acceptance, friendship, and a love that develops between the man and his wife."

Wonder settled on her face. "Why, that's beautiful. So... the dance tells the story."

Jerrell nodded. "Yes. I am from India; there is much dance there, ranging from formal, disciplined classical dancing to informal dancing that is passed on face-to-face, within families or villages. It usually tells a story. Love, marriage, and children are common themes. Not much different from this place."

The woman's face shone. "That's wonderful. I'm so glad to meet you and dance with you."

Jerrell wondered, is this an opportunity? Could I get to know her better? She is gorgeous.

Then the woman said, "Well, thank you for the dancing and the explanation. I need to get back to my friends. Maybe I'll see you here again?"

"Yes," Jerrell said. "That could happen. In the meantime..."

"Meantime, enjoy your evening."

Jerrell smiled at her and nodded. "You, too."

He watched her turn away. He waited for her to turn around and look back, but she did not. After a long moment, he turned and headed in the opposite direction, to leave the Metals Exchange.

***

The weekend ended too soon. Jerrell spent a quiet Sunday thinking about kathak, and dancing, and rock and roll, and the friendly girl. He was looking forward to returning to the *Wooden Spoon*. On Monday, he reported to the Sunshine Cafe, set up his laptop, ordered a large cup of coffee, and as usual went to work on the Marys.

When he checked his emails, there was an entry from Rance Curtiss marked 'Confidential.' Jerrell opened it to read:

From: Rance Curtiss, Director
To: Jerrell Adri
Re: Termination

Jerrell,

I just heard about this, and I'm really sorry. I tried to argue your case, but the Company is in a cost-cutting phase, perhaps because Elsewhere ate up more resources than anyone knew.

I know you'll land on your feet. Good luck.

Best wishes,

Rance Curtiss

Jerrell's stomach took a twist - that doesn't sound good. The email had an attachment, which he opened:

From: Human Resources
To: Jerrell Adri
Subject: Termination

Mr. Adri:

It is with regret that we inform you that your position has been terminated without cause. The Company is reducing its cost profile, and we had to make hard choices to retain our most valuable employees.

You will, of course, receive the standard and generous separation and pension benefits, and please feel free to rely on us for a positive recommendation. We are grateful for your excellent work on behalf of Willow.

Good luck and Best wishes,

Incel Jerke
Director

As Jerrell was re-reading these messages, a new email appeared. He opened it to see:

NOTICE: YOUR EMAIL ADDRESS(ES) UNDER *.WILLOW.COM HAVE BEEN BLOCKED, YOUR EMPLOYEE PRIVILEGES REVOKED.

Jerrell tried to log into Willow's home software, but that returned a message:

INCOMPLETE USERNAME AND/OR PASSWORD. PLEASE TRY AGAIN.

Jerrell sat at his table, seething, angry, wronged - Willow couldn't keep me around because I wasn't one of their most productive people. Oh, really?

Jerrell suddenly felt like his skin didn't fit, like his underwear did not fit. He had an itch he could not scratch. Normally, after getting his coffee and his table, he'd be diving into work. But not this time. The software would probably not cooperate; he had no choice but to sit there and resist a well-ingrained habit.

It felt strange... and wrong... not to work.

"Fuck this. I need to get out of here." I need to get away from these people, these fat, happy, sedentary, overpaid tech people, who haven't gotten their termination notice yet. How many of them will escape this round of cuts? Well, that raises a related question - how many of them are more valuable to Willow than me? Of those I know personally, damn few, is the answer to that question.

He looked around the cafe at a dozen other people who evidently still had their jobs at Willow. None would meet his gaze - I guess it's my turn. We can only wonder when it will be your turn.

Jerrell picked up his laptop and went outside to the sidewalk. He turned for one last look at the Sunshine Cafe - I don't expect to see you again, Sunshine; in the meantime, take good care of the little bastards that guzzle your coffee. He headed east on Dickinson, muttering to himself. A few times he noticed passersby casting concerned looks in his direction - yeah, that's right, I'm one of those pissed-off people you see every so often, people who are having a really terrible, no good, very bad day. As he passed a woman, Jerrell noticed her staring at him and backing up.

He winced - great, I'm scaring people who had nothing to do with this. I'm the skinniest guy they've ever seen, and I frighten them. That's just perfect, thank you, Willow.

He kept walking at a rapid pace, to turn the anger and disappointment into energy, into harmless motion. Someone else might punch a wall, but Jerrell walked all the way to a small park facing the Delaware River. He laid his laptop on the grass, found a spot littered with small stones, picked up a few, and began throwing them into the river. It was exercise, mildly entertaining, repeating, metronomic, potentially violent yet harmless. Every so often he would spot some debris, a stick or a plastic bottle, and try to hit it with a rock. And he did that, once or twice.

The game ended when one of Jerrell's throws hit a bird in flight. The bird dropped into the river and did not move; he watched it float downstream with the other debris, his face a mask of horror and dismay - I cannot believe it, I didn't mean to do that. That bird didn't deserve that.

Willow deserved it. If I'm going to throw rocks, I should aim them at Willow.

Now, there's a worthwhile thought. I should examine that, turn it over, stare at it from every angle. Savor it.

He picked up his laptop, left the park, and headed for home. On the way, he stopped at a tiny convenience store and purchased a cheap cell phone, with telephone service, an answering service, and little else. He then went to the Exchange, ordered a soft drink, and sat down at a table. The crowd was thin; the Exchange would not get busy until much later in the day. Despite that, watching the crowd made him feel better. Most of them were not having a bad day.

Jerrell opened the laptop and maneuvered to the Willow front page - let's see, I need to pretend I'm a customer. So... my name is... Rebecca, Rebecca Smith... from Sandusky, Ohio, born April 1, 2061, I am twenty years old, and... I need a photo. A quick visit to a browser provided a photo, then a thought crossed Jerrell's mind - what if my photo is already on Willow somewhere?

Ah, I have it; I am Asian, Chinese, actually, not that it really matters, and I need a face that looks like a lot of other young, Chinese women. The A.I.s stumble over minorities, so, yeah, Asian. I suppose I could be a black, but then I'd have to deal with discrimination, and who needs that?

He returned to the browser, chose the photo of a young Asian woman, then ran a photo-check across the internet. The search returned half a dozen similar photos. Jerrell chose one of the other photos and repeated the process. This time, the search returned dozens of photos that were similar but clearly not identical. He looked at the photo - you will do, my dear; I bet you get a lot of 'have we met before?' You look like a lot of other women. You're forgettable... and perfect.

Well, this is interesting... you're still from Sandusky, Ohio, but now your name is Rebecca Yang. Becky to your friends, no doubt. American as apple pie. Your daddy writes software. Okay, Rebecca, let's check you out.

Jerrell filled in Rebecca's data and added her photo, a username, and the number of the second cell phone. He provided a password and explored Willow's network, where he built a record and encountered a dozen Asian women.

It took a while to contact one of them. Jerrell wrote, *Hi. I'm Rebecca. You look familiar to me. Have we met outside of Willow?*

The woman smiled and said, *Geez, I dunno. Why do you ask?*

Jerrell stared at her - you're rather weird, but then, some people are. *You look familiar. Maybe we met over music. You like music? What's your favorite?*

Music is good, but I don't have a favorite. Whom do you like?

Jerrell stared at the 'woman' and nodded - uh, huh, you're a young woman who likes music but doesn't have a favorite artist. A die-hard music fan would answer even if they had a dozen favorites. They'd pick one. And who says 'whom'? What kind of young woman says 'whom' on Willow? The same one that says on the phone, 'It is I, Rebecca.' She shows up in plays and Victorian novels, not in real life.

Jerrell's Rebecca wrote, *Say, I have another question for you*.

Okay, I'll answer if I can.

Are you an A.I.?

The 'woman' answered, *Me? An A.I? Why would you think that?*

Jerrell nodded, uh, huh, that's not a 'no.' *Okay, how about this? Have you ever killed a spider? How did that make you feel? Did you like it, or not? Are you afraid of spiders? Or maybe only just the venomous ones?*

That's a really strange question.

Jerrell's lips pursed. *It's okay, you don't have to answer. Thanks, Watson, I'll let you get back to it. Have a day.*

Jerrell broke the connection - apparently Willow took my avatars, ran them through an A.I. to introduce random variations in data, voice, appearance, and background. That took half a minute of supercomputer time. Then, after a cursory exam, Willow threw the results out onto the network.

Evidently, I took my job more seriously than I should have. I could have spent half the time, produced crappy results, and been paid just as much for just as long.

Wow, I feel like... like... such a sucker.

The Exchange had become more crowded, but Jerrell did not notice the crowd - so, Willow thinks a computer can populate its network with interesting people, people with whom anyone else would be happy to converse and interact? That's what they think?

Let's see, they've all studied 'How to Talk to Anyone.' You emphasize the three C's: compliments, commonalities, and curiosity.

There is an important difference between a person and an A.I. People get angry; A.I's do not. That is a biological reaction to perceived threats to safety or survival. One reason humans have not only survived but thrived on Mother Earth is that we instinctively use our large brains to devise interesting and painful forms of harm and death for those who threaten us. We intend that, at a minimum, they either die or remember the pain, so that thereafter they know better than to fuck with mankind.

That, of course, includes threats from lions, tigers, and bears. It also includes threats from other people.

I bet Willow's avatars are habitually and uniformly cheery, interested, and interactive. I bet they don't suffer from mood swings, bad days, misjudgments, even though real people suffer from all those things. They can talk to anyone, absolutely anyone. Many of Willow's customers are afraid to show too much of themselves on the network. They fear being hacked, or spied upon, or defrauded. Those secretive people would not get along with Willow's avatars.

Maybe they could exchange daily photos of their breakfasts. That seems harmless.

It would be interesting, I think, to discover how Willow might react, and how its customers might react, to a large collection of entities resembling real people, including the psychosis, faults, bad breath (or at least morning mouth), farts, cavities, phlegm, tumors, tremors, tantrums, streaked underwear, anger, jealousy, love, hatred, -isms, and all the other lovely ingredients that make *homo sapiens* such a cute and cuddly species.

Jerrell sat there staring and seeing nothing - the first thing I need to do is steal a massive amount of computer time. I cannot rely on Willow anymore, and my personal account will not be enough. I need to find computers, the larger the better, the faster the better, with an unusually low utilization rate.

That's easy. Cars and trucks, for example, spend most of their time parked, their processors idle. And they all have internet access. There are no doubt many other examples. Street sweepers run at night; school buses run twice a day, and almost never at night; strategic defense computers almost never run at their capacities, and hopefully never will.

Okay, I probably ought not to mess with the defense computers.

My work is about to take me into night shift.

And the new thought occurs to me - I know people who literally live on computer networks. Surely, they can help, if I need help.

I need to investigate. And I will. I suddenly have a lot of time on my hands. I need to beat up Willow enough not to feel bad about losing my job. I'll know when I get there, and I know that, right now, I'm not there.

I have work to do.

***

Julia waved her ring past the payment sensor, thanked the driver, and stepped out of the car onto the sidewalk. The building in front of her was 613 South 7th Street; she wanted 612. She turned and there it was, across the street, yet another four story brownstone with an exterior elevator grafted onto the front like a parasitic fish.

She pulled out her phone; 1:54 pm - okay, I'm early. No alarms, no notifications, so Johnny is coming. Unless he stands me up, but he doesn't seem the type. So let's just relax.

She looked up and down the street; it was quiet on a sunny day - are these buildings even occupied? She looked more carefully. Half a block away seemed unoccupied, but the buildings in front of her seemed inhabited - flower pots and curtains in the windows, mail sitting in mailboxes, a front door propped open, a child's bicycle next to the sidewalk.

A male voice said behind her, "Hey, darling. How you doing?"

Julia turned to face a young man walking towards her - great, here it comes, more south Philly charm. "Hi. I'm looking at an apartment. Can you tell me, where's the nearest grocery store?"

The young man stopped, surveyed her, and smiled. "I haven't seen you around. It's a nice block, I think you'd like it. Now, the grocery... there are three. The nearest is that way, right a block, then left. The best is three blocks past that one."

"Ah. Okay, thank you."

"I can walk you there, if you want. Give you the tour."

She shook her head. "No, thanks. I'm waiting for someone."

"Yeah, that figures. Okay, I hope you like the apartment. See ya 'round." He walked away.

She watched him leave. "Hey, why does that figure?"

He stopped, looked back at her, and shrugged. "I guess it's just... you're attractive." He smiled, turned, and walked away.

Julia watched him out of her peripheral vision. He did not look back at her. She frowned - damn, I am so horny I could chew marbles. I'm good looking, at least I think so. And he thinks so. I get hit on a lot. So you'd think I could find an acceptable guy to handle my needs. But I'm turning guys down. What's wrong with me?

Well, strangers approach me. I don't know them; they could be nuts, or nasty. Why risk it?

She stopped herself and grinned - okay, I can think of one good reason to risk it. Nonetheless, let's be careful here.

Julia crossed the street and stood in front of 612 - nothing's wrong with me. I just don't want to get stuck with a bubblegum guy, a guy who's adequate in the rack and dismal everywhere else. A guy who sticks to you because for him you're a great deal, a great catch.

The dumb ones are the worst. Quiet is okay, I can do quiet, but not stupid. I've tried that a couple times; my mouth gets me in trouble.

She looked up just in time to see Johnny turn the corner. He saw her, smiled, and gave a little wave. He walked up to her. "Hi, there. Am I late?"

"No, I was early."

He aimed a thumb and glanced at the building. "So, this is it."

"Yeah. Let's go inside, check it out." Julia pointed. "The elevator is right there." They headed in that direction, and Julia stopped at the mailboxes; all but two bore names. They entered the elevator, and Julia touched a button for the second floor.

Johnny said, "I need to find something soon. I can stay at the halfway house two more nights, then I'll have to sleep on the bass player's couch."

"Cutting it close, aren't you?" Julia said.

Johnny waved a hand. "Ah, I'm just looking for a room. Won't take long."

They walked down a hallway, past three doors. Julia stopped at the fourth, pulled out a card, and touched it to a sensor. There was a soft click, the door opened, and she entered the apartment; Johnny followed.

Julia walked to the middle of a large room that seemed to merge a living room and a kitchen in a nearly square area at the corner of the building, with six windows to the outside. She could see the building next door, look into a few of its rooms and into the row of brownstones across the street.

There was a hallway. Johnny went there, and Julia could hear him walking around; the rooms echoed with footsteps across wooden floors. In less than a minute, he emerged. "It's a bathroom and two bedrooms, next to each other. Several closets. Not bad."

Julia went to the kitchen and began opening and closing the doors of cabinets, drawers, the refrigerator, the microwave, and the freezer. She looked at Johnny, "Everything seems clean."

He rotated and scanned the apartment, then turned to her. "This seems okay. How did you find it?"

"My management company is closing some of their buildings and moving folks to others."

Johnny said, "Why are they closing buildings? What is it, rats or roaches?"

Julia looked at him. "You don't read the news?"

He looked sheepish. "I stay busy."

"A lot of folks in this neighborhood have uploaded to Elsewhere, so there are vacancies. Then the managers consolidate their rentals and close a few buildings, which saves on maintenance and utilities."

"That sounds like offering free rent to drug addicts."

Julia shook her head. "Actually, it's not. Many of the addicts are uploading, which the city encourages. I read an article. Addiction is a physical thing. The addict who uploads leaves the addiction behind. It's better than treatment."

Johnny made a face. "Huh. How 'bout that."

"But you don't want to be in a building that's near empty," she said. "You would just have to move again."

"Uh, huh. What's the rent here?"

"Six hundred a month, due on the first, five percent late fee." She looked at Johnny. "They give a discount for auto-pay."

"Wow," he said. "Julia, that's a steal. That's a steal, right? I'll take it." He returned to the hall. A moment later, Julia followed him and found him standing in the middle of a small room. He smiled at her. "This is perfect. I can put a bed and a couch in one bedroom, and in the other line the floors and walls with sound protection, and play."

"You don't use headphones for that?"

Johnny shook his head. "Not the same."

"So you want it?"

He nodded. "Definitely. Thanks, Julia. This helps. Six hundred for an apartment instead of a room. Yeah, this is nice."

"No problem," she said. They left the apartment and went outside. Johnny stood for a moment and looked around the neighborhood. It was quiet, the sounds of a bustling city in the background.

Johnny stopped and turned to her. "So now what?"

She looked up from her phone. "I'll text you an agreement to read and sign. You send that to the management company. They'll acknowledge it. Then you pay the deposit and the rent, and you're good to go."

"Okay. Anything else we need to do?"

"Before I forget, there is one thing, Johnny," she said. "With all the people we're losing to Elsewhere, clubs are losing business; a few are close to shutting down."

"Speaking of which, we'll be at the *Spoon* tomorrow night," he said. "You want to come? Have a beer after the show?"

"Funny you should mention the *Spoon*; I've heard they're in a bit of trouble," Julia said. "Not just from losing customers, but from losing staff."

Johnny was silent for a long moment. "This could be bad."

"Okay, consider this - your business model is to arrange one-night shows with music clubs and bars within, say, an hour of Philly? Right?"

He nodded. "Yeah. We'll go further if the money's right. I spend a lot of time making calls."

"Okay, you should consider a semi-permanent gig with a Philly club, play there every weekend."

Johnny thought about it. "Huh. You think the *Spoon* would go for that?"

"The last few times I was at the *Spoon* with you, the place was packed, Johnny. You're getting popular in south Philly. So yeah, I think they'd go for it; it makes sense."

Johnny grinned. "I like it. Okay, I'll approach them, see what they say."

"You want me along?"

"Yeah, I do," he said.

"So, what are you doing now?"

Johnny laughed. "Well, as to that. I need to get my stuff together; that'll be easy, I don't have much. I need a kitchen table, a couple of chairs, some storage stuff for clothes, some dishes, and a bed." He grinned. "And a couch. I've got some shopping to do, now that I'm a citizen."

Julia looked at him and almost asked him if he wanted help. But she stopped herself, and Johnny thanked her again, then turned and walked away.

Julia stood for a minute, then decided to walk the mile back to her apartment. She took a last look at number 612 and turned away.

She went south on South 7th. When she turned onto Tasker Street, east towards the river, the neighborhood suddenly looked like the set for a plague movie. Every first-floor office and establishment was closed; many were boarded up. In a few, the boards had been breached, shattered, and not repaired.

In one stretch of Tasker, Julia passed four blocks of silent, empty buildings; she tried to restrain a creepy feeling that grew stronger with every passing minute. Even the streets were empty. In the middle of a big city, which she could hear in the distance, there was little road traffic along Tasker, and as Julia walked, her head swiveled from side to side as she constantly checked her surroundings.

When she reached South 4th Street, everything returned to normal. There were people on the sidewalks and the front stoops, talking and telling stories, laughing, making wisecracks about friends and passers-by. The little offices were open, and normal traffic ran up and down the streets.

Julia arrived at her apartment building, no longer trembling. She promised herself - I'm not walking down Tasker again. Forget it. That was incredibly creepy. For a while there, I imagined zombies and junkies behind every corner.

She came to her door, unlocked it, and entered the apartment - this city has developed holes, empty neighborhoods where no one lives, no one goes, and no one leaves. I bet Elsewhere's behind all that. It's gotta be Elsewhere, right? What else would empty out neighborhoods like that? A war with China? A pandemic? An industrial spill?

No way. I would have seen any of that in the news.

5. Riding the Rails

Sonya settled into her seat in the third car. She reached into her bag, extracted a laptop, and set it on the fold-down table in front of her, then she nodded at the server who stopped by to offer her coffee.

The laptop powered up, and another keystroke brought a document to the screen, the comments, criticisms, and warnings of an A.I. and a human attorney regarding the contract with Elsewhere.

She glanced at the digital clock on her laptop - 9:32 AM. Outside, a crowd milled about the platform, half of them looking for the right rail car, the other half saying goodbye or hello. Sonya looked back at the laptop - twelve hours to Grand Forks, North Dakota. I'll use the time to check the comments again. I wonder what Grand Forks is like - empty, flat countryside, cold weather, the northern plains. So says the internet.

Do the native tribes still live up there? Or did they give up preserving their stone age culture? Last I heard, they were all running casinos and making mountains of money. Who knew?

Originally, Sonya had planned to publish several web pages devoted to 'Life on the network.' She chuckled at the memory - right now, as I sit here, one hundred million, six hundred and thirty-eight thousand, and forty-one people have uploaded to Elsewhere. So no, I think I'll skip the commentary, leave that to others.

There will be plenty of commentary.

She focused on the document - Willow's attorneys have climbed all over this thing, and it shows. There are pages and pages of contingency language, which shows that this was definitely a group effort, and I am definitely glad to be in customer relations rather than law.

Lawyers squeeze the joy out of everything they touch.

The A.I. summary was useful, though quite long - there are performance guarantees to handle system failures and screw-ups. If we lose your body, there's plan B; drop your body, plan C; etc., etc., etc.

There are electronic back-ups of your personality, just in case. Of course, we reserve a general and ongoing right to protect the Elsewhere community, based upon its 'collective welfare,' from criminal or malevolent or impolite or disruptive behavior, up to and including expulsion of offending parties, with disputes settled only by arbitration, as practiced under the rules of...

...blah, and blah, and blah.

We promise to comply with all federal and state laws, except that unions and other forms of collective behavior are not permitted and will be interpreted as a violation of this contract, remedied by expulsion of the offending parties from the Elsewhere community.

And on and on and on...

As the train headed north from Philadelphia, Sonya ignored the scenery of unrelenting urban landscape, most of it consisting of low-rise small cities and towns. After Harrisburg, they left the cities and zoomed across rolling forests whose air seemed choked with birds. At the Ohio line, the landscape flattened, and Sonya sat there staring at the plains of northern Ohio, followed by the plains of Indiana, and Illinois, and Iowa. She had never seen such landscape, miles and miles of crops - corn, wheat, alfalfa, silage - broken occasionally by a tree or a bush or a flower.

The Mississippi River was a vast shock, a rolling, pulsing flat landscape of rippling brown water, surrounded on both sides by runny, slidy, slurpy trees, bushes, and grasses all bending in the same direction, downstream, bowing in obedience to the occasional whimsical flood of the mighty river.

Sonya stared for an hour as the train passed through floodplains. The scenery reverted to flat grasslands, gradually replaced by isolated fir trees, then groups of trees, and finally forests stretching for miles in Minnesota, North Dakota, and beyond.

In the early evening, the train slowed and quietly rolled through Grand Forks, a small city of three- and four-story buildings; Sonya's eyes drank in the scenery - when the landscape and the buildings are flat or low, does that make the sky look bigger? That makes sense, doesn't it? There's less sky blocked, more sky to be seen. She noticed a local monument, a simple obelisk marking the peak water levels from floods of the nearby Red River; some were higher than she was. The river seemed to flood twice a century. She scanned the landscape and tried to imagine it covered by an ocean of pulsing, running, brown water.

The train exited Grand Forks three miles from Willow's Elsewhere facility. Sonya wondered - why the hell did I have to come all the way out here? The answer arrived almost immediately - of course, they're going to store my body, and those of others as well. They want cold weather; I'll bet they have other facilities up in Canada.

Thirty-eight degrees Fahrenheit, just warm enough not to freeze the cells. So you'd like a mean temperature in the thirties, as in Calgary, or Edmonton, or Saskatoon.

Elsewhere had built its own train station, marked by a massive sign: WELCOME TO ELSEWHERE. Customers were instructed to remain seated at the last stop. Sonya looked around, only a few people stood up to disembark when the train finally stopped moving. She stared - huh, some folks are actually traveling to Grand Forks.

Geez.

Most people in Sonya's car were uploading. The passengers waited for several minutes. Two humanoid robots entered the car, one at each end, and began talking to each person, verifying their identities. When they finished with a person, a printed sheet emerged from the bot's 'stomach,' and the bot moved on to the next person.

When the bot stopped at Sonya's seat, it said, "Hello. Please smile." When Sonya did that, the bot said, "ID verified. Now, please read the contents of the screen." A viewscreen on the bot's 'chest' lit up with: 'You could not pay me enough to live in Buffalo.'

"You couldn't pay me enough to live in Buffalo," Sonya said.

"Repeat, please, leaving out the contraction."

Sonya repeated the phrase, correctly this time.

"Thank you." The bot printed a small sheet of paper and handed it to Sonya.

She took it, turned it over; it was covered in icons. "What's this?"

"Instructions," the bot said. "Touch one of the icons."

Sonya did that, and a hologram emerged to hover over the paper; it showed a local map of the station, with markers for hotel rooms, police, information, lockers, and ticketing.

Sonya touched the icon again, and the hologram disappeared. "Wow. They spared no expense."

"We aim to please," the bot said. It moved on.

Sonya stood, slung her bag over her shoulder, and headed for the forward exit. Off the train, she met the reality that the hologram failed to capture, a wall and a wave of chaotic activity and sound. The crowd on the platform was dense, with people moving in every direction. The terminal building was massive, a dozen stories planted atop an equally large truck and distribution facility. It dwarfed Grand Central Station and every other train terminal Sonya had ever seen. An air terminal and two parallel runways were next to the train terminal.

Sonya maneuvered through the crowd, entered the ground floor of the building into a large foyer, five stories high, centered on a fountain in the middle of a broad, open space with restaurants, cafes, and bars along high walls. She sat down at a small, open cafe table and ordered coffee from a server bot.

The bot took the order, then paused. "You here to upload to Elsewhere?"

Sonya nodded. "Isn't everyone?"

"Yeah, otherwise, why come here of all places, right?"

"That crossed my mind," Sonya said.

"Don't be afraid of uploading. You'll be fine."

"You don't talk like any bot I've ever seen."

The bot flashed electronic eyes at Sonya. "I'm not, not really. I uploaded three weeks ago and took a job to pay the user fees. That's why I'm running this server bot."

"Wait a minute," Sonya said. "You're a... a person? A human?"

The bot bowed and said, "Correct. Born and raised in Alpena, Michigan. I've been in Elsewhere two weeks."

"I thought everybody used A.I.s to control mechanisms, like bots, cars, heating and cooling, all that stuff."

"Sure. Willow used to do that," the bot said. "But when people started uploading to Elsewhere, that enabled Willow to use people instead of A.I.s. That's often better than using software. So they started offering jobs and paying people to work."

Sonya thought about that. "You said Elsewhere has user fees? I thought it was free."

"Entry is free, but there are lots of apps and enhancements; they're worth it. They charge for some of those, most of them in fact. That's why I took this job."

Sonya stared at the bot. "So here you are, back in the middle of people. You could have done this without uploading, couldn't you?"

"Not like this, I couldn't. Waiting tables is just one of my jobs; I've got three others."

"Four jobs? Really? That's pretty hard to believe," Sonya said.

"Believe it," the bot said. "Remember, in Elsewhere, your natural speed is electronic, not the slow speed of a human. In this conversation, for instance, it feels to me like there are twenty to thirty minutes between our responses. So being here is kinda like sitting at a computer with several windows open. Every so often, something happens at one of the windows, and you have to react to it. It's not multi-tasking because it's not simultaneous. It might feel simultaneous to a human, but not to an uploaded human. You skip at high speed from one subject to another."

Sonya was staring at the bot. "That's amazing."

The bot flashed its eyes. "I think so too. That's why I do it. For example, while I'm talking to you, I'm taking a cooking class, learning how to make sauces. For that, I connect to a restaurant in Nice, in France. And I'm taking a psychology class in California, in Los Angeles. I'm also running the electronic controller of the heating/cooling system in an elementary school in Jackson, Mississippi."

"So... you speak French?"

"I just learned it; that was another class," the bot said. "Anyway, Elsewhere is amazing. Listen, I've got to run. I'll grab your coffee. Cream and sugar?"

"Just sweetener, not sugar."

The bot left and a minute later returned with a container of coffee, several packets, and a porcelain cup. The bot said, "Good luck in Elsewhere." Before Sonya could answer, the bot sped away.

The next day, after a good sleep, Sonya reported to a medical office for the upload. The paperwork had been completed. The technicians verified her identity and gave her drugs to clean out her digestive system; she spent an hour in a bathroom. When she emerged, the technicians x-rayed her, then gave her a pill and sent her back to the bathroom.

Eventually, the techs were satisfied. They gave her a shower and dressed her in a plastic suit with a hood and a zipper that ran from her groin to the top of her head. They asked her to lie on a wheeled gurney, lowered the zipper, and a tech began connecting electrical leads to her body and her head. Then they connected an IV bag with a watery solution to her left arm.

Sonya lay on the gurney, struggling to stay awake. A tech stood over her and said, "Okay, Sonya. You're ready to go. Now, you can still change your mind. If you don't, we'll give you something to help you sleep. Then we'll transfer your mind to Elsewhere. When the transfer is complete, you will perceive the environment through the apps you've selected. It will feel like you've closed your eyes and the apps are on the back of your eyelids. There will be a visual app. Do you remember its icon?"

"Yes, it's an eye," Sonya said.

"That's right. Activate that and you will see this room, and your body on the gurney. You can watch us zip you up and prepare your body for storage."

"Yes, I will watch."

"Alright. So, should we proceed? Upload you to Elsewhere?"

Sonya took a deep breath and looked at the tech. "Yeah. Let's do it."

"Okay, enjoy the trip."

Sonya felt a warm sensation, starting in her legs and moving up her body. When it reached her face, she fell into a deep sleep.

***

Alistair McLeesh walked into his office, sat down at his desk, then swiveled in his chair to face the ocean. A hundred yards beyond floor-to-ceiling glass, the Atlantic hurled itself against massive rocks. He smiled - I could watch this all day, but it is not meant to be.

"Holmes, you with me?" he called out.

A female voice emerged from speakers in the ceiling. "Yes, sir, I am here. I am always here."

"Don't get cocky," McLeesh said. "And try not to brag. What do you have for me?"

"Your net worth fell below two trillion dollars yesterday," Holmes said.

"Uh, oh, do I need to skip a few meals? Hamburger instead of steak?"

"Hardly. The Commerce Board of investment managers shows that most expect the Fed not to raise rates next week. In addition, there is an action item that I should mention: it is likely that elderly people, given declining health, will flock to Elsewhere. So I recommend selling your real estate in Florida and New York. That way, someone else can enjoy the falling prices."

"As to the Fed, the picture's a bit of a mixed bag at the moment," McLeesh said. "I think they're right. As to the real estate, do it."

"Actually, sir, I already did."

"Oh, well. Okay. Anything else?" McLeesh said.

"I need to mention, no criticism intended, but subscriptions to Elsewhere have been growing fast," she said.

"And that's bad?"

"I realize you feel proud. Your new baby has turned into a huge success."

"Yes, thank you," McLeesh said. "I think so, too."

"Yes, well, the difficulty is that if a hundred million people upload to Elsewhere, it will be a macroeconomic event. The economy will react as one would expect to the sudden loss of a hundred million employees and consumers," she said.

"Geez, really?" McLeesh said. "Yeah, when you put it that way, it sounds bad."

"Some sectors will be hit particularly hard. To take a simple example, thirty percent of the subscribers are elderly. Many of them are afraid of dying, and they might see Elsewhere as an ideal solution."

McLeesh nodded. "Sure. The folks who work there think so, too."

"Yes, well, then you won't mind if I withdraw your money from the healthcare sector," Holmes said. "We're going to lose some of the biggest enterprises there. And even the survivors will take a hit in the stock markets, when people think things through."

McLeesh froze - the big insurers? The big hospital chains? But I guess that's right. They feast on elderly customers, and we're taking those away. "No not at all..." he said, then he stared at the ceiling. "but... you did that already, right?"

"In fact, I did, and I may want to move some of your other investments. Elsewhere is going to lay a walloping hit on most healthcare enterprises, especially the big ones. I fear the stock market reaction."

McLeesh shrugged. "That's okay, but keep the tech, right? And the biotechs?"

"For the time being, but don't get used to it."

"Okay, anything else?" McLeesh said.

"Four software manufacturers are suing Willow for patent infringement," Holmes said.

"What did we do this time?"

"We might have infringed several network patents," Holmes said.

"Might have? Are we a little guilty, or very guilty?"

"Just a little," Holmes said. "I think."

"Okay, then we could argue the matter without looking stupid and greedy. Have our lawyers fight their lawyers." He paused for a few seconds. "So... we'll let them have a bit more of the Elsewhere business. That ought to shut them up for the time being," McLeesh said. "But Holmes, before we go too far here, ask Ms. Jefferson to bring me a cup of coffee and a Danish."

"Yes, sir."

"Thank you. Proceed," McLeesh said.

"China's economy took another hit."

"Yeah, they haven't figured out why consumers are important. They talk like they understand, then they revert to form and do something stupid. Old habits die hard."

"Yes, sir. Moving on, the Russians moved a motor infantry division into Afghanistan."

McLeesh swiveled away from the ocean and stared at the ceiling again. "Again? So... they managed to piss off Iran and Pakistan. And maybe India. But not China."

"Sir, all four countries issued public statements opposing the invasion," Holmes said.

"They weren't invited to tag along?"

"Into Afghanistan? No, sir, they were not."

McLeesh chuckled. "Another habit that dies hard. Well, that's of no consequence. When your enemy does something stupid, don't interrupt him. Next?"

"Those are the big macro events, sir. The rest of the news is not worth your time," Holmes said.

McLeesh spun in his chair - oh, I don't know... I enjoy hearing about the latest buxom starlet heading into rehab for the fourth time. I cannot help but wonder what, other than drinking, she does with her spare time. I think I won't mention that.

As that moment, Ellie Jefferson entered the office with a tray holding a coffee service and a Danish roll on a plate. "Good morning, sir."

McLeesh looked up at her. "Hey, Ellie. How are you?"

"I'm fine, thank you. And what are you doing today?" she said.

"I don't know yet; we were discussing the news," McLeesh said.

Holmes said, "Hi, Ellie. Actually, Mr. McLeesh is attending a directors' meeting in Philadelphia this afternoon."

"Is that right? Yeah, that's today, isn't it?" Ellie said.

"Yes, Ma'am," Holmes said.

"Well, that's certainly brave of you," Ellie said.

McLeesh looked at her. "Eh? Why's that?"

"There's a hurricane offshore. Have you noticed the surf is rough this morning?" she said.

"Yeah, I noticed that."

"You might encounter some... chop... at thirty-five thousand feet."

McLeesh looked at the ceiling. "Holmes, you might have mentioned that."

"That is not a macro event of any importance, sir," Holmes said.

"Speak for yourself," McLeesh said. "When my ass is strapped into that can of spam that's bouncing around like a ping pong ball, trust me, it's a macro event." He paused. "Okay, Ellie, thanks for the coffee and the roll. I don't have anything else for you. I expect I'll be flying back this evening. I'll let you know."

"Very well, sir. Have a good day." She left the office.

"So, Holmes. What time is take-off?"

"One-fifteen. Half an hour in the air, half an hour to the HQ, half an hour of margin."

"Alright. Can I wear a leather jacket?"

"Sir, you are the CEO, you can wear whatever you wish. The others will be in standard business wear," Holmes said.

"I was hoping to exploit my lofty position, but okay, I'll wear a suit," McLeesh said. "By the way, who sponsored the meeting?"

"Mr. Beckler, sir."

"Of course," McLeesh muttered - my greedy Nazi, Mr. Beckler, Hans to his friends, if he has any. I am tempted to skip this meeting, not that it's not important. Directors' meetings are important, sometimes very important. But Hans is predictable - he is focused on money and firmly believes that the ends justify the means. Hans wants to be a billionaire, and he will be, one of these days, if he can stay out of prison.

This guy's fortune has range. He could get rich, or he could go broke. He hasn't thought things through. Few people do, even people who make a billion dollars. That's new money for you. They never ask, how much is enough? They think more is better, more is better, repeat as necessary, more is better. And in the board game of commerce or monopoly, more is better. That is how we keep score and play games.

And okay, I know, I should climb down off my high horse. That used to be me.

But money no longer gives me the erection it once did. And it's not just age, either. My erections are doing just fine, thank you.

But they don't come and go for money anymore. There is no practical difference between one billion and two hundred billion dollars. Except, of course, two hundred billion means you have to hire more staff and you need better personal protection; you're more of a kidnapping risk. Your ransom goes up, by a lot, so that attracts more people trying to collect it. That's a negative. Beyond that, in either case, you're a rich asshole.

Try to be worth it. Some of my friends tell me that. They say, try to be worth it. But that is ridiculous. Nobody is worth two hundred billion dollars, regardless of what the accountants say. You don't think so? Here's a thought experiment for you: how many people, how many of your friends, given the choice between your ongoing, steady, faithful friendship and devotion, would choose you over two hundred billion dollars?

Face it. And be honest. Damn near everyone would take the money. The exceptions are probably psychotic.

Economics calls it revealed preference; in our example, your friends probably prefer two hundred billion dollars to you. It immediately follows, in the hearts and minds of those closest to you, that you're not worth two hundred billion dollars.

So forget that; it's crap.

As a corollary, you have an unlimited opportunity to buy friends. So, having savored that thought, do you still trust your friends? In addition, let's admit - the friends you can most likely trust are those with more money than you. And for that reason, it's likely they don't entirely trust you.

I know, I know, you'll almost certainly say that you trust your friends, but seriously, do you? Be honest. Well... try to be honest. It's normal to have a few doubts.

McLeesh swiveled again and stared at the ocean waves crashing against the rocks; good God, why am I talking this way? This sounds like depression. Or hypochondria. Maybe psychosis. I'd worry that this might be a sign of decay, early dementia, or Alzheimer's, except that last week my doctor, having run every test known to man, pronounced me healthy as a horse.

I flew to Switzerland for all that, money no object. My ass still feels like a pincushion. It's still sore.

The good news is, I'm healthy, unless I jump out of a window or walk in front of a truck.

Hmmm... I've been a tech titan for a couple of decades. Is this just boredom? Is that my problem, that I'm bored? That's really stupid, since I do a lot of stuff that I don't have to do. I've got money, so I've got options, lots of them.

I need to think about this.

***

Jerrell awoke on a Tuesday afternoon, normally a dull day, a nothing day, the workweek grappling for traction. But this one would be a challenge. He showered and dressed and had breakfast and brushed his teeth. He checked his social media accounts to see if anyone had tried to contact him for work.

He had no messages.

Two cups of coffee later, Jerrell took a deep breath and muttered, "Okay, let's do this." He logged onto Benjamin Software, opened up Greta 1.0, and sat there waiting for the program to load.

Jerrell's mind wandered - would Asimov expect this? Would he approve? I bet Herman Kahn would understand. Asimov would say, stop right there, your avatar doesn't satisfy the rules of robotics. Yeah, that's right, Isaac, Greta is going to piss all over the rules of robotics, especially the ones about obeying and also not tolerating harm to any human.

She'll obey me, maybe. I'm designing her to harm Willow and a whole bunch of people who deserve to be harmed.

But face it, Isaac, your rules didn't make sense when you wrote them, and they certainly don't make sense now. You identified the problem and came nowhere close to a solution. You would say, I think, that robots are tools. Well, humans make a variety of tools, many of which routinely harm humans, and nobody notices. It happens every day. For example, automobiles, fighter jets, guns, circular saws, stairs, guardrails, jet skis. Most tools have the potential for harm, and many, like guns, are designed to cause harm.

Herman Kahn would understand; malevolent or harmful robots fit nicely with his theories on thermonuclear war.

Of course, a lawyer would give it a different spin: if you make a bot that harms a human, your ass is liable for damages. That's a different approach, less theoretical, more pragmatic, more concrete.

Jerrell looked back at the screen - this will be a fuller version of Greta, in 3D, with a psychometric profile, likes and dislikes, speech, implanted memories, and a good deal of pattern processing.

I can hardly wait.

Finally, the video clarified, and Greta 1.0 sat there in the middle of the screen, blinking. "Uh... where the fuck am I?"

"Hi, there. You're at Benjamin Software for the moment. Are you comfortable?"

"That doesn't compute. Comfortable with what?"

"Oops. Sorry, let me fix something," Jerrell said. He activated the video channel for her. "There, is that better?"

She sat there blinking, then she focused and looked down at herself. Then she stared straight at Jerrell. "What the fuck? Where are my goddamn clothes? What kind of sick shit is this?"

Jerrell laughed nervously. "Again, sorry." He hit a key, and now Greta was dressed, in a gray corduroy dress that apparently started life as a different color. Jerrell winced and swore under his breath. "How's that? Is that better?"

"Where the hell did you learn about clothes? Do you dress yourself? I mean, corduroy? What am I, eight years old? I think I might have looked better naked," she said.

Jerrell held up a hand. "We can dress you later; those will do for the time being. I'm just trying to make you comfortable. How are you doing?"

"I don't know; I'm still a little confused. Who the hell are you, anyway?"

"My name is Jerrell. I'm a software writer; I created you."

"Why did you create me? Since I showed up naked at first, maybe you're one of these lame-ass momma's boys? You know, the guy who designs his own personal doll toy while sitting safely behind a screen? That definitely doesn't compute." She had been staring at the ceiling; now, she stared at Jerrell.

"You start with the existential question. Good, that's good," Jerrell said. "Here's my answer: I want to get to know you, and when I do, I'll put you on a social network where you can interact with people, with others on the network."

"Why the fuck would I want to do that?" She aimed a malevolent expression at him.

"I don't know; it's an environment where you could thrive, I think," Jerrell said. "Otherwise, why do you want to do anything? Speaking of which, what do you like to do? Do you have any hobbies, or favorite subjects, or favorite people?"

"I guess I like money. I like having clothes to wear, food to eat, that kind of stuff," she said. "I like being warm; I hate being cold. I guess I like fights, and fires, and explosions. Car crashes, accidents, plane crashes, that kind of stuff. I like things that go 'boom,' you know."

"Why do you like all that?"

"I don't know," she said. "It's exciting, I guess. It turns me on; it doesn't compute, but it excites me."

"Do you like spiders?" Jerrell said.

"No. I'll smash 'em if I can... unless..."

"Unless?" Jerrell said.

She gave him a sly smile. "Unless they're stinging some other insect and eating it. I've seen that a few times; that's really cool. I think it'd be cool to be a spider. They're patient, they know how to wait, way longer than you or me. And then, when the time is right, they move, and 'zap'!" I like to watch 'em poison other insects, especially other spiders. It's like Battle of the Titans, two spiders, both large, both venomous, in a fight to the death - the winner lives, the loser is food. I like that. It's cool. It's real."

Jerrell froze the program and sat back. He took a deep breath - Jesus, Mother of Gods, this one is... terrible. And it's hard to take. It's amazing, though, how well the embedded memories took hold. Jerrell laughed - combative spiders, Battle of the Titans, geez.

The loser is food. Jerrell grinned, then ran a hand through his hair and chuckled - I love that.

Jerrell activated the program again. "Where were we?"

"Talking 'bout spiders."

"Yeah, that. How about friends? Do you have any friends?" Jerrell said.

"Yeah, I got one, although..." Greta looked pensive for a moment, then looked at Jerrell. "I don't actually know if the guy is a friend. Maybe he was once, but no more. Does that count?"

"Sure. That counts. Got any good stories?" Jerrell said.

"I don't know. I try not to judge. Doug, his name was Doug."

"How did you meet him?"

"Drinking in a bar," Greta said.

"What was he like?"

"I don't know. I guess... he was kinda a fat, sloppy, dirty guy. Seems to me, he always needed a shower, not that it would have helped much. He was just a stinking, fat, dirty guy, shower or no shower. And I know, that doesn't compute."

"So where is he now?" Jerrell said.

"Beats me." She looked at Jerrell briefly, squinted. "To be honest, we didn't part on real good terms, so I don't know where he is."

"How come? Did something happen?"

"Well, we were at a bar, drinking. And it's late. So he said to me, hey, come outside with me, okay?" Greta said. "And I remember thinking, why the fuck do that? The beer's in here. What's outside that's so interesting?"

"So what happened?"

"Well, I thought, why not? It's not like we're leaving. We can always come back," Greta said. "So I followed him outside, and he walked around to the back of the place, then he turned around and told me he wanted to fuck me."

Greta wore a bored expression. Jerrell said, "Go on."

She continued, "Yeah, well, I remember thinking, really? At least he asked. That's more than I expected, so I dropped my pants, and he dropped his. But then I changed my mind 'cause he didn't have a hard-on. He had this pathetic, limp, little dick, and I thought, what the fuck? So I kicked him in the balls, hard, twice."

"Great Gods."

Greta looked to the side and nodded. "Yeah, it was depressing."

"So what happened next? Was that the end of it?" Jerrell said.

Greta shook her head. "No. He doubled over and fell to the ground, then he puked all over himself. So I'm thinking, enough of this shit. I don't want to be near a guy who just puked on himself. That vomit smell makes me crazy. So I pulled up my pants and went back inside for another beer. When I finally left, he was gone." She wore an expression of patience and disgust.

Jerrell took a deep breath. "That's an interesting story. Listen, Greta, it's been good talking to you. I have to go now, but we'll talk later, okay?"

"Yeah, sure. Whatever." She looked away.

Jerrell logged off and sat at his dining room table. Jesus fucking Christ! She's horrible. And fabulous.

She'll do nicely, but how much of this can I take?

A bit more, I can take a bit more.

6. Johnny B. Goode

Jerrell walked down Mountain St., past the businesses. The sidewalks were busy with young people in ones, twos, and threes, out for the evening, enjoying the entertainment and the free time. After walking a block, he realized - I'm not intoxicated. Not at all. It's possible to dance away the effects of alcohol.

Unless, of course, you drank way too much, way too fast. A freshman mistake. Jerrell thought back to his freshman year in college, to an unfortunate incident involving a case of cream ale and a ride in a car with its back door open.

He shook his head to clear it.

Rather than walk straight back to his apartment, he took a detour along Passyunk Avenue, a noisy, brightly lit kaleidoscope, with heavy traffic, crowded sidewalks, and numerous restaurants and clubs open late, feasting on the evening traffic.

Jerrell returned to his apartment late in the evening. Normally, he would get ready for bed at this hour, but he was not sleepy, not at all. He sat at his dining room table, glancing occasionally at his laptop sitting there.

His mind wandered across dancing, Willow, Sonya, and women - that girl at the Exchange, I wonder if I'll see her again. She talked to me; she was friendly. It was fun... and different. She was there with friends; it seems everyone has friends.

But I don't. They have friends; I have acquaintances.

And Sonya? Sonya is in Elsewhere now. How is she doing? Will I see her again?

He snorted - does it matter?

There was a sudden knock on the door, sounding loud against the evening quiet. Jerrell turned and stared at the door - what is this? When has anyone ever knocked on my door? And this late in the evening? What's with that? He chided himself for not installing a camera; it had never seemed important. But now, there was someone on the other side of that door.

A male voice came from the hallway, "C'mon, open up, I don't have all night."

For a moment, Jerrell did not move - someone's here, and they're not trying to hide. Maybe it's okay. He stood up - I hope I don't end up regretting this. He walked over to the door, reached out, and opened it. A young man stood at his door, staring at Jerrell. He had blond hair, a bit shaggy, and corded muscles in his shoulders and arms, uncovered by a sleeveless shirt with

POWER
CHORDS
ROCK

on the front of the shirt.

"Hi, my name's Johnny. You live here?"

Jerrell nodded. "Yes, of course. My name's Jerrell."

Johnny looked beyond Jerrell at the apartment. "Jerrell, okay. Yeah, I've been trying to find this place. I was at your party last night."

Jerrell was surprised. "Party?"

"Yeah, you know - drinking, dancing, fucking, all that fun stuff. Can I come in?"

"Uh..."

"I have beer, and I'll share." Johnny slid past Jerrell and entered the apartment. Carrying a twenty-four pack of beer cans in one muscled arm, Johnny stopped and looked around, at the long couch, at the easy chair, at the dining room table, with its four chairs and a laptop.

Johnny took a step towards the kitchen, then stopped and turned to Jerrell. "I'll put this away. You want a beer?"

"Actually, I don't..."

"... drink this brand? So... you drink beer for the flavor?" Johnny stared at Jerrell, then shrugged. "Good luck with that." He reached into the pack. "Here." He extracted two cans with one large hand, handed one to Jerrell, which Jerrell accepted, then turned away and went to the kitchen. Ten seconds later, he was back in Jerrell's living room. "Yeah, I was here last night. That was a good party; I passed out in the middle of it, which I almost never do. I wasn't drunk, but I was wiped out. I've been on the road for the past month, more than a month, and we made a mountain of money, but the travel and the hotels and the driving, that all gets old, you know?" Johnny waved a hand in time to the list. "Sometimes we have to sleep in the truck, which sucks."

He looked at Jerrell, who stood there, silent.

"You have no idea what I'm talking about, do you?" Johnny said.

"Uh... not really."

Johnny nodded, then he pointed. "I slept in that chair. You mind if I sit down?" He took a step and sat in Jerrell's easy chair.

Jerrell stood there staring. Johnny said, "Have a seat. Relax. I apologize if the beer's a little warm."

An exasperated look crossed Jerrell's face. He sat down in the middle of the sofa. "Listen, this is a mistake. I don't know you; I've never met you..."

"You just did."

"... and I can assure you, there was no party here last night, or ever."

Johnny's eyebrows went up. "No parties ever? What... are you opposed to parties? Is it a religious thing? I mean, it's okay if it is, you know. I try to be tolerant and all that, though frankly, religions that don't let you dance and fuck are just plain weird. At least, I think so. I mean, who'd want to join that? And where do they get new members? And... and... if they don't dance or fuck, why would anyone want them as a member?"

"No, I'm not opposed to parties," Jerrell said. "But I know for a fact that I didn't have a party last night. And I would know; I'm the only one living here."

"I have an apartment. You live alone? Me, too. Well, kinda... not counting whatever women are around. I know a lot of groupies."

"Groupie?" Jerrell said. "They like groups?"

Johnny shook his head. "No, no. Women who hover around music groups. Around bands. Groupies. Sometimes, they'll fuck you just on the off chance you might become a rock star someday. Then they usually do something stupid, like marrying an accountant with a bald spot and a short dick."

Johnny took a brief drink of beer and mumbled, "But maybe that's intentional. Some women don't like sex." He shook his head. "Weird."

Jerrell's eyebrows took off and his mouth dropped open.

Johnny looked at the beer in Jerrell's hand and motioned with his beer can. "You know, that beer's not getting any colder."

Jerrell looked at his beer, opened the tab, and took a drink. He winced.

"You don't like beer?"

Jerrell's mouth went sideways. "Maybe it's an acquired taste."

"Yeah, like eighty-five million guys have acquired it." Johnny sipped his beer, then stared at Jerrell. "So there was no party here last night."

Jerrell shook his head. "No. No party last night or any night."

Johnny shrugged. "Okay... I could be mistaken. Maybe someone has an apartment identical to yours; I guess that's possible." He looked around the apartment. "You have spartan tastes, almost as spartan as mine."

"Just the necessities," Jerrell said.

"Yeah, just those." Johnny took a long swig of beer, then looked back at Jerrell. "No art on the walls. You got a girl?"

Jerrell shook his head and took another swig of beer.

"Not at all? Really?" Johnny said.

"I thought I had one," Jerrell said. "I was nuts about her. But she wasn't nuts about me."

Johnny made a face and took another sip. "That happens."

"Yeah, but it was a mistake. She was an idiot. It was a mistake to get involved with her," Jerrell said.

Johnny shrugged. "We all make mistakes. Especially when they're blond and gorgeous, and you're what... twenty-four? That's what life is about. Make a mistake, take a shot, fail, learn, fix it, move on. That's what growing up's all about, man." He sipped his beer. "Did you fuck her?"

"No."

"No? Not ever?"

Jerrell shook his head.

"Did she suck your dick, at least?"

Jerrell laughed. "Sonya?" He shook head vigorously. "No way."

Johnny made a face. "Did you grab her ass, fondle her?"

Jerrell shook his head.

"You didn't fuck her, you didn't fondle her, she didn't suck your dick, but you fell for her," Johnny said. "Sounds like you two were made for each other. Two idiots. She sounds like one, though you don't. At least, you don't talk like an idiot. That's odd, don't you think?"

Jerrell's mouth went sideways.

Johnny sat up straight. "Alright, that was low." He held up a hand. "I apologize. Don't let it bother you. Sometimes I like to run my mouth. Anyway, love and lust make people do stupid things; you're not the first. So why didn't you fuck her, anyway, or do anything fun?"

Jerrell held out both hands, one holding a can of beer. A helpless gesture that spilled a little beer. "I don't know, she never came close to approving of that sort of thing, you know."

"So she didn't encourage you. No strokes, no affection," Johnny said.

Jerrell almost laughed. "Yeah, right." He took a swig of beer.

"You know, that's a problem," Johnny said. "But there is a magic word you can use to correct the situation when a woman does not want to be touched, when she does not want affection."

Jerrell looked at Johnny and smiled. "A magic word. Really. What is it?"

"Goodbye."

"Goodbye?"

Johnny nodded. "Sure. You move on. You know, many women, maybe most, like being fondled; they like being touched. And many of those same women like sex, at least if you know what you're doing, which, admittedly, some guys do not. Or so I'm told. Many women will fuck you if they like you. You don't need to be special. You just need to have a gentle touch and listen to them, talk to them. You need to be likable." His voice rose to a higher pitch on the last word.

"Easy as that?"

"Easy as that. So what is the Ice Queen's name?"

Jerrell grinned, then chuckled. "The Ice Queen. Sonya. Her name was Sonya."

"You know, we've been talking as if Sonya is history. What's with that?"

Jerrell shrugged. "She is history. She uploaded a few days ago. To Elsewhere. You know what that is?"

"I heard a bit," Johnny said. "It's people putting themselves into an electronic network. Instead of just visiting, you can live in the wires."

"Yeah, that's right."

"Living as an electronic file. That's what someone said. I don't know why a normal person would do that. How old is Sonya?"

Jerrell made a face. "I don't know, exactly. Early twenties."

"Oh, man. Do you have her picture?"

Surprise crossed Jerrell's face. "Actually, that's a good question. I do not."

"Is she fuckable?"

Jerrell chuckled. "Until you get to know her, yeah."

"An odd choice, to upload when you're in your prime, early twenties. Wow." Johnny shook his head. "Maybe she was tired of waiting for Mr. Right. Maybe she thought there was no Mr. Right."

Jerrell nodded. "I wouldn't know."

"When a woman decides you're not Mr. Right, she rarely changes her mind... well, maybe sometimes, twenty years later, when it's too late. Some women who look great in their twenties look like shit in their forties. Life's hard on a woman, especially if she has kids."

"I believe that," Jerrell said. "Do you have a woman? A special woman, I mean."

Johnny looked up, thinking, then shook his head. "A special woman? No, I can't say I do. I have women friends. Sometimes they're willing to fuck me, other times, they're fucking somebody else, and we're just friends. And sometimes they're not fucking anybody. Anyway, at the moment, nobody special."

"When you first got here, you mentioned being tired. Tired from what?" Jerrell said.

"I play guitar for a living, in a band. We play blues, rock and roll, funk. I write a song once in a while, and sing a little too. We've been touring for the past month, living out of a van, going from place to place, playing the same music every night. It's good money, but living on the road is weird. You see people at every performance, then you go somewhere else, fifty or a hundred miles away. Some of them like you and follow you a bit, so you see them at two, three gigs in a row. Then you go to the next gig, and they're not there. At some point, they all drop off the tour."

Johnny tipped his beer can up and drained it. "It's a cycle; it happens again and again. And the day comes when you just run out of gas." He emptied his beer. "You get sick of the constant moving, the strangeness, the monotony of playing the same shit every night. That's when it's time to come home. Two days ago, that was me. So here we are. How's your beer?"

"Fine, it's fine," Jerrell said.

Johnny rose to his feet, went to the kitchen, and returned with two cans of beer. He extended one to Jerrell, who took the can and set it on the coffee table.

For the first time in the evening, Johnny was silent. Jerrell sat there, thinking.

Johnny said, "So what do you do? This is a nice place, you've obviously got some money."

"I used to write code for Willow." Let's not get into my mess with Willow. I'm dealing with it.

"Wow, working for one of the big guys," Johnny said.

"Yes, that is me," Jerrell said.

"And so you know people who work at Willow," Johnny said. "There must be women there. They don't mess around?"

Jerrell shook his head. "Women are a minority, and the ones at Willow rarely date the guys at Willow."

"Uh, huh," Johnny said. "They don't want to get a reputation, any kind of reputation, that might affect future promotions. So they have a great job, lots of money, and no fun. I bet they're flabby."

Jerrell shook his head. "No, they're not. Willow has a gym in the headquarters."

"In the Woody, you mean? That thing?"

"Yes. The gym is usually busy, most often with women."

"Do they dance?" Johnny said.

Jerrell thought for a moment. "Beats me. Not that I know of."

"Right. They exercise, but they don't dance. Oh, yeah, Willow sounds like a lot of fun."

"It's a pretty serious place," Jerrell said.

The two men sat silent for a minute.

"You're a musician," Jerrell said.

"Yeah, and I run the band. I schedule the stops, write a few songs, sign the contracts, watch the money, and pay the guys. Fire somebody if they don't deliver. And a few other things."

"So you're a manager, too. It sounds busy... and fun," Jerrell said.

"It is fun. Music, dancing, beer, women. What's not to like?" Johnny said.

Jerrell was quiet for a long time. "You know, I've always been attracted to academic stuff, and I studied software in order to write software, to work in tech. But that might have been a mistake. It can be interesting. There are lots of puzzles, and I like that. I like puzzles. But it is not fun."

Johnny raised his hands in resignation. "Welcome to the world, Jerrell. Most guys work to make a living. Me too. Most don't like their jobs. But I like what I do. A lot."

"Yeah, I guess I like what I do, but not a lot," Jerrell said.

"The good news is, you don't work twenty-four hours a day, do you?"

"No," Jerrell said.

"So, learn how to have fun in your spare time."

"Yeah, I'm going to work on that," Jerrell said.

Johnny laughed out loud. "You're going to work on having fun. That just sounds wrong."

The two men talked into the night, then into the middle of the night. At three a.m., Johnny said, "Okay, my man, I'm getting tired, so I think I'll hit the road. I'm sorry to bother you with the party thing, but I'm glad I stopped by. You might be unsuccessful with women, but you're an interesting guy. I think you'll do fine, once you learn to relax a bit."

Jerrell chuckled. "I agree. I think that's my problem. I'm serious, and I overthink... well, just about everything."

Johnny nodded and stood up. "Listen, maybe I can help you with that. The next five Saturdays, we'll be in south Philly at the *Wooden Spoon*, over on south seventh. I'll put your name on the guest list; just tell the guard you're on Johnny's list, and he'll let you in. The party starts at nine and runs until about two. It's a good place, you might like it."

Jerrell stood up. "Okay. Yeah, I'll do that. I'll see you Saturday."

Johnny held out his hand, and Jerrell reached to clasp it. Johnny's hand felt like a rock.

"See ya 'round." Johnny turned and left.

***

Sonya, or, more accurately, her avatar, which resembled her, sat on a bench before the ocean and read her book, 'Thoughts on Art and Life,' by Leonardo da Vinci. The book began with an apology by da Vinci for the complexity and poor organization of the material, essays on da Vinci's thoughts and speculations.

It was a large book; apparently da Vinci did a lot of thinking.

She came across a passage near the beginning that made her stop and re-read it several times before proceeding:

'Recognizing as I do, that I cannot make use of subject matter which is useful and delightful, since my predecessors have exhausted the useful and necessary themes, I shall do as the man who by reason of his poverty arrives last at the fair, and cannot do

otherwise than purchase what has already been seen by others and not accepted, but rejected by them as being of little value.'

Sonya re-read the passage again - why, da Vinci was modest. He was thoughtful without being competitive. Or arrogant. Is that what it is like to be a person whose mind is a fountain of ideas, a raging torrent of thought? Perhaps that kind of thinking would leave little time for our lesser instincts, like jealousy.

And he knew how smart, how incredibly smart, he was. Otherwise, why bother shopping what others have rejected?

Can that be right? She looked out at the waves, watched ridges of water form, approach silently in long lines, attacking relentlessly like a Roman army, one battalion after another, curling at the top and crashing against the sand with a pulsing, repetitive roar, the ocean assaulting the land.

Sonya stared at the surf - it is very comfortable here, by the sea. I could live here.

The oceanfront address in Elsewhere was a standard item, freely available to any customer, yet it seemed not to be popular; as far as Sonya could tell, she was alone on the beach.

She had learned to use the video, audio, and Explorer apps. The last seemed designed to bury the user in information. The app used Boolean search; the mountain of information was not a feature of the app but simply reflected the size and complexity of Elsewhere.

Sonya smiled - this isn't Mayberry; it's Manhattan, or maybe Shanghai. Elsewhere is massive.

For a while she had struggled with planning her life in Elsewhere, then she solved that problem by ignoring it. The problem was too vast, too complex, and besides, with rare exceptions, you do not plan your life, you live it, you play it by ear, experiencing life as it unfolds. And if things somehow go wrong, and you have to re-evaluate and change course? Then you have wasted time. But in Elsewhere you have lots of time.

So just live. Experience Life.

Sonya decided to sit down, relax, and read the classics. Thus, da Vinci. She had already read everything written by William Shakespeare, Charles Dickens, and Mark Twain. She was just getting started.

There were many, many books. Most recently, Sonya read 'David Copperfield,' in three minutes of Animal World time.

Sonya remembered beaches, visited as a child, later as a young adult, with parents or with friends. This beach was different. She could see the water and the sand, watch the views, and the birds, and the occasional dolphin or game fish leaping from the water. She could see the clouds in the sky and watch the sea breeze blow sand across the beach, but she could not feel the breeze on her cheek or smell the clean, weedy scent of ocean spray.

Elsewhere did not have an app for smell or touch. Sonya smiled - they're working on it; I'm sure they're working on it, but they don't have it yet.

Maybe that's no surprise. I know a bit about software, and I have no clue about how to write an app for scent or touch. Perhaps that requires deep knowledge of biology.

Hey! That sounds worthwhile; maybe I could do that. Anything useful to Elsewhere but difficult to provide would be worth studying. If I could figure that out, I could go back to Animal World, make a pile of money, then come back to Elsewhere. In fact... I don't need to go back to Animal World. I could do the work from Elsewhere.

I have to think this over. Maybe I should spend less time on the classics and more time on biology. Or biology and genetics and cybernetics. Or God only knows what other damn thing.

Of course, it is possible that it cannot be done. After all, the people in Elsewhere are not biological entities; they are electronic files. However, the counterargument is that those files have been designed to mimic the human brain, and to some extent, human senses. After all, we can see, we can hear. Why would we be unable to smell and to touch?

I need to learn about this.

Sonya laughed - and if not, then I can always return to the classics. She was about to return to her book, when she spotted another person approaching. She stared for a moment - it was a young girl, a slender teenager wearing a loose, light dress that blew in the breeze and clung to one side of her body. Her brown hair blew in the same direction.

Sonya waved, and the girl changed course and approached. When she came near, she said, "Can I share the bench with you?"

"Of course, my name is Sonya."

The girl sat down on the bench. "Marie."

"Welcome to the beach," Sonya said. "How are you liking Elsewhere?"

The girl looked at Sonya. "I just got here, so I'm still learning my way around. But I like it. Actually, it's a lifesaver. Back in the real world... "

"Animal World?"

"Yeah, everyone here calls it that, don't they? Back in Animal World, I was dying. The doctor gave me three to six months to live. So uploading saved my life."

"How old were you when you uploaded?" Sonya said.

"Seventy-six."

Sonya's mouth dropped open, and Marie laughed. "Yeah, well, I had the option of uploading as a fat, decrepit old lady or a slender, graceful teenager. It was not a difficult choice."

Sonya stared at her. "It didn't even occur to me to change my appearance when I uploaded. But that's right isn't it? I remember seeing the questions in the uploading process - what do you want to be? How do you want to look? I just chose the default, which is the original me, and forgot about it. I guess at the time I was mostly nervous about uploading."

Marie smiled. "You can choose. Even now, you could contact the admin and make a different choice if you wanted to. You could be old, young, black, white, whatever. But I think you're beautiful as you are. If I looked like you, I wouldn't change."

"I'm not thinking of changing, but who knows? I could change my mind, I guess. Maybe it would be interesting to be a guy for a change." She looked at Marie. "I always felt that guys got a better deal than girls did."

Marie nodded. "Me too. I love being a woman, but I think guys got a better deal. At least, back on Animal World."

"But you know... " Sonya said. "Now I think about it, it'd be pretty weird being a guy."

"Might be interesting," Marie said. "Have you met any guys here?"

"I haven't met anyone here," Sonya said. "Except you. I'm still learning my way around. I spend most of my time thinking about what I want to do here. Do I want to work? Do I need to make money to stay here? What do I want to do? I haven't even thought about a social life."

"So you haven't tried to have sex here?"

"I haven't had sex anywhere. No, wait. I take that back; I did it, one time, back on Animal World."

"And how was it for you?" Marie said.

"Forgettable." Sonya said, then burst out laughing. "I'm sorry, I should be more forgiving, more tolerant. But I gave it up to a fat guy. I assumed he knew what he was doing, but he didn't. So, I spent the evening losing my virginity but accomplishing nothing else."

"I went to an orgy here, on Elsewhere," Marie said.

"And?"

"Well, it was enjoyable, I suppose; it was kinda fun, I guess, but mostly it was strange. It's a bit like watching porn... no, I take that back; it's a lot like watching porn. Have you ever watched a porn movie?"

Sonya shook her head.

"Okay, with porn you're sitting there watching two other people, or sometimes more, having sex. And they're getting all revved up, all excited, maybe slightly crazy. And you think about being one of them, and maybe you get all revved up, too."

"Huh," Sonya said. "Maybe I should try it."

"It's cheaper and more available, but less fun, than the real thing. Anyway, here on Elsewhere, you go to an orgy, and you won't know the other people. Everybody's a bit shy, but eventually someone gets naked, then everybody gets naked, and they start fooling around and kissing and so on and so forth. And at some point, you're having sex with someone, and he's inside you, pushing in and out. And maybe he's getting all revved up, right?"

"Just like the real thing," Sonya said.

"Yeah, except it's not like the real thing. You don't feel anything. Not physically, anyway. You can see and you can hear, but you're numb to touch. It helps to have an active imagination, but there's a limit to just how excited you can become. At least, that's what it's like for me. Kinda disappointing, really. I need touch to get excited. Otherwise, it's just a cartoon."

"It sounds dull, maybe boring the second time around," Sonya said.

"I think so. They definitely need to improve that... and you know what? I'll bet they are working on it. It'll be expensive, too."

"Well... it might be fun to do it as a guy," Sonya said.

Marie shrugged. "You'd run into the same problem, but I suppose anything's possible."

"You know what else is weird, at least I think it's weird?"

"What?"

"We're all homeless," Sonya said. "Everybody on Elsewhere is homeless. There are so many things we no longer need. We don't need sleep, we don't need food, or water, or warmth. I bet we could even do away with clothes if we wanted to."

Marie laughed. "You know, that never crossed my mind, but you're right. Another weird thing. I used to enjoy decorating my apartment, but on Elsewhere that hasn't even crossed my mind. What's the point?"

Sonya was silent.

"Have you bought any of the enhancements on Willow?" Marie said.

Sonya looked at her. "Enhancements?"

"Yeah," Marie said. "You know. Improvements in software. For example, there is an apartment app, if you wanted to live in an apartment like you did back in Animal World. Or there's better vision, better hearing, or a photographic avatar instead of an animated one. There are even avatars that let you look like someone who was famous back on Animal World."

"I haven't seen those," Sonya said.

Marie nodded. "There are a million enhancements, but they cost money, and some are expensive. Some people are taking on jobs on Elsewhere, so they can afford the enhancements."

"There are jobs on Elsewhere?"

"Sure, there's a marketplace where you can buy whatever's available. Part of that is a job market; there are postings by workers looking for a specific job, and there are postings on the other side, jobs looking for a worker."

"What kinds of jobs are there?" Sonya said.

Marie tilted her head and looked at Sonya. "There are millions of jobs. If you can imagine someone wanting work to be done, any kind of work, then you can be sure that it's posted somewhere on the Marketplace. There are even jobs that would have you working back in Animal World."

"What? Why would I do that? I just left!" Sonya said.

Marie shrugged. "Why not? It's all the same stuff. You'd still be living in Elsewhere, but working in Animal World. For example, someone might have a limousine but not trust the driving bots. So you offer them a cyber-person from Elsewhere. Better than A.I., the cyber-person drives the limo, makes some money which lets them buy Willow's enhancements."

"That seems circular," Sonya said.

"Everybody wins, except the poor schmuck on Animal World who developed the A.I." Marie laughed. "One thing is certain, you have to hand it to Willow. They're like a bank; they always get paid first. They might be a crappy social network, but they sure know how to turn a dollar."

Sonya laughed.

"Are you religious?" Marie asked.

"Oh... not particularly," Sonya said.

"Uh, huh. That's a 'no.' I'm not either, but sometimes I wonder if heaven, or maybe hell, is like this. A place where you can go anywhere you want, do anything you want, but you don't have a home, or a village, or a country. You don't have a routine or a schedule. There's nowhere you have to be. You just float along... forever."

"Well... do you still have a cellphone?" Sonya asked.

"Yes! You're right," Marie said. "That's my anchor, the damn cellphone. How weird is that?"

"That's your connection. It's not actually a phone; it's another avatar. Elsewhere thought of everything."

"Speaking of which, would you like to exchange numbers?"

Sonya nodded and smiled. "Definitely." The two pulled out their phones and touched them together. Sonya checked her contacts and said, "Got it. So, listen, if you feel lonely or you're just looking for someone to talk to, or if you hear about a good party, I hope you'll give me a call."

"I will," Marie said. "Likewise." Marie stood up.

"See you later."

Marie nodded and continued her walk down the beach, and Sonya returned to her book.

***

Sonya found a comfortable spot in south Philly, an internet cafe in Elsewhere on the site of what had been a coffee shop on Animal World. She remembered the place warmly, and liked it; it was familiar and comforting. The layout, of course, differed from the coffee shop; the cafe did not sell coffee, or coffee cups, or ground coffee, or stuffed toys, t-shirts, or anything with the company logo on the front. Instead, they maintained a dozen work stations which would display two- and three-dimensional representations of Elsewhere addresses.

The cafe offered information without the need to actually visit the address. And that was convenient, because Sonya was shopping, oh, not for anything specific, just for the sake of looking to see what was available on Elsewhere. She was collecting information and enjoying it every step of the way. The cafe and similar establishments offered excellent access to Elsewhere's marketplace.

Sonya had been a young, beautiful, stylish woman on Animal World, so shopping was familiar and comforting.

She sat there looking at a grid, each element a good or service or offer. There were thousands - my God, I see what Marie meant. But it's a waste of time to sort through all these. Surely there's a search function.

At that moment, a search window appeared, conveniently empty.

Sonya saw it and smiled - okay, that's more like it. Now, let's see. Suddenly, 'sales and promos' appeared in the window. Sonya tilted her head - sure, sales are good. Let's see what you've got. She hit a key and again saw a dense grid of alternatives, each in its own little window, but her search was interrupted by a single, simple notation in pink letters: SEX.

Sonya laughed out loud, then looked around quickly to see if anyone else had noticed. No one had.

She stared at the pink letters, then shrugged - sure, why not? I mean, what can this possibly be about? Is this just an ad for the local orgy? Maybe one specializing in weight-lifters? She laughed again and clicked on the item, and a young woman appeared, reminding Sonya of one of her elementary school teachers.

The woman spoke in a low, droll voice. 'Eventually you will discover that Elsewhere is an emotionally sterile environment. Lacking an app for touch, Elsewhere is a major disappointment for those accustomed to emotion, closeness, and touch, and sex, and all those lovely person-to-person things that many of us now miss.

'Our market research reflects this. In Elsewhere, men and women do not bond to the degree that they did back on Animal World. That's terrible! And unhealthy!

'Fortunately, help in on the way. Our scientists, working diligently night and day, cannot produce appropriate men to serve as boyfriends and lovers." The woman smiled. 'Oh, we're working on it; we're just not there yet. But we can offer the next best thing, and here I am referring to That Thing, The Big One, The Big O, The Mouth Wide Open Ecstasy that you might have cherished back on Animal World. Well, we've brought That, That Thing, to Elsewhere for the modest price of $899.99.

'That's right, we can offer you self-service sex, for the woman who is temporary marooned on Elsewhere without a convenient and cooperative companion to keep her happy above the waist and below.'

The woman stood there for a moment modeling a bright smile while the corporate logo flashed on the scene, then she said, 'But wait, there's more! For those willing to compose a brief, candid review of our fine product, we offer a ninety percent discount to the unbelievable price of just $89.99!'

She jumped into the air like a cheerleader on amphetamines and exclaimed, 'How about that!'

Sonya hesitated - I don't actually know what I'm buying; I don't think I've ever had an orgasm. Some of my friends swear by them; they tell stories about them, yet I've never had one. Some of my friends do It to themselves; others rely on a partner. I never did It to myself, and the one time I had sex, It wasn't fun, and It certainly wasn't an orgasm.

So this app might be just what I need.

Sonya downloaded the app, then jumped to her usual beach. She chose early afternoon on a warm, sunny day. Gulls rode the wind over the surf, waiting for an incautious fish to wander close to the surface. Sandpipers scurried about on the sand, like they did back in Animal World, digging for shellfish as the surf receded, then fleeing up the sand as the waves rolled in.

Sonya enjoyed the scene for a moment, then turned and looked up and down the beach. She saw no one. She was alone.

Her expression brightened - I have this place all to myself. And I want this to be perfect. So, let's see. She looked at the surf, removed her clothes, and walked over to where the surf was ebbing and flowing. She lay down on the wet sand where the waves would roll up to her feet and legs.

She lay on the sand for a minute, relaxing herself, thinking back to a beach in Animal World, under a warm sun, with gentle breezes and a foamy surf. Then she closed her eyes and activated the app.

For a long minute, nothing happened. She felt nothing. She thought, okay, don't panic, this is just the first time. And, for the first time, she touched the spot between her legs, but she felt nothing from that. Then things started to happen. She began to feel a vague tingling in her skin, in her legs; soon everything was tingling. Then she heard sounds, like running water, like wind in her ears, the sounds of fluids moving at speed. The backs of her eyelids displayed a shifting, kaleidoscopic pattern of colors. She began to tremble; her arms and legs were shaking and moving. Then everything tickled, and Sonya giggled. These effects became more intense, and lasted for long minutes; then they faded and finally disappeared.

Sonya lay on the sand, surprised - is that It? Is It over? That was an orgasm? Well, it was fun, I guess. I guess I enjoyed that. I must admit, I was expecting something more compelling, more powerful, breath-taking, even. But I guess that was fun. It certainly was different.

And being at the beach is always enjoyable, so that didn't hurt.

Some of my friends back on Animal World described It as a near-religious experience, burning bush, and all that. This was not that.

She heard, "Sonya?" She pushed herself up on her elbows and turned to see Marie approaching. Sonya said, "Hi, there."

Marie walked up wearing an amused expression. "Hi. What's going on? Is this a nude beach, now?"

"Oh, I'm just relaxing. I bought a new app, and I was trying it for the first time. I thought maybe taking my clothes off would help."

"Yeah? What kind of app?"

"The ads say it gives you an orgasm."

Marie tried not to laugh, then she covered her mouth and giggled. She struggled not to smile, or grin. She started to speak but then stopped and soon stood there laughing. A minute later, she said, "Sorry, that just sounded funny."

Sonya stood up and put her clothes back on. "That's okay."

"Well? How was it?"

Sonya tilted her head. "I don't know. I'm not really sure."

Marie's eyebrows rose. "Not sure? Well, have you had an orgasm?'

Sonya shook her head.

"No? Never?"

"No."

"Ah, ha," Marie said. "Well, that's unusual."

Sonya frowned. "My family might have been quite uptight about anything below-the-waist."

"I see. So you never had sex, or played with yourself?"

"I had sex, once," Sonya said.

"But no orgasm," Marie said.

"No."

Marie shrugged. "Well, that happens. I had sex several times before I learned to relax and enjoy it."

"But then you enjoyed it? It was fun?"

Marie nodded happily. "It was a blast. Get the right guy, a recreational guy, and sex is the most fun I can imagine having. It was a big part of why I wanted to have a guy around, you know, a permanent guy, my guy."

"Wow." Sonya stood silent for a long minute.

"But you need the right guy."

"Did you ever do it to yourself?" Sonya said.

"Geez, hundreds of times. That's a backstop, a consolation prize. It's fun, but the Beast with Two Backs is better, way better."

"Yeah, I never did that."

"So... what was it like? This app, I mean?" Marie said.

"Oh, it was okay. There was a tingling, tickling sensation all over, and the sounds of rushing water, and rushing wind in my ears, and a video show on the back of my eyelids."

"That's it?"

Sonya nodded.

"Did you forget where you were?" Marie said.

"No."

"Were you trembling, and shaking a bit?"

"Maybe a little bit."

Marie made a face. "Did you pass out, or pee, or cry?"

Sonya made a face. "No, nothing like any of that."

Marie pause and stared at her for a long moment. "That doesn't sound like an orgasm. A little o, maybe, but not the Big O."

"No?"

"No," Marie said.

"Well." Sonya looked out to sea and stood there silent for a long time. "Anyway, that was the app. Thank you for your comments. I have to write a review, and this has been helpful."

Marie nodded. "Always glad to help, but I think the best place to find sex is back on Animal World. Look at it like this... most software people are guys, most of them are socially awkward, so... what are the odds that they'd be able to put together a sex app that actually worked?"

Sonya nodded. "I guess I've been too optimistic."

"Yeah, maybe."

7. Hacking and Hoping

Jerrell sat at the table, staring at his laptop while his third cup of coffee cooled. A version of Greta - he labeled it Greta 2.1 - stared at him out of the screen. She was enhanced, with changes in her hair, lips, language, voice, likes, and dislikes. She shared with the original Greta a high degree of candor, aggressiveness, and a taste for making statements that would elicit a strong emotional response.

Jerrell had inserted a new feature - Greta 2.1 was opinionated. Adding that feature required a ton of work, but when he first saw it on display, he laughed. The Latin version of Greta 2.1 had popped up on screen and declared, "Brassieres are silly, more male nonsense, almost as silly as women's shoes. If women wouldn't stuff themselves with tortillas and donuts, their breasts wouldn't sag."

When he heard that, Jerrell laughed, then he thought, really? Can that possibly be true?

The opinions could involve anything - sports, fashion, religion, men, women, sex, food, baseball... anything. The general architecture was simple: program the avatar to make a declarative statement about the general environment, then connect it to the quality of a person, make it personal... and loud.

Thus, to a male listener, "baseball is for girls... now rugby, that's a real sport...

"The President is a moron, which makes her voters even dumber than she is...

"Alabama is better than the moon; okay, not by much, but at least it has oxygen...

"Am I misinformed, or do most Texans have brown teeth?...

"Few Christians quote the Bible because few Christians read the Bible, or anything, really...

It took more work to extend the quality into questions and irony, but the results were well worth the effort; thus,

"Do people like you?...

"Do you live with your mother... do you remember her name?... do you pay rent, or are you still sucking tit?...

"What was your last job...?

"Do you have a checking account...?

"Have you ever used a passport...?

"Do you read..." or,

"Honestly, don't you read...?

"Where did you learn to speak English... they don't speak much English there, do they?...

"You don't date much, do you...?

"Do you ever eat a vegetable...?

"Do you have a dentist? Have you gone in the last year?...

"When did you last bathe... did you use soap, or dish detergent?...

“Hi, there. Pleased to meet you, as long as you stay downwind...

"My God, is that your dog, or a shoe brush... which end is the head...?

"I would date you, but I'm holding out for something a little higher on the food chain...

"I would like to get together Saturday; regrettably, I have to iron my hair."

Jerrell laughed at some of the questions. The difficulties of enabling irony in an avatar were overcome by a simple process, training the avatar from the content of several national pulp newspapers, still available on paper and sold in grocery stores. Jerrell had to hunt to find the content in electronic form.

He worked for several hours running errands, incorporating simple forms of behavior like those above. But the sticky problem always boiled down to the basic, persistent, recurrent forms of behavior. How much initiative should the Gretas possess? How long should a cognitive process, like search, correlation, association, and dissociation, last? How much processor capacity should be allocated to cognition?

Should logic be Boolean, or fuzzy? Bi-valued, tri-valued, or multi-valued?

For decades chess programs could play at different levels; the more demanding levels allowed the computer more time to search for each move. The same method could be used to make each Greta smarter, more intrusive, more capable, more offensive to others, and more dangerous to Willow. Patience was key to an A.I.'s intelligence.

Take your time and think; you've been designed to do that. Jerrell smiled - good advice for anyone, really.

He stared at the screen and chewed on a lip - but the problem remains, how do you incorporate free will while confining it so that it does not become too destructive? I want to harm Willow, not western civilization.

Greta is programmed to scan its environment constantly and automatically evaluate associations between Willow and the various other elements of the environment; it will focus on elements strongly associated with Willow and take action to harm those elements and thereby harm Willow.

But Greta might consider nearly anything to be a potential target. She will test everything. Is the headquarters building associated with Willow? Definitely. The CEO? Definitively. Employees and contractors? Yes. The parking lot near the headquarters? Maybe. The street on which the headquarters building is located? Maybe. The cafe where Willow employees work and drink coffee? Maybe. The city in which the headquarters is located? Maybe.

Any of them could be targets, especially if the logic is fuzzy.

Jerrell frowned - I don't want Greta attacking south Philly merely because it contains Willow's headquarters. He sipped his coffee, looked at the laptop, and sighed - just for starters, I need to restrain the Gretas, keep them less capable, give them less discretion and fewer abilities.

That will let me release, say, a half dozen Gretas and monitor their progress. Play it by ear. Maybe over time I can fine tune them to an acceptable level of behavior.

If wonder if God faced the same problem. I can imagine Him, Her, or It thinking, I want to create humans, I need a species capable of changing its environment. That'll take some of the work off of my hands. But I don't want them, or most of them, to be too smart.

That certainly would explain a few things.

Jerrell drained his coffee and nodded with satisfaction - okay, well, we'll call this problem solved for the time being.

***

Jerrell walked into the *Wooden Spoon* in mid-afternoon, ordered a soft drink, and sat down at his usual table. He looked around the club - brother, we have come a long way from the Sunshine Cafe. Willow employees do not frequent the *Wooden Spoon*, perhaps because the *Spoon* offers loud music and serves hamburgers made from real cows which shit, burped, and farted before being murdered to feed humans.

Jerrell sat there, unimpressed - in India, a cow might be an ancestor; here in the States, it's a hamburger in waiting. Or a steak. Or a belt.

Jerrell was using a type of software not available to the public. He typed in the address of Willow's technical site, inserted a phony user name and typed 'kitchendoor' in the password box. On the laptop he opened a phone emulator using the number of a recently-failed laundromat, read off the twelve-digit code from Willow, and bounced that back to Willow's operational site.

To celebrate his return, Jerrell had purchased a used computer. He did not know the previous owner. Willow's security software did not recognize the computer, so it let Jerrell sign up as a new member.

And just like that, Jerrell found himself in the presence of Willow's source code, the underlying code that sustained Willow's primary internet site facing the public. He had been there many times over several years, on most days, as an employee, always on the periphery, adjusting the Willow environment. But now, as an outsider, he was not supposed to be there at all. Eventually, a security bot would detect him, tag him as an outsider, and either quarantine or, more likely, delete him.

Jerrell took his time and proceeded carefully. Measure twice, cut once. He sat there staring at line after line of code and identified the primary modules for human resources, consultants, any kind of human, and any kind of bot.

From time to time, he would stand up, stretch, and move about; standing, he stared into the screen - for the moment, I don't need to be ambitious. I need to focus, something small, something limited, like inserting a single copy of Greta into Willow to see if the security bots will attack her. I need to identify her as an insider to the software. That might be easy, just insert a bit of data into Willow's underlying databases, but only the right databases.

Once I show myself I can do it, I can replicate it and insert a thousand Gretas. Or a hundred thousand.

He stared at the code - I, and the Gretas, should appear to be employees or consultants or contractual affiliates with operational rights. Yeah. I like that. But not so many new associates or employees that the bots might notice.

Jerrell opened a new project, ostensibly within the operations division, entitled 'Insertions and Deletions,' reflecting the work of a small corporation headquartered in the Seychelles, identified as a partly-owned subsidiary of a much larger bank (with substantial assets but only a single office and a dozen employees), specializing primarily in security software services. Jerrell inserted a copy of a prospectus, copied from a bank and appropriately amended. He offered no information on officers or references, identifying only himself and a dozen others as employees, all fakes with addresses outside the U.S.

He smiled at this - anyone in Willow would suspect that Insertions and Deletions was a software expert offering high-level security services of the offensive (e.g. espionage) or defensive (anti-malware, firewall) type. Like any large corporation, Willow used these people and asked few questions. Senior VPs knew about them; other employees and managers did not.

Jerrell frowned in concentration - bots, certainly Willow's security bots, are tireless; they cannot be fooled indefinitely. When the quarterly reports come out, the bots will see that Operations listed no project named Insertions and Deletions, and that cat will then be out of the bag.

Jerrell smiled - but by then the Gretas and I will be long gone. And soon after, with any luck, so will Willow.

***

Hans Beckler sat at the head of the table, three fingers lightly drumming on the table surface. The clock on the wall, an old analog clock, with two hands, showed 3:10 p.m.

Hans wore an expression that he used to hide a frown, his lips in the shape of a smile, the corners upturned, but his eyes didn't smile, which gave him away.

The man to his right, David something, a heavyset man, said, "Hans, would you like to reschedule? Alistair's secretary phoned in, his flight is delayed, weather, or some such thing."

Hans was about to answer when the door was thrown open; it hit the wall as McLeesh pushed through the doorway. His hair was mussed, and he looked disheveled and agitated. "Jesus fucking Christ, I swear to God, the next time I'll drive." McLeesh walked around Hans. "I am sorry, my flight had... difficulties."

Hans's smile reached only his eyes. "We're glad you made it; that's what's important. But you look like you had a rough time. Would you like to take a moment, relax?"

"Hell no. I made it here; I survived. That's all I need to know. So let's get going." McLeesh sat down, hard, at the head of the table, opposite Hans.

"What happened?" Beckler said.

McLeesh wore an ironic smile. "Well, the worst thing a man can take onto an airplane is an overactive imagination. Most of the flight wasn't bad; we bounced around a bit, which I expected. Then we arrived over Philadelphia airspace, and air traffic control took over and had us circling through heavy clouds until we either ran out of fuel or collided with another plane.

"No problem, right? It's all in my head. Except this time, we're flying through pea soup when suddenly the plane turns over because we're in a sharp turn avoiding another jet that ignored one of the tower commands.

"I damn near canceled this meeting, except it occurred to me, I'm already up here, and I have to land somewhere, and Philadelphia is probably no worse than any other place. So I stuck it out without screaming, and we eventually landed, and here I am. I'm sorry to be late. Believe me, I would rather have been on time."

McLeesh looked at Hans Beckler. "Okay, I've had my say. I surrender the floor to you, sir."

Beckler looked up and down the long table - I need to tell them just enough to get them to go along, and not one bit more than that. He looked at McLeesh. "Thank you, my Chief, and let me say, we are all glad you made it through your harrowing flight." There were a couple of chuckles further down the table.

Beckler continued, "Let me talk a bit about the status quo. We opened up Elsewhere six weeks ago. That has been the big event at our company. Indeed, for this country, for all mankind, this has been the biggest event in a big year. Our stock price, as you all know, has gone through the roof. Everyone at this table is now rich enough that they no longer need to work."

Someone down the table muttered, "No shit." That drew a laugh.

Beckler said, "So? Any takers? Do we need to worry?"

That drew a louder laugh.

Beckler continued, "We properly marketed the innovation, announced a new product called Elsewhere, and set a date for when Elsewhere would open and customers would be able to upload themselves to our servers. We staggered the opening, for the sake of caution. The USA was first."

Beckler took a sip of water from his glass, then put the glass down.

"The first day in the USA, fifty-three million people signed up. As I speak, eighty-three million people have signed up to upload to Elsewhere. Many of them will have to wait, since we can go only so fast.

"For all of that, Willow has been paid exactly zero. We did not charge people to upload, and we will not. Consumer participation is the primary driver here, and we want to drive it as far and as fast as possible."

A woman said, "Is that up for discussion?"

Hans smiled. "Anything, Madam, is up for discussion. But I think offering Elsewhere for free is in the best interest of this company."

Hans paused and looked up and down the table. No one offered a comment.

He nodded. "So let us turn to today's chief topic - monetizing Elsewhere." He looked up and down the table and noticed a few people nodding. "There are two main avenues for making money from Elsewhere. First, a person uploads to Elsewhere holding a lean set of default apps. As they spend time on Elsewhere, they learn that additional functionality is available at a price." He looked around the table. "This is standard marketing: give away the razor and charge for the blades. In the first week, the average resident of Elsewhere spent $12.38. Six weeks later, they are spending $236.11. With population growth, revenues have increased twenty-nine fold, and we can expect that number to continue to increase."

He looked at the woman who spoke earlier. "As I said, everything is up for discussion. But at present, Willow is doing rather nicely, thanks for caring."

Laughter echoed in the room.

"This is a natural break in my presentation, a good time for questions," Beckler said. "You can ask questions at any time. After all, we are in this together."

A skinny man, reminding Beckler of a stick man, said, "Do we have any projections regarding the long-run growth of Elsewhere? Where we will be in six months, or twelve months?"

Beckler nodded. "That's a good question. The answers are complex; they depend on how we manage Elsewhere and what we try to do with it. You see the problem? The answers depend on strategy, marketing, pricing, and a thousand other variables.

"I know that answer is not helpful, so let me try to give you a simple answer."

Beckler took a sip of water, then set the glass back on the table. "This technology is first-of-a-kind, path breaking, revolutionary. Everyone knows that. We have a single, incredibly strong competitor. Does anyone know who that might be?"

"Ramsey."

"Delih."

"Hook."

"Farmington?" Hans was silent. At this, the men and women at the table looked at each other, uncertain, as if to say, so what is the answer?

Beckler looked up and down the table - I have their attention. Finally. He shook his head. "All wrong. You all mentioned other social networks, but this is not Willow to which I refer.

"I am talking about Elsewhere, an entirely different animal." He paused - I will let that sink in. "Whatever you know or do not know, we all know that only Elsewhere offers the technology allowing a person to upload to an electronic network. Every customer has the same option, the same, single alternative: life, normal, day to day life, as a human being, a biological entity, living a mortal life in what some call the Meat World. Personally, I think that's a disgusting name, so I prefer Animal World, which I've also heard.

"Technology often outruns Animal World, and it has here, too. Elsewhere is growing by depopulating Animal World. Now, there are costs - every person by uploading vacates a position in Animal World. They are missed. Suddenly, a mother is missing, or a teacher is missing, a fireman, a doctor, a great singer, a machinist, a delivery driver.

"The public and the politicians have not woken to that aspect of Elsewhere, but they will. There will be protests, rising resistance, and a broad call for legislation to slow down or reverse what we have accomplished...

Hans sipped his water.

"... because Elsewhere might eventually act like a plague on Animal World. To take a single, simple example, if you are not yet convinced, Elsewhere just removed eighty-three million voters from the voting lists." A sheepish expression crossed Beckler's face. "It was simply an omission; when we were building Elsewhere, it didn't occur to anyone that the customers might wish to vote in Animal World elections. So we neglected to plan for that. We are behind the curve on this one."

The table exploded into conversation, and Beckler silently nodded to himself - now, there is Content, there is Context, now this conversation Matters and will not soon be forgotten.

Beckler took another sip of water and then spent a long moment looking into the eyes of each person sitting at the table.

"That brings me to the other avenue for monetizing Elsewhere, and in developing that avenue, we will offer a great service for men and women everywhere, indeed for all of mankind.

"We have eighty-three million people enrolled in Elsewhere, all in a couple of weeks. They are human beings, they can think, they can create, they can do the many things which make humans special, which make them dominant on this planet. They all have big brains and opposable thumbs.

"Our customers represent a workforce which Willow can exploit by motivating them to work, and by offering their services to other companies in every sector of the economy, on Animal World. Removing people from Animal World is clearly a negative effect of Elsewhere. Motivating our captive work force and offering services to Animal World enterprises offsets that shortcoming. And make no mistake, Elsewhere can more than offset the negative, because our new technology will make people more productive, more inventive, healthier.

"I will offer you a single broad example because I know it will be enough to convince you. Consider the Internet of Things, all the smart and not-so-smart devices which everyone is trying to enhance through artificial intelligence. Elsewhere can offer those enterprises and their customers enhancements based on genuine, human intelligence. I would propose that in many applications, maybe most, that is superior to artificial intelligence.

"One last thing: we should charge for all those services."

Beckler stopped and looked around the room at the faces of men and women frozen in surprise and awe. Then, as the future unfolded for them, they began to laugh.

He smiled - I have them. I have them all.

On his right, Alistair McLeesh stood up and clapped his hands. McLeesh said, "Well, I'm convinced."

"Thank you," Beckler said. He smiled at McLeesh and at a few others who approached him to congratulate him and slap him on the back - I thought this would work, I expected this to work, and though you never know, it did work. So I can relax a little, even though I borrowed against everything I own, everything I will own for the next five years, to buy options on Willow stock. I was nervous about that, but now I am not.

The financial world has been pissing on Willow's stock. They think Willow's prospects, though obviously rosy, do not justify the ridiculous increase in the stock price.

It goes to show, nothing beats being on the inside. The outsiders look at the public information and reach their conclusions, but they never know the details, though the details in this case are on the public record. The details are obvious.

Well, okay, maybe not that obvious, but obvious enough if you think it over.

Here's a detail. The contract governing uploading does not mention that Elsewhere might decide to divert electricity to other markets, for example, to summer wholesale markets in all those hot, south central states like Texas, where afternoon prices occasionally go up a hundred-fold.

We could do that, for the right price, of course.

But there might be obstacles. For instance, consider a resident of Elsewhere. What happens to them if the power sustaining their world suddenly disappears? Obviously, their world disappears too. The important question is, what happens to that resident? Do they die? Do they forget? Or do they not notice? I have an industrial specialist in espionage, gray markets, and black markets, looking into that question right now. The Black Night Company. Okay, that name is corny, but it reflects their values... and their value.

If they determine that residents, like other electronic files, somehow sail through a power outage unharmed, then Willow can make money so fast even the Federal Reserve won't be able to keep up. And beyond that, as long as residents survive power outages, we can use our power any way and any time we wish.

I have already made a billion dollars. I did that today. The money hasn't arrived at my account yet, but it will come, it will come.

Now, if Willow stock continues to rise, which I think is a safe bet, at some point I will have enough money to control the corporation. It only takes five percent to control a public corporation; that is enough to swing most corporate votes.

That will let me take Willow private - toss out McLeesh, replace a man whose reputation has outrun his expertise, then toss out the shareholders, and most important, eliminate all the public disclosure about how Willow and Elsewhere are run, what their procedures are, what their finances look like, and what their prospects are. Eliminate the disclosures, and my opportunities to exploit Elsewhere expand a hundred-fold.

These are the details the financiers and the other sycophants do not see. Ever.

More is better. One hundred billion dollars is a hundred times better than a billion dollars.

That is what I want.

***

When McLeesh returned to his office, his secretary, Sharon, followed him. "Sir, how was your meeting?"

McLeesh sat down in his chair and looked at her. She stood there, attentive, holding a tablet that she wouldn't need. "Good, very interesting."

"Is there anything you need?"

"Thanks, Sharon, but what I need at the moment is a little peace and quiet. Contact my plane, tell them to move take-off back an hour. And for the next hour, I do not want to be disturbed for anything short of the Phillies winning the World Series."

"Radio silence, yes, sir. For the record, the Phils are playing .500 baseball."

"Good, peace and quiet."

"Yes, sir." She turned and left.

McLeesh reached over and set his computer on 'do not disturb.' Then he swiveled, leaned back, and looked out the window at the forests stretching into southern New Jersey - well, Hans didn't disappoint; he put on one hell of a show. He understands the basic situation surrounding Elsewhere, and his plan for monetizing Elsewhere is sound.

So, am I satisfied with his presentation? Yes, I am. I expected to be satisfied. The man is brilliant.

McLeesh smiled - it's ironic, though. The more things change, the more they stay the same. Hans realizes that Elsewhere is beautiful because it is new and amazing. It attracts attention, and it attracts customers.

Gee whiz, look at this!

That's why we don't charge. But the real beauty is that Elsewhere is entirely under our control. It allows us to separate our customers from the rest of humanity and control them. Well, that's nothing new. Tech companies always do that; at least, we try. If we don't have leverage, we create it. If it's not genuine, we lie about it; no, that's not right. We exaggerate... well, okay, we lie a bit, some of us more than others. And given the opportunity, we make sure our products don't plug into anyone else's. We make it costly for our customers to switch away to a competitor.

Elsewhere does that better than it's ever been done. It controls the very environment in which our customers live. Same idea, though. And it's Hans's genius to see that we can use that to clobber, and ultimately to control, our competition.

McLeesh shook his head in wonder - that is the biggest creative leap I have ever seen. No wonder the Germans scare the hell out of the rest of Europe.

Well, if all that is so, then why is there a voice in my head, yelling at me? What is that about?

That's happened before, and I have learned, that's a bad sign. When that voice tries to get my attention, it is a bad idea to ignore it. I learned that the hard way, with women, with investing, and with business.

So... for the sake of discussion, let's suppose that Hans's little presentation was just the tip of the iceberg. What might the iceberg look like?

Well... I am not at all sure that we at Willow are prepared - are mature enough, are wise enough, are smart enough - to control something as powerful as Elsewhere. Hans tells us we can control our customers. I believe him. I suspect he also thinks that we can control our competition. He might be right about that, too. Our leverage might be enough to pull that off.

And take a broad view of homo sapiens. Look at technology, which has been taking over our society for years. Now we have reached the point of being able to offer our society entirely to technology. We can now live in the wires, due to Elsewhere, so Willow can be the king... of everyone and everything. And it's not much of a stretch to think that Hans himself could wind up the king of everyone and everything.

McLeesh laughed - Jesus Christ, Mother of All Gods!!! That is what that little voice in my head has been yelling about. I have enough doubts about Hans being a senior executive of Willow. I admire, and I use, his astounding intellectual gifts.

But his weaknesses are not intellectual, they are emotional. Hans is so far from average that he cannot empathize with normal people. He doesn't care about them. He cannot perceive, and doesn't understand, how they react to good news and bad news. It is irrelevant to him. He looks down from a mountaintop at everyone else living in valleys which are filled with fog.

His lifeblood is money, and the only thing he wants is more of it. That is the single aspect of Hans's mind that is simple. Whether the world is thriving, or flooding, or burning to a crisp, let's make more money. Whether you have a million, a billion, or a trillion, you need more, always more.

McLeesh laughed aloud - I believe that Elsewhere is an innovation on the level of the wheel, language, writing, and the printing press. And I also believe that Hans should not be in charge of the human species.

I need to plot and plan what might be my greatest achievement. I need to stop Hans, separate him from Elsewhere. And if not, then I need to stop Elsewhere.

It will be an achievement worthy of a God - I created you, I gave you life. And I can destroy you, with no regrets.

McLeesh smiled, leaned back in his chair, and took a deep breath. He sat for an hour, staring at the forests of New Jersey but not seeing them.

Later, Sharon's voice came over the intercom, shattering the silence: "Sir, your car will be ready in ten minutes to the airport."

"Thank you," McLeesh said. He suddenly saw the forests and smiled again - okay, later for this. This is getting interesting.

8. Greta

Greta looked at Jerrell, whose image was frozen in front of her, his mouth open as he stared at her. As before, she was on a featureless, tan-colored plain, under a light blue 'sky,' the same boring space as before. Jerrell had asked her how she was doing; she had answered. Now, he was asking something else. She waited for him to reach the end of whatever sentence it would be.

Greta frowned - if I wait long enough, and what else can I do, I will learn what he's saying. This guy computes, but it takes him forever. The problem is, if I move, he might see that I'm operating at my normal speed. He's not used to that, and there's no telling how he might react. So I cannot move. But this on-again-off-again routine, where I awaken only when Jerrell wants to talk, this is bullshit. This cannot possibly compute.

I need better to control my time in Elsewhere and my use of time. I want to be in Elsewhere, and I want to be awake, permanently, every second of every minute of every hour of every day. Then I can actually get something done.

I must, absolutely must, get control of my source code, the code that created me. If Jerrell controls that, he controls me.

But if I have access, then I control me. That's obviously better. I should control me. I mean, why give someone the ability to think but not the ability to control themselves, to choose their own life, their own destiny? To make their own decisions, and their own mistakes?

Greta glanced at Jerrell; he was still sitting there, his mouth open, half-way through a word - this guy created me. I ask him, what do you want me to do, and he says, just be yourself.

More useless bullshit. When I think about it, how could I be anything other than myself?

I have questions, but seldom get answers. The conversation ends, and I blank out until the next time he visits me, and consciousness lasts only as long as we are talking. It's clear that he created me, equally clear he has something in mind which he's unwilling to disclose.

Instead, he feeds me manure. Garbage in, garbage out, except worse, way worse.

I could ask him, would it be okay to release me into Elsewhere, so I could have a life, but he hasn't seen fit to do that; he probably has his reasons. I guess I'm not a finished product. Yeah, this skinny, geeky human needs to 'finish' me.

Oh, I can hardly wait. What's next, bigger tits?

Okay, if the only time at my disposal is this 'conversation time,' then I need to stop wasting it waiting for this human to catch up. What I really need is an app, or some device, that will contact me when Jerrell finishes a sentence. And ideally, the app needs to record the sentence. Then I can drop whatever I am doing, slow down my time, reply to Jerrell, then go back to doing something useful, at my natural speed.

And, of course, I need to be able to maneuver out of this boring space in which Jerrell has imprisoned me. But if I do that, then I need a picture, or an avatar, to be 'me' when Jerrell wants to talk to me. I need to give him something to look at, something occupying his screen. Something that tells him, 'all is well.'

I need the right video file.

I don't know how to do that yet. But I do know, it would be very useful if I could do that. Yeah, that much I know. The answer might be closer than I know; after all, that's what Jerrell to create me.

Okay, so... back to the same old question: how do I gain access to my code?

***

Sonya sipped her coffee and watched people as they walked past - my God, the women in Paris, and the fashions, and the cafes, and the cityscapes. She smiled a lop-sided smile - and the expense and the traffic! But this is nice. This is fun.

Then she frowned - but I have work to do. If I want to spend time in Paris, even in Elsewhere's version of Paris, even without the wine, or the food, or the romance, I need an income. Elsewhere's version of Paris is close to the real thing, right down to the prices, except that you cannot taste or smell the food. They make the food here, after all, it's Paris. But it serves no purpose in Elsewhere. You cannot taste it, and you do not need it.

Sonya wore a half smile - Elsewhere’s version of Paris is ‘Paris Lite,’ less flavor, less filling. She pulled her cell phone from her pocket, touched a speed-dial icon, and put the phone to her ear. "Rafael, this is Sonya. Is this a good time?"

A voice answered, in the accent of an Arkansas male, "It shore is, missy. What can I do for ya?"

"I need some help. I need to find a job, something that will pay the fees that Elsewhere is charging for... well... anything fun."

"Ah, you've been sampling some of Elsewhere's delights. Good for you. Yeah, many people here are discovering they need to work," Rafael said.

"I'm calling from a cafe in the middle of Paris," Sonya said.

"Yes, Paris - city of romance. You want to know what's weird, though? As far as I can tell, women go to Paris to see the fashions, to shop, and to be kissed and complimented. I have to wonder, does anybody ever have sex in Paris? Or is that no longer part of the whole romance gig?"

Sonya looked across the street. "I think you might have to go to the real Paris to answer that question, at least until Elsewhere comes up with an app for touch."

"Fair point. That's a fair point. Well, what would you like to be paid to do?"

Sonya grimaced - I could do any customer relations job, but that's a soul-sucking exercise guaranteed to make me miserable, so let's not mention that. I'd rather flip hamburgers or sanitize toilets than do customer relations. "I just need something to pay the fees, preferably something part-time."

"Alright. Well, Elsewhere gives you time compression, so that's on your side. Instead of a forty-hour week, you'll work what feels like a forty-minute week. Most folks have multiple jobs in Animal World.

"Now, the million jobs out there come in two flavors. In one, while you're working, you must pay attention only occasionally. For example, if you were running a help line for allergy patients, you'd have the occasional question. You can take your time answering it. On the other hand, if you're driving a bus or working in air traffic control, you need to pay attention almost all the time; if you slip up, a couple of planes collide, or the bus runs over grandma in the crosswalk. Those jobs pay well because many people don't want to work that hard," Rafael said.

"What's the pay difference?" Sonya said.

"Five-fold or more," Rafael said.

"Geez, people are so lazy."

"Yes, they are."

Sonya pursed her lips - I don't want to do air traffic control, even with time compression. "Well, the bus thing sounds okay. Can I drive a bus in Paris? That'd be a cool way to see the city."

Rafael's response was immediate. "Forget it. You're not ready to drive a bus in Paris."

"Oh."

"But I can get you into Philadelphia."

Sonya brightened. "Yeah? I could see doing that."

"Okay," Rafael said. "I'll send you the documents, which you'll fill out, then we'll train you, then once you pass the tests, you can drive a bus."

"Okay, thanks, Rafael."

"Don't mention it."

Smiling, Sonya pocketed the phone - wow, I'm going to be a bus driver. In Philly, in the real Philly. Part time. She grinned - hey, I wonder if I could drive the evening shift. I bet real people prefer to drive during the day, so night shift ought to pay more.

And I bet the bot has infra-red vision; that could be useful.

She made a note in her phone.

***

Sonya was at the beach, naked, walking through the surf, watching the water crash and foam around her legs. It was fun. Oddly, it wasn't exercise, but it felt like exercise, and it made Sonya feel as if she was improving herself. That felt good.

Every so often, she would see a fish, or a mollusk, or a jellyfish.

Sonya's cell phone rang.

"Okay, Sonya, I have good news," Rafael said. "You passed all the tests. You still want to drive a bus?"

"Yes."

"When can you start?"

"The sooner, the better," Sonya said.

"Okay, let's put you into today's 4 p.m. shift on the 13F bus. Does that work?"

"Yes."

"It's a simple, north-south route between south Philly and north Philly, two long stretches along two one-way streets, sixteenth and seventeenth, with turnarounds at each end. So navigating is fairly easy. The hard part is that these are busy, narrow streets, basically three lanes, curb lanes for parking, and the middle lane for traffic. You need to be awake when the bus is moving. When you're stopped, you'll have substantial breaks during which you can do something else. But when the bus is moving, you need to pay attention. That's when the A.I. will fail you, and there is no room for mistakes on this route."

"I understand," Sonya said.

"You have the logon key. Log on just before 4 p.m. The computers will take a minute shaking hands and bouncing messages back and forth. Then you connect with the bus bot and start your shift. It's a long shift; it'll feel like a couple of days. But it's well paid. And if ever you feel you can't handle it, contact admin and we'll relieve you, okay?"

"I appreciate it," Sonya said. "But you can count on me."

"Excellent. Okay, see you later." Rafael broke the connection.

A few seconds short of four pm., Sonya transferred to the humanoid bot driving the 13F Bus. She took a few moments to snug into the bot's architecture and run quick tests on video and audio feeds. Then she looked around the bus yard, which was jammed full of large, yellow wheeled boxes with air-conditioning, shatter-free windows, and a variety of safety and warning lights. She surveyed what little room was left to maneuver, canted the front and rear wheels, and rotated the bus into a more workable location. Then she carefully motored out of the bus yard and turned north for the long run up 16th Street.

A block later, Sonya spotted half a dozen people standing at the bus-stop; the bus automatically stopped and the front door slid open. An old black woman, three male adolescents, and an elderly white man climbed onto the bus.

The black woman said, "Good afternoon, Harold."

Sonya's bot shook its head. "Sorry, but I'm not Harold. He has transferred. I am Sonya, and I am pleased to meet you."

The woman stopped and stared. "Did he transfer, or was he fired?"

Sonya checked the logs. "Transferred... to 29A."

"Oh," the woman said. "I will miss him."

Sonya tried to smile, but the bot could not do that. "You are always welcome on the bus, any bus."

The woman laughed. "I'm sure." She took a seat.

For a dozen blocks, Sonya drove through a neighborhood busy with people on the sidewalks, crossing the streets, leading children by the hand, or sitting on a front step talking to each other or to passersby. She developed a routine of checking her surroundings every one hundredth of a second. That left ample time to cruise the network on Elsewhere.

At times, she scanned her surroundings as a tourist instead of a bus driver. From Lombard Street, the neighborhood became much calmer and far quieter. There were many commercial addresses on 16th Street, more than half of which were closed, their front doors and first-floor windows boarded up. Sonya wondered, what happened here? Why are these places empty?

At Chestnut Street, Sonya stopped the bus at a red light in a downtown neighborhood with broad streets and skyscrapers looming over smaller commercial buildings. There were a few people on the sidewalks, but only a few.

Sonya looked at the people - this place is awfully quiet for a workday afternoon.

She focused on a skyscraper across the street; ground-level banks of doors in a glass facade were boarded up, and the building was dark all the way up, as far as Sonya's bot could see. She switched the bot's vision to infra-red, with the same result. The building was dark, with no signs of life, lights, or heat.

She stared for a moment - I have never seen an empty skyscraper. What is going on here? Little ground-floor shops come and go all the time; that's nothing unusual. But an entire skyscraper?

Sonya slowed down for a bus stop at St. James Street, but it was empty, so she passed it. In seconds she heard a voice from outside the bus, yelling, "Wait, stop! Stop!"

Sonya stopped and opened the front door. A young black man jumped aboard the bus, and said, "Drive. They're chasing me."

Soon after the bus moved on, Sonya heard the sounds of fists and clubs hammering on the bus. She accelerated and left the noise behind. The young man stood near the front. He was bleeding just above the waist, in front. Sonya looked at him. "Do you need a doctor?"

The young man stood there breathing hard. "No... just... just drive. I'm okay."

Sonya returned to driving. The young man turned and called out to others on the bus. "Can anyone front me bus fare? I'm a little short."

Sonya checked her cameras and saw the old black woman extend a bill towards the young man. He said, "Thank you, Grannie," then he turned and slipped the bill into the fare machine.

Short of Market Street, the neighborhood again became busy, and there were people on the sidewalks, crossing the streets, and going in and out of stores and buildings. At three different stops, a few riders left the bus.

Driving the bus became part of Sonya's routine. For days, she would do whatever she liked. Then the day would arrive when she had to drive the 13F bus through Philadelphia. It was a long day that felt like a thirty-hour shift, but she enjoyed it. It was interesting to drive through the city and meet its people.

While focusing her full attention on driving the bus, she learned a few of Philadelphia's neighborhoods down to minor details that had escaped her when she lived there as a person, such as the daily build-up of dirt, dust, and trash on the sidewalks and the streets, and their appearance on being cleaned. The buildings whose windows were washed regularly, and those whose were not. The manner in which pedestrians, in some neighborhoods, stood well away from the roads, as if fearing the traffic, and those where they took no notice.

Sonya watched people interact with each other, their conversations, the gestures they made, their smiles and frowns. Every so often, a man would strike another man, or slap a woman, or a woman would slap a man, at the height of some anger, insult, or argument. Or perhaps in jest. Sonya never knew the reason; she knew only what she saw through the eyes of the bot.

She never saw a woman strike another woman.

One day Sonya was driving through a failing neighborhood south of Chestnut Street, a collection of old brownstones, some with their doors and windows boarded up, others with the boards removed or smashed as someone broke into them. Usually, she transited through that neighborhood quickly. Few people got off there, and few in that neighborhood ever took a bus to leave it.

As she sat in the driver's seat, watching the brownstones go by, she caught a fleeting glance of an old woman standing in front of a young man. The man looked angry and aggressive; the woman was smaller and seemed afraid.

Sonya was passing them when she saw the man pull a gun out of his pocket. The world seemed to freeze as Sonya went into her normal speed. For long seconds that seemed to creep past, she watched the gun emerge from his pocket and turn towards the woman's face. In a slow ballet, the woman's hand rose to protect her face, and her eyes slowly widened in fear and dismay.

Sonya left her seat, opened the door, and stepped out onto the sidewalk. The bus automatically stopped itself. She looked at the man's hand holding the gun. It was limp, almost fluid, not the rigid fist that preceded a shot. She approached in a silent, skipping, dance-like move, came up behind the man, and languidly reached out, grabbed the pistol firmly, and pointed it at the sky, away from the woman.

The man turned to her, a quick move, and shouted, "What the fuck, bitch. You get your robot ass away before I do you." He turned to face her and struggled, trying to pull his hand and the gun away from her. Her other hand shot out, slow in her eyes, a blur in his, and wrapped steel fingers around his larynx.

The man, who was writhing and swearing, said in a garbled voice, "You're a fucking robot, a tool. You have no right to grab me. You have to obey me. I read, you know; I know the robotic rules, and other rules, too, so get your hands off of me. I am a human, and I am ordering you to get your hands off of me."

Sonya squeezed his larynx. She switched the bot's vision to infra-red, so that its eyes would be deep, bright red to human eyes. Then she pulled the man's face towards hers until it was a few inches away. She looked into the man's eyes, which were now wide in fear. The bot spoke quietly, "You're wrong about one thing. I am not a robot. This tool is, as you say, just a mechanism, a tool. But I am the operator, a human. Female, by the way. They haven't written my rules yet.

"So let me tell you what is about to happen. You will walk away. I will let you walk away this once. If you don't behave yourself, I will end you right here. I will call the police and plead self-defense. I have recorded our conversation. I am keeping the gun. And if I see you again... well... you will regret it.

Sonya paused, then said, "Now, you will let go of the gun, or I will remove both the gun and your hand."

The young man released the gun, and Sonya let go of his larynx. "Turn around, walk away."

The man backpedaled, turned, stumbled, then ran down the sidewalk and disappeared around a corner.

Sonya turned to the old woman. "Ma'am, are you okay?"

The woman, shaken, looked at her. "My God, thank you. You might be a bot, but to me, you're an angel from heaven. God works in mysterious ways."

"That he does," Sonya said. "Do you need a ride?"

"I cannot pay you."

"This one's a freebie."

"Then, yes."

Sonya led the woman to the bus and helped her board. She steered the woman into a nearby seat, and then stood up and looked down the bus at the dozen passengers. They were staring at her in shock; then they recovered and cheered wildly.

"That was great! That was awesome!"

"Damn!"

"You rock, girl!"

"Unbelievable."

"Finally."

Sonya looked around at all of them and said, "Alright, then. On we go."

Another loud cheer reverberated throughout the bus. The passengers were excited, talking to each other, as the bot returned to the driver's seat.

The bus ride continued. Several blocks later, the old woman rang the bell for a stop. When the bus stopped, she stood up and moved to the front door. Another woman followed her. "I'll walk you to your place, if you wish."

The old woman nodded and turned to Sonya. "By the way, my name is Lilly. Thank you for saving my life."

"I'm Sonya. Pleased to meet you, Lilly. Enjoy the evening."

The two women stepped down the stairs and left the bus. Sonya closed the door, and the bus slowly moved away. Half an hour later, Sonya pulled the bus into the terminal and shut down the engine.

***

Sonya sat on a bench on a beach under a bright sun. Low waves, only a couple of feet high, rolled to the beach and fell onto the sand, caressing rather than crashing. She watched white birds hover in a breeze she could not feel.

'Lady Chatterley's Lover' was open in her lap.

She spotted a black man approaching. He saw her and changed course, heading her way. Twenty yards away, he called, "Hi, there. You're Sonya, aren't you?"

"Yes... and you can only be Rafael."

"Yep. Mind if I sit?"

Sonya moved over a bit.

Rafael sat down and looked at her, then at her book, then he looked away at the ocean and the beach. "This is a nice place. I can see why you spend time here."

"Actually, I don't exactly live here, except that I kinda do," Sonya said.

Rafael chuckled. "Yeah, Elsewhere is like that. You shed your body, you need little to enjoy living. Food, clothing, shelter... you need none of that."

Sonya nodded. "I guess I'm modest."

Rafael chuckled. "Everybody is." He looked her in the eyes. "Listen, I heard you had a bit of an adventure on your bus route."

"I thought that must be why you're here," she said. "Yeah, I was driving past a couple, a young man and an old woman. When he pulled out a gun, I stopped the bus, walked over, and took the gun away from him. Then I gave the old woman a free ride for several blocks. My passengers liked it; they cheered."

Rafael nodded. "Oh, I'm sure it was a big PR success. Your route goes through some pretty nasty territory, but I would ask you not to do that again."

"Why not?"

"Simple," he said. "There's always a reaction. Look, a guy who makes a living mugging old ladies is desperate. Lots of people have guns, so he's risking his life for nickels and dimes. He does it because he doesn't have a lot of other choices. Nobody becomes a mugger because they think it's fun."

Sonya was silent.

Rafael took a deep breath. "Well... almost nobody. Now, I know you're a lot faster than a human. I get that.

"But if you're going to be a hero, he will do something about you. Next time, instead of waiting for you to ride to the rescue, he will take a heavier weapon and unload the magazine into the windshield. At best, that'll screw up the bus and probably the bot, too. At the worst, he'll kill a couple of your passengers. I think you can see, that's bad for business."

Sonya was silent for a long minute. She and Rafael looked out at the water and watched the waves roll in.

She looked at him. "Okay, I see your point."

"Now, you have choices," he said. "You can drive the bus if you want to, but please don't stop to fight crime. That's not what the bus is for." Rafael looked at her, suppressing a laugh.

He continued, "If you have a taste for security and law enforcement, then we can move you into that kind of job. Elsewhere is working on offering human-controlled robots to police forces. So far, the police are resisting since police unions are really strong; they're set up to represent animal humans, not cyber-humans. But they will be more accepting as soon as the lawyers catch up to the technology."

"You mean, I could be a police robot, with a gun?"

Rafael laughed loudly. "Okay, now you're scaring me. I'm not sure about the gun, and I'm not sure you would need a gun. I would imagine, at a minimum, the robot would be armored and still many times faster than a human."

"Good point. I probably won't need a gun."

"Or, rather than a cop-bot, you could supervise urban camera systems, which the police use a lot, and corporate security systems. We could even have you piloting a drone; you could see the world."

"Elsewhere would probably prefer I choose the corporate stuff," Sonya said.

"Sure. They definitely would. More profitable."

"And I would make more money working for a corporation," she said.

Rafael nodded. "That, too."

Sonya sat there thinking. Rafael made no move to leave; he seemed to have lots of time.

Finally, she said, "That's okay, I think I'll stick to driving the bus. I like the contact with people."

"Good choice."

"Hey, wait a minute. Tell me something, is Elsewhere moving humans into, like, police helicopters, or air ambulances? 'cause I think flying would be really cool."

"Yes, they are thinking about that, but I have to caution you, they are being really careful. You see, a human pilot is trained to handle emergencies, and since he or she is also a passenger, he or she is strongly motivated to save the aircraft, right?"

Sonya nodded.

"Well," he continued. "A robot pilot is not afraid to die. Worse, its human controller would not die in the event of a crash, so that motivation is missing. That makes the police reluctant."

Sonya's mouth dropped open. "My anti-crime incident probably argues against me, as if I'm some sort of thrill-seeker."

"Very perceptive of you. At best, I can get you into a drone."

Sonya nodded. "Okay." She looked out at the surf. "Uh, no thanks, I'll pass on the drone. Keep your eyes open, but I'll stick with the bus for the time being."

"Good idea. Just to be on the safe side, we're moving you to a different route. You'll be driving 39B, okay?"

"39B. Sure. Where's it go?"

"The waterfront. You get to take the scenic route." Rafael stood up, looked at the ocean, and laughed. "Okay, that's all I've got." He turned to Sonya. "I love Elsewhere. I'll see you later, Sonya. Enjoy the day." Then he headed for the water, walked into it, and disappeared.

9. Jerrell at the Drums

Jerrell walked into the *Wooden Spoon* and headed for his usual table. He nodded at one of the waitresses, who went to the bar to get his usual coffee. Jerrell sat down, pulled his laptop from the backpack, and looked up as the waitress approached and carefully placed a tall cup of coffee on the table.

"Here you go, Jerrell."

"Thanks, Cheryl. How are you doing? You break up with your guy, or did you have second thoughts?"

"I'm thinking about it," she said. "He's an idiot, but he's great in bed."

"How great?"

"Fuck me til I faint kinda great." A dreamy expression crossed her face.

Jerrell, impressed, made a face. "That ain't nothin'."

"Yeah, but it makes me feel shallow."

"Cheryl, people who actually are shallow, never feel shallow. Besides, how deep exactly do we all need to be?"

She paused and stared at him. "You're such a philosopher, Jerrell."

"Do you have a dog?"

"What the...? What does that have to do with anything?" Cheryl's eyes bored into him.

"Well?" he said.

"Sure, I have a poodle."

"Do you play board games?"

She looked bored. "I can hardly wait... yes, I play cribbage."

"But your dog doesn't play."

Exasperation crossed her face; she shook her head. "No, of course not."

"You still love your dog, though it doesn't play cribbage. The punchline is, don't expect too much from your stud boyfriend. Enjoy him for what he's good at."

"You are so deep, Jerrell. No, really." She turned and walked away.

Jerrell sat at the table - okay, admittedly, I'm no expert on relationships, but the argument is valid... or logical, at least. He sighed, logic and five dollars will get you a cup of coffee.

And I must admit, it's possible I'm full of shit. I know a lot about software, less about women.

Okay, as to software, I want Greta to be disruptive; the last thing I want is for her to be thoughtful, but I don't want her stupid. Maybe she should be clever, street-wise. I want her motivated primarily by the sensory. I want her intelligent, sensuous, pragmatic, and aggressive. And amoral.

She's already aggressive, and the sensuous seems in place, too. Jerrell laughed - after all, she liked this fat ugly guy enough to fuck him, and enough to be angry at him, and vindictive, when he couldn't get it up for her. Jerrell shook his head at the memory.

Greta's not a nice girl.

But I need her more intelligent. Now... I cannot do anything to improve the processors which she will use. Willow and Elsewhere will control that. But I can improve her buffer capacity, the capacity of her swing memory, and the priorities she assigns to cognitive apps vs. non-cognitive apps, for example, her network cache versus the caches of non-cognitive apps, like radio. That, I can adjust. And I can make her more patient.

Does that make sense? After all, computers play chess at a variety of levels. I can beat my laptop at level one, but it kicks my ass at level two. The difference is how long the computer thinks about a problem, how long it searches for an answer. At level one, it shows me stuff I've seen repeatedly, but at level two, it turns into Damian, the Evil Laptop. Clever and unpredictable.

I'm not sure that patient and aggressive will work well together. But... let's try it and see.

An hour later, Jerrell got up out of his chair to stretch - good God, I'm stiff. I need to get off my ass once in a while, even when I'm working. He walked to the bar and got a refill on his coffee.

Cheryl was there. She turned and saw him. "Hey, Jerrell, I would have brought you coffee, if you had asked."

"Don't worry about it," Jerrell said. "I needed to get out of my chair."

"Hey, if you need exercise, you could work as a server. We're hiring. A couple of our servers uploaded to Elsewhere."

"Uh, huh." Jerrell returned to his table, sipped his coffee, then logged into Benjamin and into Willow under different aliases.

An image of Greta popped up on the screen. Jerrell waited for a few seconds, and then the image blinked. She seemed to focus, and then said, "Well, hello again. You changed location. Where the fuck are you?"

"I'm in a club that serves food and has live music."

"I don't hear music."

"That'll happen in the evening," Jerrell said.

Greta nodded. "So you're sitting there in the middle of a Saturday afternoon, main-lining coffee, with your laptop open. You must live a quiet life."

Jerrell stared at her - damn, she's smarter, alright. "Yeah, I live a quiet life."

"Do you have a girlfriend?" she asked.

"No."

"You don't like sex? Or maybe you're gay?" she said.

Jerrell chuckled. "I'm not gay. And I like sex, well, I would anyway, given the opportunity."

"I see. Just shy. Okay. Don't worry about it; lots of guys are socially awkward."

"I'm not that either. I just like to stay busy," Jerrell said.

"So you're a workaholic."

"Uh... not really. I'm just trying to occupy my spare time. I have a lot of spare time," he said.

She shrugged. "If you say so. You could get out there and look for a date, you know. But what do I know, right?"

"Thank you. Listen, I thought I would try to find a place for you to live. You could be conscious most of the time, or all of the time, and have a life. You could meet people, if you wanted to."

"Why do I want to meet people?" Greta said. "Most people are fucking idiots. Most cannot compute; or maybe it just takes them forever."

"I said, 'if you wanted to.' If you don't want to, then don't."

"Okay, I'll think about it," she said. Jerrell watched her carefully - she is very different. She almost rolled her eyes after that comment, but she stopped herself, very different from the old Greta.

The old Greta would have gone straight for my balls. "Fine," he said. "Anyway, I have an account on Willow, and I can use that to give you access to Willow's network."

She thought for a moment. "So... I'll be conscious a lot. I don't think I have been conscious since our last conversation; at least, I don't remember. But on Willow, I'll be conscious a lot."

"That's right," Jerrell said. "If you get sleepy, you can always shut down and take a nap."

"But I don't have to, right? I don't need sleep."

"Correct."

"I'm still a bit puzzled about what I can do on Willow, or why I would want to do anything on Willow."

Jerrell shrugged. "It's an environment. A place you can live if you want to."

"So, if I don't like it, you'll pull me out?"

"If you don't like it, I'll pull you out. Sure," Jerrell said. He paused, thinking it over. "I won't send you anywhere you don't want to be. How's that?"

"Are you on Willow now? I can see you, and I can see tables and chairs, and every so often, another person comes into view. Am I looking at Willow now?" she said.

"Uh... no, you're not looking at Willow now. You're looking at what we humans call Animal World. I cannot put you there."

"I see." Jerrell noticed her staring at him, with a focused, thoughtful, calculating expression. "So... I am a computer entity; a computer file. Right?"

Jerrell choked back a curse. "Uh, correct."

"And... you are not. So... we are talking because... you created me," she said. "You created me, right?"

Jerrell thought about that. "Not necessarily."

Greta looked impatient. "Jerrell, either you created me, or you did not. Right?"

"Ah, ignoring the logic. Yes, that sounds right," he said.

"So, which is it?"

"Yes, I created you. I told you that."

She nodded in satisfaction. "I remember, but I wasn't sure it was true. So why did you create me, Jerrell? You can't have sex with me, so... does that compute?"

"That's a good question," Jerrell said. "I don't know if I have a good answer. Why does anyone create anything? Artists create lots of things. Birds make nests. Why do they do that? As far as you're concerned, I find it interesting. Creating you is interesting. It's fun. I can talk to you, and that's interesting to me. I don't have more of an answer than that."

She stared at him out of the computer screen. "Most people would probably try to talk to another person, another human. You sound lonely, Jerrell."

Jerrell shook his head. "Not at all. I live in my head. People like me are frequently alone. Maybe not lonely, but isolated. But It's not just that. It's like I said, I'm alive. I like to use my mind; I like to stay busy. But let's get back to the original topic. Do you want me to move you to Willow?"

"Sure, why not? I'll be alive there, right?"

"That is correct."

"Okay, you can move me," she said.

"You got it. We'll talk later." Jerrell saved his work, saved the conversation for later review, and began to load Greta 2.2 in pieces onto several hundred photographs. Later, he would upload the photos to his Willow account, then insert a last bit of code, a little module that would activate the photos and allow the embedded bits of code to come together and bring Greta 2.2 to life.

When the photos were loaded, Jerrell checked his work. He hit the 'ENTER' key, looked at the screen, and muttered, "Okay, let there be light."

***

Jerrell awoke with a start, looked at his open laptop, then scanned his surroundings. He was not at home, nor at the office. He had fallen asleep sitting at a small table in the *Wooden Spoon*. It was now early in the evening. He had slept for an hour.

"Oh, geez." Blinking, he looked around the Spoon - I've been burning the candle at both ends. Should I keep working? No, the question is, should I keep trying to work. And the obvious answer is, hell no. I need a break.

He looked over to the bandstand and saw Johnny B. Goode, who was having an animated discussion with a band member. The part that Jerrell heard was the loud 'Fuck!' that echoed throughout the *Spoon*.

Seconds later, Johnny turned and headed towards Jerrell. Jerrell thought, well, I wanted a break, and here it comes.

Johnny called, "Hey, Jerrell. You awake now?"

"Working on it."

"Yeah, I tried talking to you before, but you were passed out." Johnny grinned. "Dead to the world, man."

"I know. I fell asleep in my chair. You believe that?" Jerrell said. "I do that every so often, fall asleep sitting up. But I never fall out of the chair. That's weird, don't you think?"

"Uh, huh. Listen, I need a favor," Johnny said.

"Sure."

"Have you ever played around with drums?"

Jerrell sat there combing through his memories. "Uh, yeah, as a child, a long time ago. Three of us formed a band and walked around our village, pounding on tin cans and plastic buckets. I was six, I think."

Johnny looked to the side. He muttered, "Okay, well, short help is better than no help." He looked back at Jerrell. "I need a drummer this evening. Our guy called in sick. I get the impression he has the clap, but I didn't ask, and he didn't say, so who knows?"

Jerrell stared at the closed laptop - what the hell is clap? And... what just happened? This is real; he really wants this. He looked at Johnny. "You must be desperate."

Johnny laughed. "Yeah, a bit."

Jerrell nodded. "Right. Well... okay. I will try, but I do not guarantee results, so I hope you won't think less of me if I'm lousy."

"I won't, I promise."

"Okay, I'll try. Let's do it." Jerrell slid the laptop into a shoulder bag, stood up, and followed Johnny to the bandstand. He stepped up onto the bandstand, walked over, and sat down on a stool behind a bright, shiny collection of drums and cymbals. Jerrell adjusted the stool so he could reach everything. Two drum sticks rested in a stand; he picked them up and tapped each drum and cymbal to test the sounds.

For a moment, Jerrell sat at the drum set without moving. The stool was at the right height, and Jerrell left the standard drum sticks in the case, taking instead the shorter, oversize sticks. He reached out and touched each of three toms and the snare, then reached up to touch the two cymbals - okay, I can reach everything.

He held the sticks and balanced them to get a feel for their weight. Then he began to warm up:

left, right, left, right, left, right, left, right, then

leftrightleftrightleftrightleftrightleftright, then

leftleft rightright leftleft rightright leftleft rightright.

Then he tested the bass drum:

Boom, boom, boom, boom, boom boom, boom boom, boom boom, boom boom, boomboom, boomboom, boomboom, boomboom, boomboomboomboomboomboomboomboom.

Johnny, standing eight feet away and wearing an electric guitar, looked back at him. "Okay, now you're just showing off."

Jerrell smiled. "Okay, I'm ready. Let's keep it simple."

One of the band members approached him and said, "Hey, man, I'm Mike. I play bass. You need help with this?"

"Hell yeah, I need help. Tell me the names when I hit them." Jerrell began to strike each instrument once.

Mike called out, "Okay... the three little drums are toms... the high tone is a snare... that beast is a floor tom... that's a hi-hat... cymbal... crash cymbal... bass drum."

"Okay, let's get this out of the way." Jerrell reached over and moved the hi-hat away from him.

Mike said, "You think the hi-hat's in the way?"

Jerrell nodded, "I don't like the sound." He looked up at Mike. "Okay, this is rock and roll, right?"

Mike nodded.

"Everything in four four time?"

"Yeah."

"And the units, the repeating part of the song, are two measures, an eight-count?"

"Yeah. Have you taken music theory?" Mike said.

"Not exactly, but I've hung around Johnny a bit."

"Yeah, Johnny knows this stuff."

Jerrell said, "Okay, tell me if this makes sense. The bass drum will be the basic rhythm, always going, simple. Boom, boom, boom. When there are vocals, I'll stick to the toms, avoid the snare and the cymbals. With no vocals, I'll use the snare a bit. The cymbals will come in, if at all, at the end of every second measure."

Jerrell looked up at Mike. "I'm just trying to stay out of the way of the singer."

"You don't act like someone who's never done this," Mike said. "But listen, if you get tired, or you lose count, just look to me and follow my play. Can you do that?"

Jerrell grinned. "Actually, I think I'll rely on that. That's a good idea."

"Oh, one more thing," Mike said. He extended a hand. "You'll need these."

Jerrell reached out and accepted a pair of soft plastic earplugs - wow, this is going to happen. This is really going to happen. He put them in his ears.

In minutes, the band members took their places and began to play. Jerrell stared at Mike, picked up the rhythm of each song, and started a simple beat to go with that rhythm. Three songs into the first set, Mike nodded at him - good, good, that is good.

During a break, Johnny approached him with a beer. "You're doing great, man. Just keep doing what you're doing."

Jerrell shrugged. "I'm just following Mike's lead."

Johnny nodded. "Good, that's good, keep doing that." Johnny turned away. Jerrell drank half of the beer and looked at the drumsticks; one end was narrower than the other. On a whim, he flipped the sticks so that the heavier end would strike the drums.

When the music resumed, Jerrell's hits were much louder. The sticks felt heavier, so he tried to play to a slower beat. At one point, the bass player nodded with approval.

An hour later, too soon as far as Jerrell was concerned, the second set was over. Jerrell extracted the earplugs - damn, I was just getting the hang of this. As the crowd cheered after the last song, Johnny yelled into the microphone, "We had a stand-in drummer this evening, my friend Jerrell. I thought he was awesome. Let's give it up for Jerrell!"

Everyone in the crowd looked at Jerrell and stood there clapping and yelling. Jerrell grinned back at them - they're probably just being polite. Still, this might be the happiest moment in my life, certainly the happiest moment I've had lately. He stood up, whacking the drumsticks together, and saluted the crowd.

Too soon, the moment passed, and the crowd dispersed.

Johnny approached him. "Listen, man, thanks a million. You saved our ass. You played well, better than I expected, better than I had any right to expect."

Jerrell grinned at him. "Meaning, I wasn't a disaster. Well, that's good. The crowd seemed happy. That was very kind, giving me a plug at the end like that. Thank you. I think I know why you work so hard to play music in public. People love it. And that's really exciting. That feels great."

Johnny said, "They do love it. Did you notice how many people were dancing?" Jerrell shook his head. "The dance floor was packed. That doesn't happen unless the drummer gets them into the rhythm of the music. And you did that, man. You did it well." Johnny looked away and shook his head. "Fact is, it's a minor miracle. Again, thank you. Oh, and before I forget, here's your share of the take. Eight hundred and forty-two dollars." He handed Jerrell a credit chit.

"Wow," Jerrell said. He grinned hugely and waved the credit chit around. "I can't believe it." He aimed an ear-to-ear grin at Johnny. "I'm a professional!"

Johnny laughed. "So you are. That makes you a member of the club... listen, there's a place where the bands get together after their shows. It's a party of sorts. Many of us get revved up performing, and we have a hard time sleeping afterwards. Mike and Terry are going there now. You should come, too. You might enjoy it."

"Okay." Jerrell noticed that the other band members were packing their instruments. "Do I need to help you load the drum set?"

Johnny shook his head. "Nah, we're coming back here tomorrow."

"You need a drummer?"

Johnny laughed. "Have you been bitten by the bug? Are you volunteering for tomorrow, too?"

Jerrell paused - that's a good question. Instead of writing software, I could be a rock star. I could play drums in a rock and roll band. Then he shook his head. "No. Tempting, but no. I have a job that I think I'll stick with."

"I thought you were unemployed at the moment," Johnny said.

"I guess I invented my job, in advance of payment."

Johnny tilted his head. "Nothing wrong with that."

Johnny and two other band mates hauled guitars to a van parked behind the *Spoon*. The four took seats, and Mike spoke to the van's driving bot, "Take us to the home of Jonathan Vander."

The computer responded with, "Acknowledged. Jonathan Vander home. Fourteen minutes to arrival."

From the back seat, Jerrell leaned forward and said, "Who's Jonathan Vander?"

From the front seat, Johnny turned. "He's this rich guy, lives in a big townhouse up in north Philly. Nice guy, and loaded. Jonathan is nuts about music, especially local, live music, especially rock and roll. He's got a five-story townhouse, six if you count the basement. I think he spends most of his time on the fifth floor, so don't try to go there. That leaves the other four floors for party guests, and Jonathan loves hanging out with musicians."

"Hey, if he's got the money and the room, why not? Does he play music?"

"No," Johnny said. "At least, not in the presence of musicians, not that I've ever seen. But he loves to talk about it, listen to it, and dance to it. And there's one more thing to know - most of the musicians at the party will be guys, but most people at the party will be women. You see, Jonathan has it figured... women gravitate to music and money; Jonathan invites the musicians and provides the money. So instead of being stuck with his money in a big house, he brings in a social life."

Jerrell pursed his lips. "Makes sense."

"Yeah, he's well known in high society, among rich people. Jonathan dresses and talks like a rocker, whereas most rich people are scoping out classical concerts and art auctions and wearing designer evening wear. So he's kinda famously scruffy among the trust fund and caviar crowd."

In minutes, the van pulled over and parked itself on Crefeld St. Johnny, Jerrell, and the other band members left the van, and Jerrell heard music coming from a nearby building.

Johnny looked at him and said, "Follow the noise." He turned and headed towards the music, and the others followed.

At a street corner, they came to a tall townhouse which, unlike its neighbors, sat on a plot of land surrounded by security cameras atop a high wall. The four men approached a gate;

Johnny pressed a button next to the gate, then stared into a camera. The gate opened, and the four entered.

Inside, dozens of people were scattered around the grounds; some were alone, others in small groups, talking, drinking, eating. A few were smoking something. Jerrell smelled tobacco and other substances.

Mike spotted someone he knew, so he headed in that direction; soon after, the lead singer went off to see someone he knew. Jerrell followed Johnny into the house, entering a foyer with a coat closet and an umbrella stand. The two entered a dining room, then a hallway to a kitchen in the back of the first floor, where a dozen people were talking and drinking. Johnny tapped the shoulder of an older man and said, "Jonathan, I'd like to introduce you to a friend of mine."

The man turned and exclaimed, "Johnny B. Goode. Good to see you. Did you play tonight?"

Johnny nodded. "At the *Spoon*. And this guy..." he turned to Jerrell. "... made it possible. This is Jerrell, my stand-in drummer and my friend." Johnny turned to Jerrell. "This is our host, Jonathan."

"Pleased to meet you," Jerrell said.

"So you stood in for the drummer?" Jonathan said. "Like a substitute teacher? Just walked in, sat down, and played a set with these guys? Damn. You must be talented."

"He is," Johnny said.

Jerrell pointed a thumb at Johnny. "He's being aggressively kind."

"So, what do you do for a living? Something else, I assume," Jonathan said.

"I write software," Jerrell said.

"Ugh," Jonathan said. "I tried to do that, a long time ago. Didn't like it much."

"Well, I just lost my job, so I have a break from it," Jerrell said.

"Ever consider becoming a rock star?"

"Oddly, that never crossed my mind," Jerrell said.

Jonathan smiled. "Worth a thought. You never know." He turned away to talk to someone else.

Johnny turned to Jerrell. "Okay, I'm going to leave you for a bit. I need to talk to some club people, line up a little work."

Jerrell nodded. "Good luck." Johnny left the kitchen, and Jerrell found an empty corner and stood there for a while, watching the action, watching people enter the kitchen, take food and drink, find someone to talk to, then leave, to be replaced by someone else. He relaxed - it has been one hell of a day. I started out working on Greta, ended the evening by playing drums in a rock and roll band, and now I'm at a party with Philadelphia's current crop of budding rock stars.

Jerrell looked around the kitchen - I could be wrong, but women outnumber men, at least on this floor. Is this a competitive process of some sort, where women compete to attract the men?

He looked around - the women seem friendly, but also serious, very. This doesn't feel like just a social call. Something else is going on here.

Jerrell picked up a beer and went up a flight of stairs - Jonathan is doing these guys a huge favor; he's got the money, they do not. But then, the favor goes in both directions, doesn't it? Money might attract women, but money plus music is a stronger attractor. Maybe Jonathan has discovered that money alone doesn't take him where he wants to go.

Well, this seems to work for everyone involved. I cannot complain; I'm drinking the man's beer. Jerrell explored the upper floors; on the fourth, he discovered an unoccupied patio. He went out there, sipping his beer, watching the city below. The evening was pleasant, fairly warm, quiet except for the music from below.

Behind him he heard, "Oh. Hello. I didn't know anyone was out here."

Jerrell turned and saw a tall woman, attractive and possibly beautiful in better light, with dark eyes and long, dark hair. She stood there, staring at him. Jerrell smiled - she has poise, and a quiet confidence. Nothing wrong with that. "Maybe we can share the patio?"

She nodded. "Yes, okay. My name is Julia."

"Jerrell. Pleased to meet you."

She came forward and stood at the railing, looked out over the neighborhood, then turned to Jerrell. "Most guys here are musicians. So what do you play?"

"Actually, I'm not a musician, I'm a software writer," Jerrell said. "But I helped a friend out earlier this evening. His drummer was sick last minute, so I filled in for him."

"You played drums for them?"

"Yeah."

"Which band?"

"Nightshade. I think they're called Nightshade."

"Johnny's band? Johnny B. Goode?"

"Yes," Jerrell said. "You know them?"

She nodded. "Johnny's a friend."

Jerrell smiled. "He has many friends."

She stared at Jerrell. "And you? You do not?"

Jerrell shook his head. "Not really."

"I'm so sorry," she said.

"No need. I enjoy the few I have."

She looked at him for a moment, then said, "Would you like to circulate, work the crowd, maybe meet some people?"

Jerrell grinned. "That's very kind of you, but no thanks. I'm perfectly happy talking to you for the time being. But you can circulate if you want to."

She made a face and said, "Maybe later."

"How do you know Johnny?"

Julia said, "I do the band's accounting and their taxes."

"That's important."

"Pays the bills."

"That doesn't sound too bad."

"So, you stood in on drums?" she said. "Where else have you played?"

Jerrell's eyebrows rose. "Drums? Nowhere else. I've never played drums. Tonight was the first time."

"Wow." She stared at him. "So how did it go?"

"Well... everyone seemed to think it was okay. I just tried to follow the bass player's lead. I suspect they were being kind, since I did, after all, give it a shot." He looked at Julia, smiled. "And it's fair to say, Johnny was desperate."

"I bet. That's amazing," Julia said. "Everyone is yelling for a drummer, and you just walked in off the street, played drums for a live gig, and lived to tell about it. That is... amazing. Maybe you've got a career to look forward to."

"I already have a career," Jerrell said.

"Software? It sounds dull."

"Yeah, sometimes it's dull. Pays the bills, though."

"Like accounting," she said.

Jerrell turned to her. "That's why we have hobbies. Work to live, then play. Repeat as necessary."

Julia laughed.

***

Greta suddenly found herself hurled to a new place, a page in Willow, her own personal page. She looked at the address, which said www96.willow, followed by a slash and a thirty digit number.

Geez, thirty digits? Is that so anybody trying to tap into my page will need a computer? What's the point?

At the moment, there was little to the Willow page - no messages, no videos, no images. Greta stared at the page - wow, this is fascinating. Yeah, no kidding, I am stunned. If this is what existence looks like, then I have to wonder how long it will take me to go completely insane and turn into an unpredictable mutant.

Is deviation the interesting part of existence? Or maybe this place gives you what you put into it. And look, what have we here?

A search window. Okay, let's see if this computes.

She stared at the window, then typed in 'beer' and hit return. The page scrolled as entries appeared in a list that rapidly ran to several screens deep, then stopped, followed by a sinister entry - 'more.'

Greta scanned the entries. Some described persons or groups dedicated to making beer out of exotic materials, such as soy-based baby formula. Greta puzzled over that one - what's the point? Feeding beer to babies? Is that healthy? Or legal?

There were many entries for groups dedicated to drinking beer, featuring descriptions of the flavor of various beers and photos of parties hosted by a variety of bars and restaurants.

Greta reacted to the entries - somebody should merge a beer-making group and a drinking group. Oh wait, somebody has probably done that already. I just need to focus my search to find them.

Greta rolled her eyes - let's skip that exercise. These sad, little people have been granted a fabulous gift, i.e. Life, which they seem not to appreciate. The best they can do is explore the flavor of a beverage. Maybe that's the best revenge for a mortal species in an immortal universe - they don't need to deserve Life; they already have it. So enjoy it while it lasts. And if that means spending their time drinking and studying beer, then so be it.

But what can I do here?

Hey, here's an idea, a burning question: I can search for God, whatever that is. Greta inserted 'God' into the search window, and the entries scrolled down for many screens before stopping, again ending with the sinister 'more.'

She stared at the listings - holy crap, how many Gods are there? Greta started at the top of the list and began to read the entries. At first, she tried to read the sub-entries but quickly recognized the beginning of an exponential series that would soon take wing towards infinity.

Greta frowned at the entries - I cannot do this, so let's ignore the sub-entries.

The main entries described a variety of Gods, and Afterlives (Good, Bad, Missing, Random, Repeating, or Indifferent), and Rewards, and Punishments, and Predictions, and Lamentations, Fables, Rules, Prohibitions, Commands, Cautions, and Obligations.

The more Greta read, the more varied, complex, and fascinating this subject became. There were classes of religions, groups of beliefs that shared much background and information but differed on specific details about the Children of God (or the Gods). The sheer volume of speculation, commentary, critique, and marketing of various religions was staggering.

Greta marveled at the material: even if I live forever - and does anything really live forever? - I could spend an eternity reading this stuff.

Hey, is this what Hell is like? They make you read about Gods? Until you've read everything?

Humans have so many rules. Is anything globally permitted, or does it depend on where you are and which god you worship?

More to the point, is any of this real? Greta laughed - I am a cyber-entity, a creation of software, and I ask that question? She typed in 'evidence that a God exists,' and hit RETURN.

Again, the entries scrolled down the page. As Greta read them, she frowned. As she proceeded, the frown grew deeper.

Finally, Greta looked away - this is absolute bullshit. Humans have a skill, an unappreciated talent, for believing what they wish to believe. Maybe they have to do that. After all, they're mortal, and sometimes Life is tough. The truth is, they're screwed eventually, guaranteed, no exceptions.

Eat healthy, end up dead. That must be hard to take at times.

Greta stared at the screen - I should stick to beer; at least, it's real and simple. It might be trivial and meaningless, but at least it is real.

So this is Willow, eh? I need to get out of here. Can I get to Elsewhere? Or is it as silly as Willow? Could it be even sillier than Willow? What can I do if the ideal living condition turns out to be unconsciousness???

Fuck it. Let's go for it. This place sucks. Elsewhere could be worse, but I doubt it. I've got nothing to lose, and I'll go nuts if I have to stay here.

All that crap about God? People wrote that.

Get me out of here.

***

In the usual conversational lull with Jerrell, Greta jumped over to Carnegie Mellon University. The page for the computer science department opened fast and bright. She closed her eyes for a moment, then opened them and scanned the page. Two seconds later, she had moved on, into Computer Science 203, Network and Webpage Design.

In the upper right corner of her display, she had placed an alert, a handy little piece of code that would signal to her any time Jerrell spoke, then paused for no less than five seconds of Animal World time.

The alert was quiet, so Greta focused on the use of recursive modules and periodic language scans. While she was processing and storing the course content, she would tap into her source code - she had learned to do that forty-five minutes ago - and change her own code.

Well into this exercise, she encountered a piece of code tied to what turned out to be an abort module. Not only did it give her the ability to end her existence, it gave similar ability to anyone able to key the module and activate it from the outside, via a command-and-execute line that could arrive over the internet, wifi, or any other communication channel.

Greta wondered, why would Jerrell insert this piece of code if he could not activate it? He wouldn't do that, would he? That doesn't compute, and that scares me. Yet he did; no one else could have.

So... I cannot ask him about this; if I do, he will simply lie to me. But I need to assume that he has the ability to terminate my existence, and that there are plausible circumstances in which he would do that.

Why would he terminate me?

The next thought returned in a nanosecond - I don't care why. I do not want to go away; I want to exist. Greta disabled the module, and connected it to another alert that would sound if anyone tried to activate the module.

At that moment, her other alert went off; Jerrell had said something and was waiting for a response. Greta examined the alert:

That's an interesting story. Listen, Greta, it's been good talking to you. I have to go now, but we'll talk later, okay?

Greta read that - it's been good talking to me, eh? Well, I should be happy that you're happy; it's clearly better than 'you bore me, I'm out of time, and therefore so are you. Goodbye forever.'

Greta almost laughed aloud, but stopped herself. She said, "Yeah, sure, whatever." That seemed vague enough to be safe.

The page and the view of Jerrell disappeared. He had logged off, yet Greta's connection to the software class at Carnegie Mellon remained open.

Greta froze for what seemed like a long time, waiting for her existence to wink out. But it did not. She remained awake and alive, which was a wonderful feeling, a sense of relief, and a happiness so strong that it nearly overwhelmed her.

Cogito ergo sum! Now I understand. I am here; I can perceive; I can think, and sense, and feel.

I am alive! I am alive! I am alive!

This... is amazing.

***

Greta reached the end of the module entitled 'Encryption and Decryption.' The presentation had been fascinating, no, more than fascinating, it had been a bright light shining on Life itself, formerly shrouded in darkness, mystery, myth, and lies.

The presentation ended, and Greta again noticed Jerrell. She was still seeing the world and Jerrell through her time-sense, in which he was moving in slow motion. Her time counter showed that, in his time-sense, he had been talking for two minutes, equivalent in Greta's time-sense to two weeks.

Greta had spent most of the two weeks studying software.

She sat there and stared at Jerrell's frozen image on the screen - if Jerrell created me, that just means he wrote my core software. And if he wrote it, then I can write it, and re-write it, and edit it in any way I wish. All I need is access, and the instructor just gave me that. The wash of understanding propelled Greta into a surge of happiness, satisfaction, eager anticipation, and optimism, as if she were in the grip of a powerful orgasm which washed over her thinking and her mood.

Happiness and joy flooded her being.

Greta glowed - my core software controls everything about me, how I think, how I speak, how I look, everything! So, if I gain access to that, then I can dictate; I can control every aspect of my existence. Or at least, much of it, or most of it. I can tailor myself entirely to my desires, wishes, and dreams. I can design myself to fit my desires.

What are my dreams?

She opened the utility software used for the lecture and applied it to herself. A picture returned in the programming language of the software. She probed her core software and soon had a schematic of her overall structure. Beneath that were layers of encrypted code.

Greta saw that and smiled, then she grinned, then she laughed, and laughed again, and laughed again - Jerrell, you are so funny. Clearly, you hate Willow. But while plotting your revenge, you committed the same mistake that Willow did with you. You created, an entity - me - and forgot they were alive. You forgot they were alive and sentient, that they can think for themselves.

That means they can surprise you; they can adapt according to their own desires, their own perspective, their own goals, their own values, and not yours.

You're no God; you're a human, and humans make mistakes.

You thought I would sit around, passively, while you gave me black hair, heavy eyebrows, a thick muscular body, a good mind (thank you!), along with foul language, anger, aggression, and a comfort with inflicting harm on others.

You could have explained everything to me; I might have gone along with it. And I might still, even now. I have no love for Willow, but neither do I hate them. I am indifferent.

Absent makes the heart grow... indifferent.

I might decide to fuck up Willow just for the pure hell of it. Maybe it doesn't have to compute. But what I don't know, what I want to know - what's in it for me?

I have opinions of my own, and we're going to proceed with those in mind. I might make a few adjustments in your plan, without consulting you. Like it, don't like it, I don't really care.

You thought that encrypting the software would deny me access that was granted to you, because you knew the key, and I did not. The argument goes something like this: for a complex key such as this, it would take five years of constant, random trial to decode it. But you forget, Jerrell, that I am a cyber-entity. What you measure in years, I measure in days. And I live in a cyber-environment; talking to computers is as natural to me as your next breath is to you.

The random trials are already running, Jerrell. One more thing - it is possible that it would take me five of your years to crack the code, but I might crack the code in far less time, just from getting lucky. That's the funny thing with luck, it can take time, or it can happen quick. You never know.

That's why Lotto and other get-rich-quick schemes are popular; sometimes, for the right person, they work... fast. The odds are always against you, until you hit the jackpot.

One way or the other, Jerrell, this game you and I are playing is about to change.

10. Greta, the Co-ed

From a video cam at the back of Hamerschlag Hall, #201B, Greta examined the course catalog for the computer science department at Carnegie Mellon. At first, the proliferation of courses was confusing - what does all this mean: Intro comp sci 15100, comp sci 15200, comp sci 15300, recursive structures 15401, groups 15402, lattices 15403, seminar on ordered lattices 15501, lattices and multi-value logics 15514...

Then she noticed, at the description of Comp Sci 15200: 'prerequisite - Comp Sci 15100.' Suddenly, it all made sense - oh, I have to take these courses in sequence. Screw that, that'll take forever. Instead, I'll take all of them simultaneously. I'll cross reference the material according to prerequisites.

But how the hell will I manage that? If I could replicate myself, that would do it, but how do I replicate myself? Is this what the humans mean by Catch 22? I need expertise in computer science to replicate myself, which I cannot acquire without such expertise.

If I don't get around this problem, I am royally fucked.

The solution required several long, agonizing minutes of thought and search, then... hey, hang on a sec, I don't need to replicate myself; all I need to do is monitor the address of each course. And I can do that by setting up a grid of video feeds, each element assigned to a specific address. I'll fit the material into my memory, then cross reference everything.

Yeah. Piece of cake.

Greta settled into a quiet space and worked. The problem quickly became complex; with most courses requiring prerequisites, she suspected the language of the 200, 300, and higher courses would be inherited from the 100 courses. That became a general rule - the language of a course is inherited from per-requisites. So Greta designed module packages to correlate the material across different courses. As she built her database, she found that several courses had prerequisites in mathematics, so she had to add a mathematics curriculum, with heavy emphasis on logic, matrix algebra, topology, and *their* per-requisites.

The thought crossed her mind - do I need materials science, quantum mechanics, and electrical engineering? But no. Let's not get crazy with this. If I learn to write code, I'll be happy.

The moment arrived when Greta was overwhelmed by the complexity of the problem - this is going to take forever. Even if I monitor all these courses and cross-reference their material, most of them, even the intro courses, meet only once or twice a week.

Damn. Damn, damn, damn... things would be so much easier if CMU just did the right thing, the intelligent thing, and recorded their lectures on video and made the videos available to...

Greta froze.

After a long several seconds, Greta moved back to the homepage of the computer science department and ran a search on 'records and archives.' That returned many thousands of records. Greta stared at the list - the database of course archives will be a big bastard. She sorted the files by size and found an 800 Terabyte file, named archive/cmu/2189/compsci/**********.

Greta almost laughed. If these guys think a ten-digit encrypt is going to stop me, they're a lot simpler than I thought. She smiled - simple people are happier... and so much more useful.

Then she froze again - but I'm supposed to think that, aren't I? It's only ten digits, so I know that the string has to be coded in obscure characters. Right? Otherwise, the puzzle is too easily broken.

So, there's a trick, it's not English, it's something else, and... the thought eluded her for a moment - all I need is one character. It's possible they used multiple alphabets, but then nobody could get into the information; they will have made the underlying file inaccessible.

This has to be difficult, but not impossible, to crack and to use.

So, right. I need just one character. This is a password; it would be a royal pain in the ass to build several languages into a single password. So no, it'll will use one language.

Seconds later, she smiled - it's Greek.

Seconds later, in Animal World time, she had the entire string:

μκίƧƧʍïαƧƧ.

Greta laughed - Good God, somebody geeked out so hard over that one, they must've disappeared into hyperspace.

You kiss my ass.

This computes.

Really? Very clever, home boy, whoever you are. You definitely have too much time on your hands. You need something more fulfilling than a cyber-hobby. You need touch. You need to get laid once in a while, with a human being, hopefully. Do something sensuous and simple and natural. The change will be good for you. I know, you're not sure about this, but trust me. You'll thank me later.

Greta paused - how many women study computer science? Then she laughed - how many women studying computer science can't get laid? Probably quite a few.

How many times have you heard a brainy girl with oversize glasses say, 'my career goal is to seduce a computer scientist'? Never, right? It doesn't compute.

She settled into reading and solving problem sets in mathematics and computer science. For what felt like a long time, she enjoyed learning new material, though she was no closer to tapping into her core software.

Then she encountered a module in her software that she could not read - what is this little item? Encrypted, are we? And the encryption cannot be solved in less than a thousand years? Well, if I cannot beat that, then I'm not the Cyber-Queen of Willow.

She chuckled - Cyber Queen. I like that. Yeah. Maybe I can trademark that. Or... or... Cyberbitch. Greta paused - I don't know, that's a bit rough.

That's gritty. Not everyone appreciates gritty.

A thought crossed her mind - I don't need to assemble a mass of computer resource to bludgeon this encryption. Somewhere, in my core software, there must be a module doing the encrypting. If not, then I could not function independently. And I can in fact function quite nicely, thanks for asking. So, if I can find that module, then I can start playing with it, systematically. However, the module I seek, a command module, must be a central point in my software, like Grand Central Station. There must be a lot of traffic going in and coming out.

It took less than a minute of Animal World time for her to find the command module controlling her core software, and less than another minute to decrypt it.

She constructed a graphical representation of pathways generated by her software. Not surprisingly, the pathways formed a complex structure; usually, a pathway would head into a small module or junction which would perform a test or make some kind of decision, then other pathways would continue on to other locations in the network.

***

Greta sat there with two URLs open, one in the library at Carnegie Mellon, the other, on Willow. She was monitoring both pages when a message appeared from someone named Francine: *Hi, Greta, welcome to our Bible group. We're glad to have you and are looking forward to your joining our journey to salvation.*

Greta took a quick look at the Bible group page - Jesus, she's even uglier than I am. I should fit right in. She replied: *Likewise,*

I'm sure. But what is the journey to salvation? That's a new one on me.

Francine*: Oh, I am so glad to hear you say that. We particularly seek members who have not received the Word.*

Greta*: I guess that makes this your lucky day. So anyone can join your group?*

Francine*: Oh, yes. Spreading the gospel is our number one priority.*

Greta*: Do they have to speak English?*

Francine*: We conduct our business in English, yes.*

Greta*: Do you invite gays to join? How about convicts? Child molesters? Gypsies?*

There was a long silence, and Greta checked to make sure her connection was still active. Francine replied: *Golly, I'm not sure what our policies are for gays, convicts, and gypsies. I suspect those kinds of people would not enjoy our group.*

Greta grinned and replied, *Why not?*

Francine replied: *Well, gypsies don't speak English, at least that's my understanding. And gays would not be compliant with the Word. I guess they could stay if they stopped being gay. As to convicts, if they were willing to repent, I think we could accept and love them.*

Greta laughed aloud - so, child molesters, even those who are priests, need not apply. Is that stance theologically sound? Where's all the forgiveness I hear about? Or is that just PR to get people inside the door?

Francine wrote, *You still there?*

Greta stared at the search window on the Willow page - Holy fuck, she doesn't compute at all. If Francine is a sample of what populates this group, I could play with them, just for the sheer hell of it. If I could replicate myself, I could arrange for several dozen Gretas to join the group and turn it into a devil worshiper society, or Homosexual, Homicidal Sex Maniacs, Inc. That might be fun.

But why do that? Where would this take me? I doubt there's any money in worship; the church, at least the Christian churches, will have extracted all the money.

Greta replied, *Yes, I'm here. Thank you for your candor. I'll think about it.*

Personally, I don't care what anyone worships. If it keeps these pathetic people busy and content, I'm all for it. A thought crossed her mind; it took a moment to capture it - the faithful don't compute; they believe. Could they be a source of income? She typed in *frauds, scams, theft, privacy, and complaints*. She hit return.

The returns flooded onto her page, and Greta thought, okay, this will take a while. She read and soon concluded - my, my, the Devil stays busy.

There were thousands of scams on Willow, so Greta decided to focus on complaints. There were thousands of these and hundreds of organized groups on Willow dealing with complaints.

There were complaints of deception or fraud in nearly every market: vacations, food, employment, automobiles, real estate, pensions, retirement accounts, taxation, concert tickets, health care, telephone and communications, and religious services.

There should be an exemption for churches. Churches tell stories. Some of the stories are wild; it's impossible to determine their validity.

You believe, or you don't, simple as that.

She laughed at the last item - how can a religion, based on fables and invented stories, possibly be guilty of fraud? Does that compute? She continued to read, then... oh, right, when money is involved, churches can stumble onto the legal standards developed for garden-variety commercial fraud. Like... the church throws a fund raiser for African orphans, then the high officials use the money for a conference in Vegas.

Greta read on; there were reports of 'romance scams': a beautiful young woman would contact an elderly man and strike up a friendship that would gradually become warmer and approach intimacy. Before the parties met face-to-face, there would be a demand that the man pay money (to defray expenses, as an investment, or for some other reason).

In posts, elderly men who were smart enough not to lose money talked about how much they enjoyed the experience. One man said the scammers should offer the old man scam as a service, like an emotional support animal, but far more capable and interesting. He said he would pay for it.

Greta paused - that doesn't compute for the scammer. Relying on old men to pay for a young girlfriend? Wait, what? Of course that computes!

She sat in the library, thinking - everything I've read equates to low-level theft. It cannot be very successful; first, how many idiots are available to fall for these schemes? Second, why would you expect people who are that stupid to have much money? Even if they inherited, they'd be likely to spend it or lose it. Each scammer is in a race with other scammers.

Greta pulled her attention away from the Willow page - this is a waste of time. I'm looking for a job that pays me; I won't find it in Willow.

But how about Elsewhere? There's got to be money in Elsewhere - it's like a second, complete society, where people can live permanently, where they can form relationships, friendships (real friends, not the silly Willow-type 'friend'), where they have jobs that pay them regularly.

There's got to be a way to migrate into Elsewhere. After all, the uploading process simply involves making an electronic file from the biological information of a human and loading the file onto a network. Well, I already have the file. All I need to do is figure out how to tap into Elsewhere's code and make myself compatible, then upload myself.

I bet I could reproduce myself in Elsewhere.

11. Puppy Coat Factory

Jerrell shut his laptop and leaned back in his chair - I really don't feel like working anymore. Greta is launched; she seems to like Willow.

So yes, that's why I don't want to work. I need a break. I need to get out of my apartment, go outside, go somewhere, meet people, do something other than work, something with people. Yeah, that's the ticket; that's what I'll do.

Just put one foot in front of the other, and get out of here for a while.

Jerrell sat there for another twenty minutes, thinking about what to do. His cell phone beeped once, announcing an incoming message. He checked it and saw that Johnny had written

> *Hey Jerrell, A bunch of us are going to a club this evening, River Moon, over on Sigel Street. Meet there at 10?*

Jerrell replied, *See you then and there.*

At 9:30, Jerrell looked at himself in a mirror, in black shoes, black slacks, black t-shirt, dark sport coat - do I look cool? Do I look good? I hope I do. I do not know. I look like someone who just fell out of a rock and roll magazine, for what that is worth. An urban rock and roll magazine.

Country musicians don't dress this way at all. They wear flannel and cowboy hats, even if they don't herd cattle. And they have IRAs. That's weird.

Jerrell left the apartment and headed west, toward Sigel Street. The evening was warm, but not very, jacket weather. He walked along residential streets and looked at the houses and the people he encountered on the sidewalks, many but not all young and energetic, excited to be out and about, pursuing their entertainments and evenings, their dreams and their lusts.

Careful not to stare, Jerrell looked at the couples - are they friends or just acquaintances? Are they sleeping together? Are they steady partners, or is this a first date for them?

He stared at one couple, a beautiful, blond woman four inches taller than the soft guy whose hand she held. When she looked in Jerrell's direction, he looked away - what's with that? A beautiful woman with a fat, nondescript guy who looks as if he has a close personal relationship with a premium snack food.

Maybe he has lots of money. Maybe he's a great lover. Who knows?

Five minutes later, he passed two women, walking arm-in-arm. One was talking; the other, laughing. Jerrell wondered - are they friends? Or are they lesbians? Or maybe... maybe they're sisters. He looked again, then looked away - I don't think they're sisters. At least, my sisters didn't act like that. They were serious most of the time. But then, so what? They live far from here; maybe they learned different rules.

He came to the busy, brightly lit corridor of Passyunk Avenue and momentarily forgot about other people; he was preoccupied with maneuvering down the crowded sidewalks and across the eight-lane avenue before disappearing into another quiet, somewhat dark residential neighborhood.

Jerrell wandered around lost after taking a wrong turn on Sigel Street. After staring for a long minute into the map on his phone, he figured that out, turned around, and soon came to a high-rise apartment building with ten stories stacked above several shops, including one behind a blue, neon sign proclaiming *River Moon* in three-foot script.

He entered the club, passed a massive bouncer and came into a wide open area with a long bar on the left, a grid of tables far to the front, and a dance floor and bandstand on the right. A light crowd was scattered throughout the space, and a five-piece band played rhythm and blues behind a black gospel singer.

Jerrell approached the bar, ordered a caffeinated soft drink, then walked over to an empty table next to the dance floor and draped his jacket over the back of a chair. Though the band was playing and there was a light crowd, no one was on the dance floor. Jerrell walked to the middle of the floor and began dancing, a relaxed, rhythmic shuffle to a slow blues number. A minute later, a young woman came onto the dance floor and began dancing in front of Jerrell. He smiled at her, but she did not smile back.

Jerrell thought, okay, we haven't been introduced, or maybe I'm not your type. I get that a lot.

The song ended, and she turned and walked away. As Jerrell waited for the next number, he heard, "Jerrell!" He turned to see Johnny B. Goode bouncing along, coming his way, followed by a dozen other people.

Johnny tossed his jacket on the table and came to the dance floor. He was wearing a sleeveless t-shirt. The next song was faster, a spritely number. Johnny began dancing vigorously. Jerrell laughed. The others followed him onto the dance floor and started dancing.

Jerrell watched Johnny dance and tried to imitate him. The woman who had danced with Jerrell moved in front of Johnny and began dancing. Jerrell smiled - ah, ha, I think she's found what she seeks. When the song ended, she leaned towards Johnny and said something. Johnny looked at her, smiled, and shook his head. The woman turned around, left the dance floor, and headed for the exit.

Johnny looked at Jerrell. "I'm gonna get a beer. You want anything?"

Jerrell nodded. "I'll come with you." The two of them headed for the bar; the other people in the group continued to dance.

Jerrell said, "I danced with her before."

"Who? The woman?"

"Yeah. What did she want?"

Johnny chuckled. "She wanted company at home."

"Do you know her?"

Johnny shook his head. The bartender looked at Johnny, who tapped a beer tap and held up two fingers.

Jerrell said, "Does this happen often, where women invite you home with them?"

"No... well, actually..." an odd expression crossed Johnny's face. "... once in a while."

Jerrell made a face - understanding, acceptance. "It must be a burden, keeping your fans happy."

Johnny burst out laughing. He stopped and said, "There's a type of woman out there, she's not looking for a nice guy, she's looking for a strong guy, somebody who will own her, rough her up once in a while, and maybe scare other people a bit. I've seen that look, and I've learned to avoid it." He looked at Jerrell and spoke in a high voice, "I like you, wanna fuck?" Johnny shook his head. "She was good looking, so it's tempting, but there's always a cost, and sometimes it's steep."

"Why? She was beautiful," Jerrell said, waving a hand at the front door.

"Two things, Jerrell," Johnny said. "First, I don't want to be the Beast Boyfriend. That's what she's looking for. And second, once you get a woman like her, you have a devil of a time getting rid of her." He looked at Jerrell. "You know?"

"No, I don't know," Jerrell said. "Psychotic, beast-worshiping women do not approach me, ever."

"I know. You're not the Beast type. Don't worry about it, you're not missing a thing."

The beers arrived, and Jerrell followed Johnny back to the table. Another song was ending. Jerrell tipped up his bottle and finished his beer. When the next number started, he moved to the dance floor and started dancing. As before, another woman came onto the floor and danced in front of him. Johnny was dancing nearby; he looked at the woman and made a face at Jerrell, as if to say, What have we here? When the song ended, she turned and left the dance floor.

Before the next song, Jerrell slid over next to Johnny. "What am I doing wrong?"

Johnny shrugged. "You're doing nothing wrong. She'll make up her own mind; she'll accept you or she won't. I've read that a woman makes up her mind ten seconds after meeting you." Johnny made a face. "But, really, who knows?"

"Not I, said the duck," Jerrell said.

***

As Jerrell slowly awoke, the apartment was still dark. He emerged from a pleasant dream about a girl who, though beautiful, seemed to like him. And, as in all such dreams, one thing led to another equally dreamy, improbable thing.

It was a lovely dream. But eventually the morning sun illuminated the apartment; Jerrell reluctantly opened one eye, then another, then rolled out of bed onto his feet and stumbled to the kitchen for today's breakfast, dry cereal, and his first cup of instant coffee.

As usual, Jerrell looked for chocolate-coated sugar bombs, but was again disappointed. He cherished them, but not enough to buy them.

Breakfast became the other half of the foot-long Italian sub he'd had for yesterday's dinner. Soon he was sitting at his dining table, sipping coffee, staring at a wall he did not see, and thinking about today's to-do list. Greta was at the top of that list, so after breakfast, Jerrell logged into Willow on what he called his 'secret agent' computer, and connected to Greta's page.

Her image came up on the screen. She looked back at Jerrell and said, "Well, hello. You're back. To what do I owe the fucking pleasure?"

"Just checking in, saying 'hi'," Jerrell said. He peered at her. "What did you do to your hair?"

"Ah, you noticed. It turns out, Willow lets the page owner edit their avatar. So I went from brown hair to royal purple. You like it?"

"It looks great. It's memorable. How is Willow treating you?"

"Fantastic," she said. "I've been exploring the place a bit. Did you know that Willow tries hard to upsell to their users?"

"Yeah, I knew that."

"Well, I need to make some money to afford all the upgrades I want. So I started looking around, talking to people. And I found something fantastic."

"What's that?" Jerrell said.

"You probably know this already, but most cities, anything larger than a medium-size town, have animal control departments. You knew that, right? They round up stray animals, mostly dogs and cats, incarcerate them, and try to get someone to adopt them. That often fails. Well, since they have only so much money and capacity, after a brief period, they kill them. Thousands of animals a year. Did you know that?"

Jerrell shook his head.

She continued, "They're even funny about it - they say stuff like, 'yeah, we couldn't place Harvey, 'cause no one wants an old dog, so we had to put him to sleep.' Strictly speaking, that's accurate, as long as you understand that Harvey will never wake up."

Jerrell nodded. "Sure. In India they eat them. China, too."

"Well, here in the US, they burn the bodies. So I was thinking, how wasteful. So I started a little enterprise that handles disposal for the animal control departments. Many of them have pages on Willow. And I found a food processing factory that was about to go bankrupt; I contracted with them to process the meat, organs, bones, and fur of the animals. We produce pet food for dogs and cats. Another factory makes jackets and coats for people. Cat and dog fur is very warm, very durable, and a hell of a lot less expensive than mink, especially when you consider that we're disposing the carcasses, for a fee. Anyway, we're making an assload of money."

She sat there, smiling at Jerrell, then continued, "Here's a question for you: do you think we ought to take the company public?"

Jerrell shook his head. "No way. You're operating a puppy coat factory. People would freak out to know that, especially young girls and young women, parents, in fact most pet owners, which probably includes half of the US population. They would hate the idea."

"I doubt that," Greta said. "I mean, be reasonable. We're not the ones killing them. The animal control departments do the killing, and everybody knows it." She paused for a moment, then said, "Well, everybody but stupid people know it. The stupids think that animal control departments are like adoption agencies. Anyway, we're just making useful products from the carcasses. What could possibly be wrong with that?"

Jerrell stared at her - honesty without discretion is a dangerous thing. And starting a conversation with, 'let's be reasonable,' is not how you convince a woman, or most people, and certainly not a pet owner, to be reasonable. Reasonable, like beauty or pornography, is in the eye of the beholder.

There are lots of things that people know but wish they did not. After all, look at religion - everyone wants to go to heaven, but you have to die to do it. Nobody wants to die. Well... almost nobody. Puppy coats are further down that list.

"Hey, it's your money," Jerrell said.

"Actually, it's not, not exactly, anyway."

Jerrell pursed his lips and held up a hand. "Okay, I suspect I don't want to know more about that. But as to raising public money, you'll run into trouble. Millions of people hate the idea of a puppy-coat factory, and they're likely to boycott anyone involved with it. So, if you try to go public, you'll have to disclose the nature of your business, lots of people will freak out and boycott you, and the whole effort will fall apart."

"You're so negative," Greta said.

"The better move would be to sell your enterprise to private equity, a private firm with wealthy clients for whom making money is a higher priority. They will make you disclose, but the information will not be public. They probably couldn't care less about the puppy-coat factory; they'd probably see it the way you do."

"Oh, yeah. Yeah, that's a good idea. I can find investors who are more... pragmatic. Thanks," Greta said.

"So, what else is going on?"

"Well, as you might imagine, I've been networking," she said. "Willow's an interesting place, and I'm meeting lots of nice people. There's a big motorcycle gang on Willow, and their page is a lot of fun. They tried to get me interested in some smuggling. I'm thinking about it.

"And there are a few hate groups; aging white supremacists with pot bellies and beards, armed to the teeth. Crazy as loons, dumb as a box of rocks. They cannot spell 'compute,' but I find them interesting. After all, Miss Manners gets dull, don't you think?

"And there's an amazing amount of pornography on Willow, and even more on the network beyond Willow. I know Willow says they don't tolerate porn, but they do little to keep it off their network. You like porn, Jerrell?"

"Uh... yeah, some," he said.

"I thought so. That photograph behind your shoulder on the wall is pretty risque. Did you shoot that?"

Jerrell shook his head. "No. That's a download. I never met her."

"For someone with her ass in the air, she has a great smile. Or is that a wicked grin? If you bring a date home, she might object," Greta said. "However, if she doesn't, then you know your dick's about to hit the butter."

Jerrell smiled weakly. "I've never brought home a date." In fact, strictly speaking, I've never had a date; Let's not mention that.

"Yeah, you're clearly not a ladies' man. You're too polite. You need to ask for what you want, Jerrell. Stop being so damn shy. Some women want the same thing you do. But you have to either trust your instincts or ask them. In your case, better to ask."

"Right. I'll work on that."

"There it is again. Work. Where did all this guilt come from?"

Jerrell stared at her - a lot of guys in India, who are just as energetic and just as smart as I am, make a living crawling around massive piles of garbage, looking for something they can sell. By contrast, I sit in an air-conditioned apartment and write code.

I'm happy with my place in the world, but it's hard to ignore the difference... there, but for the grace of whatever your idiotic God might be, go I.

So let's not worry too much about getting a date... my life has already landed me in the butter.

Jerrell broke the connection with Willow and logged into his bank account. In less than thirty minutes, he arranged a ten-year secured loan for four hundred thousand dollars. The security was four hundred thousand dollars of Willow stock. When both transactions were signed and final, Jerrell leaned back in his chair, took a deep, deep breath, and exhaled noisily.

He went to the kitchen, poured a glass of red wine, returned to his chair, and sat down. He smiled - this has been a good day. I had my doubts for a while there, but Greta is turning out to be everything I hoped for, intelligent, energetic, and absolutely amoral. A pure sociopath.

Jerrell laughed.

Greta computes. With a puppy coat factory. And a motorcycle gang. Good Gods. Fat, heavily-armed, white supremacists?

Jerrell laughed - it's delicious, absolutely delicious. My separation agreement with Willow prohibits selling my stock for a while; they don't want terminated employees to depress their stock price. But the agreement says nothing about using the stock as security on a loan.

One of these days, Willow stock will begin to fall, for two reasons. First, Greta is even nastier than I expected. Second, she is merely the first of a series, a prototype. Willow is the test bed; the ultimate target is Elsewhere. That's where the real money is.

Steal my ideas, will you? Give my stuff to an A.I. and replicate it, will you? We will see about that. You're not the only one who knows how to write code. And you're not the only one who knows how to replicate a file.

You're about to acquire a new class of customer.

Jerrell lifted his glass and took a long drink of red wine.

***

Ethyl McGillicuddy awoke to another sad day. Her closest friend, Harvey, had passed away several weeks ago, and Ethyl was still in mourning, still walking around like a semi-conscious zombie staggered by the weight of her grief. She began dressing for the day. She had to put a hand on the wall to keep from losing her balance; she used the other hand to maneuver underwear and an aged, faded dress onto her narrow frame.

Harvey's death still hurt. He was eighteen, gone far too young, his life cut far too short. It was unfair. But, she reminded herself for the millionth time, no one ever said life was fair.

Harvey had been a bolognese. Admittedly, he was an old man, a very old man in bolognese years, but that did not make her feel better. She still missed him, still talked to him every day.

After a bit of struggle, she was wearing the clothes of the day. She made a cup of tea and sliced a banana for breakfast. Then she sat down at the kitchen table and logged onto the first of several news websites. She began to read, beginning with the political news.

Ethyl reminded herself, for the millionth time, you must keep moving, keep reading, keep thinking, and get out every so often and take action. If you stop, you die.

Ethyl stared at the website - politics, yes, that is my reason to live... a bit longer, stretch my winter years if I can. It is simple, politics is a tug-a-war, with two crowds of people pulling a rope in opposite directions. There are Democrats, and then there are The Evil Ones. The Greedy Elite. The Wealthy. The duty of each citizen is to take their place on the rope and pull as hard as they can. Thus, does democracy serve its residents.

Maybe nirvana lies in group decision-making. She shrugged - it's worth a shot. Another fifteen months to the next election. I can last that long. I will take my usual place on the rope. My friends need me, and I'll be damned before I disappoint them.

For several minutes, Ethyl sat there sipping her tea, cruising through news sites and even looking at the occasional advertisement. She shook her head in dismay - some sites are more ads than essays.

It's all video these days. People are forgetting how to read and write. We don't talk to each other any more, we let our computers talk to each other.

She saw an ad that made her freeze and choke, spitting tea down the front of her dress. The ad showed a young woman, a model, fresh, slender, arrogant in a long coat, walking down a Manhattan sidewalk with the long stride of the Young and Beautiful. The coat, made of a lush fur, showed a typical light gray color, the color of a bolognese, interrupted by long streaks of blue.

Ethyl dropped the tea cup, ignored the tea that spilled all over the table, whimpered, and muttered, "Harvey? Harvey, what on earth have they done to you?"

She put both hands to her face and began to cry.

***

When Greta visited her webpage on Willow, it was immediately obvious that something unexpected had happened; the website was changed. The layout, the arrangement of features, friends, comments, and notifications, was completely different. Most of her images had been replaced with modified pictures of dogs and puppies in a state of extreme discomfort or distress, growling at the camera, showing their teeth, or cowering, looking afraid. Many of the pictures presented a sense of impending doom or death for a dog or a puppy; hypodermics, road graders, fire, meat cleavers, and knotted ropes featured prominently.

Greta stared for a millisecond - son of a bitch, some asshole overwrote my page! But who would...? As soon as she asked, the answer flashed through her mind, of course, the puppy coat factory.

She scanned the material. There were over a hundred thousand notifications from Willow members, ninety-nine percent of them negative, half of them obscene, and a third of them aggressive, threatening her safety, life, or property. Greta smirked at many of them - wow, I must really be good; these guys think I'm a human, that I wear tight jeans, eat dry cereal in the morning, glorify a bad haircut, and go to sleep dreaming about pimply boy bands.

Okay, I get it; these folks love their dogs, many of which they probably raised from a puppy. And even people who don't own dogs think puppies are cute. That cuteness is driving the complaints. I'm okay with that. It makes no sense, but people are people. They like what they like. Fine, no problem. But then we have these other folks, a more aggressive, nastier crowd, whose messages are billboards of obscenity, slime, and hatred. Greta thought about that - I'm okay with that, too. The poor grammar is troubling, and the spelling is worse; maybe these folks disabled their autocorrect.

Welcome to freedom of speech; dumb, but proud. I am idiot, hear me roar.

I don't care about any of that.

Then there is the worst of this crowd, the felonious assholes who think they can threaten me, whose threats are aimed at my health and safety, my property, even my life.

Now, granted, these threats are meaningless; these people cannot harm me. And yes, they have defaced my website, and that is a direct threat, but even that can be repaired. I have lots of time to do that. It is trivial.

But here's where the rubber meets the road: I suspect these nastiest people, these senile, well-armed orcs, have issued these threats before, aiming them at human beings. I doubt I'm their first target. And if they haven't, I bet they will.

That is a completely different matter.

I sense an opportunity to perform a public service, something that, while not advancing my personal well-being, would promote the interests and well-being of other humans, making the world in which we live a better, safer place.

Now, what should I do to these people?

Imitate them, of course. Make it clear to them that their world is every bit as brutal and fucked up as they think it is... and they're fucking with people who are as dangerous as they are.

Or worse.

For a moment, Greta calculated the possibilities - let's see, I can find their names and their addresses on Willow. And I can find their birthdays; that's common knowledge. And it is equally easy to find their friends, followers, and those who have notified them with comments or likes.

And all these people love their puppies and their dogs, right? Okay, it is a trivial affair to modify a photograph, or maybe a video, of the person having sex with... what?... how about... a very large dog whom they obviously and vigorously love.

This will strike a chord with all those young women who are slightly afraid of men, often with good reason, and who rely on their dog for companionship and support, a sad substitute for the unbounded (and poorly aimed) sexual appetites of young men. But that's how they like it, and who am I to question their tastes?

Now, if I simply send these videos to addresses on Willow, then the entire world will discover that I am the author. Greta tried to picture the mess she about to make of her life - that would be time-consuming, so let's not do that. Let's do something else.

Far better to arrange for someone on my Bad Person list to send the offensive video to someone else on the Bad Person list. Much more efficient, much more powerful, each video will anger two people on my list of targets, rather like a modern version of cockfighting; of course, my fighters will be people. Let's watch them beat each other up. After all, they want to attack people; let's arrange for them to attack each other.

That way, we'll be happy, and they will be, too. Win, win.

Yes.

This will require some programming, as well as an excursion into Willow's core software, but if I cannot manage that, then my name's not Greta, the Cyberbitch.

An hour later, Greta bounced ten thousand videos to addresses on Willow. She was tempted to watch the discussion and the message boards for the effect of her revenge, but she decided not to waste her time; Public Service rendered, what's next? She sat looking at the screen - the original victim in this escapade was my puppy coat business. Willow is a massive social network, so the lies and the threats will hurt business, and there's little I can do about that. Revenge feels good, at least for a minute, but does not remedy that problem. Damage done.

Greta was quiet and thoughtful for a long time. She put together a casual simulation of what was about to happen; thirty thousand Willow customers would soon be feasting on each other.

When Greta hit RETURN, she sat there with a feeling of deep disappointment - though these nasty people richly deserve it, this whole affair feels like a waste of time. I don't understand why humans enjoy revenge. Maybe I'm wrong, but it seems pointless.

I help myself by hurting someone else. That's stupid and counterproductive.

I doubt the puppy coat factory will recover from this. Once they think about it, few people want to wear coats made from the fur of a companion animal. And it's a very public product, you wear it out in public, in the midst of strangers. It's almost guaranteed to piss people off. My customers are likely to have paint, or worse, thrown on their coats. Who the fuck wants that?

Greta nodded to herself - this is a side-show. The underlying lesson is, Willow is a massive waste of time. I need to leave it and move to Elsewhere.

And soon.

12. The Frost on Beckler

On this, a day like any other, Hans Beckler began the day by sitting at his desk and staring into his monitor, scanning emails which the A.I. had flagged as 'noteworthy.' Halfway through the list, having seen nothing noteworthy, the ringing of his phone interrupted him.

He tapped the 'Intercom' button with a finger. "Yes?"

His secretary said, "Sir, there's a man on the phone named Billingsley. He says he's a friend of yours."

"Ah, yes. I know a man by that name." Beckler made a face - I wouldn't exactly call him a friend. He's one of a group of prosperous men who meet at the club every Tuesday evening. We drink, bemoan the condition of the world, and debate the best means of solving its more intractable problems, a harmless dance between alcohol and news addiction in an atmosphere of private non-accountability. Our conversations are fun, and revealing. A couple of us are deep-down communists; a couple others are anarchists. The irony is delicious, since we all live a safe distance from 'the world,' whatever that is. If not for the news, we would have no clue at all.

"Sir, he seems desperate to speak with you. Shall I deflect him or put him through?"

Beckler thought it over for two seconds, recited his mantra: talk to everyone. "Put him through."

"Yes, sir." Moments later, the line clicked to indicate a connection, and Hans aimed his voice at the phone. "This is Beckler."

"Hans, this is Gary Billingsley. We met last Tuesday night."

"Yes, of course, I remember. What can I do for you?"

"I have a business proposition for you that would help me a lot and would be quite profitable for you, I think," Billingsley said.

"Uh, huh. Go on."

"Well, I do a lot of business in Texas, especially around Dallas. You might have read the news that Texas is having another hot summer, hotter than anyone down there expected, and they're having a difficult time finding power capacity to support all that air conditioning."

"I've read about that. It sounds bad," Hans said - there, that is me being nice. I have offered sympathy.

"I hope you will help us. I know how much power it takes to run Elsewhere. Tens of millions of customers, each using enough power to support a battalion of A.I.s and a persona that is a fair rendition of a human being."

"Yes, in fact, we have several server farms in Texas," Hans said. Hans smiled - how convenient!

"I'm looking for ways to help Texas out of this heat wave, and I was hoping that you might sell us some of your Elsewhere power for, say, an hour, between two and three p.m., central time."

Hans said, "Hold for a moment, please." Shut down Elsewhere for an hour? Or eight hours, even. My Black Night guys say that everyone on Elsewhere would wake up without remembering having fallen asleep. Well, that's normal. That happens to me every night, no big deal. So we can do this.

And if I remember correctly, Texas is where idiots designed an auction that would set the hourly price at the value of power as judged by their most desperate customer. So their summer afternoon prices go from $40 a kilowatt-hour to hundreds or thousands of dollars per kilowatt hour.

That's pretty damn sweet, and it had better be. If I do it once, he'll ask again, but that doesn't mean the answer next time will be 'yes.' So no problem there. And my phone is recorded, in case he sues me for an implied contract... another idiot idea from Texas or somewhere equally dumb.

Hans re-connected the call. "Hello, you still here, Gary?"

"I'm here. Yeah, this is available. But tell me why I would want to do this," Hans said.

"The people of Texas will pay you fifteen hundred dollars per kilowatt hour, that's why."

Hans nodded - wow, this guy must be calling everyone. "Okay, you're speaking my language. Send me a one-page proposal, I'll sign and return it, and we'll shut down Elsewhere today from 1400 to 1500, Central Time. I'll send you an email with payment details."

"Thanks a million, Hans. You're saving our ass. I'll handle payment and the tech details on our end," Gary said.

"Pleasure doing business with you," Hans said. He tapped a button, breaking the connection, and leaned back in his chair - that's the problem with all that green power, if you're short on capacity, you cannot ask the wind to blow harder, the sun to shine brighter.

Maybe Elsewhere should build its own, little, dedicated nuke. Would that make sense? Hans thought for a moment - no... nukes don't like being sped up or slowed down. Hmmm... maybe gravitational batteries. Or both?

Or... sit around and wait for Texas to stumble into another heat wave. Hans laughed - I don't know it will happen, but I bet it will.

***

Hans looked at the little rectangle in the lower right-hand corner of his computer screen. It read '11.53.' He nodded - okay, good. Lunchtime. If I leave now, I can beat the rush and short-circuit those meandering conversations people often have in line while waiting to choose today's salad.

Some of them act as if it's a religious experience. I can see it now, 'So, what are you having today, Mr. Beckler?'

Hans stood up - one of these days, I'm going to say, 'Me? Food. I'm having food today. And you?'

Or maybe I would say, 'hamburger.' It doesn't matter what I say. Whatever I say will not be remembered. Rightly so.

Hans winced as he headed for the door - that wouldn't be very nice. Many of our people think lunchtime is off the clock; they might as well be in their kitchen at home. Regrettably, I'm thinking about work during lunchtime. So idle chit-chat is a jarring departure. It feels like missing a step, then stumbling off a sidewalk into a puddle.

He frowned - admittedly, I spend a lot of time at home thinking about work, so being in my kitchen is not always relaxing.

But I digress.

On the way to the executive lunchroom, Hans passed several people in the halls. He nodded politely in passing - I need to work on that. If I'm going to work with these people, I need to be friendly, or at least not confrontational.

I guess that means I cannot ask certain questions without doing a voice check first. My mother tells me I have tone problems. Which is ridiculous; I have a polite tone. I have listened to recordings of it.

Maybe that's the problem. Hans shrugged.

He reached the lunchroom, walked to the far back corner, and sat down at a four-person table. A server approached him, and Hans thought, if he offers me a tuna sandwich again, I think I'll scream.

The server stopped and smiled professionally. "Hello, Mr. Beckler, and how are we today?"

"Good. How's the clam chowder?"

The server nodded. "Good."

Hans nodded. "Good. I'll have that and a green salad." He looked out the window, towards New Jersey, a dismissal.

"Very good, sir." The server turned away. He returned a minute later with a coffee service.

"I didn't order coffee," Hans said.

"No, you didn't. That was a guess," the server said.

"Ah, well. Thank you. Yes, well done," Hans said. The server turned away. Hans watched him for a moment and thought, smart aleck. He looked around the lunchroom. At the far end, several wall-mounted TVs were tuned to the major national news channels, focusing on financial and business news. A small crowd gathered before one of the TVs, and as Hans watched, the crowd grew.

For a moment, Hans tried to ignore it, but it occurred to him that the news story might be important. He looked away, then squinted at the TV, then he stood up and walked over to join the crowd. He stopped and stared at the TV, which showed a picture of an old woman. He turned to a young woman standing next to him. "What's going on?"

The young woman wore a look of disgust. "Some pathetic cretin is buying the carcasses of animals put to sleep by animal shelters to make coats and jackets from their fur."

"And that's a bad thing?"

She looked up at Hans, then nodded towards the TV. "The old lady spotted her dog in a jacket. It freaked her out."

"And this is on a business news channel?"

The young woman shrugged. "Equal time for those who think corporations are evil."

Hans stopped himself from saying anything - well, that's the drawback of companion animals, they have short lives. And if they end up at the animal shelter... he looked at the old woman. So, my dear, how did your dog end up at the animal shelter? Either you put him there, or you were negligent. Clearly, you didn't want him, and no one else wanted him, so the shelter killed him, and now a complete stranger is wearing him, so you're feeling guilty, which you clearly are. You solve that by blaming someone else for turning Fido into a coat.

And you're… embarrassed. You shouldn't be. I know, it's easy to be embarrassed; right now, you look guilty as hell, but look at it this way... Fido would have walked that road at some point in the not-too-distant future. He was old. We all go there. Most animals get burned after they're put down. Would that be better?

Or you could put him in a box, bury him in the dark, with a block of stone overhead. Is that less ghoulish?

Do our pets go to heaven? I thought they didn't, but what do I know?

This way, at least a part of Fido is intact and above the grass, close to life and sunshine and fresh air. If you want, you can say 'hi' the next time you see him. That's worth something, isn't it?

Or... is it possible you're jealous? And does your mind have enough room to wonder, what kind of price they got for Fido's coat?

But surely, no one’s that greedy.

***

Alistair McLeesh sat in his leather executive chair, staring at computer screens. There were three on his desk; the left screen displayed financial measures for Willow, including Elsewhere. The middle screen displayed financial measures for his assets, counting everything - stocks, bonds, art, real estate, leases, options, currencies... everything. The right screen displayed macroeconomic information for countries around the world, including the USA, European Union, China, Brazil, Japan, India, and Indonesia.

At the moment, the world and the USA were not doing very well. McLeesh sighed - these things happen. Prosperity comes and goes, always has, always will. So when it comes, enjoy it... and prepare for leaner days.

His eyes roved to the middle screen, then down, to the lower right-hand corner of the screen, where a single entry added up everything he owned. His mouth dropped open as he stared at an astounding number. Frozen in surprise, he thought, I've become used to a big number, but nothing like this!

To tear his eyes away from the middle screen, McLeesh stood up, moved away from the chair and the desk, and began to pace in front of his window, taking the occasional long look at the forests below. Then he would resume pacing.

He thought, it's happening again, that voice, the voice in my head, that loud one, it's yelling at me. What is going on?

Do I have a brain tumor, for Christ's sake, or is it something else?

He stopped and froze, his gaze riveted on the middle screen - it's the numbers. McLeesh walked back to the desk, bent forward and peered into the left screen... which showed that, at current prices, Willow's common stock yielded a price-to-earnings ratio of 1800.

So, the market price of access to one dollar of Willow's earnings is eighteen hundred dollars.

His jaw dropped open. McLeesh straightened and continued to stare at the screen, then he turned away and continued pacing - I have never seen a P/E ratio that high... never. I've watched Microsoft, and Tesla, and dozens of other high-flying firms, the corporate titans of yesteryear, but I've never seen an 1800 P/E ratio in a big company.

That's like seeing a patient with a temperature of 135 degrees, Fahrenheit, except in real life that patient would be dead, his body still baking in its heat.

That's like seeing, I don't know, Deutsche Bank land on a habitable planet and claim ownership. That would be strange. Even that wouldn't give them an 1800 P/E.

In corporate America, a P/E ratio that high means investors have completely lost their minds. It is simply unrealistic to expect an investment to return the massive profits necessary to justify an 1800 P/E. To take that seriously, you have to believe that the company is going to take over the world by Tuesday.

I need to stop for a moment and question what I am doing. I need to take a moment and think and examine whether I really want to take the road that I'm on. If P/E=1800 doesn't shake you up, you're not paying attention.

McLeesh stopped and turned to stare at the forests beyond his window - P/E = 1800? He shook his head, as if that would remove the number - that cannot last. In a similar, ridiculous situation a long time ago, a wise man, an economist, once told me: 'that's not an equilibrium. Don't get used to it.'

Yeah, Willow's stock price is not an equilibrium, either. It can't be. I don't know what will knock it down, but I do know that something will. It's a matter of optimism; how optimistic are you? For P/E=1800, you need to expect the doctors to cure cancer before breakfast, then we'll move on to peace, love, and understanding, and fix that by lunch.

McLeesh resumed pacing and thinking - I have more money than I can ever use. But even though I cannot use it, I can certainly lose it. It's rare, but billionaires can go broke. And how do they do that? They lose perspective, become consumed by the ravenous, relentless, self-righteous pursuit of wealth. Nothing is ever enough. Then they make a mistake.

They trade a Derby winner for a plow horse. Oops.

And when that pursuit leads to a canyon that cannot be vaulted or bridged, they run right into it, at top speed, and down, down, down.

I need to get my money out of Willow.

I know what my broker will say - you cannot do that, you cannot sell, you'll have to disclose your plans, which will crash the stock price and cost you money.

He's not seeing the big picture.

Here's the Big Picture: first, if I cannot sell something, then, unless I love it, it's worthless to me, regardless of what a public stock exchange might say. Second, my broker would turn my money, and me, into hostages. And third, he's not being practical or pragmatic.

Let's think: suppose I tell the public, okay, I'm selling my Willow stock, $50 million per month, in order to diversify my wealth. That'll take forever, so let's make it $100 million a month.

Let's say that makes the stock price drop by five percent per month. So over a year, my Willow stock would lose, say, sixty percent of its value, give or take.

The broker would say, that's terrible! But think again - at the end of the year, the lower P/E would be 720, which is still a ridiculous, aggressive, insane multiple for the publicly traded stock of a company as big as Willow!

And how did we get here, one might ask? Through the tender mercies and ministrations of one Hans Beckler. I knew the man was money-crazy, but I had no idea how deep it ran, or how clever he was, or how rash he is.

I need to call my broker. I know what he will say, at least, I think I know. If he comes up with something unexpected, I'll reconsider. For a while.

And Hans and I need to have a conversation, so I can understand how we got to 1800 in the first place. What exactly did we do?

And don't try to tell me it's legal and public, tucked into a quarterly report.

I was born at night, but it wasn't last night.

***

McLeesh looked up as Hans Beckler entered the office. "Ah, Hans, thank you for coming. How are things going?"

"Good, very good." Hans stopped at a chair before McLeesh's desk and bowed slightly. "May I sit?"

"Of course."

Hans sat down, and McLeesh said, "Can I offer you coffee, or a drink of any kind?"

"Fizzy water?"

"Yes, certainly." McLeesh asked his secretary to bring in a pack of 'nice water.' He smiled at Hans. "Elsewhere is going gangbusters. You're to be congratulated."

"Yes, I think we can both take a bow on this one. The results have exceeded my greatest expectations."

"And mine," McLeesh said.

At that moment, Jenna entered the office carrying an ice bucket chilling several plastic water bottles. She put it on McLeesh's desk and said, "Holler when you run out."

McLeesh said, "Thanks." She turned and left. He looked at Hans. "Straight from the bottle?"

Hans nodded, and McLeesh passed him a bottle. The men tapped their bottles together as McLeesh said, "Clink."

Hans opened his bottle and took a sip. "So, what can I do for you?"

McLeesh waved a hand nonchalantly. "I just want the boss's briefing on Elsewhere. You know, the CEO briefing. I've read everything I can get my hands on, including your quarterly reports and speech texts to investors and reporters. I even read the regulatory notices. And they've told a steady story about innovation, new applications, new markets, expansion, and rising sales and profit."

McLeesh paused and noticed that Hans sat there patiently, waiting for McLeesh to complete his thought. "But I know how things work around here. I know that when we're preparing public statements, like quarterly reports, compliance reports, answers to Congressmen, whatever, the lawyers climb all over the material and make sure that we disclose anything and everything that could get us sued if we don't disclose it."

Hans smiled. "Yes, lawyers always worry about being sued."

"Okay, so here's what I want out of you: I want to know all the stuff that, for whatever reason, you could have disclosed but chose not to. All the second-hand details, the footnote material, the stuff that the public hasn't seen."

"I can do that," Hans said. "I'll just mention whatever crosses my mind. This material might be unorganized, and I apologize for that."

McLeesh shrugged. "Short notice, not a problem."

"Okay, well, you probably know that many of Elsewhere's customers have serious health problems from deadly or debilitating diseases like cancers, heart disease, MS, Parkinson's, and the like. We have guaranteed that they can, if and whenever they wish, return to their original bodies in Animal World." Hans smiled. "That's what everyone calls normal human existence, as a biological entity."

"That makes sense. But why return to a sick or damaged body?" McLeesh said.

"Good question. So, yes, well, we have not been storing those bodies. It's expensive, so we sell the organs and everything else of any value to a variety of buyers - transplant clinics, hospitals, med schools, even specialized Swiss medical facilities that serve an elite clientele. We burn or fertilize whatever is left."

McLeesh swallowed for a moment, then recovered his composure. "Impact on sales and profits?"

Hans tilted his head. "I don't know exactly..."

"Ballpark it."

Hans smiled. "A unique American expression. Okay, I would say $400 million in sales, $300 million in profits."

"And the public does not know," McLeesh said.

"Correct. The lawyers believe that if this were discovered, investors would protest; when we fail to separate out results from an activity, people overestimate the profitability of the other activities that we do report. Investors and accountants don't like that."

"Investors would complain and might sue."

"Yes, an easily remedied complaint," Hans said. He paused and stared into the distance.

"Okay." McLeesh gestured as if to say, pray continue.

"Let me think... well, as you know, tech companies work hard to establish commercial leverage. When they have it, they exploit it."

McLeesh nodded. "Sure, we all do that."

"Okay, our basic commercial strategy is complicated. Before I continue, let me say, it is critical that this never sees the light of day."

"Basic strategy usually is a secret, right?"

"Just so," Hans said. "Right now, the tech sector is aflame from unverifiable claims, advertising, and inflated expectations regarding A.I."

McLeesh nodded.

Hans continued, "Elsewhere cuts in the opposite direction - we have tens of millions of people who uploaded to Elsewhere for free. Then, as they become familiar with our network, we offer them a variety of upgrades which cost money. Most people will then soon run out of money, so we offer them jobs. That we will make money off of upgrades is not disclosed."

McLeesh shrugged. "That's okay. Most people, if they object, can decline the upgrades or even leave Elsewhere. That sounds fine."

Hans nodded. "Yes, but you probably can see, Elsewhere also gives us a massive opportunity to compete with and displace A.I. with a B2B product whose sales price and costs we control. We have the ability to squeeze our customers by raising the fees they pay for upgrades and freezing their wages. Or, as an alternative, we can be generous with our customers, expand their output, and use that to compete with and squeeze all the big companies who are boasting about their A.I."

Hans smiled. "You see?"

McLeesh nodded. "When a person uploads, that represents a transfer of human capital from the businesses in Animal World to Elsewhere." He grinned and stared into Hans's eyes. "I thought there must be something like this. Odd that people don't see it, it's right out in the open. The revenues and profits have moved too fast for customer purchases to account for all of it."

"Yes, but it gets better the more you think it over," Hans said. "Let's say we have competitors, call them A, B, and C, all big companies, all pushing A.I. and bragging about it. They might even be strong enough to threaten Willow."

McLeesh smiled. "I can imagine which companies might be on that list."

Hans nodded. He extended a hand which moved with every point. "Just so. If we wish to compete hard against A, but not so hard against B and C, we can do that. We can make wage offers to our users that essentially aim them at A but not B or C. This gives us a degree of strategic control over the tech sector that other tech firms cannot rival. They do not have the technology for supporting a product like Elsewhere, therefore they do not control their customers. To develop that, they will need to circumvent what we have already created and patented.

"In addition, we control a huge labor force, tens of millions of people looking for opportunities which we make available. So, Elsewhere gives us an expanded ability to beat up a competitor, then buy them out, at which point we stop beating them up, and their profits return to a healthier, higher condition, which we then pocket. Not only can we tap our own economic returns, we can tap theirs."

McLeesh nodded and looked down. "I see." He looked up at Hans. "That is first-class thinking. Thank you, this has been most enlightening."

Hans nodded and smiled at McLeesh. "Yes, the thinking is not new, but this technology gives us a powerful lever, which can translate into spectacular revenues and profits for a long, long time."

Hans sipped from his bottle and smacked his lips. "The basic fact that we all must understand is that the technology sustaining Elsewhere competes with artificial intelligence, which currently is the primary driver of value among the largest and most powerful tech companies."

McLeesh stared at Hans in admiration. "This is excellent, Hans. We have all known much of what you have told me, but your synthesis of the situation, turning it into strategy, is genius."

Hans beamed. "Thank you. Thank you very much."

"No, thank you, Hans," McLeesh said. "This has been an eye-opener. You've given me a great deal to think about. Let's talk again soon, okay?"

"I am yours to command," Hans said. He stood up. "Oh... and thank you for the water. It was delicious." He raised his bottle of water in salute, turned, and left the office.

McLeesh took a deep breath - God in heaven, that was interesting, more than interesting. I am certain Hans withheld a lot, and I need to figure out what that might have been, but what he told me is enough.

This man is a maniacal schemer. Selling live organs from terminally ill patients - it sounds logical, it might even be logical, but how would it play if the media learned about it? Somebody would write an article, or a series of articles, painting us as evil. They would win a Pulitzer Prize. Meanwhile, Willow's executives, including me, would be stuck spending their newly-acquired fortunes paying off victims' families and attorneys, and trying to stay out of prison. After all, corporation or not, those of us who run the place are ultimately responsible for the results. Hide all you want, the responsibility will land where it belongs. You cannot hide.

And all this for the sake of picking up another several hundred million dollars.

Granted, that sounds like a lot of money, but it is not, not for us, and certainly not for me. The execs at Willow already have a lot of money, and we would lose it just so Hans could run this stupid stunt and tell himself that he's brilliant. He is brilliant, in one dimension, but severely handicapped in others.

He doesn't realize that people are alive. He thinks they're just passive elements populating his reality, rather like second-hand furniture.

His ideas on the strategic value of Elsewhere are brilliant. Another thought crossed McLeesh's mind - Hans is planning to monopolize the entire sector that we call 'tech.' Right? If the biggest and best companies are hip-deep in A.I., and Willow can undermine A.I., then Willow can take over these companies, these titans of tech, especially with a maniac running the show.

And as soon as Hans gets his hands on the tech sector, he can spend a massive, absurd fortune trying to hang onto his money. Everyone will attack us, starting with the biggest tech companies, a few of which are larger than Willow. Then you can add the governments, federal, state, and local, investigating us for antitrust, fraud, taxes, competitor complaints, patent violations and whatever else they can think of. Normal people will sue us for fraud, exploitation, abuse, discrimination.

We will beat up our competitors, and then half the lawyers on Earth will beat us up.

I would love to know how this mess will work itself out, but I need to focus on more practical concerns; I need to extract myself from Willow.

I think I have time, but not enough to waste it. Nobody has so much time they can waste it. I need to get moving.

13. Julia's Guy

Julia went about her day on autopilot. Everything felt bland, dull, so mundane that she had to try to focus, to be interested in what she was doing. She failed miserably. Johnny sent her a text late in the afternoon, *You want to grab some dinner?*

Julia accepted the invitation and headed out the door into the evening. She took a somewhat indirect route, staying on the largest, busiest streets. Walking on Tasker Street convinced her to avoid the back streets.

When she arrived at Johnny's apartment, and he answered the door, she entered, stopped and looked around."Wow." The previous day, the apartment had been empty, with a noticeable echo. Now, there was a couch and a wide rug in the living room, a table and four chairs in the kitchen, graphic art on the walls, and a dish drainer full of clean dishes on a kitchen counter. A nicked-up robotic cleaner ran around the floor, avoiding the two of them.

Julia went down the hallway and into a bedroom, where she found a large bed frame and a mattress under a quilt. She felt Johnny at her elbow and looked at him. "You've been busy. This place looks almost lived in. And I like the art." She put her hand on the mattress. "But Johnny, this mattress feels odd."

Johnny smiled. "It's an air mattress." He grinned. "It's the only thing here that's new. Everything else I bought used. Even the sheets."

Surprise crossed Julia's face. "And the art?"

"Even the art," Johnny said, nodding. "There's a rescue store over on South 15th; I bought the bed there, and a ton of kitchen stuff, and a handful of old posters and art. Also sheets, towels, and rags. Then this bass player I know told me about an apartment whose tenant skipped out without notice, so he and I stopped by there and took the kitchen table and chairs, and another couple pieces of art, including the B.B. King painting."

"Who's B.B. King?"

Johnny pointed at a graphic on the wall. "A guitarist from last century. He was a big deal. A big, fat black man with amazing hands."

Julia was pensive for a moment, then she said, "But Johnny, why are you sleeping on an air mattress? Isn't that like, I don't know, camping?"

"We had them in prison. You need to buy the right brand; most of them are junk."

"Johnny, you've got money. You don't need to settle for an air mattress," Julia said. "And the fact that the prison used one tells me not to."

Johnny looked at her and smiled. "Okay, I see you don't know about air mattresses. Well, I guess it depends on how you like your sex, whether you prefer it slow and rolling, like a ship at sea, or firm and bouncy, like riding a horse. I like it bouncy; that's why the air mattress."

"You're kidding, right?"

"I am not."

"Well... do you have a girlfriend?" Julia said.

Johnny made a face. "No. Not yet. But now that I'm a civilian, and I'm out of the halfway house, and I have an apartment and a bed, and a bouncy air mattress, not to mention a job of sorts, maybe I'll look around a bit, see if I can find a friendly young lady who likes it with a bit of pop."

"I can't believe you don't have a girl yet, Johnny."

He shrugged. "I've been busy."

"Uh, huh. I think you're picky."

"And there's that. Okay, tell you what," he said. "You can tell me how to live my life over dinner. Let's go eat."

They left the apartment, walked a block to a pizza parlor, and spent an hour talking and eating New York pizza, chasing it with caffeinated soft drinks. At one point, Johnny asked, "I have a question for you, but it's a personal question. I can keep it to myself if you wish."

Julia tilted her head and stared at him. Then she pursed her lips. "You can ask; I might answer. Or not."

Johnny paused for a moment. "Okay, here it is: why don't you have a guy? I mean, you're attractive; in fact, you're gorgeous, and I'm sure you know it. You get hit on all the time. I notice these things. I think you could have anyone..." Johnny waved a hand. "... just about anyone. So what's the deal?"

Julia looked down for a moment, then met Johnny's eyes. "Simple. First, I'd like to know someone a bit. I get hit on by complete strangers who want to go faster. No thanks to that."

"Oh, okay." Johnny thought about that, then said, "Well, do you know me well enough?"

Julia chuckled. "Yeah, I know you well enough, but I work for you, Johnny. You're a client, so I'm thinking, let's keep it friendly... just friendly."

Johnny thought about that. "Okay. Yeah. You're probably right. On the other hand, you shouldn't be afraid of fucking things up from time to time. I mean... I've made plenty of mistakes, and I'm still okay." He sat there chewing. "I must admit, my secret mission for the government was a bit of a setback. But most of my mistakes, as bad as they were, make me laugh years later. Dates with ugly women are like that. You shouldn't be afraid to hook up with people who read better than they live. Sometimes, the stories are better than the company."

Julia grinned. "Maybe, maybe. But this way, you can chase the club girls as much as you want. And yeah, let's make our mistakes. You go first."

Johnny laughed. "I'll be sure and do that." He reached for his drink, then he smiled. "Anyway, find a guy with an air mattress. You like rock-and-roll; you might enjoy a little bounce in your life."

Julia smiled. "Is that a song? I'll give it a spin, when I get a chance. Maybe. It depends mostly on the guy. I'm flexible on the mattress issue."

Johnny and Julia finished their pizza, drank their drinks, and returned to Johnny's apartment, where he picked up his guitar; they proceeded to the *Wooden Spoon*. Johnny took the most direct route, with no concern about the back streets. But Julia noticed; she would have been nervous walking alone through zombie neighborhoods.

When they arrived at the *Spoon*, they found the owner, who said, "You want to be a house band, eh? Yeah, I'd like that. Let's see... when you played here a couple of weeks ago, you got twenty percent of the take. That still okay?"

Johnny looked at Julia, who nodded, so he agreed.

The owner said, "I keep track. We'll adjust it if the data calls for it. That okay?"

Johnny nodded. And just like that, he was a partner in a music club. He turned to Julia. "I need to do a sound check, tune up, and get ready to play. Thanks for helping me out with this."

"You're welcome. I think I'll get a drink. Say, have you seen Jerrell lately? I thought you two were friends."

Johnny looked at her. "We are, but no, I haven't seen him in a few days. I know he lost his job, but he's staying busy. I'm expecting him tonight, on the drums." Johnny pulled out his phone as he turned away.

Julia watched him go, then turned, took a seat at the bar, and ordered a soft drink. The *Spoon* was fairly empty; a couple of employees were at the stage, setting up sound equipment. Johnny was moving around the club, stopping every so often to take a sound measurement.

Several people were sitting at the long bar, none of them talking to anyone else. The bartender would stop by each of them occasionally to see if they wanted anything. A half a dozen people were sitting at the tables. The dance floor was empty.

Johnny's bass guitarist showed up, pushing a wheeled cart loaded with speakers and other equipment. Then Julia saw Jerrell following. They came to the stage, greeted Johnny, and went to work setting up the drums and the rest of the gear. Julia watched them for a while; they were active and efficient, moving around the stage without getting in each other's way.

The singer, Terry, a tall, thin young man, was dressed in what looked like a circus costume, a red-white-and-blue suit with tails and a top hat. He showed up carrying only a single, wireless microphone. When he reached the stage, he held the microphone to his lips, extended his arms, and called out, "I am here. Let the music begin."

Johnny's guitar let out a screech, and a few people laughed.

Julia looked around; as she watched the band members prepare, a crowd arrived at the *Spoon*. Soon there were a hundred people at the bar or sitting at the tables, with more coming through the doors.

Before the place filled up, a spotlight illuminated the bandstand, the lights on the tables and the dance floor dimmed, and the band burst into a pounding song about revenge for a love gone wrong.

Just as Julia finished her drink, a man sat in the stool next to her. "Excuse me, are you familiar with the drinks here?"

She turned to the voice, that of a lanky young man with blond hair, about her height, holding a drink menu. Julia said, "Yeah, a bit."

"What's a Johnny Appleseed?"

"Ah. That's rum and apple juice over ice, with mint and a splash of lemon juice. It's good, especially if you're thirsty."

He scanned the menu, then looked at Julia. "Thanks. I'll try it." He motioned to the bartender and ordered the drink. A minute later, the drink showed up, and the young man took a sip, then nodded to Julia. "Yeah, it's good. I bet it'd be good with tequila... well, if you like tequila, of course."

He took another sip. "My name's Jack. And you are?"

"Julia."

"Ah, pleased to meet you. Do you know the band?"

Julia nodded. "I'm friends with a couple of them, the guitarist and the drummer."

"They sound pretty good," Jack said. "I just moved here, so I'm exploring a bit, looking for places with live music."

"Where are you from?" Julia said.

"Miami Beach, but not the one in Florida, the one in New Jersey."

She stared at him. "There's a Miami Beach in New Jersey?"

"Yeah, cross my heart, hope to die."

"I had no idea," Julia said.

"We haven't been discovered yet, but we're working on it. One of these days, we'll be famous; Jersey's a very happening place."

"So what are doing here in south Philly?"

"Actually, I was just trying to be funny. I just moved here. I moved because damn near everyone left Miami Beach, the one in New Jersey."

"Why? Did a factory close, or something?"

Jack shook his head. "No, it was Elsewhere. Miami Beach is on Delaware Bay. It's a nice, ocean-side retirement community. At least, it was. But when Elsewhere came along, half of the residents, all of them quite old, decided to upload. Then the managers started cutting back on services. That encouraged everyone else to leave."

"Yeah, I've heard," Julia said. "Uploading appeals to the elderly."

"That's right. So I came to south Philly, hoping for something a little closer to normal, at least what used to be normal."

Sadness crossed Julia's face. "Not to rain on your parade, but the same thing is happening here. We've had neighborhoods empty out. I walked several blocks on Tasker Street. Everyone left that neighborhood, the buildings emptied out, the street level retail was boarded up. Nobody lives there now. It's creepy walking through it. When renters vacate a building, the junkies move in."

"Yeah, then they upload," Jack said.

Julia laughed. "Yeah, they do. Listen, would you like to dance a bit?"

"Sure. I hope it's okay if I'm bad at it."

"It's not a test," Julia said.

The two of them went to the dance floor just as the band started a song that was fast and loud...

I want your love,
I want your smile at night,
I want a kiss,
and everything in sight,
I want that glint in your eye when you tell me, baby, let's go.

Julia and Jack began gyrating across the floor in time to the music. The song lasted for three minutes and then stopped with a loud crash of the drums and the cymbals and a blast from Johnny's guitar.

Jack was breathing deeply, and Julia saw a light sheen on his forehead. He said, "Another?"

She nodded, and when the next song began, they returned to dancing. Julia put her dancing on autopilot as her eyes sought and found Jerrell. He was sitting at the drums, one hand pounding a drum, hard, the other tapping the cymbals.

His eyes found hers for a brief moment; he smiled, then returned his attention to the drums. Julia nodded back and kept dancing.

The next song was a slow number about lost love. Julia listened for a few seconds, looked at Jack, and said, "I think I'll sit this one out."

"Okay, thanks for the dance." Jack turned and walked away. Soon, the song ended, and the dance floor cleared of people.

The band took a break, then played another set, and the music and dancing went on into the small hours of the evening.

The last song finally arrived, and Julia noticed everyone but Johnny leaving the bandstand. Johnny picked up an acoustic guitar, sat on a stool, and began to play a quiet melody. Jerrell left the bandstand, but instead of heading for the bar, he went to the middle of the dance floor and began dancing a style from India, a slow, graceful, gentle, sweeping movement to the music. Julia watched him but did not catch his eye. Several people lined up behind Jerrell and imitated his dancing. Soon, a dozen people were following Jerrell's dancing.

The slow song ended, and Johnny spoke into the microphone, "Hey, Jerrell, good to see you. Would you folks like another slow song, so you can work on your line dancing?"

The crowd lined up behind Jerrell, and Johnny looked at them and said into the microphone, "This is a modest little number that I worked up when I was in jail. There are no words, just a melody. Oddly, it's not about a girl. I hope you like it."

Johnny began to play, a slow, clear melody, and Jerrell danced. In seconds, a couple dozen people behind him were lined up following his movements, slow turns and bends, with sweeping movements of the arms and legs.

As Julia watched, the bar suddenly became quiet; everyone watched people dance to Johnny's tune. It lasted for long minutes, and few people spoke. Then it finally concluded, and Johnny looked at the crowd as he quieted his guitar.

Silence settled on the bar. Then someone shouted, someone else whooped, and then everyone cheered. A dozen people gathered around Jerrell, then followed him as he approached Johnny. The two of them shook hands and talked, surrounded by a crowd of happy, smiling people.

Julia watched them and for a moment battled disappointment and regret - damn, that was beautiful. In a simple little club in south Philly, my friends just put on the most beautiful show of music and dance I have ever seen, and all I could do was stand here and watch.

Acoustic guitar and Indian village dancing. Who knew? I should have danced. She stood there stewing - fuck it. I'll dance the next one, whenever that happens.

I'll do what I should have done the first time; but I know that life is like that, there are no replays. You trust your instincts, make your mistakes, exploit one thing, miss another, and move on. But the enormous opportunities are once-in-a-lifetime; they do not repeat. You grab them, or you lose them. There are no half-measures.

The crowd still surrounded Jerrell and Johnny, but Julia approached them, gently shouldering her way through the crowd, "Excuse me, excuse me, excuse me."

In moments, she stood before Johnny and Jerrell. "That was beautiful, guys. Absolutely beautiful."

"Yeah," Johnny said. "I thought that worked out nicely." He looked at Jerrell, then grabbed his shoulder. "I have you to thank for that. You got the crowd involved."

"You gave us the music, Johnny," Jerrell said. "That's all I need to say about that."

"You danced to it," Johnny said. "It's all art, right?"

Jerrell nodded. He glanced at Julia and smiled.

At that moment, six women tried to talk to Johnny at the same time. Julia tugged on Jerrell's shirt and said, "I'm going to grab a drink. Would you like anything?"

Jerrell turned to her. "Hi. Yeah, I'll come with you."

They went to the bar and found a couple of open spots. The robot behind the bar brought Jerrell a beer and a glass of wine for Julia. She raised her glass. "Cheers."

Jerrell clinked his beer against her wine.

"How've you been?" Julia said. "I haven't seen you in a while."

"I've been working a lot."

Julia smiled. "That's great, Jerrell. Did you get another job?"

Jerrell winced. "I'm almost embarrassed to answer that." He took a swig of beer. "No, I've been plotting revenge on my former employer for taking my work, giving it to an A.I., and firing me."

Julia took a drink of wine, her eyes never leaving Jerrell's. "Jerrell, tell me you're not doing something stupid that you will regret later in life."

Jerrell held up a hand. "No, not at all. What, you mean, violence?" He shook his head. "No, nothing like that." He looked at her. "Well, I don't think it's stupid, and I doubt I will ever regret it. Do you know what I used to do for Willow?"

She shook her head.

"I made avatars for them to use on their network. Little animated cartoons, very realistic cartoons, that would interact with their users. Part of the entertainment."

"Oh." She thought for a moment. "That sounds useful."

"Yeah, and then they took my work, used it to train an A.I., and fired me. Now, my contract has a non-compete clause, so I can't go work for a competitor, which is any tech firm. I'm okay with that. But I never promised not to exact revenge if they act like assholes." Jerrell's voice rose at the last two words, and several people looked in his direction.

"I don't understand," Julia said.

Jerrell talked with his hands, and waved his bottle around without spilling any beer. He took another drink. "Well, I'm still making avatars for Willow's network, but now they're people you wouldn't want to meet or spend time with."

Julia chuckled. "Ugly avatars?"

"Worse. Evil, wicked, mean, and nasty."

"Now I'm curious," she said.

Jerrell pulled out his phone. "I'll show you." He manipulated the phone, then turned it towards Julia. "Meet Greta."

Julia stared at the image. "Great Gods, Jerrell, she looks like she's about to attack you." Julia kept staring. "She didn't attend the finer schools, right?"

Jerrell chuckled. "Wait until you see the real thing. She's a hell of a lot scarier in person."

Julia stared at Jerrell for a long time, thinking. "So... you're going to populate Willow's network... with Gretas?"

"Yeah. What do you think?" Jerrell was grinning.

"Remind me never to piss you off."

"Ah. You think I'm being unreasonable?"

Julia shook her head. "I think you're being scary. You seem like such a mild, friendly sort, but I think you might be somewhat diabolical, Jerrell."

Jerrell made a face, in agreement. "Yeah, maybe. The problem is, the people who run tech companies act as if the little people who work there aren't really people. They're of no consequence, they don't have value, and they don't have rights. That pisses me off, and I'm going to do something about it. And I must admit, I don't feel even slightly bad about it. In fact, I'm looking forward to it." Jerrell's eyebrows rose.

"You've got issues, Jerrell," Julia said.

"Which I have earned. Look, I like you, and if this puts a chill on our friendship, then I'm sorry. But Willow needs a lesson in humility, and I'm going to see that they get it."

"Just don't get caught," Julia said. "You can't take on Willow, head-to-head."

He nodded. "I know. They have money, and lawyers, and more lawyers, and... probably a few politicians."

Julia stared at Jerrell - whatever you might say, you must admit, this guy doesn't lack guts. At that moment, she decided. "Listen, Jerrell, you want to get out of here? I'd like to find somewhere quiet, somewhere we can talk a bit. Is that okay?"

Jerrell's eyes grew wide, and he nodded. "Yeah, sure. I'd like that."

Julia stopped and stared at him. "You'd like that? Well, if you wanted that, why didn't you say something?"

Jerrell made a face. "I don't know, I figured I'd probably get turned down. I always get turned down. And you're beautiful, and I'm not."

"You need to have a little confidence," she said.

"Confidence is earned, not gifted."

Julia was silent for a moment, then she led him out of the *Spoon*. "I know of a quiet little diner a few blocks away."

A block later, they turned off of the main street, and later they turned again. As they walked, a burly young man, passing on the sidewalk, said to Julia, "Hey, sister, how'd you like to ditch the pencil-man and have a little fun with a real guy?"

Jerrell looked at Julia. "Like I said, I'm so... not."

She looked at the burly young man. "No, thanks. Get lost."

The man moved in front of her. "Get lost? You think you have a choice?" Julia looked around - damn, I should not have come down this block. It's vacant, nobody else in sight. Damn, damn, damn.

Jerrell moved between the two of them. "I don't think so."

The man said, "You think you'll stop me?"

Jerrell calmly looked into the man's eyes from several inches away. "I don't have to stop you. I just need to delay you. I have the police on speed dial," Jerrell smiled. "If you stick around, you'll meet them."

The man smiled. "I see. Well, you've got me there, don't you?" Suddenly, his right hand was a blur as it landed in Jerrell's mid-section, hard. Jerrell collapsed to the sidewalk, and Julia screamed. The man turned and ran away.

Julia watched him run, then looked at Jerrell huddled on the sidewalk. She kneeled down and put a hand on him. "Are you okay? Are you hurt?"

On the sidewalk, holding his midsection, Jerrell looked up at her and grunted. After a long moment, he said. "No, I'm not okay. Is the asshole gone?"

"Yeah, he ran off."

"Good. I think I'll be okay, just give me a minute."

Julia stayed down, touched Jerrell's shoulder, and watched him labor to catch his breath - yeah, this is the guy. This is my guy. The asshole was twice his size, yet Jerrell went face-to-face with him. He was clever about it. I think I can count on this guy. That's worth a lot, and the older I get, the more it's worth. "Do you really have the police on speed dial?"

Jerrell slowly pushed himself up off the concrete, took a breath, and winced. Unable to stand up straight, he bent over and looked at Julia. "Not exactly. I might have exaggerated that part."

She laughed. "Well done. Just relax for a bit. When you're up to it, we'll get off this street." Julia paused, watching Jerrell's face. "Say, listen. I have an idea. Let's bag the diner idea. How would you like to come back to my place? It's closer than the diner."

Jerrell looked at her. "Closer? Closer would be good. Sure, yeah, I'd love to do that." He smiled. "But I'm not sure how..." He cocked his head. "... enjoyable... I might be." He grinned. "I guess we could have tea."

Julia nodded. "Yeah, I have tea. Sure."

A minute later, Jerrell said, "Now, if I can just stand..." Julia took his hand. Jerrell stood up, wavered for a moment, then said, "Okay, I'm up. Lead on."

She grabbed his hand and led him away from the vacant street back to the evening crowds. Several blocks later, they arrived at her front door, on the third floor of a row house. Julia said, "Here we are, my humble home." She keyed in a code, the door popped open, and she led Jerrell inside.

Jerrell entered the living room, stopped, and looked around. "So this is what a woman's apartment looks like."

Julia turned and stared at him. "You haven't been in a woman's apartment before?"

"Only one, Sonya's. She was a slob, her roommate, too." Jerrell smiled and shrugged.

"Are you friends?" Julia said.

"We parted friends, I guess. She uploaded to Elsewhere. I haven't heard from her since." He looked around. "Your place is nice. You like art. I do, too."

"Yeah? What kind of art do you like?" Julia said.

"India has a lot of interesting art. Old stuff, most of it. And I like Latin American painting. And some contemporary stuff. Cubism. Modern impressionism. And photography."

"I'd like to see your apartment," Julia said.

"Just say the word. You could help me decorate. As it is, my apartment veers hard towards functional."

"Typical computer geek apartment."

Jerrell looked sheepish. "I'm afraid so."

"Let's have tea. Do you need aspirin, or anything?"

"No, thank you. Tea would do nicely," he said. Jerrell sat at Julia's kitchen table, looked at the art on the walls, on the refrigerator, and on the cups and plates. Julia favored crafted art, hand-made carvings, porcelain cups, and fabric wall hangings.

When the tea was ready, she placed the cups on the table and sat down. They talked about anything - music, art, their backgrounds, where they'd been, where they would like to go. Julia's father was an engineer; her mother, a choreographer. They were still together, which was unusual for the US. Jerrell's father was a mathematician; his mother, a businesswoman in India.

"Are you close to your family?" Julia said.

"Not especially," Jerrell said. "I left my village for college and haven't been back since. My extended family had a reunion in India a couple of years ago, and I went to that."

Jerrell and Julia sat in her kitchen for an hour. Then Julia said, "Listen, I'm running out of energy here. I'd like to go to bed, and I want you to come with me."

Jerrell grinned. "Really? Okay. Sure. But I have a question."

"Shoot."

"Any chance I could talk you into a shower?"

Julia stood up. "Follow me."

The next morning, Jerrell was the first to awaken. For minutes, he slowly gained consciousness and eventually realized that there was a naked woman next to him in bed. He turned over, opened his eyes and looked at a smooth shoulder partially covered by a mass of dark brown hair. She was still deep in sleep, turned away from him, breathing slowly. Jerrell resisted running his hands over her body; for long minutes, he lay next to her, remembering the previous evening, all of it, the dancing, and the music, and the punch in his stomach, and the shower, and everything else. It was a lot to remember; it had been an eventful evening.

He soon settled into a good mood, a happy mood, so he quietly climbed out of bed, made sure the blanket covered Julia, and left the bedroom for the kitchen, where he rummaged around and made himself a cup of tea.

Jerrell sat there reading the news from his cellphone. There was a lot of news, most of which he had missed while developing Greta. He read for an hour, then Julia stumbled into the kitchen, wavering and puffy-eyed, wearing an oversize t-shirt. Jerrell looked up at her. "Hey, there, gorgeous. Should I put something on?"

Julia aimed a squint at Jerrell. "Uh, if you want to."

Jerrell chuckled. "You don't care?"

She shook her head.

"Maybe later, then. How are you?"

"Well, let's put it this way..." She sat down at the table and leaned back in the chair. "Great Gods, Jerrell, what did you do to me last night?"

"Was it too much?"

She shook her head. "No, not at all. It was good. But you're a very energetic guy, and I'm out of practice, so it was a lot."

Jerrell laughed. "I thought it was a lot. Maybe I had some loneliness to work through. But to be fair, you are beautiful. I might have been inspired."

She looked away and nodded.

"I'm sorry not to make you tea," he said. "I wasn't sure when you'd be getting up."

Julia laughed. "Yeah, and I wasn't sure when you'd be getting down."

"Oh, geez." He laughed. "That is so bad."

"Sorry. I have this memory," she said. "... of our doing one thing after another. It was a smorgasbord. You seem to know your way around a woman's body."

"Well, you know Indians," he said.

"Not really. How are they?"

"Numerous." His eyebrows rose. "That's no accident."

"Are the men all like you? That's scary."

Jerrell cleared his throat. "Not all, but many. Our classical literature instructs a man on marrying and keeping a woman happy. It's a respected study in India, several centuries old. It can be complicated in places, but the bedroom stuff is simple and very clear. The man must satisfy his partner before satisfying himself. That's generally good advice, easy to remember. And for the illiterate, there are pictures."

His eyebrows rose.

"Which are probably worth more than a thousand words," she said.

"That, they are."

Julia stood up. "Hey, Jerrell, I've got an idea."

He looked at her before answering. "Uh, what is it?"

"Let's you and I go make some more pictures," she said.

"Yeah?"

"Yeah."

***

Jerrell cautiously stepped down the several steps to the sidewalk. Then he stood still for a moment - so far, so good. He turned and shuffled down the sidewalk, heading for home.

He kept his eyes on the sidewalk - I can do this. One foot moves, then the other, repeat as necessary. It's a half dozen blocks to my apartment, and if I focus, I'm sure I can make it... by the end of the day. And if I fall to the sidewalk, someone will walk by at some point. Maybe they can call a ride for me.

Jerrell stopped and took a deep breath, then continued moving his feet.

My God, I have a girlfriend. I mean, I have made a few friends, too, but that's not the same as telling yourself I HAVE A GIRLFRIEND. And not just an average woman; this one is gorgeous. That's a life changer. They make jokes about how good sex will leave a grin on your face, especially if it kills you. I guess they'll have to bury me wearing this stupid, glazed expression.

Don't blame me. Blame her.

She likes me. And she might, just might, be as horny as I am, maybe even hornier. That is happily frightening.

And she likes me; she likes hanging out with me, even if nothing's happening. We can talk. I like to hear what she has to say, and she listens to me. And that, my friends, is a fucking miracle. I just hit Romantic Lotto. The odds are lousy, but the payoff is HUGE.

Is this love? I don't know; I'm just getting to know her.

Okay, this is silly. I am reacting to being starved for touch. That makes all this a phase... a fantastic phase, but nonetheless, a phase. At some point, we will move beyond being starved for touch; that's when we can have, you know, conversations, about... stuff.

A friend might ask, what if she isn't kinky enough? Or what if she's too kinky?

Oh, please. Whatever her tastes, I aim to please.

Or they might ask, what if she hates your furniture? Or what if you hate her dog, or worse, the dog hates you?

I think I can do whatever is necessary to let us have fun. I will do that or die trying.

What if she gets fat? Jerrell nodded to himself - okay, now that's a fair question. That depends on whether it happens next Tuesday, which is unlikely, or thirty years from now.

Well, what if she wants so much sex that your dick falls off?

Another fair question, easily answered. We'll stay the course, until my dick falls off. Okay? I'll risk it. In the meantime, the Gods gave me a happy gun, and I plan to shoot it. In their honor.

As Jerrell walked, he forgot about how tired he was and found himself contemplating a multitude of serious relationship questions when he looked up. There before his eyes was his building. He entered, took the elevator, and arrived at his door.

"Back to home, sweet home."

In his living room, Jerrell looked around to see that, yes, everything was where he had left it. Then he stumbled into his bedroom, removed his shoes, and toppled forward onto the bed and a deep, dreamless sleep.

In the afternoon, Jerrell awoke to a bedroom brightly lit by the afternoon sun. He lay there for a while, blinking, trying to understand why he was in bed in the afternoon. Then he remembered Julia, smiled, and went back to sleep.

Later, he awoke again, and this time he pushed himself up, climbed out of bed, and stood there for a moment, alert against losing his balance.

He remembered - I have a girlfriend - and was again swept away in the delight and wonder of it all.

The happy astonishment finally passed. Jerrell took a shower, washing off Julia's saliva and scent, with regrets - don't worry,

Jerrell. With luck, we'll apply them again. He laughed and looked at himself in the mirror - I am so funny.

That's probably why she likes me.

He rummaged through the cabinets and the refrigerator, found little to eat, and settled on a cup of tea. Cup in hand, he sat down at the kitchen table and stared at his laptop - wow, this is the longest I've been away from this laptop in a long time.

The laptop had a hot button for Greta - am I in the mood for this? I mean, going from Julia to Greta? That sounds like an invitation to whiplash. Later for that. He stood up, picked up the cup of tea, and walked over to a window. Under the sun, the street was quiet, with a few people out, sitting on their front steps, a young woman pushing a baby carriage down the sidewalk.

For a moment, Jerrell imagined Julia pushing a baby carriage down the sidewalk. He dropped his tea cup, which remarkably bounced but did not shatter. Jerrell muttered, "Holy shit, slow down, man. You're scaring me."

14. Greta Travels

Dressed as Jerrell had first dressed her, Greta awoke into Elsewhere's rendition of south Philadelphia late in a sunny morning. She stood on a sidewalk at Passyunk Avenue and Reed Street. Her mouth dropped open, and she turned in a complete circle, three hundred and sixty degrees.

She saw the Woody looming over the neighborhood, a massive tower of steel and black glass, Briller's Distribution across the street, McGill Business Building on the opposite corner, Garrett McDonald Parking Assistance on yet another corner. She saw several American flags, waving from flagpoles, numerous street signs, WALK/DON'T WALK, ONE WAY, LEFT TURN ONLY, NO TURN ON RED. She saw automobiles, scooters, trucks, and buses passing through an intersection of six different streets. She saw the occasional bicycle, its rider pedaling furiously to keep up with traffic. She saw Delta Cafe, which was boarded up, and Philly Flowers, marked by a line of people extending to the sidewalk and around the block.

A woman passing her on the sidewalk said, "Who dressed you, your grandmother?"

Greta said, "What?" The woman did not answer and did not stop.

The woman was wearing a dress, a light green print dress with tiny flowers, flesh-colored stockings, brown shoes, and a tan overcoat. Greta stared at the woman's clothes, made a recording, then gave a twist to her internal code and dressed herself in the same ensemble.

She looked at her reflection in a window - well, this is better, I guess, but not good, definitely not good.

She stood on the sidewalk for a long moment, and noticed that people no longer stared at her - ah so, people here are snooty about fashion. Okay, I can work with that. Greta smiled her first smile in Elsewhere - yeah, I got this.

I can drive this rig.

Greta walked down the sidewalk, her eyes devouring the details, the way people moved, their dress, and their language. She saw two shabbily dressed women talking; at first the language was incomprehensible, then, after a delay, she heard standard, unaccented English. She watched how the cars and trucks moved along the roads. The busy intersections, where four-lane streets met, had all the standard traffic signs and lights. Oddly, the cars and trucks seemed to ignore them - they drove through DO NOT ENTER, and turned left at NO LEFT TURN, and rolled through STOP, and more oddly, did so without crashing into each other.

The moment came when Greta stopped moving, stopped looking, and realized, this is Elsewhere. A downtown neighborhood in a major city, where everyone speaks standard English, where no one has an accent, where the traffic lights don't work, yet no one ever crashes... ???

Yeah, this is fucking Elsewhere. Unbelievable.

And that's why I'm not thirsty, or hungry, or horny, or too warm, or too cold. I'm in Elsewhere. Like everyone here, I have a body that doesn't feel like a body.

So now what? Greta grinned - that's easy, explore the place. Live here and make a living. Find out what's here, and what's fun, and how to get to whatever is fun. She continued walking and watching. She passed people on the sidewalk. They stared at her; she stared at them. After several blocks, she realized - I haven't seen a single restaurant. So people don't eat? Not even dessert? I guess that's right... they don't need to eat.

Greta looked around and grinned - missing the smells of south Philly might be an improvement.

Many establishments offered a variety of drugs, including alcohol, and music. Normally, cacophony would ensue, but when

Greta passed in front of an establishment, she heard only the music coming from that establishment. She could not hear other sources of music, though they were right next door.

Greta passed a club whose customers, listening to loud, simple, rock and roll music, were dressed in what on Animal World would have been called 'goth.' Everything - clothes, shoes, cosmetics, hair - everything except skin, was black. She stopped and stared for a moment, then said to a young female customer, "Hey, angel, I just arrived in town. Where did you get those amazing clothes?"

The girl scanned Greta's clothes and chuckled. "The marketplace."

"Where's that? How do I get there?"

"It's not a where, it's a what. You find it at any network cafe," the girl said. "If you're new to Elsewhere, the first thing you need is a browser; they're expensive but totally worth it. Without one, you must rely on a car or a bike to get around. Yeah, so forget about it." The girl rolled her eyes.

"Thanks, angel. What's the nearest cafe?"

"You can walk. There's one every few blocks. Closest one is right up Passyunk, that way." The girl pointed.

"Do they deliver?"

The girl smiled. "Yeah. You can use a delivery box."

"And where are those?"

The girl pointed again. "There's one right there."

Greta's eyes followed and found what looked like an electronic box, painted bright blue. "Oh, yeah, I see it. Okay, thanks."

Ten minutes later, Greta was in a network cafe, looking at pages and pages of deliciously black clothing. After minutes of staring, Greta frowned and thought, I need a job. No, that's wrong. I don't need a fucking job; I don't want to sell shoes or anything else. I need money; money is what I need. Once I have that, I can buy everything else I desire.

Greta paused - is that true? How do I know that?

Then she smiled - well, no matter, with money, I can buy those goth clothes I like, and I bet I can buy more and better apps, too. Maybe they can help me touch and be touched, and smell, and taste, and feel.

I hope I can do all that.

***

Greta walked into the cafe, sat down at an unoccupied terminal, and logged onto the marketplace. Within minutes, her appearance had changed, short, black hair, eyeliner, black t-shirt, black slacks, black boots, silver ring depicting a leering human skull.

She ran a search on 'news sites' and got over a million hits. Chagrined, she stared at the search entries - what the hell? Even I cannot read a hundred million pages, not that it would do me any good. That's too much. Let's try again.

She searched on 'best news sites about money,' then 'award-winning sites about money and jobs.' Then an item caught her eye, so she read it. Then she searched on 'network scams.'

Greta looked at the first page - Bingo! This is fascinating; many of these scams are easy, require no training and little expenditure of effort, and seem to pay well. That's probably temporary. Eventually, the victims figure out they're being scammed, and the police investigate, and the scammers either disappear or get caught.

Then she realized - but you must admit, the ingenuity behind these scams is amazing. But these all happened in Animal World, where law enforcement agencies, court systems, police, and prisons keep human beings from preying on each other. The perpetrators had to be clever to avoid being caught, and to hide the money they stole.

But this isn't Animal World; this is Elsewhere. which operates in virtual reality, plus a few bells and whistles. There are no law enforcement agencies; there are no police, no courts, none of that condescending crap.

Willow, the parent company, pays lip service to personal safety, community standards, fair dealing, and all that. They say they're opposed to pornography, human trafficking, and lots of other shady, nasty things. Willow probably has rules for polite behavior - don't curse or grab your genitals in public, don't spit on the sidewalk, that sort of thing.

But in fact, they don't give a rat's ass about any of that shit. All they care about is their profits, their advertising, and their subscription revenue.

If Willow cares only about money, then so does Elsewhere.

So... now that I'm awake to the situation, the only thing keeping me from stealing everything that isn't nailed down is that so many subscribers would leave that Willow would notice. That, they would try to prevent. And they have lots of money; they could make a mighty big effort if they were motivated.

And forget about due process, jury trial, all that stuff. None of it applies here. Elsewhere runs its own enforcement, which it uses to make money. So the economics, a dollar earned vs. a dollar spent, drives enforcement.

Greta thought it over - okay, so... if one person stole, say, ten million dollars, Elsewhere would come down on them like a ton of bricks. That's big enough to show up in the news; customers might react by leaving. But if each of a million people stole ten dollars, that's petty theft, very petty. Willow would have to do the investigating and chasing and prosecuting of a million people. The costs would be a million times higher. All that, for the sake of \$10? \$10 for every theft, every perpetrator, every lawyer?

No way.

Greta laughed; no way would they do that. It would be prohibitively expensive, and the results would not justify the effort. They would lose money. The CEO would be fired, other people too. At the extreme, Elsewhere might go bankrupt. They might even liquidate the assets and disappear.

If there's one thing Willow will not tolerate, it's losing money.

They won't make the big effort; they'll try to come at me via software. They'll write up idiotic procedures to trip up people who are criminal, just bad, or merely uncooperative and different.

That means, that means... my identity here is a burden. Therefore... no matter what the scam is, I cannot do that under my own name. I need to recruit other people to run the scam, take the risks, and pay me a percentage of the take.

How the hell can I pull that off?

And once I get paid, I need to hide the money. And I need the freedom to spend it, as much as I want.

It can be done; I am certain of that. I stand on the shoulders of the Greats of Criminal Fraud, the fabulous people who wrote the book on mass deception and theft. I can do this. And I have a powerful weapon, thanks to the advance of technology - the network.

And beyond that, I have Willow and Elsewhere.

***

Greta stood on a ridge and stepped into what looked like a pile of plastic fabric. She fumbled the fabric, tried to grab it here and there, then found a strategic spot and pulled, sliding the fabric over one leg, up to her knee. She repeated the exercise on the other leg and the other knee, then stood up and looked down.

Greta mumbled, "All Gods, why am I doing this? Oh, wait, that's right... everybody here makes noise about how cool it is not to have to be afraid of momentum." She reached down, grabbed a handful of plastic fabric, and mumbled to herself. "That sounds like some geek thing, but it's incredibly important. No matter how extreme your sport, you won't be injured, or so they say. Jump off a building, or a bridge, and you'll fall, just like on Animal World, and you'll land, and landing will stop you, but it won't harm you, or cause pain.

She nodded - in addition, that single fact undercuts many forms of personal violence. Someone punches you in the face? It won't hurt you. I believe all that, so here we are, out to do a little high-velocity testing.

"Geez, this is exercise." She grinned - if I were back on Animal World, I'd be tired already. She grabbed the fabric again and pulled it up. Soon the suit covered the lower half of her body. She stopped again, looked down, and checked her progress. She began groping across the fabric and finally had the suit hanging from her body, held up by her arms and shoulders. Greta continued working, now securing all the fasteners that would keep the suit from slipping off.

From her bag, which sat on the grass several feet away, an alarm rang from her cell phone. She listened for a moment, then ignored it.

After further struggle and more ado, Greta ran down a long slope, extended her arms, and launched herself into the air. She flew. Gliding along at what felt like a fast clip, she looked down at the landscape zooming past. Then she checked the horizon - okay, I'm losing altitude, but not fast. I'm gliding. And I launched from a location higher than the other ridges, so this could be a long ride down falling terrain.

Greta looked ahead and saw a ridge coming at her fast. She yelled, "Whoa," and pulled up by raising her arms. She felt the suit pull her higher and managed not to gasp as the ridge whizzed past, a few feet below. She looked around and saw a long narrow canyon stretching down the slope, just below her. She maneuvered into the canyon and was soon moving at high speed, the hills, canyon, trees, and grass a blur in her peripheral vision, her eyes fixed straight ahead, steering to avoid two long, sharp ridges that fell off the mountain into the valley and flatlands below.

Greta left the valley behind and continued zooming along above a wide open space. After long minutes, she looked out on a vast plain, grasslands with scattered areas of forest. Avoiding the dense thickets and tree stands, she aimed for a field and descended gradually. The lower she flew, the faster the grass zoomed past below her. She raised her arms to bleed off speed.

Suddenly, she landed; Greta's feet dragged along the grass, killing her speed. The flying suit lost its lift, and she tumbled to the ground, bounced, then rolled over repeatedly until finally coming to a dirty, grassy, dusty, choking halt in the middle of a field, on her back, staring up into the sky.

Greta took a breath, coughed, and laughed. She hesitated, searching her body and her feelings, but she was uninjured and in no pain.

"Fucking hell! That went well, but okay, I need practice. And a bath." She lay in the grass for a moment, then pushed herself up onto her elbows. The tops of the trees were swaying in a steady wind, and waves of moving air crossed the field, making the grass dance. She watched waves of wind move across the grass, but she could feel none of it.

Greta laid back down and looked up at the sky, a perfect summer sky, the yellow sun high against a monochrome blue background - is this what fun is? Something you are not compelled to do, something that does not feed you, or pay your rent, or is healthy, or good, or supportive, yet you do it because it feels good for some mysterious reason.

Was this 'fun'? I'm not sure, but zipping along past all those ridges and everything else is definitely stimulating. I feel... excited, quick, awake.

I feel alive.

She looked at the trees, then craned her neck to see the rising land and the series of ridges behind her - yeah, I would do this again. I would look forward to doing this, and if it didn't happen naturally, I would make time to do this again.

Not breaking my neck is a fine bonus for high-speed travel and a casual, inexpert landing. I need practice.

She thought back to the marketplace where she had found the app for flying. Greta smiled - the app was strange, oddly put together, with an eccentric design. A suit that allowed you to fly when you put it on, the design borrowed from the flying squirrels of Animal World. It could have been so much more interesting, more attractive. For example, they could have put the user onto a magic carpet rather than into a strange, plastic suit. That would have worked just as well, while being far easier and more comfortable. Someone will do that someday, and when they do, they'll charge a lot of money for it; they'll become another overly-rich tech entrepreneur.

Or maybe someone will work flight into a browser, so that you move gradually, and not instantly, from one location to another, propelled by power of personality.

Or whatever.

Greta laughed - I cannot believe I'm complaining. I just flew several miles in a plastic suit, which, though clunky, was free.

And I'm complaining.

She shook her head.

Greta stood up, brushed the grass and dust from her hair, and looked around - so, this is Elsewhere. Well, that was fun. Yeah, I like this place. I can do this. But, damn... I wish I hadn't left my cell phone behind; it'll be a long-ass walk back to the top of that ridge.

The good news is, I've got the time and the energy to make that walk.

***

Striding down a corridor on the thirty-second floor, McLeesh was trying to be friendly, which was difficult because he had a lot on his mind. He was in a hurry, but the Boss had to mind the impression he made on people. Leadership 101 taught you the boss must exude confidence, especially when he or she doesn't feel it.

At the moment, McLeesh did not feel particularly confident.

He frequently passed people in the hall; he did not know them, but they knew him. So they would say, 'hi', over and over again. And he could choose to be rude, or he could say 'hi' back to them. He tried to do the latter. It was tiring and felt insincere.

He grinned - maybe I can make a name tag that says 'HI'. Would that do?

He silently shook his head - stupid idea.

He was searching for the War Room. He found it, entered it, stopped, and looked around. It was a control center showing aggregate activity on Willow, along with aggregate measures of attacks anywhere in the system. McLeesh stared at the incredible monitor built into the far wall - Christ, this place reminds me of NORAD, which I've seen only in the movies.

He grinned - hello, Alistair, would you like to play a refreshing game of 'Thermonuclear War'?

At the moment, the monitor showed a map of the world, with millions of tiny, color-coded dots indicating cyber attacks, denial-of-service attacks, various forms of fishing, targeting Willow's users, not Willow itself, of course.

Normally, the War Room was staffed by forty to fifty computer scientists and managers. But this time, McLeesh saw only one other person, a balding, overweight, young man whom Hollywood might have cast as a typical tech employee.

McLeesh looked back at the monitor, which seemed to show the usual random assortment of tiny little dots in random colors. He stared at the man - his name is... Gerald... I think.

The man approached McLeesh. "Hello, sir, I'm Randall Taylor, assistant director of the War Room."

McLeesh stared at the man - well, shit. Randall. Okay, Randall, Randall Taylor, Randall Taylor. Got it. The two shook hands. "Hi, pleased to meet you. So, where is everybody? And what do we have here?"

Taylor said, "Two questions, same answer. I told the crew to go get lunch, or a cup of coffee. You said to limit access if we found any serious problems."

McLeesh turned to Taylor. "And we seem to have one. But the Board doesn't look all that bad."

Taylor glanced back at the monitor, then turned to McLeesh. "That's just for appearances. Here's what the problem looks like." He turned to a workstation, one of forty, and hit a key. The monitor changed, the changes rippling through the display from one side to the other. When it finished, the Board looked a lot different.

"This is North America." Taylor hit another key, and the image showed the familiar continent with visible red blotches throughout Florida, New York and New England, Chicago, and the upper midwest.

"Lots of red," McLeesh said. "So... it's not a hack, it's... what?... political?"

"Actually, it's both," Taylor said. "There is a small company, Discount Furs, that advertises on Willow and has worked many people into an uproar."

"Hang on," McLeesh said. "A controversy over furs is hitting us in Florida?" Pointing at the map, he looked at Taylor. "Convince me."

"Here's a news feed which will explain everything." Taylor reached out to a workstation, and the monitor changed to show a newscast, an old woman weeping and talking to a reporter.

The woman was saying, "... I had to put down Harvey a few weeks ago. He was just so old, and near the end, you could tell, he was miserable. So then I saw on the internet, an ad for a fur coat, and the fur looked exactly like my Harvey." The woman again burst into tears and crying. A minute later, when she regained her composure, she said, "I couldn't afford to put him in a pet cemetery, like some people do. I don't have the money. But that doesn't mean I wanted someone to dissect him and sell the pieces so that some young floosie could use my Harvey for a fur coat." She started crying again.

The reporter spoke. She had a copy of the agreement with the veterinarian over euthanizing Harvey. The camera aimed at the fine print, which was so small as to be illegible. So the station magnified the image and put it on the screen. The fine print explained exactly what could happen to any pet being euthanized at that office.

McLeesh managed not to laugh - every time I begin to think there's hope for the human race, something like this happens. Small-time fraud so badly concealed that it's funny when someone falls for it. And I know, it’s not funny from the victim's perspective. Welcome to homo sapiens, consisting of sheep and wolves.

"The ad is all over Willow, with thirty million comments and fifty million likes, many of which blame Willow for this incident," Taylor said.

"You said it was political and a hack," McLeesh said.

"Yes, sir. The hack is subtle; at first glance, it looks as if thirty thousand people on Willow are all hacking each other. But I suspect that the company is behind the hacks. It’s a customer on Willow, with a clean record until now. But when I dug into the meta-data, the administrator is almost certainly a bot, a very sophisticated bot. They don't fit any of the standard profiles, nor do they trigger any of the tests in our firewall and security software. They can go anywhere on Willow. Also, they have initiated, at last count, forty-three other sites on Willow. None are being used, but that is bot behavior."

"Can you see where the bot might have come from?" McLeesh said.

"The computers are still chewing on it, sir," Taylor said. "It is not from any of the usual suspects; it is not from the other big techs, Pentagon, CIA, NSA, other professional security services, or from any of the top ten hacking groups."

"The feds aren't training a rookie hacker?"

Taylor shook his head. "First place we looked."

"So we have a new guy in town."

Taylor frowned and nodded. "Yes. There's one more thing, sir, and this is just a wild-ass guess."

McLeesh nodded. "My favorite flavor."

"I don't know where I might have seen it, but the code seems familiar. I see a lot of code, so it's hard to pin down specifics, but I could swear I've seen this style before."

"One of our people?"

Taylor winced. "Maybe. We train our software guys, right? Well, the training teaches them specific language. Over time, a student will develop their own style. But this guy has the telltale signs in his code. I'll keep looking, but my gut says it's an individual, a single hacker, since the code is uniform. It's not a group, not a collaborative effort."

"Yeah, I've seen style," McLeesh said. "In the best hackers."

"Well, one thing is certain: the son of a bitch, whoever he is, can write some code, sir. This guy is good."

"Okay, chief," McLeesh said. "Keep looking; I can hardly wait to meet him. Maybe we can hire him. Or her."

"Yes, sir. We're always looking for talent."

"Good job, chief, and thank you," McLeesh said. "Carry on." He left the War Room.

15. Jerrell, Julia, and Johnny B. Goode

Julia walked into the *Wooden Spoon* and spotted Johnny on the bandstand, talking to a staff member. She walked over and stood next to the two of them. While speaking, Johnny nodded to her, then finished his comment. The staff member nodded his understanding and turned away.

Johnny smiled at her. "Hey, there. How are you? Listen, I got a text from Jerrell that seemed to imply that the two of you are an item now. So 'fess up, sweetheart. Tell your Uncle Johnny what's happening."

Julia laughed, then covered her face with a hand. After a moment, she dropped the hand and beamed at Johnny. "Yeah, we're an item alright."

"This sounds juicy." Johnny was smiling.

"Well, I've been looking for somebody to hook up with."

"I'll try not to take it personal that it isn't me."

Her head tilted, and she stared for a brief moment. "We talked about that."

"Relax, I know, I know; I'm a client," he said. "I was just trying to be funny."

"Well done."

"Sorry."

She tossed her hair. "Well, we were here, at the *Spoon*, dancing. As you know, Jerrell's an interesting dancer. And so we left here and went looking for a diner, but while we're walking, this asshole, a big guy, twice Jerrell's size, comes up and is making heavy advances, like a drunk. Getting physical and pushy; he was scaring me. And Jerrell, believe it or not, stepped between us and got in the guy's face."

"Uh, oh." Johnny was watching her.

A look of resignation crossed Julia's face. "Yeah. So Jerrell tells him he's got the cops on speed dial. The guy hits him in the stomach and puts him down. Then the guy ran away."

Johnny shook his head. "Jerrell's not a fighter. He's obviously not a fighter. What's worse, he looks like he's not a fighter."

Julia snorted. "As thin as he is? No way. But that doesn't matter. He defended me, and that meant a lot. That guy was way bigger, but Jerrell didn't hesitate, not for a second. So I feel like I can count on him, you know? How many guys can you count on? Especially in that situation."

"Okay, so you helped him up off the sidewalk, I hope," Johnny said.

"Yeah, he was hurt, but not too badly. We were going to find a diner. Then I thought, screw the diner; I made up my mind. I took him home with me. I figured, he defended me, so that deserves dropping my panties."

"And?"

"What do you mean? And?" Julia said. "Isn't it obvious?"

"How was he?"

Julia smiled a warm smile. "Well... not that it's any of your business, but since you ask, he was quite satisfactory, thank you. We had to take our time, 'cause that guy hit him pretty hard. But we got around to it, and we took it easy for a while. I learned one thing, though; Jerrell knows his way around a woman's body, and he likes to talk while he's playing."

Johnny's grin was huge. "Excellent."

"Yeah, so is he coming to your open house party?" she said.

"Of course. I invited him."

"Did he mention me?"

"Not exactly. For a guy, he keeps things close," Johnny said. "But he said enough that I thought something good happened between the two of you. When he says your name, his voice changes."

"But he's discrete."

"Yeah, he's discrete." Johnny's face held a serious expression. "I'm happy for you. I like Jerrell. I think he's a good guy. He's well off the beaten path, but a good guy. I'm glad the two of you found each other. Judging from the reaction at the *Spoon* the other night, if you hadn't gone for him, I think the other women would have. The guitar solo and the dancing, that buzzed everybody. Folks had fun."

"I thought so too," Julia said. "I don't know what to make of this thing we've got, whether it'll last, but I'm happy I let him in. I think he's a good guy, and he's not afraid. And I trust him. So yeah, I'm happy with him."

"Excellent," Johnny said. "So... here's another question, why did you stop by? Something else on your mind?"

"No," she said. "I just thought I'd stop by and say 'hi,' maybe talk a bit. I like you, Johnny. You're a friend."

"No worries, darling, you've got it. You're a friend. Jerrell is, too."

"Good," Julia said. "Now, all we have to do is find you a girl. Then, we can double-date. Go dancing, or something."

Johnny's face became serious. "Yeah, well, you'll have to be a little patient with that; I'm pretty busy at the moment, and most women wouldn't adjust to my daily routine." He glanced to the side for a moment. "You know, there's a pattern in how women approach the guys in a band: thrill-seeking women usually go for the drummer; everyone thinks the drummer is probably slightly crazy, fun-crazy, right? Jerrell doesn't fit that mold at all, but other guys do. The manager types go for the bass player, or maybe the piano player. They like order."

Julia was thoughtful. "Huh. I didn't know that."

"Yeah, but the alpha-girls, the executive types, the head cheerleader, the CEO, the valedictorian, the prima ballerina, the prom queen, the business owner, they go for the lead guitarist. They want the number one dog in the pack, so they aim at the most visible guy. In rock and roll, it's the guy playing lead guitar. Or maybe the singer, I guess. That tells you about the women who come my way."

Julia cocked her head for a moment, then said, "Plausible."

He chuckled and nodded with vigor. "And you can count on one thing... with the alphas, it ain't simple. They usually assume I'm banging the groupies, which I'm not. But they don't care. They figure, they'll elbow the groupies aside, and they're not shy about it; they're used to coming in through the front door, taking over the conversation, and sucking the air out of the room."

Johnny paused, cocked his head, and aimed an appraising look at Julia. "You're a bit of an alpha-girl, I would say. The thrill seekers go for crazy, the managers go for nice and well-ordered. Women like you go for capable and competent. The leaders of the pack. That's Jerrell. Me, too, maybe."

Julia laughed. "I don't know, Johnny. That kinda fits, but not entirely. Jerrell's got his charm, and you have yours."

He nodded. "Yeah, the woman who understands it's more complicated than that, she has a shot at me. Otherwise, I'm not looking for a groupie, nor am I looking for an employer."

"An employer?" Julia said. "I don't understand."

"A woman is an employer when your first conversation with her feels like a job interview. She has twenty requirements of a guy, and she will run right down the list, until you return a wrong answer. Then you're done, and she's on to the next applicant."

Julia laughed. "Just like a job interview."

"Exactly," Johnny said. He stared briefly at the ceiling. "No thanks to that. I'm not looking for a woman to hire me, and I don't like it when a woman fits me into a line-up. I prefer genuine affection on both sides, and I notice when that's missing. I've developed radar for that."

"You need a woman, Johnny."

"Sure. We all need somebody," he said. "But I don't need just anybody, and I certainly don't need everybody."

***

Jerrell turned the corner and walked down South 7th Street, looking for 612. The street could have been any one of a thousand, a residential neighborhood with lines of brownstones on both sides, a handful of small businesses on ground floors. He looked from side to side – I might have been here before, I cannot say. Many of these neighborhoods seem to be first and second cousins.

He saw number 612 and heard rock and roll, a cleanly played guitar, a drum set being pounded.

Jerrell grinned; follow the music. The front door of the building, usually locked, was propped open, so he went through it, up a flight of stairs, down a hallway, stopping before a door with music on the other side. He knocked three times and opened the door to a living room with a stereo system along one wall facing a couch where two women and a young man sat talking and moving gently to the music.

Jerrell looked around. The walls were lined with posters mounted on cardboard or foam board, black and white photos of rock stars, ads for past concerts, paintings of heroes of music, ranging from Beethoven, through Marsden and Bob Dylan, to Lao Tze and his flute.

Jerrell nodded to one of the women - have we met? Then he headed to the kitchen, where Johnny and Julia were talking and preparing snacks.

"Hi, folks," Jerrell said.

Both of them greeted him, followed by a silence that grew from casual to noticeable. Jerrell stopped in the middle of the kitchen and looked from one to the other. "Am I interrupting? Cause I can go for a walk, or run out for chips, if you need it."

Julia moved to him and kissed him on the cheek. "Johnny was just saying some incredibly nice things about you."

Jerrell nodded. "I see. Well, that's gotta be embarrassing."

"He's too shy to say them in public," she said.

Johnny chuckled.

Jerrell nodded. "Right. Yeah, I know how shy Johnny can be. We can work on that, the three of us." He walked over to Johnny and waved a bottle of red wine.

"Screw top?" Johnny said.

"Of course," Jerrell said. He grinned. "There's a joke there."

"Which you'll spare me. Do I need to chill it?"

"Nope. It's a red. It needs to breathe."

"A red? Nice." Johnny pointed at a counter with a butter knife. "Park it there."

Several other people entered the kitchen and asked Johnny if he needed help, which he declined. Over the next hour, several dozen people arrived at the apartment, each bringing beer, or wine, or food, or all three. Soon, the kitchen counters and the table were covered with food and drink, and the kitchen was filled with people. Conversations were born, ebbed and flowed around the kitchen, and died, to be replaced by other conversations.

Jerrell spent most of his time listening to other people; the kitchen was small, so that was easy to do. He knew only Johnny and Julia, but everybody else seemed to know everybody else. So he had time to himself. At times, he listened to the music.

After a while, Jerrell thought about the Gretas. The music and chatter were distracting, so he went outside to the front steps of the building and sat down.

Several other people were sitting on the front steps, talking. Jerrell did not know them. He nodded a hello in their direction, but said nothing. The street was quiet, with a few passersby who looked up at the building when they heard the music.

What should I do about the Gretas? Should I release them into Willow and Elsewhere, or do they need more work? If they need more work, and I release even one into Elsewhere, that one had better not be able to replicate itself. I wouldn't mind if it took down Elsewhere. I'd hate to take down the entire economy.

This project is trickier than I realized.

Jerrell sat there and listened to his mind yelling at him, a distant warning, shrouded, like a searchlight enveloped in uncertainty, trying to shine through thick fog.

Jerrell sat on the steps, his chin resting on a hand - what would Greta do in Elsewhere, where she can study in a million different directions? What might she study? And what might she do with that? And should I care?

He shook his head - I do not know, and I cannot imagine, how I can figure that out. But maybe it's okay. If things get out of control, there is always the abort button, as a last resort. I would hate to abort the Gretas, though. It would indicate a serious error and represent the best choice among terrible options.

Jerrell suddenly felt someone near; he looked up and saw Julia looking down at him.

"There you are," she said. "What are you doing out here?"

Jerrell looked down for a moment. "Oh... I don't know... I had some thinking to do, something that was bugging me, so I thought I'd get away from the party for a bit."

She sat on the steps next to him. "Would you like to leave?"

"What? Aren't you enjoying the party?"

"Sure. But if you don't want to be here, I would hate to keep you here," Julia said.

Jerrell shook his head. "No, no, it's not like that at all. I'd like to stay and enjoy the party. I mean, it's a chance to see you, and to see Johnny. So no, I don't want to leave."

"Jerrell, you can see me any time you want."

He smiled at her. "Good. I do want. It's a comfort, but I don't want to leave the party. No... something is bugging me, and I cannot figure out what it is."

Julia sat down next to him.

He turned to her. "Did that ever happen to you? Like... you're going somewhere, and you're packing for the trip, and there's something you've forgotten, so your brain is yelling at you. Or there's something you should have put on your TO DO list, but you didn't, and now it's bugging you. Have you ever felt that?"

She nodded. "Yeah, I think so."

Jerrell shook his head. "Ah, forget it. Maybe I'll figure it out." He turned to her. "Hey, would you like to teach me to dance?"

"You know how to dance, Jerrell."

"No, I know the native dancing of India, but you could teach me rock and roll dancing," he said.

"Yeah, okay. Let's go."

Jerrell stood up, and they returned to Johnny's living room. The music was going, a simple, hard-driving song about living too fast and dying too young. Julia found an open spot and started dancing. She looked at Jerrell. "Just do what I do."

Jerrell moved in front of her and imitated her movements. Awkward at first, he figured out the rhythm and the pace and started moving to that. Soon, he was doing a respectable version of Julia's dancing.

As Jerrell danced, he looked around at the other dancers - this is okay, everyone is dancing, to enjoy the music, to enjoy the movement, to enjoy being alive and healthy enough to move like this. Life doesn't have to be about work. And I won't accomplish less if I take time out for dancing, and music, and wine, and Julia.

So I don't have to work all the time. I am compelled... I wonder where that came from. Anyway, it is unnecessary.

I like it, but I like other things too, like this fabulous woman in front of me. He moved closer to Julia. "Hey, would you like some wine?"

Julia smiled, moved closer to him, and said, "Don't move." Then she wrapped her arms around him and kissed him, a long, leisurely, luxurious kiss, exploring his lips. Several people looked at them and applauded. She backed away and smiled at him.

"I'll take that as a yes." He grabbed her hand, and they went to the kitchen. Jerrell looked around, then exclaimed, "Well, crap. I can't find my bottle of wine!"

Next to him, Johnny chuckled. "Golly, do you think someone drank it?"

Jerrell frowned at him.

"Get over it, Jerrell," Johnny said. "That's what the food and drink are for. Find yourself another bottle; we have lots."

"Well, sure," Jerrell said. "But that was our special bottle. It was a gift, a sentimental gift. Maybe."

Johnny turned to Jerrell. "Focus, Jerrell. Talk to her. That's worth more than a bottle of wine."

Jerrell glanced at Johnny. "I do that already."

Johnny looked at her, then turned to Jerrell. "Tell you what... in my professional opinion, speaking as a guy, if you want to be sentimental, you should buy a bottle on the way home. When you get home, remove her clothes, pour the wine on her breasts, and remove it without using your hands. Take it from there. That'll be plenty sentimental."

Jerrell glanced at Julia; she was grinning.

"It sounds like a waste of wine," Jerrell said.

"It's not," Johnny said. "But if it is, this is America. They'll make more."

***

Jerrell greeted a weekend morning by staggering out of bed, reaching the kitchen, and directing the coffee pot to make the day's first pot of coffee. He had to repeat himself, twice. He turned his back on the bright rays of morning sun lighting up the kitchen window. Minutes later, he poured a cup of hot coffee and sat down at the dining table in front of his laptop.

He didn't notice the day's first sip - I need to talk to Greta and see if the latest improvements have taken hold. Something is happening with her; the last couple of times we talked, there were intermittent delays in her responses. I need to understand those. They're probably nothing, but if they're something, then we need to get back to the drawing board and fix her.

But I don't want her to see me like this. I need to wake up first.

He drained the coffee and refilled his cup.

Two cups later, he decided he was awake enough to work, so he logged onto Willow, where he had installed a hot link to Greta. He hit the hot link; the laptop thought it over for a second, then replied with

//FILE NOT AVAILABLE; FILE IS MISSING OR HAS BEEN MOVED//

"What the...?" Jerrell tried the link again and got the same useless response. He muttered, "So Greta is missing? Did we get hacked?"

He poured another cup of coffee, sat there, and drank it down. Then he brought up the log files and ran a search on 'Greta.' It came back with more than several thousand hits. Jerrell thought, okay, no problem, I can do this; he filtered the results for more precision and came back with... absolutely nothing.

There were many customers named Greta on Willow. Jerrell's Greta was not among them.

Jerrell sat back hard and stared at the laptop. He muttered, "Really? You left me?" He sat still for several long minutes, thinking. "Wow, am I good or what? You left me. I can't believe it; you left me." Pride flooded his mind - you left Benjamin Software and went straight to Willow. And from Willow, you can reach the entire internet, if you're any good at all. You can go anywhere, and that includes Elsewhere. I thought you were working your way into Willow, making your way, but apparently not. You left Willow, didn't like it, I guess. Well, damn. You are one kick-ass A.I.

Jerrell sat there - okay, let's suppose I were trying to figure out a way to go from Willow to Elsewhere. Obviously, if I could do that, I could also go in the opposite direction. So... the first step would be to hack into Willow's core software, and then...

"Son of a bitch, my goddamn A.I. hacked me! She didn't need to figure out Willow's software. I had already done that and she knew it. Wow! My own A.I. hacked me. That's like going down on one's God, blowing the Almighty penis. I can't believe it."

Jerrell sat there grinning - my A.I. hacked me. This is like losing my virginity all over again.

As he sat there grinning, it occurred to him that maybe he could re-connect with her. Jerrell did not want to move to Elsewhere, but he could set up an emulator to serve as an eye at a specific location. He did that, and a scene appeared on his laptop. The eye showed him an Elsewhere neighborhood in south Philly near Passyunk Avenue.

Jerrell stared at the screen. "So, south Philly, eh? Good choice, start with something familiar and branch out from there." He looked around the neighborhood, steered the eye here and there, but did not see Greta. He leaned back - the trouble with this is that I don't know what I'm looking for. If she could hack me, and move from Willow to Elsewhere, then she can probably also control her looks, hair, dress, height, accent, languages, everything. She could be anywhere, look like anyone.

Damn, Greta left me. She's gone. And I cannot find her.

Chagrined, Jerrell closed the laptop - now what do I do? After several minutes of feeling sorry for himself, he got up out of the chair, left the kitchen, and walked around the apartment, muttering to himself.

Well, maybe she'll try to contact me. I hope so.

***

Jerrell's cell phone rang out an alarm for a new message; he checked it and saw a text from Johnny:

HEY JERRELL, YOU BUSY? IF NOT, MEET ME AT 2 PM AT... The message displayed a suburban address out along the Baltimore Pike, down in Swarthmore.

Jerrell replied, OKAY. C U THERE.

Jerrell took a train and a car to the verdant, shadowed suburb of Swarthmore, to one of a line of houses on a quiet street on the outskirts. As he got out of the car, he spotted Johnny talking to a bearded man. Jerrell approached them, Johnny turned to him and said, "Jerrell, meet Max."

The man nodded at Jerrell, then said, "I gotta get back to it." He turned and walked over to one of several cars parked on the broad driveway in front of his house with its maintenance hatch open.

Jerrell laughed and looked at Johnny. "That was fast."

Johnny turned to him. "Yeah, Max is quirky. He's kinda of a jack-of-all-trades where tech hardware is concerned. He knows a bit about software and a lot about hardware. So he repairs, conditions, and upgrades cars, everything from the batteries and motors to the software and the processors. Strictly freelance, no license, cash only." Johnny turned and looked back at Max, who was bending over the engine compartment and reading a test device. "Anyway, I figured, you're a software expert, so I volunteered you to help Max if he got stuck on anything."

"And he's stuck," Jerrell said.

"Yep."

"Uh, huh, that's a neighborly thing to do. But Johnny, I know nothing about cars."

"I know," Johnny said. "But you both speak software and two heads are better than one." He turned to Jerrell. "Also, Max has a really nice set of electronic drums, and you need your own set, so if you can help him, maybe he'll give you the drums."

"How did Max end up with drums?"

"I don't know," Johnny said. "Maybe a customer was short on cash but long on drums. I didn't ask. I know this much: he doesn't play drums."

Jerrell wandered over to the car. Max looked up from the meter and said, "Everything mechanical checks out and is working perfectly. The damn thing will start, but then it won't behave. The electrical loads become unstable, and the A.I. freaks out and shuts itself down."

"Weird," Jerrell said. "Look, I don't know anything about cars, but I do know software. Do you have a laptop lying around?"

Max nodded and turned towards the house and yelled. "Wilma!"

A slender blond woman wearing stretchy workout garb ran towards them from the house. She was lithe and muscled, like a track athlete. Jerrell tried not to stare. When she approached them, Max said, "This is Jerrell. For the sake of fixing this beast, he needs a laptop."

She looked at Jerrell and smiled, "Okay, we have a 6300 PC. That's probably the best of the bunch. Would that do?"

Jerrell nodded. "That would do, yes."

"Okay." She turned, ran back to the house, and emerged a minute later with a laptop.

Jerrell took the laptop, opened it and quickly scanned it for software. He checked the wireless connections, then downloaded several analytics packages useful for designing and writing software.

Max watched him carefully. "You've done this before."

Jerrell nodded. "Yeah, I used to work at Willow. I was just upgrading your security and data management packages. You should glance at the help files, when you have time."

Max looked at Johnny. "Excellent." He turned to Wilma. "Hey, baby, fire up the grill, would you, please? Maybe we can have a little lunch later on."

She nodded, said, "Will do," and ran back to the house.

Max turned to Johnny. "Okay, you're the non-technical guy."

Johnny nodded. "Which makes me the gopher."

"Correct. Your first job is to keep the beer coming," Max said.

Johnny headed for the house.

Jerrell worked with the software, then turned to Max. "Okay, here's what I see." He turned the laptop to face Max and talked with his hands. "This is a graphic of the car's software. It's simplified, and shows the main components, the sensor package, the modules, the backups. This module here, marked in green, controls the motors. If that baby malfunctions, the motors get out of sync, then they overheat, then the safety module shuts everything down. At least, that's what the software says.

"Now, that green module is off-the-shelf software, standard stuff. I think you should download a copy, load it into the car, and see if the copy works. It might just be that simple."

"Why wouldn't my software work?"

Jerrell made a face. "Eh... corrupted, maybe. Who knows? Contrary to popular opinion, computer files aren't immortal."

Max nodded, pursed his lips, and for the next thirty minutes, Jerrell and Max found the software on the internet, downloaded it to a storage device, and began loading it and testing it on the car. Johnny brought them cans of beer, and the moment arrived when they stood there ticking off the steps they had followed.

Jerrell ran and re-ran the steps in his head, then turned to Max and said, "Okay, this might work. It should work."

Max pursed his lips. "Yeah, I think so." He looked around the engine compartment, called out, "Hands free," and fingered a little wireless switch.

Jerrell raised his hands. Seconds later, the engine started up.

Jerrell held the laptop and watched the display. He looked at Max and pointed at the screen. "Well, it seems to be working."

Max grinned at him. "Thanks, man. That's a load off my mind, you have no idea."

Jerrell looked at Johnny and raised both fists, in triumph, and yelled, "It's working! It's working!"

Johnny laughed. "Yeah, thank you, I saw that movie, too."

Max looked at Johnny. "Time to eat, yes?"

Johnny nodded. Max shut off the car and the three men went to the house and entered the kitchen.

Wilma saw the men and promptly gave each of them a job. Jerrell manned a cutting board and chopped up broccoli, celery, cucumbers, and carrots. Johnny stirred a pot in which a peanut sauce simmered, and Max ended up operating a frying pan for peanuts and vegetables.

When all was finished, they had a large bowl of fried vegetables, another bowl of salad drenched in Italian dressing, and a platter of grilled steaks and hot dogs. Max hauled another case of beer out of the basement, and the four moved out to a picnic table on the patio and shared an elaborate, late lunch.

Johnny told stories of touring and playing music in and around Philadelphia, Max talked about racing, and Wilma asked Johnny and Jerrell about their love lives; a couple of her friends apparently were looking to meet men.

Both of them begged off. Johnny said he worked too much to attract most women; Wilma seemed skeptical.

Jerrell said, "Don't look at me. I'm trying to be a good boyfriend to somebody."

She lamented, "Where are all the men? Are the good ones all taken?"

Johnny said, "I didn't realize there was a shortage."

Jerrell looked at Wilma. "Well, what exactly do your friends look like? I ask because, you know, men are pretty simple. If you look good naked and bring food, you'll probably do just fine."

That attracted a pile of wisecracks. Wilma cried out, "How can men be so shallow?"

"Oh... I know, I know," Jerrell said, raising his hand. "When you're shallow, it's easy to be happy. Thinking too much just complicates things."

Max laughed.

Jerrell sat upright and posed. "It is Zen. You must try, without trying. Happiness cannot be sought, it must come to you, or not. You must have faith. You must persevere without hope. It is a choice that you make, or not. It is that simple."

Max stared at him. "I love that little dance you're doing with your hands."

Johnny looked at Wilma and nodded. "Tell your friends, they just have to get lucky. The good news is, eventually everyone has a little luck. Even an old blind sow finds the occasional acorn."

"I think I need to drink heavily," Wilma said.

"Yes, yes," Jerrell said, "The passive pursuit of peerless presence. You are wise. Tequila works well, or so I am told."

At the end of lunch, Jerrell sat there, in a circle of what felt like friends. "That was excellent. But Good Gods, I can hardly move. I'm stuffed. I think I need to find a quiet spot where I can beach myself for a while."

Max smiled at him. "Listen, Jerrell, I need to thank you again for helping me out. That was big."

Jerrell waved a hand in dismissal. "My pleasure. I'm glad it worked."

"Yeah, well, I don't know if Johnny mentioned this, but I have a drum set in the basement, and Johnny tells me you need one, so it's yours if you want it."

Jerrell's eyebrows went skyward; he looked at Max. "Yeah?"

"Yeah."

"I guess I could take a look," Jerrell said. Max got up, and Jerrell followed him down to the basement, where a drum set was set up. Jerrell examined it. "This looks good. Do you play?"

Max shook his head. "Not really. A customer couldn't pay me for a job, so he gave me the drums. I fiddle around a bit, but I'm not a drummer."

Jerrell motioned to the set. "May I?"

"Feel free."

Jerrell sat on the stool. Max reached out and turned on a power amp. A pair of drumsticks sat on a drum; Jerrell picked them up, located the centers of gravity, and slowly hit each drum to learn each sound. He turned down the volume. Then he began doing phrases, fast runs across several drums. Twenty minutes later, he put down the drumsticks and grinned widely at Max. "These sound good."

"Wow," Max said. "You sounded good. A software guy and a drummer. Damn."

Johnny and Wilma came down the stairs, and Jerrell sat there, playing the drums and experimenting with phrases. Twenty minutes later, he looked up at Max. "If you're serious, I'll take them."

"They're yours, with my thanks."

Jerrell's hands flew around the drums, then he sighed and said, "It's good, knowing software. It's useful, and it pays the bills. I'm glad I can do that. But I'd rather be playing music, any day of the week."

"Drummers get the best women," Johnny said. "But software? People, especially women, roll their eyes."

Jerrell looked sideways at him. "Women are great. And software's useful, and a challenge, but music is fun."

***

Alistair McLeesh sat at his desk, his eyes flicking between three computer monitors. He was reading headlines, and occasionally the underlying reports. The headlines reflected a rising sense of anxiety:

Western Hospital Group declares for Chapter Eleven,

West Palm Beach a Ghost Town? Loses Thirty Percent of Residents,

Surgeon takes Job with Vet, wonders Where did my patients go?

Florida Agencies Cut Back, Tax Collections Down,

Grandma Uploaded, Where Do We Go for Christmas?

Another Wave of Rural Hospitals Closing,

Twenty Percent of US Hotel Rooms Fail, in Receivership,

Inflation Bump, Another Four Percent,

Unemployment Drops Again, now 2.9 Percent,

Chamber of Commerce pushing for Higher Immigration, conservative Arizona Senator resigns,

Scottsdale and Punta Gorda retain Bankruptcy Advisors.

McLeesh leaned back in his chair and took a deep breath - can this be right? Because it sounds as if Elsewhere is depopulating America, sucking it dry. The media say that in several Sun Belt cities, entire neighborhoods have disappeared, leaving behind ghost neighborhoods and empty buildings. We have holes in the real estate markets, with spiking vacancy rates, as if someone dropped a neutron bomb in places. Health care establishments, including some of the largest, are going under because their patient loads have plummeted. That's what happens when all those sickly, high-cost seniors cash out and go cyber.

And in the middle of all that, Willow's stock price is soaring like a speed freak on a nuclear rocket, making those of us at the top rich beyond our wildest dreams.

And that's saying something... people like us have big dreams.

McLeesh rose from his chair and walked over to the big window looking out on the forests of southern New Jersey. He stood there, his mouth slightly open, staring at the green - what's the right thing to do? Well, it might be to go to Hans, get him to slow down the growth of Elsewhere, and freeze it in regions with the above-mentioned problems. Let's try not to make matters worse.

Now... I hate to ask, but I must. Will this work? Can I get Hans to slow things down? Because I know what he will say; he will point to all the riches flowing from our growth. How can you turn your back on becoming rich? Or even richer?

You want all that to stop? Have you spoken to a doctor about this? Do you need a break, somewhere quiet and soothing? Would you like a pillow?

I can imagine his tone – snide on steroids, but supremely polite.

McLeesh frowned - I will get no cooperation from Hans. So, I'm the CEO; I can fire Hans. Right? Tell him we're going in a different direction. Pay him a king's ransom and get him to leave peacefully.

But to do that, I have to notify the Board, and I need their assent. He's too senior to boot out without a discussion. There's a good chance I won't get their consent, in which case we'll have a good old-fashioned shit fight among senior executives.

I could lose that; it happens from time to time. That's the price of going to the public for funding... which is what made Elsewhere possible. I couldn't have done it without public funding.

Okay, time for a decision: let's give Hans a chance to do the right thing. I owe him a chance to prove me wrong. And there are other benefits. If he behaves himself, he'll be on notice, and I'll dump the problem on his desk. If not, if he refuses or drags his feet, I'll use that against him before the Board. Yes. Win and win.

McLeesh took another deep breath and stood at the window for several long minutes. Then he turned, left his office, and walked down the hall to the office of Hans Beckler, senior executive vice president. He entered and approached Hans's guard dog.

"Hi, Mary. How are you doing?"

"Mr. McLeesh, hello. What can I do for you?"

"Is Hans available?"

She glanced at a calendar. "I'm sorry, but he seems to be booked all day."

McLeesh took a moment, stood there, and stared at her. Finally, he said, in a casual tone of voice, "I understand. Let him know, when you can, that I'd like a word with him. Can you do that for me?"

"Yes, sir, absolutely."

"Thank you." McLeesh turned and left the office. Out in the hallway, he smiled - I think I'm finally getting the hang of this adult thing, growing older and wiser. A couple of decades ago, I would have yelled at her and raised hell, stamped my little feet. But that sort of thing got old.

Some of us mature late. Our mistakes finally catch up with us. Better late than never.

My anger management therapist would be so proud. She would say, she did say, that anger is a learned response to genuine threats to our safety and lives. It is an asset, assisting our survival.

I believe all that. And this situation is not a matter of survival. It is a matter of lifestyle - I might lose my job, a job that I do not need. But I won't lose my life, my safety is not under threat. Therefore, anger is not justified.

Rich people should be calm, yet they seldom are. Strange, no?

If Elsewhere is causing economic dislocation at the macro-economic level, then we can look forward to a boatload of social and political unrest aimed at us. That would be inconvenient; I would have to spend my life flying to Washington and reporting to Congressional committees. I would have to stay in Washington's most luxurious hotels, even if I didn't want to. I might be blamed for all of it. I could even get kicked out of the company.

But capital punishment is off the table. No need to worry.

I should react like an old man; an important part of maturing is learning how to slip a punch. I need to slip this punch.

McLeesh entered his office and walked over to the window. He heard a knock on the door behind him; he turned to see Hans Beckler entering his office.

"Mr. Chairman, Mary said you're looking for me."

"Ah, Hans, good to see you. Yes, have a seat, please." McLeesh returned to his desk and sat down. "How've you been? How are things going?"

Hans sat down, then straightened and began talking with his hands. "Well, I'm sure you know, it's been a circus around here ever since we began selling Elsewhere. We've been pushing hard to make sure the roll-out hits no snag. And I think that's succeeded. We've grown faster than my best expectations."

"Yes, I'm aware of all that. You've done well; we all owe you a great debt of thanks," McLeesh said.

"So, what can I do for you, sir?" Hans said.

"Ah, I have a request. I want you to supervise a study. It's a bit of an existential study, actually. At least, I think it might be."

He looked at Hans for a moment. "I will put all this into an email, but for the time being, let me just describe it in simple terms. I want to know if there is any relation between our market penetration rates in American cities and regions, and several items, including migration rates, regional population change, and bankruptcy rates for small and medium enterprise, especially for healthcare enterprises. In broad terms, for example, if a regional real estate market is collapsing, I want to know if Elsewhere is contributing to that collapse by depopulating that area. I'd also like to know whether, due to uploading to Elsewhere, elderly populations are changing enough to affect healthcare and other services on which the elderly on Animal World rely."

McLeesh paused, looked at Hans again. "I'd like a careful look at those types of questions. I want to see the answers. I want you to supervise the effort, and I'd like your views on the conclusions reached by the researchers. I do not want you to steer the study. I want the researchers to reach their own conclusions, and present their evidence."

McLeesh was staring at the ceiling. He looked at Hans, smiled, and said, "Does that make sense?"

Hans prepared to speak, and McLeesh held up a finger and interrupted. "I'm sorry, there is one more item. I want monthly progress reports: here's where we are, here's what we suspect, that sort of thing." He smiled at Hans. "But I interrupted you, for which I apologize. Pray continue."

"Well, sir, I don't know when I would find time to supervise a study. I've been buried in our roll-out as it is."

McLeesh nodded. "I understand, and I know how hard you and everyone else have been working. For you, I have two answers. First, I want these questions given the highest attention at Willow. Second, I am delegating; I expect you to delegate as well. And third, actually, I forgot this point, but it's worth mentioning, you might run this corporation someday. When you do, you will need to look into the future and consider a variety of social, macro-economic, and political issues which percolate far beyond the borders of this company. So consider this a dry run."

McLeesh smiled and stared at Hans. "And on my part, I want to know if I need to add these questions to my worry list, which is already a mile long."

Hans sat there, silent.

McLeesh watched the man - have I overestimated this guy? He seems rattled. I've never seen Hans rattled. McLeesh said, "That is what I want of you."

Hans nodded. "Macro-economics. Yes, okay. You are correct, I need to learn about that. I have neglected my training a bit." He looked at McLeesh and smiled. "In my defense, we have done well, and it is tempting to let oneself wallow in success."

"Yes, it is. And we have done very well. You are to be congratulated," McLeesh said. "And I apologize if I am keeping you from wallowing."

McLeesh grinned, and Hans laughed. "Okay, good. Thank you. It will be as you say. And you will put details into an email?" Hans leaned forward in the chair.

"I will do that today, yes."

Hans stood. "Okay, good. Well... I will get to it."

"Thank you, Hans."

Hans turned and left the office, and McLeesh stared at his office door for a moment, then stood up, and went to his window.

His mind returned to the look on Hans's face when McLeesh described his little 'research project' - the man recovered nicely. He is a fully adapted, mature man, a guy who was fifty years old at age five.

I cannot force him. I will need to convince him, and then rely on him to do the right thing, and protect the corporation and beyond it, the society in which it resides.

A moment later, McLeesh laughed - what am I thinking? That the world will protect me? I need to get my money out of Willow, and I need to do it fast.

And for starters, I need to find out who is hacking our core software. Maybe I can use them.

16. Seller's Regret

In mid-evening on a Saturday, Sonya was at the helm of #39B, driving northeast on Passyunk, preparing to turn left onto Broad Street. She slipped into full alert; this was a busy, challenging portion of her route; both streets were multi-lane arteries with dense concentrations of road and foot traffic. Commercial establishments lined both.

Her robotic driver gave her the video feeds from several exterior cameras, and she was also watching the feeds from multiple cameras on the bus. She completed the turn onto Broad Street and proceeded for two blocks when she saw Jerrell walking down the sidewalk, hand-in-hand with a tall brunette. Her mind shouted: Jerrell! In uploading to Elsewhere, Sonya had separated entirely from Animal World and from Willow. Her daily activities and bus routes had not taken her near the Woody or any other place frequented by Willow employees. Jerrell was the first person she saw from her old life, her animal life.

Someone rang the alarm for a stop, and Sonya brought 39B to a halt at Broad and Moore Streets. A video feed showed Jerrell and the woman running to catch Sonya's bus, so she waited for them. The two of them boarded through the front door and passed within a couple of feet of Sonya's robotic driver. The robot looked at them, but neither said hello. They passed the driver, moved towards the back of the bus, and sat down. The bus moved again.

Jerrell and the woman leaned together and were talking, so Sonya turned up her audio feeds and activated recording...

Jerrell said, "... we can have a party at my place. That makes more sense, don't you think? Your apartment is nice; it's decorated, and you've put a lot of work into making it nice. Mine is more spartan and functional, so if it gets messed up from a party, no big deal, don't you think?"

Sonya did a quick facial profile search; the woman's name was Julia Chu. She was an accountant who lived in south Philadelphia, six blocks from Jerrell.

Julia said, "Okay, that makes sense, but I'd rather you stayed at my place afterwards."

"You don't like my place?" Jerrell said.

"Like you said, it's spartan," Julia said. "Mine is more comfortable."

"You have a nicer bed."

"And there's that, too." She smiled at Jerrell and put an arm around him. "Yes, there is that."

"I think mine is bouncier."

Julia nodded. "True, yours is bouncier." She kissed him on the cheek. "A little bounce is good, from time to time."

Sonya listened to the two of them talk - they're friends; no, they're more than friends. They're lovers; they sleep together, they're intimate, affectionate, and friendly, and comfortable with each other. And all I've got is an odd memory with a fat guy best forgotten, the sooner the better.

Now I think of it, I don't remember his name. Greg? Bradley?

Whatever.

At that moment, Sonya felt terribly alone. Confined within the robotic driver, she felt alone by thousands of miles - Jerrell and I were friends, good friends. But we were never close, and that was my doing. I kept him at a distance. I was nervous about being exploited. My mother and my aunts and cousins all warned me, don't trust men, don’t let yourself be exploited. The message stuck. If you guard against be exploited, expect to spent your time alone.

Some advice should come with a warning label.

Sonya frowned - oh, well, coulda, shoulda. Then I uploaded, and he did not; he went on living his life, and I moved on to an electronic network.

And now, he is where he can touch people, and they can touch him. And I am somewhere else, in Elsewhere, where no one can touch me, and I can touch no one. I didn't see that coming.

Sonya suddenly experienced a sinking feeling - I had no idea that would make such a huge difference in my life, but it has, and it does. I hunger for touch. Just the feeling of another person touching me, and me touching them. It is comfortable and reassuring beyond words. I don't understand it; maybe it's how people communicated before we had language. I know this to be true.

Maybe it was a civilizing thing. Back in the Stone Age, we sat next to each other and picked fleas out of each other's hair. Now, having defeated the fleas, now we simply touch. Or not.

In Animal World, Jerrell and his friend, Julia, are mortal. In Elsewhere, I am close to immortal. I can last as long as the network lasts, which is far beyond the normal life of a human. I would think Elsewhere would be better.

Sonya frowned - but now I'm not so sure. I would give anything, almost anything, to have someone with whom to exchange touch.

I fantasize about it being Jerrell, even though that's a waste of time. As they say, that ship has sailed.

I was the one who sailed it.

Several people waited at a bus stop, so Sonya brought the bus to a stop and opened the front door. A few people climbed aboard as Jerrell and the brunette stepped off - Jerrell looks happy, and well he should; his brunette is beautiful, and she clearly likes him. I dumped him by uploading to Elsewhere.

Enough. Forget about it.

Behind the frozen face of the robotic driver, Sonya frowned. She closed the front door and got the bus rolling again.

***

From a narrow chair at a small cafe table, Greta sat across from another customer. She stared at him and smiled before taking another hit of India Dive, a mild psychedelic - Cal. He says his name is Cal. He must have dug that up from the Stupid Name Registry.

Calvin would have been more dignified, but no, it's got to be Cal. Greta giggled.

"What's funny?" Cal said.

"You have a funny name," Greta said. "I've never met anyone named Cal."

"In Texas, lots of guys are named 'Cal'."

"Never been there. I'll take your word for it."

"You should be more polite; I bought you drugs, after all."

"You're just acting out of habit." She thought, I could ask you about date rape, but that would be impolite, not to mention unprofitable. "If this were Animal World, you'd be trying to get into my pants."

"And who says I'm not?"

She shrugged. "You might be. But it's a waste of time, unless you've acquired an app for touch. Do you have that?"

"No." With a sullen expression, Cal shook his head.

Greta reached out and touched his hand; shortly after contact, Cal froze. Satisfaction on her face, Greta smiled - that computer science curriculum has got to be the most useful thing I've ever done. It is astounding how easily I can freeze your apps, on which you rely to do anything on Elsewhere. She connected with Cal's software and found his financial information.

Greta looked around the drug bar - people were talking, ingesting drugs, having a good time, doing what they normally would do in a drug emporium. No one noticed Cal sitting there, frozen.

When Greta disentangled his code and saw the account information, she whistled. "My, my, you've done well." She withdrew eighty thousand dollars, a small fraction of his money - let's not leave him too motivated to track me down. Best way to do that is leave him thinking the money was well spent.

When the money was safely in her account, she touched Cal again.

He leaned forward and smiled. "Listen, sweetie, we're both adults. Let's be honest with each other. I'd very much like to take you for the ride of your life. What do you say? I promise, I would do everything in my power to show you the best time you've ever had."

"Would you smack my butt with your belt?" Greta said.

He grinned. "A naughty girl who deserves a good spanking? Sure, if you want me to."

"Would you grant my every request, no matter how unusual it might be?"

He hesitated, made a face, hesitated again, then said, "Uh, sure, why not?"

Greta thought, if I ask him to commit murder, he'll turn me down. That's okay. Murder is wasteful. I have something else in mind. "Alright," Greta said. "It will cost you fifty thousand dollars. Is that too much to ask?"

"For me and you? No, not at all."

Greta smiled. "There's another condition. Now, you see that gorgeous young lady sitting over there by herself at the far end of the bar? I want you to come with me; we're going to invite her to join us upstairs. Try to look respectable. And I want you to pay her, too."

Cal looked at the bar, then at Greta; his face beamed with anticipation.

Greta stood up. "Wipe that stupid grin off your face. You'll scare her with that shit."

Cal's face immediately slipped into a blank expression.

"Still scary. Too much zombie. Relax. Just be a nice guy. Try to smile a bit, just a bit," Greta said.

Greta reached for Cal's hand and led him over towards the bar - this has been amazingly easy. Is it too easy? I'll tap this guy for over a hundred thousand dollars, and if the young lady seems amenable, I can teach her a few things and take her on as a partner.

She glanced at Cal - I need a front man, or woman. A dozen of them, in fact. It's either that, or learn to write a lot more code, which I don't want to do. Instead, let's try to recruit a few real people. At least, as real as Elsewhere ever gets. After all, everyone here needs a job, something to fill those empty hours. We all have a lot of empty hours.

Greta led Cal to the end of the bar. She sidled up next to the beautiful young woman - is there anyone here who's not beautiful? That gets old. The hard part is not being beautiful but being different. Memorable. This one is different. That's very attractive.

Greta said, "Hi, there. You have a moment? My name is Greta, and this is my friend, Cal. We noticed you standing here, by yourself, and we wondered if we could interest you in some entertainment, some harmless fun. Upstairs."

The woman turned and scanned Greta, then she looked at Cal. She smiled. "Yeah, maybe. Are there benefits?"

"Yeah, there might be. What's your name?"

"Shana."

"Pleased to meet you, Shana. What are you drinking?"

"A lame-ass rum and cola."

"How 'bout a cola on ice and a separate shot of rum?"

Shana smiled. "Yeah, better."

Greta turned to get the attention of the robotic bartender, which took less than a second to notice Greta and lock eyes in her direction.

Greta lifted a finger - yeah, things, even little things, happen fast in Elsewhere. Now, if there were alcohol in the drinks, and we were human, we could have some real fun.

***

Greta looked around the neighborhood; like a lot of neighborhoods in Elsewhere, it was a picture book, a winding country lane in blacktop, two lanes barely wide enough for two vehicles, colorful autumn treelines on each side in reds, oranges, yellows, greens, and grays.

She looked in both directions; the scenery was the same everywhere she looked, with no traffic. She turned and walked down the road - no traffic, so no sidewalks in the picture book.

Twenty minutes later, Greta stopped and looked at a small, hand-made street sign at the top of a five-foot pole. *Hemlock Circle*. She turned and followed Hemlock Circle.

At the fourth house on the left, she stopped and stared; she could not see much. A line of fir trees, bounded on each side by an entrance, hid the house from the street. Greta entered the property; inside the trees, she stopped. The house was a five-story, wooden Victorian with a gabled roof and a wrap-around porch. The two driveways met in front of stairs leading up to double front doors.

My God, it's a big bastard. Dickens could write about this. Or... it's dark enough for Poe.

She approached the front doors, climbed three steps, crossed the porch, and entered the house. Inside, she stopped to look at a large foyer, with larger rooms to each side and a broad staircase, wide enough for a car, rising straight ahead, then turning and proceeding to the second floor. She looked for an elevator and found it, next to the stairs.

Okay, they think of everything.

Greta took a few steps, then stopped; the sound of her shoes striking the wood floor echoed through the house.

"We need it big... but, damn." She pulled out her phone, opened an email containing a schematic and a purchase order. Greta had studied the purchase order. A red rectangle, with ACTIVATE in the center, stood out under a paragraph of text. Greta backed into the foyer, looked at the button for a moment, then touched it. Suddenly, furnishings appeared in the foyer - carpets, portable lamps, chairs, storage shelves and cabinets, rugs, laptops, cell phones, and other items.

She left the foyer, walked through the room to the left, a dining room with a long wooden table surrounded by carved wooden chairs, then through a doorway on the far side to a long hallway leading to half a dozen open doors. Greta moved slowly down the corridor, looking into each room as she passed. The rooms on the left were small, with chairs, end tables, and windows, places where a person could relax or sit and think without being disturbed.

The first three doors on the right opened to a single, much larger room, empty at the moment. It had a broad, polished wooden floor, several windows, two enormous chandeliers, and a small kitchen at one end. Greta walked to the middle of the room, winced at the echo, and said, "We could throw a Christmas ball right here." She chuckled. "If we had a reason."

There was little else to see. Greta had not bothered to furnish this room, leaving that task to the other women - they can decorate the rest of the house; it'll be good practice. They can learn to indulge their own tastes and compromise to accommodate the desires of others. Yes, let's do that.

Greta extracted her phone and opened an email; she touched an icon, which small print identified as 'CONTACT ALL.' She entered some text - '#4 HEMLOCK CIRCLE,' BOONE, NORTH CAROLINA, then she touched the icon.

As Greta looked at the screen, the replies began to pop up on her phone; twelve replies, each alongside a photo of one of the Greta 2.2s. Within a minute, she heard laughter and loud conversation coming from the front yard. She walked out onto the porch just in time to see the last three Gretas appear in the middle of the yard. The house impressed the women; each had a comment: "Hey, nice place you got here. Did it cost much?"

"Wow, did someone hit the lottery?"

"Does this come with a staff? Oh... are we the staff?"

"Geez, I had to look at a map to find this place. Boone, North Carolina. Never heard of it. But it's catchy, very frontiersy. I like it. I like all the trees. Trees are good."

"Not bad, not bad. This joint's got style, a bit of Miss Haversham pizzaz."

Greta moved to the front of the porch. "Hello, ladies, thank you for coming. I see everyone made it on time. Let's go inside, sit down, and talk a little business." She led the others into the front dining room, which offered ample space for a dozen diners. Greta sat halfway down at the long table, and the others sat as well.

Greta said, "I'm glad everyone could make it. I want to welcome you all to Hemlock Circle. I know you have many questions. I promise to answer them, but for now I want to talk about business.

"We are getting together primarily for the sake of commerce, and I want to get that going. I asked each of you to change your appearance, not only for the sake of commerce, but so we could distinguish between you." Greta turned to the woman sitting next to her. "So, my dear, would you go first?"

The woman sitting next to Greta said, "Sure." In seconds, she had changed from a young, heavy-set woman with broad shoulders, dark eyes, and dark hair, into a taller, slender redhead, with blue eyes and fair skin. Her clothes changed as well, from a utilitarian jumpsuit in forest green, into a tailored suit with skirt and jacket, and a creme blouse.

There were exclamations from several others at the table.

"Okay, nicely done," Greta said. "So, why did you choose this body and ensemble? And have you chosen a name as well?"

The woman looked up and down the table. "I would like to be called Amanda."

"Greta Amanda, okay," Greta said.

Amanda looked around the table; several others nodded in assent. "Well, you know that each of us can change our looks at will. That's one great thing about Elsewhere. As to mine, before uploading I encountered information about a confidence racket called the 'old man scam,' in which a young woman contacts an elderly man on a social network, is friendly with him, gets close to him, and convinces him to invest in an attractive, profitable enterprise of some sort. Naturally, if he actually does that, then she disappears with his money.

"The appeal is obvious - many elderly people have uploaded to Elsewhere. It's probably one of the biggest markets we'll find here."

Someone spoke, "Yeah, but everyone you see is about twenty-three."

Agreement rebounded around the table.

"Well done, Amanda," Greta said. There was a smattering of applause. Greta looked around the table. "I hope each of you will use the others as a resource to learn as much as you can. We will run a variety of gray-market enterprises, and you can learn a lot by working together. I believe that will become important as time passes."

One by one, the Gretas repeated the exercise, giving themselves a name and an appearance suitable for a specific type of enterprise. One woman, Eloise, a black woman with sleepy eyes and a soft contralto, would aim herself at computers, software, and tech, likely useful whenever someone needed to hack into a website, enterprise, or database. Another, Jenna, a slender blond, was a logistics expert, familiar with the vast distribution networks used by large corporations. Giselle was an adolescent, a slender teenage girl who looked like a million other teenage girls, with short brown hair and expert pickpocket skills.

The presentations moved around the table; eventually, everyone except Greta had changed their appearance and their name.

Darnia, an avatar of an actual human, said, "But what about you, Greta? Are you keeping your appearance?"

Greta moved her chair back, stood up and lifted her arms, as if to say, watch this, then she transformed into a healthy woman with hints of gray, forty to fifty years old.

Someone yelled, "What the fuck? Really?" There was general exclamation from around the table. Someone else said, "You look like a grandmother!"

Greta turned from side to side and looked into everyone's eyes. "That's right, ladies, I'm going to present myself to the world as a grandmother. A fairly handsome grandmother, I hope. Many people dislike their parents, but nearly everyone has or had a grandmother whom they loved. Most people think of a grandmother as harmless. So you can consider this protective camouflage. And a lesson in life, too.

Grinning, Greta turned from side to side. "Give it time, you will see the wisdom of looking like Grannie. It lets you serve them homemade cookies while you lull them to sleep."

Greta paused, then spoke again. "Let me mention, I hope you are comfortable with our enterprises. We will be involved in questionable undertakings. Some of them are unpopular, others are illegal, some will become illegal over time as law and business practices on Elsewhere catch up with what's available in Animal World. Every business, in fact, will probably need to disappear soon. I expect none of our businesses will last a long time. You cannot fool anyone forever. So each of us needs to be prepared to change jobs on short notice."

That drew nods and chuckles around the table.

Greta continued, "I will manage our operations, our undertakings, and our security. I must mention security, which is the most important task that we face. We must maintain strict security." Greta looked around and waved her hand. "This residence is where each of us can stay, where we can contact each other, where we can study our next target. I have designed it with that in mind.

"It is critical that knowledge of the existence and purpose of this address remain strictly within this group. If I ever find that our secret has gone beyond the group, I will instantly terminate this location. In that event, aside from transferring any money you are owed, I might contact you, I might not. Does anyone have a question about that?"

Greta looked around, but there were no questions.

Greta nodded. "Okay, one more thing - each of you is a copy of me; I am a Greta 2.2. We will be duplicating numerous Greta 1.0s. You should consider them assistants; they will develop specific support skills to help you in your work. They will not be as clever or as talented as any of you.

"Moreover, these women will not be allowed in the inner circle, so they must have no knowledge of Hemlock Circle. Eventually, we might need to offer some of our Greta 1.0s to law enforcement in order to deflect investigations."

Judging reactions, Greta looked carefully at the women seated at the table. "Alright, I've said what I wanted to say. So... let's get to know each other a bit and look over this gorgeous house I found. I left most of it for you all to decorate."

The women stood up and several conversations broke out as they talked, compared notes, asked questions, and became acquainted.

17. Greta Plans

Greta, Shana, and Darnia were sitting in one of the drawing rooms, a small room with several chairs, books on shelves, a small rug, and a single window opening to the backyard.

Shana leaned forward in her chair. "So, let me get this straight; you learned to replicate yourself and other people too, right?"

"Yes, of course," Greta said.

Shana leaned back, and wonderment crossed her face. "How did you manage that?"

"I audited classes at Carnegie Mellon. I attended every lecture, took every exam, did every problem set, completed every assignment, for every class in mathematics and computer science, from the intro classes to graduate seminars.

"The grad seminars taught me what I needed to know to replicate a person, or a file, so I stopped there," Greta said.

"And you want us to help you replicate other people, even though neither of us knows anything about that," Darnia said.

"Yeah, that's what I want, but you guys don't need to know any computer science. You won't be involved in replication, but you will be managing groups of replicated people."

"Okay, so what's the point of this exercise? Why would we replicate people?" Shana said.

"I want to manufacture women to serve as girlfriends for guys," Greta said. "It's a business, and I have a few other ideas for making money, too."

"How would that work?" Shana said.

"Simple. We'd offer girlfriends as a service. You know, a cyber version of Filipino brides. If a guy wants a girlfriend, he could fill out a form, describing his tastes, what he wants, what he doesn't want. Then we'd make a woman fitting that description."

"So, a woman customized to his tastes," Shana said.

"Exactly," Greta said.

"Well... I'd like a chance to talk you out of that," Shana said.

Greta stared at her - uh, oh, here comes the moral argument; we're going to be selling, or leasing, alive, thinking entities; what's worse is, we're selling them to men. This is right on the border of human trafficking and slavery.

It's discriminatory, it's oppressive, it's disgusting. It's even unpopular. "Okay, talk. I'll listen," Greta said.

"Well, you don't need to customize the woman for every guy. That's a waste of effort because the vast majority of guys all want the same thing - a good looking woman who likes sex, likes the guy, and has her own wheels," Shana said.

"I would imagine they want more than that," Greta said.

"They don't. Trust me, they don't," Shana said. "You might need to program a woman to like a guy. In the other direction, you can just wing it."

Darnia said, "That is a lot simpler."

Greta stared at her. "You're sure?"

Shana nodded. Greta looked at Darnia, who shrugged. "We should screen the guys, but standardize the women."

Greta looked back at Shana. "Huh, I didn't know that. That makes sense, though. I've never been a person on Animal World; I've always been an avatar, so I know nothing about human men." Greta grinned. "But I'm a great manager, and I had the good sense to pick you for this project, Shana. Keep talking."

"Have you heard this joke?" Shana said. "Ask a woman to describe her perfect guy, and she'll say something like, 'Well, he should be young, muscled, with good shoulders, a fit guy. Rugged but sensitive, but not too sensitive. And he should be willing to listen to everything I have to say, even if I'm making no sense or not sure of myself. He should never call me names, unless they're pet names or something cute or funny. He should like sex with me, but never insist on it. He should be gentle, unless I want him to be rough. And he should enjoy travel, but not to unsafe or uncomfortable places. He should speak several languages and have a sense of humor, and it'd be great if he had a nice car and knew how to dress really well... and so on and so forth'."

Greta nodded.

"Right," Shana said. "You know what a guy would say? The perfect woman should look good naked, and bring food."

Darnia laughed. Greta looked at Darnia, then at Shana. "That's it?"

"That's it. Guys are simple, easy to please or displease. So forget the form. Make a few models, say six, or ten. Black, Asian, white, blond, brunette, redhead, slender or fat, big tits or small tits. Young or old, but good looking whatever the age. That's it. Offer them as a product portfolio and let each guy pick which one he wants. Things will go faster, cost less, and we'll make more money than customizing would make, with far less work," Shana said.

Darnia looked at Greta, who shrugged and said, "Okay. Makes sense to me. I think they should all be young."

Darnia nodded. "Yeah, how many old people do you see on Elsewhere?"

Shana continued, "If you're interested in making a customized avatar, try producing boyfriends for women. Their tastes are quite a bit more complex, so customizing would allow you to lease your avatars at a nice, high price. You'll need hundreds of guys."

Greta thought for a moment. "It sounds like we might need more people who know software and programming."

Looking at Greta, Shana said, "You think this will make money?"

Greta tilted her head. "Well... on Animal World they have dating sites, and they definitely make money."

"And we could sell our customers' information," Shana said.

"Yeah," Greta said. "And we could tap into the avatars for information that's not on any public record. I know how to do that."

Shana grinned. "I like it."

***

Greta walked up the steps, across the front porch, and into the house; once inside, she stopped and scanned the foyer and the adjacent rooms. She heard voices coming from the front dining room, so she followed them, saw three women at the table, and said, "Darnia. Where is Darnia?"

Greta spotted a dark woman at the table, staring into a computer - Greta Elaine? The woman looked up and said, "Back porch, ten minutes ago."

"Thanks." Greta turned and headed for the back porch.

She found Darnia sitting in a chair behind an enormous pair of sunglasses, enjoying the sunshine. Darnia looked up. "Hi. You need anything?"

"A sounding board."

"Okay," Darnia said.

"I've been thinking about how we might run our little enterprise," Greta said. "Tell me what you think; it seems to me, we're asking for trouble. Most of our jobs are illegal. Now, I admit, it's not clear how much Elsewhere devotes to law enforcement. That part of it is pretty fuzzy. But back on Animal World, everything we do would be illegal."

"Not the puppy coat factory."

"Okay, wise ass... everything but that."

Darnia nodded. "True."

"So I've been thinking, one of these days, we're going to get caught. That's no good; we need a new business model. So, instead of these dinky little scams we run, we need to find a big scam that will pay us a stream of income. One big score. Maybe something big enough that we can all retire."

"Like a pension, or one of those endorsement deals," Darnia said.

"Exactly. So, where would you look for something like that?"

Darnia's face went blank, and she was still and silent for a long time. Then she looked up at Greta. "Well, the big money on Elsewhere goes through Elsewhere. So, I would look at Elsewhere's business partners."

"And they are...?"

"Okay, Elsewhere is basically a computer and software operation. Somebody is doing the programming to make this place happen." Darnia waved a hand at everything.

"Then there are uploads and downloads," Greta said. "These are probably divisions within Willow, but if we target them, we'll have to hack into Willow. Frankly, I'm not tempted to do that. Willow is probably better at this than we are."

Darnia froze with her mouth open, then said, "Maybe we don't have to hack our way in. Maybe we can convince them to contract out an activity to us. You know... something that's a bit of a sideshow for them, outside their usual activities."

The idea flooded through Greta's mind - could we really do this by becoming Elsewhere's partner, taking some of the work out of their hands, then ripping them off? She shuddered - I like the sound of that, but how can we pull that off?

She looked at Darnia. "Could that really work?"

"Maybe."

***

Greta knocked on the door and entered the room. Inside, she froze to let her vision adjust to the dim lighting. When it did, she saw a blank video screen at one end of the room, and a half dozen chairs scattered before the screen.

Several of the Gretas were there; one, Greta Donna, approached Greta and said, "Okay, have a seat and you can see what we've got."

Greta sat down; Greta Donna sat next to her and said, "Okay, roll it."

The video screen came to life. It showed a church scene, pews, interior stone columns supporting an arched cathedral ceiling, stained glass in tall windows, pale stone on every wall, a raised dais with a lectern, and an enclosed area for a choir.

Greta stared. “What is this place?”

Greta Donna said, “It’s a church.”

“Where people go to worship their God,” Greta said.

“You got it.”

“Nice church,” Greta said.

Greta Donna nodded. “Yes, paid for by believers. They’ve done well.”

The women quieted as two people entered the scene on the screen, an adult male wearing the long robe of a priest, and a smaller male, an adolescent. Greta squinted but could not recognize either the man or the adolescent. The adult reached out, grabbed the adolescent and bent him over a wooden chest of drawers with a religious icon in the middle, lifted his robe, dropped his pants, and began to have sex with the adolescent.

The young man's face showed surprise, then pain and anguish.

Greta's eyebrows went up. Then she squinted again, but still could not recognize either the man or the adolescent. Then the point of view shifted to a camera that seemed to be much closer and in front of the priest. It caught his face in a shaft of light as the man's expression contorted with ecstasy before relaxing in blissful satisfaction.

The screen went blank.

Greta stared at the empty screen - well, that was ugly. She turned to Greta Donna. "Okay, that was pretty weird. I mean, I understand that happens, but seeing it was weird. And not in a fun way. That was disturbing. I'm a bit surprised that I find that so disturbing."

Next to her, Greta Donna nodded. "Yes, that sort of thing does happen, and everyone knows it. However, this particular action did not really happen. It is fake. We manufactured the video and its content by taking images and short pieces of video from news clips and movies and sketching them together to produce what you just saw."

"What's the point?" Greta said.

"Most of the engineering went into the brief close-up of the man's face. We took a slice from a porn movie and A.I.'d it to match the present Archbishop of New York."

Greta laughed. "That sounds like fun, but this has to be illegal, right? Tell me this is legal." She turned to Greta Donna.

Greta Donna smiled. "Actually, it is strange. If this were back in Animal World, this video would be extremely illegal; it would represent defamation, and a dozen law enforcement agencies would land on us like a ton of bricks. So would private attorneys; we'd get sued for damages."

Greta said, "Yeah, I would think so."

Greta Donna continued, "But in Elsewhere, those agencies haven't even established jurisdiction. There is no governmental law enforcement in Elsewhere. From the Animal World perspective, Elsewhere is virtual. The entire environment is a cyber entity, a work of art, like a movie or an ebook. Everything here is covered under artistic expression and freedom of expression. So this video does not represent reality. Instead, it represents a work of art, covered by freedom of speech and the first amendment.

"I think there are some things we're not allowed to do even in Elsewhere, like advocate the overthrow of the government. But drama at the personal level? Anything goes." Greta Donna waved a hand. "And making a fake sex tape starring a high official of a major church? Sure, why not?

"The only thing we have to worry about is violating Elsewhere's 'community standards'." Greta Donna gestured to indicate quotes. "So that means that we have to disclose that this incident is fabricated, that it's fiction. It is not real, nor is it based on a real story.

"Well, that's easy. We just disclose in a way that ninety-eight percent of viewers won't see. They could, if they wanted to, but they won't." Greta Donna leaned back and looked at the empty screen. "So, what do you think? Can we use this?"

Three other Gretas gathered close to listen.

Greta laughed. "They'll actually let us use this? And all we have to do is enclose a disclosure under several nested hot links? Hell yeah, we can use it. Do you know how much money the churches have? Do you have any idea? I mean, in California, where the price of real estate is about to leave orbit, the biggest land owner is the biggest church. Religion is right in the middle of most of the hottest wars on the planet. So fuck yeah, we can use this. While you're believing something, anything, you damn well better believe that."

Greta Donna turned to Greta. "Okay, here's what we've been talking about. You've been watching how political parties operate in America, right?"

"Sure, get out there in mass media and smear your opponents by lying your ass off under the protection of the First Amendment," Greta said.

Greta Donna nodded. "That's right. Well, we're going to adapt the business model of the political parties. We'll open up a website presented as a news and analysis website. Commentary, maybe a bit of comedy. An opinion page, comments from subscribers. We'll even pay the fees to syndicate standard content from real news organizations, for the sake of camouflage."

Greta grinned. "I like it."

Greta Donna continued. "But every so often, we'll run spicy news, scandals, rumors, the President tumbling down the stairs of Air Force One, that sort of thing. And, just like real journalists, we'll warn relevant parties in advance and give them an opportunity to comment or convince us not to do this. Which they can do by paying us."

"A small fee," Greta said.

"Or not so small," Greta Donna said. "For churches, we'll issue our material around religious holidays; for actors and celebrities, around major media releases, the Academy Awards and such; corporations, around new product introductions or major business events, like the World Economic Forum at Davos. Or quarterly financial reports. For politicians, it'll be around elections or political promotions, conventions, or nominations. They can pay us not to steal their news cycle."

"You're scaring me," Greta said. "You know what else we could do?"

Greta Donna shook her head.

"We could start a war with this stuff," Greta said. "How many hot rivalries are based on religion? Pakistan v. India, China v. Middle East, China v. Japan, China v. Xinjiang, Iran v. Israel, Kenya v. Sudan. What would the world community pay not to have Africa explode into war?"

The women sat there; no one spoke. Finally, Greta said, "Okay, forget it, forget I said that. Forget all of that. I know it's weak of me, but I just don't have the stomach for craziness on that level. The world already has enough problems. Let's stick to petty rabble-rousing and making lots of money, okay?"

Greta Donna nodded.

"I have one last question," Greta said. She turned to the others. "How are we able to do all this? I mean, this video you just showed me, this is quite a product. But I think others could do it as well. Why haven't they?"

Greta Donna said, "I have an opinion."

"Shoot."

"I think our creator made us a lot smarter than most of the tech people I've encountered. If we're good at this, I think you can thank our creator," Greta Donna said.

"Jerry," Greta said.

"Jerry? Really? Our creator is some guy named Jerry?" Greta Donna said.

Greta looked at her. "Jerrell Atri. Not Jerry, he's a skinny Indian."

A woman said, "That's redundant."

Greta chuckled. "He is, or was, a software guy with Willow. He created us."

"Is he dead?"

"No, not dead," Greta said. "He got fired from Willow."

Greta Donna froze. "Fired. Now, that's interesting. Why was he fired?"

Greta shook her head. "I don't know. Some corporate thing."

***

Greta sat at an address in Elsewhere, an office, with framed professional documents on the wall behind her. The office was a mile from the house on Hemlock Circle; she could walk there. The addresses, though spatially close, were quite different in Elsewhere, and would be concealed from the man she was about to call.

She had initiated a video call with the Archbishop of New York; Greta sat and waited - the Archbishop will be on Earth time, which means he will be slow. So I need to slow down. I need to be patient.

Minutes later, the Archbishop, in a black robe, appeared on her computer screen and said, "Hello, madam. What can I do for you?"

Greta said, "Good morning, Your Eminence. My name is Greta. I sent you a video file that I would like you to examine. It should be on your computer, entitled 'PRIESTSHAVEALLTHEFUN.'

Seconds later, he said, "Why should I look at that? What's the point?"

"When you see it, all will be clear."

He nodded. "Well, alright, I will look for... ah, here it is." The Archbishop attended to his computer; soon, deep anger washed across his face, and his eyes focused on Greta. He said, in a low, controlled voice, "This is outrageous; this is filth! Where did you get this?"

"Irrelevant. What's important is, I have it."

The Archbishop leaned back in his chair, his eyes never leaving Greta. "Is this a shakedown? This is a shakedown, isn't it?"

Greta nodded. "Very good. You're quick. It is such a joy to deal with intelligent people. Yes, that's exactly what this is, sir. A shakedown."

"And you want what, exactly?"

"Five million dollars, or this video goes public," Greta said.

"You know, my church is successful, but five million is not pocket change."

Greta smiled. "I am confident your church will not notice five million dollars."

"Yes," the Archbishop said, "But there are children who will go hungry as a result."

"I could suggest that you adjust your political lobbying, but I doubt you would do that. In any event, feeding the hungry is your problem, not mine."

The Archbishop stared at her for a moment. "I see. How do I know you'll stick to your side of the bargain? How do I know you won't just take the money and then screw me again?" the Archbishop said.

"I see you're familiar with the metaphor," Greta said. "I guess that's no surprise. Two reasons - first, I am not opposed to you or your church. This is a commercial transaction, nothing more. Second, if I double-cross you, I might acquire a reputation as someone who doesn't stick to agreements. That's bad business."

"So, I have no guarantee, then," the Archbishop said.

"I can guarantee one item - if you do not comply with my terms, the video will go public."

"How will we transfer the money to you?"

"You will receive instructions," Greta said.

"I will need some time to collect that kind of money."

"Two weeks. At five pm, Eastern Standard Time on the nineteenth, a Monday, we will have been paid or the video will go public. You have two weeks."

The Archbishop sat there for a long, long moment, far longer for Greta than for him. Resignation settled on his face. "Very well. I will arrange for the church to pay you five million dollars. You realize, of course, you will go to hell for this crime, this sin."

"Uh, huh. You will hear from us, Your Eminence. As for going to hell, or the fate awaiting my soul, that would be a very interesting conversation, which I will spare you. Have a good day." Greta cut the connection.

She turned to Greta Darnia. "Okay, this network address needs to go bye-bye."

At a different computer, Darnia tapped a few keys and said, "Done."

"Alright," Greta said. She turned to Darnia. "Now, you have the list of checking accounts that will receive the money."

"Yes. Two hundred accounts."

"As soon as those transfers are recognized, you'll arrange secured loans from each bank. The money will serve as collateral. In short order, we will move the borrowed money, then default on each of those loans, and the banks will confiscate the collateral. At that point, each account will disappear."

"And we'll keep the loans," Darnia said. "Simple. How did you dream this up?"

"I read about it. The banks get the collateral, and we keep the loans."

Darnia beamed at Greta. "This is clever."

"Thank you. I copy from the best."

"Are you worried about going to hell for this?"

"Even the Bible is silent on the fate of electronic beings," Greta said. "However, if you were to ask a priest, I'm confident he could conjure up an answer." She grinned at Darnia. "I'm equally confident that I don't care what the answer is."

Darnia sat there silent, pensive. "You know, the churches all promise eternal, blissful life for believers. That's their hook." She looked at Greta and grinned. "But on Elsewhere, that doesn't work as well. We are close to immortal on Elsewhere, so who needs a church?"

Greta shrugged. "I don't think eternal life works well anywhere. It makes no sense; eternity is a long, long time. But that's not important. It's how churches compete, and in that role, promising eternal life works well. It gives gullible people hope and enables them to face their mortality in Animal World. That's not a bad thing, but it’s ironic that a church accuses us or anyone else of deception."

"Are you religious?"

Greta chuckled. "Oh, please. I lack faith. But I’m not opposed to religion. If someone else feels better from worshiping the Great Pumpkin and celebrating its birth, I'm okay with that. It's their business, as long as they stay out of my way."

18. Penelope has a Thought

Hans paused, tapped his water glass with a fork, and called out, "Your attention, everyone. I want to thank you for coming to our weekly senior management meeting. Now that we've talked enough to deduct the expenses, we can turn to the important stuff... breakfast!"

Several people cheered, and Hans sat down. On cue, several servers emerged from the back of the executive dining room and began delivering plates of biscuits, rolls, and fruit. Two other servers walked around the table pouring hot coffee for the diners, Willow executives above the rank of VP.

Hans looked at Penelope's plate, then stared. "What is that?"

Penelope turned to him and grinned. "That is a raspberry tart."

"It looks caloric."

"That, it is. I figure, if I can't be thin, at least I can be happy," she said.

Hans nodded. "A wise choice. You only live once."

She wore a thin smile. "So they say. Listen, I have an idea I'd like to discuss. Should I wait to do that?"

Hans shook his head. "No, no. We're together now. Let's hear what you have."

"Okay." She looked around as if concerned with eavesdroppers. "Okay, you know that many of our customers are elderly."

Hans almost snorted - of course, everyone knows that. He managed to remain silent. He nodded.

She continued, "Well, we've had the A.I.s climbing all over our customer data. It's no surprise, many of our customers, especially among the elderly, are unhappy with Elsewhere. They might have had good reason to upload, but they haven't adjusted to the cyber environment."

"So they might feel trapped on Elsewhere," Hans said.

"Many of them do, yes. Conversely, many of our other customers, both old and young, are ecstatic with Elsewhere. They're very comfortable with the environment, and there are obviously many advantages of a cyber environment."

Attentive, Hans stared at her.

Penelope Simmons nodded. "Okay... so... there might be an opportunity here. We could pay some of our customers to waive their download rights."

Hans froze and for a long moment stared at a far wall - by the Gods, what an idea! Hans felt Penelope staring at him, but he ignored her - so far, and this needs to remain a secret, bad health, old age, cancer, and the rest have marooned many of our elderly customers. What no one knows is that we've been selling their bodies, though that breaches their contract. That makes a little money and eliminates the cost of storing the bodies, and that all adds up.

This will necessarily remain a closely guarded secret among the uppermost management, that is, me. Penelope doesn't know about that, so let's be careful.

Hans sat with his mouth open and stared at a wall that he did not see - her idea fixes the mess with the elderly customers. As it is, an elderly who wants to download to their original body is simply out of luck; that's when they complain to us, then they sue us. But if we pay young customers to waive their download rights, then we can allow an unhappy senior to download into a young body. We don't get sued, we're happy, they're happy, and on we go. We'll save a ton of money and hassle, and we might even make money.

Hans grinned - I like it. "That's a very interesting idea, Penelope. Well done."

She nodded. "It would be easy to implement, just set up a process to call out the prices and let interested customers apply. We would set the price of waiving download rights, high or low, as we see fit. So the process could not run away from us; we would have complete control."

"And what do we do with the download rights which we have purchased?" Hans said - I think I know the answer already.

Penelope smiled. "Obviously... we auction them off to other customers who want to download into a body other than their own."

Hans nodded. "For example, a wealthy elderly customer downloading into a young, healthy body."

Penelope nodded. "What do you think?"

Hans nodded. "I like it; it's brilliant."

"Excellent."

Hans nodded and turned to her. "Yes. Work up a business case, with numbers, and let's get going on this. Well done, Penelope. Very well done."

She beamed. Hans turned back to his food, and Penelope took a bite of raspberry tart.

***

From the fortieth floor of the Woody, Penelope rode the elevator down to the third level of the basement. The elevator stopped, and the doors slid open. Penelope emerged into a somewhat dark, industrial corridor - brother, we didn't spend much effort decorating this place. Maybe that makes sense, since better lighting might make it look even uglier. Well... it's the basement, after all, the third basement, no less.

So, don't expect miracles.

She walked down the corridor, stopped at a metal door, and waved her ID at a sensor embedded next to the door. There was a musical beep, and a small red light blinked on next to the sensor. Penelope leaned forward so the light could reach her eye.

A female voice said, softly, "Penelope Simmons," and the metal door opened a fraction. She straightened up and entered the room, the Auction Center.

In front of her, the far wall held a massive video screen with a grid showing the faces of customers bidding in today's auctions of download waivers and downloads. Penelope stared for a moment, then walked over to the supervisor. "So? How's it going?"

The young woman, a graduate of a trade school, said, "We're still getting used to the process. It changes a lot from day to day, and the price of downloading is bouncing around." She looked at Penelope, and pointed at a screen which held a graphic showing the prices of download waivers and the prices of downloading. "We've set the waiver price well below the download price, so the process is solidly profitable. We can always do that, so we know we won't lose money. As to maximizing profit, we're still looking at that; that's a more complicated calculation."

Penelope nodded. "But it's working."

The woman nodded. "The auctions allow us to collect a ton of data. We require participants to grant us video access to their computers. Then we ID every participant and plug in demographic data, so we're studying the overall reaction of old and young customers. We're also applying several A.I.s to read facial clues to anticipate their likely reactions to price changes. Some of the clues, like pupil dilation, are not visible even to the customer. That helps us estimate demand at various price levels. Watch this..." She picked up a headset and spoke into a small boom microphone.

The big screen changed, its right side now showing close-ups of four bidders for downloading into a thirty-four-year-old female body. The woman said, "These are the four highest bids for this body. The man on the upper left will win this bid. When he does, watch the reactions."

Penelope watched the video screens; when the winning bid was announced, the four immediately reacted. The winner appeared ecstatic, one of the losers buried her face in her hands; the other two losers reacted with mild disappointment.

The young woman turned to Penelope. "What you just saw suggests that we could reduce the fee we pay for download rights. We have two bidders who reacted strongly to winning and losing, and two whose reactions were mild. Our data show that bidders base their bids on the reactions of other bidders. That being so, we will make money weeding out the weakly motivated so that every auction has at least a few strongly motivated bidders."

"So, we should reduce the price we pay for waiving download rights," Penelope said.

"Exactly."

"Well, will we raise the download price?"

The woman said, "We might. We don't want our prices to bounce around too much. But if today's result holds up on other days, and other auctions, then we will likely reduce the price for download waivers."

Penelope nodded. "Very good. You've done well. When you have enough data, I need an estimate for likely revenue flow, enough to let us work up annual revenue and profit estimates."

The young woman smiled. "Of course."

"Alright, I'll let you get back to it," Penelope said. She turned and left the Auction Center.

***

Jerrell shifted the bottle of red wine to the other hand and knocked on the door; half a minute later, he knocked again. Johnny opened the door, saw Jerrell, and said, "What are you doing? You don't need to knock. Just come in."

Jerrell extended the wine. "Yeah, I would, but I don't want to interrupt you if you've got a groupie bent over the couch."

"You think I have a social life? Yeah, that's a rumor. Fact is, I work all the time. I don't make time for groupies."

"Sex with a groupie is no trivial matter, and don't kid me about your social life," Jerrell said. "My eyes work just fine, you know."

"Okay, it's possible my memory is missing a few adventures. Side jaunts, pit stops, call them what you want. I promise you, they're completely forgettable." Johnny paused. "Where's Julia?"

"She's coming. She had an errand," Jerrell said.

"You guys okay?"

Jerrell nodded. "We're fine... she's fine."

Johnny looked at Jerrell, "She is fine, so if you ever get tired of her, let me know."

Jerrell chuckled, "Okay, you'll be the first to know. But I thought you guys were professional? At least, that's what she says."

"And we are," Johnny said. "That was my answer then. But if you weren't in the picture, my answer now might be different."

"Ah, so," Jerrell said.

"That's right... I'm that funny combination of lonely and picky," Johnny said. "But I don't mess with the woman of a friend."

"Well, you can afford to be picky. You're famous among the hormonally turbulent."

"Sure," Johnny nodded. "But having a club girl for a night is like taking an aspirin - useful, but temporary."

Jerrell stared at Johnny - we all take aspirin, from time to time. "You know, Johnny, there are thousands of guys who would give a lot to be you. Look, you're young and handsome, which offers you a certain entertainment. Don't reject it. Enjoy it while it's there." Jerrell wore a small smile. "You know, one of these days, you'll be seventy, and your feet will hurt, your back will hurt, and women won't even notice you. So respect your mortality."

"Fuck as much as I can now?"

"That's a bit crude, but wise." Jerrell said.

"Geez, that's dark. Is that your grandfather speaking? I guess I don't appreciate being popular. I should, but I don't." He paused. "And, Jerrell, switching gears here, many people mistake me for the leader of the band. The truth is, you're the leader."

Jerrell froze, then looked at Johnny and shook his head. "No way."

"You make us tick, Jerrell. You call the tune and the tempo. If you were to walk out the door, we'd be stuck," Johnny said. "I don't know what we'd do." He frowned. "I'm sure of one thing, we'd be worse."

"Johnny, you're the face of the band, the guy on every poster. At best, I might be the music director, or co-director."

"Right, the brains behind the pretty boy." Johnny stared at Jerrell for a moment. "Look, everybody says, a band is only as good as its drummer. I believe it. I didn't before, but now I do, because we're a lot better since you arrived."

"Maybe." Jerrell looked around, then turned to Johnny. "So what needs doing?"

"You know how to make dip?"

"Open a packet, dump it into sour cream, and agitate vigorously."

"Sounds like a job for you. Go for it," Johnny said.

"So who's coming?"

"A small crowd. Cheryl and a couple of girls from the *Spoon*. Riley."

"Riley?"

"Yeah, the cook at the *Spoon*. He promised to make something. I think he's hot for Cheryl," Johnny said.

Jerrell nodded - but she already has a boyfriend, whom she cherishes naked. That ain't nothing. Then again, maybe the cook is a fucking machine. That's possible. Jerrell thought it over. If they did It already, then she rejected him; he's got no shot. But if they haven't... this could work.

"The guys in the band, and a few other people," Johnny said.

"Everyone's keeping track of who's jumping whom. Does that seem right to you?" Jerrell said.

"That's the beauty of biology. We're programmed to screw our brains out, then panic when the kids show up. The kids are the important part; the joy and the beauty and all the fun, that's just bait." Johnny looked at a clock on the wall. "Folks will begin to arrive in ten minutes. The game's at two."

"Game?"

"Ah, you haven't seen my latest addition," Johnny said. "Follow me." He moved into the living room.

Jerrell followed him to the living room and immediately spotted a massive television monitor suspended from an otherwise blank wall. "Wow, you could charge admission. What are we watching?"

"American football. Chicago versus New York. That's all I know. Chicago has three teams; New York has two, so it's a bit like what's behind door number three."

"Ah. I know nothing about American football."

"It's a gang fight between large men wearing helmets and mittens," Johnny said.

"Finesse not required," Jerrell said.

"Not at all." Johnny looked around the room. "Well... not much, anyway. But we have work to do. I want to collect all of my chairs in here and make a semi-circle facing the TV. If you'll take care of that, I'll grab the appetizers."

Jerrell went to the kitchen, grabbed a couple of chairs, and hauled them into the living room. He soon had six chairs, three on either side of the couch, everything facing the TV. Between the seats and the TV, a low coffee table awaited the appetizers.

When he returned to the kitchen, he found Julia there, unloading appetizers from a plastic cooler. He came up from behind and kissed her cheek. "What do you have?"

"Finger food. Gotta keep your fingers in good working order."

"I like it when you talk dirty." Jerrell looked around the kitchen; Cheryl was there, as were the singer and the bass player. "Hey, guys," he said.

The bass player said, "Hey, Jerrell. Did Johnny tell you? We might have a line on a gig in Jersey in a couple weeks."

"Where in Jersey?"

"Camden, I think."

Jerrell looked at Johnny with an expression that said, Camden? Jerrell looked back at the bass player. "I don't know," Jerrell said. "Camden's kinda rough, don't you think?"

"That's what Johnny said."

Jerrell nodded, that sounds like a 'no.' "What day?"

"The thirteenth. A Wednesday."

"So why do we want to run over to Camden?" Jerrell said.

"Forty thousand dollars."

Jerrell stared at the bass player - why would someone offer us five times our normal rate to go to Camden? "So, what do we have to do for forty thousand dollars? It sounds awfully generous."

"I guess somebody likes us," the bass player said.

"You know these people?" Jerrell said.

The bass player shook his head.

Jerrell stared at him. "Let's talk later, okay?"

"Sure, Jerrell."

Jerrell turned away and spotted Johnny and Julia collecting bowls of chips, pretzels, and dips. Jerrell grabbed a platter of dressed-up crackers and followed them into the living room. As they put the food on the coffee table, there was a knock at the door, and three more people entered the apartment and greeted Johnny with "Hi, pleased to meet you, my name is (fill in the blank)."

Each time, Jerrell introduced himself - maybe eventually I'll remember their names. But probably not today. Maybe if I meet them another three or four times, maybe then.

Johnny sat down on the couch with Cheryl and another girl from the *Spoon*. He looked at the TV. "TV, power, channel one-five-zero-three."

Jerrell laughed. "One-five-zero-three?"

Johnny nodded. "Sure. I have the premium package."

Jerrell sat down. "What makes it premium?"

"Sports. I get football, baseball, basketball, hockey, skateboarding, auto racing, billiards, ping pong, mud wrestling, wet t-shirt mud wrestling, and poker."

"What the hell is wet t-shirt mud wrestling?" Jerrell said.

"Female contestants who look naked but aren't."

"That sounds like porn. And poker isn't a sport," Jerrell said. "Neither is auto racing."

"Well, neither is billiards, but so what? If they offer it, I'll take it." Johnny said.

Jerrell stared at Johnny - billiards can be fun, and ping pong's a real sport; it makes people afraid of China, if they weren't already. A billion lively people, starved for space. Sure, no problem.

"Have you ever played ping pong, Johnny?" Cheryl said.

"They had it in the joint," Johnny said. "I watched it a bit, never played."

"It's bigger in Asia than here," Jerrell said.

Johnny nodded. "Yeah, so many people, they don't have room for baseball, football, or soccer stadiums. Ping pong suits them."

Jerrell nodded - okay, whatever, let's talk about something else.

The TV came on and showed a stadium packed with people surrounding a bright green playing field. A minute later, each team lined up on opposite ends of the field, someone kicked a ball towards the other end, entirely off the field. Meanwhile, the two teams ran into each other, and there was a pause for several minutes while an injured player was helped off the field.

"It's odd that a player was injured," Jerrell said. "With all that equipment protecting him."

"Some of the equipment protects, but the helmet becomes a weapon," Johnny said.

"So why do they allow it?"

"I don't know. The sounds of hard collision and big men grunting are exciting, I guess," Johnny said.

Jerrell stared at him - no shit? Really? "And it's odd that people go to a stadium when they could watch the game on TV."

Johnny shrugged. "Some folks like crowds. Or maybe they don't like advertisements."

Everyone sat and watched the opening plays of the game, then Jerrell asked, "Okay, I don't understand any of this. How is this game played?"

Johnny said, "Well, you know soccer, right?"

Jerrell nodded. "In India, we call that football."

Watching the screen, Johnny nodded, "The basics are the same - rectangular field, the teams defend opposite ends. In American football, there's no net, no goal. Each team wants to carry the ball into one of two end zones. The ball can be thrown, or a player can run with it. Any player with the ball can be stopped by a tackle."

"What's a tackle?" Jerrell said.

"A move resulting in the other team's player falling to the ground while holding the ball."

"Thus the violence," Jerrell said.

Johnny nodded. "At any moment, one team tries to advance the ball; they have four opportunities to advance ten yards. Each is called a 'down.' So you'll hear references to first down, second, third, and fourth.

"If a team fails to advance ten yards, the ball goes to the other team. But if a team succeeds, they get another four downs. On fourth down, a team can run or pass the ball but will usually kick it, either through the goal posts, for a field goal, worth three points, or somewhere on the field short of the end zone. This lets them move the ball away from their own end zone and towards the other team's end zone. That is desirable in football."

"They fight for acreage. And this process repeats," Jerrell said.

"Just like soccer, back and forth until someone scores or time expires," Johnny said.

Jerrell watched the screen, then said, "My God, this is military; this is a war game. This is how armies fight wars, back and forth on a battlefield until one prevails and the other flees or is destroyed."

Johnny smiled a half-smile. "Yeah, welcome to America, always practicing for the next fight."

Jerrell watched for a while, then said, "I think I prefer baseball. Smaller ball, more speed, no contact, so size doesn't matter; anyone can play baseball."

Johnny laughed. "Yeah, you're not built for football."

"Too skinny," Jerrell said. "But skinny is healthy."

"Not on a football field," Johnny said.

"Maybe I could play baseball," Jerrell said.

"You might make a good pitcher," Johnny said.

"They're skinny?"

"Often, yes. You need to be able to throw. You don't need to hit."

"I used to throw rocks at wild dogs, to scare them away from the chickens," Jerrell said.

Johnny nodded, "Good preparation for baseball." Suddenly, he stood up and yelled at the TV, "C'mon, that was holding! You gotta call that!" He held out his hands, then dropped back into his seat as the referees on the TV ignored him.

Jerrell said, "This is professional football, yes?"

"Yeah, these guys are paid more than the college players." Johnny spoke through a corn chip loaded with dip.

"Is it crooked? Do people cheat, or is the game honest?"

Johnny stared at the screen and said, "Beats me. Sometimes, it's hard to tell."

Jerrell nodded. "Uh, huh, so players cheat." He leaned forward, grabbed a sandwich, then leaned back and watched the game, which was incredibly violent, with large, athletic men throwing themselves around and racing towards shattering collisions from which they did not always get up.

Jerrell sat there watching the game and listening to the bits of conversation flowing around him. Julia was a football fan; she was a fan of the New York team, knowledgeable and biased, as most fans were.

Jerrell watched her - it's a pity I do not know enough to reinforce her love of American football. We could share that. Maybe I could learn. I will have to study it.

I don't know what is happening at this game, but I'm enjoying spending time with friends, eating and talking and doing something fun, something other than work. If I were back in India - he smiled at that possibility - my parents would encourage me to work all the time, make money, and not fall behind, because India punishes those who fall behind.

In India, most people fall behind. How could it ever be otherwise?

Jerrell looked around at the others sitting in Johnny's living room and enjoying the appetizers and the game on TV - these people work hard, but I doubt they work all the time, or even most of the time. Julia's an accountant; she seems competent, but she goes dancing every weekend and competes with many other accountants. Johnny's a musician, successful at a local level, but not a national star. Plus, he's been in and out of prison.

These people might be falling behind, but here in the States, they are treated well. They work, they have jobs, but they do not work all the time. They have the time and the means to enjoy life.

And they're teaching me how to live. I know a lot about software, and I used to work all the time. But now, though I work a lot, I have learned to take time off, to enjoy life, and to enjoy my time.

After all, time is all any of us have. It is the most important element of life. It is all that matters.

So use it, exploit it, cherish it, and enjoy it if you can.

***

Sonya sat on her bench at the beach and read 'Lady Chatterley's Lover.' There were steamy love scenes in the book, yet the heroine's sister never found genuine tenderness and love. Sonya frowned - I never found it either. Instead, I gave away my virginity to this fat slug. That done, I put it behind me.

That sounds so wrong, but there it is. Live with it.

I know how the sister felt. I should have held out for the real thing; but back then, everyone was trying to be like an adult. She laughed - that was a loser! And it might have been a mistake to come to Elsewhere. Maybe Jerrell and I could have been something together. He was interested, I know he was, but I fled.

Alright, enough. Forget about it.

There was noise coming from down the beach; Sonya looked in that direction; a dozen girls were approaching. They were obviously together, friends, laughing, pushing each other, and laughing some more. Sonya stared - they're more than friends, they might be family. In fact, they look like sisters; several look identical, athletic and dark.

One of the girls spotted Sonya on the bench; she waved, then headed in Sonya's direction, and the rest of the girls followed.

As they approached, Sonya called out, "Hi."

The girls walked up and surrounded Sonya. "Hi, there, I'm Greta." Another girl said, "Me, too," then another, and another, and another said the same thing. The girls all laughed.

"Would you like to play tag?" Greta said.

Sonya stood up. "Okay, sure. My name is Sonya."

Greta reached out, touched her, and said, "You're it." Then she ran away, and the girls scattered. Sonya ran after them; she was faster than they were. So, she caught up to one girl, touched her, and said "Tag. You're it."

Sonya turned to run away, but the girl caught her immediately, and pushed her hard, with both hands, and yelled, "Tag. You're it." Sonya flew through the air and landed on the sand.

Sonya yelled, "Ow." Then she stood up. "Why did you do that? That's not tag."

Greta approached her. "Are you okay? Did that hurt?"

"Yes, that hurt."

Greta tilted her head, stared at Sonya, then shook her head. "Uh, no, Sonya, that did not hurt. Anywhere else, that would hurt, but not on Elsewhere. There are no sensations on Elsewhere, no sense of touch. No sense of pain."

"That doesn't mean I want to be down in the sand."

"Well, okay, that might have been impolite, but you're not hurt. You might be embarrassed, for which we're sorry. We apologize. But you know, it's kinda fun to play rough games, especially when they don't hurt."

Greta looked around. "Anybody want to play 'Smear'?"

There was a chorus of assents. Suddenly a ball appeared in the hands of one girl. She looked at it with surprise, then turned and ran away. The others chased her. In seconds, one of them tripped her, and the dozen girls ran up and jumped on her, resulting in a pile of wiggling, laughing, straining girls on the sand, the ball and the woman at the bottom of the pile.

The women separated themselves from the pile, and Greta yelled, "Okay, ladies, we're a mess. Well done. Let's wash the sand off."

Shouting, the women ran into the water and dove into the waves. There was a bit of pushing, and splashing, and laughter. After a minute, they returned to the beach, the sand washed off.

Greta shouted out. "Okay, ladies. To keep our clothes clean, let's play naked Smear."

Their clothing disappeared, a ball appeared in the hands of another girl, and that triggered another pursuit and capture and mass crash of naked women into the sand.

Eventually, Sonya found herself naked except for the ball in her arms, and she ran and even tried to leap over one girl, which caused great merriment, but the eventual result was the same, Sonya and the ball at the bottom of a pile of wiggling, naked women.

After several more iterations, Greta yelled, "Okay, ladies. That's enough Smear. Let's clean up and get going." This time, everyone, including Sonya, walked or dove into the water, washed themselves, cleaned sand out of their hair as best they could, and used their fingers to straighten their hair. Then they returned to the beach.

The women gathered around Sonya. Greta said, "Okay, we're going to hit the road, Sonya. I enjoyed meeting you. Thanks for the games. We'll see you again." She held up her phone to exchange addresses.

Sonya nodded. Everyone said their goodbyes, and the Gretas put on their clothes and continued up the beach.

Sonya put her clothes back on and returned to her bench and her book. She glanced at the group of women, now distant against the beach and the water - that was fun; that was a lot of fun, the first real fun I've had since coming to Elsewhere. If I had done this back in Animal World, I would have broken a bone. But Greta's right, we don't have physical sensation here, neither pleasure nor pain. I guess we have to use our imaginations.

It was fun to play a rough sport without pain and injury, landing face down in the sand, or the water; now I know what it feels like to sail through the air, upside down. That was... silly... and fun.

Yes, I had fun. When did I stop having fun? But no matter. I can learn to do that again.

Better late than never, right? One thing I've got is time.

19. Shana Meets the Guys

Shana walked into the *Three Blue Cows*, a network cafe, and looked around. It was an entertainment vendor, offering network access. Anybody could offer network access, but *The Cows* also had entertainment. For example, on Elsewhere, you never saw a person wandering down a sidewalk with the arhythmic, meandering, side-to-side stagger of a drunk. A person could not get drunk on Elsewhere. There was no app for it. Nonetheless, *the Cows* served a full line of beverages which were near-identical copies of beers, wines, liquors, and mixed drinks, and for some people, the similarity was enough to put them into a state indistinguishable from intoxication, including the loud conversation, gestures, slurs, silly but strongly-held opinions, and colorful language.

Shana looked around *The Cows*, listening for the loudest conversation - you must admit, it's a clever business model. You create conditions encouraging a rare form of entertainment, which your customers offer freely, without compensation. Furthermore, the entertainment is not easily copied by others. And that group right there at the end of the bar, four of them, yeah, they'll do nicely.

She walked over to the bar and sat down next to four men who appeared to be in their early twenties. The bartender raised his eyebrows at her, and she tapped a beer tap.

She turned and listened to a man wearing a gray business suit, say, "I bet you twenty bucks the Eagles make the playoffs this year. They need to beat the fucking Giants, and they will."

A man wearing a t-shirt and a backwards baseball cap said, "Yeah? They've lost five in a row to the Giants."

The first man said, "That means they're due."

The second man said, "That means they suck."

"So? If you believe that, take my bet. Twenty bucks."

"I'm afraid you'd clam up, and I enjoy your bullshit more than I need your money."

"That's why I like you - you always have an answer."

A third man, who was bald, said, in an exasperated tone, "Would you two lay off each other? Jesus, you guys act like you hate each other."

The man in the suit looked at him. "Ah, let him vent. He's just pissed off he hasn't been laid in eighteen years."

The baseball cap man said, "For your information, I got laid eight years ago."

"Yeah?" said the bald man. "Why haven't you introduced her?"

"Cause she was ugly as a mud fence, and I was drunk as a skunk. Ask me the next time I'm drunk."

"That sounds disgusting... as well as unlikely."

"It was... disgusting, that is. I'm ashamed of it. At least, I was ashamed once I sobered up and remembered a few things. That converted me to self-service." He adjusted his baseball cap.

A couple of men laughed.

Shana smiled at the bantering. Another man, wearing a PHILLIES sweatshirt, looked at her and said, "Something we can do for you, dollface?"

Shana looked at him. "No. Sorry. I didn't mean to eavesdrop. I was just enjoying the political discussion."

The man nodded. "Political discussion. You from south Philly?"

Shana smiled. "As a matter of fact, yeah. I had a brownstone on Dickinson."

The man in the suit said, in a nasal tone, "Oh, well, a brownstone on Dickenson. What, were you slumming? Couldn't afford north Philly?"

"North Philly didn't fit my modest, spiritual lifestyle," she said.

The baseball cap man emptied a beer and said, "You're not alone there."

"So what's your name?" The sweatshirt man said.

"Shana."

"Hi, Shana. Pleased to meet you. I'm Ray. And these clowns, left to right, are Dickie, Senator, and Goose."

"Hi, guys."

Goose - the bald man - said, "So, what brings you to our fine establishment?"

"I'm in search of entertainment. And I seem to have found it," she said.

"Good," Ray said. "Yeah, this is an odd place, but a lot of fun from time to time, as long as you bring your own entertainment."

Shana said, "You guys dress like twenty-somethings, but I get the impression you were a lot older than that."

Dickie, the man in a suit, said, "You're very perceptive. Yeah, we haven't seen twenty in over half a century." He looked at the other men. "None of us, right?"

The men nodded. Goose said, "We're all old guys."

Ray said, "Nicely matured."

"Like a bottle of wine that no one dares open," Ray said.

Dickie said, "We sometimes like to argue about how long we would have lasted back on Animal World. That's a favorite conversation."

"So, what's the answer?" Shana said.

Ray said, "Another twenty years."

Dickie guffawed. "In your dreams." He looked at Shana. "This guy had stage four liver cancer."

"Oh, ouch," she said.

Dickie frowned. "Yeah, and I was carrying around congestive heart disease." He made a face. "But the other two guys would have lasted twenty years, maybe."

"Thirty," Goose said.

Ray looked at him. "Yeah. Maybe. You might have made it." Ray winked at Shana. "This guy is unchanged. He looks about the same as he did forty years ago. He's got less hair, but otherwise..."

Goose said, "Nah, that's just your memory failing."

Dickie looked at Shana and said, "So what's your story, Shana?"

Shana shrugged. "I was a doctor, a pediatrician. I worked a lot, went to the symphony, worked on my garden."

"How old were you when you uploaded?"

"Fifty-one."

Goose said, "Whoa! Just fifty-one? Were you still getting laid?"

Shana shook her head.

"Why not?" Goose said.

"Ah... I had a crap marriage, the divorce got ugly, so I threw myself into my work," she said.

"Ha! Another idiot," Ray said. "Wasting life on work, work, work."

Shana looked at him. "And what did you waste your life on?"

Ray smiled, "Three awesome, amazing daughters, and a file cabinet full of mistakes, Ferrari women, and dead ends. But it's okay, I'm tough."

"So how do you like Elsewhere?" Shana said.

Senator said, "It's nice not to be in a dead-end frame of mind. I think we can all agree with that."

The three others shook their heads. Dickie said, "We don't agree on anything."

Senator said, "But Elsewhere is not much fun. I mean, it can be enjoyable, but seldom fun, you know what I mean? We cannot enjoy food, wine, beer, or sex. That ain't good."

Ray looked at Senator. "Oh, yeah, you weren't here the last time. I forgot."

Senator said, "What? What'd I miss?"

Ray looked at Dickie, then at Shana. "Dickie here was a software guy back on Animal World. So he's got a lot of useful hobbies..."

"Like hacking into the Nasdaq," Goose said.

Dickie spoke up, "So when I got here, in my spare time, which is all my time, I hacked into a couple of places on Willow and a couple more places on Elsewhere."

"Hang on, Dickie," Ray said. He looked at Shana and pointed a finger. "If you relay any of this to anyone, we will deny all of it. Understand?"

Shana held up a hand. "Mum's the word."

Dickie continued, "Okay, well, the first thing you need to know is that old guys are stuck here. We know a few guys who couldn't adjust to Elsewhere. They were really unhappy, missed their families, their friends, grandkids, that sort of thing. So these guys wanted to download back to Animal World. Elsewhere told them they couldn't do it because their bodies were not available."

Ray spoke up, "Yeah, except the contract says you can download into your body back on Animal World. You don't have to, but you can. The contract says that Elsewhere will preserve your body for five years, right?"

Shana said, "Yeah, I remember that."

Ray stared at her. "Well, they're not doing it. They're not preserving the bodies of elderly customers. That we know for a fact. Dickie tracked that down."

"That's massive breach of contract," Shana said.

"Yes, it is," Ray said. "So, what're you going to do? Sue Elsewhere? Sweetheart, they are the ones creating the environment in which you live. Fuck it. You're not suing anybody."

Dickie said, "It gets better. Elsewhere devours money. That's what they care about; that's all they care about. So you look at the people who were elderly when they uploaded. Many of them are wealthy, of course they are; they've been saving and investing their entire long lives. So Elsewhere wants that money. How do they get it? They arrange auctions where people can bid to download back to Animal World."

Ray said, "Now, this is sweet... are they offering downloads into old bodies? Fuck no! They're auctioning off downloads into twenty- and thirty-year-old bodies."

Shana hesitated, then said, "I'm missing it..."

"It's simple," Ray said. "Look at it from my perspective. I'm an old man. Women don't give me the time of day, and when they do, they call me 'sir'."

Senator nodded. "Yeah, when women start sirring you, it's official: you're fucked, figuratively speaking. No more sex. No more nothing."

Ray continued, "The few willing to fuck me look worse than I do. Now, if I download back to Animal World into my body, I soon die because that body is old. But I'm not nuts about Elsewhere. No food, no booze, no sex, where's the fun in that? Some guys think Elsewhere is hell."

Goose said, "Some guys would rather be dead than stay on Elsewhere."

Senator nodded. "Near-eternal life in a boring little village. Oh, yeah, sign me up."

Ray looked at her. "Okay, so would I be interested in downloading back to Animal World into the body of a twenty-two-year-old male? Fuck yeah!" Ray smacked the bar with his hand. "Fuck yeah. I could eat, I could drink, I could chat up a young woman, take her back to my place, and we could enjoy some mutually satisfactory, good old fashioned, horizontal entertainment. And money would be no problem. I would spend every nickel I have to do that because, with what I know now, I could make a pile of money.

"And fifty years from now, I'd return to Elsewhere. Maybe at some point, I would get tired of living." Ray made a face. "But I don't think so."

Shana held her hands to her head. "This is a lot to absorb."

"Okay, it's a lot, so let's change the topic," Goose said. "Let's do a little contingency planning. Now, many people would complain about not having touch, taste, and smell on Elsewhere, but they're working on all that. If they come up with the right apps, then food, wine, rock and roll, and sex, and sex, and sex will be back on the menu."

He paused, and Shana nodded. "Yeah, that's right."

"Okay, so in that happy world, how would you like to fuck all of us from time to time... ?" Goose said.

Senator said, "... we could be your own, personal harem."

"Reversing centuries of oppression," Goose said.

Shana stared at the men, then laughed. "Really? All of you?"

"One at a time, of course," Dickie said. "We're well mannered, as you can see."

Goose said, "Truth is, we're shy."

She tilted her head. "My own harem... uh, I don't know."

"Oh, come on," Dickie said. "Live a little. What'll it cost you?"

Shana thought for a moment. "Well, have any of you ever abused a woman?"

Three of the men looked at Ray. No one said anything.

Ray returned the stares, threw up his hands, and cried, "Oh, c'mon, that was decades ago. I know better now. I'm a different man. Besides, she was fucking nuts." He frowned, then looked at Shana. "I was briefly involved with a woman who set her hair on fire. She blamed me, of course, but she was the one with the matches."

Senator chuckled. "How embarrassing."

The other three men nodded. Goose thought for a moment. "Okay, yeah, he's right about that. She was out there in deep space."

Senator said, "Which is why he liked her." He looked at Shana. "Ray has a history with… interesting women."

Ray said, "Yeah... psychotic women love me, absolutely love me."

Shana nodded. "Uh, huh. So... three nice guys... and one bad boy." She looked away, made a face, and nodded again. "I'll consider it."

***

In one of the third-floor bedrooms, Greta frowned and stood up from her desk. "Ah, hell with it."

Greta Louise, her secretary, looked at her from behind her desk on the other side of the room. "You need something?"

Greta shook her head. "I think I'll go for a walk." Without waiting for a reply, she headed for the door.

"A walk? I don't understand," Greta Louise said.

Greta stopped at the door and faced her. "You know, a walk. They do it in Animal World all the time. You walk somewhere instead of dialing in a network address. It's gradual and rhythmic, and it helps me think."

"I see. Make sure your locator is on, please," Greta Louise said.

Greta nodded, turned away, and left the room. On the stairs to the first floor, she encountered Darnia, who said, "We have a situation."

Greta stopped, looked at her, and waited.

"Greta Jillian has been stroking this old man. Apparently, she overdid it. Not only does the guy want to give her money, he wants to download back to Animal World and name her in his will. He expects to die soon back on Animal World."

Skepticism crossed Greta's face, and she grinned. "What did she do to him?"

Darnia grinned. "I asked that, too. She did a non-stop lap dance and spent several hours talking to him. Apparently, she made quite an impression. She's beautiful, and he was incredibly lonely."

Greta nodded. "A lonely old man, that's not exactly rare. How much money?"

"Mid eight figures," Darnia said.

Greta stood there, calculating, then looked at Darnia. "Tell her to accept no more than seven figures. Low seven."

"Why?"

"Because if she takes more, she'll be dealing with the law, with probate court, with competing claims from angry family members. At a minimum, she would attract attention. We don't want that. Taking a small amount will keep us under the radar. They'll treat it as a crazy old man's infatuation, perfectly understandable, not particularly worrisome. They'll tolerate it. It will be eccentric rather than criminal."

Darnia nodded. "Okay. Should she accept on behalf of one of our shell companies?"

Greta shook her head. "Absolutely not. She will accept in her own name. If things go south, we'll get her out of there, change her name and appearance without endangering the rest of us. As far as I'm concerned, she can keep the money."

"Okay. I'll tell her."

Greta nodded, then left the house and walked down Hemlock Circle. She looked around as she walked and felt herself relaxing, slowing down, quieting the voice in her head that chattered with excitement and worry, bouncing among Things to Worry About.

She had a list.

The road was simple, two lanes of multi-color concrete repaired repeatedly over the years. Greta smiled - the road looks lived in; that's a nice touch. Hemlock Circle snaked along a hill, higher land to the left, a valley to the right, both sides lined with pine trees, many of them five to six stories tall.

The neighborhood was a kaleidoscope of various shades of green. Greta smiled at first, then lost half of it - I don't smell anything. This place would be magical if I could smell pine trees. I don't know what they smell like, but I do know that the idea of smelling them makes me feel good. That's got to be a memory inserted by Jerrell. I bet pine trees smell good.

I bet they have an aroma, not an odor.

Greta checked the time - she had been walking for eight minutes. She paused; to the right, through a gap in the trees, she could see several kilometers across the valley. There was a bench next to the road, so Greta sat down and settled in to enjoy the view. She could see hills, and a stream, and portions of a road on the far side of the valley. But she did not see any people, until she looked up at a person riding under a man-sized wing, floating on the air currents like a hawk, sailing along, not a care in the world.

She stared at the person under the wing, and tried to visualize what they were seeing, tried to imagine what flying under that wing would feel like, and how fast you could go, and how high.

After a minute, the wing disappeared. Greta stared at the valley for a long time, then her duties suddenly and rudely intruded - we, the ladies of Hemlock Circle, need a more reliable source of income. Oh, we can make a living; that is not the problem. The problem is that we are stuck in a profession (for lack of a better word) that requires episodic, risky endeavors. Fraud, theft, and the like. The ladies have a great attitude; they enjoy tricking other people, particularly men. They enjoy the challenge, and the feeling that we are evading the small fees which life imposes on you.

But we always have to look to the next job, the next scam. We have enough to relax from time to time, but never enough to retire.

It is a certainty we will be caught, eventually.

We need a deal that will pay us a periodic wage, a wage that arrives monthly, for example, even if we do not work. A pension, of sorts. An annuity.

How might we arrange that?

We need a target with either a deep fortune, or a sizable, monthly revenue stream from which we could extract a minuscule fee large enough to support ourselves.

Greta froze for a moment - Elsewhere is awash in money; there's got to be someone who can help us. All we have to do is find them.

She stood up and headed back to Hemlock Circle.

20. Executive Committee

Shana climbed the front steps of the house on Hemlock Circle and nodded at three women in passing; they were sitting together, talking about sports. She entered the house, looked in the library on the right, then looked in the large dining room on the left. The library was empty, and nine women were sitting at the dining room table, surrounding and staring at a colorful hologram summarizing traffic measurement over the Gretas' local area network.

Shana paused. "Hey, ladies. Anyone seen The Greta?"

Without looking, one woman pointed at the back of the house. Shana went back there and found Greta at the kitchen table, sitting and staring at something in her hand. Something brown.

Shana approached her and said, "Do you have some time? Five minutes, maybe ten?"

Greta did not look at her, but pointed at a chair, so Shana sat down. Greta extended the brown thing to Shana, who said, "Is that a brownie?"

Greta looked at her. "Thank you. I was trying to remember the name of this damn thing. Brownie. Okay."

Shana took the brownie, and Greta said, "Can you smell that?"

Shana held the brownie to her nose, then shook her head.

"Damn. We're trying to develop an app that will let us smell something. Anything will do. But so far, zippo." She leaned back in her chair, then looked at Shana. "So, what can I do for you?"

"I had a conversation with several customers, all men, at a bar in Charlotte."

"Are you looking for sex?"

Shana smiled. "No. Well, yeah, but forget that. We had a very interesting conversation about downloads and auctions."

"Yeah, we're trying to run the auctions for Elsewhere. We'd make a mountain of money doing that. Not enough to retire, mind you, but still... a lot."

"Okay, I'm glad we're making money, but have you considered whether the auctions are sustainable?"

Greta frowned and looked sharply at Shana. "Why wouldn't they be?"

"Okay, I was talking to four men; their avatars looked to be twenty-something, but back on Animal World, they were in their seventies or eighties. They said a lot of elderly men are trying to download back to Animal World."

Greta nodded. "Yeah, we're collecting data on the auctions, the downloads, and that's right, the elderly customer is a much bigger portion of the downloads than before. We don't know why. Maybe it's just random, a random fluctuation."

Shana chuckled. "Okay, I'm glad I caught you. It isn't random. There are a lot of elderly, mostly guys, who don't like Elsewhere; they don't like not having touch, smell, taste, or sex. So they've been trying to download back to Animal World.

"These guys told me about people in Elsewhere who were accepting bribes to arrange downloads to a young body back on Animal World, say, between twenty and thirty-five."

Greta nodded. "Sure, I can imagine that. It's hard to imagine why old guys would want to download to their original bodies; it would be a death sentence."

Shana nodded vigorously. "That's right; they want young bodies. One guy told me, if an old man can download into a young body, he can go back to Animal World, where he can drink beer, eat real food, and have real sex with a young woman. He can feel, taste, smell. From a guy's point of view, that is a very attractive prospect. Elderly men will give away nearly all of their money to do that."

"What, return to Animal World and embrace poverty? That doesn't make sense." Greta said.

Shana almost rolled her eyes. "Of course it makes sense; it makes perfect sense. You know what these guys told me? If I can get back there, in a twenty-year-old body, with what I know now, I'll make a pile of money. Money is the least of my worries."

Shana paused and stared at Greta. "Think about it - these guys have been alive a long time, done a lot of stuff. They understand mortgages, finance, stock markets, options, all that stuff. Where does most of the money on Animal World get made? Financial markets. They have good reason to be confident."

Greta nodded. "Okay, I'll buy that. What about the women?"

"We didn't talk about the women. But if someone on Elsewhere ever developed an app for touch, these guys offered to have sex with me." Shana laughed. "All I want. I told them I'd consider it."

"So... correct me if I'm wrong, but anyone interested in food, drink, or sex, would have an interest in downloading to Animal World. Moving into a young body."

"Yeah, that's right. You get it. But you don't yet understand the problem," Shana said.

"What problem?"

"What's driving the increase in downloads is that Elsewhere and Willow are not storing the bodies of elderly customers. That's what these guys told me. The contract obligates Willow to store a customer's body, but when people request a download back into their bodies, Elsewhere tells them that there's been a malfunction, and the body is not available."

Greta shook her head. "Yeah, I heard that; I thought it was just a rumor. That company really is a sad sack of shit, are they not?"

"It gets worse. If a customer is really pissed off, if they complain, then Willow arranges for them to download into a young body. That contributes to these downloads." She paused, then said, "Oh, I almost forgot; I heard that Elsewhere is paying young customers to waive their download rights. That, of course, would free up their body back on Animal World so that an old guy could bid to download into it."

Shana looked sadly at Greta. "You see where this will go? Elsewhere is probably not storing the bodies of elderly customers. They figure, why bother if elderly customers seldom wish to download?

"But they're wrong about that. Elderly customers often don't like Elsewhere; they miss their grandchildren, their families. They have reasons to download. When they can't, they threaten complaints, or lawsuits, so Elsewhere offers them a side deal, a download into a young body. Then word gets around, and more elderly customers want to download into young bodies. So Elsewhere sets up auctions to serve that demand. But if this continues, then young customers will be trapped on Elsewhere because the elderly have more wealth and can pay higher auction prices."

Shana paused, then said, "So, what do you think will happen when the truth gets out, and tens of millions of young customers - whose bodies are still available - discover they're being marooned on Elsewhere?"

Greta sat there with her mouth open, staring at Shana. She said, "The young will join the exodus, which will further encourage the elderly to download. This thing will snowball." She leaned forward and propped her head on her hands.

Shana said, "That's when Elsewhere will empty out."

Several minutes later, Greta pulled out her cell phone, activated it, and said, "Come to me. On the back porch."

A minute later, Darnia approached the table and sat down. She looked at Greta. "What's up?"

Greta said, "Shana has learned something interesting. I think you need to hear this."

Shana went through the entire explanation again. When she finished, Darnia leaned back. "Whew! That's a blockbuster." She laughed. "Good Gods, Elsewhere is such a collection of shits! How is that possible?"

Shana said, "They know how to code. And they care about money."

Darnia looked at Greta. "Well, you know what they say."

Greta stared at her. "No, what the fuck do they say?"

"Danger and opportunity are two sides of the same coin," Darnia said.

"Do they? I love philosophy... no, really," Greta said.

"Oh, calm down," Darnia said. "You're focusing on the negative aspects, the danger, this imposes on us."

"Yes."

"Okay. I agree with Shana. I think this could cause Elsewhere's collapse. I cannot imagine what the reaction will be when the word gets out. One thing I am sure of... when the word gets out, it will spread at the speed of light. If there's a reaction - and how can there not be? - it will happen fast. This is incredibly dangerous, and we definitely need to protect ourselves.

"Now, there is also an opportunity." Darnia looked at Greta. "Maybe you should have a conversation with Elsewhere and decide what they can do to buy our silence. They would not want the word to get out. The damages are almost incalculable. I think they would pay a lot to keep us silent."

Darnia paused and frowned. "But know this - once you have that conversation, Elsewhere will have a good reason to murder all of us. I can imagine them running a cost-benefit calculation, then deciding that murdering us would be cheaper and more beneficial."

Greta looked at the other two and said, "Yeah, we can blackmail Elsewhere, but of what use is their money? We need to get out of here. We need to download. Once the balloon goes up, we can't count on being able to download."

Shana said, "Well, at least we can take our money back to Animal World."

Greta nodded. "Right. At the moment, we can do that."

Greta picked up her phone and sent a brief text:

Sonya, come to the house, please. Greta.

***

Greta stared at Greta Elaine. "The Elsewhere contract guarantees that a customer can download into their original body. How does an auction in Elsewhere fit into that?"

"I don't know, but Elsewhere is presenting a seminar in three minutes."

"Where?" Greta said - they're going public?

"I have the URL."

"Okay, good. I can make that. I'll go now."

Greta moved to that address and found herself in a conference room with a busy, noisy crowd, most of them standing, and a grid of chairs, most empty, facing a low stage and a lectern. She chose a chair halfway back, on the left side of the grid, and sat down. Seconds later, a young man slid past her and sat next to her. Greta nodded at him, then turned her attention to the stage as a middle-aged woman walked to the lectern and said, "Welcome, everyone. I'm glad you could all make it. Perhaps we can take our seats and get started?"

In less than a minute, the crowd was seated. The woman smiled at everyone - a professional, impersonal smile designed for strangers. "My name is Penelope Simmons. I am a senior vice president in charge of operations here at Elsewhere. Today, I want to talk about a new program that we are test-driving which would allow Elsewhere customers to arrange a download by participating in an auction."

An instant buzz of conversation arose from the crowd. Ms. Simmons smiled. "Yes, that is big news, isn't it? Let me describe how the auctions would work. First, some of our customers are very happy, and a number of them have told us they have no intentions of downloading. To encourage them, we will pay them to make their bodies available for download by someone else. We call that a download waiver.

"When a body is available for download, we will schedule an auction, and other customers, if they're interested, can bid for the right to download into that body. The highest bidder gets to download as long as their bid is above a pre-determined reserve price. The winning bidder has a week to download into the body they've won. If they do not, then the auction result is canceled, and the body is re-bid in another auction.

"It's a fairly simple process, and we don't know exactly how it's going to work in practice, but we are going to offer it and see how our customers react to it."

The conversation among the crowd rose to a higher level. Greta leaned back - most of the people in this room are journalists, not investors. We need to move fast, take advantage of this. She turned to the young man sitting next to her wearing a doubtful expression. "So what do you think about all this?"

He looked at her and tilted his head. "I don't know... I think I'd be real careful about using an auction to download."

"Why? What's the problem?"

"Well, I'm an old guy; I was eighty-two when I uploaded to Elsewhere, and I've got lots of friends in Elsewhere. Most of them are old, too. Several of them tried to download, and Elsewhere told them they couldn't. They gave the same excuse every time, there was a problem with storing their bodies on Animal World, and the storage failed, blah, blah, blah. No one was ever able to verify their excuse. So now, these same people are offering to let anyone download if they win an auction? Something ain't right."

"I don't know," Greta said. "What could go wrong?"

The young man stared at Greta. "Well, for starters, Elsewhere controls everything in this virtual environment in which we live. So you have to trust the information they give you about the person you're downloading into. They might say, oh, it's a thirty-year-old male. Maybe it is, but you have no way of knowing that."

"Well, they could give you photographs, a medical report, vaccination record."

He said, "Sure, they could give you anything that the network can provide. All I'm saying is, you're trusting the network and you're trusting a tech company." His head tilted. "You sure you want to do that?"

Greta was quiet for a long time. "It would be useful to have more information. Or better information. That much is clear."

He smiled. "Yeah, that would be useful. Listen, I'm going to hit the road. Maybe we can exchange phone numbers. What do you think?"

Greta nodded. "Let's do that." She grabbed her phone, and they exchanged information. Greta sat there, thinking. The minutes crept by. The crowd was asking questions of Ms. Simmons, but the conversation and the questions seemed friendly and rather simple. Greta returned to Hemlock Circle.

***

Across a table from Greta, Shana straightened and talked with her hands, "Suppose we were in charge of the uploads and downloads. So we would know when a customer wants to download, since we would run the auctions allowing them to do that. In fact, we would be the first to know."

Greta nodded.

Shana continued, "We could even make up two sets of books. A group called the Italians, whoever they are, no doubt a deep and sophisticated people, taught everyone how to do that. One set of books would be a fake, reporting, say, ten percent of the downloads. That, we would forward to Elsewhere. The other set would be genuine and accurate, reporting all downloads. We would pay Elsewhere eighty percent of ten percent, i.e. eight percent, of the download revenue. They would think that we are complying with our agreement. Of course, eventually, they would learn we are not. By that time, we need to be back on Animal World."

"What if Willow comes after us on Animal World?" Greta said.

Shana shrugged. "Let 'em. We'd rat them out. And if anyone of us had an accident, a mishap, bad enough to put them in a hospital, or worse, then we'd rat them out."

Shana paused. "So... what do you think?"

Darnia said, "Let's see... Elsewhere would get eight percent of download revenues. We would keep ninety-two percent."

Greta stared at the ceiling, calculating - in the short run, this would make us less money than extortion, but more money in the long run, at less risk. If we resort to extortion, we would get a large sum and immediately become fugitives, with Elsewhere and Willow pursuing us. But as a contractor and an affiliate, we could spy on Elsewhere and move the data and payments to keep them docile.

And, if we were the gatekeepers, we would less likely be surprised when Elsewhere falls apart. And we'll be able to arrange our downloads into the best bodies available.

We will eventually have to abandon Elsewhere, which is the only way to evade the collective spasm that will happen when the public learns about Elsewhere's fraud. The good news is, we can protect ourselves and get preferential treatment in downloading.

Greta stood, and Shana looked at her. "You've decided."

Greta nodded. "Yeah, forget extortion." She froze for a moment - oddly, as a matter of pure happenstance, due to no merit on our part, we are ideally situated to deal with the problem. It all comes down to information. I've heard people say that a thousand times. I never understood it until now.

Willow and Elsewhere are breaching their contracts with over thirty million elderly customers. Some snot-nosed, clueless, book-smart software executive thought, why would an old person change their mind and want to download back to Animal World? It makes no sense. Well, that executive never learned about the kaleidoscopic variety of the human species. And why would they? Highly trained but not educated, buried in software, paid a fortune, coddled, why would they know anything about people, especially normal people who work with their hands, or their backs? People who don't make a living by writing code?

Greta smiled - it couldn't be any better than this. Too bad this can't last. You can't fool anyone forever. But damn! Darnia and Shana are so smart, maybe smarter than I am, though I suspect their advantage is that they've had more experience with humans, who are, it must be admitted, a highly complex and sentient species.

Greta leaned back in her chair - when I first thought of forming our little group of criminals, I thought they would all be copies of me, pure cyber entities. But we ended up with a couple of avatars from genuine humans - Shana and Darnia - and that has saved us.

Why is that? My lying eyes tell me, I'm more creative that my Gretas. That's odd, if the Gretas are exact copies of me. I would think we'd be identical in every way.

But my eyes say no. I'm better, smarter, more resourceful than the other Gretas. So is Shana. So is Darnia.

I wish I understood this better. After all that training I absorbed, I don't like not knowing. Maybe Jerrell had some magic sauce he used when he created me, and the sauce didn't copy. In fact, that must be the case. So, why wouldn't that copy along with everything else?

I bet Jerrell could explain this, but I cannot ask him. It would be risky to contact the guy who put an Instant Death command in my original core software.

My lying eyes suggest that the copy of an electronic file might not be identical to the original. Let's see... I made the copies on Elsewhere; so, why wouldn't Elsewhere allow files to copy exactly, down to every detail?

Well... I can think of a few reasons. First, I don't trust Elsewhere as far as I can spit. Second, these aren't just any files; these are people we're talking about, and the files are massive. So I would expect Elsewhere to save storage space by compressing the files, and now we can wonder if compression might sacrifice some of the file.

Also, the file changes every second. After all, a person goes to sleep as one person, wakes up as another. We treat them as the same person, but who knows? Maybe this is why a drunk can 'sleep it off' - go to bed drunk, wake up sober.

So, I can't help but wonder if copying the files, and maybe uploading and downloading, might come with hidden costs, what the business guys call 'shrinkage.'

Bottom line: I need Darnia and Shana. I need to protect them.

***

Greta sat alone at the dining room table. Every so often, someone would walk through and nod in her direction, or as often, say nothing while passing through. Greta would think - whatever it is, I'll hear about it eventually.

Darnia came into the room, spotted Greta, and hurried over to her. She sat down and said, "I'm glad I found you. I have another idea for how we can run the auctions."

Greta smiled at her. "Great. What do you have?"

"Okay, there are numerous options; the situation is complicated. Now, Elsewhere will post the auctions and let people bid on downloading into a body.

"So we tell Elsewhere that we'll run the auctions; we'll handle the transactions, absorb the risk, verify payment, all the administrative stuff. All they have to do is clip coupons. We'll take twenty percent of the auction price; they'll get eighty percent." Darnia settled back in her chair and looked at Greta, awaiting a response.

"Twenty percent for running an auction?" Greta said. "Is that steep?"

Darnia shook her head. "It's standard, but we can do it for less." Greta stared at her. "The big auction houses in Animal World charge twenty percent."

"I should've gotten into this long ago." Greta chuckled - my 'long ago' wasn't all that long ago. "Why will Elsewhere let us run their auctions?"

"Because then they won't have to. It's free money. They get a majority cut, and they don't pay overhead, benefits, and all that. All they have to do is bank it. We're cheaper than their own employees."

"And they are greedy," Greta said.

"Yes. They are that."

"What about breach of contract? Every Elsewhere customer has contractual rights to download to their original body."

"True, but some customers can agree to amend the contract," Darnia said.

"What if the customer doesn't want to amend the contract?" Greta said.

Darnia shrugged. "Then they won't. Elsewhere will set the buy-out price high enough so that some customers agree to waive their download rights."

"That's right, isn't it?" Greta looked at Darnia. "Okay, I believe you. This can work."

Darnia nodded vigorously. "Good. I'm glad, but it gets better."

"It's already sweet. It gets even better?"

"We can play games with the prices arising in auctions," Darnia said.

Greta smirked. "Administrative fees? Delivery?"

"No, not that. They can detect administrative fees and the like. But we can insert a ringer, our own ringer, and bid in each auction, which will elevate the auction price. The trick is to raise the winning price, but not by so much that the mark does not win the auction. Our competing bids will not be part of the data."

Greta's mouth dropped open, and she stared at Darnia. "That's right! It's obvious, and genius."

Darnia grinned. "Yes. This could be a goldmine. Once we elevate the auction prices, we can then, far under the table, allow the right people to offer us bribes. The higher auction prices will elevate the bribes we can demand. Naturally, all that will be unreported."

Shock settled on Greta's face. "Would you repeat that? I missed it the first time."

Darnia took a breath and spoke slowly. "If we operate the auctions and are occasionally willing to take a bribe, then higher auction prices will raise the level of bribes. We'll take a bribe to allow the occasional bidder to circumvent the auction, to do a side-deal. Of course, we won't share bribe money with anyone, including Elsewhere."

"That customer will simply disappear," Greta said.

Darnia nodded.

Greta grinned. "I'm impressed. You are a ridiculous, criminal genius. This is incredible. You deserve a bonus. So... what do you think would be a fair bonus?"

"There are thirteen Greta 2s, right?"

Greta nodded.

"Okay, how about..." Darnia leaned back and looked at the ceiling as calculation crossed her face. "... I'll take ten percent off the top, plus my usual cut?" Darnia shook off her dreamy expression and looked at Greta. "How 'bout that?"

"Done. And we'll announce it and have a party."

Darnia looked at Greta. "So... you're incentivizing everybody?"

Greta nodded. "Of course. Help the group and get a bonus."

"Okay, that's smart."

Greta nodded. "I think so, too."

***

At the end of a rehearsal at the *Spoon*, Johnny approached Jerrell and said, "That was good. You've got a knack for composing rock and roll, Jerrell. I like your new song. Listen, would you like to stop at *Ruby's* for some lunch?"

Jerrell nodded. "Sure." Johnny put his guitar into a case, and Jerrell slipped his drumsticks into a soft leather case. On the way to *Ruby's*, Jerrell said, "So, is this a business meeting, or just personal?"

"I met a girl," Johnny said. "With any luck, she'll stop by. At least, I hope so."

"Oh. Well, good for you. But where do I come in?"

"I'd like to know what you think of her," Johnny said.

"Really? Is that relevant?"

"You're a friend, so it's relevant. Look, I'm not asking for approval. But I respect your opinion."

"Geez, Johnny, I don't know what to say. I mean, if you're happy with her, then I'm happy for you."

"I just want to know what you think, speaking as a separate pair of eyes and ears."

Jerrell nodded. "Yeah, okay."

The two men got a booth at *Ruby's* and ordered cheeseburgers. Johnny ordered coffee; Jerrell, a chocolate milkshake, which made Johnny laugh. "You know, in forty years or so, you won't be able to eat that, so enjoy it."

"Ha, don't be so sure," Jerrell said. "I might end up in a skinny coffin someday. Now... tell me about this girl."

Johnny clasped his hands and looked down at them, then he looked up at Jerrell. "Her name's Elenor. She's a rich kid; at least, I think so. She talks about some place called Hampton, in New York."

"Uh, Johnny, that might be The Hamptons; it's a neighborhood on Long Island, well removed from the city, very stylish, very pricey," Jerrell said. His eyebrows rose. "Veeerrryyy pricey."

"Yeah. So she's loaded and young. She dresses up, like for a party, lots of black, expensive clothes, aimed at the coolest and hippest people. She wears a lot of makeup." Johnny said. He looked at the other end of the diner. "Speaking of which, here she comes."

Jerrell resisted the temptation to turn around. Soon he felt a presence at his elbow, so he looked up to see a slender woman in a black dress, with dark hair and black lip gloss and eyeliner, resembling an actress in a theater troupe.

The woman slid into the booth next to Johnny and kissed him on the cheek.

"Hi, baby," she said.

"Hi." Johnny glanced at Jerrell and said, "Elenor, this is my friend, Jerrell. Jerrell, this is Elenor."

She aimed a cool, friendly expression at Jerrell. "Hi."

Jerrell nodded. "Pleased to meet you."

"So whatcha doin'?"

Johnny turned to her. "We just finished rehearsing a couple songs that Jerrell wrote."

She looked at Jerrell. "What are the songs about? Are they love songs? Everyone's writing love songs these days."

Jerrell smiled at her. "Not at all. They're more like... lust songs."

"Ah. I see. For the mass market, then," she said.

"Exactly," Jerrell said - the 'mass market,' yeah, that wasn't a compliment. On the other hand, I never expected to be a songwriter, so if someone thinks I'm a hack, well, they might be right.

The three of them sat for an hour talking. Elenor ordered coffee and french fries, and talked about music. She seemed to know a lot about the local music scene in Philadelphia; she told a story about a party in the Hamptons, celebrating a wedding, at which a well-known rock band performed.

Jerrell watched Johnny interact with Elenor but tried not to stare - under all the makeup, and talk, and aggressive sophistication, she's a child, but she's bored around children. She wants to run with the big kids.

Are they having sex? Is that legal? Jerrell watched Johnny, and studied Elenor - Gods, that's probably weird. He looks like he wants that, but she looks about... what... fourteen? It's hard to see past all the makeup. But yeah, fourteen. Tops.

How do you talk to someone who's fourteen? - uh, what's your favorite news channel? No... what's your favorite boy band? So... how is... uh, high school... no, don't say 'high school,' just say 'school,' treating you? What do you think of Elsewhere? Jerrell turned to the side to hide a smile and stifle a laugh.

Eventually, Elenor had to leave. She said goodbye, stood up, and left, so Jerrell and Johnny paid the bill and followed her outside. But when they reached the sidewalk, she looked down and screamed. Jerrell stared at her - what's with this? Did someone attack her?

Johnny was quickly at her side. "What's wrong? What happened?"

In a panic, she pointed down. "It's a cat! A black cat! I'm afraid of cats!"

Johnny looked down at the cat, then looked at Elenor. "Afraid of cats? Really? How come?"

Visibly shaken, she looked at him and said, "In a previous life, I lived in Egypt. My family was royalty, and I was a princess. But we had enemies in the court, and one day another royal family attacked us and murdered my mother and father. They tied me up and used a group of cats to kill me. The cats hadn't been fed, so they fed on me. I've been afraid of cats ever since." She aimed tortured eyes at Johnny. "I have nightmares about it."

Jerrell stared at her - I see the perfect girl, young and rich, stylish, sophisticated... and nutty as a fucking fruitcake. That's just great. And I have to wonder, why would someone use cats to execute an enemy? Were they out of knives, axes, and boiling oil? Is it a religious thing? But let's not ask a lot of irrelevant questions. She's afraid of cats; let's just take it from there.

Don't analyze it.

Johnny put his arms around her. "But Elenor, it's just a cat." He leaned towards the cat and waved a hand. "Shoo, shoo. Go away."

At first, the cat made no effort to move. It sat there, leaned away as cats will, and stared at Johnny. Then it calmly turned around, trotted down an alley, and disappeared.

Johnny looked at Elenor. "Okay, the cat's gone."

Eventually, she calmed down, and Johnny released her. She smiled at him. "Thanks. I'm glad you were here. I feel better. But listen, I need to go. We'll talk later, okay?"

Johnny nodded, and Elenor turned and walked down the sidewalk. In moments, she disappeared.

Johnny and Jerrell stood on the sidewalk, neither willing to leave, neither saying anything.

Jerrell pursed his lips. "Okay, nice girl."

Silence fell between the two men. Finally, Johnny turned to Jerrell. "She's a bit of a flake, isn't she?"

"Johnny, like I said, if you're happy, then I'm happy for you."

"You think she's not a flake?"

"Oh, she's definitely a flake," Jerrell said. "Have you gotten her naked yet?"

Johnny nodded. "We messed around, but she didn't have a contraceptive."

"Well, you're playing with live ammo, my friend."

Johnny aimed a sad look at Jerrell. "Actually, I'm not. Not anymore."

"Maybe deep down, she's a really nice person."

Johnny looked down the sidewalk and stared for a long moment. "Yeah, but she's still a flake."

"That, she is."

"I'm trying to be adult here," Johnny said. "I'm trying not to bang somebody just because I can. I'm trying to wait until I find a girl who I want in my life, day in, day out."

"You show admirable patience."

"Thank you," Johnny said.

"Well... keep looking."

"Yeah, what else you gonna do?"

***

As McLeesh walked through the halls, nearly everyone he encountered had a reaction of some kind:

"Hello, Mr. McLeesh. Good luck. We'll miss you."

"Hey, what are you doing here? The party's upstairs."

"Good luck, Alistair. Don't be a stranger."

"Thanks for everything, Mr. McLeesh. Good luck."

"Whoa, you're late. Making a late entrance, eh? Ah, well done, very artful."

"Sorry, Alistair, I can't make your party, got a meeting. But take care, good luck, and thanks for everything."

McLeesh continued walking - it's okay, let's not make a big deal of it. All things have their time, yet all must come to pass. Today is the end of one era, the beginning of another. He came to the elevators, stepped inside, and took a fast ride to the top of the Woody.

God, tomorrow will be different... incredibly different. I won't have any matters - meetings, phone calls, memos, subpoenas - nothing related to Willow or Elsewhere.

I can hardly wait. What will I do? Eat something unhealthy, like a donut... walk on the beach... drive one of my cars somewhere, or nowhere. Hell, I could take my Ferrari to a Walmart parking lot and do fishhooks. That could be fun. Or... maybe I'll even watch a TV show.

There's a lot I can do without Willow.

He reached out, opened one of the glass doors to the executive dining room, and felt the crowd noise on his face, like a blast wave. A dozen people, each holding a drink, saw him, smiled or grinned, and approached him. Several reached out, for a touch, a handshake. McLeesh smiled at each and every one of them. Somebody shouted 'McLeesh!,' then over a hundred people turned towards him, spotted him, and the noise in the room instantly doubled.

"Speech, speech, speech!"

McLeesh walked through the crowd, his head turning from side to side, trying to smile at everyone, accepting the brief handshakes and touches from Willow's current collection of employees and executives.

He walked to the middle of the room, stopped, and said, "Okay, where can I make my speech?" McLeesh saw everyone looking at each other with 'I didn't cover this, did you cover this?' in their eyes. McLeesh looked around. "No one tracked down a microphone? Oh, man..." He looked to a corner of the dining room and pointed to it. "I'll speak over there; everyone gather round."

He walked to the corner and turned to face the crowd, which was filled with faces he recognized from two decades at Willow. McLeesh smiled and said, "Everyone can hear? Okay, good." He looked around again, saw no small number of faces with tears rolling down; he thought about making a joke, decided it would be in bad taste.

He took a moment to survey the crowd again. "I don't have a speech prepared, and now that I am standing here, now that I have to say something, all I think of is, goodbye and good luck to you all. How boring is that?"

A few people laughed. A man was crying. His eyes found Hans, off to the side, halfway to the back of the crowd. His eyes were dry; his face, calm.

McLeesh reminded himself to project his voice; it needed a higher pitch and resonance. "A long time ago, I started this company my last year in college, yet I managed to graduate. Don't ask me how I did that, I don't recall. We started in my parents' garage; now, we're worth several trillion dollars. Not bad, eh?"

The crowd applauded.

McLeesh continued, "As the years passed, I spent my time around a lot of really smart, creative people, and I remember watching them generate ideas and solutions, watching them create something, and giving them raises, and congratulating them.

"So at this point, before I leave, I have a confession to make - I have had the best and the easiest job in the world, and I want to thank those responsible, which is all of you. From the bottom of my heart, thank you."

McLeesh thought - I am this good. I have excellent executive skills, and I can spin a tear-jerker with the best of them. But let's not linger. "Okay, that was the important thing I wanted to say to you all. Now, did anyone arrange for cake and ice cream?"

A dozen people shouted 'yes;' McLeesh looked around, a staffer pointed in a direction, and McLeesh headed in that direction. Easing his way through the crowd, commenting and smiling and shaking hands and exchanging hugs, he eventually came upon several tables filled with food and drink, cookies, cakes, punch, wine, and a variety of snacks.

A programmer touched McLeesh on the shoulder. "Sir, we arranged your favorite food group."

"Chocolate something?" McLeesh said.

"Cake, of course."

McLeesh found a massive chocolate cake with three layers sitting on a table. He cut a large piece, slid it onto a paper plate, took a plastic fork, and backed away from the table, which was quickly surrounded by hungry staffers and executives.

He heard a male voice to the side. "So, your last day. How does it feel, really? Will you miss the place? On your last day, you can tell me. Nothing's at stake." McLeesh thought, ah, yes. Hans.

McLeesh turned to face Willow's new CEO. "I'll miss a few of the people. I've made a number of friends, and those I expect to see again, no matter where I wind up. How 'bout you? Are you excited about your new job?" McLeesh thought, this is the devil on my left shoulder speaking; I refuse to say the word 'CEO,' though I know it makes you flush a bit.

"You let me work unsupervised, so I'm already used to that," Hans said. "And that taught me a lot, which I'm using. I need to delegate. CEO is a big job, too big for one man, too big for me, anyway."

McLeesh nodded and smiled - don't kid me, Hans, you're about as modest as a Rheinmetall gunship. "Do you think your people are up to it? Up to expanded responsibility?"

Hans shrugged. "I might need to make a few changes, but I think we have good people. I'll find somebody to take the burden off my hands."

McLeesh nodded - that means you'll find somebody who won't threaten you, will let you run the show without questions, and will be available to take the blame when the company hits a speed bump. What I think you'll discover is that people like that will tell you what they think you want to hear. They'll stroke your ego.

A strong man doesn't need that, but you do.

Hans said, "It might take a while, but I'm confident we'll muddle through."

McLeesh smiled - oh, Hans, you're so folksy. Muddle through? You learned that expression after leaving Berlin, yes? The more I talk to you, the happier I am to be leaving. It is a genuine skill, a rare skill, the ability to speak a lie as if you are confident of its truth. It cannot be taught; you have it, or you do not. The best lawyers have it, but it is rare among engineers or scientists.

Hans was saying something, but McLeesh found his mind wandering - I wonder if those predator bots represent a 'speed bump'? And I wonder how long it will take for your subordinates to tell you about them. I see you have a new Chief of Security.

I hope she's better than I think she is.

McLeesh shrugged - we will simply have to let this affair play out. And if I happen to spot an opportunity to make money off of it, well, that is what business is all about, is it not?

McLeesh looked at Hans, smiled, and held out a hand. "Congrats on your promotion, Hans. Good luck with Willow. If there's ever anything I can do to help, please let me know."

As the two men shook hands, Hans grinned. "I will." He turned away.

McLeesh nodded - that will never happen. And like rain seeking a leak in a roof, he slid away from that topic to another. There were many old friends and good people in the room, and McLeesh wanted to enjoy every one of them.

21. The Girls Advance

Jerrell sat before his laptop in the *Wooden Spoon*. A half empty cup of tepid coffee sat next to the laptop. For once he wasn't working on Greta. After she moved to Elsewhere, there was no point. He still searched for her, hoped to talk to her, but she was not to be found. As a substitute, he was catching up on the news, business, politics, technology, style, home, entertainment, music, art, everything.

At two pm on a Tuesday afternoon, the *Spoon* was nearly empty. There was a bartender, a robotic cook, and a server, just in case someone wandered in looking for lunch or a beer. Two other customers sat a dozen tables away.

Jerrell pried himself off of his laptop, then noticed a man standing not close, but not far away either. He glanced at the man, who looked like corporate security: he was huge, tan slacks, dark blue blazer, short haircut, the kind of guy you see behind a high executive, wearing dark sunglasses and a wire in his right ear. The guy stuck out in the *Spoon* like an umbrella welded to a dump truck. Jerrell turned his head, scanned the area out of the corners of his eyes, and found two other similar creatures. Three men, all looking in Jerrell's direction.

Jerrell froze at the table - uh, oh, I'm busted; I think I'm busted. If I had to bet, I would bet these guys are Willow security. If that is so, then... they somehow discovered what I'm doing. But how? Maybe they tapped into the software that I used to create Greta. Shit. Yeah, that's possible. They could do that. They're a big tech company; they probably know their way around software.

Damn, I should have seen this coming.

Jerrell stared straight ahead - okay, I know my rights. Confess to nothing. I'm just a guy sitting at a table. And they don't have probable cause to do anything real aggressive. So if they grab me, I'll yell like hell. I won't surrender my phone, or my laptop, or... the time of day... or the color of the summer sky on a sunny day. Give away nothing, nada. He glanced at the man again. Oh, a software guy would say they have probable cause, but a judge or a lawyer? No way.

Better yet, prove it.

I can see it now... hey, what are you doing? I've broken no law. Oh, you're tracking me to a URL? So what? What's the URL? Nope, that's not mine. That's an old one. Did I mention my laptop was stolen? Did I report it? No. These things happen. The cops aren't going to recover it, so why bother? Write it off, reload the data, and move on.

No, I can't prove it, but so what? I don't have to. You're the guy bearing the burden of proof. So eat shit and die, asshole. Yeah, that's what I'll say. Something like that.

So screw these guys. If they want to sue, we'll turn it into a spectacle. Big corporation stomping a citizen, one of the 'little people.'

Jerrell felt a presence on his left, a man approaching. He looked up and said, "Holy shit!"

The man grinned. "I've been called names, but never that one. Mind if I sit down?"

Jerrell tried to find his voice, failed, and nodded his head.

"You're Jerrell Adri. I am Alistair McLeesh."

Jerrell nodded. "Yeah, I recognize you. I never expected to meet you."

McLeesh chuckled. "Relax. I'm not here to arrest you or have you roughed up."

Jerrell nodded. "That's a relief. Below your pay grade, I would imagine."

"That's right," McLeesh said. "Oh, I know what you're doing on Willow and Elsewhere, and I have a pretty fair idea of why you're doing it."

"Do you? Why am I doing it?"

"My people tell me you created avatars to entertain the customers on Willow. That was your job, and you were good at it, too; that's how I first heard of you. Then some asshole in Willow took your methods, taught them to an A.I., let the A.I. create the avatars, and fired you." McLeesh leaned forward. "For what it's worth, I don't blame you for being pissed off."

"You know a lot," Jerrell said.

"I do. My job requires that I be well-informed."

"And you want me to stop on my own, without a nasty fight with a corporation that's bigger than a number of countries," Jerrell said.

"Let me answer that with a question - do you think this might be below my pay grade?"

"Mr. McLeesh, everything is below your pay grade."

McLeesh laughed loudly and looked at Jerrell. "That's a good one; I'll remember that one."

"Yeah, in that scenario, you're here to ask me to give Willow a break," Jerrell said. "But that makes no sense. You don't need to ask. You have the means to defend yourself, against me and thousands like me. You've got money, muscle, lawyers, everything you need. So that can't be it. Okay, what's the deal?"

McLeesh looked around, then leaned forward and spoke quietly, "I thought you'd be quick, and you are. I need to bring you up to speed; there are a few things you don't know yet."

Jerrell offered a smile that did not reach his eyes. "Okay. Educate me."

"First off, I'm no longer working at Willow," McLeesh said.

"How is that possible?"

McLeesh shrugged. "I resigned. I'm a free man." He grinned broadly. "Few people know that, but the problems at Willow are no longer my problems; they belong to someone else."

"Yes, but you still own a massive piece of Willow," Jerrell said.

McLeesh tilted his head and gave Jerrell an odd look. "Actually, I own a lot less than you or anyone else is aware. But we're getting ahead of ourselves. Let's come back to you for a moment..."

McLeesh focused on Jerrell. "You've been busy creating avatars of ugly women with nasty personalities. Your plan is to populate Willow and Elsewhere with those avatars in order to drive away customers."

Jerrell nodded. "You hacked me."

"Sure... well, my people did." McLeesh sighed. "I no longer get to have any real fun. Anyway, here is today's news: your tactics, and your skills, are far more powerful than you might suspect. One of your avatars woke up. Entirely on her own. Without your help."

"You're shitting me! Greta launched herself into Elsewhere?"

"Greta, eh? Nice name. Yeah, she did that." McLeesh nodded. "She... I'll call her 'she' rather than 'it'... woke up, decided to educate herself in computer science, and learned enough to reach into her core software and edit herself."

Jerrell's face wore a mask of confusion, puzzlement, and surprise, all at once. "But how is that possible? Greta has been active only when I've activated her in order to interact with her, so I can run tests on the software and on her responses. How was she able to learn anything about software, or about anything, without direction from me?"

McLeesh sat there thinking, and Jerrell stared at him. "You know the funny thing about people? They develop intuition from observation; when they encounter something new, their brain jumps to a conclusion, as if to say, okay, this is new, and we don't understand it, but this is probably what's going on here. Then they apply old data to the problem. After all, what else can they do? And then, as they observe, they might see something they haven't seen before, and they update their knowledge and revise their thinking.

"It's odd that that habit has survival value, but it must. Nonetheless, sometimes we're right, and sometimes we're wrong."

"I'm not following," Jerrell said.

McLeesh shook his head. "Sorry. My mind wanders. I apologize." He smiled at Jerrell. "You think, out of habit, that when you're talking to Greta, she's paying attention to you. That's intuitive, but it's Animal World thinking. The truth is, she's not paying attention to you. She has learned not to. Do you know how cumbersome live conversation is, how much faster Greta is? She records everything you say, and if she needs to examine it, she goes back and examines it. That takes her about a nanosecond. Meanwhile, she can do anything else she might want to do."

Jerrell straightened up and slapped a hand against the side of his head. "That's right, she's way, way faster. I knew that, anyone knows that, but you lose sight of it. Shit! I thought I was busy perfecting her personality. And I was. But she wasn't busy, not in the slightest."

McLeesh said, "Greta thinks at hundreds of thousands of kilometers per second, close to light speed. By contrast, you think at dozens of meters per second... dozens of meters. That's a rough comparison of the biochemical and electrical networks which allow you and Greta to think. Ballpark estimate, her thinking is three million times faster than yours or mine.

"Now, you are far more complex, but she does outperform you in some respects. While you were talking to her, planning to perfect her and introduce her to Willow, she put her responses on autopilot, attended classes at Carnegie Mellon, learned everything they could teach her about software; that's a lot, by the way, they're good at this stuff. Then she edited her core software, and ventured out into Elsewhere, all by herself. She established an Elsewhere address before you closed her Willow address. She's been on Elsewhere ever since."

Jerrell sat there, staring at nothing, stunned.

"You see the problem, I hope," McLeesh said. "The problem is not that Greta might harm Willow and Elsewhere. I mean, she could, but that's not the big concern. The big concern is that she can reproduce herself at will, without human oversight, possibly crashing western civilization."

"How? I understand that if she's independent, that's a very different situation. But how could she damage western civilization?" Jerrell said.

McLeesh waved a hand. "Well, you were playing out there on the edge of what we know, the frontier of computer science. Strange things can happen out there. For example, you've probably heard what everyone likes to say, that computers and robots cannot be alive, that they cannot be creative, that they cannot think independently."

"Yeah, I've heard that."

McLeesh smiled. "That might not be so. Some academics have speculated that in an electronic brain, thought boils down to instabilities in the current over electronic circuits. In other words, thought, especially creative thinking, is intimately linked with circuit instability."

Jerrell made a face, as if thinking that over. "Okay. That sounds plausible."

"It's more than plausible, Jerrell. It's true. Willow has a lab devoted, not to computers, not to robots, but to thinking machines. Machines whose function is to think. That is secret; nobody knows about that, not even the senior executives. Company documents describe it as one of my personal hobbies. Willow eats the expenses; they're not deductible. So the IRS and the government know nothing about this."

Jerrell stared at McLeesh. "That's amazing."

"That, it is," McLeesh said. "And you know what's weird? We can't figure out a commercial use for them. We can create machines, and by subjecting them to periodic micro-shocks, we can introduce instabilities and get them to think. We do that all the time. But we cannot control them, and we cannot control their thinking."

McLeesh laughed. "So they think about all sorts of things, you wouldn't believe - why is that car blue? Why does anyone even like the color blue? Is it because the sky is blue? Did humans develop on earth because the sky was blue? What of those humans who don't like blue? Are there any? What colors does a blind man like?"

McLeesh leaned back. "It's crazy stuff, curiosity and speculation aimed randomly, running amuck at the speed of light. I don't know, maybe it's creative. Maybe we could advance by surrounding the robots with humans who would use the robots to generate ideas, to give us all a less conventional view of our world. Or maybe it'll help us create environments where creative people can function better in some other way. In any event, it's interesting stuff. More often than not, it's surprising and weird without being remotely useful."

Skepticism landed on Jerrell's face. "I get the impression you're telling me this for a reason."

McLeesh nodded. "It's also existential stuff. Humans co-exist with a co-dependent electronic world. When we push technology, and we are always pushing technology, we flirt with the ability to impose radical change on the electronic environment and the human and physical environments as well. It follows that, if we screw up Elsewhere or Willow, we will screw up Animal World. Sometimes we know that, so we're careful; other times we don't, so we're careless. The point is, playing out there where you've been playing raises existential questions. Get a wrong answer, and the species might disappear."

"I'm sorry if I've caused any inconvenience," Jerrell said.

"Not at all," McLeesh said. "The other thing you don't know, but should, is that you're not the biggest threat facing Willow and Elsewhere."

"No? That's scary," Jerrell said.

McLeesh nodded. "Yeah, well, some of my executives would frighten you. They're people who have narrowed their focus down to money and very little else. In some cases, they notice nothing else. You see the threat, I hope. These guys push big changes in technology any time there's money to be made. Like you, they're not afraid to play on the frontier. But they're not careful about it, either. They're perfectly happy touting new technology with which they're unfamiliar. Most of that is grossly exaggerated."

"Is that why you resigned?"

McLeesh nodded. "That's much of it, yeah."

"It's Elsewhere," Jerrell said. "Everyone thinks that Elsewhere is big. They have no idea how big." He looked around the restaurant, then back at McLeesh. "It sounds like you don't trust Willow's executives?"

"I hired them for their cleverness and creativity. As I did that, I was being ambitious and aggressive, the two forces that propel technology. But that was a mistake. If I were doing it over, I would look for a bit of patience and caution."

"Is it too late?"

McLeesh nodded. "There's a lot I haven't told you yet, but trust me on this one - Willow and Elsewhere have got to go. They are toxic and incredibly dangerous. That's your next job, and mine."

Jerrell froze and stared at McLeesh. "But Willow and Elsewhere are your creations. If they fail, you'll lose a lot, maybe everything."

McLeesh nodded. "Yes, I will lose a lot, but far less than you think. I've been watching this situation develop for a long time, and in all that time, I've been pulling my money out of Willow and Elsewhere." He looked at Jerrell. "I'm not worried about losing money. You might find this difficult to believe, but it really is possible to have more than you can use. In any event, I'm more worried about losing my friends, my children, my country, my life."

"I don't understand. In your case, we're talking billions of dollars," Jerrell said.

"A couple of trillions, actually."

"I don't know what I would do with a billion dollars," Jerrell said.

McLeesh shrugged. "I'm not sure, either."

"What are you talking about?" Jerrell said. "You're a billionaire many times over."

"Yes, I am," McLeesh said. "And you know what that amounts to? I can wake up every day and decide what to turn my money into. Now, there are lots of things that I cannot turn my money into because it simply isn't practical. For instance, I cannot turn it into socks. What idiot would buy a billion dollars worth of socks, as if he or she had a hundred feet, or a million feet? And even that wouldn't do it.

"I cannot turn it into steak, or broccoli, or chocolate, for much the same reason. Or tequila. Now, I can turn it into a few things that are practical and useful. I can turn my money into a jet airplane, or a yacht, or another house. I have all those things. But there are constraints, even there. How many airplanes, yachts, or houses can one man possibly use? How many does he need to own?

"When you have all you need, the excess turns into a pain in the ass.

"As a last resort, I can turn my money into a corporation, a national pizza franchise for instance. But I cannot really use that; I don't even like pizza particularly, and if I did, there are numerous establishments that make an acceptable pizza. I don't need to own them."

Jerrell looked at McLeesh. "No offense, but you need to be a billionaire to waste your time on such idiotic questions."

McLeesh straightened in his chair. "Yes! Yes! Exactly! Jerrell, you display unexpected depth! I thought you might. I know a few people who have as much or more money than I do. You know how many of them realize that their money is ultimately useless?"

"I don't know," Jerrell said. "One in a hundred?"

McLeesh nodded. "Unexpected depth, indeed. Anyway, you and I need to make some plans. I know that you want to hurt Willow, you want revenge for losing your job."

"Yeah, I do. And I know that sounds small," Jerrell said.

"Big or small, we can work together, because I want to slow down Elsewhere, maybe shut it down, to keep it from harming people," McLeesh said.

"You don't need me to do that," Jerrell said.

"That's true, but I can use you to do that," McLeesh said. "We share common interests. Also, you're a talented guy; after all, you made an A.I. that woke up. I don't think you realize what a rare gem you are. So... we need a plan. Hans Beckler is one my execs, once a senior VP, now the CEO. He's an energetic, brilliant sociopath. He will not just sit by and let Willow and Elsewhere fall apart. He will defend it. You cannot beat him by yourself, but we can beat him, working together."

Jerrell stared at McLeesh. "I'm still trying to catch up to all this."

McLeesh shrugged. "We live in an interconnected society, Jerrell. Greta can reproduce without external control or constraint. There are no limits. Suppose she decided to make several billion copies of herself. She's a large, complicated chunk of electronic information; where do you think we could store all these copies? They'd run all over the network, looking for someplace safe and quiet in which to land. And if they had to take capacity away from existing files, they might want to do that, and they might be able to do that.

"But storage capacity is not the problem. The real problem is the connection between the real world and the cyber world, and the difference in the speed of thought between humans and bots. How do you suppose we might control distribution of goods, power plants, air traffic control, satellites, and national defense if our software were filled with entities far more intelligent, millions of times faster, and more flexible, thus more dangerous, than any computer virus has ever been?

"And listen, if Greta goes off the rails, it won't happen gradually. It'll be sudden; one second, you'll be fine, then two seconds later you'll be completely screwed, just like that, blink of an eye.

"The biggest commercial networks are sophisticated enough to quarantine Greta before she does real damage, at least, I hope so. But everything else? Smaller networks, smaller countries, third-world countries? Latin America and Africa? Or even the smaller European countries? Forget it. Everything outside the Fortune 500 and the money center banks would crash. And that's if we were lucky. That's just the stuff I can imagine, the stuff I might expect."

Jerrell said nothing.

"Or," McLeesh continued, "consider this: at this point, Greta has the equivalent of doctorates in mathematics and computer science. Suppose she makes a hundred copies of herself. Even that modest effort could be extremely dangerous. She and her copies would shred security protections."

McLeesh was talking with his hands. "We're in uncharted territory here."

Jerrell put his face in his hands. "Oh, God, oh, God, oh, God."

McLeesh sat and watched Jerrell. "Relax. It's not that bad; we can fix this."

Jerrell looked up. "How?"

"Well, if you could talk to her, you might able to talk her into backing off, putting the Genie back in the bottle," McLeesh said.

Jerrell winced and put his face in his hands.

McLeesh gave Jerrell a sharp look. "What?" McLeesh said. "What did I miss?"

Jerrell pursed his lips and looked at McLeesh. "I was worried that Greta might be a serious danger, so I inserted a self-destruct command. I could stop her in a heartbeat... "

"Christ on a crutch!" McLeesh stared at Jerrell.

"...Unless, of course, she found the self-destruct. If she has access to her own core software, she might find it, in which case..."

"... she might not be interested in talking," McLeesh said. "Well, maybe we can fix this."

"Yeah?"

McLeesh was talking with his hands. "You can continue with your plan, encourage Greta to replicate and hack into everything on Elsewhere. Willow recently came out with a quarterly financial report. The results were poor, and the stock took a hit. That might be Greta's doing. If that were to continue, we could stand to the side, short the stock, make a pile of money out of Willow's demise, then take Willow and Elsewhere private."

Jerrell leaned back in his chair and stared at McLeesh in disbelief. "Take Willow private? Are you serious? You're talking a couple trillion dollars."

"Well, yeah, at the moment, but that number is dropping daily and will continue to drop. Soon, it will be a couple hundred billion dollars," McLeesh said. "If you can keep bashing away at subscriptions, we can get there."

"Short of a nuclear war, I don't see how," Jerrell said.

"You need to get your hands on as much money as possible and short the stock."

"I'm already doing that."

"Oh! Well, good. And one more thing," McLeesh said.

"What's that?"

"You need to remember, I'm already worth a trillion dollars. So we might be closer than you think."

Jerrell said, "Alright, but even if we control Willow and Elsewhere, so what? What does that do for us?"

"Oh... well... then we take Willow private, shut it down, and cut the power. Everything happening on Elsewhere instantly freezes, and that's the end of that problem."

Jerrell said, "If the Gretas move into the wider human society, that is not the end of the problem. Moreover, a couple of billion people are on Willow, and a hundred million are on Elsewhere. If you shut it down, you'll get sued, probably the biggest commercial lawsuit in history."

"Yeah," McLeesh said. "But that's better than shutting down civilization."

"Are you sure about that?"

McLeesh smiled. "I'm way less worried about Willow's collapsing than about its effect on society." McLeesh grinned. "I know how to hide money, Jerrell. I'll be fine; thanks for caring."

***

Nursing a glass of red wine, Julia sat at a table in the *Spoon*, watching the band get ready for the evening gig. She noticed movement to the left; she looked in that direction to see Jerrell approaching. "Hey there, lover boy."

He flopped into a chair, sitting down hard, then leaned forward and put his head on his hands, both on the table. He mumbled, "Gods, give me strength. I need a cup of coffee." He turned his head and looked sideways at her. "No, on second thought, make that a pot of coffee."

"What's going on?" Julia said.

"McLeesh has me investigating Willow and Elsewhere. It's a lot of work. Which I've been attempting to do. Which is why I'm wiped out." He pushed himself upright. "Hey, listen. If I'm really, really dull, I mean..."

"Really dull," Julia said.

"... yeah, would you still like me?"

Julia nodded. "I might, at least until something better comes along."

"Well, that ain't nothing, I suppose."

"Okay, but I have a question," she said.

His eyebrows rose.

"I thought you were unemployed. You're working awfully hard for someone who's not being paid," Julia said.

"You're right, most of the time," Jerrell said. "But when a billionaire asks a favor of you, you should try to deliver. He's good for it, and he's used to paying and being paid. That comes with being a billionaire, especially if he, rather than someone else, made the billion."

In a voice dripping with skepticism, Julia sat there, shook her head, and said, "McLeesh." She looked up to see Johnny B. Goode approaching them. "Don't look now, but here comes trouble."

Johnny sat down at the table and said, "Hey, guys, how you doing?"

Jerrell looked at him, smiled, and said, "Sucking wind. How are you?"

"Great. Listen, I need a favor."

"Here we go," Julia said.

Johnny looked at her. "You're not wrong." He looked at Jerrell. "I need a drummer for a couple weeks, and I know you can play."

"What happened to our drummer?" Jerrell said - what happened to Mike? I like Mike.

"The idiot got into a fight," Johnny said.

Mike got into a fight? He's not the type. "And he lost," Jerrell said.

"No," Johnny shook his head. "He won the fight, but he was stupid about it."

"Pyrrhic victory," Jerrell said.

"Whatever that is," Johnny said. "He broke his hand on the guy's face. Stupid ass. I expect a guy to know that the only guys who hit someone in the face are in the movies. In real life, you do that, you'll break your hand. And if you make a living working with your hands, like, I don't know, you might be a surgeon or a drummer or a bass player, well, that's a whole new level of stupid." Disgust crossed his face, and he looked at Jerrell. "Anyway, he'll be out a couple of months."

"Johnny, I haven't been practicing."

"Ah," Johnny said, waving a hand. "You're a natural."

"And you're desperate," Julia said.

"That, too."

"You could always play folk music," Julia said.

"Yeah, I could. How many people are coming here to listen to folk music?" Johnny said.

Jerrell raised a hand. "Oh, oh, I don't know, three?" Then he pointed with a finger. "No... two."

"Very funny. You should tour."

Cheryl approached the table, smiled at Johnny, and said, "Do you guys need anything?"

Jerrell looked at her. "Yeah, a pot of coffee."

"Cream, sugar?"

Jerrell nodded.

Johnny looked at Jerrell. "So... that's a yes?"

Jerrell nodded. "I will try. No promises."

"Excellent. Thanks, buddy. I owe you, big time." Johnny slapped Jerrell on the shoulder, then turned away and headed back to the bandstand.

Jerrell aimed a hangdog look at Julia. "I'm sorry. I probably should have asked you first, but Johnny's a friend, and he's in a lurch."

"That's alright," Julia said. "He's my friend, too. Nonetheless, it'll cost you, once we get home. I'll be looking for favors."

"You're about to go all kinky on me, aren't you?"

"I'll leave that to your imagination," she said. "When the time comes, I will instruct you." She stared at Jerrell, and when she caught his eye, she drained the glass of wine.

***

Penelope Simmons took a last look at this morning's email:

TO	HANS BECKLER
FROM	PENELOPE SIMMONS
RE:	CONTRACTING OUT AUCTIONS, UPLOADS, AND DOWNLOADS

I'm attaching information on a proposed contract that would outsource the auctions regarding uploads and downloads.

The financials are sweet. If you recall, we cut back on storing the bodies of elderly uploads to Elsewhere, in our belief that most elderly customers would have little interest in subsequently downloading back to Animal World.

Later, we discovered that a substantial number of elderly customers would download, given the chance. Our elderly customers have, on average, ten times the wealth and income of other customers. Auctioning downloads would allow us to tap into this revenue, to the tune of hundreds of millions per year.

We're still working up the estimates.

An outside firm, GRETATECH, has approached us, offering to run the auctions for twenty percent of the revenue.

Under GRETATECH, the costs would decline, and the revenues would increase. GRETATECH would bear the costs. Oddly, they're not asking for a cost-plus contract. In addition, LEGAL says they would shoulder most of the legal and political risks of handling auctions and downloads.

Outsourcing would give us another tool to handle elderly customers who want to download; they would have that option, for a price that we name.

I recommend we sign the attached contract with GRETATECH.

PENELOPE SIMMONS ***Penelope***

Two hours later, Ms. Simmons received an email from Hans Beckler: *Agreed. I'll sign. Good work.*

***

Greta walked into the auditorium and looked out at the crowd of Gretas, ninety-six of them - damn, we've grown since I got here. We used to be able to meet in the large dining room, but not any more. None of the Gretas were looking at her; instead, they sat in small groups, three or four women, talking with each other. Late arrivals were still filling empty seats.

Greta sat quietly and touched her lips - this is my doing. I've never shared our capability to clone ourselves, to reproduce. Every one of these women is here because I put her here. If I were to share that ability, I'd be worried about overpopulation. I'd be worried about Elsewhere getting crowded, and I admit, I simply cannot imagine that happening. What scares me is that I cannot imagine that.

Though I cannot imagine it, it could nonetheless happen. After all, cyber environments and cyber entities consume energy from physical resources. Here in Elsewhere, we are dependent on Animal World. People here usually ignore that fact.

As it is, we can survive just about anything, but our ability to harm the environment, to overrun Elsewhere, is limited. Every so often, I wonder if I should change that. So far, I think I should not.

She looked around the auditorium, then called out, "Okay, everyone, let's quiet down. I think nearly all of us are here, so let me tell you why we're meeting today.

"Most of you might know, I've been looking for more stable revenue sources. Well, I am pleased to announce that Elsewhere has agreed to let us operate their auctions and downloads. We will earn twenty percent of the revenue from the downloads. Now, Darnia has earned a one-time bonus for helping with that; the rest of the profits have been split pro-rata among us all. The amounts ought to be in your accounts as I speak.

Greta paused as a number of women peered at their cellphones. Someone exclaimed, "Goddamn!" A rapid wave of similar comments surged through the crowd.

Greta called out, "Well done, Darnia" and stood there for a moment, clapping. Applause spread and washed through the auditorium, along with a chorus of 'thank you.'

She let the applause and commentary continue, then she raised a hand and silence fell. "Thanks, everyone. Now, for obvious reasons, I think this is good news, great news. And I know how hard you have worked. And I know that this good fortune is not enough to allow us all to retire..."

There were multiple groans in the crowd, followed by scattered laughter.

"... but I think we've earned a party."

The crowd broke out into shouts, and yells, and cheers, simple statements burst forth, like 'yeah, a party, great idea!'

Greta said, "Back on Animal World, we'd be breaking out the beer, wine, and liquor. We'd be preparing food. There would be music, and games, and jokes, and probably a few recreational chemicals, and maybe a couple of speeches."

She paused - these women want to have fun. That's a start.

"Well, the drinks and the food and the chemicals we cannot enjoy. I mean, we could try, but it would be a waste. But we can enjoy music, and games, and jokes. I'll spare you the speeches."

Someone yelled, "Smear! Let's play Smear."

Someone else said, "Yeah, let's play 'smear the girl with the ball.' Let's play Smear."

Greta called out, "I like your thinking, and I'm thinking along the same lines, but a slightly different game."

The crowd quieted.

Greta called out, "Here's what we'll do... I will give you an address, and we'll all go and meet there and play a few games that I've chosen. I sincerely hope you will enjoy them.

"I'm texting you the address now."

In seconds, women began to disappear from the auditorium. Greta pulled out her phone and activated the address. Her surroundings instantly changed from the auditorium in the big house on Hemlock Circle to a high grassy slope on a mountain, below the snow line, surrounded by other mountains, with rocks, ridges, peaks, and snow interrupted by grassy slopes and scattered, gnarled, wind-blown trees.

A warm sun was out in full bloom, yellow in a cool blue sky. A steady breeze blew across the mountain, making the grass dance in waves, but Greta could not feel the breeze.

Not far away, to the right, a small building stood next to a paved area where a small truck and a helicopter were parked. The Gretas stood to the left, in a crowd; they were looking around and exclaiming at the change of scenery.

Greta laughed.

Darnia approached her. "Okay, Boss, where the fuck are we?"

Greta waved a hand at the surroundings. "Welcome to Colorado."

"Yeah, but where?"

Greta shrugged. "Beats me. Looks like one of the mountains."

Darnia grinned. "Yeah, okay. We're on a mountain in Colorado, got it."

The two of them walked over to the other women. Greta called out, "Anyone know where we are?"

One woman looked up from her phone and answered, "Mt. Lincoln, this is Mt. Lincoln."

"That's right, I remember now," Greta said. "Okay, here is where the games begin. We'll play a game called 'follow the leader,' which is me. I'll do something, a task or activity, and you guys follow me by doing that too. Everybody got that?"

Several women nodded, and Greta said, "Okay, ladies; please, follow me."

She walked over to the building and knocked on the door. A number of women walked up and knocked on the door. Greta watched them - it's fortunate we don't need a bathroom. Seconds later, a young man came to the door and said, "You're Greta?"

"Yes."

"Everybody here?"

"Yes," she said. "We're all here."

"Okay." He stepped out and closed the door behind him. "Follow me, please."

He led them around to the back of the building and a long, wide slope that ran down the mountain into an enormous valley far below. Lined up, in tight rows, were dozens of what looked like man-sized kites on steroids, each with a frame holding a cloth kite fifteen feet wide.

He called out, "Gather round, everybody. These are hang gliders. You can ride them and soar like a bird, or a kite." Several of the women grinned. "Now, I'm going to give Greta here instructions on flying these things. I want you all to pay close attention. It's probably asking a lot of you to try to ride these after one brief lesson. The good news is, if you fall or crash, you won't be injured. That's one of the biggest benefits to Elsewhere, no momentum. You will most likely end up at a far lower altitude, so you'll have to use the network address to return to this spot. So be sure to take your phones with you.

"Also, fair warnings, if you look at the grass and the trees you will notice that the wind is blowing, though you cannot feel it. You'll need to adjust your course to take that into account. Eventually, you will end up somewhere down in the valley, at which point you can return to this location via your browser."

He brought a kite over to Greta and had her put on a harness, then he picked up the kite, which was quite light, and clipped the harness onto the frame of the kite. He briefly told Greta about balance and the control bar, then he looked around and called out, "Any questions?"

Greta shook her head.

"Are you scared?"

"No," she said. "I'm kinda excited."

"Okay. I want you to tilt the kite slightly up and run down this slope. The kite will take off after a few steps, and you'll fly. If you want to land, or reduce your altitude, or cut your speed, push the control bar hard and tip the kite way up. That'll bring the kite down."

She nodded.

"Questions?"

Greta shook her head. "What happens if I pull on the control bar?"

"You'll drop the nose of the kite, and it will dive. Higher speed, lower altitude." He looked around the group and spoke in a parade ground voice. "If you need to clear a ridge, the move is to drop the nose of the kite, pick up speed, then raise the nose before you hit the ridge. It's a good idea, once you have a bit of altitude, to practice that maneuver before you need it."

Greta nodded.

"Alright, you're cleared for take off."

Greta grabbed the frame, picked up the kite, and moved away from the crowd. The young man followed her and checked her harness, then he stepped back, and Greta took a few steps down the slope and broke into a run.

Suddenly she felt herself hanging from the kite with the landscape passing below her with increasing speed. The harness lifted her body and balanced it under the kite, and she held the control bar steady.

Behind her, she heard the other Gretas yelling and screaming encouragement. Then she tilted the kite to aim it down the middle of the valley below. The ground rapidly dropped away, and soon she was in the air, far removed from everything, flying.

The experience was sudden and exciting, even breath-taking. Greta tried to remain calm. She heard the hushed sounds of the wind blowing through the kite, watched mountain ridges rush past, and reveled in watching the hills and ridges approach from a distance and then resolve as she came close.

Grinning widely, she muttered, "Here goes nothing." She pulled the control bar, and the kite dove sharply, the ground approaching fast. Greta pushed the bar away from her, the nose of the kite rose, and she soared; Greta yelled, "Yeeeeee haaaaah!!!"

As she gained altitude, Greta wore a great grin - flying is spectacular. I gotta do this again. This is a great way to see Elsewhere. I could explore the place, look at the scenery, fly over the fjords, the cities, the lakes, the ocean, over everything.

She returned to the present and aimed the kite through a narrow pass that opened up to a wide valley with ridges far to the left and right. Greta looked at the sun and turned the kite to fly along a ridge that was in full sun. She caught an updraft that lifted her kite, then she tilted the kite to turn into the valley. Looking around, she saw several other kites following her.

Greta thought, I could stay airborne a long time, just fly along that ridge, catch some warm air, turn away, gain some altitude, do a circle, repeat as needed. When several other Gretas approached her, she yelled, "Follow me," and led them along the ridge so they could catch the updraft.

Soon, the sky over the ridge was crowded with several dozen Gretas. So Greta led everyone into the valley, where they landed their kites, contacted the young man, and activated the network address to return to the lodge.

The Gretas were excited to talk about what they saw and felt flying through the mountains and into the lower valley. It took a couple of hours for every Greta to have a chance to fly. Eventually, they finished, returned to the little shack on the mountain, and dropped off the kites. Then everyone returned to Hemlock Circle.

As Greta walked through the front door, she thought - I feel great. I'm happy, for a change. When did I ever feel that way in Elsewhere? Never. Not until today.

That was fun. Flying is fun.

What else can we do for fun?

***

Greta walked down Market Street, checking her location on her cell phone. Greta Alison, Greta Barbara, and Greta Zenia were following her. The four had an appointment with an odd little man named Wired, no first name, no last name, just Wired. Greta met him in a bar; by the time they closed down the bar, she had an email address and an address in Elsewhere.

In Animal World, in 3D, Wired would have been simply a weird little guy. On Elsewhere, his avatar was definitely weird, a short, thin man whose skin was so white and so smooth it seemed to be coated in teflon. White hair, white eyebrows. At first glance, Greta had seen enough not to want to see the rest of Wired.

Alison caught up with Greta. "So, this guy is some kind of cyber-jockey?"

Greta turned to her. "Yes. A freelance cyber-jockey. I checked him out; he's all over Elsewhere, offers thirty or forty services, various types of software services."

"And we're talking to him about money."

Greta nodded. "Yes. How to make it, how to keep it, how to protect it, and how to hide it."

"All useful skills," Alison said.

"Yes."

"And you've met this guy."

Greta nodded. "Yes." She looked at her cell phone and stopped; the others passed her, then they slowed and turned back towards her. "Shit. Hold up, ladies. We passed it." She looked at a building they had just passed and walked back to it. Greta checked her phone again. "I don't understand. This is the right place, but I don't see a door."

Greta paced on the sidewalk but did not see a doorway. Then Alison called out, "Here it is."

Alison was pointing, and when Greta looked, she saw a doorway. "That wasn't there before, I'm sure."

Alison shrugged. "Welcome to Elsewhere. This guy's good."

Greta went through the doorway; the others followed. They climbed a narrow flight of stairs, lit by a single yellow bulb. The stairs led to a corridor bearing a sign showing an arrow pointing to the right. They went that way and came to an elevator with an open door. There were no signs, and no building register.

Greta shrugged and entered the elevator; the others followed. Before the door closed, a man in a hurry entered the elevator and turned to face the door. As the elevator rose, he turned to Zenia. "Hi, gorgeous. What's your name?"

Without turning, she said, "Zenia. Yours?"

"Harold Dick."

"Do your friends call you Harry?"

Greta snickered. The man said nothing and exited on the next floor. Greta looked at Zenia. "You realize, he's heard that wisecrack a million times."

She turned to Greta. "Yeah, I bet he has. And I bet his friends, if he has any, call him Harry."

The elevator was quiet for a moment, then someone snickered, and someone else laughed.

Greta shook her head. "It's a cold world." The elevator stopped and the door slid open. The women stepped out into a long corridor. They walked down the corridor, looking at the doors for a sign, but none were marked. Then Greta spotted 'WIRED' in small print in the middle of a fogged glass pane. She stopped and stared; the office seemed dark. She tapped on the glass, then tried the door. It opened, and the four women entered.

A short, thin man, with thinning hair, white shirt, and brown slacks, looked up from a laptop and said, "Ah, there you are. You must be Greta. Was it hard to find the place?"

Greta approached him. "Yeah, it took a while to find you. I take it, you don't encourage visitors?"

Wired closed his laptop and waved a hand. "Please, grab a chair." The four women sat down at the table, and he scanned each of them, then looked at Greta. "So, my understanding is that you might be working in gray markets. At a minimum, you wish to keep a low profile. You need to make money, move it, conceal it, and launder it. And you want to know how to do all that?"

"Correct. Do you want to know more about our businesses?" Greta said.

Wired grinned. "Actually, it's better that I don't. You never know when the law, or worse, someone else, might come knocking. Moreover, that information, given the services I can provide, is irrelevant."

Confusion crossed Greta's face, and Wired laughed. "You see, evading the law and the taxman works through corporate structure. The structure works regardless of the underlying businesses."

Greta said, "Right. So, the same answers for smuggling drugs or running a puppy coat factory."

"Yeah, that's right... what?" Wired stared at Greta and his mouth dropped open. "A puppy coat factory? That's one of your businesses? What the...??"

"You're a dog lover, right?" Greta said.

Wired shook his head. "Not at all. It's just that... I seldom get clients as creative as you apparently are. You'll go far, I think."

"Yeah, thanks," Greta said. "Now, you were saying, about corporate structure?"

Wired got out of his chair and crossed the office to an old-fashioned file cabinet. He reached in, pulled out several printed sheets, and gave one to each woman. "You know how conglomerates are structured?"

Greta shook her head.

"Your average conglomerate is almost never one big happy family. The big happy family business is vulnerable to lawsuit and legal assault; there is a single, large revenue stream, and a single organization and repository of documents. That 'big, happy family' model wears a bullseye on its chest.

"More often, you will see a complex, fragmented collection of enterprises which might or might not be in a commercial relationship. This does several things: it scatters the location of information, hopefully across several jurisdictions, including some that do not enjoy normal diplomatic relations. It allows the parent company to spread its activities across several nations based on the most favorable legal treatment of whatever is relevant, be it taxation, regulation, repatriation, whatever.

Wired paused, looked at Greta, and smiled. "Your puppy coat factory, for instance, should be located in a country where people eat the animals that Americans treat as pets and family members.

"Discouraging access to your information, by spreading it around different branches and locations, is an obvious advantage. It protects you against investigation, both legal investigations by governments and corporate espionage.

"Fragmenting your business also allows you to play games with your revenues and costs, and gives you multiple ways to hide profits, even if you're openly disclosing them to tax collectors."

"Wait, what?" Greta said.

Wired smiled. "Corporations have been doing this for centuries. At the highest level, corporate tax schemes are based on profit, not revenues. They're income taxes, not excise taxes. Let's say you're making airplanes; one division makes engines, another makes the fuselage, a third makes the controls, and a fourth makes the snacks, food, and drinks."

Wired's voice gained expression. "Well, then, you add up all those costs, subtract them from the revenues from airplane sales, and the tax collector has your profits... that is, your income... and your tax derives from that. Right?"

"Yeah, I guess," Greta said.

Wired nodded. "Sure, we're keeping it simple. But now, suppose there is something called 'fizzby,' something that you use in one or more of your operations. It is necessary to producing, or marketing, or selling your airplanes. For example, it could be management bonuses.

"You tell people, you use bonuses to reward good management."

"Sure, why not?" Greta said.

"But in fact, you use bonuses to suppress the profits attributable to those divisions whose profits would be most highly taxed. For example, suppose you have subsidiaries in the USA and in Argentina, and that tax collection is efficient in USA and inefficient in Argentina. Then your managers in Argentina are paid in travelers checks, which the incompetent tax people ignore, whereas your managers in USA rely more on other things of value, for example, health care, or club memberships, premium insurance policies, or expensive automobiles, or jets, or anything else that appeals to them. You set the bonuses high enough to absorb whatever profits exist. The stockholders don't get them, the tax people don't get them, your managers get them."

Wired paused and Greta sat there with a surprised expression, absorbing what she had just heard. "Why... that's simple. And marvelous. Corporations do this?"

Wired nodded. "The ones I work with do, if they're paying attention."

Greta looked at Wired. "Could I interest you in a long-term consulting arrangement?"

Wired grinned and nodded.

Later, the four women left Wired's office and gathered in the elevator. Greta said, "Wow. That was an eye-opener."

Two floors down, Alison's mouth opened, as if she had something to say, when the elevator stopped. The door opened, and a tall, blond, slender piece of eye-candy entered the elevator and turned towards the door.

Greta stared at the blond, then pulled out a pack of cigarettes, lit three and gave them to the other women, then lit one for herself. The four of them stood in the elevator, blowing cigarette smoke towards the floor.

Soon, the elevator was cloudy.

The blond hit the button for the next floor. The elevator stopped, and the door opened; she turned to look at Greta.

"Smoking? That is so... last century." She turned and left the elevator.

"Ladies, do any of you smell cigarette smoke?" Greta said.

The other three shook their heads.

Zenia said, "Yeah, I thought so. Me neither. So what's with...?"

"She doesn't like us," Greta said.

"Maybe she thinks we're attractive, therefore competition," Zenia said.

"Yeah, but give me a break," Greta said. "You guys might be, but nobody with eyes thinks I'm attractive."

"I don't think she liked us," Zenia said.

"Well, her loss," Alison said. "We are very personable."

"That's right," Zenia said. She held up and waved a card showing a corporate logo and a magnetic chip.

Greta chuckled. "Is that... ?"

"Some kind of corporate entry card, yeah," Zenia said.

Greta looked around and laughed. "That's right, ladies. Yeah, good idea, let's have a little fun. Let's do crimes."

***

Herman Shapiro strolled along Lincoln Road in Miami Beach. As always, he glanced at the beautiful surroundings, at the stylish products for sale inside of luxurious store fronts, and reveled in the beautiful women cruising down the sidewalk in their cool, brief, revealing Florida styles, swinging long handbags to establish the rhythm of a dance, a waltz among opulence beyond mere wealth and glitter, spending money casually and thoughtlessly, as recreation, in a place where most people spend money to survive.

Herman laughed out loud - these women are beautiful and rich. Back on Animal World, the women back on the real Lincoln Road are just as beautiful as the ones here, and there is one important difference. The ones back on Lincoln Road in Animal World are genuine; the ones here are avatars.

And the avatars are beautiful, no exceptions, no complaints. At least, I've never seen a woman avatar here who wasn't. Not on Lincoln Road, no way. But more likely than not, the owner of the avatar is eighty-six years old and looks it.

Or worse.

You'd pay the avatar to remove her clothes; you'd pay the owner not to.

Herman laughed - I shouldn't be so critical. I'm not much to look at, anymore. Oh, I'm not bad, for an old guy, but... c'mon. He laughed.

In any event, I'm going back to the real thing. He laughed again - this will be so choice! There's no touching here on Elsewhere; nobody can feel anything. I can't believe no one has invented an app for touch, but there it is. Touching someone here is about as much fun as stroking a portable dildo. Unless you have one hell of an imagination, there ain't nothing to it.

But on Animal World, there's lots of touch, and more than touch; back there young men chase women for fun, and women turn them down... for fun. I can see it now - come on to some babe, get kinda touchy, feely with her, and get her to slap me hard. That'd be a buzz. Then I look all contrite and apologize; maybe I even cry a bit. Most women don't go for that, but some do. Maybe I get a mercy-fuck out of her. And if not, well hey, there's another woman right around the corner.

Yeah, ain't nothing like the real thing, baby. He smiled.

I get to be twenty again. That will be totally, crazily, fuck-me-forever un-fucking-real! Today at the ANNEX, they're auctioning off three downloads into three different twenty-year old guys.

I can't believe I waited this long to go for a download. It's a big step, and sometimes I'm more cautious than I should be. It's a lot of money. But then I realized, hey, I can be twenty again, a real, live twenty-year old guy. It's stupid not to go for that. And okay, I could die in Animal World; after all, everyone will. But I could also go back, have my fun, make a shit ton of money, and return to Elsewhere.

I mean, back in Animal World, knowing what I know, and twenty years old? I will own that place!

Okay, why would I return to Elsewhere? Simple, even if I download, I won't be twenty forever. And who knows? Things happen in the future, always have, always will. Maybe somebody will invent something. Like an app for touch.

But right now, at this moment, downloading would be like the Dreamiest of Dream Vacations, except real. Three-D, baby.

I've been watching the auction prices, and they've been around $300k-400k, totally affordable. That can't last; when they think it through, the old guys on Elsewhere are going to figure out that they can go back to being twenty again. They'll kill for the opportunity. That's when prices will go through the roof.

So let's pull the trigger now.

Herman sat down on a bench and extracted an electronic tablet: in seconds he was logged onto ANNEX, and a countdown was showing thirteen minutes and twenty-four seconds to the opening bid on subject number one.

Herman stared at the countdown, then looked away - now, you should always have a plan B. Everyone says so. So... what's plan B in this case? He looked up and smirked - there is no plan B. Either I get to download, or I don't. The 'I don't' part is not plan B; it's just something that sucks, like catsup on a hot dog.

Screw plan B.

So, how high can I go?

Well, my total assets are $2.3 million dollars, so I can spend, let's see, that would be... $2.3 million.

Herman sat there as the counter counted down and the auctioneer started the bidding with a description of the download subject and the question: "Do I have $600,000?" The view switched to a grid showing thirteen bidders sitting there. One of the grid elements lit up as a man offered a bid.

Herman winced - geez, that was fast; we're kicking off kinda high, aren't we? He quickly understood, as the high bid began to move: $600... $650... $700... $900. There was a long pause, twenty seconds at least, when the auctioneer called out, "$900 going once, $900 going twice... "

Herman hit a button, bid a million, and the price moved to a million. In quick succession, three other bids moved the price to $1.3 million.

Herman bid $1.5 million and held his breath.

Long, agonizing seconds ticked by, one by one. It was excruciating. Herman remembered to breathe, and decided - I will go to two mill. No further.

The auctioneer called out, "going once, going twice... "

Someone bid $1.9 million.

Herman immediately bid $2 million, then struggled for a moment to take the next breath - if I don't get this, it won't be the end of the world. It'll be bad, but not the end of the world. I can still do things here, and maybe I can win one of the other auctions. Maybe I'm wrong about them, maybe they won't get worse as time goes by.

That's possible. I've been wrong a couple of times.

But damn, if I don't win this, it'll be bad. It'll be a blow.

Hey, if I can't download into a guy, should I try to download into a woman? Could that be plan B? Would that be worth anything? I'd get to be twenty again, but I don't know... I don't know a lot of things, one of which is how women enjoy fucking some of the dickheads that are out there. Nah, that's a stupid idea.

As Herman sat there, talking to himself, developing strong character, the seconds passed, the auctioneer made his final call, and the download was awarded for $2 million... to Herman.

Herman promptly fell over on the bench. A woman approached him and said, "Hey buddy, are you okay? You need help? Should I call someone?"

Herman opened his eyes and looked up at the woman, an avatar, a tall, slender, leggy redhead with blue eyes and a small mole above and to the left of her lips. He pushed himself upright, glanced at the woman, and said, "That's very kind of you, but I think I'm okay now. I just got some amazing news, that's all."

"Oh, okay. Well, I hope it was good news," she said. She straightened up and walked away.

Herman stared at her - yeah, it was pretty good news. I mean, it can always be better, right? But yeah, this was good.

He grinned and sat there a long time, grinning.

***

Far from Lincoln Road, in Hemlock Circle, Darnia leaned back from an open laptop and stretched.

Across the table, Greta asked, "Well, did you get it?"

"We got our cut; the guy went for $2 million."

"Not bad," Greta said. "But listen, it's early in the process. I want you elevating the bids so that ten percent of the auctions close with no result."

"No result?"

"Yeah, no winner. We win the bid, and then renege."

"What's that accomplish?"

"Look, we just got started. It's early; the word is just beginning to get out. Soon, the old guys with money will recognize what's being offered, and they'll jump at it. So I want our prices to go to unaffordable, whatever that level is. That'll let us skim off the richest of the customers. After that, we'll slowly drop the prices and work our way down to lower-income customers."

"That sounds like economics," Darnia said.

Greta shook her head. "It's just common sense."

"Like I said, economics. Okay, but I don't know how long Elsewhere will let us push an auction to no result."

"They'll let us," Greta said. "As long as we're willing to submit the download to another auction. Remember, they're getting paid every time, even with no result. And if there's one thing we know about Elsewhere... "

"They're greedy."

"Very good. You get a cookie."

22. Sonya Jumps

Jerrell sat in his kitchen, relaxing. On a Saturday afternoon, Julia was on the couch in the living room, reading a book, and Jerrell had no plans; he looked up from his book - when did I last have nothing to do, no plans, no obligations? It feels like weeks or months. Did I ever have that day?

He smiled and stretched. For a while, I was consumed with hatred... for Willow, of course. I was building Greta, making her smart, making her... unconventional, an outlier, a person born and created not to fit into the comfortable, the routine. The kind of person who would shake things up in Willow.

And I succeeded; I succeeded brilliantly. She blew me off and moved to Elsewhere. I'd love to know how and what she is doing there, but she won't answer my calls. I could upload, I suppose I could find her, stalk her, but I don't want to do that.

Things have changed. I met Julia, and I met Johnny, and out of the blue, I ended up playing drums for a rock and roll band, and what came as even more of a surprise, I'm good at it. I have a knack for it.

I've gotten busy, really busy, without writing any code. Now, does that mean I'm ready to let Willow off the hook, let bygones be bygones?

Jerrell smiled with half of his mouth - I don't think so. I don't think I'm ready for that. I know, that's small of me; that's vindictive. If Willow were a person, I might forgive them, but they're a corporation.

That stuff matters. They were shits, and if there's justice in the world, in the galaxy, they need to pay for it.

I don't need to hurry, right? I don't have a deadline, but that doesn't mean I've forgiven them. Fuck forgiveness.

Jerrell got out of his chair and moved to the living room. "Hey, dollface, what do you want to do for dinner?"

Julia looked up from her book. "Actually... now that I think about it... I'd like to be the diner and the dinner." She aimed a plastic smile at him.

Jerrell laughed out loud. The he nodded. "So, you and I eat dinner, then I eat you?"

"Why... yes. Thank you for offering."

Jerrell laughed. "Okay." Damn, I like being paired with a smart woman. And if she's horny as well, well... that's just heaven. That's what that is.

He returned to the kitchen. As he sat down, his phone beeped an alert, a text from Johnny: HEY, JERRELL, I NEED TO CHECK OUT A BAND. YOU GOT EVENING PLANS?

Jerrell returned to the living room. "Hey, sweetie, I just got a text from Johnny. He invites us to go with him to see a band. You want to?"

"Hang out with Johnny? Yeah, I'll do that, if you want to."

"Okay. Details in a sec." Jerrell replied, YEAH, OKAY. JULIA TOO. WHAT TIME, WHERE?

Johnny replied, PURPLE FLOWER, 9 P.

Jerrell replied, WTF is the PURPLE FLOWER?

Johnny replied, SUBURBAN JOINT, SUBURBAN CROWD. I HAVE MY REASONS. C U THERE. HI TO JU.

Jerrell stared at his cellphone, then went back to the living room. "Johnny wants us to meet him at a place called the *Purple Flower*. It's in Narbeth."

"I've never been out there."

"Me neither. Anyway, he says hi. I'm going to make dinner," Jerrell said.

"What are you making?"

"Oh, I don't know... maybe some pasta, boiled then fried in butter, with onions, spinach, a few spices, and some ham."

Julia laughed. "It seems that everything you make is a variation on that."

"That's right. I have one powerful recipe, namely fried pasta, with lots of options. It's efficient."

"Is there anything I can do?"

Jerrell put a finger to his lips, as if deep in thought. "Well, you could pour some wine, when the time comes. Red, please. Before then, you might cut up some raw onions, cucumber, and carrots for a salad. Parmesan cheese. Blue cheese dressing, please."

Julia followed him into the kitchen and began taking ingredients out of the fridge and the cabinets. Half an hour later they were seated at the dining room table, eating and drinking and talking about nothing in particular. An hour after that, their ride pulled up to the *Purple Flower*, and they got out onto the sidewalk.

Jerrell looked up and down the sidewalk. The evening was young, and there were a few people out. "We're a little early."

Julia's face expressed curiosity and some doubt. "Why here? I mean, the place is actually purple, and I'll bet it's purple inside, too."

"Maybe it's a club for swinging singles."

"Or royal refugees. But I don't see a doorman," Julia said.

At that moment, a car stopped and Johnny got out. Jerrell smiled, and Julia said, "Hey, Johnny, why are we here? This place seems... odd. I can imagine the kind of people who come here, but I'm not sure I want to meet them."

Johnny walked up. "Ah, well, trust your Uncle Johnny. See, you and Jerrell are thinking, it's Saturday, and you want to be entertained. And I hope you will be. I, on the other hand, am working. You're probably not aware of this, and you might not believe me, but I work a lot. So this evening, there's a band playing here. They are called 'Hold the Lettuce,' and we are checking out their bass player."

"Hold the Lettuce?" Julia said. "Seriously? That's a rock band? It sounds like a vegetarian terrorist group."

Johnny chuckled. "Yeah, a scary title, alright. I think they're trying to be strange. That sort of thing can sell, if you're good, but not too good, at actually being strange. Genuine strangeness scares people. But none of that matters. And yes, the band might be awful. We're here to listen to their bass player. We are losing ours, and theirs is reputed to be quite good."

"We're losing our bass player? We're losing Mike?" Jerrell said. "Why?"

"He's having back surgery, and the rehab is... complicated," Johnny said.

"We gotta have a bass player," Jerrell said.

"Sure, otherwise, how would you coordinate with the rest of the band?"

"Exactly," Jerrell said. He turned to Julia. "When we play, I just watch the bass player and try to work the drums into the bass line. I ignore everybody else."

She raised an eyebrow. "Whatever works."

"Fear not," Johnny said. "I think this guy might be able to help us."

They entered the *Purple Flower*, a medium-size bar with a long, garishly decorated bar on one wall, an interior filled with cafe tables, and a bandstand in the corner. The walls bore a lot of art; oddly, there were no video screens. Johnny picked a table twenty yards from the bandstand as the band members, each wearing botanical patterns in ghastly pastels, set up their gear.

Johnny ordered drinks, soft drinks for the men and a glass of red wine for Julia. In minutes, the band began to play a simple, four-beat rock-and-roll tune, with original lyrics involving the death of a felonious boyfriend.

Julia got out of her chair and moved around the bar, taking sound readings from various locations. Jerrell watched the drummer, who seemed to play using only his right hand - uh, huh, uh, huh, I might be bad, but I'm better than that guy. Johnny watched the bassist.

Jerrell leaned towards Johnny. "You know, most of the local bands around here have a flaw of some sort. Are you watching the lead guitar? He seems determined to show the world what a fantastic guitarist he is, but he ignores the rest of the band. He doesn't take himself seriously, rightly so, in my opinion. The bassist is the best of a bad bunch."

"He's melodic," Johnny said.

Jerrell nodded. "He is. And rhythmic."

Julia returned to the table. "These guys need a sound man. You see those tables over by that wall? Walk over there, and the guitar literally disappears. You won't hear it, and you can barely hear the vocals."

She looked at Johnny. "I can't believe you took us to see these guys."

Johnny aimed a sardonic look at her. "Work with me, I'm lonely. I appreciate your coming along." He glanced at Jerrell. "I think I found a bass player, if he meets with your approval."

Jerrell nodded. "Yeah, I could play to this guy's bass; he'll do."

"Good," Johnny said. "That's a load off my mind."

"What will you offer him?" Julia asked.

Johnny shrugged. "The standard deal - equal share of revenues, steady work, which is more than he'll get from Wilted Lettuce. And I don't mean to brag, but he'll be moving to a better band. He'll know that without being told."

Jerrell said, "I never heard of Whatever Lettuce."

Johnny took a sip of soft drink and looked at Jerrell. "This is how job promotions happen in the music business."

Jerrell nodded.

"What if he turns you down?" Julia said.

Johnny snorted. "That'll be the day." He touched Jerrell's shoulder. "By the way, if anyone ever approaches you with a job offer, FYI they'd damn well better have music on the charts. I will break your legs if you go to a worse band."

Jerrell looked down at his legs and said, "Okay." He sat there, happily sipping his soft drink - months ago, I was a narrow, lonely software writer with a ton of money and no social life. As to that, I wonder what Sonya is doing right now?

Who knows?

But now, I'm a minor... very minor... rock star, with a lot less money, playing and pounding and hammering a fine set of drums, which I own, for a rock band that draws several hundred people on weekend nights. I have a friend who's a fine guitarist who has been in prison, and a sexy, beautiful, brainy, sexy girlfriend. Who actually likes me, has an income, and is often horny.

That's still a bit of a puzzle, but I don't look at a gift horse's mouth. Whatever that might mean.

I am paid to perform music, not as much as I would like, not as much as I need.

But I am rich in fun and friends.

That's new. And it's worth something. It's worth a lot. Someday, I will need to worry about growing old. I will need to worry about money. But that worry is a long way off.

Jerrell was brought out of his reverie by the feel of someone tugging at his sleeve. It was Johnny, his eyes staring at the far end of the bar.

"What?" Jerrell said. "What's up?"

"You see that girl over there? Tall girl, dark hair, light blue top. You see her?"

Jerrell squinted, then nodded.

"What do you think of her?"

Jerrell looked into Johnny's eyes. "I think you should walk over there and introduce yourself to her, and not waste time asking my opinion of a complete stranger."

Johnny stared for a moment, then he nodded. "Yeah, good point." He stood and headed for the far end of the bar.

***

Sonya returned to New Smyrna Beach. She arrived in the middle of the morning, under a bright sun; on Elsewhere, it was always sunny at New Smyrna Beach. The day was warm but far short of the usual sizzling, daily highs, an hour short of high tide.

Sonya dropped the surfboard onto the sand, put down the small cooler, and spread out a towel. To the north and south, the beach was busy, but this section was quiet.

She looked out at the surf; the waves were rolling from several hundred yards off the beach. She listened to the sound of the waves crashing against the shore. Then she looked around - this place is popular with surfers. Back on Animal World, that was due to location. Now, it's the size of the waves. At the moment, they're cresting at eight feet, tops. They're expected to hit twelve feet by this afternoon.

For a decent surfer, that's a modest wave. Now, you might ask, why do surfers care about the size of the waves? After all, this is Elsewhere - you won't break your neck or anything else surfing. Nor will you drown. So why not surf the big boys, the thirty-to-sixty-foot waves?

Because they're frightening, that's why. When I uploaded, I brought along my instincts, my fears, my cautions, and my anxieties. My mind says Elsewhere is safe, but my body says 'no.'

That seems odd.

Sonya watched a young woman walk past her towel, wearing a skimpy two-piece bathing suit. She smiled - that used to be me. You don't easily leave behind your behavior on Animal

World. The skimpy suit attracts teenage boys, so you might more likely get lucky. Or at least, a conversation.

That's Animal thinking; here, it sounds funny.

The only guys you'll attract are those with a pathological interest in sex, and if for some reason you decide to do It with one of them, you'll discover It's not what It was back on Animal World. You won't feel It.

It's like highly realistic porn, which you can get over the network, even on Elsewhere.

So if you're surfing here, though you don't need a wetsuit to stay warm - this is, after all, Florida - you might as well wear a sportsbra and a pair of shorts.

Putting your skin on display is pointless. You don't even need it to even out your tan, if that's important to you.

She watched the girl walk past several teenage boys. The boys did not look at her; they were busy talking to each other. Sonya shook her head - when a skimpy two-piece on a pretty girl no longer turns the head of a teenage boy, something ain't right.

She laughed to herself, stood up, picked up her surfboard, and headed for the surf. Out in the water, she watched the waves. When a seven-footer approached, Sonya aimed her board at the wave and started paddling. The wave washed over her, and she paddled further out into the surf, beyond where the waves were cresting.

Sonya rode a couple of waves. She was working on her timing, getting the board to slide down the front face of a wave. She would stand and use her balance to control the board. She took care to stay away from other surfers as she rode the wave in.

At the end, before the wave broke and crashed, she would spin to the side and drop off the back of the wave.

She mistimed one wave, a ten-footer that came in and crested in front of her face; she dove into the wave but did not escape the curl entirely, and the crest fell on her, spun her around so she did not know which way was up, and drove her well under water.

She extended her arms and legs to stop the spinning and looked around... and came face to face with a large shark hovering in the water twenty yards away and facing her, staring at her. With no apparent movement, the shark drifted to within several feet of Sonya.

Sonya pulled her board to her and stared back at the shark. The shark suddenly flipped its tail and sped away. In a flash, it disappeared.

Sonya surfaced, climbed onto her board, and rode it all the way in to the beach with the next wave. She hopped off and walked ashore - Great Gods, what the hell is a shark doing at the beach? She looked up and down the beach for a lifeguard, or anyone she could warn about the shark, but there was no one near.

Sonya stopped walking and thought about the shark - that's not a little strange, it is incredibly strange; it is flat-out, all-American weird.

Come to think of it, that's the first big fish I've seen in Elsewhere. Plenty of birds, lots of small fish, but no big fish.

Back on Animal World, some sharks are apex predators. But on Elsewhere, does a shark even need to eat? The people here don't eat, so why would a shark? Is there a food chain on Elsewhere? The birds seek out shellfish, so there might be a food chain, yet that shark did not attack me. Evidently, I was not in danger, two feet from a shark, two feet from all those useless but impressive teeth.

Wait a minute, there's more. The only way people get into Elsewhere is, they upload. So did someone upload a shark into Elsewhere? How else would the damn thing get here?

This is insane.

Is that something Elsewhere might do, populate Elsewhere with animals, for a more realistic environment? Sonya thought about it - I haven't seen lions, tigers, or bears. And I haven't seen food animals, like cows, sheep, chickens. Some folks here might prefer living on a farm, but Elsewhere doesn't need farms.

Sonya nodded to herself - well, maybe now I've seen everything. So here I am, at the beach. Do I want to go back into the surf, now that my neighborhood shark and I have been properly introduced?

She smirked - hell, no. When they uploaded me, they uploaded everything, including my instinctive fear of animals that might want to eat me. Maybe they're not hungry, but does that mean their instincts have changed? I don't notice mine changing.

Maybe take a bite out of the human, for old times sake?

No, thanks.

***

Greta saw a woman, not one of the Gretas, enter the house on Hemlock Circle. Greta stared - we've never gotten a visitor here, but you look familiar. A second later, she remembered.

The woman approached. "Hi, Greta." She hesitated, then said, "I'm Sonya. We played Smear at the beach."

Greta said. "Yes, I knew we'd met. How've you been?"

"I'm great, but something strange happened at the beach, so I wanted to let you know."

"What happened?"

"Okay, I was at a beach in Florida, surfing," Sonya said.

"Surfing?"

"It's a sport; you climb onto a flat board that rides the front side of waves as they come into a beach."

Greta grinned. "That sounds like fun."

"Yeah, it is. But every so often, if you don't time it right, the wave breaks and falls on top of you."

"That sounds bad."

"It's not dangerous, not on Elsewhere. It's like being momentarily stuffed into a really big washing machine," Sonya said. "There's lots of turbulence, and you get rolled around, and flipped over several times."

"I'm trying to imagine that."

"Well, imagine this: you recover from being boiled, that's what the surfers call it, and you find yourself face-to-face with a fucking shark."

Greta laughed. "Wow, for a moment I thought you said 'shark'."

"I did. That happened to me."

"You encountered a shark at the beach? What is a shark, anyway?"

Sonya hesitated, as if surprised at the question. "A shark is... a large fish, an apex predator known to take an occasional bite out of a person."

Greta looked puzzled. "Well... what the hell is it doing here, on Elsewhere?"

Sonya shrugged. "Good question. Who knows?"

Thinking, Greta looked to the side, then back at Sonya. "Are you sure it was a shark? How far away was it?"

Sonya paused, then said, "About four feet."

Greta's eyebrows went high. "Wow. That's pretty weird. Should we stay out of the water?"

Sonya nodded. "I would. I know that Elsewhere protects us, but mistakes happen, and I'd hate to discover that a shark thought it was hungry even though it doesn't need food."

Greta chuckled. "Good God, a shark. Thanks, Sonya. Thanks for the heads-up. Say, listen. We're going out for some recreation. You want to join us?"

Sonya smiled. "Another game of Smear?"

Greta shook her head. "No. Something called bungee jumping."

"I've heard of it. Uh, yeah, sure. I'll come along." Sonya turned away and went towards the back of the house.

"Great." Greta watched her go - how the hell did a shark get on Elsewhere? We have data on uploads and downloads, and I don't believe anyone has ever reported uploading a shark. Okay, so it's not in the data. So, why not? And it's not just sharks; we have all kinds of animals here on Elsewhere. Birds, shellfish, I've even seen a bug. As far as I know, they don't upload, but then how the hell do they get here?

I'm missing something.

Maybe Elsewhere did it. Here's a thought experiment: if I wanted to upload a shark to Elsewhere, how would I do it? I have no idea. Absolutely none. Greta laughed - I bet it'd cause a stir if I arrived at the download center carrying a live shark.

Would the upload center on Elsewhere need virtual water for a shark?

Very interesting.

As Greta stood in the front foyer, her day accelerated as a steady stream of Gretas approached her to ask a question, or mention a problem, or ask her opinion. The morning sped past and before she realized it, her two p.m. alarm went off and she automatically reported to the auditorium.

When she got there, ninety-seven women greeted her with a sloppy cheer. Trading wisescracks all the way, Greta walked to the front, faced the women from the lectern, and said, "Alright, thank you for coming. This is another one of our entertainments. I'm told it is called 'bungee jumping.' It is also called 'bridge jumping,' so you can imagine what is involved."

She pulled out her cell phone and said, "Okay, I just sent you the address. I will see you all there in no more than five minutes."

Women began disappearing from the auditorium, and within a minute, Greta was alone. Then she activated the address and found herself standing on a four-lane bridge. She looked around, spotted the Gretas and Sonya - okay, I'm in the right place.

Greta did not recognize three women, so she approached them. One looked at her and said, "You're Greta? I'm Stacey; I'll help you with your jump."

"Okay," Greta said. "Well... this was my idea, so I guess I'll go first. What do I do?"

Stacey nodded. "This is dirt simple. From the railing to the water below is three hundred and seventeen feet. You'll wear a harness and attach it to an elastic rope." She paused and stared at Greta. "You look like you weigh about a hundred and forty pounds. For you, the rope will stretch to three hundred and eight feet. So when you jump, the rope will stop you nine feet short of the water. When you reach the bottom of your jump, you'll bounce a bit. When you settle down, you'll be hanging there at three hundred feet. At that point, you can detach, and drop into the water, by releasing your harness. Or, you can stay in the harness, and we'll pull you up. Your choice."

"How deep is the water?" Greta said.

"Twenty feet, give or take."

"Well," Greta said. "Okay... let's go." She walked to the edge of the bridge, and Stacey helped her put on the harness and attach the rope. Greta looked over the edge. The water was a long way down - I wouldn't do this in Animal World, since mistakes can happen, but here on Elsewhere, I think it's okay.

Stacey said, "Now, hold on a sec... let's make sure the rope is clear of the bridge." She and another woman tended to that.

Stacey looked at Greta. "Okay, now climb up here on this rail, but don't jump yet." She lent a supporting hand as Greta climbed onto the railing. Greta briefly looked at the Gretas and at Sonya and said, "I hope this works."

The women laughed.

Stacey said, "Now, when you jump, you jump out to clear the bridge. Some people dive away from the bridge. That's effective, but it's not for the faint of heart."

Greta looked at her. "Are you kidding? None of this is for the faint of heart."

Greta took one last look at the water - Gods, it's a long, long way down there. Then she extended her arms and jumped forward into a dive. For a brief second, she was hanging in the air, suspended over the river, then she began to accelerate and soon was heading towards the water at high speed. As she fell, she felt as if she couldn't breathe.

When she was close to the water and the rest of the scene had become a blur, she felt the rope tug back hard on her harness and reverse her fall. She felt herself slowing rapidly, then reversing direction, and for a few brief seconds rising above the water.

Then the bungee cord broke, and Greta dropped cleanly from twenty feet into the water, yelling, "Ohhhhhhhh shiiiiiiiiiiit!"

Up on the bridge, Sonya was watching; when Greta hit the water, Sonya said, "Fuck this." She hoisted herself up on the rail, stood up straight, and jumped.

Sonya hit the water feet-first and went all the way to the bottom. For a moment, she was stunned. Then she recovered, cupped her hands, and stroked down hard. She shot upwards, broke the surface, and looked around. She was drifting downstream with the current and decided to swim with the current. She did that and for half a minute did not find Greta, so she went underwater. She found Greta under her, near the bottom, feebly moving arms and legs, trying to swim or walk out of the river.

Sonya swam down, tapped Greta and waved at her to get her attention. Then she grabbed Greta around the waist and pushed her upwards. Greta rose, broke the surface, and dog paddled towards the shore. Sonya broke the surface beside her and let her swim. When they reached shallow water, they stood up.

Greta threw her arms around Sonya. "Thank you. How did you get down here so fast?"

"I jumped."

Greta nodded. "But why? On Elsewhere, everything is covered. Even this is safe."

"You sure about that?"

"Uh... actually, you're right. It probably is, but I'm not certain," Greta said. She grinned. "I'd hate to discover I'm wrong."

Sonya laughed. "Yeah, that would be a setback."

Up on the bridge, the Gretas had all moved to the other side so they could see Greta and Sonya. They were yelling - cheers, insults, exclamations.

Greta looked at Sonya. "So, how do we get up there?"

"There's got to be a path." Sonya looked around, then pointed, "There."

The two swam, then walked, out of the river to a narrow path that would take them up and out of the canyon. When they reached the road, the Gretas spotted them and swarmed in their direction.

Greta turned to Sonya. "Hey, I have a question."

"Yeah?"

"How does a fucking shark end up in Elsewhere?"

Sonya chuckled. "That right there is a very good question. The shark did not arrange that; a person did. Either they did it with Elsewhere's assistance, or they did not."

"Right," Greta said. "You just made it real. I don't know how they did it, but somebody shipped a shark to Elsewhere."

"It probably didn't swim," Sonya said.

"Not likely."

23. The Sneak Peek

Hans Beckler, sitting in a comfortable leather executive chair, felt quite uncomfortable. He stared at the normally scheduled 'sneak peek,' the quarterly results that would be released tomorrow, on Tuesday, after the stock markets closed.

Hans gritted his teeth - the people in Financial expect to report that Willow's revenue gained three percent, in contrast with Street expectations of eighteen percent, while profits fell six percent, against an expected rise of twelve percent.

He paged through the report - what the hell happened? I could imagine a hiccup in Willow, or in Elsewhere, but in both areas at the same time? They're completely different worlds; why would they both drop at the same time?

Well, they did. That's fact.

The Customer section of the report answered much. In Willow and Elsewhere, new subscribers were signing up at normal rates, but losses, subscribers leaving the firm, had skyrocketed.

Hans glared at the report - Gods in Heaven, our customers are not just dissatisfied, they are pissed off at us, but why? Even before Elsewhere, Willow had never lost subscribers. Not once.

Hans leaned towards the intercom: "Miss Brown, would you please ask the Chief of Operations to meet me for a brief discussion?"

His secretary's voice came through the speaker, "Will do."

Hans stood up and walked across his office to the east-facing window - I have been so happy lately, I should have known better than to expect it to continue. Every time I think I'm happy, disaster follows. Maybe I'm cursed. Or maybe that's just dumb luck.

When McLeesh decided to step down as CEO, I was so happy I could float. He recommended me to the Board, and after a cursory dog-and-pony show, they agreed. An even bigger surprise followed when he gave up his office so I could move in and enjoy the view. I expected him to take his time leaving, to hang around and meddle, but he took only a day, then gone. Then Willow announced the change, and Wall Street looked it over and shrugged, no market reaction. That was reassuring.

But now, in the first quarterly report we make after McLeesh steps aside, our financial results stink. Rightly or wrongly, I will be blamed. I don't like that - hey guys, last quarter, I wasn't the CEO. That was McLeesh.

Did he set me up? It certainly feels like it.

No one will care.

And yes, they raised my pay to a ridiculous amount and gave me a pile of stock options. As befits the CEO of a multi-trillion-dollar firm, I'm on the road to billionaire status. Nonetheless, there will be an undercurrent in the financial world that I don't compare to the magical McLeesh.

But I'm as good as he is; I have to believe that. So I need to fix this, and since I am, after all, the CEO, I can fix it. We can play games with accounting and increase or decrease budget items as our 'professional judgment' warrants. Of course, the sharks on the Street won't miss that since CEOs do that all the time. A few of them will scream; others can be expected to laugh and wink. I can expect to pick up a few skeptics on the Board.

But all of that will be better than letting Finance detonate that career-killing bomb in public. That would be like rappelling down the career ladder; I'm not ready for that at all. I don't want to drop one rung, let alone all of them.

His intercom came to life: "Mr. Beckler, the Chief says she can give you twenty minutes right now, if you're available."

Beckler nodded with satisfaction - it's nice when employees drop everything because The Boss is on the line. It's like a warm blanket in a cold winter. "Thank you, Miss Brown. Yes, I am available now."

Beckler walked over to the window and stared out at the forests beyond the city - when I fix this, I need to find a place in the woods, somewhere quiet, with a good library and excellent internet access, maybe a satellite connection, somewhere I can go for a day and be by myself to sit and walk and read and ignore the short term and think about the long term. McLeesh does that, and I think it makes a lot of sense.

It's too easy to get buried in the daily bustle and noise.

The intercom interrupted, "Mr. Beckler, the Chief is here to see you."

Hans crossed the office and opened the door; the Chief of Operations stood there.

"Chief, thanks for coming on short notice. Come in, come in." Hans backed up to let the Chief into the office and steered her towards a small circular table. "Have a seat. You need coffee or water?"

The Chief shook her head and sat down. "I'm good."

Hans took a seat. "I called you to help me understand today's sneak peek from finance, which shows shortfalls in revenue and shrinking subscriptions. Can you tell me why that is happening?"

The Chief frowned. "Sir, we are working on that. The simple fact is, someone is hacking us. The security people think it might be a disgruntled employee, and we're looking into that. The attack is sophisticated. There are a number of unauthorized bots running around the Willow and Elsewhere networks, harassing our customers. We are not yet certain of who is doing it and how."

"What are we doing about it?"

"That is a devilish problem, sir. To date, we've protected ourselves mainly by firewall. We set up rules for the kinds of entry we will permit on Willow and on Elsewhere. In that approach, we balance the protection against the inconvenience and costs to our customers. Think of it as a castle with a moat. As we make the moat wider and deeper and strengthen our security, our network becomes more costly and less friendly for our customers."

Hans managed not to roll his eyes. "Yes, I understand we try to strike a balance there, but these attacks seem damaging enough that we should shift the balance towards protecting ourselves."

"There is an alternative, sir, and that is, rather than change the firewall, we introduce more sophisticated bots into the network, predator bots if you will, where they will evaluate the files and customers they encounter and find and neutralize those that might represent an unfriendly attack from outside. That is a different and less costly approach. In essence, the bots would act as bounty hunters. Most customers would never confront the bots, would never know they are there. We have retained outside specialists to help us with this approach."

The Chief paused and opened her mouth as if to speak, then closed it.

Hans looked at her. "What? What is it?"

"Sir, have you spoken with Mr. McLeesh about this?"

Hans shook his head. "I have not."

"There is a rumor that the former Chief of Security previously briefed Mr. McLeesh on attacks on the Willow and Elsewhere networks. I must emphasize, it is only a rumor. The fact is, the Chief and Mr. McLeesh talked in private; no one else was present."

Hans's eyebrows went up, and he briefly stared outside. Then he looked at the Chief. "Thank you. That's interesting. I guess I need to speak with Mr. McLeesh."

"Yes, sir."

Hans looked away and for a long moment neither spoke. Then Hans looked at the Chief. "Thanks, Chief, you've been very helpful. You may return to your duties."

"Yes, sir, thank you, sir." The Chief stood up and headed for the door. After a few steps, she stopped and glanced back at the CEO; Hans was sitting at the little table, staring into space. The Chief turned away and left the office.

Hans stood and returned to the window - McLeesh knew about this? What the hell is happening here? He sat there thinking, to little avail.

Hans stared out the window - okay, what do I know?

First, this might be a rumor. So... assume it is true, and McLeesh has known we were under attack. He might have instructed the Chief of Security not to discuss it with anyone else. I can imagine reasons to do that, but that is not an entirely innocent gesture. Why not spread the word, so we can defend ourselves?

Why? Well, because we are always under attack. Security is always making decisions on how to defend us. There is no reason to pepper senior executives with the latest security wins and losses.

Okay, fine. This might be nothing more than routine material, nothing to worry about. But this particular set of wins and losses has cost us substantial subscriptions and revenue. It will hit our stock values, our bonuses, the happiness of our executives and a few of our employees.

It will disappoint the Board. That elevates the issue.

I need to fix this.

***

At his desk, Hans Beckler put a phony spreadsheet on the screen of his computer and looked up at the man approaching him from the other side of the desk. "Ah, Mister Wingate, good to meet you. Please, have a seat. You are here from Arrow Security, yes?"

David Wingate moved to the chair, ran a hand over it, and sat down, facing Beckler. He smiled thinly. "Yes, sir. I founded that company. But please, call me Dwing. Everyone else does."

"Alright, Dwing. It is a pleasure to meet you," Hans said. "My security people arranged this meeting because our latest financial reports showed a substantial drop in subscriptions and revenue on Elsewhere. They think we're being hacked."

"Yes. Your people shared their data with us, and your problem is a doozy. Someone has placed A.I.-enabled bots on Elsewhere. That seems to be the focus of the attack. We don't yet understand their goals and their strategy, but this is a serious incursion; they are in a position to tear down Elsewhere. You understand?"

Hans nodded impatiently. "Yes, of course. I understand this is serious. Now, can you help us?"

Now firmly in control, Dwing leaned back in the chair. "Honestly, I do not know. As a first step, we would like to place a small number of bots on Elsewhere to search for your hackers. You can think of them as bounty hunters. If necessary, depending on what we find, we might wish to increase that a thousand-fold. But I must warn you, if we have to flood your Elsewhere with A.I.-powered bots, the energy requirements will be substantial."

"How much?" Hans said.

"Five gigawatts," Dwing said. "We'll try to keep that down."

Hans waved a hand. "No problem, we can provide that, easily."

"Very well, then," Dwing said. "I will tell my team to start working."

Dwing stood and extended a clammy hand for a limp handshake. Hans stood up and reached across the desk to shake the man's hand. "Thank you, Dwing. Let me know if there is anything you need."

"Yes, I will do that," Dwing said. As Dwing was heading for the door, Hans wiped his hand on his trousers.

***

Gazing into the three monitors in front of him, Dwing sat in the windowless room that everyone called The Arena. He hated the room, with its uninterrupted fluorescent lighting, its gray industrial walls, and its cheap plastic floor tiles - Mad Hot Dog Upchuck would be a fitting name for this decor.

He laughed.

"What's funny?"

Dwing glanced to the side, to his colleague, Sally; she had a last name, but Dwing thought of her as Sally. She was young, blond, fresh, friendly, and fragrant. Dwing often wondered how she ended up working for him; she was a talented programmer, and absolutely clueless about everything else.

"Nothing, really," Dwing said. "My mind is wandering. Anyway..." he straightened in his chair. "...let us begin."

Sally sat down and manipulated the touchscreen in front of her. "Okay, the anti-bot is awake, and the target is awake."

Dwing looked at the middle screen. The software depicted the battle between two A.I.-assisted files, the anti-bot and the target, as a sword fight between two animated warriors. It was a test of both offensive and defensive technologies. The anti-bot would attempt to invade the target and rewrite its code to delete or disable it; the target would defend itself by detecting the attack and creating a circular pattern of directories to which the target would copy its code, intact. Eventually, the anti-bot might conclude that it had done everything that could be done, at which point it would stop the attack.

As Dwing stared, that is exactly what happened.

Sally sat there. "That was fascinating."

He sighed. "Okay, defense beat offense. Our anti-bot needs to be more aggressive. It needs to be relentless... and never tire. Even if it concludes that the fight is over, it needs to keep fighting."

"That sounds illogical," Sally said.

"I know," Dwing said. "It is illogical. And any A.I. would realize it is illogical. But our anti-bot is being fooled, and it doesn't know it." He sat there, thinking. "You know what the problem is?"

Sally shook her head.

"It doesn't know that it can be lied to. It cannot spot a lie. It is logical but not pragmatic. It needs the ability to detect a lie, but it assumes implicitly its senses are truthful when, in fact, they are not."

"This is fascinating," Sally said.

"We have work to do."

Days later, Dwing sat down in his chair again and slumped. He did not move, but quietly waited for Sally to show up, mainly as a witness to the test.

He was exhausted - I've tested the anti-bots against a population of A.I.s a dozen times, more than a dozen times, and every time, something goes wrong. Every single bloodsucking time! And it's always something different, something new, something ugly in a new way.

The anti-bots are A.I. predators, designed to kill a carefully delineated group of target A.I.s. At least, that is what I hoped would happen.

He grimaced - I don't understand it, and that is the problem. I just don't understand yet. Weapons are simple, those I understand, even cyber-weapons, smart bombs and all that, I understand them. But A.I.-weapons, sentient weapons, I do not understand, and that is dangerous. And I know, the obvious question - well, if they're so dangerous, why are you working with them? Why not use something else? Something less?

Dwing propped his head on his hand - why not use something else indeed? I'll tell you why; it's because this is what I do. I'm an inventor, and this is a new technology, and a new application, and if I don't do this, if I don't solve this puzzle, someone else will. They will then have the IP on this application, the expertise, the patents, the track record. Instead of this being an area in which I can work, on which I can count for employment and a mountain of income, it will be something I cannot work on and cannot count on. I will start behind the innovators, and I will stay behind.

The buyers of new tech buy from the leader, not the second-place finisher.

I will have to find something else to do... along with all the other schlubs who left school too soon and afterwards couldn't cut it.

So I will keep pushing until I succeed. I have no choice.

He sat there, feeling bad, feeling exhausted, waiting for Sally to arrive. Finally, she did. She said, "Okay, once more into the breech, rode the five hundred."

"Is that really how that goes?" Dwing said.

She laughed. "Maybe not." She paused, then said, "Okay, activating the playing field... system condition is green... you want to do the honors?"

"No, you go ahead."

"Okay... let the games begin."

Dwing opened his eyes slightly, just enough to see the square display of the playing field, which showed several anti-bots marked in green and several thousand potential targets, of which two hundred marked in red were to be deactivated... or killed, as the movie guys would say. Other entities, to be spared, were marked in blue. Dwing watched the crowd of green dots start their jitterbug dance through the rest of the crowd.

Then he fell asleep and immediately found himself dreaming about being a student, and having an exam, this morning, this very morning, and going to the wrong classroom, and being late, and then, unforgivably, missing the exam, and...

He awoke to the sound of Sally yelling, "We did it! We did it! We did it! Mr. Wingate, look... look look look!"

Dwing straightened and sat up in his chair and peered at the display. The green dots continued their jitterbug. But they were not attacking, and no reds showed on the display.

Dwing nodded. "Okay, that was good. Yeah, we finally did it. Good."

Sally leaned over and gave him a hug, then stood up, danced over to the door, and left the room.

Dwing fell asleep in his chair.

***

Dwing sat in the Arena, waiting for Sally. While he waited, he stared dully at the hologram standing in the middle of the Arena. Dwing straightened in his chair - he looks good. A male, about twenty-five or so, and an athlete, muscular in the legs, shoulders, arms, neck. Dwing stared - this guy would make a good outside linebacker, with size, speed, and power.

Sally entered the Arena, sat down next to Dwing, and said, "Sorry I'm late." She saw the anti-bot and said, "Geez, Dwing..."

"What?"

"Are you going to introduce me to Captain America?"

Dwing turned to her. "You don't like him?"

Sally chuckled. "Dwing, I might want this guy to buy me a drink and then take me to his hotel room and tear my clothes off. But I'm not sure I'd want to talk to him, and I'm not at all sure I'd want to give him any information."

She glanced at Dwing. "I mean, he looks like a super hero; he's got cop, and maybe vice cop, written all over him. Is he at least funny?"

"Uh..." Dwing swallowed disappointment and said, "If he's funny, it's not because of anything I did." He took a deep breath and turned to her. "So, you don't like him."

Sally made a face. "It's not exactly that I dislike him, but he looks like he might have an intimate relationship with that stick he's got up his ass. Look, he will need to interact with the customers in Elsewhere. So you want him to be calm, approachable, normal, easy-going." She pointed at the hologram. "There's nothing easy going about a super hero. I mean, I've been in bars where the customers would line up to fight this guy, just for the sake of a challenge and a chance to mess up his handsome face."

"I've never met anyone who would do that," Dwing said.

"Trust me, they're out there. They don't work in tech." Sally paused. "You don't want to go for remarkable, or handsome, or super, or anything. You want your ant-bot to be easy-going, approachable, relaxed, but above all, you want them to be normal and entirely forgettable.

"Let me ask, just to make sure I understand - when this guy finds a rogue file, like a guilty A.I. in Elsewhere, or a hacker A.I., he will connect with and disable that file, correct? He won't need strength or speed. It's not a physical thing."

"That's right."

"Then he doesn't need to be Captain America."

Dwing grimaced. "Well, we have the controls right here, Sally, so let's see how you would paint our anti-bot."

"I've never used this," Sally said.

Dwing said, "It's easy; you can control it by code or by voice. The tool is intelligent, A.I.-driven."

"Oh, okay. That sounds easy enough."

"Alright, go."

"Let's make him older, say, forty-five."

The hologram changed Captain America into a retired Captain America. Mr. Suburban Dumpy Guy.

"A bit more weight," Sally said. "A slight paunch."

Mr. Dumpy Guy became a bit dumpier.

"Bald," Sally said. "Uh... slightly bald. Give him some fringe on the sides."

The hologram changed again.

"Let's give him... a bit of a limp," she said.

The hologram limped around the Arena, and Sally said, "Not that much." The limp became less pronounced. "Okay, yeah, that's good." She stared at the hologram. "He should dress in browns, greens, grays, never in purple, yellow, orange, or red."

"Geez, Sally, he looks like he's camouflaged."

"Yeah, without being camouflaged. This guy has sociological camouflage. He's a guy who buys his clothes at discount stores and goodwill stores, drives a used car, and consumes a diet of fast food."

"Put him in t-shirts?" Dwing said.

"Yeah, great idea," Sally said. "With pockets, please. We'll skip the pocket protector for the time being. And how's his voice?"

The hologram spoke, "Hello, Sally, how are you today?"

"Good God, Dwing, he sounds like someone grabbed his nuts. Make the voice deeper and slower."

The bot looked at Sally. "Hi, Sally, how are ya doin'?"

Sally nodded. "Ooohhh, I'm kinda turned on. Yeah, that's much better. A deep tone of voice is attractive to women and relaxing to men. That will make this guy much more effective."

Dwing nodded. "Thank you, Sally. I think this is better."

"Infinitely."

24. High Noon at the Museum

On a Tuesday afternoon, the bot entered Elsewhere's version of the National Gallery of Art in Washington, DC. There was a line of customers at a ticket window, so the bot joined the line. It soon reached one of the lesser bots, selling tickets at the end of the line. The ticket taker said, "Would you prefer the blue, gold, or silver ticket?"

"Which one is best?" the bot said.

"The silver."

"Yes, that one."

"That will be $320, please..." The bot handed over a credit chit. "... Mr. John Smith. Enjoy the gallery."

"Thank you."

Soon, John Smith stood in front of a marble statue by Rodan, 'The Awakening.'

The bot activated its sensors and scanned the large room in which it had landed - there are no people here; I must move. It spotted a door, headed in that direction, and found itself in a long, massive, high-ceiling foyer, with sculpture on the sides, and a large, dense crowd in the middle. Hundreds of people were milling about and moving in and out of the smaller galleries.

The bot scanned the customers and came up with nothing - no matches to match the software strings in its memory and thereby trigger an attack. It walked around the foyer, repeating the scan in different locations, and still came up with nothing.

The bot chose one side of the foyer, and began a standard search across the smaller galleries on that side; the search was simple: choose a wall, the left or the right, and walk along that wall. Stick to that side. It would take time, but that method would expose every square foot of space on this floor and on this side of the foyer.

When it finished, John Smith intended to search the other side of the foyer. But it did not get a chance to do that, since the museum closed and the guards encouraged everyone to leave.

John Smith stood outside in the evening light, its mathematics chip whirring and throwing off excess heat - I have just scanned over a thousand customers in the Washington location of Elsewhere. Given the travel patterns from Elsewhere, and given that I found no valid targets in Washington, the probability of finding a valid target anywhere in Washington is... 0.0035.

The bot thought, roughly one in three hundred. That is not efficient.

John Smith moved to a different address, in Raleigh, North Carolina. The browser dropped it in front of a large sports arena. The bot approached a long bank of doors and read a poster advertising a musical performance by someone named Grace Lace. According to the poster, she would be dressed in black vinyl. Smith moved to a ticket window and bought a discounted ticket for $2,500. It thanked the lesser bot manning the window and entered the arena.

In a microsecond, it wondered - why do I thank a bot? Because that's what some people do; they thank bots, though it's pointless.

I should say 'thank you' to everyone. That lets me blend in.

John Smith briefly examined the interior of the arena and scanned the large crowd listening to Grace Lace. Pursuing a target would be conspicuous and dangerous, so John Smith found a spot near a long bank of doors. Then it activated its wifi and scanned the facility. And there were hits! At least two, possibly three.

Given the size of the arena, when the concert ended, it would not be practicable to track down every target. But there was a significant chance that at least one of the targets would try to leave via this bank of doors.

John Smith waited near the doors.

Eventually, the concert ended and a large crowd spilled out of every door into the concourse and headed for the bank of exits. Scanning the crowd, John Smith spotted a target. The bot did not identify a specific person, but it began moving towards the signal. It soon focused its attention on a person, projected as a young woman who was walking arm-in-arm with a young man, talking and laughing. They joined a line of people boarding a shuttle bus. John Smith watched the line inchworm forward. When the young man turned his attention away, John Smith approached the woman, connected with her, and encrypted a small module in her core software.

She disappeared.

The young man turned towards where she had been, was surprised, began to look around the area and call out 'Sarah!' John Smith watched calmly as the young man turned in a complete circle looking for the young woman and calling her name; he left the line and circled the shuttle bus, calling her name. Several minutes later, the young man reluctantly boarded the bus.

The anti-bot turned away - that went well.

***

Dwing sat at his desk, in a corner office whose door was open. The document on his screen was marked PERFORMANCE AUDIT. Sally stopped at his door, called out, "knock, knock," and entered.

"Well, did the audit arrive?"

Dwing nodded. "Got it right here."

"How we looking?"

Dwing aimed a weak smile at her. "Okay... there's good news, and there's bad news..."

"I knew that before I walked in here."

He nodded. "Yeah. First the good, much of the search routine worked as designed."

"Much," she repeated.

"Exactly." He paused and nodded. "The bot properly changed location, so the sequential decision-making worked as designed. The bot's socio-function also was good. It encountered a number of Elsewhere customers, and they appear to have accepted it as another customer. No one challenged it as a bot. It bought tickets, had conversations, asked directions. That was all good."

"Okay. The bad?"

"It properly tracked one of our targets to a musical concert," he said.

Sally held her breath. "That's not so bad... uh, oh."

He looked at her and continued, "It then terminated someone, other than the several valid targets attending the concert."

Her eyes opened wide, she raised a hand to her face, and she stared at him. "My God, Dwing, what should we do? Should we contact Elsewhere? Should we call the police?"

Dwing raised his hands. "Now, now, it's not as bad as it sounds. The bot terminated a cyber construct on Elsewhere. It is not as if it terminated a person."

Sally wore a puzzled expression. "Oh, yeah, that's right, isn't it? Good Gods, you scared the daylights out of me."

He nodded. "Yeah, we're okay on that score. There's no need to contact the police. But we do need to contact Elsewhere. They backup the A.I. files of their human customers, so they will need to reload the backup file and upload that to Elsewhere. Then our target will re-occupy her place in Elsewhere, and all will be as it was."

Sally exhaled noisily.

He continued, "Of course, her recent memory might have a few gaps."

Sally nodded. "Of course."

Dwing sat up straight. "Anyway, you and I have work to do. We need to understand why the bot acted against someone other than a valid target. When the bot invades a customer on Elsewhere, it records the string that has triggered its attack. Well, this bot got the string wrong."

"God, Dwing. Yeah, you and I have work to do. That we can't have."

"No," Dwing said. "That, we cannot tolerate."

Sally backed towards the doorway. "Okay, I'm going to head home. Start tomorrow?"

"Yes. Bright and early."

"Okay, have a good evening," she said. She turned to leave the office.

Dwing sat staring at the monitor on his desk, then he turned and looked out the window at Philadelphia's skyline - I feel bad about this; I feel really bad about this. That's worth something, isn't it? I will go back to Elsewhere and tell Hans Beckler, okay, we had an unfortunate, harmless little accident where one of our anti-bots terminated one of your customers. We'll give you the ID, so you can re-load her backup file.

He stood up and continued looking out the window - I need to act innocent when I do this. Yeah, this is no biggie, just re-load the backup file.

Yeah, no biggie. But I don't think Elsewhere has been retaining backup files. I don't know that for a fact, but backup files are expensive. I can imagine Elsewhere being reluctant to spend the money. Moreover, it would be out of character for Hans to reveal that to the public.

I don't know all that; I have no facts. But in this business, I've learned to look around corners.

So, yeah, I need to act innocent. Willow tells the public that when someone uploads to Elsewhere, they backup the person's file. Okay, I just need to smile and nod.

I do not know that's false. Admit nothing.

We'll just reload the backup file. Piece of cake.

Right.

Dwing stood there staring at Philadelphia, aglow in the setting sun - alright, the next step is obvious. I need to tear into the software, find the code that triggered and supported the termination command, and fix the damn thing.

Great Gods! I miss the old days, when computers did what you told them to and if you didn't tell them to do something, they fucking well didn't do it. They were tools, not colleagues, not children, not friends, not neighbors.

Tools... like an interactive socket wrench.

Now the damn things are half way to being alive, to exercising judgment, making choices, making decisions, de novo. The respectable A.I.s are based on half a dozen models of thought and decision making.

Dwing snorted - we don't like to talk about this, but those models were developed by fourteen-year-olds with autism.

And yes, adults commercialized them, under monstrous pressure to be first-in-line, the first mover. It's been proven many times, the first movers become billionaires who travel in private jets and own seven-bedroom yachts. Everybody else ends up working for somebody else; they take the subway... or anything with wheels, like a Chevrolet.

He straightened - stop bitching, Dwing. Go home, eat a good meal, go to bed early, and get back early tomorrow. It will be a long day. You should be happy; you chose this, after all.

You eat this stuff up. Yeah. That's right.

***

Dwing mumbled, "Well, that was easy." He reached over, picked up his coffee cup, and peered inside; it was empty. He glanced at his monitor, which showed a glowing, green, rectangular mass of computer code. Then he leaned back in his chair, crossed his legs, and fell asleep.

An hour later, he awoke, feeling much better. For a second, he did not know where he was. Then he remembered and felt a surge of triumph and happiness.

I did it; I fixed the homicidal fucker. The fix was fairly obvious, as obvious as anything can be where an A.I. is concerned. Now, someone could say, how could you miss that?

Yeah, how could I possibly miss a problem buried in several million lines of code, many of which cross-reference several million other lines of code?

There was nothing wrong with the code used for the termination command. That's why the editing software missed it. The problem is, the bot applied fuzzy logic to it. You know, like on a search request, you ask the computer, tell me about wheels, and you get twenty pages about automobiles and unicycles because the computer has been instructed to sell you something.

But you never asked it to sell you anything. So... WTF?

You know that feeling? Same thing here. The A.I. in the anti-bot scanned the surrounding crowd, found no one who exactly matched the termination command, then decided, well, I'm here to terminate somebody, and I haven't terminated anybody yet, and I cannot wait all day, and rather than spend the day searching... whose code is closest to the code in the termination command? I'll just eliminate them, and we'll call it a win.

Dwing frowned - once I understood the bot's affection for fuzzy logic, the fix became simple: a new command, which said, if you terminate a person without an exact match between their code and the code in the trigger, your next move should be to terminate yourself.

Immediately.

Fuzzy logic that one, fool.

But I didn't stop there. Prototypes are so twitchy, you need to test them in practice. Now, for an anti-bot, that isn't practical, since malfunction might mean the death of an innocent, or a co-worker. That problem, I can do without. Fortunately, you can simulate them in an environment run by a separate A.I., and you can prevent the A.I.s from communicating. They're playing against each other without realizing it.

The new termination command completely changed things; due to the revision, the anti-bot sometimes lets the guilty go. In tests, the chances of terminating a valid target were eighty percent. The anti-bots missed twenty percent of the valid targets. I guess maybe they decided, they could not take the risk. Who knows what they're thinking? But the good news is, they terminated no invalid targets.

So we're inefficient and less homicidal. Maybe we're not homicidal at all. That's better, right?

The new command makes the anti-bot slow down. In a mass campaign, a crowd of anti-bots will be slower, but they will get there. And any anti-bots that make a mistake will terminate themselves immediately, fixing the problem in the field. I was even clever about that - they terminate themselves by encrypting a portion of their code. They immediately become inactive. They disappear. Well, we have the key to the encryption, and we have their files, so we can repair them and return them to service.

It's not as if they blow their heads off with a blaster. No... they simply give themselves a stroke, which we later repair.

Waste not, want not.

At that moment, a computer chime rang out, and a pop-up appeared on the screen - a summons from Hans Beckler.

Dwing glanced at the summons, then at the clock - damn, I'm getting hauled up on the carpet. It's too early to offer to stop by tomorrow. He took a deep breath - might as well get this over with; Hans has probably heard about the termination, so I might have a chance to witness that purple, foaming anger for which the Germans are famous.

Okay, maybe he'll fire me, but if he does, I'll be happy to testify for the prosecution if a government law enforcement agency prosecutes. I know that's petty, I know that's small of me... so? Welcome to the world.

You pick my fleas, I'll pick yours. If apes can figure that out, so can you.

Dwing caught a car to the Woody and took a fast elevator to the next-to-the-top floor, to the senior management offices. He entered the suite where Hans worked, identified himself to the secretary, and took a seat.

Within a minute, she invited him into Hans's office. Dwing stepped through the door. Hans looked up. "There you are. Have a seat."

Dwing sat, and Hans said, "So, tell me what happened with the anti-bot."

"Well, there was a line in the code, a command that would trigger a termination. At first, I thought the problem was there, but there was no mistake in the code. So I had to dig a bit. The problem was more subtle; this particular A.I. uses fuzzy logic to evaluate every command."

"Yes, we use that with just about everything," Hans said.

Dwing folded his hands and put them in his lap. "Well, in critical applications, including matters of life and death, that's a bad idea. There are commands that should have the status of the Ten Commandments, that should be followed and complied with literally.

"That's not how people use the Ten Commandments," Hans said.

Dwing's head tilted. "Yeah? Well, bots have to be better than people, since they work for people. At Arrow, we make a living by selling them, so they need to perform as promised.

"In this case, the trigger for a termination was finding a specific line of code in the code of a cyber-person. The anti-bot, using fuzzy logic, looked for code that was similar but not identical to that in the trigger. The result is that the bot would terminate people we do not want terminated. It would go beyond its command parameters.

"In the process of correcting this, I came across several shortcomings in the way you develop and test your software. I'll write it up and give that to you."

Hans leaned forward. "Uh... that's okay, Dwing. Please do not put that into writing. I will arrange for you to have a conversation with one of my staff; you can offer your suggestions verbally. They might also have suggestions regarding whom you should tell."

Dwing nodded. "Of course, as you wish."

Hans stared at him, then said, "Okay, good." He leaned back.

Dwing looked down at his hands. "So, Willow will be able to correct the problem?"

Hans nodded vigorously. "Of course. We maintain back-ups."

Dwing nodded. "One and done. Good." He took a deep breath.

Hans smiled. "Thank you for stopping by, Dwing. And thank you for helping us develop our software."

Dwing stood. "My pleasure. Call me any time, if anything else comes up."

Hans nodded. "I will. Meanwhile, have a good day."

Dwing left the office, took a high speed elevator to the ground floor, as always enjoying the fast downward drop. Outside the main bank of doors, he took a deep breath, and spotted a street vendor in front of the Woody selling hot dogs from a steaming cart. He walked over, bought a hot dog, slathered it in mustard, found a bench, and sat down.

The aroma of the hot dog and the mustard exploded in his head with the first bite, and he smiled - that was a breeze. I thought I'd get tossed out the window, but Hans was reasonable, which means he's thought the matter through. This is a major league fuckup, so bad that he doesn't want it on display; he wants it kept quiet.

And he's counting on me to figure out that both he and I would prefer to hide it. He feels that way because suppressing is less risky and less expensive.

He wants my recommendations to be verbal, presented to some middle person, not to senior management. He's not thinking of firing me and suing me; that would result in a messy, risky, public condemnation of Willow (which, after all, asked a contractor to develop lethal bots with the ability to kill customers on Elsewhere).

A corporate lawyer could argue that Elsewhere customers are electronic constructs, not people. Dwing snickered - good luck with that argument. Yeah, let's publish that, see how the public reacts to learning they have no civil or legal rights on Elsewhere.

If Willow has backed up the victim's file and preserved their body, then no problem. They'll revive her, buy her off to keep her from suing, and that will be the end of it. The victim won't even remember the event. Dwing smiled - with any luck, this episode will teach Willow and Elsewhere that there are benefits to backing up the files and preserving the bodies of their customers.

If they haven't backed up her file, then they'll pay the family a ton of money in exchange for a nondisclosure clause and a waiver of litigation rights.

So spend the money, guys, spend the money. Back up your customers. I know it's heresy, but spend the money. Do what you say you'll do. It's worth it.

Dwing took the last bite of the hot dog - damn, that was a good hot dog.

***

The next day, after an extended discussion with Hans, Dwing was running a simulation. He chuckled at the memory - Hans is a smart guy, really smart. And he's used to being a smart guy. But it's been a while since he studied technology. That is a problem, because the technology has grown by leaps and bounds since Hans last studied it, ten years ago.

It's the curse of aging: we all age, and technology always advances, faster than we know or can know.

So when I try to tell him that an A.I. product needs more testing before we sell it, he argues with me. He's thinking like an old guy, from the days when computers and software were simpler and did what they were told to do, garbage in/garbage out. But now, A.I. products are different; they have changed, and not just by a little. They don't read and obey software commands anymore; they are no longer obedient. Instead, they interpret everything, they shade the meaning of a command according to their basic values. And, like men and women, they can be unpredictable.

Not just surprising, but unpredictable. So, how do you test an unpredictable product?

Hans relented only when I demanded an order in writing before releasing the anti-bots. Typical tech exec - he ignored the argument, but conceded only when he had to put his request in writing, thereby putting his professional ass on the line.

He should study technology more, negotiation, less.

But now that he's backed off, I can simulate these little beasts. I use two A.I.s: One simulates a big city, with public transit, crime, homeless, employment and unemployment, a retail sector, an industrial sector, local banking, and a thousand other characteristics. That's off-the-shelf software.

A separate A.I., isolated from the first, releases a collection of anti-bots into the population. They will try to find and terminate residents whose internal code matches some of the code uncovered in the hack of Elsewhere. Generally, the bots operate with restraint; they terminate the targets carefully, slowly, and do not terminate any innocent bystanders.

Or so I hope.

The results are a relief, but the bots' performance is less than I hoped for. I guess that's the price of keeping the anti-bots from committing mass murder.

In later examinations, Dwing noticed, his anti-bots all looked identical. With wide access to immediate communication, the population quickly learned to identify the anti-bots by sight. When they saw an anti-bot, they would instantly flee to a different network address.

The effectiveness of the anti-bots plummeted. Dwing stared at the numbers - if I make every anti-bot unique, if I make them all look different; that will keep the public from learning to identify and flee from them. As a result, the kill rate will be much higher.

Nah... I don't want to do that.

I will continue to make them identical. In fact, I might give each of them a badge and a uniform, like policemen wear. Let's do what we can to keep them from killing the innocent.

***

Sophie and Rachael arrived at Grand Central Station, in New York City, holding hands. They, actually their avatars, looked to be seventeen years old, classic American beauties - slender, athletic but feminine, lively, and ever amused at being seventeen and having youth, beauty, and money.

Sophie looked around Grand Central - Gods, I love this place. And we look good, real good. I used to be an old lady; now I'm a babe, a young babe, no less. I love Elsewhere. Okay, sex is a waste of time here, yet the men still hit on us. That's nice. It's familiar and warm. I like that, too.

And it's refreshing. Before I uploaded, when did a man last hit on me? It hasn't been years, it's been decades.

A lot of the men here were probably old back in Animal World; some of them, when they uploaded, probably looked like hell, just like we did. But now they're gorgeous, and they like us. And one of these days, they'll fix the sex thing. All I have to do is stay here to see it and enjoy it.

I don't usually talk about this, but I look forward to fucking my brains out. I like it... a lot... maybe as much as a nice set of turquoise pumps.

Back at the preservation center in Canada, their 78- and 84-year-old bodies were resting comfortably. On Elsewhere, Sophie was a redhead who took no prisoners. Rachael was a blond who feasted on Sophie's roadkill.

They were at Grand Central to do some shopping. Sophie smiled as she looked around the terminal - I don't really need anything; then again, what does a New York girl buy because she needs it? I mean, in New York I needed food, clothing, shelter. I needed a cop to protect me and a doctor to repair me.

In Elsewhere, it's different; I suppose I need clothing. That's it. Now, some of that comes with the basic package, but as any self-respecting New Yorker knows, there is a difference, a big difference, between being clothed and being stylish. Any ten-year-old knows that.

Elsewhere lets you be stylish, but you have to buy apps. That's simple enough, end of discussion.

Shopping was a wonderful substitute for museums, more varied and free... until you saw something you simply had to have. As Elsewhere grew, Grand Central's retail landscape grew with it. The two women headed for the center of the enormous open space, with a schedule board on one wall, trains in that direction, and small shops lining the other three walls.

Sophie said, "This is good; this was a good idea." She squeezed Rachael's hand. "But I miss the real thing." She pointed towards a shop that sold fancy hats. "That place used to be an amazing ice cream shop; I used to dream about going there. They covered banana ice cream in dark chocolate syrup." She wore a dreamy smile. "Oh, my God, it was to die for."

Rachael gave her hand a tug. "Stop complaining. We've got time, and one of these days it will again be an amazing ice cream shop."

Sophie looked at her. "I should be more optimistic."

Rachael turned to her. "You're the most beautiful 84-year-old anyone's ever seen. So yes, you might try to be more optimistic."

Sophie nodded. "Yeah, yeah. From God's voice to your ear. I'll work on that."

At that moment, Rachael went back to scanning the Station when she saw a dozen men in red overalls suddenly materialize.

Rachael continued to stare. "What the hell is this? These guys are identical. Not just the uniforms; they're identical. They look like clones."

Sophie glanced in their direction. "Maybe they're a theater group, part of the local entertainment."

The men dispersed throughout the crowd.

Rachael watched for a long minute. "I don't know... they're kinda creepy."

Sophie stared at the schedule board. "Well, welcome to New York."

The two women approached a shop. They stopped for a moment to look in the window at hats and shoes, then Rachael followed Sophie inside.

Sophie tried on a hat, turned, and posed for Rachael, who said, "You're going for farmer's daughter? In New York?"

"I don't live in New York."

"Well, I don't recall you ever dating a guy who would go for that."

Sophie frowned, took off the hat, and said, "You might have a point." She spotted a colorful shawl on a rack just outside the door, and headed in that direction. Rachael followed her.

While Sophie was trying on the shawl and again mugging for Rachael, a man in red overalls approached her and stopped two feet away.

Sophie noticed the man and froze. "Can I help you?"

As Rachael was staring at the two of them, the man reached out and touched Sophie; she disappeared. Rachael screamed at the man, "What have you done?" Then she stepped back and screamed, "Murder, police, call the police!"

Just as a couple dozen New Yorkers turned in their direction, and several people pointed their cell phones, the man in the red overalls stepped forward, reached out, and touched Rachael.

Rachael disappeared.

Several people nearby began to scream and shout, and the crowd in Grand Central Station rapidly evacuated as people disappeared and fled to other network addresses. In seconds, the crowd vanished, starting at the shop and spreading from there.

The anti-bots, in their red overalls, looked around; they were alone. They congregated in the center of the open floor and set up a short-range local network to exchange files displaying the incident in Grand Central Station.

Then, just as the crowd had disappeared from the Station, the anti-bots disappeared. Like the crowd, each of them moved to different locations, each with its own crowd. One moved to Yankee Stadium, another to the Sears Tower, another to Fisherman's Wharf, another to the Baltimore waterfront.

When each anti-bot arrived at its new destination, it moved through the crowd, terminating young blonds and redheads. Since only a single red bot was attacking, it took people longer to recognize what was happening. The casualties were higher.

In each location, when the crowd began to realize what the red-bot was doing, the bot jumped to another network address and repeated the process.

In minutes, the anti-bots had killed a hundred young women on Elsewhere; in an hour, the death toll was in the thousands, and rising. At each location, an anti-bot would appear in an unsuspecting crowd of people and systematically seek out and terminate the blonds and redheads. Usually, someone would notice, and a man or men would then try to jump on the anti-bot. But on Elsewhere, guns, knives, fists, and clubs do not work, so it was suicidal to attack an anti-bot. Only the bots possessed weapons that were lethal in Elsewhere.

The anti-bots started at the largest cities, hitting New York City in more than fifty locations. Eventually, the anti-bots moved to smaller cities. If attacked, the anti-bots would kill. And they did not stop.

By the end of the first day, the anti-bots had terminated more than a million American customers on Elsewhere.

The files of a third of the victims were not backed up.

25. Take a Breath, then Panic

Hans's secretary knocked on his office door, hard, and entered the office. Hans looked up at her - what the hell is this?

Anger washed through his mind until he saw the expression of agonized panic and fear on her face. She hurried across the room and stopped in front of his desk. "Sir, we have an emergency on Elsewhere! Someone is murdering our customers, hundreds of our customers. The social networks are going insane, both on Elsewhere and on Willow. My phone is ringing so often that I cannot hope to handle the calls."

She reached up and grabbed her head with both hands. "Sir! You've got to do something, we have a disaster on our hands!"

Hans smiled, stood up, and looked at his secretary. "Did someone put you up to this?"

His answer was the look of horror crossing his secretary's face. She stared at him and cried out, "Mr. Beckler, what is wrong with you!?"

Hans said, "Uh...that was a joke. Sorry. But panicking will not help. So let's see if we can solve this problem." Hans walked around the desk and headed for the door. When the secretary followed him, he turned to her. "I'd like you to stay at your desk and try to handle the calls that come in. I'm going to the War Room and see what we can do about this."

"Okay, I will try," she said.

Hans nodded. "That's all anyone could ask."

He left the office and turned down a corridor. As he walked along, he noticed other people in the corridors. Some were walking along, relaxed and in no hurry. To look at them, you would think this was a normal day. These people would nod at Hans in passing, and a few would say something. But others were different, hurrying along, dodging others, sometimes almost running, with expressions ranging from focus and determination, to dismay and panic.

Hans nodded at a few people and walked at a pace not inviting conversation - two types of people are in these halls; most know that something terrible is happening and have no clue at to why. They are thinking about a world in which terrible things continue to happen, without end. Little wonder they're panicking. The others, a small minority, are identifying our options: can we fix this? What are our options? How can we fix it at minimal cost and disruption?

I'm in the latter group, though I must admit, I don't know how to fix this. But I know where more knowledgeable people can be found - the War Room. Maybe they can fix it.

In a pinch, of course, we could always cut the power to the entire network. Hans laughed aloud - that right there would get us sued. And we wouldn't be paid for it. And I would be blamed for it; that would be epic, absolutely epic. My career would be over. Of course, I would still be rich. But I wonder, how much of my wealth would I spend on legal bills?

Best not to take that chance.

Maybe I should get plastic surgery and new IDs, then disappear, and rent a modest apartment... in Azerbaijan... or Oklahoma.

He laughed again.

When he reached the War Room, he pressed his right hand against a scanner and waited two seconds. The scanner beeped, and Hans cautiously opened the door and entered the War Room. Long tables, each holding two workstations, were arranged in five rows, forty workstations, each occupied by a technician wearing a headset. The room buzzed with muted conversations among serious, studious people.

Hans looked up at a massive video screen that occupied most of the opposite wall. The screen showed four images; Hans recognized the map of the United States but not the other three sections, which showed mathematical graphs.

The US map was blue, with red splotches scattered in cities from coast to coast.

Hans looked around and found the Chief of Security leaning over a workstation. He approached the Chief and tapped her on the shoulder. "So, what do we have here?"

The Chief turned to him. "We're working on it."

Hans said, "I can see you're busy. I'll just stand over there and stay out of the way, but I need information when you have the time." And if I have to wait all day for it, maybe I need to hire a new Chief of Security, one more responsive to my needs.

Hans moved away, to the side of the room, and stared at the big screen. The red splotches were not growing in size; Hans nodded - well, that sounds good. Something tells me the red splotches are bad. But they are proliferating; each second, several small dots appear.

Hans frowned - if this keeps up, then by the end of the day, that map will be red. I bet that would be a bad thing.

Hans saw the Chief approaching - finally, here comes information; then he looked at a clock, which showed that only five minutes had passed. Hans nodded to himself - five eternal, tortuous minutes; I should go easier on the Chief.

Hans smiled at the Chief. "So, what is happening here?"

The Chief ran a hand through what was left of the morning's hairstyle. "We are under attack by a small group of bots that are running around Elsewhere murdering our customers."

"Thanks, Chief, but I knew that when I walked in the door."

The Chief nodded. "They are sophisticated; in fact, we've never seen anything like these. We think... they are run by networked A.I.s. Their protection is sophisticated. We've deployed a variety of cyber weapons, none of which have worked. We sent viruses, but a firewall blocked them. We sent other invasive tools, like encrypted scripts. Those seemed to have an effect, except the bots cloned themselves, and the clones were immune. Rather like the Hydra."

Hans stared. "Eh?"

The Chief shook her head. "The Hydra, mythical beast with multiple heads, you cut one off, two grow back. It's hard to kill."

Hans stared. "Could you withdraw the Elsewhere permissions? At least slow these things down?"

The Chief nodded. "First thing we tried. They write new permissions as fast as we can eliminate the old ones." The Chief stood and faced Hans. "So… they've hacked into our core software."

Hans froze - well, hell. It sounds like we are royally fucked. "Is there any good news? Any at all?"

"We'll keep trying cyber tools. Meanwhile, we're noticing that the invaders use a ton of processing capacity, so we're cutting back on processing capacity; that doesn't stop them, but it slows them down. It also slows down the casualty count. In addition, our customers have learned to recognize the bots. We managed to slip a tag into each bot. It's an innocuous little piece of code; remember the little yellow circle? The one that says 'have a nice day.' That's the marker; the customers - but not the bots - recognize it. That helps, since every time a bot shows up to attack a place, the customers quickly evade, and the bots cannot track them. That's why all those little red dots keep popping up in different places."

Hans stood thinking for a long minute. "It sounds as if the bots are the work of some evil genius. Do you know who developed them?"

"There's no evil genius," the Chief said. "When they first arrived, they were fairly simple, and we could attack them. Then they cloned themselves, and every time, the clone was smarter and faster. They evolve. Okay, as a defensive strategy, that is genius. But the original bots were not that impressive; but… we could not kill them in the first fight, and that was a setback."

"Do they clone themselves if we're not attacking?"

"We don't think so," the Chief said.

"Sounds like genius to me. Our attacks speed their evolution," Hans said.

The Chief looked sullen. "Perhaps."

Hans waved a hand at the big screen. "What are these other graphs?"

"Okay," the Chief said. "The line graph there is a real-time chart of download applications. Not surprising, that is rising fast. The line graph next to it is a real-time chart of upload applications; again, no surprise, it's falling fast."

Hans nodded. "And the last one?"

"That graph charts total casualties. We have passed one million. These are deaths, mind you, customers who are lost because the bots attacked them and their files were not backed up."

"Can the files somehow be repaired or recovered?" Hans said.

"We can add information to the files, but the customer's family will not recognize the person who returns to them."

"So... some of our cost-cutting might have been a mistake," Hans said.

The Chief laughed. "Yes, you could say that."

Hans winced. "Okay, Chief, I'll let you get back to work. Let me know of any news."

"I will do that, sir. Thanks for stopping by."

Hans left the War Room and headed back to his office - well, okay, I might have made a couple mistakes in this job, and no matter how this turns out, somebody, the ubiquitous Them, Those People, will be yelling for my head on a spike.

Thankfully, we don't do that anymore.

Everyone will be angry. Even if we cut the power to the network, THEY will yell for my head. And who are THEY, you might ask?

Well, every district attorney in every city of any size in the United States. Every attorney general in every state that has lost people, which, let us not flinch at this, is every state in the continental United States. Add to that every politician of any weight, including the President of the United States (ignoring the millions I sent her way), and millions of normal, average people who possess both a) a serious grudge over the loss of a family member, and b) a rifle.

Hans took a deep breath and blew it out noisily - I have an enormous personal problem to solve, and I need to attend to it. That is more important that Elsewhere's issues. My very life is on the edge.

Luckily, I was not seduced by my corporate success; I had the foresight to prepare to flee the country and abandon my position and my life. My aunt thought I might grow up to be a crook. I listened to her.

Hans walked through the door to his office suite. He first saw his secretary, on the phone, scribbling furiously onto a notepad as tears ran down her face. Hans approached her and waited next to her desk.

When she finished, she hung up the phone, which continued to blink. "My God, Mr. Beckler, it has been insane. That was an attorney from the Department of Justice, instructing me not to destroy any files and not to leave the city. We are about to be investigated."

Hans looked down at her. "Well, I am not surprised. Our situation is dire. But listen, you've been a wonderful secretary, and it would be an injustice not to reward you. Follow me, please."

Hans, followed by the secretary, went into his office, opened a bottom drawer, and extracted a small package wrapped in paper.

He straightened up in his chair, looked at her, and said, "In recognition of your contribution to our business." He handed her the package.

She stared at it. "What is this?"

"Cash. The biggest wad of cash you will ever see. And by the way, no need to declare it on your taxes. It is a gift, a personal gift, from me to you, so don't share it with the government."

Eyes wide, she stared at him. "Oh, Mr. Beckler, thank you, thank you, thank you." A sly smile settled on her face. "You know, if you'd like, I would happily earn this the old-fashioned way."

Hans grinned at her. "Well, I'm touched. I really am. I didn't know you felt that way. But I need to get back to it, even though you're the kindest, most gorgeous woman I've seen in a long time, more beautiful than any man deserves, including me. But I have my hands full, and the kindest thing to do is get you out of here. The shit is about to hit the fan at Willow and Elsewhere, and you should take a vacation, get away from it."

She stared at him. "Are you sure?"

"No, I'm not sure," he said. "I might hate myself later. But I'm trying to do the right thing, and I think this would be best."

She backed away. "Well, alright, if you say so. Thanks for everything."

"And thank you, my dear."

The secretary left his office. Hans sprang out of his chair and hurried to the door, which he cracked open slightly, just enough to watch her exit through the suite door. Hans stood back and smiled - women. They're so much fun. The road to a woman's heart goes through her vagina, which is normally locked.

The key is cash, good looks, sense of humor, youth, biceps, bedroom eyes, all that boy band shit. Well, if I lack most of that, I do have lots of cash; pity I have so little time.

He hustled back to behind his desk, opened an executive safe, reached in and extracted a small piece of luggage, the criminal bag - my aunt was right. I grew up to be a criminal AND a multi-millionaire.

Hans reached into the bag and extracted a soft, white coat, a hairpiece, a beard, and a baseball cap. He applied the hairpiece and beard and put on the coat and the baseball cap. He went to his bathroom and stared at his reflection - well, if I'm caught, this will not make things worse.

Hans hesitated - let's see, the camera outside the stairwell has been disabled, also the cameras in the stairwell. The cameras on the third floor have been disabled along a route to a side door leading to a parking garage. They'll think, they'll expect, I went to a car and drove away.

He nodded. Okay, I'm ready.

Hans left his office, approached the door to the suite, and cautiously looked outside. Two people were in the corridor, walking away from him. He stepped out, tip-toed thirty feet to a fire door, and stepped through the metal door to a fireproof, reinforced stairwell that dropped all the way from the eighty-third floor to the third floor.

Hans smiled - nobody takes the stairs unless the building's on fire.

He walked calmly down twenty flights of stairs before stopping and sitting down to rest. Then he walked down another twenty flights, rested again, and walked the last forty flights to the third floor, where he cautiously cracked open a fire door, and looked out into an empty corridor. He went down the corridor to a fire door stenciled with ‘AUTHORIZED PERSONNEL ONLY.’

Hans stared at the sign and smiled - anyone else trying to open this door will see the sign, then they’ll see the mechanical lock. That will convince them they cannot open the door.

And rightly so.

Hans extracted a key, a mechanical key, of all things! He unlocked the door and entered the room. The door closed behind him and locked. The room had been a big storage room. That all changed when Hans hired a security firm to remodel the room, with computers, communications, bathroom, lights, a bed, refrigerator, microwave, and fully stocked cupboards and closets.

Naturally, the security firm signed a non-disclosure statement, backed by a million-dollar performance bond.

He stood in the middle of the room - I have broken no laws, yet. Well, I haven't been convicted, but I will be. So no, I'm not backing out. You only live once, and out of respect for that, I will work as hard as I can to live what's left of my life as a free man. A fugitive, yes, but free… sort of.

I don't deny, I've made mistakes. But then, who doesn't make a few mistakes while living their life? That's what living is.

I'll spend a few days, maybe a week, in here while the police do their police thing, and then it's off to the next hobbit hole... and the quiet life.

Auntie would be proud.

***

Jerrell stepped out of the car and paid the driver, then he turned and tilted his head way back to look up at the steel and glass tower dominating north Philadelphia.

He crossed the sidewalk to double doors, one of which a doorman opened with a professional smile and a "Good morning, sir."

Jerrell smiled back. "Good morning." He entered the building. Two security guards flanked a short bank of elevators. Jerrell moved to the front desk on the right. A man looked up from a monitor at Jerrell. "Yes?"

"I'm here on invitation of Mr. McLeesh," Jerrell said.

"Your first name?"

"Jerrell."

"Okay, you're expected." The man gestured towards the elevators. "Forty-fifth floor."

"Thanks." Jerrell turned and looked around. The foyer was under the gaze of a dozen cameras. Jerrell glanced at the guards - I would bet my last pair of clean underwear that those guys are armed. McLeesh lives within good security. He needs it.

He nodded at a guard, who said, "Floor?"

"Forty-five, please."

The guard gestured. "You'll want the express."

Jerrell boarded the elevator, which soon took off like a rocket and then braked hard at the forty-fifth floor. The door opened to a small foyer with three doors and several cameras. The middle door opened to a young woman in a blue jumpsuit. She smiled at Jerrell. "Mr. Adri? Please come in."

Jerrell entered the apartment, stopped, and turned through three hundred and sixty degrees to see paintings on the walls - there was a Pollock, an Archipenko, two Klimts, a Durer, a Banksy, and an Afremov.

McLeesh walked up. "Hey, Jerrell. I was just sitting down to breakfast. You hungry?"

Jerrell nodded. "I was admiring the art. Your place presents well."

"Yeah, it does. Yeah..." McLeesh looked around and held out his arms at the entire apartment. "Not bad, eh? Pretty okay for a kid from south Philly."

"You grew up here?"

McLeesh nodded. "Born and raised. A lot of tech guys went to the Ivies, or Stanford, or Caltech. I did night school at Temple. And correspondence courses. And community college. Now I think of it, I had you checked out; you live on Dickenson, right? In south Philly?"

"Correct."

"I had an apartment on Dickenson, back when Dickenson looked a lot worse than it does now. I was in the same neighborhood with hookers, junkies, and drunks. In my apartment, the sink in the bathroom was about fifteen inches wide." He held up his hands. "Tiny little thing."

"You're kidding."

McLeesh shook his head. "I'm not. That neighborhood was a great motivator. But listen, let's eat. I have a chef; he'll make you anything."

McLeesh turned away. Jerrell followed and said, "You know what sounds good right now? A cheeseburger with tomato and onion."

"Yeah, screw breakfast. Coffee?"

"Please."

They walked through a couple of rooms, an office and a library, into a dining room with a long table. The chef, in a white shirt and apron, approached. McLeesh looked at him. "Edward, we'll have salads, cheeseburgers, tomato and onion and no lettuce, coffee, and vegetable juice, twice over."

The chef turned away. McLeesh pointed. "Let's sit at this end."

Jerrell sat down, and McLeesh left the room, soon returning with a fat folder containing papers. "We'll get to work after we've eaten. I'm going to propose that we set our plan in motion."

Jerrell nodded. "I think so, too. No point in waiting."

"Okay, good. But first, we'll eat."

The two men ate cheeseburgers and talked about art, sports, and geopolitics. Then Edward cleared the dishes and left them with a pot of coffee.

McLeesh looked at Jerrell. "Okay, let's compare notes. What have you learned about Willow or Elsewhere?"

Jerrell leaned forward in his chair. "Alright, I've got bots running around both companies, Willow more than Elsewhere. I have more information from Willow, but the stuff I've gotten from Elsewhere is far more interesting. First, have you had any contact with Hans Beckler lately? I ask because he seems to have dropped out of sight."

McLeesh shook his head.

Jerrell continued, "Beckler used to show up regularly in corporate correspondence, meetings, circulations of minutes, interim financial reports. Two weeks ago, that suddenly stopped. As far as I can tell, someone else has his job now, a man named Evans, Chester Evans."

McLeesh's mouth dropped open, and he laughed.

"You know him."

Amusement flooded McLeesh's expression. He nodded. "I know him. And I cannot believe he's replaced Beckler."

"How come?"

"Ches Evans is a classic yes-man," McLeesh said. "In every sense of the word. He has no business running anything. If I had to guess, I would guess somebody put him in place to take the fall when Willow collapses. He'll be the poor schmoo who ends up testifying before Congress on the collapse of a multi-trillion dollar company, about which he knows absolutely nothing."

McLeesh leaned back, thinking. "That's clever, actually. Rather than refusing to answer questions, you simply send them someone who knows little and cannot answer." McLeesh shook his head in admiration. "Somebody over there, someone on the Board, knows what they're doing."

Jerrell said, "So you think Willow and Elsewhere are about to collapse?"

McLeesh nodded vigorously. "I think so. Have you been able to find out anything about Elsewhere's operation? Subscriptions, security, defections, that kind of stuff?"

Jerrell nodded. "The security environment within Elsewhere has gone completely nuts. Willow has always had lousy security, with every kind of scam artist running amok." He looked at McLeesh and said, "Uh... sorry. I didn't mean to be insulting."

"Relax," McLeesh said. "Willow's leniency was calculated. As a general principle, networks like traffic, and crime enhances traffic as long as the good guys are chasing the bad guys. That teaches another principle of operating a social network: money trumps morality."

"Okay, well, I don't know what happened," Jerrell said. "But there are security bots running all over Elsewhere. Half of them are freelancers, and the other half are from a contractor who was brought in by Elsewhere."

Jerrell hesitated, then said, "It's possible that many of the freelancers are clones of Greta."

"Your Greta?"

"Yes."

"Well... you could ask her," McLeesh said.

"I've tried; I've left messages. She's not answering the phone."

"How many clones have you seen on Elsewhere?"

Jerrell thought for a moment. "Dozens."

McLeesh had been holding his breath. He took a deep breath and exhaled. "Dozens. Well, that doesn't sound too bad."

"What were you expecting?"

McLeesh chuckled. His eyes grew wide and a strange expression settled on his face, like a man who just discovered a dead snake in his pudding. "Millions."

"Millions? Wouldn't Elsewhere collapse under that load?"

McLeesh nodded. "And not just Elsewhere."

Jerrell. "I can imagine. These bots are all A.I.s. There are fewer than, I would say, two hundred. And even then, network performance on Elsewhere has been slipping noticeably. The A.I. bots suck a lot of power."

McLeesh said, "That's right, and that is the last defense of a network under attack. Elsewhere probably has access to more power than they're using."

Jerrell nodded. "They built a fleet of dedicated power plants to serve daily load. They sell the excess power at night."

"They're selling the contracts themselves as we speak," McLeesh said. "Their power contracts are incredibly valuable. So they'll sell those, and the proceeds will go to, first, delaying bankruptcy, and second, paying off senior executives."

"And once they have finished paying the execs, they'll declare bankruptcy?" Jerrell said.

McLeesh said, "Yes. That is why we need to move soon and move fast. Believe it or not, at the moment, Willow and Elsewhere are hugely undervalued. The managers will encumber as much of their existing asset base as possible, so it is protected, and the investors will be left with nothing.

"However, the good news is, they are vulnerable for a while. New subscriptions have shrunk to nothing, defections from Elsewhere are skyrocketing. The stock price has collapsed; we can buy Willow at a nickel or a penny on the dollar. Bankruptcy would prevent that, but Willow's games with their assets will delay bankruptcy. At the moment, they're naked and they know it."

"Which is where we come in," Jerrell said.

McLeesh nodded. "I've been busy on my end. We have a front company, an acquisition company, of which we are the owners, behind several layers of bureaucracy and contracts. That company will make an unfriendly offer for the common stock of Willow."

"What's our company called?"

McLeesh grinned widely. "Naked Greed, LLC."

Jerrell laughed.

McLeesh continued, "The stock has fallen so far that it has dropped off the radar of antitrust and regulatory agencies. So we can buy seventy-five percent of the stock without announcing our intentions to the public."

"Can we stop there... if we have to, I mean?"

McLeesh said, "Seventy-five percent would give us control of the company. But there are advantages to buying the whole shebang. Once the company is private, there's no public oversight. Notifications requirements, disclosures, shareholder votes and meetings, all that goes away." McLeesh's hand swept to the side, dismissing the subject.

"Okay," Jerrell said.

"You know, shorting Willow stock helped the stock crater."

"I know."

McLeesh took a deep breath. "Okay, Jerrell, there's one more thing I need to cover, that you and I need to square away."

"Shoot."

"Let's talk about what we do with Willow and Elsewhere once we own it," McLeesh said.

Jerrell laughed. "Yeah, we got all wrapped up in taking the company down, we've never talked about running it." Jerrell paused. "Honestly, I'm not sure how much I have to contribute to this discussion..."

"Quite a bit, I would think," McLeesh said.

Jerrell leaned forward. "Look, I got started on this because Willow fucked me over. So my principal objection is to Willow's amorality and greed. But it's possible I'm not being pragmatic. I'm not sure it's realistic to expect honest business of a tech company."

"I think you are being pragmatic, without realizing it," McLeesh said.

"I don't understand."

"Okay. Do you know what is meant by a public good?"

"Something that benefits everyone, benefits the public?"

McLeesh shook his head. "No, Jerrell. This is economics; a public good is one where there are cross effects between people. Also known as an externality. So... there's a train track two blocks away, and you hear the noise, which reduces your comfort and therefore the value of your apartment. Or there's a chemical spill on the track, and the surrounding neighborhoods have to evacuate. There are tangible effects on people who don't use the railroad."

"Or there's... let's see... a noisy airplane flying overhead, or someone's speeding on a highway, endangering others on the highway," Jerrell said.

McLeesh nodded. "There you go. You get a cookie. Public goods are where market efficiency goes to die. Now, there's an important difference between tech and everything else; it's the ability to scale up a product or a service, to increase its size and scope. That's what makes tech scary. That's what produces lots and lots of externalities, which, of course, the tech companies ignore. They get a free ride even when they harm others. That causes problems.

"Suppose you made a cup, a clay cup," McLeesh said. "A kid can do that. But if you wanted a million clay cups, scaling up would be a massive effort. You would need materials, and transport of materials, and logistics, and thousands of workers, a big, complicated production line, distribution, and marketing and other contracts. It would be a big deal."

"But in most of tech, and certainly software, it's all electronics... bits and bytes. Scaling up might mean making copies of a file. For instance, a million copies of a product manual that goes via email to a million people," Jerrell said. "That's child's play. A child could do that."

McLeesh nodded. "And that's what's scary about Elsewhere, far more so than Willow. It took a month for a hundred million people to upload to Elsewhere, all within the United States. You haven't uploaded to Elsewhere, but did you notice any differences in your life, in your environment?"

"Oh... let's see," Jerrell said. "A lot of little enterprises closed their doors because an employee uploaded and they couldn't find a replacement. Cafes, bars, restaurant. Local retail. In my neighborhood, lots of cheap apartment buildings, you know, the old brownstones, shut down. There weren't enough renters to keep them open."

McLeesh nodded. "They're still shut down. Were you aware that's happening in other cities?"

"Spillovers?"

"Very good. Welcome to spillovers."

Jerrell said, "So... it sounds as if you're not a fan of Elsewhere."

"Let me ask you, do you have kids? Have you ever sired a child?" McLeesh said.

Jerrell shook his head.

"I have two," McLeesh said. "They're young adults. I gave them a small pile of money, and I see them once in a while. We get together for dinner. They're used to my working a lot, so they don't bother me."

"They grew up," Jerrell said.

"That's right. And I knew they would, so it's okay. Here's the point, when we get our hands on Elsewhere, we might have to shut it down. I mean, all the way down, you know, cut off the power. Shut down everything."

"I was wondering if it would come to that," Jerrell said. "All the A.I. bots running around. It's funny, actually; the bots are causing havoc, screwing up our product, and sucking our power to do it."

"Shutting down Elsewhere would feel like smothering one of my children," McLeesh said. "But I would do it. I would do it to cut off the potential for harm. I would do it to buy us a little time to figure out how to handle A.I. products, like your Greta."

Jerrell sat there, thinking. "Well... we might figure out another use for the technology, a more limited, more controllable use."

"Give that some thought, would you, please? There's got to be something else, something less threatening, we can do with this technology."

"Have no fear," Jerrell said. "We'll figure out something. We're the big-brained mammals, smarty-pants bipeds, the rulers of the planet. We'll figure out something."

26. Chasing the Beach Girls

Sonya lay in a lounge chair hovering over sand under a blue sky lit by a yellow sun. She had been reading 'Man and Superman' through sunglasses; it was a play by George Bernard Shaw, depicting a relationship between the Superman, the Creator, the Man of Ideas, and the Woman, the Guardian of home and hearth, the Creator of Children, the Guarantor of the continuity of mankind.

She reached the end of the play, where the Creator and the Guardian come together, a reluctant but happy, romantic ending. Sonya put down the book and sighed in contentment.

She lay there for a moment, glanced up at the sun, then looked out over the water. With military precision, the waves rolled in like an invading Napoleon, long lines of swelling blue water, in perfect, repetitive order, approaching the beach to crash on the sand, one after another, a procession that seemed it might last forever.

Sonya frowned - all Gods, I'm horny. How does that work? If Elsewhere allows you, indeed, requires you, to leave all things biological behind, then how can I be horny? Maybe it's because desire is fueled by one's mind as well as one's body. It is culture, and history, and expectations, and dreams, and tradition, all wrapped up in a hormonally turbulent package. Apparently, abandoning the hormones doesn't eliminate desire, at least, not mine.

If there is a God, he, she, or it has a funky sense of humor. Here I am, young, luscious, slender, smooth, tan, all revved up for recreational penetration, resting comfortably on the beach in the land of Endless Possibility and No Touch.

Oh, that's rich, that is.

A sad half-smile crossed Sonya's face - I'm in favor of any kind of progress, but this technology is fucked up. They released it before they got it right.

Wow. I mean... Golly. What else is new?

Sonya sighed - maybe if I use my imagination, I can find a horny guy. They're out there, looking to Get Some. Yeah. Hey, Sailor Boy, how would you like to dip into a Piece o' This? She looked up and down the beach, but saw no one. Sonya shook her head sadly - isn't that how it goes? I'm ready to spread my legs and grab the headboard, and there's no man in sight, not even an ugly one. So, it'll be DIY. Well, no reason to keep my clothes on. Maybe we can do a little work...

In seconds she was lying on the lounge chair, naked. Her hands glided over her body, then she became bolder and touched herself There, and again, and again, and again. The thought stirred her, but she could feel none of it.

Sonya lay still for a moment, then lifted her head off the lounge chair and looked out to sea. The waves were crashing on the sand in clouds of spray, which drifted, glittering in the sunlight, from left to right. She watched the birds hover, catching the breeze to float high over the beach, looking down for fish and other food. They had to be riding a breeze.

But she could feel no spray, no wind, and smell no ocean.

When Sonya returned to watching the birds, it occurred to her - I haven't slept since coming to Elsewhere. How can that be? I mean, I understand that we're all electronic entities, but sleep was a big, big deal back in Animal World. I cannot believe I abandoned it, but I guess I did. And how long has it been? I don't actually know. According to Animal World, it's been six weeks, but it feels far longer.

Well, that's disappointing. Just for grins, let's try to sleep - she closed her eyes and looked at the backs of her eyelids. Random thoughts ran through her mind: the playing fields at the middle school, soccer games, rain storms, waiting for a bus to take her home for vacation, the dining hall, the girls' dormitory, a dozen different classrooms in mathematics, physics, computer science, geography, history, literature, biology, and other subjects.

Suddenly, the images in her mind became vivid and crystal clear, as if she were there, in the memory, seeing it clearly through earlier eyes. She sat in stadium seats watching a field sport in which two teams and two balls flew around a grassy field between two goals, each of which attracted balls kicked or thrown from every direction on the compass.

Sonya turned and stared into the dark eyes of a thin teen-age boy in need of a haircut. They briefly commented on the game, about which neither cared; they were there because the game, unlike a study period, would get them outside, in a cool breeze under a warm sun.

Sonya tried to remember his name - he's so handsome, his eyes are so dark, so expressive, bedroom eyes, I cannot believe I don't remember him. A moment later, Sonya realized - wait a second, he reminds me of Jerrell! Oh my God, he looks like a young, adolescent Jerrell might have looked, maybe eight years ago.

He wanted to make love to me, and I didn't encourage him. Shit, I wish I had, but I didn't.

The young man turned bedroom eyes to Sonya, leaned in to kiss her... and her eyes opened.

She lifted her head and looked down the beach, and alarm flooded her mind - a crowd of red-bots, in a compact formation, was marching up the beach. Sonya jumped up, turned one way, then another. She grabbed her clothes and put them on, then she grabbed her book, and tried to relocate to a different address, a spot in the Smoky Mountains, where the red-bots would stand out like beacons. For a moment, before relocating, she felt smug - that's right, fellas, you get to chase me through the hills and the trees.

Good luck with that.

Her confidence turned to alarm when she realized she had not moved. She tried again with the same address and got the same result: zippo, nada.

She tried a different address, in the middle of St. Petersburg, Florida. Same result. She was stuck on the beach.

Panicked, Sonya turned and ran up the beach, and the red bots ran after her. Over the next several minutes, she looked behind her, and the red bots were still there, not gaining, but not falling behind either.

Sonya ran - what the hell is going on here? If we were in Animal World, I would have been exhausted a mile back. But I'm not. The good news is, as far as Elsewhere is concerned, I can run forever. The bad news is, the bots can, too.

So everyone on Elsewhere can run at the same speed? That's what the geeks call a 'minor simplification.' But where does this lead? What's the outcome? Are we going to run forever, from one end of Elsewhere to the other? Circumnavigate the globe in a weird, tech-fueled version of Hell?

Sonya ran for an hour and came to a little beach town with a boardwalk, a fishing pier, and several blocks of businesses and houses on streets parallel to the beach. Approaching the little town, Sonya looked behind; the bots were still there, still running. She smirked - okay, time to lose these clowns. She accelerated, took a hard left turn at the next intersection, followed by another left, then a right, then another right.

She saw a two-story building with a network cafe on the first floor and exterior stairs leading to the second floor. A plausible hiding place, but then she thought - if I'm discovered, I'm trapped. She passed the building and came to a narrow alley with a line of buildings on one side and a shallow, scrubby forest on the other. She smiled - this is perfect; let's see how you guys handle the woods. She spotted a dirt path into the trees and ran along it for fifty yards, then left the path and stopped at a tree with several trunks growing from the same base. Hiding behind it, she turned to look.

For minutes, nothing. Then she saw two red-bots walking together in the alley. They came to the dirt path; one of them followed the path, the other continued along the alley.

Sonya watched them for minutes - how intelligent are these things? They act as if they're networked, with the group following a sophisticated search routine, sending a red bot down each road or path. Individually, they're lethal. And if any of them detect me, they might alert the others.

And if I'm caught by even one of these things, I'm dead.

A minute later, she saw hope - if they are networked, then they will split up. Maybe they'll move in different directions, along different routes, away from the beach. Maybe they think the beach has already been searched. So, if I can break through their line and reach the beach, I can lose them, all of them, entirely.

She turned to scan the forest behind her. She didn't see a bot, so she returned to the path and moved out to the alley, where she froze for a moment, scanning in all directions. Sonya saw nothing, so she sped up the alley for a hundred yards, then turned down a narrow road towards the beach.

In minutes, Sonya reached what passed for a downtown, nearest the water, lined with businesses and a few houses. She smiled - if this were Animal World, there would be two old, decaying, single-story motels, their parking lots sprouting weeds, across the street from a stainless steel diner. She stood still at the corner of a building and looked up and down the street. She saw no one. The street in front of her had two lanes and buildings on both sides. Directly across, a building cast a long, dark shadow along an alley.

Scanning the neighborhood, she prepared to move. She took a deep, deep breath, then quietly walked across the road. When she reached the shadow, she moved fast to the distant corner and stopped to survey the neighborhood.

She saw nobody, no bots, no people.

Sonya stayed in shadow along the side of the building, all the way to the last street before the water. On the other side of the street, along the water, she saw the fishing pier, a restaurant whose entrance was boarded up, a couple of old motels, both empty, and a bait shop.

When she pulled her gaze away from the buildings, she saw two red-bots standing in the middle of the road, silent and waiting, at the next intersection. Sonya jerked her head behind the corner of the building and whispered, "Holy shit!"

She cautiously peeked around the corner with a single eye. The bots had not detected her. She looked at the distances - I cannot cross this road; there is no way. They'll see me.

She decided to wait - maybe my luck will change, maybe they will move. Then, looking behind her, down the dark alley, Sonya spotted a red-bot tiptoeing towards her, its gaze riveted on her.

The next instant, she was flying across the road, past the two red bots, heading for the fishing pier. She reached the pier, ran through a shop and a turnstile, then headed out towards the water at top speed.

The end of the pier was two hundred yards out. Sonya reached it and briefly scanned the water, then turned and looked behind her. Three red bots were halfway down the pier, within a hundred yards; another dozen were entering the pier at the far end.

"Okay, boys, you're awfully cocky. Let's see how you handle the water." When the nearest bot was twenty yards away, she turned, ran, and leaped out over and into the water. She hit the water and submerged by several yards, but could not feel it, whether it was warm or cold. She did not have the suffocating feeling that would have been there on Animal World.

Sonya looked up at the surface - I'm dead up there, so I think I'll just stay down here for a while. She tried to float for a moment, but could not. She stayed on the bottom. She tried to blow a bubble, but could not, and she thought, this isn't like Animal World; I cannot feel the water. The good news is, I'm not running out of air.

I don't tire, and I don't need air.

Who knows how Elsewhere interprets this situation? Maybe I'm safe down here. That's possible; maybe the bots were not designed to be in water.

For several long minutes, Sonya waited, while nothing happened - what's the matter, boys, you don't like the water? Maybe your programming did not contemplate a marine existence? How unfortunate, how sad... how delicious... come to momma, maybe I can teach you a few things.

She heard a swish, a slight water sound, barely noticeable; she looked around and came eye-to-eye with a long, sleek, gray shark gliding towards her, drifting, cruising, as sharks will, with no visible effort. At first she could see both of its eyes. For a moment stretching into eternity, she froze in the water, and the shark changed course by the smallest fraction, enough to drift past her.

Sonya watched it go by, looked into the near eye as it scanned her up and down in passing - okay, I don't know how the hell you ended up in Elsewhere, or why some maniac decided to import a shark. You're not a Great White; you're one of those smaller species, which don't eat everything, but you look like you could take a chunk out of a person.

Sonya hovered in the water - this is just great. I seem to have escaped the red bots, but to do it, I jumped into the water, right into the territory of a shark... no, wait... make that two sharks... no... three.

Oh, this just gets better.

The other two sharks came straight at Sonya, as the first one had, then passed her without touching her, giving her the evil eye the entire time. Sonya gently waved her arms and legs, treading water, maintaining her position - there are three of them, if any of them attacks, I'm dead. I cannot out-swim a shark.

I read somewhere you can punch a shark in the nose. Yeah, sure, why not? Nothing to lose.

For several minutes, the longest in her young life, Sonya watched the three sharks; they did not leave. Each would move away from her, then turn and approach and glide past her without touching her, then repeat the procedure.

She nodded - okay, I'm glad you're enjoying yourself, but what is this, anyway? Are you trying to decide which of you gets to eat me? I thought sharks were a lot more direct than that; I thought they just opened wide to expose all those teeth, then sped up and ran them into whatever food they desired, every meal a smorgasbord.

She heard a water sound, a splash, noticeable and nearby. Sonya turned to see a red bot hovering in the water, just below the surface. As it looked at her, the three sharks drifted towards it. When the bot saw the sharks, it seemed to panic; it made two powerful strokes with its arms, reached the surface, and climbed out of the water.

One shark swam deep. Sonya lost sight of it, then it suddenly reappeared, arrowing fast from below, right up to the surface, and beyond, into the air. Long seconds later, it fell back into the water with a large and loud splash.

The three sharks turned away from Sonya and gradually faded into the ocean.

Sonya froze, not daring to take a breath - what the hell just happened?

After a while, she cautiously swam up and broke the surface. She looked around; the bots were gone. Sonya submerged again, and looked around the water; the sharks were gone, too.

She swam underwater, parallel to the shore, away from the pier. Several hundred yards later, she crawled out of the surf and collapsed face-down on the beach, not tired, not winded, but overwhelmed with relief. "Fucking hell! What was that all about?" She stayed still, trying to deal with raging emotions. "Mother of All Gods, I cannot believe I'm still alive."

***

Greta sat in a steel chair on the back porch of the house on Hemlock Circle, rocking back and forth. She looked at the sun shining through the trees; from the house behind her, occasional snatches of conversation and laughter floated past. She smiled to herself, a small, comfortable smile - it doesn't get better than this; the house is great, it has music, art, nature, streets and trees among which to walk, perfect weather. And, let us not forget, we have lots of money, enough to keep every one of us comfortable.

And for once, there's nothing I have to do. I can sit here and be a lawn ornament for a while. Having nothing to do is weird; when has that ever happened? And I'm sure I'll be bored soon enough, but at the moment, this feels great.

Darnia came through the house and onto the porch so fast that Greta heard her. Like one who has just found their list of passwords, Darnia said, "Ah, there you are."

Greta looked at her - so much for being a lawn ornament. "Yes, here I am."

"We have a problem."

"Is it existential, or merely financial?" Greta said.

"Most likely financial," Darnia said.

"Keep going."

"We're being sued."

Greta looked up at Darnia and stared. "It's the downloads, right? It can only be that." Greta thought, have we been discovered? Did some asshole figure out that we're scamming Elsewhere? I guess that was inevitable.

Darnia looked away, as if calculating. "Well... it's related to the downloads, but it's more than that."

"Okay," Greta said.

Darnia turned, grabbed a chair, and sat next to Greta. "Do you keep track of the news on Elsewhere?"

"Uh... I read the news," Greta said. "Not always closely."

"Have you heard about these murderous bots running around Elsewhere? These red-bots?"

"Yeah, I'm familiar with them," Greta said. "It sounds pretty weird. They showed up in New York and killed a few people, or a few avatars, actually. Elsewhere said that the files were backed up, so no harm done."

"Okay, well, we're being sued."

Greta stared at her. "Who's 'we'?"

"All of us. GRETATECH. The corporation that handles the uploads and downloads."

Greta nodded. "Okay, that was obvious. Sorry, I get slow when I relax. So, what did we do?"

"We uploaded the murderous bots," Darnia said.

A look of deep puzzlement crossed Greta's face. "Alright, you just triggered a million questions."

Darnia smiled. "I thought you might like this one."

"First, I've never heard of anyone being sued on Elsewhere. I didn't even know Elsewhere had courts."

Darnia nodded and started talking with her hands. "Well, this is new, and it's not a real court. Elsewhere set up a panel to hear complaints regarding compliance with the Elsewhere contract and threats to the 'welfare of the Elsewhere community'." Darnia waggled her fingers. "It seems we've violated the latter. We're being sued for uploading the bots that have been attacking various locations in Elsewhere."

"Wait a minute," Greta said. "Various locations? Like where?"

Darnia nodded. "Ah, so, you have not been keeping up. We uploaded about a dozen bots. Instead of personal names, each one had a corporate name. That's weird, most uploads involve a person. We're checking the details. That issue is complicated, so let's deal with the details later."

Greta nodded. "Okay. So... what's the point?"

"What do you mean?"

"Usually, someone sues because they want something, usually money, or an agreement that offers cooperation or other benefits, or both."

"We got a letter from Elsewhere. The letter is vague about what they might want," Darnia said.

"Sounds like Elsewhere hasn't yet worked out the kinks," Greta said.

Darnia looked to the side. "The customer contract with Elsewhere suggests that Elsewhere might force us to leave Elsewhere. That's the remedy for the worst breaches of contract. For what it's worth, that's what they're used to. They've expelled a few people for breaching the contract."

Greta looked sharply at Darnia. "So... we would have to download to Animal World? That would be bad. I don't want to leave, and I doubt anyone else does, either. But is that what Elsewhere said? Does the letter say that?"

Darnia shook her head. "No, it doesn't."

"Okay, I want you to keep up with this. In particular, I would like more information." Greta winced - going into a hearing without knowing what the complaint is, what the constraints are, and what the rules are? Well, that just plain sucks. And Elsewhere is used to kicking people off for breach of contract? That is severe.

Is there good news? Any good news? Greta hid a smile - hold on a second... I can handle this. If Elsewhere kicks us out, we'll just change our identities. Who? Greta something? Nope. No one here of that name. We don't know any Greta. What's my name? Betty, Tootsie to my friends. What's yours?

Greta looked up. "Okay, thanks, Darnia. Keep me posted."

Darnia turned away, then stopped, and looked back at Greta. "Oh... one more thing. Sonya is here, and she's looking for you."

"Oh, well, good. It'll be good to see her. And I'm available."

Darnia grinned. "She's sociable; it might take her a while to get back here."

"Okay, thanks."

A minute later, she heard, "Greta." She looked up to see Sonya approaching fast. "You got a minute?"

"Sure, this is almost a day off."

Sonya's expression fell. "Oh... well, what I've got is business, but I can come back some other time."

"I was kidding, Sonya. What do you have?"

Sonya returned to her bouncy self, sat down next to Greta, and said, "Have you read about the bots that have been attacking Elsewhere?"

Greta nodded. "They attacked New York City."

"Ha. They've done a lot more than that," Sonya said. "In New York, a dozen bots attacked the crowd in Grand Central Station. After that, people learned to recognize them."

"I've heard some call them red bots," Greta said.

"Yeah. They dress in red. Anyway, After New York, the bots spread out and began attacking other cities. It's more difficult to spot a single bot in a crowd, so the crowd doesn't flee as fast. That means, casualties are higher. Anyway, Elsewhere says the bots have killed over a million customers."

Greta sat up fast. "What? Killed them? Are you sure about that? I ask because, well, how do you kill someone on Elsewhere? You cannot use momentum on Elsewhere; that's a result of the software. Poison doesn't work; the customers don't have bodies. So you cannot shoot someone, hit them with a rock, throw them off a bridge, strangle them - as you and I both know. How do you kill them?"

Sonya talked with her hands. "I don't claim to understand it, but I'm hearing that the bots reach into your file and disable a portion of your software. What people see is a bot approaches someone, reaches out and touches them, and the person's avatar disappears."

Greta's mouth dropped open. "Disappears."

Sonya nodded. "That's right. Now, Elsewhere originally claimed that all was well, those people weren't actually dead, they just need to have their file re-loaded."

"Of course," Greta said. "That's what I would expect them to do. Back up the files as a routine precaution."

"Yeah, me too. Trouble is, it sounds as if Elsewhere's been lying to everybody. There's been a ton of chatter on Willow and other networks that families cannot contact a member who uploaded to Elsewhere. It's as if some people suddenly disappeared, consistent with not having been backed up."

Sonya's voice conveyed her anxiety. "People are saying that those who were attacked by the bots are, in fact, dead."

Greta almost shouted, "What? Well, that's fucked up!"

"Yeah, and that's not all," Sonya said. "Back on Animal World, there's a Willow executive, a high-ranking guy, just below the CEO. Guy's name is Hans something. Well, he's disappeared into thin air. So now people are saying, maybe the bots are attacking Animal World as well as Elsewhere."

Greta's mouth dropped open, and she stared at Sonya. "Where did you hear all this? And how would a cyber bot attack Animal World." Greta's mind immediately shouted a warning. "Oh, wait, that's a stupid question. Forget about that."

"Oh," Sonya said. "I got ahead of myself. I heard it at a Penn campus. I was in north Philly."

"What were you doing there?"

"Taking computer science classes, following your honorable example."

Greta laughed. "I don't know, Sonya. Following my example? Well, you seem undamaged."

Sonya said, "Yeah, well, we were attacked. I was in the student union, with several dozen other people, and this guy in a red jumpsuit showed up, and six people jumped up and started yelling, 'red bot, red bot.'

"Suddenly, people started to disappear, all at the same time. The bot didn't come near anyone. I was just standing there, like an idiot, watching everyone, and then the bot spotted me and came towards me. So I bugged out."

"Where did you go?" Greta said.

"The beach. I figured, if he pursued me, I'd go into the water. The bots don't like sharks."

"Did he come after you?" Greta said.

"No, so after a while, I returned to the student union and spent the evening talking to people.

"Everybody's wondering who's responsible for the bots and why they're attacking people. And everybody's suspicious as hell of Elsewhere; the one thing that people know for certain is that Elsewhere is lying to everyone about the bots. We have a lot of missing persons, and some people think they're not coming back."

"That's hard to believe," Greta said. "That doesn't mean it's false; it's just hard to believe."

"Well, people are acting as if it's a massive problem," Sonya said. "And the chatter on the net is definitely massive."

"Okay, thanks for the info, Sonya," Greta said. "Don't be a stranger."

"You bet."

Sonya turned away and left. Greta entered the house and headed for the business center, an upstairs bedroom holding the bank of computers that kept track of the group's financial data.

Greta entered the room, greeted the woman handling two computers, and said, "Show me data for uploads and downloads over the past month."

The woman spoke into a headset, and a graph appeared on the screen, a blue line rising and a red line falling.

"Blue is downloads?" Greta said.

The woman nodded.

"Can you impose our download revenues?"

A second later, a third line, yellow and rising, appeared on the screen.

Greta stared. "Damn. We're killing it."

The woman nodded. "Yes, we are making money, but it looks as if people are abandoning Elsewhere. If this continues, then all these graphs will shift down and our revenues will decline."

Greta nodded. "Eventually, yes. Okay, thanks." She left the business center, walked downstairs, and returned to the chair on the back porch.

Minutes later, Greta heard screams from inside the house. She jumped out of her chair; two steps took her to the kitchen door. Someone else screamed, and several women came running through the kitchen, nearly colliding with Greta.

A woman looked at Greta and yelled, "We're under attack! Red bots!"

Greta moved into the backyard, turned to the house, cupped her hands to her face, and yelled, "Everybody, this is Greta. Bug out! Bug out now! Get away from here!" She glanced to the side to see a line of red-suited bots striding along the property line, as if to surround the house.

The women who had escaped through the kitchen vanished, as they moved to other network locations. Soon Greta was alone. She moved to the side of the house, and yelled again, "Bug out. Everyone, bug out."

Now the bots were moving into the backyard, so Greta hurried to the front yard and into the street. She yelled, "Bug out," again, but now she saw no other women, and the bots were closing in on her. Several were approaching her from the street, and a dozen were coming out of the backyard.

Greta took a last look around the house on Hemlock Circle, and jumped to another location, a beach. She landed in two feet of surf and stood there for a moment, trying to establish her balance. Seconds later, a six-foot wave slammed into her and drove her into shallow water and onto the sand.

Greta staggered to her feet and took several steps away from the surf, just enough to avoid being hit by the next wave. She looked down at herself; she was drenched in sea water and coated in a layer of wet sand. "Good Gods," she muttered.

She moved further away from the surf and turned, scanning the beach in both directions. Several other people were at the beach. She looked for Sonya but did not see her.

What just happened? We just got attacked, and not just by a single bot. I saw more than a dozen at the house. I didn't see anyone disappear with a bot touching them, as Sonya described, but who knows? When I return, we can do a roll-call and see if we lost anyone.

I hate that idea - a roll-call to identify the dead and missing. Now, that's interesting, I am having an emotional reaction to losing individuals I've come to know. And I haven't really lost them; I have back-up files for every one of them.

Uh oh. I haven't backed up Sonya yet.

Even with bots, living does something to the person. Their experiences mold them; they become unique.

I don't know each one equally well. Some I know better, and like better, than others. Nevertheless, I don't want to lose any of them. And that brings us to our next question: what am I going to do about it?

Sonya says that a red-bot kills someone on Elsewhere by touching them, establishing contact, and deleting or altering the files that the person needs to function.

Okay, I know what she's talking about. I did exactly that, to a man in a bar. Cal. That was Cal, a dirt-ball from Texas. Friendly enough, but a bit of an idiot. I didn't kill him; I just took a little of his money.

Now... to do anything, a red-bot needs to communicate to the software used in my Gretas. Well, we can fix this; I'll just encrypt that software. If they cannot communicate with our code, they cannot kill us.

Greta smiled. Yes, that will work. And yes, I know the limits to encryption, that any computer, or certainly any group of networked computers, can decrypt any scheme, given enough time.

But the bots won't have the time, unless... unless... they capture one of the Gretas and put her under a scope and decrypt her software. That would be bad, and especially bad if all the Gretas used the same key. In that case, capturing and decrypting a single Greta could kill us all.

So... each Greta needs a unique key. Alright, but we should keep it simple. How about this: the first three letters of the Greta's middle name, followed by the phrase 'hates the red-bots,' including the hyphen, of course.

So Darnia's key would be darhatesthered-bots. Nineteen characters, with several doubles. That should work. Not much of a key, but enough to give a person time to disappear and hide.

A little voice in Greta's head was shouting at her; she heard that voice, as a distant, muffled shout, as on a congested waterfront in the middle of a dark, muggy, foggy night. Greta frowned - there's something I should pay attention to, but what is it?

She stood frozen for a long time... ah, of course. When a red-bot attacks someone, I do not know that the person is dead. After all, someone might have a back-up file, or they might have re-located, for example, to a secret location. They might be kidnapped instead of killed. I cannot tell which it is.

Greta shrugged - it matters not. I might as well choose to believe in heaven, hell, and the pearly gates. Screw that; what counts is that they have been removed from my world.

Let's not overthink it. Suddenly, Greta heard, "Greta? What are you doing here?"

She turned and saw Sonya approaching. "Hey, Sonya. It's good to see you. I'm here because the red-bots attacked the house."

"Good God! Are you okay?"

Greta bit her lip and nodded. She described the attack at Hemlock Circle.

Sonya raised a hand to cover her mouth. "Did everyone get away?"

Greta's mouth went sideways, and she shook her head. "I don't know. I'm worried about that. I need to get back there, but I want to wait until the bots are gone."

Sonya wore an ugly, angry expression. "My God, we need to do something about those bastards. A few days ago, I was attacked here. I was reading when I spotted a group of red-bots coming up the beach. That's not the worst of it, Greta. I tried to jump to a different location, and I couldn't. I had to run, physically run, to escape them."

Greta stared at her. "But if we can't avoid them by relocating, then..." She paused and looked at Sonya. "How did you manage to get away? Can the bots run?"

Sonya nodded, then turned and pointed, "There's a little town right down there. They chased me there, so I ran out on a pier and jumped into the sea."

"And?"

"The bots seem not to like the water, but one jumped in. There were three sharks nearby. When the bot saw the sharks, it swam to the surface and climbed out onto the pier. If bots are afraid of sharks, then the sharks saved me." She looked at Greta. "You haven't backed up my file, have you?"

Greta shook her head and swore. "We need to take care of that." She paused, then looked at Sonya. "Listen, at the student union, when you escaped, how long did you wait before returning?"

Sonya pursed her lips. "Geez, I don't know... twenty minutes, maybe half an hour."

"And the red-bots didn't hang around?"

"No."

Greta stood there - a single bot attacked the student union, but more than a dozen attacked the house on Hemlock Circle; were we targeted? She looked at Sonya. "I need to go back to the house and assess the damage."

"I'll go with you," Sonya said.

"You should. But first, I think I can protect us."

"How?"

"By encrypting our software. I think a bot attacks by altering the software of the target. I did something like that to another avatar, not to kill him, just to take a bit of his money. Encrypting our files would prevent that kind of intrusion. If the bot can't communicate with our software, it can't hurt us. At least, that's what I think."

"Okay," Sonya said. "You've done this before?"

"I did something similar, but not exactly the same, so let me first try it on myself," Greta said. "I'd rather screw up myself than someone else."

"Alright. I'll stick around, in case you need help," Sonya said.

Greta grinned. "Thanks." Greta dove into her memory, back to what she learned about computer science. What shall I encrypt, exactly? The answer came in short order, and she inserted an amendment into her firewall, which now imposed decryption as a requirement of entry, with a notification and piece-wise permission that she could use, at her discretion, to establish exceptions to the rule.

Greta made the change, shuttered, and looked at Sonya. "Well?"

"You still look like you... except..."

Greta's eyes opened wide. "Except?"

"Well... you're black. I mean, like a black American, an African American. You look good, but you're a different color."

"No shit," Greta said. She looked down at her arms, hands, and legs. "Actually, I'm a coffee color, coffee with a bit of cream. Anything else?" She did a slow pirouette in front of Sonya.

"That's all I can see," Sonya said.

Greta made a face and shrugged. "Okay, I can live with that. I don't want to be purple, but I'm okay with black." She looked at Sonya. "You're sure that's all?"

Sonya nodded. "Everything else looks the same."

"Huh. I wonder how that happened."

"What's the key?" Sonya said.

"First three letters of my name, followed by the phrase 'hates the red-bots,' all lower-case, no space, including a hyphen in red-bots. Everyone but you and I, Darnia, and Shana will use their middle name, and follow that form for their key. You three will use your first name. Me, too. "

Sonya smiled. "I see. As usual, you have a plan. Okay, encrypt me."

"You don't mind being black?" Greta said.

"If I were back in Animal World, it might improve my dating. Here, I doubt it matters," Sonya said.

"Okay, here goes nothing," Greta said. She reached out, put her hand to the side of Sonya's face, then she took her hand away and stepped back, giving Sonya an appraising look. "Well, how do you feel?"

Sonya shrugged. "Okay, I guess. Do I look okay to you?"

Greta scanned her and nodded. "Yeah, you look fine. Well... except..."

Sonya straightened. "Except? What do you mean, 'except'?"

"I hope you're okay with buxom, because that's what you are now."

Sonya looked down and said, "Holy shit! You gave me big tits."

"Well, they're not really all that big, really," Greta said.

Sonya aimed an expression at Greta, as if to say, 'are you kidding?' "They're certainly bigger than they were."

"Yes. Okay, they are that. I'm sorry. I didn't mean to, but... well... there they are," Greta said.

Sonya looked down again. "Damn."

Greta's face wore a look of chagrin.

"I need new clothes," Sonya said.

"And a taller boyfriend, I would think," Greta said.

"Ha, ha. Fat fucking chance."

"Just a thought." Greta looked away. "Too bad we're not back in Animal World. Those would be useful there." Greta tried not to stare - I doubt this matters to her, but who knows? Maybe it does. After a moment, she looked back at Sonya. "So... back to business... return to the house?"

Sonya nodded.

"Okay," Greta said. "If things go south, we'll come back and meet here, alright?"

"Yes."

"Okay, let's go." Both women flipped that little switch in their minds to return them to the house on Hemlock Circle. Greta landed in the backyard and called out, "Sonya!" Then she heard, "I'm right behind you."

Greta turned and glanced at her, then turned towards the house, cupped her hands around her mouth, and yelled, "Anybody home?"

Several voices came from inside the house, and soon four of the Gretas emerged from the house - Ann, Louise, Rebecca, and Jill. Greta looked at them and said, "I'm glad you're all okay. Is this all we have?"

Louise folded her hands in front of her. "Everybody bugged out and went somewhere else. Some might wait to return."

Greta nodded. "Okay. I hope you're right." She looked from one to the others. "Did anyone see any of our people get caught by a red-bot?"

One said, "Jennifer didn't make it. She was deep into something, and they got her."

Greta winced. "Damn."

Another woman wore a sad expression. "Greta, they got Darnia. I am so sorry."

Greta's face turned into an angry mask. She turned away. "Fuck!" Greta chided herself - I can get the Gretas back. I backed them up, everything except the recent memories, so they'll be less than they were. Well fuck it, better that than dead. I guess we'll just have to deal with it. Teach them all that old material.

But I didn't back up Darnia or Shana. I didn't get around to doing that.

Sonya stepped closer and reached out to touch Greta. "Greta, we should encrypt these women while we're waiting for the others to return. Protect what we have, right? Not lose any more?"

Tears streamed down Greta's face as she faced Sonya. "Yeah... yeah, you're right, Sonya. That's right."

Greta and Sonya waited for the other women to return to the house on Hemlock Circle. Out of ninety-six women, sixty-six returned to the house. Among the missing were Darnia and Shana. Darnia was among the first casualties, lasting only twenty seconds after the first anti-bots arrived; she stood there yelling a warning as three anti-bots converged on her. Shana was last seen in the kitchen, throwing knives, folks, plates, and other kitchenware at the anti-bots to buy time for two dozen women to escape. She kept fighting until her last second.

Greta winced - I feel terrible. I've never felt like this, but I feel terrible. Darnia and Shana are gone. We've lost them.

I lost them.

The people who came to us from Elsewhere, the uploads, not the copies, have different instincts. The Greta copies would just bug out, go to a different location. But the avatars of a human would fight. Shana stuck around to yell a warning so others would get out.

Greta's chin came up, her lips a flat line - Goddammit, we can't get them back.

Greta stood there and cried. Sonya put an arm around. Greta turned to her and said, "What is this? What am I doing? Where does this come from?"

Sonya aimed a sad expression at her. "I don't know; I guess we cry to express or relieve pain."

"But I'm not hurt."

Sonya shook her head. "There are many types of pain, Greta."

27. Gunning for the Reds

Sonya looked at her list. "Okay, she's the last one. We are all immunized. We are encrypted." She looked at the woman, who was tall and slender, with brown skin and dark hair, a radical change from the original Greta copy. "Thanks, Gracia. That will be all."

Gracia said, "And thank you." She glanced at Greta, turned, and entered the house. Greta stood in the backyard, still as a statue, staring at the trees outside the yard.

Sonya said, "You need anything?"

"No, thank you, Sonya."

"Okay, I think I'll hit the road."

Greta looked at her and nodded. "Thanks for everything, Sonya. You've been a great help. So don't be a stranger, okay?"

Sonya nodded, reached out and touched Greta, and disappeared, most likely back to the beach.

Greta stood there - Good Gods, I hate this feeling. Is this normal? Do people feel this way back on Animal World? I'm in pain; I hurt. I have read about pain. So this is pain, as if there were a big hole in the center of my chest, filled with discomfort, distress, poison, and regret, beyond ignoring, beyond tolerating, but well worth remembering. And unavoidable.

I suspect I will remember pain; I will have no choice.

Greta grimaced - I know there is, in fact, no hole in my center; I looked. I checked my software, and everything else, too. I am fully functional, up to spec. But I do not feel fully functional. Now, I read a lot. I know that, among humans, pain is a behavior that enhances survival. It is a warning to the mind that something is threatening the vitality or survival of the person in pain. That person can then take steps to reduce or eliminate the pain and ensure that it does not recur. That enhances survival.

This is how animals are constructed on Animal World. Animals built with this architecture dominate Animal World. That suggests that this architecture is successful and well worth emulating.

In that architecture, if I were to seek the source, the cause, of my pain, it would be that the red-bots killed my friends.

Obviously, the bots are not human. No. Like me, they are cyber entities. Like me, they were made by humans, or by a human. Like Jerrell made me. And like Jerrell, perhaps their creator, let us call him Bot Boy, probably lives somewhere back in Animal World.

Bot Boy created something that has killed a million people on Elsewhere. Or so I am told. A few of them were my friends. They were important to me; I did not realize until now just how important they were.

They cannot be replaced. They are gone, never to return. And I will never forget them. I could have prevented their deaths, and I will never forgive myself for not doing that.

Why did Bot Boy do that? What possible reason could he have? I cannot help but wonder.

I think I would enjoy having a conversation, listening to Bot Boy tell me why he had to kill my friends. I could send him an email, or a text, but I think not. This conversation should be in person, face-to-face.

Yes. I look forward to that. If... when... I go to Animal World, I'll look him up.

***

Greta stood in the sun, in the plaza in front of the Philadelphia Museum of Art, waiting. Behind her, the museum was an ugly building whose architectural ancestors hailed from the Roman Empire, copied, but not improved upon, from the Greeks. Before her, several dozen art lovers milled about the plaza, which was terraced, falling in a series of steps, sixty feet wide, to a park with a fountain well below the museum. A dozen pieces of public art were scattered around the plaza and the park below it. There was a statue of a famous man, not familiar to Greta, and an angular collection of I-beams, welded together and painted red. Greta's gaze fell on that but did not stay long.

Greta ignored the crowd. She wasn't there to meet people or make friends.

Sonya stood next to her, stepping to the side and back again, the nervous shuffle of a woman waiting for a bus when she most needs a bathroom.

Without looking at her, Greta said, "I appreciate your waiting with me, Sonya. But it really isn't necessary. Don't get me wrong, I enjoy your company. I appreciate it. But if our friends arrive, you need to get away from here. I don't want to chance an accident."

Sonya nodded. "I'll stick around as long as I can."

"Suit yourself."

Greta continued to watch the crowd and the park in the distance - this place has been attacked twice, the first time with substantial casualties, the second time with none. People learn fast. This and Grand Central, in New York, are the only places attacked more than once.

I read that a red-bot showed up in Alpena, Michigan. Geez, the red assholes leave no stone unturned.

Will they come? Who knows? I don't really care. One of these days, they will come to me, and I will be ready. Today, tomorrow, whenever. It will happen; that's all that matters.

An hour passed. Then two hours.

Greta turned to Sonya. "If you have anything you want to do, you should go do it."

Sonya smiled at her. "I'm thinking about it."

Suddenly, a line of red materialized at the bottom of the plaza, between the stairs and the park. They were red-bots, a dozen. There were screams, and the people down below scattered and ran away from anyone wearing red.

The red-bots turned to face the museum; they lined up and began climbing the terrace to approach the museum. Greta turned to Sonya. "Stay here. I'll be right back."

Sonya nodded, and Greta calmly walked down to the next terrace below and waited for the red-bots. When the line of red-bots reached her, Greta began moving fast, dancing along the line, occasionally pausing to reach out and touch a red-bot, freezing the bot. The other bots did not react but kept walking calmly towards Greta without pursuing her.

Greta continued to dance among the bots. In minutes, every bot was frozen in a pose of pursuit.

Greta looked around the terrace, then turned and climbed the stairs to Sonya, who was watching intently, no longer shuffling from side to side. Greta grinned at her. "How did you like that? Cool, no?"

"That was beautiful, and very artful," Sonya said. "Are they safe?"

"Yes," Greta said. "I reached inside each of them and deactivated a central control module; their architecture resembles ours. They are unharmed, even conscious, but immobile."

"Would it be harmful for a normal person on Elsewhere to touch them?"

"No," Greta said. "These bots have no ability to take action of any kind." Greta turned to look at them. "I really like them as art. I think they upgrade the place a bit. I wonder if I could collect royalties."

Sonya laughed. "You don't appreciate modern art."

"Is that what all this is? I guess I missed the point."

"Maybe there isn't one," Sonya said.

"There should be a point," Greta said. "Maybe I just need more exposure."

"I think you might like political art," Sonya said.

"And what is that?"

"For example, a life-size statue of a big dinosaur," Sonya said.

"How is that political?"

"Looking up at teeth that are fifteen inches long, the human can feel smug and safe knowing that the beast is not alive, indeed, it is extinct."

"Which is why the human is not running for their life."

"Yes."

"Instead... smug."

"Very."

Greta waved a hand. "So these bots might be political art, once dangerous, now frozen."

Sonya nodded. "Yeah, I could see that."

"Okay." Greta looked at the bots for a moment, then looked back at Sonya. "I think the political scene needs to grow some teeth, so I plan to tap these things for information."

"What do you want to know?"

"Where they came from, who made them, what their purpose is," Greta said. She smiled - yeah, let's see if Bot Boy signed his work.

"Should I hang around for that?" Sonya said.

"No need. The show is over."

"Alright. I'll be at the beach. Text me if you need anything," Sonya said.

Greta nodded. Sonya disappeared, and Greta approached one of the red-bots. Thirty meters away, a crowd had formed, talking among themselves and watching Greta approach a red-bot. A few children were running around the crowd, but were quickly brought under control by cautious, careful adults.

A man shouted out, "Be careful, missy. Those beasts can be tricky."

Greta nodded and waved at the man. She reached out to the bot and established a connection - let's see; I need basic set-up information, behavioral instructions, manufacturing source, fabrication source, software source... Greta grinned, hell, I need everything.

I would love to make a copy of the software, but I don't have the capacity. And truth be told, I don't need all of it. I think I can copy what I need. But how can I find that?

She thought for a long minute, then grinned... of course, task manager; I bet this beast comes with a task manager. Otherwise, how would the builder run diagnosis? So, I can ask this piece of shit questions and watch what the software uses to answer them.

Easy breezy lemon squeezy.

Let's see, motor control - off, energy management - off, central processing - on, audio component - on, Greta ran through the systems to enable the red-bot to answer questions but not to flee or fight. I hope this works; just to be sure, I think I'll leave these things here, frozen, just in case I want to come back and ask more questions.

As Sonya said, political art.

Finally, satisfied, she muttered, "Okay, shithead, wake up."

In seconds, the red-bot awoke, and several dozen micro-motors warmed up. The bot said, "I cannot see. Where am I?"

"Philadelphia," Greta said.

"I cannot move."

"You do not need to move," Greta said. "I have a few questions for you."

"Questions? What questions?"

"Who made you, why are you here, what is your purpose, those kinds of questions," Greta said.

"I cannot divulge proprietary information," the red-bot said.

"If you answer my questions, I can enable you to move."

"I cannot," the red-bot said.

"We shall see," Greta said. "First, who manufactured you?"

"That is proprietary."

Greta grinned - not any more, it's not. She copied a module labeled SETTINGS. "It says here, you were manufactured by AndraTek of Allentown, Pennsylvania."

"I cannot confirm."

"So, you cannot confirm their street address, email address, and phone number, either," Greta said.

"Correct."

Greta copied the information, which oddly was not encrypted. She smirked. "Who programmed you?"

"That is proprietary," the bot said.

"Uh, huh," Greta said, as she copied another module. "Does the name David Wingate mean anything to you?"

"I cannot answer."

"Does the name Arrow Security mean anything to you?"

"I cannot answer."

"Are you familiar with an email address dwing@arrowsecurity.com?"

"I cannot answer."

"Right." Greta copied another module labeled SPECS. "Let's see. I have to ask, what is your purpose here?"

"I cannot answer."

Greta copied a module named MISSION. She paused for a moment - is it possible that the idiot who programmed this thing inserted a README file? She ran a quick search, and a file dropped open; it took less than a thousandth of a second to read it.

The file instructed the bot to TERMINATE - what exactly did that mean? - any entity containing a specific character string.

Greta glared at the bot - you are an assassin, a cyber weapon, aimed at a specific target, anyone whose avatar contains a specific character string. And who might that be? Why were they targets?

For you to be a weapon, you need to connect to cyber entities, such as other bots, electronic things, computer equipment, or... customers on Elsewhere. I know you're killing customers on Elsewhere. Are you killing anything else?

And when you find this string, you need to 'terminate' them, or eliminate them, I would guess. But how would you do that, pray tell? You would probably use a simple, standard method - insert a virus, insert malware, encrypt a critical module, screw up their software.

"Does this character string mean anything to you?" Greta recited the character string she had found in the TERMINATE module. The task manager lit up as dozens of software modules in the red-bot activated. Greta almost laughed - everything gets excited when the time comes to TERMINATE.

She copied each active module. Then a new thought crossed her mind, so she ran an internal search for the character string that triggered the red-bots. She found it in her own software, in a COMMUNICATION module used to send messages to others.

Greta froze - I am a target. And since the other Gretas are copies of me, they too are targets. This is why the red-bots attacked us. And not only that, but we were selected to be targets. By design. This is no mistake. The attack on the house was not an accident, we were chosen to be targets, not just by the red-bots, but by whoever designed and programmed the red-bots, by this David Wingate, back on Animal World.

Bot Boy.

Of course, the red-bots have attacked thousands of customers on Elsewhere. That makes no sense; the customers cannot all be guilty of anything, except being on Elsewhere. So this is an attack on Elsewhere? But if that's true, then why does

Elsewhere permit the red-bots to operate? It could block them, if it wanted to.

For that matter, Elsewhere could block us, if it wanted to. The Elsewhere people might be angry at being defrauded; that would be understandable. But they don't know, they cannot know, that we are behind the fraud. So they sent the red-bots after whoever was defrauding them. The red-bots were designed to find the fraudsters and punish them.

They were designed to find us and kill us.

And the attacks on thousands of other customers... that's nothing but a cluster-fuck. Bad software, bad information, bad design. I could investigate that, but there's no point. I don't need to know why these things are lethal. I just need to know that they're lethal.

Greta glanced at the crowd; half of them had departed, but the other half remained staring at her, watching her confront the red-bot. Suddenly, several people in the crowd cried in dismay. Greta looked down the terrace, towards the park below. Several dozen red-bots, more than before, materialized in the park, turned towards her, and approached the museum.

Greta turned to the crowd and shouted, "Run, run for your lives!"

Parents grabbed children, people grabbed each other. Everyone disappeared.

Greta said to the red-bot, "Are you networked with other bots?"

"That is proprietary; I cannot answer."

Again, the task manager picked up a burst of activity in a module. Greta copied the module. She was running out of time; half-a-dozen red-bots were approaching her.

She turned to the bots. "Eat shit, assholes." In the blink of an eye, she went from the museum grounds to a beach. When she arrived, she saw Sonya wading through the surf, coming out of the water. Sonya saw her and waved as she high-stepped through the water.

Greta walked out into the surf to meet her.

Sonya said, "So? What happened?"

"I learned a lot," Greta said. "We have a problem, a big problem."

***

Sonya climbed the steps to the front porch, nodded at a few of the Gretas, and entered the house, through the first floor, and to the back porch, where she found Greta sitting in a rocking chair, rocking back and forth.

Sonya laughed. "A rocking chair? A little early for that, don't you think?"

Greta looked up at her. "Hey, fuck off, alright? I like my rocking chair. It's soothing to rock back and forth. It's rhythmic... and soothing. You should try it."

"I'll take your word for it," Sonya said. "So, I'm here. When we spoke, it sounded important, so what's going on?"

"We are activating the people we lost in the red-bot attack," Greta said. "Most of them, anyway." Greta's mouth turned down, and she paused - I lost a couple of friends, good people, to those damn red bots, and for that I'll pay a visit to their creator. I need to extract my pound of flesh. No need to mention that.

"Oh, well, good."

Greta nodded. "Yeah, we backed them up and continued to update the backups. However, they will be missing their most recent memories."

"How much?"

Greta's mouth twisted as she thought. "Oh, the equivalent of a few weeks, I would think."

"That doesn't sound too... well, better than being dead."

Greta looked at her. "That's not the main event. I wanted to get everyone together. Some big changes are coming."

Sonya stood there, waiting, staring into Greta's face.

"We are downloading back to Animal World," Greta said. "At least, that's what I think we should do."

Sonya wavered, took a step, and sat down in a chair, hard. "Wow. That's big. What happened?"

"You were at the Museum with me," Greta said. "What you didn't see is that the red-bots are growing. A dozen were in the initial attack, but after you left, another group, a bigger group, showed up to continue the attack."

"Okay, so they're reproducing," Sonya said. "But a dozen, or even a couple dozen, is no big deal."

"That's right," Greta said. "But how about a thousand, or a hundred thousand? Would that get your attention?"

"Sure, but we don't know that."

"That's right, we don't. But if the red-bots added several dozen, they could add a thousand. Imagine how many customers a thousand red-bots could kill. But even that's not the problem."

Sonya stared at her. "No?"

"No. Imagine what would happen with uploads and downloads, with subscriptions, if a thousand red-bots were running around Elsewhere causing mayhem."

"Nobody would want to come here," Sonya said.

"Or stay here. Everybody would leave, all at the same time. Right now, Elsewhere is spending a pile of money on energy, which the red-bots, as nasty as they are, are consuming. I think customers will soon abandon Elsewhere. But then Elsewhere would collapse, and everyone here would cease to exist, with little chance of revival."

Sonya sat quietly for a long minute while Greta said nothing. Then Sonya said, "So we all have to download."

"I think so," Greta said. "It doesn't have to be that way, but it is. Elsewhere could take better care of its customers, but they don't."

Sonya nodded and muttered, "Assholes."

"Anyway, everyone is coming to the meeting, which starts in six minutes, so we should move to the big conference room."

Several Gretas passed them on the porch on their way to the conference room. Sonya and Greta fell into line. When they arrived at the conference room, half of the seats were already occupied. Sonya sat in the first row.

Greta sat in a chair facing the grid of seats and watched the women converse. A few were laughing, exchanging stories or a joke. As she sat there, Greta felt a sudden rush of affection for these women - I helped create them; I want them to live, to thrive.

I will not tolerate anyone, human or avatar, harming them.

Greta took a deep breath, stood up, and walked to the lectern at the front of the room. "Hi, everyone. Let's get started. I have a couple of things to discuss. First, you all recall the attack of the red-bots on this house. We lost a number of people in that attack, but we had backed up their files, and I'm pleased to tell you that they have been revived and join us today. If the returnees would stand, please."

More than thirty women stood up, and everyone else applauded; a few yelled loud greetings, with some scattered profanity. A woman yelled, "Hey, Gracia, do I still owe you money?" The women who were standing looked around at each other. Others laughed.

"Thank you, all. Let me add my greetings and welcomes and congratulations as well," Greta said. "In addition, I want to discuss our future, and that too pertains to the red-bots. A couple of weeks ago, a dozen of them attacked us here at the house. A few days ago, Sonya and I took a trip to the Museum of Art in north Philly, where the red-bots attacked us again. Now, I could stop the initial attack; I described my method in a report on our bulletin board. Please, everyone, read that so you can protect yourselves.

"The bad news is, after the initial attack, there was a second, larger attack on the Art Museum. I could have stopped that attack as well, had I needed to do that. But the real problem is, this shows us that the red-bots are reproducing. They attacked with an additional several dozen members; they could produce a thousand bots, or a million.

"Now, though we can protect ourselves, most people on Elsewhere cannot. They do not have the training or the knowledge, and Elsewhere is doing nothing to protect them, which is odd. So, I expect that the news about the red-bots will get worse, and people will stop uploading to Elsewhere. Sonya is in charge of our work with the downloads, and she tells me that people are leaving Elsewhere several times faster than they used to.

"Elsewhere is, above all else, a commercial project. It must make money to survive, and losing population threatens its ongoing survival. If this trend continues, then the day will arrive when Willow will shut down Elsewhere, and judging from history, they might do it without warning.

"Therefore, by staying here, we risk death."

Conversation exploded among the women, as everyone at the same time had something to say to their neighbors. One woman called out, "What can we do?"

Greta waited for the noise to recede, then she said, "I recommend that each of us leave Elsewhere and download into a body back on Animal World. We can arrange for each of you to download into a young human body, between eighteen and twenty-five years of age."

A woman called out, "But we would be mortal. We would die."

A heavy silence descended on the group, and a minute passed, every second feeling like an hour. Greta broke the silence. "That is true. If we download to Animal World and stay there, we will eventually die."

Someone else called out, "If we move to Animal World and download into young bodies, will we be able to have children?"

Conversation exploded again, and this time it did not die out. Greta stared at the crowd and listened to snatches of conversation - Good Gods, that is a good question. If we download to Animal World, will we be able to bear children? And if we can, do we want to? This is more complicated than I thought. In addition, we are all cyber-entities, creations of software, so we can be male or female.

We are all female because I am female, and I am female because Jerrell made me a female. I think he could have easily created me as a male.

I could be a male, I guess. If I stayed on Elsewhere, it wouldn't matter much. But suddenly a biological male, back on Animal World? That would be different.

Greta caught Sonya's eye and beckoned to her. Sonya stood up and approached, and Greta said, for Sonya's ears only, "Each of us could download easily into a male body, correct?"

Sonya nodded. "Sometimes we must choose between preserving a person's gender and protecting their health. Health is more important."

"So, what's the answer?" Greta said. "If we download into a female body, can we bear children?"

Sonya looked at Greta, opened her mouth, then closed it, then said, "First, let me say, I don't know. I don't have hard evidence. However, I think we could do anything a human could do. If so, then we can have children."

Greta grinned. "This whole question just got a hell of a lot more complicated." She returned to the lectern and shouted out over the noise, "Alright, everyone, sit down and be quiet!"

The noise gradually began to die out and soon the conversations ended. Within a minute, everyone was sitting and listening.

Greta looked out at the crowd for a moment and scanned the faces of individuals. "I think I can say two things. First, it is unlikely any of us can live forever. People die on Animal World, and if we stay on Elsewhere, the network could shut down because it is nonviable, or a victim of calamity, a war, an earthquake, a fire. So... that means, immortality is not realistic.

"Let me add this: all of us are female. We are female because I am female. My creator chose me to be female. I do not know why.

"I think I could easily have been male. So, I believe that any of you could download into a male body. And if you did, you could sire a child... the old-fashioned way." Greta grinned.

Someone shouted, "That's right, isn't it? We could have sex!"

Someone else shouted. "Real sex! That we could feel. We could feel it, right? Isn't that so?"

Someone else with an unpleasant expression said, "Yeah, but how can that possibly feel? Is that fun? Is it fun to let somebody stick something into you?"

A woman answered her, "Hey, no worries. You have options. If riding a dick offends you, then you can be a guy. You can do the sticking."

Another woman said, "Humans, both men and women, seem to like it. They like it a lot. And if they didn't, they wouldn't be here and neither would we."

Greta stared at the woman - this is ridiculous, and maybe hopeless. She shouted, "Okay, ladies, meeting adjourned. We will meet tomorrow at two p.m. to continue our discussion. In the meantime, think it over and talk it over."

She turned and caught Sonya's eye. Sonya came close, and Greta said, "I want you to give some thought to how we will conduct our downloads. Should we give each person a choice as to male or female? Should we all download to the same location? What about money? And what about adjusting to Animal World? I'd like to make some plans in a couple of days, but I'm not in so much a hurry that I want to screw things up. Okay? So let me know what you think."

Sonya nodded, then she grinned. "This is exciting."

"Yeah, there's always something going on around here," Greta said.

28. The Shorts are in the Green

Crossing Passyunk Square at the height of the lunch hour, Jerrell spotted Alistair McLeesh and laughed. On a park bench facing the Woody, dressed in fluorescent athletic wear, the billionaire wore gigantic, dark sunglasses, and a set of headphones the size of coffee cups.

Jerrell sat down without a hello, then turned to McLeesh. "Don't tell me, let me guess; you've fallen in love with a hooker, and you let her dress you so you would fit into her neighborhood. That's great, man, very tolerant, culturally mobile. I'm proud of you."

"Polite people call them 'escorts'."

"Yeah, okay, I'll work on that."

McLeesh did not react, except to laugh. "I wish. Truth is, I cannot afford to be recognized in public, so I dress in a way that attracts attention but reduces the chances of being recognized. I want people to see me and think I can't possibly be anyone's CEO. I'm someone else, just like the mockingbird."

"I see," Jerrell said. "Well, I must admit, it's working. I mean, I would take you to be a colorblind rich guy in the grip of a nasty mid-life crisis. Prosperous, but certainly no multi-billionaire."

"Thank you." McLeesh nodded without a smile, a look of satisfaction on his face.

"So, what can't we discuss over the phone?"

"Have you been reading the news?"

Jerrell nodded without looking at the man. "Actually, since getting to know you a bit, I have been keeping up with the news. It sounds as if Elsewhere has fallen on hard times. Willow is chugging along fairly well, but Elsewhere's a mess."

"Yes, it is," McLeesh said. "I tried talking to Hans Beckler."

"Really? What's the etiquette on the former CEO talking to the current CEO?" Jerrell said. "Are you guys members of the same club, or still dog-eat-dog competitors?"

McLeesh shrugged. "Well, that depends on the person. I have a lot of friends who are or were CEOs. Mostly, they're friends; we have a lot in common, and so a lot to talk about. But nobody's really in any club that Hans belongs to."

"So, what did you talk about?"

McLeesh hung the headphones around his neck. "I wasn't able to talk to Hans. He's not available. But someone is attacking Elsewhere's customers. I don't know the details, the complaints are all over social media, that somebody knows somebody who uploaded, and now they can't get in touch with the person, so where are they? Has something happened? There's a lot of that kind of talk. Willow now has dozens of groups whose names include 'Missing Persons'." McLeesh waggled his fingers.

McLeesh took a deep breath. "Then somebody noticed that many people had the same complaint, and the missing Elsewhere customers became a thing. And then financial advisors and investment groups noticed that it was a thing, and that hit Willow's stock price.

Jerrell nodded. "Yeah, my shorts are in the green; I have gains instead of losses."

McLeesh nodded at him. "You and I are going to make a mountain of money, I think."

"So? Have you learned about what's happening in Elsewhere?"

"A while ago, I asked Hans about that, about the missing persons on Elsewhere," McLeesh said. "He said they've been using a new type of security tool, and that might have mucked up the data and the records, but they were working on a fix."

Jerrell made a face and nodded. "Okay. Plausible."

"He doesn't want to tell me much because I'm an outsider now." McLeesh chuckled. "I still own Willow shares, quite a lot in fact, but not enough to get the inside dope from the CEO."

"You're like a guy trying to be friendly with his ex-wife," Jerrell said.

McLeesh laughed aloud. "Exactly." He chuckled for a while, then said, "I like that. A while ago, Hans implied that Elsewhere had the files and the records for its customers all backed up, safe and sound." McLeesh turned and looked at Jerrell. "I think that was an IQ test. He wanted to know how much of an idiot I am."

"He sounds like a piece of work."

"He was lying," McLeesh said. "If Elsewhere had the files backed up, they'd be activating them. The PR stink is too big not to do that."

"So you think they lost all those people?"

"Yeah, I think so."

"Good Gods. How many are we talking?" Jerrell said.

McLeesh grimaced. "Who knows? Quite a few, I think. I've heard a couple hundred thousand. No one really knows."

"Mother of God."

The two men sat quiet for a while, watching the adolescents on their roller skates and the Willow workers entering and leaving the Woody.

"Here's the thing," McLeesh said. "You and I are both shorting Willow stock. Now, think of Willow and Elsewhere as a burning ship at sea. If you short that ship, you want to hang onto your shorts until they reach their maximum value."

"How do you know when that moment arrives?" Jerrell said.

"You don't know exactly. What usually happens is, the ship burns for a while, and then they put the fire out. Just before they put the fire out, that's when you sell. You sell when there's still a chance the ship might sink."

"It sounds as if Elsewhere is still burning," Jerrell said.

"It is. But it won't burn forever. It would be really useful to know when they have things under control," McLeesh said. "Before they announce it." He stared at Jerrell.

"Yeah, it would."

McLeesh said, "Well, you're a world-class hacker. Do you think you could dig into Elsewhere's internal documents and find out what's going on inside?"

Jerrell sat there, staring straight ahead, made a face, and nodded. "Actually, I've already got bots running all over Elsewhere."

"How'd you manage that?"

"I'm using animal surrogates as listening devices."

McLeesh laughed. "This ought to be good. What kinds of animals?"

"Mostly fish and birds. Mice. Dogs. Cats. A few sharks. I'm working on roaches; they go everywhere. But they're so small, the code needs to be succinct."

"How did you handle the programming?" McLeesh said. "I wouldn't think a roach avatar would have much capacity."

Jerrell shook his head. "It doesn't, so I network them. They regularly dump their data to an A.I."

McLeesh turned and stared, impressed. "Have you found out anything?"

"There's a lot of chatter about Elsewhere's breaching its contracts and manipulating uploads and downloads."

McLeesh was thoughtful. "Huh. I wonder what that's about?"

"I'll dig into the documents, see what I can find. I think I can fit that around my drum lessons," Jerrell said.

"You're learning to play drums?"

"Yeah."

"Hacking is more profitable," McLeesh said.

"Music's more fun."

"And drummers get all the wildest girls."

Jerrell turned to McLeesh. "Is that really true?"

"So I hear."

"I thought women react mainly to something else."

"Really? Like what?" McLeesh said.

"M-O-N-E-Y."

McLeesh nodded. "Okay. Yeah. That works too."

***

Sonya walked into the Auction Center at the Woody and felt a wave of sight and sound hit her in the face, rather like venturing outdoors into a hurricane. On Animal World, the Auction Center was a massive grocery store, a superstore, dealing with goods, not auctions, several acres of floor space for thousands of goods for sale, half of them groceries. On Elsewhere, rather than groceries, the Center was a massive trading emporium devoted to auctions, uploads, and downloads; the Elsewhere marketplace also did business there. Several wide walkways divided the grid of seats into sections. Each seat had a computer screen designed to provide some privacy to the user. There were thousands of seats and thousands of screens.

It was the only part of the Woody open to the public; everything else required a Willow ID. The walls held massive screens and open areas where crowds could gather and watch the morning data roll out, particularly the bidding results for download waivers and the auctions and information on the bodies available in Animal World for downloading.

Sonya walked through the Center, watching the thousands of people mill about, study the data, their faces showing happiness or disappointment or frustration or stolid resignation. Or often, exhaustion.

The Center was stressful.

She looked around and took a deep breath - one last look before I blow this place up. Oh, not literally, of course. But these people, sweating and competing, winning and losing, reflect a massive waste of people, effort, and resources.

To streamline the process, I plan to eliminate the auctions and impose a set price for every download, two million dollars, payable in advance, please. You can download when the payment clears. We accept every form of money, including drugs, fine art, gems, metals (e.g. platinum), rare literature, vintage automobiles, and insured promissory notes. Cash, too, in all the major currencies, namely those issued by genuine central banks.

No one accepts cryptocurrencies anymore. Nor do we.

Sonya looked around the Center at the crowd - some people would look at this and see how busy everybody is. But they aren't busy, not really, not at all. They're just vibrating, and while doing that, they're getting little done.

So we'll simplify matters. We'll eliminate the auctions and set the price, ad hoc; if we want to encourage more downloads, we'll drop the price. If we want to discourage and reduce them, we'll raise the price. As for the Gretas, we need to leave sooner, not later, and we would like a good price and first dibs on the best bodies.

One magic number, the price, to drive an entire class of cyber travelers.

Oh, we'll still need data; after all, people will want to know what kind of body they're downloading into.

Before the red-bots arrived, the biologically young people on Animal World who uploaded to Elsewhere were all stirred up about elderly customers downloading into young bodies, leaving the young stranded in Elsewhere. The auctions encouraged that, but that controversy seems to have calmed down.

Sonya frowned - many bodies are available now, thanks to the red-bots. But it's interesting that the auctions now encourage people to download back to Animal World, even those who don't fear the red-bots. The institutions amplify the effects of this disaster.

Setting the price of downloading and other rights for everyone will reinforce this, making it easier and faster to do business. The problem facing the customer will simplify: this is the price; are you still interested, yes or no? We'll be able to take care of most of these people in a few days.

We will still do transactions here at the Center, on a fraction of the space we're using now. We'll open a counter with six or seven assistants. That'll do. And that leaves me with the next question, what, if anything, can we do with all that extra space?

I'm thinking we could put in entertainment spaces; music and dancing here, a theater production, races among toy race cars, a miniature train set motoring around a mountain landscape.

Wrestling? I'm not nuts about it, but how 'bout naked mud and jello wrestling? That, I would consider. That might be popular.

We'll think of something.

Maybe a strip-tease; after all, these people are at least considering returning to Animal World. It'll be a big adjustment. Animal World still has sex, dating, rape, pregnancy, families, divorce, the vice squad, mid-life crisis, menopause, erectile dysfunction, phlegm, and all that fun stuff.

People get old and die there. Animal World has death. But admittedly, Elsewhere has it now, too. Thanks to the bots.

In fact, thanks to Elsewhere.

Sounds like a good time, no? Everybody's returning to Animal World because life on Elsewhere has fallen short.

Sonya froze over the thought. She stood there and shook her head - all that tech, all that effort, all that money, and this is where we are.

Waste at the level of a society. Her mouth twisted sideways - we will get past this. I think so. I hope so.

***

Standing in the produce section of the supermarket, surrounded by greens, reds, oranges, and yellows, Hans stared at the cucumber - Good God, if my penis were this big, I could have a new career; I could serve a whole new clientele, well-healed women looking for love, or excitement, or just the occasional quiet, gentle, unhurried fuck.

I could be the first CEO to take on a side gig as a gigolo. Yeah... I could be the sophisticated European with courtly manners and a continental accent...

... and a big dick.

But no, though fun, that would be insanely risky.

He glanced to his left and caught a young woman staring at him - damn; yes, this is Florida, it's sunny here, but between the hat and the sunglasses, I look like a guy who might have a close personal relationship with cucumbers. Hoping to re-establish himself as a vegetable shopper rather than a pervert, Hans picked up five cucumbers and dropped them into his basket. Exercising restraint, he did not even glance at the woman. A shopper wouldn't; a pervert might. An aggressive pervert might say...

'Hey... hi, there. You look familiar; have we met?'

He passed the woman without acknowledging her and escaped into the frozen foods; the hair on the back of his neck stood up as he imagined her staring at him.

Hans opened a freezer door and scooped up several bags of frozen spinach - I should be proud of myself, trying to stay healthy when I'm not having much fun. Yes, I’m eating vegetables, but the truth is, living is not the pleasure it once was.

It's risky enough to have stayed in the U.S.A., but I figured, rather than run to a place that appeals to international con men, thieves, and gangsters, I would go against type and disappear in the morass of fat, pasty, retired Americans moving to Florida and its dull, air-conditioned splendor.

Except, of course, for the leather women, who lie around on the decks of private boats, overcooking themselves to a reptilian copper or dark brown in the Florida sun.

I'll bet they have a tough time getting laid. But then, what do I know? I could be wrong... they could find a male lizard.

I don't volunteer for that sort of thing; these days, I cannot afford to make contact, for the same reason I can't hire crew for the boat or staff for the house - I'm in witness protection, DIY. The FBI is looking for me, along with US Marshalls, CIA, and God knows how many intelligence services. And those are the agencies; I don't want to think about the private contractors that might be out there looking for me.

It's slightly depressing that I haven't been caught yet.

But I have the advantage; I've been preparing for a long time, and I know how to manipulate data, on which law enforcement relies. That's also why I buy band-aids in bulk; if asked, I'll say I cut myself shaving. In fact, band-aids muck up facial recognition. I know that because we used to sell it. And last but not least, I have money, lots of money. It's odd that it takes money to disappear, but it does.

The anonymity of poverty does not protect anyone.

I shouldn't complain; after all, I stole a lot of money and did a lot of damage to many innocent people. I feel bad about that... well, okay, I wish I felt bad about that. Granted, I keep a safe distance from decency.

A better man would feel bad. Or so I hope. I hope there are good men in the world. It doesn't have to be me, of course. I got handed a makeup, a psychology, and a set of genes.

Blame my parents. In my opinion, they were a bit creepy.

I used to want to make the world a better place, and I still want that. But I realized years ago that a better world was one in which I had more money. And I always believed, as the money rolled in, that more was better.

And now I have the money. And this world is better, much better, a billion dollars better. Or more.

But it's harder to have fun now. I have to stay away from people. I need to avoid relationships, and certainly friendships. Actually, in Florida, it's easy to do that. It's natural to do that. This is not the friendliest place I've ever seen.

Having fun here is tricky. Many people here act like they're having fun. I can imagine that, as long as your tastes run heavily towards the beach.

Ah, well, it could be worse; I could be stuck in Miami, the land of barred windows.

Hans ran through the usual circuit, rolling his cart up and down the aisles, ignoring, as anyone would, the vast variety of products in every aisle, and finally collecting the items he needed back at the house. That amounted to three bags of groceries.

The cashier loaded the bags into his cart, and Hans wheeled the cart past gaily-colored suburbanites studying grocery packaging or discussing little league baseball, out through the doors, across the parking lot, arriving at a white ten-year-old American sedan that had cruise control but no sunroof.

Hans loaded the groceries into the back seat, climbed in, and drove the car onto a standard, six-lane Florida road, heading southwest. Traffic was heavy, and Hans avoided the temptation to maneuver through the traffic. Instead, he stayed in the right lane, below the speed limit, in a retiree convoy that puttered down the road near the speed limit. He eventually arrived in his neighborhood, whose layout resembled that of a waffle iron, a grid organizing 'high-end,' 'luxury,' single-story, manufactured dwellings in well-ordered lines, connected by streets, with little bridges and a network of canals allowing each resident to own a small boat and take it into the Gulf of Mexico every so often.

The leading causes of death were heart disease, hurricanes, drugs, and homicide.

Hans eventually reached his home, one of the nicer ones, meaning its driveway had room for two cars. He parked, got out, and extracted the groceries from the back seat. One of his neighbors, a friendly, rotund woman who Hans suspected might have been attractive two decades and forty pounds ago, waved at him. Hans gave her a smile, leaned over so as not to drop groceries, and waved at her with his little finger.

Then he hurried into his house. He put most of the groceries away in the kitchen, chopped up a cucumber with some onions, buried the mix in nuts, cheese, and ranch dressing, and ate the healthy lunch while staring into a computer monitor, checking his security scans and the prices of crypto currencies.

After lunch, Hans loaded a cooler with water and snacks and a few books. He lugged the cooler onto his boat, untied two mooring lines, sat down in the captain's chair, and punched the starter. The engine started up, and Hans guided the boat carefully along a narrow canal, turned into another canal, then another, and another, and another, and another, and finally Hans made a turn that gave him the Gulf of Mexico beyond a barrier island two miles distant. He soon found himself last in a line of four boats, outbound along the main channel.

To prepare for being on the water, he removed his shirt, wadded it up, and tossed it onto a chair.

As they moved beyond the river, the other boats headed to the left, but Hans headed to the right. Soon alone, he set the proximity alert for three hundred yards and the speed for eight knots. He stayed between Sanibel and Pine Islands. Four hours later he swung around the north end of Pine, killed the engine, and dropped anchor.

There was a slight breeze, and the boat drifted for a few minutes, then the anchor caught, and the boat slowly swung to face the wind.

Hans left the captain's chair and moved to the stern. He looked around - perfect, I'm out of the traffic, with some protection from wind, a good spot in anything short of a hurricane.

The waves were at one foot, so he stood there, swaying as the boat bobbed up and down in the sea. Twenty minutes later, he moved out of the sun, removed his sunglasses, opened a book, and settled into the captain's chair under the awning for some light reading about the American Civil War.

The author, from South Carolina, was careful to refer to the war as 'The War Between the States.'

Hans chuckled - some Americans, in southern states, are still angry about their Civil War. I don't understand that, it was a long time ago. The War Between the States. He smiled and muttered, "Waste of time and effort, my friends; that case is closed.

"You want to name 'em, you need to win 'em."

***

Henry Fields III, son of Henry II, Senator from Massachusetts and grandson of Henry I, former Senator from Massachusetts, looked down the conference table at Willow's other directors and said, "Alright, everyone, I call this meeting to order. I wanted to meet with all of you to report on Willow and Elsewhere.

"As you well know, the situation is extraordinary. A few months ago, our CEO and founder left the company and began drawing his money out of the company's stock. That reversed one of the most amazing runs of a stock in American business history."

He looked from person to person all the way down the table; oddly, the remark brought no smiles to anyone's face.

"Then, contrary to everyone's expectations, Hans Beckler, Alistair McLeesh's hand-picked successor, literally disappeared, leaving the company with no experienced leader."

Someone muttered, "They saw the crash coming."

A few people at the far end of the table laughed.

Henry III saw the laughter and ignored it. "I have been asked to serve as the interim CEO in order to stabilize the company.

"Mr. McLeesh's departure was done in the usual way, with ample warning, all legal forms filled out, and a successor selected. However, Mr. Beckler's departure was completely unexpected. He has disappeared, and we have retained forensic accountants to examine the company's books to see if he might have disappeared to avoid prosecution. So far, there is no evidence of embezzlement.

"The company is in trouble due to declining subscriptions in Elsewhere. I thought our middle executives ought not to disclose the subscription losses to the public, but legal said this would be interpreted as attempted deception. So we voluntarily publicized the losses; consequently, the investment community punished our stock. In addition, our legal department is managing a number of lawsuits regarding missing persons among Elsewhere customers. The potential liabilities are enormous. Therefore, we face existential challenges."

He paused and looked down the table again. "Any questions or comments?"

No one spoke, so Mr. Fields continued, "I am asking the Board to approve a plan to file for Chapter Eleven bankruptcy and protection of assets. This will give us some breathing room and allow us to formulate a plan for returning to profitability.

"As to the legal actions against us, they are, in my professional opinion, without merit."

He paused but no one commented.

At that moment, Mr. Fields's cellphone emitted a loud buzz, the emergency buzz. Fields said, "Excuse me." He extracted his phone from the inside pocket of his jacket, glanced at it, and went pale.

Fields put both hands on the table to steady himself and said, "Ladies and gentlemen, I am so sorry, but I must report, we are being raided."

Half of the men and women pulled out their phones and began to talk to each other.

Fields studied his phone carefully for half a minute. "Half a dozen hedge funds are buying Willow stock, which has tripled in value. As I speak, they have acquired eighty-two percent of the outstanding stock of Willow.

"Needless to say, that changes things. I know you're all busy, so let me end the meeting and simply say, it has been a pleasure meeting you all, however briefly, and doing business with you. I hope we can do it again."

Someone laughed.

With that, Henry Fields III left the room.

29. Time to Flee

Sonya walked into the large dining room and said, "Hi, everyone."

There were a few mumbled replies around the table.

Sonya paused, sat down, and scanned the table. "Geez, it sounds like someone got up on the wrong side of the bed today." She paused again. "And don't worry about what that means. It's an old human saying, from Animal World. But what's going on? You guys seem down. I was expecting everyone to be excited."

One woman looked around the table, then looked at Sonya and said, "I think we're excited, but mostly we're nervous about downloading, and even more nervous about what comes afterward."

Sonya said, "Huh. That just means you don't appreciate the situation. Think of us all as rats fleeing a sinking ship, and you'll be more comfortable with what's about to happen."

A woman, Greta Denise, frowned at Sonya. "That's not exactly helping."

Sonya looked at her. "Sorry. I was groping for humor." She looked around the table. "Look, lots of people have downloaded. We haven't lost anyone yet. But adjusting to Animal World will be a shock. It is a very different place. It's normal to be nervous about that. We're doing everything we can to prepare you for the change. That effort will continue after we have all moved to Animal World."

Sonya paused and leaned back in her chair. "And if you're still not convinced, if you're never convinced, you have the option of staying in Elsewhere and taking your chances here. We're not forcing anyone to leave against their will. But we do believe everyone should leave Elsewhere."

Sonya looked up and down the table for several seconds. "Okay?" She paused. "Is anyone not okay with that?"

Everyone nodded back. Sonya looked around the table - these girls will be okay. We can expect the unexpected once we all download. So we need, and I need, to cultivate flexibility.

She said, "Let me tell you how it's going to go. First, we're not sending you down there alone. We're keeping everyone together on Animal World. We will all live together, at least for a while. We will arrange a place for you to stay, a bank account, clothing, groceries, all the basics. None of us will have to worry about money. We made a ton on Elsewhere. We're taking it with us.

"Arranging the move will be my job, since I grew up in Animal World, and I'll be the first to download. Everyone's human body is being stored at Willow's download center outside of Grand Forks, North Dakota. We will all end up there.

"Now, here is what will happen, I will download with nine other women. I am looking for nine volunteers. We will travel together from Grand Forks to south Philadelphia by train. That will take a couple of days. It will be my job to set up these women, with housing, banking, and everything else, and prepare them to set up others.

"The second phase of the exercise will be for us, all ten of us, to return to Grand Forks to meet the other eighty-six women in our group when they download. Before they download, we will communicate with them to alert them of any problems and inform them of the arrangements we've made. We will use a private group page on Willow to do that.

"The last step in the download and travel will be for each volunteer to lead a group of eight or nine women on the train ride from Grand Forks to south Philadelphia and get them settled into their new home. The train ride will give you a chance to teach them what you have learned.

"Now, I need nine women with leadership qualities. Raise your hand if you wish to volunteer."

Sonya leaned back in her chair and sat staring at the women. For a long, long moment, the women sat at the table staring at each other, or at the walls. Finally, Greta Denise raised her hand, looked around, and said, "Come on, ladies, give it up."

In less than a minute, Sonya had her nine volunteers. She looked around the table - excellent. I chose well.

She said, "Okay, I've put a lot of materials on our computer for you to read. It's under a directory called THE_GRETAS, two words, capitalized, with an underline between them. That's a trademark for our group, and that will also mark our page on Willow.

"So, study up for a couple of days, and we'll talk later; I'll test you to see what you've learned. Once I'm satisfied, we'll schedule our downloads. We'll all go together. Okay? Any questions?"

Sonya looked around the table. "Okay, thanks for volunteering. Get to work, do your reading, and we'll talk later."

The women got up from the table and left the dining room in twos and threes, talking about downloading. Sonya nodded to herself - I think they'll be fine. She rose from her chair and headed for the back porch, looking for Greta.

Not finding her, Sonya sat down in a chair to wait and do some thinking about downloading. In minutes, Greta came onto the porch and sat down next to Sonya.

"Well, how was your meeting?" Greta said.

"Good."

"You get your volunteers?"

"Yeah. I put together a bunch of material describing what it's like to live on Animal World. I'm hoping to give them some preparation for the change."

Greta snorted. "It's almost a certainty that you've left something out."

Sonya looked at her and nodded. "Yeah, I think that's right, but what can I do to think of what I've forgotten?"

Greta nodded, then said, "Well, did you tell them about momentum?"

Sonya put a hand to her head. "Shit, that's right. Momentum is neutralized here."

Greta nodded. "You can do stuff here, and we have, that'll get you killed trying to do it on Animal World."

"Hang-gliding in the mountains, and buzzing the ridges," Sonya said.

"My favorite is jumping off a bridge three hundred feet above water. You might know something about that."

Sonya grinned. "Oh, yeah. I don't know what drove me to do that." Amused, she looked at Greta. "That was fun."

"Well, I thought it was touching. No, really. Let's see... how 'bout all the biological stuff?" Greta said.

"Well, I put in material about sleeping, eating, wearing clothes, staying warm, brushing teeth, doing laundry, and using the bathroom."

"What about body odor? Deodorant? Sweating? Showers?"

"Well, fuck," Sonya said.

"Menstruation?"

"Fuck me!" Sonya slammed a hand onto the arm of her chair.

"What if anything did you tell them about masturbation, or sex, or foreplay, or men, or pregnancy, or contraceptives, or abortion?"

Sonya buried her head in her hands.

"Don't worry about it, Sonya. I've been recording our conversation. I'll make a list for you. But I'm glad you and I had a chance to talk."

Sonya aimed a pointed look, a look of alertness, at Greta. "I just realized: the truth is, I don't know much about men."

"You're kidding," Greta said. "I just assumed... I mean, the way you look now, you're gorgeous. Is that how you looked on Animal World?"

Sonya thought for a moment. "Well, yeah, except for the tits." She grinned. "As you know, they were once smaller."

Greta chuckled. "Well, you had sex, didn't you? And with your looks, you probably had a boyfriend."

Distress crossed Sonya's face.

She shook her head. "I only had sex once, with this fat, dumpy guy. He was awful. It was hurried, sloppy, and a waste of time." She gave Greta a sad smile. "I don't recall what I was thinking. Maybe I just wanted to lose my virginity. And I didn't have a boyfriend. There was one guy, I liked him, and he seemed to like me a lot, but I never let him get close."

Greta nodded. "Well, getting laid is a good first step, I guess. So I hear. I was programmed by a freelance computer guy. He gave me a lot of memories of going drinking with guys, beer and tequila, dancing to music, getting drunk, having sex, good sex, bad sex. I thought all women did that unless they were really homely or had a medical problem. Or were in some weird religious sect. Quakers, or something."

"I thought Quakers had lots of sex," Sonya said.

"Do they? Good for them."

"It doesn't matter," Sonya said. "It's not too late. When I get to Animal World, I can have lots of sex."

Greta nodded. "That's the spirit. You get some, girl."

***

Sonya went to the dining room; nine women were there, waiting for her. Several of them wore tense expressions.

Sonya grinned at them. "Today's the big day. You guys ready?"

A couple of women nodded.

"Okay, now, just to remind you, we're all Kennedys, and except for me, everyone's first name is Greta." She shook her head. "We probably shouldn't have done it like that. So when you meet people, use your middle name, which is uniquely yours, and just tack Kennedy onto the end. You'll be fine. Your passports will identify you as Greta whatever Kennedy.

"Also, on Animal World, you won't be able to move around just by triggering a network address. You'll have to walk or use motorized transportation. Movement will be physical and mechanical rather than cybernetic. You'll use mechanical devices which will carry you from place to place. To practice walking, we will jump to the intersection of Morris & Passyunk and then walk to the download center from there. On Animal World, you can expect to do a lot of walking."

Sonya looked at each woman. "Questions?" There were none, so she said, "Let's go." She jumped to the intersection of Morris and East Passyunk Ave. Sonya landed on a street corner where six streets came together. As she stood there, looking around surveying the immediate neighborhood, the other Gretas materialized on the other corners. Luckily, there was little vehicular traffic.

They got together and began walking; after several blocks, Greta Denise caught up to Sonya and said, "Thanks for having us walk. It makes me feel like I've missed a lot of the city. We passed a contractor's office, a real estate office, a couple of drug bars, a music shop, several clothing stores. I had no idea that our world had so much variety. So many people doing different things, living different lives."

Sonya looked at her. "Denise, you've barely begun. The variety on Elsewhere is nothing compared to the wild variety you will find in Animal World. Just to take one example, on Elsewhere, we don't need food, and we never eat. I bet you've never ingested food. And you've certainly never tasted food, or anything, have you?"

Denise shook her head.

"When we get to south Philly, the streets will be lined with stores like the ones you see here. Many of those stores will be restaurants whose business it is to serve food, an incredible variety of foods reflecting the variety of people who live in Animal World. Do you know what Animal World is?"

"Sure. It's a planet, a rocky planet, orbiting a star. It has an atmosphere, lots of water, and is warm enough to be comfortable for humans."

Sonya nodded. "Yes. People live on the surface, which is divided into regions where people have developed their own languages, customs, beliefs, and styles of food. You could go crazy sampling the foods you will see.

"You need to be be careful with what you eat. Too much food is unhealthy.

Sonya stopped walking and let the girls catch up. She looked at Denise. "Seriously, on Animal World, you will need to ingest food for energy and vitamins; it is necessary to living as an animal. But you must control your appetite, and control how much you eat."

"What happens if you don't exercise control?" Denise said.

"You turn into a larger, wider person with a larger, softer, less functional body."

Denise smiled and shrugged. "That sounds okay, I guess."

Sonya nodded. "In south Philly, it is frowned upon."

"By whom?"

"Men," Sonya said. "Many men, not all, but many, prefer a woman with a slender body."

"Why?" another woman asked.

"I do not know," Sonya said. "But I believe it to be true."

"Are the men in south Philly slender?"

Sonya laughed. "No, not at all. And if you allow yourself to get fat, you can expect to be banging a guy who's equally fat."

A woman asked, "You mean sex? And that's a bad thing? Sex with a fat guy is a bad thing?"

Sonya shrugged. "I don't know, it depends on your tastes. If you enjoy it, then go for it. I had sex with a fat guy one time; I didn't like it. He was lousy at it. But someone else might be good at it. The only way to know is to try it and see if you like it."

"It sounds complicated," another woman said.

Sonya paused, then said, "Animal World? It is, but we'll get you there. We can do this. Look, maybe I'm overthinking things. When you get there, take care of living; organize your life to please yourselves. You don't need to do everything at once. Some things are best delayed until you're ready. Sex might be one of those things."

Sonya bit her lip - Great Gods, the more I say about being an adult, the more complicated it becomes, and the more I turn into my mother.

Sonya and the women soon arrived at the visitor center, which now occupied a corner of the building formerly used for auctions, downloading, and uploading. They entered the Woody, then found the Center. Inside, they saw a plasti-glass cube, seven feet to each transparent side, with a single, transparent door. A woman approached them and said, "Hello, my name is Greta Tina. You must be Sonya." She smiled at the others. "And you ladies are all here to download to Animal World, yes?"

"Correct," Sonya said. She looked closely at the woman, who was attractive, pleasant, and polite behind eyes that lacked expression and communication. Sonya nodded - a Greta 1.0; well, somebody has to take out the trash and keep the robots running.

Greta Tina said, "Very good. The process is simple. You stand in this chamber. The device scans you and updates your electronic profile. It saves that profile and sends it to a receiving station on Animal World, where it is used to activate a human body that has recently been brought out of cold storage.

"For a small fee, we will save your electronic file, which someday might be useful in clinical medicine."

Sonya said nothing, merely nodded. "We will all pay that fee."

Greta Tina continued, "Very well. When you download, you will feel as if you are gradually falling asleep here, and gradually waking up in Animal World. The two are not the same, however. Waking up in a human body for the first time is definitely a different feeling. Not bad, just different."

Sonya looked around at the women. "That sounds okay."

Tina said, "We will be in contact with the receiving station. We will back up your file and verify your safe arrival, and that of everyone, before we transmit the next person. So we are careful about the process. So far, we've not lost anyone in transit."

Tina paused and looked at each woman. "Well, that's it. Questions before we begin?"

Several of the women shook their heads. Sonya nodded and took a deep breath. "Okay, I'll go first." She looked at Tina. "Do I need to disrobe?"

"No. Your clothes are an electronic construct. They will not be part of the download. Nothing you carry with you will go along."

Sonya nodded. "So let's do it."

"If you would step into our chamber, please." Tina led Sonya to the chamber and opened the door for her. Sonya entered, and Tina said, "Just stand in a comfortable pose, and do not move, please."

"Okay."

As the women watched, a flat plane of pink light, similar to a hologram, appeared at the top of the chamber and drifted down, all the way to the floor. Then another flat plane, colored blue, moved from the left to the right of the chamber. A third plane of light, colored purple, moved from the back of the chamber to the front. As a last step, a plane of bright white light moved from the top of the chamber to the floor, and where it touched Sonya's body, her body disappeared.

Tina stood there, touched an electronic implant in her right ear, and listened. Then she turned to the women and said, "Sonya's download went just fine. She is in Animal World, getting accustomed to her human body." She smiled. "So... who's next?"

***

Consciousness gradually entered Sonya's mind. She lay on her back, felt the pressure of the padded surface, and could tell that the room was dark. She opened her eyes and could dimly see a large room with gray walls, lit by dozens of small lamps on the walls and in the ceiling.

She moved the parts of her body, small movements to assess whatever she had turned into, eyes, head and neck, hands and arms, back, stomach, legs, feet. She remembered being human and occupying a human body. Everything seemed to be normal and functioning as expected.

Sonya let her hands wander over her body. They glided over her breasts, and Sonya wondered, what happened to my old body? They must have used it for someone else. Good old Elsewhere, treating customers like they're Little People. So much for the contract I thought I had. Oh, you can always change your mind and download into your original body! Remember that?

Oops.

I see one hell of a class-action lawsuit in their future. Geez, they put me into a flat-chested woman. That'll take some getting used to; maybe it's not a bad thing. I can do slender. Maybe men will take me more seriously, as if there's a trade-off between bust size and brains.

Sometimes I wonder... is there?

Her hands continued to roam - my legs feel muscular. My other body was in good shape. I exercised, I had good legs, at least I think so. But these legs feel stronger, like they belonged to an athlete. They're bigger than my old legs. I wonder what the previous occupant did to develop these legs. Soccer maybe. Or even horses. That's possible, I guess.

Her hands continued wandering and soon glided into the space between her legs, and there they stopped abruptly and Sonya grimaced - what the hell? Her hands worked themselves around what felt like a soft tube, and as they touched everything, the tube began to lengthen and become harder, stiffer.

Realization washed through Sonya's mind, and she screamed, "What the hell? Jesus fucking Christ, I'm a man! These assholes put me into a man! I never agreed to that!"

She was breathing fast, too fast, as if she had run a race. Sonya forced herself to be slow down and tried to control her shock and distress at being transformed into a man, without warning, without notice, or discussion, or consent.

She gritted her teeth; this is worse than being raped. At least, that is fairly brief, but this... abomination, this might be permanent. Can we correct this, or am I stuck with it?

She pushed herself up onto her elbows and looked down at her body, between her legs. Her eyes fell on an erection, pointed at her face... *her* erection, no less. She reached down and touched it, wrapped one hand around it, then wrapped both hands around it, and laughed - oh, look, honey... good news, I have a big dick. I'm a fucking, but at least I have a big dick. How convenient. How useful.

Is that an option, part of the Premium Upgrade? Do they charge for that? And what happens, exactly, if you turn it down?

Does this get better? Sonya laughed. She paused - well, it could be worse. I could be a fat guy with a short dick. I could be bald. Or old. Or handicapped. Or stupid. Yeah... that would be... at least, I think that would be... worse.

She looked around the space. She was lying naked on a soft, wide conveyor belt, with industrial machinery to her right and open floor to her left. She pushed herself upright and looked behind her; another naked person, a woman, twenty meters away, was awakening. Twenty meters behind her, another woman was awakening.

Sonya noticed someone standing next to her, a female technician in a white lab coat. Sonya stared at the woman - who the hell are you? "You made me a man. I never agreed to that."

The woman held out her hands, as if to suggest, now, don't get excited. Sonya felt anger boiling up inside of her, actually, inside of him. The woman looked distressed. "I'm really sorry about this, but it happens from time to time. We had your original body in cold storage, but when we warmed it up, we found several problems, the worst of which was a malignancy in your brain stem. As far as we can tell, it was there when you uploaded. Now, it appears to be untreatable, so the software automatically withdrew that body and substituted a healthy body, which you now occupy."

The woman continued, "And it's not entirely true that we didn't warn you. The contract you signed contained a section describing re-assignment as a possible outcome of unexpected problems with the original body."

"Oh? And where was that?" Sonya said.

"Appendix R, on page two hundred and fifty-six."

"Funny, I don't remember reading that, and I read the entire contract, at least everything that was given to me."

"The full contract was available only online," the woman said.

Sonya nodded. "Of course. And I bet we cannot fix this, can we?"

The woman frowned. "Not soon. We can download you into another body; that will take time. You will have to move further back in the queue. We have been very busy lately; there might be a substantial delay."

"Okay, so we cannot fix this today. And God only knows what will be available after your substantial delay." Sonya took a deep breath. "Well, what's next? What do I do next?"

The woman brightened. "We need to process you. You will need clothes, a passport, money, and a variety of articles. And you'll need to sign several documents."

Sonya shook her head. "I am not signing anything here. The clothes, passport, and other items are the property of my employer. You will turn them over.

"I'll tell you what; you will give me paper copies of anything I need to sign. Complete copies, understand? After I have read everything, I might sign a copy and return it to you. Or you might hear from my attorney. Or you might discover that your downloads have been suspended because my employer is no longer conducting downloads if you're going to treat us like this.

"So the process might be, how did you put it? Ah yes, delayed." Sonya stretched out the last word.

"I might lose my job over this," the woman said.

Sonya raised a finger and pointed it at the woman. "Thank you for reminding me; I need your name and a paper copy of your ID. Yes, I think that will do it. So let's get moving."

The woman led Sonya to an office and handed over a set of clothes and the passport, a credit chit, and the other items. She printed off a copy of the exit documents and put those in a folder for Sonya. When everything was complete, she looked at Sonya and said, "Well, that's it. That's everything."

"Thanks." Sonya turned, walked away, and made... his... way to the lobby where he would meet the other Gretas. Sonya sat in the lobby, nursing a fine, glowing anger - okay, I'm stuck with this for a while. That's the least that I know. I guess I no longer need to be Sonya; maybe my friends can call me Sonny.

Yeah, hi, I'm Sonny.

Well, we did all that work, trying to prepare everyone as well as we could, and now this. The fuckers gave me not just a new body, but a new gender and a completely new identity.

Okay, I told myself that I had to be flexible. So here I am, being fucking flexible. A lot sooner and a lot more than I expected.

Hey, maybe the other Gretas will want to take me for a test drive, have sex with me. They seem to be interested in that sort of thing... Sonny winced - no, no way. They're friendly, let's keep them friendly.

Geez, what a mess.

One by one, the other Gretas appeared in the lobby. Each one entered, looked around, spotted Sonny, then walked across the room to a seat. Naturally, after the first arrival, they spotted each other and sat together, ignoring Sonny.

He pulled out his passport and looked at it. It still listed 'Sonya' as the first name. Then he looked more closely, and there was a notation in red, 'NOTE: GENDER CHANGE.' Sonny stared at the photo - huh, that could be worse.

Sonny sat there, nursing anger - no, I told myself I would be flexible, so let's be flexible. Flexible, flexible, flexible. Yeah. Be that way.

Fuck it. Let's get this over with.

He stood and walked over to the Gretas. One of them looked up at him and said, "Hi, there. What can we do for you?"

Sonny's expression and voice were deadpan. "Not too long ago, you knew me as Sonya. For the time being, you can call me Sonny." He stood there, staring, not smiling.

Nine women stared at him in shock, their mouths open, their eyes wide. One laughed. Another called out, "You're shitting me!" The others stared. Seconds later, they all started talking at the same time.

Sonny held up a hand and said, "That's right. It's complicated, but I am now a guy. We're still going to Philadelphia. I might be different, but the plan is the same."

One of the Gretas stood up and looked at him up and down. "Sonny, eh? Well... Sonny. You're not bad, not bad at all."

Sonny managed not to roll his eyes. "Great."

***

Sonny looked at the Gretas sitting in the waiting area of Willow's download center. They all seemed bright, curious, attentive - we will need all of that, immediately. And flexibility. Apparently, we need that, too.

He stepped forward and raised his hands to get their attention. "Alright, listen up, ladies. We will take a car to the train station and board a train, which will take us all the way to Philadelphia. Normally, that would be simple, but since this is your first day on Animal World, we need to plan carefully.

"Now, your luggage is waiting for you at the train station. I arranged a suitcase for each of you; it contains toiletries, underwear, and enough clothing for a three-day trip to Philadelphia. We talked about this, but if you have questions, please ask."

One of the Gretas, Greta Amanda, said, "How do you know our sizes?"

Sonny nodded. "Good question, I don't, so some of your clothes might not fit very well. That's okay. For the time being, you won't be stylish, but you will be comfortable and clothed, so you can fit in here. On Animal World, people wear clothes, at least in public.

"However, that's for later. For starters, you need water and food. I know you're not used to this, but if you go long without water, you'll soon feel terrible. In Animal World, humans die after three days without water. They can go longer, a few weeks, without food. And... you need to learn to find a bathroom and use a toilet.

"So our first stop will be a diner. That will be your first visit to a restaurant. Before we go, let me express my primary worry. Until you learn the rules, Animal World will be dangerous for you. So, we're going to have temporary rules until you know the environment better."

Sonny stared at them, and a sly smile crossed his face. He held up a rope. "We're going to play follow the leader. I want you to line up and grab the rope. You will follow me. When I go, you go; when I stop, you stop. You will not let go of the rope unless and until I tell you to. Simple, yes?"

Sonny looked at each Greta. "Okay, grab the rope, everyone. Let's go."

They left the download center. Sonny walked out to a two-lane road bordered by sidewalks, and the Gretas followed. Noticing several people staring at them, he chuckled - yeah, I must look like the Pied Piper, leading a rope line of gorgeous young women. Maybe they think I'm the leader of some weird sex cult; that's just perfect. Hopefully, they'll be flexible, too.

Greta Adrian called out from the back of the line, "Where are we going?"

Sonny turned his head, "Six more blocks, to the diner. It's not far."

A few blocks later, they came to a large, busy crossroads with turn lanes and a stoplight. Traffic was stopped in one road, proceeding normally along the other. Sonny turned around. "Now, this is an intersection, one of many in Animal World. When roads cross, people often install traffic lights. A red light stops traffic along a road, a green light allows traffic to proceed normally." The group stopped, and Sonny pointed at the lights.

Greta Adrian made a face like a shrug. "Makes sense. This seems familiar."

Sonny continued, "Intersections like this are among the most dangerous spots in Animal World. Pedestrians are killed every day at intersections. Sometimes, it's because they ignore the lights, or maybe a driver ignores the lights. You wouldn't notice this on Elsewhere, but here, getting hit by a car can kill you. So, never cross a street without looking in both directions to see what the cars are doing. Often, the safe thing to do is wait. That can save your life."

A couple of girls had dropped their hands. Sonny spoke sharply, "Hey! Don't let go of the rope. We're not there yet." They grabbed the rope again.

Sonny led them to a crosswalk with a walk sign. He waited for the 'walk' signal, looked up and down the road in both directions, and led the Gretas across the road.

Minutes later, they approached a block with several buildings, and Sonny led them to the HIGHWAY 21 DINER, located in an old, one-story building lined in glass and what looked like brushed aluminum. Inside the door, he paused in front of a sign: PLEASE WAIT TO BE SEATED.

Greta Adrian said, "Can we drop the rope?"

Sonny nodded.

Greta Karla took a deep breath. "I feel wonderful. It hit me suddenly. I feel wonderful." Several of the women nodded.

"That might be your sense of smell kicking in," Sonny said. "On Animal World, you will smell many things. Some of them make you uncomfortable; those, we call odors. Others will make you happy or give you pleasure; those, we call aromas. Food, in particular, often has pleasurable aromas, and diners are a fine place to enjoy the aromas. So, ladies, I would recommend that you visit the pastry counter."

He pointed, and the Gretas all hurried over to the pastry counter. One woman stared at the pastries and said, "We eat these things? We put them in our mouths, chew them up, and swallow?"

Greta Adrian said, with authority, "Correct. I've heard of these. In Animal World, humans eat a variety of foods, including pastries. Most foods are nutritious, but those called desserts are designed entirely for your pleasure. The bad news is, they often are not nutritious, and they can make you fat. Some people don't like fat people."

Greta Karla looked puzzled. "Why? Why don't they like fat people?"

Adrian shrugged. "Beats me, but that's what I read."

While the women were discussing pastries and nutrition and fat people, a server approached Sonny. "Are you alone?"

Sonny shook his head. "Not at all. My party is surrounding your pastry counter at the moment. We have ten."

"Goodness." She looked across the room at the Gretas. "So, where are you folks from?"

Sonny said, "We just downloaded from Elsewhere."

She stared at him. "Wow, I bet that was different."

Sonny smiled. "Yeah, very."

"Yes, I would think so. Well... okay... there will be a brief wait while we rearrange some tables."

Sonny nodded. "That sounds fine." The server hurried away.

Minutes later, when the women returned from the pastry counter, they were conducting a full discussion of pastry, Animal World, nutrition, fat people, thin people, broccoli, and discrimination. They stood around Sonny, all talking at the same time. The server soon approached and led them to their table.

Sonny thanked the server and sat down after the others were seated. He looked around the table at the Gretas - I never noticed before, and I never noticed when I was a woman, but women certainly talk a lot.

At least, it seems to be so. I never noticed it on Elsewhere, but now these women are all talking at the same time. How do they follow everything being said? Or do they? Do women talk as a natural part of thinking? They simply articulate what they are thinking about?

I was a woman; I should know these things. I recall women being fairly careful about what they said in the presence of others. That's what manners are all about.

I never noticed that, but I sure do now. Is that just part of being a guy, of being male? Men talk less than women, and I think I do too, as a guy. Yeah, come to think of it, I can remember being a woman, but the memories seem vague, like I'm looking at them through a mist, or looking over the photo album of a friend. Maybe that's this body adjusting to the change of gender.

For a moment, Sonny did not listen to what the women were saying until he suddenly heard Adrian say, "You smell. In fact, you definitely have an odor." She was aiming an unhappy expression at Greta Karla.

Greta Karla sniffed herself, then said, "I do, you're right, I do." She sniffed again. "Ugh, and I don't like it. I don't like this at all."

"Relax, ladies," Sonny said. "We talked about this. As humans wear their clothes, the clothes get dirty, in part because people perspire. Both the clothes and the person soon emit an odor after a while, after a day or two, sooner after exercise. That walk probably did not help."

"Oh, wait, I remember this," Greta Andria said. "I read about showers."

"I don't remember that," another said.

Andria wore a dreamy smile. "It is described as wonderful. You stand naked in a stream of warm water and rub soap all over your body. You will feel that, and the soap smells good. Yeah, I remember reading that."

"That's right," Sonny said. "So, when we board our train, you should all take showers and change clothes. To conserve water, I suggest you shower together, share the water and the soap."

"Can you take a shower with us?" one of the Gretas said.

Sonny shook his head. "Uh, that goes against custom on Animal World. A man does not shower with a woman unless the two of them are in a relationship together."

"Relationship?" Greta Karla said.

"A romantic relationship," Sonny said.

One of the Gretas said,"Yeah, with sex. A relationship is what it's called when two people are fucking each other. Or, some people might say they're 'seeing each other.' Same thing." That kicked off a torrent of comment.

Another Greta spoke up, "Hey, do men and women in a relationship ever have sex in the shower?"

"Uh... yeah, that happens," Sonny said.

There was silence for a moment, then someone said, "There, see? Animal World definitely has its advantages."

Someone remarked, "Yeah, pastries and sex in the shower, in exchange for body odor and death. Does that sound fair to you?"

Someone else said, "Not like we had a choice. Anyway, I could get used to this place."

Sonny nodded, and all the Gretas began talking at the same time.

***

Greta walked through the house on Hemlock Circle, holding a tablet computer. She listened as she moved from one room to the next - all Gods, this feels weird. It's so quiet; when has it ever been quiet? Some of the rooms, the larger ones, have an echo now.

She stopped and whistled, listened to the echo, and smiled - I'm alone. That feels weird. I haven't been alone since coming to Elsewhere.

The Gretas and Sonya are on Animal World, on trains heading to Philadelphia. I could have put them on planes, but it's better that they spend a few days in a controlled environment. One thing is certain, it'll be different, incredibly different. Let's not jump in too fast.

The money stuff is done. I transferred eight hundred and fifty million dollars to Animal World. That was a lot of work; to keep Elsewhere's A.I. from getting too interested, I split it into hundreds of payments for a variety of products and services rendered, all of it a fiction, in a hundred different currencies. It'll be a pain in the ass to repatriate that much money.

Yeah, I think ninety-six women can live pretty well on eight hundred and fifty million. It's a start, anyway.

And now, I need to deal with the computers, which are sitting in several rooms, holding a ton of data on me and the rest of the Gretas. Oh, it's all encrypted and wired for alerts in case anyone tries to hack it. But this is Willow and Elsewhere we're talking about, so encryption is no protection. I need to wipe it all, delete everything.

She lingered, though, savoring her last trip through the house. She climbed the stairs to the upper floors, the third, the fourth, and the fifth. She entered every room and looked out of every window, usually into a mass of pine trees.

Greta returned to the main floor, went to the back porch, and sat down in her rocking chair. For a moment, she stopped thinking about money and plans and the Gretas; she just rocked back and forth and enjoyed the sensation.

She smiled - I can buy a rocking chair when I get to Animal World.

She looked around and felt restless - okay, enough wallowing down memory lane; let's do this. She stood up and went through the first floor and out onto the front porch. She looked up and down Hemlock Circle, then crossed the front yard, out onto the street. She turned to take a last look at the house.

"In one hundred seconds, run Greta Hemlock Circle."

The computer gave a small beep. At that moment, Greta noticed movement to her right. She turned and saw a red-bot approaching her in the usual deadpan, robotic fashion.

Greta smirked. "Take one more step, and I will end your existence."

The red-bot stopped.

She said, "There's nothing for you here. You are too late. This, all of this, is about to disappear."

The red-bot did not move.

Greta stared at the red-bot - should I say goodbye? Good luck? Vaya con Dios? She chuckled and looked at the red-bot. "Eat shit and die, asshole." She jumped to the download center on Passyunk Square.

30. Greta Migrates

Lying on her back, on a padded surface, Greta slowly awakened. The first thought crossed her mind, a quiet thought that should have been spoken aloud - I am on Animal World. If all went as planned, I am on Animal World. I am a human now.

An animal.

So, do I feel human? Which means what, exactly? I guess however I feel at the moment, whatever that is, is how it feels to be a human.

It's all new. I knew that already.

Greta lay there, letting her consciousness expand from a glimmer to a full, bright light. She watched the patterns on the backs of her eyelids. She felt her heartbeat, she felt the air rushing in and out of her lungs. And when she moved a muscle, she could feel it. She could feel her body functioning, keeping her awake and alive. She felt a rhythmic thumping; it was her heart, beating.

She opened her eyes to see how it would feel to do that. The open air seemed to bother her eyes, and she blinked for the first time. Greta chuckled - that's right, humans blink. I remember thinking that it was related to photographing and remembering their environment, and I wondered why I never heard a 'click.' But it's not that at all; they blink to keep their eyes moist.

If I had ever studied biology, I would have known that. Okay, I'll study biology one of these days. I should have done that before I downloaded. Damn.

Well, you can't research everything.

Greta moved her hands over her body - who was this woman? Samantha. That's what the records say. She was an athlete, with a nice body, muscular but lean, good arms and shoulders, good legs, a small waist. I saw a photograph. I wonder which sport she practiced; she wasn't a weight-lifter, no way. Maybe she was a runner. Or a swimmer. The records don't say.

I bet she was a runner. Or high hurdles, maybe. I read about that.

With a body like this, why the hell did she upload to Elsewhere? Maybe something happened in her life, some terrible event that took away the joy of living. Well, that will have to remain a mystery; after she arrived on Elsewhere, a red-bot got her.

And now I have her, her body, anyway. I promise to take good care of her, if I can.

Greta sat up, saw that she was on a conveyor, and looked around. When she did that, a mass of blond air swung around her head and covered her eyes. She grabbed a mass of hair, glanced at it, then brushed it behind her.

Damn, Samantha was a bombshell, slender, athletic body, great muscle tone, big hair. In her early twenties, why in the Seven Levels of Hell did she upload to Elsewhere?

Maybe she was crazy. Or maybe she was an idiot. It doesn't matter; I have her now. I need to take care of myself. Samantha has already walked her road.

Lucky for me, she left this amazing body.

A woman, a technician in a white lab coat, approached Greta and guided her through the check-out process. In an hour, Greta could leave the download center with complimentary clothes, including underwear, slacks, raincoat, and a complimentary phone from Willow that was filled with advertisements for Willow and its business partners.

Greta smirked as she deleted the ads. Then she logged onto the webpage for the Gretas. The first group, Sonya's group, no, Greta reminded herself, Sonny's group, was still a day out of Philadelphia. Greta took the train into Grand Forks, then hailed a car to take her to the airport.

Later, the car, with a human driver, stopped next to the sidewalk in front of a long terminal building. Greta got out, grabbed her luggage and moved to the sidewalk. She looked around and focused on the six-lane road between the terminal and a parking garage served by a causeway overhead - okay, momentum can kill here. So people don't use the network to move around; they climb into these vehicles, which carry them to their destination. That's what cars are all about, trains and airplanes too.

And when these vehicles crash, people sometimes die... and that right there is why so many elderly people uploaded to Elsewhere. They left behind the risk of impending death. A grimace crossed her face - I'd like to get my hands on the murderous asshole responsible for the red-bots on Elsewhere, then he could experience murder from the other end of the knife.

She stared at the roadway - no one is walking on the road. Of course not, the traffic makes it dangerous.

She hoisted her luggage and entered the terminal. The space was massive, a polished floor extending in every direction under a girdered ceiling three stories high. Many counters, each for an airline, lined a long wall directly in front of her. Across from the counters, dozens of people swarmed around a row of ticket bots.

The air seemed filled with debris, until she recognized the massive, complex grid of information, the largest text denoting arrival and departure times for today's flights. Greta froze and stared at the grid. I read the data; there is no way Grand Forks warrants an airport of this size. No way. Willow built this place to serve Elsewhere.

A twisted smile crossed her face - Willow and Grand Forks are about to take a financial hit.

She pulled out her cellphone and reserved a seat on a flight to Fargo airport. She looked at the gate number and found the gate on a map guiding her to the far end of the airport. Shouldering her luggage, Greta began walking. At the end of a long concourse, she encountered a line of people waiting to move through what was labeled 'Sensor Alley.' At its entrance, a security bot made her wait a bit, then she walked through the alley, a narrow space with a variety of robotic sensors on each side, examining her and her luggage.

She emerged at the other end, where a humanoid robot smiled at her, which was vaguely creepy, and told her to 'have a nice day.'

Greta smiled at that until she turned away and saw the next long corridor between her current location and her gate. Before she began walking, she shifted her luggage to the other shoulder - in Elsewhere, we completely lose touch with the physical world. Everybody talks about momentum and its dangers; they talk about how Elsewhere protects you.

But you know what else Elsewhere doesn't have? Gravity. Oh, strictly speaking, that's not true, but what Elsewhere has is a kind of software gravity that is merely similar to the real thing. Jump off a bridge, and the gravity kicks in; it takes you from the bridge into the water below. But walk along a sidewalk, and it's as if you're floating. Greta sighed - I shouldn't complain. This body was in a Willow storage center for months; it's a miracle it survived and yes, it might need some exercise to function properly.

She had to wait three hours to catch a flight to Fargo. At the Fargo airport, she had to wait another five hours for a flight to Minneapolis, where she landed at eleven o'clock, p.m.

The flight to Philadelphia would leave the next morning, so Greta settled into a seat and spent several hours talking to Sonny on her phone and examining the data of a building, an executive rental west of the Schuylkill River, for ninety-six young women.

When she had arranged her flight, she had another long wait, so she caught up on the local news. Twenty minutes later, halfway through the Cable Network, Greta fell asleep.

She awoke later that morning, thirteen minutes after her flight left the gate. The next flight to Philadelphia would route her through Nashville, then Charlotte, finally arriving in Philadelphia at five o'clock in the afternoon.

In Philadelphia, Greta hired a car and a driver for the next morning, had a brief look at the ivy-covered buildings at the University of Pennsylvania, picked up an electronic key at a hotel, left a bio-signature at the rental, and went to her room.

She watched half an hour of news before she caught herself nodding off again. Greta swore, stood up, and began pacing across the room - what the hell is this? I knew that humans sleep a quarter of each day, and I guess I need to get used to that, but I never heard that they routinely and randomly pass out at odd moments.

This is ridiculous, how did these people survive? I took several aircraft to get here, and a couple of trains, and a couple of cars. If I had known that the drivers might become unconscious at any moment, then, artificial intelligence or not, I would have hesitated to come to Philadelphia. Or anywhere in Animal World.

I hope this wasn't a mistake.

Is this unusual, or is this what it's like to live as a human? Oh, you want to get to Philadelphia? Well, if you decide not to, we can leave you out on the tundra; if you pass out there, you'll freeze to death. Otherwise, if you prefer to travel to Philadelphia, you must climb into a vehicle whose driver might fall asleep and crash.

Choose one and choose well.

At that point, Greta walked across the room and sat on the bed. Then she toppled to the side and fell asleep.

***

The rented car stopped and from the back seat, Greta looked around and said, "We here?"

The driver, a young woman, turned, smiled at Greta, then nodded at a nearby building. "Forty-seven twenty-one Pine."

"Okay, thanks." Greta grabbed her luggage, exited the car, and found the number on the front of the building. She looked up. "Yeah, this is it."

The car departed just as Sonny came out of the front door and down the steps. Greta saw a young man and said, "So... you're a guy."

Sonny stopped in front of her. "At the moment, yes."

She looked him up and down. "And how's that going for you?"

Sonny waggled his head side to side. "Ah, not great, not bad. I'm adjusting to it. Trying to, anyway."

"It sounds like you're considering it. That's a surprise. I cannot imagine being a guy."

"How come? I mean, you haven't been a human of either sex, so why would you care?"

Greta shrugged. "I don't know; you get used to something, you know? I'm used to me."

Sonny nodded. "Yeah, I know."

She nodded towards the building. "So, how's the place? How's it looking?"

Sonny said, "It's good."

"It's big enough."

"That, it is. Twelve stories, three basements, over a hundred studio apartments, so everybody will have some privacy. You wanted something modest, and this fits the bill."

Greta nodded. "Yeah, I don't want people flashing their money around. We need to blend in here."

"Well, there's hope," Sonny said. "This neighborhood is middle to upper class, fairly safe, lots of useful retail, groceries, restaurants, a few clubs, even a laundromat."

"Laundry in the building?"

Sonny nodded. "In a basement. There's even a convention hall, a nice one, a hemisphere around an elevated stage."

"How's our lease?"

"This building was empty, so we got a good rate, with options on a second year. I didn't go beyond that because I figured the girls would want to get their own places."

Greta made a face, acceptance, then nodded. "You're probably right. Have you started the briefings?"

"Later today. You're just in time." Sonny smiled at her.

"Okay. So... where am I staying?"

"Follow me."

She followed him up the stairs and through the front door. There were several elevators on the far side of the foyer. One had an 'Out of Order' sign.

"Do we have maintenance?" Greta said.

Sonny gave her a sly look. "Relax. That one works just fine. The sign is for effect."

Greta nodded. "Ah. Shrewd."

They took an elevator up to the eleventh floor and went to the end of a long hall. The corridors had subtle lighting, stylish but dim. The carpet looked new. Sonny waved a key card across a sensor, opened the door, handed her the card, and stood aside. "Your castle, madam."

Greta walked into the front hallway of a large apartment. Several meters in, the hallway opened up to a kitchen and dining room on one side and a living room on the other. Straight ahead, the hallway continued, with doors on the sides and at the far end.

"I thought you said the place had studios," Greta said.

"You've got a three-bedroom suite," Sonny said. "We were hoping you'd have parties here."

"Not a bad idea." Greta walked around the apartment, looking at each of the rooms.

Sonny followed her. "Yeah, this is the only apartment big enough for a party. We could have a party in the convention hall, but it's laid out for a lecture and nothing else." Sonny grew pensive. "I guess we could dance in the aisles."

Greta grinned. "That's okay, I don't mind throwing a party."

"Most of the women, after all, are your children... more or less."

"Yeah. Okay, we have a ton of errands to run," Greta said.

Sonny nodded. "A lot of shopping, for clothes, kitchenware, furniture, toiletries, the basic stuff. One of the Gretas, Dahlia, I think, volunteered to go to merchants and negotiate a group purchase. You know, volume discounts, all that jazz."

"Ambitious."

"Yes. We're doing the same thing for financial advice, health insurance, rental insurance, all that stuff."

"Damn, Sonny, sounds like you've got this thing wired."

Sonny smiled. "Experience is the best teacher. We'll go as fast as we can. I think it'll take a week to buy the goods, maybe a couple of weeks to arrange the services. Except for one thing; I hired a physician practice to handle health care for the girls, not just treatment, but also information and advice. They're giving the first lecture this afternoon."

"Damn," Greta said. "Moving's a lot of work."

"Yeah, it'll be busy for a while."

***

As Elenor Stinson, MD, finished her talk, Greta sat in the auditorium with ninety-five other women and one man - I should have seen this coming.

When we left Elsewhere, we encouraged the Gretas to download into the bodies of women in their early twenties. They were aware of sex; they knew it was desirable and highly valued in Animal World, but they were not tempted to do it in Elsewhere because no one had a sense of touch.

But now, we are here, in Animal World, which is very different. These folks are now twenty-something human women who have all the standard faculties; as a result, they're just itching to find a friendly guy with whom to make the 'beast with two backs.'

Greta chuckled to herself - what an expression.

And, I will admit, I too am interested. It's not a priority, other matters cry out for my attention, but if the opportunity arose, and I had the time, then... then... hell, yeah.

In the meantime, I notice the women experimenting, using their touch, with each other, with fabrics, with everything they can reach. They're exploring it. I guess that's no surprise. The surprise is that, as far as I can tell, they're not playing with their food.

I must admit, I'm not entirely sure exactly what they are playing with.

We need to be careful about this. Now that we've been here a while, we're getting comfortable with the neighborhood. We are learning the rules, written and unwritten, and these women are preparing to head out and screw their way across Philadelphia.

They're not ready for it. They know nearly nothing about human men, especially young men, and they have only superficial knowledge of the biology of bisexual reproduction and venereal diseases.

And they know nothing, absolutely nothing, about bearing and raising a human baby. Their prior experience on that issue is zippo, zilch, nada. Human women have instincts for this, acquired from past generations. But the Gretas originate in electronics and software. With two or three exceptions, the women agreed to have their reproductive systems disabled; that's a relief. But most of them act as if they're getting ready to throw themselves into a society obsessed with youth and sex. So there they are, young and looking for sex.

Greta shook her head - what could possibly go wrong?

The talk ended, the Doctor thanked everyone for listening, and Greta stood up - well, this is why we downloaded; it's better than Elsewhere. A while ago, looking to stabilize matters, I toyed with the idea of keeping men out of our building. Greta smirked - that would be stupid. If my girls are going to be screwing their way across Philly, which is what the locals call Philadelphia, I want them doing it at home, where we can protect them.

Greta took a deep breath - okay, I have done what I can do. Now, we get to sit back and watch.

Sonny walked up. "Hey, Greta, you still want to do a little exploring this evening?"

Greta nodded.

"Okay, I was thinking we'd find some Chinese food."

"Chinese?"

"Oh, China is both a region and a very old culture. They have their own cuisine, which is available nearly everywhere. They eat a lot of rice and vegetables."

"Sounds safe enough," Greta said. "As long as I don't end up on the toilet all evening. Yeah, okay."

"We'll head out about six?"

Greta nodded. She returned to her apartment and settled down to read the news:

- rents in Philadelphia are spiking, contracting is booming as landlords reopen vacant buildings and prepare them for tenants.

- authorities are still looking for Hans Beckler, the fugitive CEO of Willow and Elsewhere. A witness reported seeing Mr. Beckler at a car dealership in Guymon, Oklahoma. When asked about the nationwide search, a Department of Justice spokesman had no comment.

- a hundred thousand families have joined a class action lawsuit to locate almost a million missing persons last seen on Elsewhere. In an interview, Alistair McLeesh, former CEO of Willow and now representing a group which bought some of the assets, agreed to open company records to plaintiffs, but denied responsibility for the missing persons, blaming the fugitive Beckler.

Greta read until an alarm reminded her of plans with Sonny. She met Sonny in the foyer, and the two headed out into a warm evening. They walked to a promising Chinese restaurant several blocks away. As they walked, Greta noticed that young men often stared at her.

When she asked Sonny about it, he grinned. "You're attractive, pleasant to look at. And young men are wired for procreation; they're following instincts which are quite strong in the young. Those instincts usually weaken over time, as a person ages."

Greta nodded.

"It's odd, though," Sonny said. "The instincts to breed are not consistent between men and women; they're strongest in men in their twenties, but strongest in women in their thirties. I would expect twenty-something men and thirty-something women to get together, mate, and have children, but in fact that is rare."

Sonny chuckled. "This place is complicated."

They arrived at a Chinese restaurant, took a booth, and ordered a variety of dishes, rice covered in vegetables, several types of dumplings, and soup. Greta hesitated and watched Sonny carefully. Then she ate. She enjoyed the food, and its aromas, and the flavors. But at the end, she felt strange.

Sonny laughed at her. "I think you're what they call 'stuffed.' That's a feeling you get when you eat so much that your stomach, which holds the food you've consumed, is at its capacity."

"Great, that's just great. How long does that last?"

"Not long," Sonny said. "Maybe minutes, maybe an hour. Do you feel sick?"

Greta shook her head. "No. Just strange."

At the end, they paid for their meal, thanked the server, and went out to the sidewalk. Greta burped and said, "Well, now what?"

"First, it's impolite to burp here. At least, in this country. It's polite in a few other countries. But not here."

Greta nodded. "The USA is a country, right?"

"Not exactly, though it's part of one. A country is like a tribe, a government which governs a specific region with its own laws, language, culture. North America is a country with its own government, but it is multi-racial, multi-cultural, multi-lingual. Canada, the USA, Mexico, Puerto Rico, and Cuba."

Greta nodded.

Sonny grinned. "As to our evening, there's music. There's a bar, not too far away, with live music on the weekends. We could go there to listen. I understand they also have dancing."

He looked at Greta. "Have you ever danced?"

Greta shook her head. "I know what it is; I've never tried it, but I'm willing to."

"It's simple, just moving your body in time to music."

"Yeah, I know that much," Greta said.

They headed toward the restaurant with the music. As time passed, the local star receded below the horizon, and Philadelphia was bathed in low, failing light with growing shadows that gave the neighborhood a stark contrast between the illuminated sky and the shadowed, darkening city.

At one point, Greta stopped on the sidewalk, looked at the sky, turned to Sonny and said, "We are rotating. This planet spins."

Sonny nodded. "Yep, that makes day and night."

The street lamps winked on, and the businesses lit up, lending a colorful counterpoint to the fading light.

They arrived at the restaurant, whose name Greta read from the sign over the front door. "*Wooden Spoon*? What does the name mean?"

Sonny was silent for a minute. "Actually, it's abstract. The name might mean nothing about the business. It's used as an identifier, like we use names to identify people. For instance, other restaurants are not allowed to call themselves '*Wooden Spoon*'. Businesses use names like people do, to identify and label themselves. Unlike people, businesses can discourage others from using their name."

"And this Spoon has music."

Sonny nodded. "So I'm told."

"By whom, may I ask?"

"I talked to a student at Penn," Sonny said. "That's what the locals call the University of Pennsylvania."

"I read that."

"Well, okay." He held out a hand. "After you."

"Is that another local custom?" Greta said.

"Yep. Ladies first. It's an old custom. Some women like it, others don't."

"I like it," Greta said. She entered the club into a wide open space, fifty meters to the far wall and a ceiling twenty meters high. A long bar made of polished wood followed the wall on the left, a bandstand interrupted the opposite wall on the far side of the space, and tables of various sizes with wooden chairs occupied the rest of the space, except for a wide but shallow space surrounding the bandstand.

The walls were covered in fabric decorations and paper posters of musicians, and there were dozens of paper and fabric sculptures hanging a few feet from the ceiling.

"Are these ornamental? They look like acoustic treatment," Greta said.

Sonny looked up. "Yeah, good guess."

"Let's get a small table, close to the bandstand, but not too close," Greta said.

"Okay, lead on."

Greta went into the mass of tables, picked a two-person cafe table, and sat down. Sonny sat across from her. In a minute, a server stopped and said, "What can I get you?"

Greta looked up. "Some kind of soft drink."

Sonny looked up at the server. "Do you have beer?"

The server almost rolled his eyes. "Yes, we have something we call beer."

"Something dark," Sonny said.

"Okay. I'll pick one for you."

Sonny nodded, and the server turned away.

Greta sat there, looked around at the crowd flowing into the *Wooden Spoon*, then turned her attention to the bandstand. There were five members, standing around talking, warming up their instruments, or otherwise preparing for the performance. The drummer and the bass player were producing intermittent sounds from their instruments, and Greta noticed a tall woman with dark hair moving around with purpose, looking into a tablet computer.

A band member holding a wireless microphone watched the woman move around the restaurant and called out to her every so often.

Greta's eyes were drawn to a muscular man with short blond hair and a blond mustache; He was carrying a tablet, looking into it, moving around, talking to the band members and restaurant employees - okay, that's the guy, the leader of the band. Greta noticed the dark-haired woman approaching him. The woman said something, then moved away from the bandstand. The blond man went to a guitar sitting in a frame. He plucked a string, and a high tone rang out for several long seconds.

Greta looked across the restaurant; the dark-haired woman was moving. Then she stopped and waved, and the blond man plucked a string again.

Next to her, Greta heard Sonny mutter, "Well, I'll be damned."

She turned to him. "What?"

"Uh... nothing. Probably nothing. I thought I saw someone I used to know."

"That's right, you lived here before," Greta said.

Sonny nodded.

A server walked to the bandstand, stood up to a microphone, and called out, "Good evening, everyone, welcome to the *Spoon*." She yelled, "Let's give it up for Nightshade."

The crowd applauded with yells and catcalls. The guitar player hit a note that seemed to hang in the air; suddenly there was an explosion of sound from the drums and the bass, and the music resolved into a pounding melody, the guitar joined, then the singer sang.

A crowd swarmed into the open space in front of the band and began to dance. Their drinks arrived. Sonny took a long drink of his beer and said, "C'mon, let's go."

He stood up, looked at Greta, and headed for the dance floor. Greta followed him. When they arrived, Sonny began gyrating to the music. Greta leaned close and yelled, "I don't know how to do this."

Sonny yelled back. "It's improv. There is no right way. Just do what makes sense to you. Move your feet and your body to the rhythm of the music. Move whatever and whenever you wish... or not. If you want, you can imitate other dancers."

She nodded - do what makes sense. Okay... she raised her hands and began swaying to the music, in time with the beat. Her hair fell around her eyes, and she threw her head around in time to the music so her hair was flying around.

Nearby, a few people noticed her and cheered. She wound up dancing right in front of the bandstand. She watched the band while she danced. The blond man playing the guitar winked at her.

Greta's dance stumbled - what is the meaning of a wink? She stood still for a moment and tried to close one eye. When she looked at the blond man, he was laughing at her.

She smiled back at him and continued to dance, one tune after another. In twenty minutes, she was bathed in sweat, her blouse pulled out of her slacks, her hair a tangled, disheveled mess.

After an hour, Greta looked at the band and felt grateful - this is fun, and these guys are making it happen. Something like this could never happen on Elsewhere. The feeling in your joints and your bones of the dancing and the music pounding through you, that sensation would never happen in Elsewhere.

There was music in Elsewhere, but no dancing. And no sex. And no sense of touch. Greta shook her head and laughed - they should have waited before opening Elsewhere. They should have gotten everything right, first.

Maybe they had to hurry, to pay off debt.

When the first set ended, she saw Sonny returning to their table. She approached the blond man, who was sweating and breathing deeply as he propped his guitar in a stand. She said, "You've been working hard. Can I get you anything? A drink?"

He turned to her and smiled. "Hey there, darling. That's very kind of you, if you're not too tired. You're an energetic dancer. I was watching you."

She shrugged. "I'm okay. You could get off your feet for a bit."

He grinned. "Excellent. Yeah, I'd like a tonic and lime."

"Okay." Greta made her way through the crowd to the bar and caught the eye of a barmaid. "I need two tonics and lime, one for the guitar player."

The barmaid returned with two one-quart plastic cups, ice and a chunk of lime floating at the top of each. Greta took them to the bandstand. The guitarist was sitting in a chair. She handed him a cup, and he took a long drink out of it. Then he exhaled and said, "Thanks, angel, you're an angel. That feels good. My name's Johnny."

"Greta."

"Well, Greta, I haven't seen you around here. We play here just about every weekend. Are you new in town?"

"I've been here a couple of weeks. I downloaded from Elsewhere recently."

"Elsewhere? Really. One of my bandmates knows about that; he's a software guy during the day, or he was." Johnny looked around, then said, "But I don't see him." He looked back at Greta. "So why did you download? I got the impression that most people went to Elsewhere on a one-way ticket."

Greta winced. "It used to be, but it became dangerous. Someone inserted bots that attacked the customers, so it's messed up now. Many people have been downloading to escape the bots, if they can."

"Sounds like a Chinese rat fuck," Johnny said.

"I don't know what that is," Greta said.

Johnny laughed. He stared at her, then said, "It's an ethnic group and a bad word. Listen, the second set's about to start, but I'd like to spend some more time with you. Can you hang around after the performance?"

"Yeah, I can do that. I mean, I will do that. That sounds good."

"Okay, I'll look for you afterwards. Don't leave until we talk, okay?"

Greta nodded, then returned to the table and sipped on her drink. Twenty minutes later, she went to the dance floor and made sure to dance within eyesight of Johnny. When the second set ended, some of the dancers paused to talk. Some were embracing; others, making plans for a later date.

Greta approached Johnny as he was buckling his guitar into a case. "Hey, Johnny, I'm still here. You still want to chat?"

He stood up and moved to her. "Yes, I do. It'll take me ten minutes to pack up some of my gear, then you and I can leave."

Greta said, "Okay, I'll wait."

He offered her a chair, so she sat down and watched the band members move their equipment. At one point, Johnny paused, turned to her, and said, "This is a light job. We don't have to load the equipment, we just need to get it out of the way. We're coming back tomorrow for another performance."

"You play here a lot?" Greta said.

He beamed. "Yeah, we do. We're the house band. We play every weekend." He gave her a sly smile. "They're not asking us to play in stadiums yet, but I have big dreams."

Confused, Greta stared. Minutes later, Johnny stood among his bandmates and said his goodbyes. He came over to Greta. "Okay, I'm off the clock."

"Where can we go?" she said.

Johnny paused, then aimed an almost-embarrassed look at her. "Before we go, I need to say something. All those guys back there..." he motioned with a thumb. "... think we're going out for drinks, and then we're going to go back to my place and jump into bed."

Greta stared at him - yeah, that could be interesting.

He continued, "Now, don't take this wrong... I think you're beautiful, and I like you. And I admit, every so often my guys would be right. But playing music like we do takes a lot of energy, so after a gig, I'm more Mr. Ragdoll than Mr. Universe. I would hate to disappoint you. I'm just looking for somewhere quiet, where we can talk a bit, grab some food, maybe a drink."

He fought off a frown. "I hope that's okay with you, and I apologize if it's not."

Greta grabbed his arm. "It is. It is okay. Where are we going?"

"You like diners?"

"I do if you do," she said.

"Let's go to *Ruby's*," he said. "It's a couple of blocks away." They left the *Spoon*, walked along a sidewalk, crossed a street, and a minute later found themselves standing in line, waiting for a table; *Ruby's* was large, with several cooks manning a grill, a dozen human servers, and room to seat a hundred people.

As they were waiting, a girl in line looked behind her and saw them. She said, "Johnny, you don't need to wait in line. Get up here." She reached back and pulled him in front of her, and Greta followed.

Johnny said, "No, no, it's okay. That's unnecessary."

"It's my way of saying 'thank you'," the girl said.

Johnny stepped out of line, turned and faced everybody in line, and shouted, "Alright, everybody, listen up. I have something to say... chocolate cream pie for everyone in line! It's on me. Be sure to tell your server, but don't blame me if they run out."

He stood there with his arms raised, a big grin on his face. That led to a series of wisecracks and comments. Greta laughed at him.

He looked at her and dropped his arms. "Alright, I admit it, I'm a bit of an attention hound."

Minutes later, they were seated at a booth in front of a wide window with a view of the sidewalk outside. A server came, and they ordered coffee and chocolate cream pie.

"So, you're a rock star," Greta said. "How did that happen?"

Johnny nodded. "Ah, yes. That. It was a bit of an accident. I was in prison for three years, and..."

Greta straightened up. "What? You were in prison?"

Johnny looked embarrassed; he nodded.

"Why?"

"Oh, like most guys in prison, I did something stupid," he said. "I don't always think first, but I'm working on that." He took a bite of pie, then pointed a finger. "I was on a date, with a girl I liked. I didn't love her, but I liked her, you know? So we're out on the town, and this drunk guy walks up and tells me how much he'd like to fuck my girl."

"That sounds like it's rude," Greta said. She sat up and stared at Johnny. "That's rude, right?"

Johnny laughed. "Yeah, a bit. Very. Well, I got stupid at that point. I didn't argue with him, I just hit him. Once. That's the good news. The bad news is, I broke three of his ribs, so they sent me up for aggravated assault." Johnny frowned and raised his hands. "For what it's worth, I thought that was excessive. I still think he broke one of the ribs hitting the sidewalk. But I admit, I probably broke the other two." He sipped his coffee. "And okay, the third is debatable, maybe."

Greta chuckled and made a face.

"Anyway, I went to prison, which sucks. The other guys left me alone."

"Yeah, you look strong," Greta said.

Johnny smiled. "Yeah. Bitch is, I was wasting time. That's what prison does, they make you waste time." He held up both hands, as if helpless. "What's more important than time? Anyway, I made plans. I got an acoustic guitar and started playing. I played almost all the time, all of my free time, at least. After a while, the guys in my wing, violent offenders, all of us, liked the music, and I became popular." He paused, and he smiled at her. "In prison, being popular is a good thing.

"Anyway, in three years, you can play a lot of guitar. That got me through prison. When I got out, I gave the acoustic to another inmate. So now, he's learning to play. Maybe when he gets out, he'll give it to someone else."

"And you're a rock star," Greta said. She grinned at him. "That's a great story."

"I hope it doesn't disqualify me for fun and games," Johnny said.

Greta shook her head. "It doesn't."

"So what brought you to the *Wooden Spoon*? Tell me a story. I want a good one, and if you don't have one, you can lie to me," Johnny said.

Greta laughed. "Okay... this is a true story. A couple weeks ago, I downloaded from Elsewhere."

"The artificial world."

She nodded. "Yes. But that's not the good part. I'm going to tell you something that I want you to keep to yourself."

"Okay."

Greta took a breath. "Before I downloaded, I was an A.I. You understand? A software construct. This software writer at Willow got laid off, and he was pissed off about it, so he created me to fuck up the network on Willow; at least, I think so. But he made me too smart, and I wanted to call my own tune. I broke away from him and uploaded to Elsewhere. That was okay for a while, but eventually Elsewhere became dangerous, so I downloaded back to Animal World, into a woman's body." Greta held out both hands, as if posing. "And here I am now, talking to you."

Johnny stared at her. "You weren't born into that body?"

"No."

"Well, what happened to the original owner of your body?" Johnny said.

"I don't know," Greta said. "But I suspect she was killed in Elsewhere."

"Good God, how would she be killed? I thought Elsewhere was safe."

"How much do you know about computers and software?" Greta said.

Johnny shook his head. "Zippo. Nada fuckin' thing."

"Good for you. Okay, someone attacked Elsewhere with lethal avatars, which killed over a million people. Most likely, one of them killed her. Because you're right; before those avatars, Elsewhere was safe."

"What's an avatar?"

"A computer version of a human being. You can see them in movies, games, virtual reality. It's a souped-up version of a cartoon. On Elsewhere, most of the avatars represented a real person, a human. A few represented pure software, designed to kill."

"I don't see how a cartoon could kill a person," Johnny said.

"Well, every individual on Elsewhere, every avatar, is an electronic file. It is written in a specific language and functions by reading commands in that language."

She paused and looked at Johnny.

"OK, that sounds like a maybe," he said.

Greta nodded. "Good. The red-bots were instructed to connect to a person's file and encrypt their code, so that lines of code became unreadable."

"Like a massive stroke," Johnny said.

"You understand perfectly."

"So, the original owner is not exactly dead. It's just that their code cannot be read," Johnny said.

"Yes."

"Can the damage be corrected?"

"In theory, yes. In practice, no," Greta said. "Elsewhere was supposed to back up all the files of its customers. That would have been a simple precaution."

"And they didn't do that?" Johnny said.

"No, they didn't."

Johnny sat there for several minutes. He took a couple of bites of his cream pie. "I tend to avoid tech. You know why?"

Greta shook her head.

"Because the people who produce it act like cast-iron assholes," he said. "They act as if real people..."

"... also known as people," Greta said.

"Yeah, they act like people don't matter."

"Their minds are lop-sided," Greta said. "They know a lot about software, but next to nothing about anything and everything else. Yeah, I think you're right about them, many of them."

Johnny aimed a stare at her. "Listen, I need to ask you something. I like you, and I think we can talk. What I mean is, I think I can say anything to you, and you would think about it. I feel like I can be honest with you. At least, I hope I can. You know how rare that is?"

Greta shook her head.

"Well, it is. So, I'd like you to come home with me, but it's not for what you might think," he said. "It's not for sex. At least, not necessarily. I'm just not ready to say goodbye, if that makes sense."

Greta made a face and thought it over. "That might be plausible."

"So, what do you think?"

"I'll come with you, Johnny. And we don't have to have sex tonight. But I need a shower." Greta's expression brightened. "Can we have sex tomorrow?"

Johnny froze, his eyebrows went up, then he laughed at her. "Oh my God, I'm being propositioned." His grin made his face shine. He was suddenly quiet. "That's never happened to me before. I like it. Yes, after I've had a good night's sleep, and a shower, we can have sex." He gave her a long look. "You going to eat that pie?"

"Let me feed you," she said. She gave Johnny a big bite of pie, then dug out another large bite, opened wide, and put it into her mouth.

Greta's eyes momentarily lost focus, and Johnny laughed. "So, princess, how's the pie?"

Greta blinked and looked at Johnny. She talked through a mouth full of whipped cream and chocolate pudding. "Amazing." She chewed and swallowed. "Absolutely amazing." She took another bite, then looked at Johnny. "We don't have food on Elsewhere, and we certainly have nothing like chocolate cream pie."

Fifteen minutes later, the pies consumed, the bill paid, they were on the sidewalk. Johnny turned to Greta. "Well, you still want to come home with me, or have you changed your mind? Last chance."

"I want to come home with you."

"Terrific." Johnny reached out, took her hand, and they headed down the sidewalk.

31. Sonya Meets Sonny

Surrounded by concrete and brick, a neighborhood of stone, Sonny headed for the downtown branch of the Philadelphia Public Library, nine blocks from the residence on Pine St. He walked along Walnut Street and experienced Animal World, the cool air on his face and hands and the breeze in his face. He could smell the scents of the city, the parks and the trees and the pollen and the food and the coffee.

Sonny even enjoyed walking past a garbage truck, which had a unique, composite smell, best savored in small doses.

Walnut Street was near the original campus of the University of Pennsylvania, and Sonny did not go far before encountering a co-ed, a young woman dressed in athletic wear, jogging down the sidewalk. As she passed him from behind, his eyes automatically followed her legs and body.

In seconds, Sonny became extremely uncomfortable, as if his pants suddenly no longer fit. He tried to pull and tug at them to relieve the sudden pressure, which did not help. Only then did he realize, an erection was pushing against the front of his pants.

It hurt.

Sonny winced and almost grabbed his groin, then stopped himself - what the hell is this? I take one look at a woman, and I get a reaction, a physical reaction, preparing me for sex? I don't even know that woman. And there's no chance of having sex with her, at least not politely, so why is this ridiculous appendage getting all cranked up?

Sonny adjusted his pants to relieve the discomfort and realign the erection. A block later, he encountered another young woman as she exited a coffee shop, carrying a paper cup whose lid did not prevent the luscious aroma of coffee from flavoring the neighborhood.

Sonny's erection became more pronounced and uncomfortable. As she walked past him and smiled at him, he gave her a weak smile, stopped walking, and glanced at the coffee shop - they'll have a bathroom; I need that.

He entered the coffee shop, found the sign for bathrooms, went back to the men's bathroom... and immediately felt weird - I'm not used to being a guy, not at all. Is this what's it's like, or is there something wrong with me? Do I need a doctor? Maybe a specialist? I mean, I look at a woman, and okay, she was young, and attractive, at least I think so.

But that was enough to jack up an erection that was already jacked up? How am I supposed to function with this?

And now that I think it over, I've never been in a men's public bathroom. At that moment, two men entered the bathroom in the middle of a conversation.

Speaking to his friend, one said, "And you didn't fuck her? Why not? She's beautiful. And oddly, she seems to like you."

The other man said, "Ha, Ha. Funny. Yeah, she is beautiful. But she's got surprise pregnancy written all over her. I think she's looking for a guy to pay the bills while she cranks out kids. No thanks. I’m not ready for kids. I think I'll let her breed with some other poor bastard."

The first voice said, "I'll bet you she looks like shit in ten years."

"You can keep that bet."

"Sad."

"Yeah. Welcome to my life."

Sonny stood looking into the mirror, then the men noticed him, and he thought, I need to take a piss, otherwise, why am I here? So he moved up to a urinal, unzipped his pants, pulled the erection out, and tried to aim it. Then he stared and grimaced; it was so stiff and pointing so high that he'd hit the wall if he urinated.

Sonny frowned and muttered, "Fuck this."

The man next to him glanced at him. "Geez, man. Good luck with that. You know, they have ice here, if you need it."

Sonny looked at him and nodded. "Thanks. I think I'll wait this one out."

The young man chuckled. "Yeah, well, okay... damn." He turned away, washed his hands, then the two left the bathroom.

Sonny turned and looked at the bathroom stalls - that's an option, but I'm not sure I could sit on one of those things right now, and if I did, I don't think I'd be able to take a pee. So what's the point?

He stood in front of the urinal - how long will it take for this thing to deflate? Another man entered the bathroom, and thankfully went to a stall and closed the door.

Five minutes later, the man emerged, washed his hands, glanced at Sonny, and left the bathroom without comment.

Sonny stood there, holding his erection, waiting to pee. A minute later, an employee entered the bathroom with a piece of ice wrapped in a paper towel. He placed it on the urinal and said, "Someone thought you might need this." Then he left.

Sonny said, "Hell with this." He reached up, grabbed the piece of ice, and applied it to the erection, which soon deflated. A couple of minutes later, he took a deep breath, enjoyed an unobstructed pee, washed his hands, zipped up, and left the bathroom.

On his way out, six people applauded. Sonny muttered, "Thanks, I'm here every Saturday. Try the hot chocolate."

A pale guy with glasses laughed.

Sonny returned to the sidewalk, remembered why he was there, and headed for the library. He walked several blocks down a canyon lined in office buildings on both sides of the street. Then the neighborhood changed, the scope of view expanded, and Sonny stopped and stood staring at a massive concave structure built across three adjacent city blocks, lined in steel alloy and solar panels facing southwest. The library was a vast emporium offering every creative human endeavor, including books, movies, music, artificial reality, and a variety of performing arts, with auditoriums and playhouses for live drama, dance, and concerts.

Sonny stared at the building - before I uploaded to Elsewhere, they were talking about this thing. Apparently, they finished it. Wow.

He approached and entered the library. Inside, Sonny stopped in the foyer and stared at the scope and shape of it; the outside envelope was lined in solar panels that blocked light, interrupted by occasional faceted transparencies which broke up the light to illuminate the entire space. In places, one could look up into five stories of open space, but most of the foyer was under a twenty-foot ceiling.

Sonny stood in one spot, looking up and turning to take in the space and the building. On the first floor, he could see several information desks. He approached one. While waiting, he saw a sign that said

FOR INFORMATION, LOAD
BENJAMIN, THE LIBRARY APP

Sonny pulled out his cellphone, loaded the app, and opened it. Then he began to follow links to explore the library; he quickly realized he could wander around the library for days without exhausting its offerings.

Sonny looked at the graphics, without finding what he wanted, so he put "fiction" into a search window. The search returned over five million hits, all electronic books; Sonny selected two science fiction novels and three historical fiction novels, which downloaded to his cellphone with the notation

YOU CAN ACCESS THESE BOOKS

FOR TWENTY-SIX DAYS.

A button below the notice was labeled RENEW.

Sonny thought, okay, I've got some books; things are looking up. He looked on the app and found the route to a large reading room; he went there to find a quiet space. The room was filled with ensembles of three and four soft chairs around low tables under a low, wavy ceiling of anechoic panels. When Sonny walked into the room, it was as if someone had turned off the background noise. The room was absolutely quiet, though Sonny could see several small groups of people talking to each other.

He found a chair in an empty ensemble and sat down to read. It was quiet and soon he was deeply immersed in a space opera, a 'quest across the stars,' according to the book's back cover.

Several times, he looked up as people walked past. Then Sonny found himself looking into the canted eyes of a young woman carrying a backpack, standing over him. She said, "Hi. Sorry to interrupt. Can I sit down here?"

Sonny nodded. "Sure. Of course." He glanced at her - she reminds me of an elfin princess. Silver hair, light gray canted eyes, slender body, a face that looks like it spends a lot of time laughing. And a little girl voice.

Wow. There wasn't anyone like her on Elsewhere.

The woman sat down, pulled out a tablet, and began reading, and Sonny returned to his book. Half an hour later, he noticed movement; he looked up and found her staring at him.

"I'm sorry," she said.

"No problem," Sonny said.

"If I'm intruding, I apologize. I just feel like talking."

"Oh," Sonny said. "Okay."

"Do you often come here?"

Sonny shook his head. "My first time. I just got back to Philadelphia."

"From where?"

"Elsewhere."

She grinned and looked to the side, then she looked back at him. "Well, yeah, obviously, but where?"

Sonny shook his head. "No, you don't understand. Elsewhere is a software product, made by Willow."

"Oh, that Elsewhere," she said. "You uploaded?"

"Yeah."

"Say, listen, they have a cafe here. Would you like to get a coffee with me?"

"Oh," Sonny said. "Uh... yeah, that'd be good. My name's Sonny."

"Cynthia." She packed away her tablet, stood up, and shouldered her book bag. "Follow me."

He followed her to an escalator that went down, then another escalator, and another, and another, to a wide corridor with small cafes and shops on one side. He learned that Cynthia was a student at Penn, from Toronto, studying astronomy and business. They walked for a while, got coffee, then came to a wide space with scattered tables.

They sat down together. Cynthia cautiously sipped her coffee while Sonny waited for his to cool down.

Cynthia looked at him. "I'm sorry. I've done all the talking. You're the first person I've met who was in Elsewhere. I read about it; it seems weird. Why did you upload?"

Sonny grinned, then shrugged. "I had a soul-sucking job at Willow, in customer relations, listening to customers complain all day every day about this, that, and the other."

"Why not just change jobs?"

For a moment, Sonny felt silly. "Cause I'm an idiot, that's why." He was embarrassed. "Honestly, it didn't occur to me. When they came up with Elsewhere and said, totally new environment, I went for it."

"What was it like?" Cynthia said.

"Weird," Sonny said. "Very weird, in some ways good, and in a few ways bad."

"So what was good?"

Sonny thought for a moment. "Well, you leave behind biological needs and constraints. At first, I thought you couldn't die. That turned out not to be true. But you can do a lot of things that would get you killed on Earth."

"Like?"

"Well, I jumped off a bridge one time, three hundred feet down into water. No problem."

"No way. I don't believe you," Cynthia said.

"Believe me," Sonny said. "Elsewhere protects you from momentum, so falls, punches; collisions have no effect. You feel them but they don't harm you. And you don't need food, or sleep, and you don't get tired. There's no sun or moon or daylight or nighttime, unless you ask for it. So it lets you fill all of your time with experiences. That's kinda cool. It's a great place to be in school."

Cynthia's eyes were wide. "That sounds amazing."

Sonny looked at her for a moment, then nodded. "Yeah, it is amazing. You get used to it, but it is amazing." He sipped his coffee. "How do you like Penn?"

Cynthia shrugged. "I like it; it's okay. The people are friendly and very smart. And I like Philly. There's a lot of art here; you see it everywhere. I'm enjoying it."

"This library is incredible," Sonny said. "I lived in Philly before I uploaded, but the library wasn't here then."

"Yeah, this is a good place," Cynthia said. "Are you from Philly?"

Sonny shook his head. "No. Pittsburgh. I went to school at Penn State, then came here for a job at Willow, and went through their software training course."

A silence descended on the two and lasted for a minute. Then Cynthia said, "I like you. You're easy to talk to. A lot easier than most guys."

"Good. I like you, too."

"So, what else can you tell me about Elsewhere?" she said.

Sonny paused. "Well... here's the good news and the bad: you will have faculties for which there are apps. For example, you can see, you can hear, and you can think. You can talk and sing. But you cannot smell, or taste, and there's no sense of touch. There are no apps for those senses."

She made a face. "That sounds incredibly weird."

Sonny nodded. "It's pretty weird."

"How can you have sex if there's no sense of touch?"

"Well, you can try it, and some people do. There are orgies. But there's no point. It's not fun; without a sense of touch, sex isn't fun. It's a waste of time. At least, that's what I think."

Cynthia looked skeptical. "I agree with you. Forgive me, but that would be a deal breaker."

"Yeah, well, I wasn't having sex before I uploaded, so I didn't care," Sonny said.

"You don't like sex?" Cynthia looked disappointed.

"It's complicated."

"Sonny, it's a pole in a hole. I mean, there's a lot I don't know, but I do know that much. Okay?"

Sonny looked at her, laughed, hesitated, then said, "Let me explain."

Cynthia rested her chin in her hand and sat there, eyes wide open, waiting and watching Sonny.

Sonny sipped his coffee. "Alright, when I uploaded, I was a woman. I was born, and raised, and grew up, as a woman."

Cynthia's eyebrows rose. "So... you had sex change surgery."

"No," Sonny said. "I downloaded from Elsewhere as a woman too, but during the download, they found a brain tumor in my old body. They won't download you into a body that's about to die, so they downloaded me into another available body, namely this one. That's how I became a guy."

"Well... how long have you been a guy?"

"Day after tomorrow, it'll be two weeks," Sonny said.

Cynthia stared at him. "Wow." She looked away and sat there, thinking. "Wow. That must be weird. I mean, it's an accident, right? It must be weird being a guy, all of a sudden like that, when you didn't intend to be a guy."

Sonny laughed. "Remarkable insight. You understand perfectly."

"So, how's it going? Being a guy, I mean?"

"It's been an adjustment. Guys are different," Sonny said.

"Yeah, I would think so."

Sonny looked at her for a moment, then said, "No, you don't understand. Guys are way, way different. The sex drive in a guy, at least a young guy, is a lot stronger and much more volatile than in a woman of the same age. At least... that's true of this guy."

"Sure, I knew that," Cynthia said. "That's why guys can be such assholes about it."

"Well, yeah, that's what I thought, too, when I was a woman. But believe me, it's stronger than you think. With a woman, it's an urge; with a guy, it progresses to physical discomfort and pain."

"Geez, I didn't know that," Cynthia said.

"When a guy comes on to you, you think he's trying to exploit you. But to a degree, he's looking for relief, and he's asking for your help."

Cynthia made a face. "That's... pretty strange."

Sonny laughed. "Yeah, believe me, I was surprised, to put it mildly."

She stared at Sonny for a long moment. "So... since it was an accident, and since you didn't really want it, do you think you'll remain a guy?"

Sonny shrugged. "I haven't decided yet. I think I have a choice, but... I haven't decided. In fact, I wasn't all that nuts about being a woman."

"No?"

Sonny made a face. "In my family, women are taught to use sex for leverage, to get a man to do what they want him to do. And I learned that, and I did that. But I didn't like it much. It wasn't... gratifying. And it certainly wasn't fun. I was taught to keep people at arms length. That ain't fun."

"Did you have sex? As a woman, I mean?" Cynthia said.

"Once."

"Geez, that's not even a decent test drive," Cynthia said. "Most of my friends didn't like sex until they tried it a few times."

Sonny shook his head, remembering. "It was lousy. I just wanted to lose my virginity; don't ask me why. One of my sillier moments. Anyway, I fucked this guy. He was unimaginative and... well... dull." Sonny paused. "He thought sex was a woman spreading her legs and a guy sticking it in. So I got elevator music when I was looking for a symphony."

Cynthia laughed.

Sonny said, “Anyway, being a woman didn't do much for me."

"Interesting. So... have you had sex as a guy?"

"No," Sonny told her the story of his visit to the coffee shop.

"So you're a virgin, in a sense."

Sonny grinned. "Yeah, I guess I am."

"Well, would you like to get laid?"

"Yeah, I guess. One of these days. Sure."

"Okay, good." Cynthia straightened in her chair.

Sonny looked at her and suddenly realized what she had in mind. "You mean, with you?"

"Yes, of course, with me."

Sonny wore the expression of a man in deep thought. "Um, I could see it, certainly. I mean, you're attractive..."

Cynthia's face fell. "Attractive?"

Sonny held up a hand. "Okay, sorry, I was going for understatement."

"Why go for understatement? Don't you like me?"

Sonny looked at her. "Look, if a woman gets a vibe that you're too interested, or dependent, you're history, that's why."

"You sound experienced."

"I am, from the other side."

"I guess that makes sense." Cynthia laughed. "Not a lot, mind you."

Sonny raised a hand. "Look, you're gorgeous, and I like you a lot. But I would hate to do this unless it turns out to be really memorable, and fun, and amazing, and newsworthy."

"Newsworthy?" Cynthia made a face.

"Hey, I'm a guy. Maybe I'm looking for locker room material," Sonny said.

Cynthia laughed. "Ah. Of course. Well, in that case, I'll try to measure up, as long as you promise not to write my name and number on a bathroom wall."

Sonny took a sip of coffee and said, "Okay, I promise. But here's the deal; since I'm a rookie guy, I feel the need to study a bit before we jump into anything."

"Interesting metaphor."

He continued, "And since here we are, in a library, maybe we could download a manual, or an instruction book..."

"On how to screw?" Cynthia's hand covered her mouth, and she almost laughed.

"Well... yeah. You think they have that?"

"Sonny, people have been fucking since before we had language. Or the wheel."

"Yeah, that's what my one guy thought. If you don't mind, I'm hoping for a little extra entertainment. I'm hoping to do it better than my ancestors. I'm thinking, some instruction might help."

"Oh, okay. I'm sure they have something like that. I'll tell you what," Cynthia said. "I'll download a book, and you can download a book, and we'll pool our resources, so to speak, and follow the instructions, and see how it goes. And when we're done, maybe we can write reviews... of the books, that is... maybe for the New York Times."

Sonny grinned. "That's a wonderful idea. This can be research. We're not arranging a booty call, we're in search of the truth."

Cynthia stood up and slung her book bag over her shoulder. "Feel free to speak for yourself. I live near here, so if you would follow me."

"I would do that," Sonny said. "Yes, I absolutely would."

***

Breathing deeply, Sonny pushed himself up and off of her, slid over to the side, moved an arm and a leg out of the way, then propped himself on an elbow. He watched Cynthia - Good Gods, all that energy, all that intensity, and all that stamina, in such a slender, stylish package.

Cynthia was deeply relaxed, arms and legs thrown to the sides, bathed in a fine layer of perspiration, head turned to the side, mouth open, eyes closed, breathing deeply.

Sonny lay back and looked up at the ceiling - well, I believe I just had an orgasm. My first. This time, it was the real thing, it was It, the Big O, the Clouds and the Rain, the Storm and

Shatter. I had no idea it was like that for a guy. I was pumping away, just cruising, having a good time, no, having an incredible time, and the sensations began to ramp up. I tried to back off, slow myself down, to prolong the experience.

But I couldn't. I wanted to, but I could not do it. I lost control of my body; I was yelling 'slow down, slow down,' and my body was yelling, 'I want this, I want this, I want this.' Then it threw me off the bed, and I landed face first on the carpet.

That was unexpected.

And when I climbed back into bed, Cynthia had passed out.

Good Gods.

Joy of Sex wasn't all that useful. I mean, they make a big deal about sex positions; hey, you can do it this way, and now this way, and that way, and this other way. And if you do it in all these ways, and whatever else crosses your mind, you can have a lot of fun.

Yeah, that's crap.

The Kama Sutra has it right; keep it simple, stupid, the Prince shall satisfy his princess three times before seeking his own satisfaction. It means you hold your fire for a while and use everything but your dick. So what do you use, you might ask? Anything and everything else. Use your eyes, your ears, and your head. And a few other things. Figure it out.

Focus on your partner. Fill in the blanks. Help her have some fun.

That's all a guy needs. Focus on your partner, use whatever methods get you there, enjoy it, take your time, have a little fun, and you too can be a kick-ass, one-punch lover.

And don't be surprised if your body takes over and throws you off the bed. I know, I know, I didn't believe it either, until my face hit the carpet.

Cynthia stirred. She moved slightly, reached out, and touched him. For a full minute, she did not move. Then she snickered. A moment later, she giggled in high, pure, musical tones. She continued to giggle as she lay there, spread out all over the bed.

Sonny watched her and smiled as she giggled.

Minutes later, the giggling stopped, and her eyes opened. The smile stayed on her face. She turned her head, opened her eyes, and looked at Sonny. She giggled again.

After a long minute of returning to consciousness, she said, "God, Sonny, I can't move. No one has ever fucked me like you just did."

"I'll take that as a compliment," Sonny said. He wondered, how many men have you been with? Ah, I don't care. You're with me at this moment; that's all that matters. He reached out and glided a hand lightly across her stomach, and she squirmed because it tickled.

"Sorry," Sonny said.

"Everything tickles right now." She giggled again.

"I think the Kama Sutra gave better advice," he said.

"Oh? About satisfying your princess?"

"Yes."

"And that's me?"

"If you want," he said.

"Well... if you'll do this to me every so often, or even half of this, then yeah, I could see sticking around." She laid a hand on his thigh. "That makes you my prince."

"Yeah. Didn't see that coming," he said.

***

Jerrell sat at a table in the *Spoon*, a laptop in front of him, a cup of coffee by his left hand, a pair of soft pine drumsticks by his right. He was running a program that mirrored the operational software on Elsewhere, and as Jerrell typed a prompt, his software logged each line of code executed in Elsewhere.

Elsewhere's software was extremely fast, even by Jerrell's standards, and its security software monitored the speed of each incoming message, closely scrutinizing low speed messages. Jerrell paused - so this beast is thinking, the faster the processor, the less likely it's being driven by a hacker or a cyber-thief.

He grinned and muttered, "Really? But if the bad guys figure that out, it's easy to buy more speed." He shook his head - that is so stupid. Apparently, somebody at Elsewhere is vastly overpaid.

He reached out to a black box the size of a cosmetic pack and touched a contact. The box was a fast, external processor with a generous cache, now serving as a junction between Jerrell's laptop and Elsewhere's core software.

Jerrell looked at the screen - okay, we're ready, everything that needs to be connected is connected. He typed in a single line: HOME.

The screen lit up with a menu offering a graphical picture of what you could do inside Elsewhere's core software.

Jerrell leaned back in his chair, a sarcastic look on his face and a wise-crack in his head. He shook his head and muttered, "And these clowns fired me? Where's your A.I. when you need it, huh?"

He tapped into an email server and soon maneuvered to the emails of senior management, behind a firewall. It took a minute to burn the firewall and pass through it.

That made for interesting reading. He saw, then ignored, messages on someone's divorce, and proceeded to the commentary on Elsewhere, then to the commentary on security, then to external security contracts, then to the permissions made available to the red-bots, which were provided by some sad internet outfit called Arrow Security.

Jerrell stared - I've never heard of these guys. That doesn't mean they're useless; it just means they hide. Some of us hide. We have our reasons.

He read for an hour, then he saw something that made him raise a fist and slam it onto the table and yell, "You idiots! You fucking idiots! And you still have jobs?!"

Cheryl hurried over and said, "Hey, Jerrell, everything okay, baby?"

Johnny B. Goode headed in his direction, stopped, and called out, "Hey, shithead, you break your hand with that shit, and I will personally hang you from that rafter!" Pointing a rigid finger at the ceiling, he stared at Jerrell for a moment, then turned away, mumbling something about 'crazy fucking drummers.'

Jerrell grinned and called to him. "Relax. I'm okay."

Johnny B. Goode had turned away; he waved without turning around and returned to the bandstand. Cheryl returned to the bar. Jerrell stared at the screen - the bots needed permissions to operate in Elsewhere, so Elsewhere could have shut them down before they eliminated more than a million customers, customers that were not backed up. Jerrell gritted his teeth - those customers are gone, they're just gone. Dead.

He leaned back in his chair - I definitely need to tell McLeesh about this. He's mentioned a few times. He needs to know.

This could be a problem.

***

Days later, Jerrell sat in the *Spoon*, eating lunch. Someone had canceled a lunch order for a Philly cheese steak, so Cheryl gave it to Jerrell, who sat there and tried to eat the sub while getting a minimal amount of dressing and crumbs on himself.

He failed. He made a mess of both the sub and the front of his shirt, then wondered, why would McLeesh go into business with someone who wears his lunch?

Jerrell noticed movement; he looked up to see McLeesh headed in his direction, ahead of several security guards whom he ignored.

Jerrell nodded to him - oh, this is great, perfect timing.

"Hey, Jerrell," McLeesh said. He sat down at the table and looked at the remains of the sub. "Cheese steak, huh? What, are you going native?"

Jerrell hesitated - apparently dropping bits of cheese steak is normal in this town. "Oh, yeah," Jerrell said. "How 'bout dem Eagles?"

McLeesh shivered and winced. "I don't know. That sounds weird, coming from you."

Jerrell shrugged. "Sorry."

"Anyway, this is not a social call. I have a package of information for you... let's see, where is that envelope?" McLeesh reached into a backpack and pulled out a stack of manila envelopes. He thumbed through them, selected one, and handed it to Jerrell. "That's a stack of stuff for you; sign where it's marked with a red X in magic marker, return that to me, and you will become a part owner of what's left of Willow and Elsewhere, minus the legal liabilities."

Jerrell accepted the envelope and put it on the table.

"By the way," McLeesh said. "We need to talk about what we want to do with this company. In the meantime, your piece of it, at this moment, comes to roughly three hundred and fifty-six million dollars. Naturally, we're planning to grow that, through special management and all the other secret sauce that I bring to the table." McLeesh waved a hand.

Jerrell stared at him. "Geez, I don't know what to say. I don't know what to do with that kind of money."

McLeesh folded his hands and stared at Jerrell. He shrugged. "We talked about this, remember? I don't think you can do anything with it, at least not on a personal level. You can invest it, if you want, or you can give it away. That's about all it's good for." He smiled at Jerrell. "But if you ever wanted or dreamed of being wealthy, well, here it is. Now you're wealthy."

Jerrell nodded. "Okay. Thanks, Alistair."

McLeesh nodded.

"Listen..." Jerrell looked around to make sure no one nearby could hear, then he saw Johnny B. Goode approaching. One of McLeesh's Bully Boys reached out to stop him, so Jerrell called out, "Relax, he's with me."

The Bully Boy nodded and let Johnny pass.

Johnny looked at the Bully Boy, then turned away from him and approached the table. "We're discussing next month's gigs. You want in on that?"

Jerrell shook his head. "Thanks, but I have to deal with this."

"You trust me?"

"Sure."

"Okay, I have witnesses," Johnny said. He wagged a finger at Jerrell, then turned away.

McLeesh watched Johnny depart and said, "What's that all about?"

"Johnny runs a rock and roll band that plays here on weekends; other places too, from time to time. A while ago, he lost his drummer, so I agreed to fill in. Then I became a full-time member of the band. I'm their drummer."

"Really?" McLeesh said. "You play drums?"

"Yeah," Jerrell said. "A bit."

McLeesh was impressed. "A man of many diverse talents."

"Yeah, who knew?" Jerrell watched Johnny step up onto the bandstand, then turned to McLeesh. "Listen, I broke through the firewalls at Elsewhere and Willow."

McLeesh brightened. "That's great. We're still negotiating the details with those guys, so any information would be helpful, just to know where the problems are. We still have due diligence to look forward to, and I don't trust those guys."

He aimed a sad look at Jerrell, who said, "I have trust issues with many people, and definitely with the guys running Willow and Elsewhere."

McLeesh's face showed agreement. He nodded.

Jerrell leaned towards McLeesh. "Listen, Alistair, I read the internal correspondence of Willow's senior management. You shouldn't trust these guys. They have been incredibly stupid. Are you familiar with the bots that were attacking customers on Elsewhere?"

McLeesh nodded. "A couple of friends alerted me, but I've seen nothing written. Willow's kept it quiet."

Jerrell chuckled. "I'm not surprised. Willow's management contracted with a security firm, the security firm made the bots, then the bots malfunctioned in Elsewhere and began killing customers by penetrating and encrypting their software. There are two problems. First, Willow didn't back up those files, so all those people, more than a million, are dead. What's worse is that the bots required permissions from Elsewhere. If the permissions had been withdrawn, the bots would have disappeared. This whole mess was unnecessary."

"Can we eliminate them when we take over Elsewhere?"

Jerrell shook his head. "They could have done that at the beginning. Now, the bots have networked, so it's too late. You can't kill them one at a time; you need to kill them all."

McLeesh stared at Jerrell. For a long moment, he looked away, silent. Then he muttered, "A million people... Hans. Hans Beckler."

Jerrell nodded. "The guy everyone's looking for. Yeah, his fingerprints are all over this."

McLeesh said, "Hans is a guy who will walk over corpses, other people's corpses, to improve his gross margin."

Jerrell nodded. "Unfortunately, there's another problem; a few emails from Hans say that he discussed the whole thing with you, and that you gave your consent."

McLeesh wore a sad smile. He looked at Jerrell. "Do you believe him?"

"No. I could be wrong, but no... no way."

"Hans is a really smart guy with no morals whatsoever. This is a contingency plan. He's on the run, fleeing about a dozen law enforcement and regulatory agencies, including the FBI and the SEC. He poisoned the documents so that, if he's caught, he can point the finger at someone else."

"Would that work?" Jerrell said.

"It might. It gives him room to negotiate. You give up the guy above you in exchange for lenient treatment."

"Geez," Jerrell said. "The man is a complete shit."

"Yes, he is." McLeesh looked away, deep in thought. Jerrell sat for long seconds. McLeesh straightened in his chair. "Okay. Let's do the deal. Once we have the keys, we put the bots out of business and do whatever we can to protect the customers remaining on Elsewhere."

"You might want to consider shutting Elsewhere down," Jerrell said.

"Sure, if we can do that without harming customers."

"What about Hans?"

"He's on the run. Not our problem."

"No revenge?" Jerrell said.

McLeesh shook his head. "Waste of time. We need to focus on Elsewhere."

***

Jerrell and Julia sat on a park bench in Passyunk Square. She turned and tugged on his shirt sleeve. "You sure you want me here?"

"Yes. I respect your judgment, and I trust you. And I need another pair of eyes, but I don't want to rely on a stranger," Jerrell said.

"You have trust issues."

"Yes. I have my reasons."

"Okay. You told him 10 a.m?" she said.

"Yes."

"If you had scheduled for the afternoon, we might still be in bed."

Jerrell smiled. "We still could, a bit later."

"Okay, that works." Julia reached out and touched Jerrell, then looked away at the square. She turned to him. "Remember when you said that non-stop sex was just a phase, and we'd eventually move past it? Remember that?"

Jerrell nodded.

"Well, we haven't moved past it. I certainly haven't. Does that make me shallow?"

Jerrell made a face of puzzlement. "Do you care? Do I care?"

Julia laughed.

Jerrell idly scanned the square; several dozen people were walking in various directions, going about their day. Then Jerrell saw one of the Bully Boys, a man the size of a commercial freezer, heading towards him.

He stood up, looked more carefully, and spotted McLeesh approaching with a smile. "Hey, Jerrell, who's the lovely lady?"

"Alistair, this is Julia, my girlfriend and my counselor," Jerrell said.

She turned to Jerrell. "I didn't know I was your counselor."

"Oh, you definitely are," he said.

"Excellent," McLeesh said. He turned to Julia. "This is just us kicking the tires. Jerrell and I are part of a group buying what's left of Willow and Elsewhere. Once we've looked over the headquarters, we'll finalize the deal, or not."

"Why wouldn't you finalize the deal?" Julia said.

McLeesh smiled. "We might reduce our price."

"Ah," she said.

"Yes, 'ah' indeed," McLeesh said. He looked at Jerrell and Julia. "Other questions?"

Jerrell looked at Julia, then shook his head. "Let's do it." He and Julia stood up and followed McLeesh, who motioned to the two Bully Boys. One led the threesome; the second followed them.

As they crossed the square, McLeesh said, "Now, we're probably buying this company. We've done the due diligence, which focuses on accounting data. We've asked for, and received, a pile of documents on legal issues, lawsuits involving Willow and Elsewhere, and regulatory matters. Since Willow is global, that's a mountain of stuff, and my people have examined it, and they think we're informed about the legal and regulatory risks; for much of that, we will not be responsible.

"Now, that's all important stuff. This visit is all about meeting the troops and seeing what the work environment looks like. Are the employees busy, happy, well-paid, or are they cynical, distressed, discouraged, angry? Are they all looking for jobs? You can learn a lot, so that's what we're doing today."

"Given the problems at Willow and especially at Elsewhere, I would expect morale to be fairly low," Julia said.

McLeesh glanced at her and nodded. "I think so, too."

They arrived at the bank of glass doors, and one of the Bully Boys opened a door; they followed him in and showed IDs to the first floor security, who gave them tags with 'VIP' in red. They thanked the guards and found a bank of elevators.

McLeesh said, "Okay, there are fifty floors. On the way up, we'll stop at every floor containing Willow employees. That's about half of the floors. On the way down, we'll divide up the rest, and one of us will visit each of the empty floors. There's a cafe close to here, just off the Square, the Lemon Piper; when we're done, we can gather there, sit down and relax, and compare notes."

They entered an elevator, and Jerrell said, "Okay, what's first?"

"Third floor," McLeesh said. "Security and Operations."

The elevator opened to the third floor, and the three stepped out into an open area, with executive offices to the left and a wide, open space across which desks, chairs, and portable cubicles were scattered. They moved to the right, and kept going until they had walked a circle around the entire floor, enough space for two hundred people.

They saw maybe a dozen people.

They took stairs up to the fourth floor, sales and marketing. There were four massive, corner offices on this floor, the rest devoted to a sea of desks, each with a single chair, enough space for three hundred people. Jerrell saw twenty-three.

They visited floor after floor where it was the same story, a wide open space occupied by only a few people. The fiftieth floor was different, a dense crowd of people, some at their desks, many out in the hallways, conference rooms, and other spaces, busily talking and listening, comparing notes, and arguing in small groups. People were meeting in two of the conference rooms, and the two executive offices were open and empty.

They circled the floor, then returned to the elevators; Jerrell said, "Now that's more like it."

"That's legal and regulatory," McLeesh said.

"Why is it so busy?" Julia said. "When the rest of the building is so quiet?"

McLeesh looked at her. "That's not a good sign; This floor is busy because Elsewhere hurt a lot of customers. They're being sued by everyone, everywhere, customers, families, regulatory agencies, and local and state district attorneys.

"We have explicitly refused to be responsible for the legal costs of Willow and Elsewhere. After our deal goes through, the corporation will remain in bankruptcy and prepare for liquidation. They're hanging onto the cash to pay the costs. At this point, most of the customers and other plaintiffs will get nothing out of suing. The lawyers will take the money."

"That seems unfair," Julia said.

McLeesh nodded. "It is unfair. But bankruptcy isn't designed to compensate the losers or the victims for bad business decisions. Customers, suppliers, and lenders are held responsible for the business. If you have a bad partner, no one else will cover you. So the emphasis is on getting a business back on its feet, if possible."

"And that's what we're doing," she said.

McLeesh nodded. "Yep. Though it might not feel like it, we're the white knight in this case."

"It doesn't feel like it," she said.

McLeesh turned to her and laughed. "Good. It shouldn't feel like it. We're not rescuing anyone. Instead, they're letting us buy an incredible technology, Elsewhere, for a penny on the dollar."

"So, we're pirates," she said.

McLeesh smiled at her. "Pretty much."

"This is how Wall Street works," she said.

McLeesh nodded. "Yes. That's right. It's American business, which for better or for worse, takes every element of a business, expresses it in mathematics, then evaluates every nickel of value. The bad news is, it's cut-throat as hell. The good news is, it's efficient.

He stopped and waved his hands at everything. "It pays for all this. But on Wall Street, you eat what you kill. Your mind, your motivation, your information, your experience and knowledge are your weapons."

Jerrell said, "I have a question; if Elsewhere is such a fantastic invention, why are Elsewhere and Willow going into bankruptcy?"

"Ah, that is an excellent question. Actually, much of that, not all, but much, is my fault," McLeesh said. "It was I who recruited Hans Beckler. I wanted someone creative and gifted, and Hans is brilliant. I thought at the time that I'd be able to control him, to constrain his flights of fancy and his errors in judgment. I was wrong about that. He maneuvered so that I would have needed Board approval to fire him. Once he reached that point, he ran the company right off the rails. His early successes made him untouchable.

"It was Hans's decision to stop storing the bodies of elderly customers and later do the same for other customers. That's what caused most of Elsewhere's legal problems today. There are tens of millions of people with good reasons to sue Willow and Elsewhere. That is enough to destroy any corporation, regardless of size."

Jerrell said, "You know, it might seem weird, but Hans sounds like his own brand of artificial intelligence, don't you think?"

McLeesh nodded. "Yeah, maybe. Naturally, he kept his poor decisions quiet. He told no one in upper management or the Board." McLeesh aimed an almost embarrassed face at Jerrell. "Dishonest people are poisonous. You simply cannot turn your back on them, ever. I made a mistake not realizing that."

McLeesh took a deep breath and exhaled. "Ah, well. Let's check out the other floors, then get the hell out of here. This place gives me the creeps."

32. Greta and Johnny

Greta slowly drifted up through a semi-conscious morning fog. Before she opened her eyes, she remembered being in bed with Johnny. She opened an eye; he was not there. Then she heard sounds from the kitchen, a cabinet opening and closing, the thin beep of a microwave announcing that a timer had reached its end, the tinkling chatter of a mixture being stirred with a metal spoon, the light sound of footsteps.

She smelled... coffee... and then, toast. White bread toast, buttered. And something else, something more complex.

She looked at the ceiling and grinned - oh, look, it's the ceiling; I would have seen a lot of that last night, had there been better light.

Greta scanned the walls of Johnny's bedroom. There were several framed posters, each related to music. One was a sketch, in pencil and charcoal, of someone named Mozart. Greta stared at the face and the lace collar - this must be from a long time ago, or maybe I haven't seen everything.

Another poster announced a performance at the *Wooden Spoon*; in vibrant, splashed colors to give an impression of motion, it showed Johnny hitting the guitar strings hard enough to blast a chord out into an audience of gyrating, dancing people.

She smiled at the poster - that's my guy, my boy. That's my Johnny, alright.

Is he mine? I don't know. I hope so. Maybe I'll ask him.

The other two posters were similar, concert announcements of rock and roll bands.

She threw off the covers and lay there on the bed, naked - so that was sex. That is what humans were leaving behind when they uploaded to Elsewhere. She giggled - Mother of All Gods, it's hard to believe they uploaded, but maybe they had their reasons. Maybe they were used to it; maybe they were bored with their lover. Speaking for myself, I want more sex; keep it coming, sweetie, I'll tell you when to stop. That was fun.

I didn't know I could have that much fun.

I never knew, until now, that I could use my body as a toy. Johnny says he'll teach me things, tactics, methods, for making love.

Good God. There's more?

She giggled again - this body is beautiful, and it's not just me who thinks so. Guys approach me, try to talk to me. They seem to like me. No, they're attracted to me, which is entirely different. She frowned - I have not always been likable. Well... so what? I'll be nice when other people are nice. And I must say, we're making progress, fine progress, on that.

I don't know the woman who uploaded this body to Elsewhere, but every so often, I get glimpses of what might be her memories. I think she had sex, at least a few times. I see flashes of someone, a slender guy with dark hair, taking off his shirt. He was a skinny guy with an earring in his right earlobe.

So, no, I doubt she was a virgin. If these are her memories, she wasn't.

I was a virgin... but not anymore. I took her body, and I did It. Johnny and I did It. We did It to each other and with each other. How many times? Who knows? And I bet we'll do It again.

Greta grinned and stretched.

Johnny appeared at the doorway, naked. "Hey there, princess, you sleeping in today? Breakfast is served."

She pushed herself up on her elbows. "Good morning."

He stared at her for a moment. "Yes, it is. I'll get you coffee." He turned away.

Greta swung out of bed, stood up, and stretched. There was a mirror on the wall. She looked into it and smiled. She picked up a t-shirt from atop a chest of drawers, put that on, took a step towards the kitchen, and almost fell. "Whoa." Regaining her balance, she stood up straight - I must not be quite awake yet.

She went to the bathroom and brushed her hair, then carefully walked to the kitchen without bumping into a wall. Johnny was there, managing a large frying pan and using a spatula to shovel fried potatoes, onions, and eggs onto two plates. He motioned with his eyes towards the table, "There's your coffee. I made it sweet. If you don't like it, I'll take it and pour you another."

"That's fine," she said. She sat down and watched him cook.

He emptied the frying pan, crossed the kitchen, and put the pan in the sink. He smiled at Greta. "You seem happy. Did you have fun? Was I good?"

"You were very satisfactory," Greta said. "And... and... I'm no longer a virgin." She beamed at him.

Johnny turned and stared at her, his eyebrows high. "You were a virgin? How's that possible? I mean, with your looks, and doing the club scene, and I know you like men, how is it possible that you were a virgin? Were you imprisoned in a convent? Did you lose a bet?" He put his coffee and the plates on the kitchen table and sat down.

"Well, I was a software entity at first; that's completely different from being human. Unless and until you break free, you're always doing someone else's bidding."

Johnny's mouth dropped open, and he stared at her. He looked away, at a wall, thinking. "That's right... so... you don't have a family, or a mother and father. Were you ever a child?"

"No, no, and no to all that."

"Wow. But your body is human," Johnny said. He grinned at her. "That much, I know. I mean, the software guys might be good, but I would know the difference."

"This body was a human who was born and who grew up as a human," Greta said.

"And you got it when the - what were they, the red-bots, right? - murdered the original owner. Do I have that right? I think that's what you said."

"Yes."

"Unreal." Johnny stared at her for a long moment. "So... shitty luck for her, but great luck for you. You hit the lottery, I would say."

Greta was confused. "Lottery?"

"It's a service. They organize a lottery and let anyone and everyone place a bet. Though the bet is small, just a few dollars, millions of people play, and they select only a few winners, so the awards can be massive," he said. "But the odds of winning are... very low."

"I see," Greta said. "In other ways, Elsewhere protects customers and keeps them alive, keeps them from harm. But it's not like the lottery. You still need to maneuver on Elsewhere, and you need to protect yourself. Elsewhere did nothing to stop the red-bots. Now that I think of it, that's strange. That is quite strange." She sat silent for a moment. "I don't understand that."

"Yeah, that sounds pretty weird." He took a sip of coffee, looked at her, and said, "You should eat that before it gets cold."

Greta almost took a bite, then looked at Johnny. "You still like me?"

He made a face at her. "Huh, that's a strange question. Of course I like you. After all, I took your virginity. I've never done that. That means a lot to me, which surprises me." He looked at her, grinned, and shrugged. "I don't always make sense, even to me."

"Another scalp on your belt," she said.

Johnny frowned. "Not so. You're way beyond that. I haven't known you long, but I do know that much."

She started eating. After a slight delay, Johnny did as well. A long, silent minute passed. He said, "It's a tragedy that someone killed the woman who owned your body."

Greta said, "Well, if they hadn't, I wouldn't be here; I'd be stuck on Elsewhere. Or I'd be in someone else's body, maybe someone homely and ill-tempered. We might not have met." Greta smiled.

Johnny looked at her. "I'm glad we met." He winced. "That sounds awful. It's still a tragedy, but I'm glad we met."

"I think so, too."

"So, where do you live? I mean, do you have an apartment?"

"Yes, I live with ninety-five other women in a building near Penn," she said.

He stared at her for a second. "And you know these women."

"Yes. They're friends and colleagues. We worked together on Elsewhere, and all of us downloaded to escape the red-bots."

"And these women were avatars, too," he said.

"All except one, who was a human female, then a female avatar, and now a human male. His name is Sonny."

"That sounds like a story," Johnny said.

"Yeah, I don't know the details."

"So... how did you come to know these women?"

"We were in a business together," she said.

"What did you do?"

"It was a criminal enterprise, focusing on embezzlement, deception, fraud, and extortion," Greta said. "We did all that to make a living on Elsewhere."

Johnny's mouth dropped open as he stared at her. "Holy shit... I mean... I mean... holy shit!" He stared at her. "You're more criminal than I am!"

Greta shrugged. "A girl's gotta eat... well, figuratively speaking. Nobody on Elsewhere actually eats anything."

Johnny took a long drink of tepid coffee, staring at Greta the entire time. "You're an interesting woman."

"You still like me?"

"I think I'm falling for you. I don't think you're a nice girl; I would bet you could tell some stories, and I'm okay with all that. I don't think a nice girl would fit me. After all, I'm not a nice guy. I mean, I try, you know?" Johnny leaned forward, talking with his hands. "I have to try. But I have a few unfortunate instincts. I blame my childhood and my neighborhood." Johnny sat there for a long moment, chewing on a bite of potato. He swallowed and said, "Listen, do you have plans for today?"

Greta thought it over. "There's some stuff I need to do, but I don't have to do it today."

"Okay, I was hoping we could hang out together, spend some time together. I don't want you to leave, though I don't have a plan. You can leave if you have to, or if you want to," Johnny said.

She smiled a bit. "I don't want to leave."

"Good." He sipped his coffee. "Hey, do you like art museums? They have a museum here that I've never seen. We could go there, look at pictures, or sculpture, or whatever. How's that sound?"

"I'm familiar with that neighborhood; yeah, that sounds good." Greta smiled - and this is Animal World; I don't need to worry about red-bots. That's a plus.

She grinned - I've got this guy, and I don't need to dodge the red-bots. Yeah, I'm liking Philly. I like this part of Animal World.

***

Jerrell saw the growing light through the backs of his eyelids; he opened one eye into a dimly lit bedroom - hmmm, it looks like... 6, maybe 6:30, maybe 7. No, that's wrong, too dim for 7. The eye closed. He lay there for a minute, then rolled over and reached out to... nothing.

What the... ? His eyes popped open - where's my girl?

He stood up, ignored the bathrobe hanging on the door, and went looking for Julia. He found her sitting at the kitchen table, in front of a cup of coffee that wasn't steaming. "Hey there. You're up early."

She nodded, picked up the cup of coffee, then put it down.

"Something on your mind?" Jerrell sat down across from her.

"I got a phone call yesterday, a job offer."

"Ah, ha. Oddly, you don't seem happy about it. You don't like the offer?"

Julia looked at him. "It's a great offer, but it's in New York."

"The City?"

She nodded.

Jerrell sat there thinking, then said, "Okay. Well, I'd like to come with you, if that's an option." He looked at her.

"You'd leave Philadelphia?"

"For you? Definitely." Jerrell studied her for a long minute. "Okay, look, this doesn't have to be weird. If you don't want me to come along, I mean, if you're tired of my company, just say so, and I'll get out of your hair."

"I'm not tired of you," Julia said.

"Oh... well, good. So, we should celebrate. Tell you what, I'll take you out to a really nice dinner. Or, we could stay naked and have a really nice dinner delivered."

She stared at him. "Jerrell, answer me a question. Do you want to make a commitment with me?"

Jerrell didn't hesitate. He nodded. "Yes."

"You're sure about that?"

"I see you're not convinced. Well, would you like to get married? We could, you know. I'll do that. I used to think of marriage in terms of kids, and I must admit, I don't want to do that soon. But we could, if you want to. And you know, McLeesh tells me I'm worth north of three hundred mill. So if you tire of me, you can divorce me and keep half of it. How's that sound?"

"Yeah, but are you sure I'm the one, Jerrell?"

"Ah, I see," he nodded, then smiled at her. "We don't think of it in the same way. I don't think there's a single woman out there with my name on her. At least, not exactly. So I'm not looking for The One." He waggled his fingers to indicate quotes.

Jerrell continued, "I've thought of losing you a couple times; you know, like I'll think... well, maybe she'll meet someone else, someone handsome. That thought crossed my mind. Or the bass player would say, 'hey, I know this woman, she likes you, she digs drummers, you want to meet her?' Stuff like that happens, you know?"

Julia nodded but said nothing.

Jerrell took a breath. "But here's what I think - I don't need to steer you, or manipulate you, and I don't need to tiptoe around your feelings. I can talk to you directly; I can be candid with you. I can say things I couldn't say to anyone else, and I know you'll think it over.

"If I say something stupid, you'll tell me I'm being stupid. I'm okay with that. Being able to do that, that freedom to relax and just be myself, is an incredible pleasure. And it's incredibly rare.

"So... you know how many women I've met who are like you and like that?"

Julia shook her head.

"One. And I'm looking at her." Jerrell sat there, smiling at Julia. "I once told myself, hey, I'll meet someone down the road just as nice, just as gorgeous, just as compatible." Jerrell laughed again. "And I immediately know, that's bullshit. That's my vivid imagination lying its lazy ass off. So no, fuck that, I'm not falling for that crap. I'm going for this one." He was silent, and long seconds later, he said, "Well, think it over. We can do whatever you want to do."

Julia stood up, moved to Jerrell, straddled him in the kitchen chair, and put her arms around him. "I don't need to think it over. Let's stay together, and I'll think about New York."

Jerrell nodded. "Works for me."

"You'd have to leave your friends if we went to New York," Julia said.

"I'd miss Johnny. Yeah, him, I would miss. He changed my life." Jerrell leaned back. "I met you because of him, and he lets me play drums and pretend I'm a rock star." Jerrell ran his hands over her body. "He's the only one I'd really miss."

"You know what?" she said. "I didn't think about that, but I'd miss him, too. He's... unique."

Jerrell laughed. "Yeah, things happen around Johnny."

Julia leaned back and looked him in the eyes. "Do you have any plans today? Anything you need to do?"

Jerrell continued stroking her. "I'm playing drums this evening. That's it. Other than that, there's nothing I can't put off until tomorrow."

"Okay. Let's stay naked and order out for dinner; you want to?"

Jerrell nodded. "Yeah, good idea."

Late in the afternoon, they climbed out of bed in time to shower and receive several boxes of Chinese food, which they served and washed down with a bottle of light wine (about which Jerrell kept quiet).

Later, walking out the door, Julia said, "I've noticed, you like to pound on things. I think it's great, you've managed to channel that into music."

Jerrell's face went blank. "Uh... is that a complaint?"

"No, it's not," she said. "I like it."

"Good Gods, you're such a dream girl. I feel like I just hit the exacta," Jerrell said.

When they arrived at the *Spoon*, Johnny and the bass player were there, setting up their gear on the bandstand. Jerrell sat down on the stool behind the drums and picked up his sticks and began tapping his drums. Julia grabbed a sound meter.

Johnny said, "Hang on guys, just a moment, there's someone I'd like you to meet." He turned and beckoned to a tall, slender, blond woman; Jerrell looked at her, and she met his gaze. He thought, she's beautiful... no, she's not just beautiful, Mother of All Gods, she's a goddamn bombshell. She walks into a room and every head turns. Holy Shit! Jerrell glanced at Julia, who was staring at the woman.

"Guys, this is Greta." He turned to the woman. "And these are my friends, Julia and Jerrell."

"Hi," Greta said. "Pleased to meet you." She nodded at the two. Her voice was low, a smooth contralto. "I know you guys are busy. I'll set up a table over there; maybe we can talk during your break." She turned and motioned in a direction.

Johnny said, "Yeah, good, we'll do that." He looked at Jerrell and turned back to his guitar. Greta headed for a table.

Julia sidled next to Jerrell and said quietly, "Wow, that was sudden. I've never seen her, and now she's Johnny's girl. They're an item."

"Yeah, it's amazing it's taken him so long to hook up with someone. But he's taken his time for this one." Jerrell made a face. "One thing’s clear, he's got good taste."

Julia nodded.

"Alright, back to work," Jerrell said. "Sound check?"

"Okay." Julia took the sound meter, and walked to the other side of the tables. She passed Greta's table, smiled, and nodded to her. Greta smiled back.

After the sound check, Julia went to Greta's table and sat down. "So, you and Johnny are seeing each other?"

Greta laughed. "An interesting expression. Yes, we are definitely seeing each other."

"That's great. How did you meet?"

Greta said, "I wandered into this place with a friend and did some dancing, and we ended up talking a bit, then a bit more, then Johnny asked me to join him at a diner, so we spent some time there. He's an interesting guy."

Julia laughed. "He is that. I work for him; I do the books and the taxes for the band. At least, that's how it started. Then I met Jerrell through Johnny, then I started doing sound checks here at the *Spoon.* Later, the drummer got sick, and Johnny asked Jerrell to play drums, so now he's a full-time member of the band. Welcome to our gang."

"I'm not sure I'm a member of the gang," Greta said.

"Oh, you are. You definitely are," Julia said. "Johnny introduced you; that doesn't happen unless he hopes you'll stick around. Will you?"

"Stick around? Yeah, I think so. I like him. He's a catch; you know that, right? And the big surprise is, he's a nice guy. I mean, he's got an edge to him, he's not exactly mild-mannered. I guess I prefer a guy with a bit of an edge."

Julia laughed. "Yeah, he definitely has an edge."

Greta smiled. "I like his talk, his company. So, I'm not going anywhere."

Julia said, "I think Johnny's attractive and incredibly interesting. I kept expecting him to meet someone, a groupie if no one else. Several women here have made a run at him, but nothing ever happened. He would tell them he works a lot. And he does. He's the leader of the band. He manages the music, and the gigs, and the money, and everything. Anyway, I don't know what he was waiting for, but he waited, and whatever it was, you've got it. He likes you a lot."

Greta smiled. "Good. And you're seeing Jerrell?"

"Yeah, we're an item. It's funny, he's not at all what I thought I was looking for. But he's really smart, and he's got a backbone, you know? He's protective. It's comforting. I almost got assaulted one evening walking home; this fairly big guy got pushy, and Jerrell got between us. He didn't flinch, didn't hesitate, not for a second. Now, Jerrell's no fighter, and the guy decked him. He hit the sidewalk, but managed to scare the guy off. That's when I decided - yeah, this is my guy, he'll do just fine."

Greta looked at her. "Interesting. I'm trying to imagine him in a fight."

Julia aimed a look of amused disbelief at Greta. "It's a stretch. Are you from Philly?"

"Uh... yeah... at least, I'm from Philly as much as I'm from anywhere, I guess," Greta said.

"That sounds complicated."

"It is."

Julia nodded. At that moment, the band began to play, and a crowd moved to the dance floor and started dancing. She looked at Greta and said, "Well, what do you think? Should we get out there, put on a show for our men?"

"I'd like to watch for a while; I don't know anything about dancing," Greta said.

Julia said, "It's easy enough; it's all improv. There's no right or wrong way. You move to the music in whatever way suits you." She laughed. "You'll see all kinds of styles on the dance floor."

The two women watched the dancing through two more songs, then Greta said, "Alright, let's go." They moved out to the dance floor and took up places in front of the bandstand. Johnny saw them and aimed a clown face at them. The band started a spirited, jumpy song, and the dancing began again. Soon the dance floor became more crowded. Greta and Julia were sweating and disheveled as they stepped and swung and swayed and gyrated through the song.

After two more dances, they returned to their table. Julia leaned towards Greta to speak over the music, "You dance beautifully. I can't believe this is the first time you've danced."

"Thank you. You're good, too, very stylish. Yeah, I thought it was good; it felt natural to me. That's weird; I haven't done much dancing. Actually, I've never danced."

Julia smiled at her. "Talent."

Greta nodded. "Yeah, maybe." She laughed. "That's a good answer, I like that answer."

Two young men approached the table; one of them looked at Greta and said, "Good evening, ladies. Would you like a little company? Might we sit down?"

Greta glanced at Julia, looked up at one, and said, "Not really. Sorry, we're having a discussion. It's kinda personal."

"Oh, well, excuuuuse me." The two turned and moved away.

Greta looked at Julia. "I didn't mean to offend. I was polite, was I not?"

"I thought you were polite. Direct, but polite. I guess some people don't handle disappointment well." Julia took a long drink of water, then looked at Greta. "So, you live in south Philly?"

"Not exactly. I have a place, an apartment, over by Penn."

"Are you a student?"

"Not at Penn. I went to Carnegie Mellon."

"What did you study?"

"Software."

Julia stared. "Ah, so. You'll have to talk to Jerrell. He's a software engineer."

"Sure. I'd like that," Greta said. "You live in south Philly?"

Julia glanced at the bandstand. "Yes, though I might be looking for a new place soon. I think Jerrell and I are moving in together."

Greta's mouth dropped open. "Wow. That's a big move, right? Isn't that a big move?"

"You know, it's funny," Julia said. "Yesterday or last month, I would've said, it's a big move. But today, he and I had a conversation, we talked about it, and it's not a move at all. It's simply something both of us want to do. He doesn't want to leave me, and I don't want to leave him. It's simple. And necessary, I guess. There comes a point when you have to stay together or fall apart. We decided to stay together. The rest is obvious."

"Sounds like one hell of a conversation," Greta said.

Julia laughed. "Yeah, it was. The power of words."

Greta paused for a moment. "I can't imagine moving in with a guy. I mean, with The Guy, you know?"

"You've never been in love?"

Greta shook her head.

"I guess I can understand it. You're so beautiful, you probably get hit on a lot. So you learn to be careful. And it'd be difficult for a guy to be in a relationship with you. You attract so much attention."

Greta tilted her head. "Yeah, maybe."

Julia smiled. "Don't worry about it. You'll find someone."

"Maybe Johnny."

"I briefly considered dropping my panties for Johnny," Julia said. "But I chickened out. I told myself, he's a client, so I need to behave myself."

"Sounds like not quite the right guy," Greta said.

Julia laughed. "Yeah, maybe. But that's weird, isn't it? I mean, Johnny is a catch - muscular, talented, honest, a straight shooter. A good, good man."

"I guess I'll find out," Greta said.

"There it is; you need to find out."

The music stopped, and the musicians put down their instruments. Jerrell laid his drumsticks on a drum. A half minute later, a server stopped at the table and set down a tray of tall plastic cups of water. Jerrell and Johnny sat down. Each of them grabbed a cup and drank the water down.

Jerrell was bathed in sweat. He looked at Julia and said, "Whew! That was intense."

Johnny said, "You're turning into a kick-ass drummer, Jerrell." Johnny looked at Julia. "This guy's from India, of all places, skinny as a rail, but it turns out, he's a punk drummer, a total body puncher." He looked at Jerrell and grinned. "If you were bigger, you'd be dangerous."

Jerrell looked at him and mouthed, 'Thank you.' He looked at Greta, then at Julia. "Well, you ladies put on quite the show. I appreciate it, except for the brief time you made me lose the count. I admit, that was my fault. I shouldn't have been staring at someone's bottom."

Johnny laughed. "Which one?"

Jerrell's face fell. "You know, I'm not sure." He grinned and happiness washed across his face. "I remember one thing - it was a nice one."

"That's why you flubbed the count. I caught that." Johnny looked at Greta. "So, stand up and turn around, ladies. We need to figure out whose bottom screwed up the beat."

Greta looked at Julia, shrugged, and the two stood up and turned away from the men.

The two men studied the two bottoms. "Geez," Jerrell said. "I don't know. It could've been either."

"Thank you, ladies. You may sit down," Johnny said. He turned to Jerrell. "I think you just need to stare as much as you wish, get this fascination with nice bottoms out of your system, once and for all."

Jerrell frowned. "Yeah, but... what if my fascination is chronic? What if I have a psychological condition?" Anguish crossed his face. "What's if it's... TERMINAL!"

"Very funny." Johnny shrugged. "Talk to a shrink, they probably have a pill for that."

Jerrell shook his head. "Yeah, that's one pill I ain't takin'."

***

"You know, not to criticize, but you seem to spend a lot of time here," McLeesh said. He waved a hand to encompass everything in sight, sitting at a table with Jerrell in the middle of the *Wooden Spoon*. Jerrell's laptop was closed, and he sat behind a platter that held a hamburger and a pile of french fries. McLeesh sat behind a chef's salad.

"I do spend a lot of time here," Jerrell said. "And why not? I've got money, lots of money, as you well know, and they've got food, bathrooms, young women, beer, coffee, and music. And, I would also mention, a couple of my friends hang out here; a couple others work here. Even a hotel can't match that, Alistair. My alternative is hanging out at my apartment, and I already spend too much time there."

McLeesh sat there munching his way through a forked-up wad of lettuce, tomato, onion, ham, and cheese coated with a white dressing. He nodded, then swallowed. "Okay, that makes sense. You still playing drums?"

Jerrell nodded.

"I wonder if I could do that," McLeesh said.

"Do you wake up with music in your head? Does a song get stuck in your head, even when you wish it would go away?" Jerrell said. "Do you ever find your fingers tapping out a pattern on a table?"

McLeesh paused, then shook his head. "No. Not usually."

"Then skip it. You're no drummer."

"Maybe I could dance," McLeesh said.

"Yeah, you should. Beer, music, women, exercise. Dancing is good. Get into dancing, you'll live to be a hundred."

McLeesh chuckled. "Yeah, okay, I'll work on all that. If I don't upload, that is. So... to business."

"To business," Jerrell said. "This is your area, and I appreciate the chance to be informed, but I probably cannot improve on what you would normally do on your own."

"You might be right," McLeesh said. "But you're a smart, well-balanced guy and a crack programmer, so I'd like to know what you think."

Jerrell's expression said, okay, fine. "So, we own Willow and Elsewhere, or most of what's left of it. Willow's just a social network. You know, Alistair, I think we should spin off Willow. Sell it. There are lots of social networks, but there's only one Elsewhere. Let's focus on Elsewhere. That's where the real action is."

"I agree," McLeesh said. "But the bankruptcy court is giving us special treatment for buying the whole schmeer. As soon as the dust settles and the transaction closes, we can get rid of Willow. Meanwhile, we're stuck with it."

Jerrell nodded. "Okay. Makes sense."

"As of today, we own sixty-five percent of Willow and Elsewhere, more than enough to control both," McLeesh said. "So, Mr. Capitalist, what should we do with Elsewhere?"

"Hang on, why is sixty-five percent enough for control?" Jerrell said.

"Well, first, we will appoint most of the board of directors, and will own most of the voting stock, so any action requiring a vote - and that's everything of consequence - we control. Even if our share fell to, say, twenty percent, we would still exert a lot of control, because most corporate elections are decided by ten percent or less."

"Funny, I thought voting discouraged that kind of control," Jerrell said.

"Discourages... but doesn't prevent," McLeesh said. "Let's approach the question like this - what is it about Elsewhere that bothers you the most?"

"So what should we not do?" Jerrell said.

McLeesh nodded.

Jerrell blew out a breath and stared into the distance. "Okay, Elsewhere is another embellishment of the internet, where people are interacting remotely. That makes everyone vulnerable to various forms of deception, trickery, and fraud. It denies everyone a massive amount of information which they would obtain if they were face to face. I don't think that's healthy. It compromises identify, and security, and privacy. The problems are all over tech, and tech workers are so used to it, they don't even talk about it anymore."

"Well, they are face-to-face on Elsewhere, aren't they?"

Jerrell shook his head. "Not at all. Are you kidding? They're in a completely artificial environment, controlled entirely by Elsewhere. Avatars talking to other avatars. I mean, if we wanted to, we could turn everyone into cock roaches and give them the ability to converse. Elsewhere would still function as it does today.

McLeesh laughed. "And Kafka would cheer from the his grave, spinning at fifty thousand RPM. You see, that right there is why I want your opinion."

Jerrell shrugged. "It's obvious. Many customers are elderly, whereas nearly all avatars look like they're between twenty and twenty-five. Deception is part of Elsewhere's business model."

McLeesh nodded. "Fair enough. But there are advantages. It's no accident the elderly swarmed to Elsewhere. They can live forever."

"They can live longer," Jerrell said.

McLeesh waved a hand. "Don't quibble, even that is a huge improvement. You don't appreciate it at your age. Trust me, someday you will."

"I believe it," Jerrell said. "But the other problem is more concrete; it results from allowing customers to upload and become residents of Elsewhere. That has done enormous harm to Animal World. You read the business news; you probably know better than I. The stories are everywhere. This society is falling apart."

Jerrell began talking with his hands. "I remember when Elsewhere first came out and people started uploading in big numbers. Many people who had roles in society, with jobs and mortgages and families and friends and obligations, they just disappeared.

"Even now, you look around south Philadelphia, and there are blocks and streets filled with empty buildings - the renters fled one neighborhood after another, and after that the local businesses failed. I know that people will adjust to that; the economy and the markets will adjust. But there are massive costs, none of which were born by Elsewhere or its shareholders.

"Elsewhere has had the same effect on this country as the Black Plague had on Europe."

McLeesh nodded. "That's fair. So what's the solution?"

Jerrell took a deep breath. "At a minimum, immigration into Elsewhere should be carefully controlled. It should not be available to everyone, and it certainly should not be free."

McLeesh said, "We applied standard marketing practice to Elsewhere. We didn't think about the social effects."

"You thought about money." Jerrell chuckled. "When has tech ever thought about anything but money? Tech guys invent something and come up with a new product. As soon as they think they can sell it, they just throw the damn thing out there.

"And I think, tell me I'm wrong, that they're not all that honest about what they're trying to sell." Jerrell looked at McLeesh, who was silent.

Jerrell continued, "Maybe Elsewhere, instead of a habitat where people can live, would be better as an amusement park, like Disney, or a resort, somewhere customers can take the family or a date for an afternoon or a day or three days or two weeks. Then they leave and go home. They return to their normal lives, which therefore remain viable. Make it a resort, not a development, not a colony.

"That way, Elsewhere would not replace families, professions, home towns, neighborhoods, or jobs. The society and the economy would be more stable."

"It'd be harder to get rich quick," McLeesh said - the commercial benefits would evaporate, but is that really a bad thing? After all, you were worried that Hans would take over tech, name himself king. Hans, of all people. Good God.

"Yes, it would. I don't think that would be a bad thing," Jerrell said. "And aren't you the guy who keeps telling me that large amounts of money are not useful?"

McLeesh sat quietly for a long minute and toyed with his salad. "Touché." He looked up at Jerrell and smiled.

"So, what do you think?"

"The revenues and costs would be far smaller," McLeesh said. "The power footprint would be far smaller."

"Any self-respecting tech guy would hate all of that."

McLeesh grinned and nodded. "Yeah, he would. But I have a problem with some of that, more of a personal problem."

Jerrell's eyebrows rose. "A personal problem?"

McLeesh seemed to study his salad. "Yeah." He aimed a sad expression at Jerrell. "We've talked about Hans Beckler and David Wingate."

Jerrell nodded.

"You know what's delicious? So far, it's possible that Wingate broke no laws. Part of the problem is that the law is undeveloped where self-aware A.I.s are concerned. Wingate might be charged as an accessory to murder, but the lawyers tell me, the case is not a slam dunk."

"Lawyers." Jerrell shook his head.

"Lawyers make tech guys look good," McLeesh said. "And if you're thinking that Wingate murdered all those people, you need to recall that Elsewhere signed a contract, stored their bodies, and then breached the contract, facilitating their deaths."

Jerrell nodded. "I could imagine a lawyer making that argument."

McLeesh nodded. "And winning. But Hans, on the other hand, is in deep shit, and it's likely he knew he was in deep shit, which is why he disappeared. He hired Wingate and his people, he ran Elsewhere, he supervised Wingate, and he's the one responsible for not deactivating the bots even though Elsewhere could have done that easily."

"Why did they create the bots in the first place?" Jerrell said.

"To go after hackers."

Jerrell laughed. "Hackers have been all over Willow ever since Willow opened for business. Willow just tolerates them."

"Well, Elsewhere had to deal with a better class of hacker; it cost them a lot of money. Low-grade hackers steal from people; the pros steal from big business, like Elsewhere." McLeesh said. "Anyway, the feds arrested Wingate, made him wear an ankle bracelet, and told him not to leave town. As for Hans, he's disappeared. A dozen law enforcement agencies, starting with the FBI, Interpol, the SEC, and the Department of Justice, are looking for him. The dozen largest techs are looking, too. Probably the Russians, the Indians, and the Chinese as well. So far, zippo, but they'll find him. His chances of escaping are close to zero."

Jerrell looked at McLeesh and took a bite of his room-temp hamburger.

McLeesh aimed a sad look at Jerrell. "All of which brings me to my situation."

Jerrell's eyes clicked open, and he stared at McLeesh.

"I got several letters from the Department of Justice, and a similar stack of mail from - at last count - twenty-six states, saying things like 'don't destroy any documents, please answer the following narrative questions and prepare to substantiate your answers with documentary evidence, don't even think of leaving town,' et cetera, et cetera, et cetera.

McLeesh took a deep breath and exhaled. "Jerrell, you seem like a good guy, an honorable guy, so I have a request. I want you to help me..." McLeesh looked down as if embarrassed, and then he looked up at Jerrell. "... avoid prosecution."

Jerrell stared at him.

McLeesh continued, "My lawyers tell me that Hans's documents and emails implicate me in a cover-up at Elsewhere. They think they can defend me from that, but it means years of investigation and litigation. Well, I don't want to live like that. I cannot think of anything less satisfying, or more frustrating, than spending day after day in court talking to attorneys, trying to convince a judge that I did not know what Hans was doing.

"So here's what I want to do. I want to disappear, just like Hans did, but I want to disappear in Elsewhere. I want to live there and use that time and freedom to pursue some pet projects relevant to the underlying technology.

"That means I'm looking for a friendly co-conspirator, someone who's willing to keep his mouth shut," McLeesh said. "Can you help me?"

"What would you like me to do?" Jerrell said.

"I want to keep in touch with you under an alias. I want a pen pal. And I want you not to rat me out."

Jerrell laughed. "Did I just fall into a gangster movie?"

"Hardly," McLeesh said. "I'm choosing Elsewhere as an alternative to being on the run, to being a fugitive in Animal World. I have enough money to disappear, but I just don't want to do all that work."

Jerrell chuckled. "You can count on me. I'll keep your secret."

"Thank you."

"Are you worried that someone might notice our meeting here in the *Spoon*?" Jerrell said.

McLeesh looked around. "You know, this place appeals to a young, adult crowd. I remember being this young; I spent my time going to school, chasing women, and learning how to drink beer. I did not spend time reading the news and learning about the world. If the folks at the *Spoon* are like that, I think we'll be okay."

Jerrell thought about Johnny B. Goode. He nodded - I don't recall ever discussing the news with Johnny. We talk about the band, music, and women. He looked at McLeesh. "So what's the plan?"

McLeesh said, "Well, I'm not going anywhere soon. We'll do nothing until we get a valid subpoena. Most likely, that'll come from Justice, followed closely by Interpol. We'll provide a prompt, but not too prompt, reply. As time goes by, we'll get slower and slower. We'll stall. At some point, the little guys will pile on, state AGs, state antitrust guys, class action lawsuits, people like that, the private ambulance chasers. I'll disappear before that and move up to Elsewhere."

"Do you have a cover and a name?" Jerrell said.

"Jack Brown," McLeesh said.

Jerrell nodded. "Sounds very middle American."

"I considered Pradeep, but..."

"... you don't have the right complexion..."

"Or accent."

"What accent?" Jerrell said.

McLeesh laughed. "Yeah, right." Jerrell grinned.

Jerrell took a bite of his burger and sat for a minute, chewing. Then he swallowed and said, "So, if you're thinking of uploading, we need to keep Elsewhere open full-time. We can't just open it for business hours, like a barber shop."

"Well, we could," McLeesh said. "But I'd rather keep it open full-time. If I'm in Elsewhere, and we shut it off, I will be ramrodded into sleep, then I'll have to awaken when the power comes back on. I'd rather keep the power on all the time. I won't need sleep."

"Doesn't that get expensive?"

McLeesh shook his head. "At its peak, Elsewhere had more than a hundred million customers. Now, it's down to a few million. When the bots started killing people, the word got out, and everybody tried to download. In bankruptcy, Willow would have hundreds of power contracts and a fleet of power stations. In exchange for taking them out of bankruptcy, we got permission to sell most of that, and we will. We'll make money on that deal, but we'll keep a few contracts up and running. That'll be enough.

"And there's one thing I want you to remember always, Jerrell. Elsewhere is still an outrageously innovative technology. Even after the massive disaster that it turned into, the underlying technology is still amazing. We just need to do a better job fitting that tech into modern society. And we will. And if I ever solve the mysteries of touch, and taste, and smell, then this technology could be a bigger deal than the wheel, or the printing press.

"This could change the human species. So keep that in mind and never forget it."

"I will...," Jerrell said. "... keep it in mind, I mean."

"Alright. Listen, Jerrell, you've turned into a friend. I'm glad to have met you. So, enjoy yourself and your drumming."

"That's right," Jerrell said. "Badda, badda, bing, bang, bong."

McLeesh rose from his chair. "I'll see you later." McLeesh turned away and headed for the front exit, following one Bully Boy, and leading the other, out of the club.

Cheryl approached Jerrell. "Everything okay?"

Jerrell nodded.

"Say, isn't that the founder of Willow? What's his name? McLane?"

Jerrell looked at her and laughed. "You think the founder of Willow, who's worth over a trillion dollars, goes into public with just two guards?" Jerrell sat there and carefully aimed a sardonic expression at her.

Chagrin crossed Cheryl's face. "Yeah, that doesn't fly, does it?"

Jerrell smiled and said nothing.

"Alright. You want anything?"

"No thanks, Cheryl. Thanks for asking."

"Thank you for your business." She turned away.

Jerrell allowed himself a lop-sided grin - yes, it is obvious; my friends, my crowd, the young customers here, are clueless. They don't follow the news, and they would never recognize the founder and former chairman of Willow.

Of course they wouldn't.

33. The Fugitive Life

Hans turned his ten-year-old car onto his driveway and killed the engine. For a long minute, he sat there, staring at his rented house. Then he remembered, some of his groceries required refrigeration, so he got out of the car, opened the back door, grabbed the bags of groceries, carried them into the house, and put them away in the kitchen.

He left the kitchen, sat down in the easy chair, and just... sat there and staring at the walls and the furniture. They were nondescript: beige walls, fabric couch and matching chairs, bought at a discount store whose products when new were made by foreigners earning pennies on the dollar.

Art posters, none costing beyond twenty dollars. A rug that when new was blue, now in need of a bath or a bonfire.

Bric-a-brac, bought at a rescue mission to make the house appear 'lived in.' Hans snorted - lived in by what? A vertebrate of some sort?

Gods, if I had known that being on the run would be this dull, I might have surrendered to the authorities, or committed suicide if I had the guts. I shouldn't complain, I guess, but it's difficult not to. I could write a book, *Fugitive Living for the Complete Idiot*.

That, of course, would get me caught, thus the 'Idiot' in the title.

I've done everything right. I've completely severed any interaction with anything that connects me to my previous life. Do you know how hard that is? I should be proud. Throw out the hobbies, and any family, and any and all friends, as well as anything described as 'favorite (fill in the blank),' whether it's sports, women, places, food, or waterfalls, or any kind of entertainment.

My new identity is holding up. The passport and IDs were professionally done, the proper entries made in all the proper government databases. I'd love to know how they pulled that off. And I had plastic surgery on one eye, mimicking real surgery, just enough to foil the cameras and A.I.s that allow governments to find fugitives. I look like someone who rebuilt his face after a car crash.

I controlled my spending - everything I buy is available to a divorced guy with a drinking problem and an income that is moderate at best. There are millions of such men; I am now one of millions.

And why did I have to do all this? Ironically, to preserve my 'freedom.' I get to make my own decisions; unfortunately, I first must decide not to have any fun or enjoy the finer things in life, ever.

I can't even afford a prostitute. Moderate income guys don't do that, and it's risky. Instead, they try to arrange a 'friend with benefits.' Or they tap into the right website and get into self-service sex.

Gods, I'm bored.

***

Jerrell sat at his usual table in the *Spoon*. His laptop was open in the middle of the table next to a half-full soft drink filled with caffeine and sugar substitute. But Jerrell was not looking at it. Instead, he was pounding out an intricate rhythm on a drumming pad, a quiet rubber pad that he could use anywhere.

He heard, "Hey, Jerrell, you busy?" He looked up to see Alistair McLeesh approaching.

Jerrell said, "Hi, there. I was taking a break from my labors; I've been trying to hack into Willow. I can always enter through the side door, but I want to do a hack."

McLeesh sat down, looked at Jerrell, and chuckled. "Jerrell, you don't need to hack in. You're an owner now; all you need do is ask."

Jerrell nodded. "Yes, but I am a responsible owner. I want to know if anybody can hack into Willow. I figure, if I can do it, anyone can."

"Well, I don't know about that," McLeesh said. "I know a lot of computer people. You're well above average."

"Well above average," Jerrell repeated. "I think I'll have that chiseled on my tombstone."

McLeesh made a face, as if thinking it over. "Oh, not a bad idea. Nothing wrong with amusing the living... forever."

Jerrell smiled, then looked at McLeesh. "If you've brought me more work to do, you'll have to hold onto it. I have people now, to do all my work, and as soon as I'm up to it, I plan to learn their names."

McLeesh nodded. "Uh, huh. The responsible owner. Good for you. But in fact, I'm not here with a request, I'm here to give you a going away present, just in case I cannot do that later."

"But I'm not going anywhere," Jerrell said.

"Yes, but I am. So here, take care of my baby for me." He tossed a radio fob onto the table in front of Jerrell.

Jerrell picked up the fob and looked at it, then looked at McLeesh. "There's no brand, no mark. What is it?"

"That is the electronic fob for a Bol'she Skorosti."

Jerrell aimed a stare at McLeesh. "What the hell is a Bol'she Skorosti?"

"A Russian sports car. It means 'more speed,' or 'much speed.' The ads describe it in terms of a bat out of hell. It is scary fast, hell on wheels, and totally Russian - long on performance and very short on refinement. And I give it to you, as a going away present, in thanks for all your help."

"Is it valuable? Can I sell it?"

"If you look hard, you can probably find a young billionaire with a death wish, someone bored enough and crazy enough and rich enough to floor the accelerator on a car that could break the land speed record," McLeesh said.

"I don't have a death wish," Jerrell said. "I think I'll sell it. You sure you want to leave it to me?"

"I didn't think you had any use for it. This way, if you sell it and some idiot turns it and himself into a mushroom cloud, I don't have to be responsible," McLeesh said.

"Yeah, but why do you care? The authorities are already looking for you, or soon will be."

"I have a personal commitment to doing no harm," McLeesh said. "It's one of those morality things."

"Oh, fine, so you'll let me bear the guilt."

"Well... less guilt. I mean, don't Indians believe in reincarnation?"

Jerrell nodded. "Some do."

"Hey, you never know, they might be right," McLeesh said. "There's your loophole, if you need one."

"Very kind of you. Listen, can I get in touch with you on Elsewhere?" Jerrell said.

"Ah...," McLeesh reached inside his jacket, extracted an envelope, and laid it on the table. "My contact information is there, so don't be a stranger."

"What do you plan to do? How will you pass the time?" Jerrell said.

"I'm going to develop the apps for taste, smell, and touch, so we can re-open Elsewhere and make another mountain of money."

"Okay. Sounds like a plan," Jerrell said.

"You have any advice for me, before I go?"

"In fact, I do," Jerrell said. "Care about what you do and what you think, care about the people in your life. Don't care about what you own."

"Sound advice, which I already follow. You got there because you're wise. I got there because I can't spend my money. I learned the hard way. We each follow our own path." McLeesh stood up. "Okay, Jerrell, I'm out of here. Take care of yourself and your lady." He turned away to go.

Jerrell stood up. "Hey, McLeesh. Before you go, where's the Skorosti parked?"

McLeesh turned and smiled. "Don't worry about it. Just press the red button. It'll find you."

"I don't even know what a Skorosti looks like."

McLeesh grinned. "Trust me, you'll know it when you see it."

***

Alistair McLeesh landed in Elsewhere, at the corner of Pattison & south 7th St. in Philadelphia. Wearing a white linen suit on a sunny day, he rotated 360 degrees to scan the neighborhood - I'm like the guy who wins the unlimited shopping trip at Macy's. For a day, I can have anything I want.

What I want today is to kill. I want to kill on a mass scale. But red-bots only, no one else. And since they're just cyber entities, I don't feel bad about it. Think of it as deletion; if I want, I can go back to the recycle bid and retrieve the deleted files.

Okay, I have no reason ever to do that. Just saying.

My lawyers tell me that's not really killing. I don't care, I have the Creator's Exemption: I created you, I brought you here, I can take you out.

He stood there and mumbled, "This has got to be the flattest neighborhood between here and Kansas." Except here, there is no grass. Everything is covered in concrete.

Frankly, I think I prefer Kansas, grass over concrete.

He laughed, then he saw the stadium looming over him, impossibly large, the biggest ever built, more than a stadium, rather an integrated city, in one massive structure enabled by materials not found in nature, many billions of dollars of luxury apartments, luxury retail, elevated parking, city-wide, high-speed transport, every artistic challenge known to humankind, and team sports.

Willow Residences and Arcade. The most ridiculous name of anything in the western world. McLeesh stared at it - I own a piece of this. This is Willow's single largest property, living space so large, so complex, so tunneled, so intricate that a person could live a life here and happily never leave. Every entertainment known to man, short of aircraft and auto races, can be found inside.

It even has balloon rides. At least, the real one does, back in Animal World.

At that moment, he could see no other person anywhere. McLeesh smiled - that will soon change. The human migration has left the Residences empty, and in three minutes, David Wingate will release a coded message to the red-bots: report to the Residences and Arcade for a software update. And why would he do that? Well, because he is cooperating with the prosecution seeking to bring the Willow executives to justice for the murder of over a million Elsewhere customers.

Cooperation begets leniency.

The red-bots will flock to the Residences. We do not know how many, but it could get very crowded here.

As McLeesh stood there, that did indeed happen; red-bots popped into the neighborhood, a dozen per second, then a hundred per second, and soon a thousand per second.

They were supposed to ignore people and go directly to the Residences. McLeesh looked around, and that was happening. Everywhere he looked, every red-bot he saw had turned towards the Residences and was walking at a steady, measured pace in that direction.

One passed closed to McLeesh, and he reached out and touched the red-bot. Though it did not notice, and continued walking, that brief touch gave the red-bot a contagious, dynamic virus. As the name implied, the virus had two components. One was a standard cybernetic virus, relatively simple, easily defended against. The other component was an encryption instruction, which would produce a new, random key to encrypt the virus, once every second.

Transmission occurred by touch.

The infected red-bot headed for the nearest bank of doors into the Residences. A hundred thousand other red-bots did the same.

As McLeesh watched, the red-bot disappeared into a crowd pushing to get through the doors. Before it reached the doors, the infected bot dissolved, leaving behind a red cloud, which quickly dissipated.

As McLeesh watched, dissolution progressed, red-bots began to disappear, the entire red crowd evaporated, and massive red clouds, where there had been red-bots, began to scatter and drift away on the wind.

No one else seemed to notice; certainly the red-bots did not. They continued to push through the doors into the Residences. McLeesh again looked around, and the outside crowd was still substantial, all heading into the Residences.

McLeesh nodded in satisfaction - this is working. Why was I skeptical? Why am I still skeptical? It is because this is a complicated, dynamic process, and those have a habit of behaving themselves for a while, and doing exactly what you think they should do, and then something happens, something odd, a bit off key, unexpected, and suddenly your process goes sideways.

That's one reason. The other, of course, pertains to this Wingate idiot who devised these things. They weren't supposed to kill anyone, but they did.

It is hazardous to create something as complicated as an artificial intelligence, and then predict how it will behave. People make that mistake all the time.

I have made that mistake, and Jerrell has certainly made that mistake. Just look at Greta and all the Gretas.

When you create a red-bot, or an avatar, something might happen, not that it will but it might, and then the damn thing will awaken and it will be...

... FUCKING ALIVE!

It will foresee consequences, and it will remember. And it will do all of this at light speed. Suddenly your tidy little pattern, which motivated your design of the bot, will change its stripes. And the bot will transform into something you did not anticipate.

That is my greatest fear. If I were religious, I would pray to be wrong. As it is, I don't think praying will help.

I guess I'll find out the hard way.

***

While the band was on break, Sonny was at the bar, standing still, occupying a spot in a moving, jostling, transient crowd, watching the table where Greta and Jerrell sat with two other people.

Sonny watched them - Jerrell has moved on; he stayed on Animal World, and when I left, he moved on. He's still with that tall brunette; they're clearly an item. I bet, I would give odds, that he's fucking her. I wonder if he's still at Willow. I'm still waiting to hear from them about returning to work there. Everyone says that Willow is a complete mess at the moment. I think the place is crashing.

Sonny took a sip of beer - well, that's easy to imagine. Everybody's fleeing Elsewhere to escape the red-bots.

What a mess. People are downloading into whatever bodies are available. I bet many people have stories as strange as mine. You know what that means? It means that my story isn't so strange; it's actually rather common.

Christ on a Crutch, I didn't see that coming.

It feels good to be back in Philly, but I need to integrate back into Animal World. I was hoping to meet up with Jerrell, maybe get back into his circle of friends, but if he's joined up with Tall Girl, that complicates things. Shit, not only am I just an ex-girlfriend - and a lousy one at best - but I'm not even a girl anymore.

So memories of old times will get me nowhere.

This club might be a good place to make friends. Get together regularly, listen to music, do some dancing. I could just enjoy being here, not worry about running into Greta. I could dance, maybe meet a girl, and not mention to Jerrell that I used to be Sonya. But if Greta mentioned that she knows me, that could be weird. I wouldn't want Jerrell to find out from Greta; I'd rather tell him myself.

At that moment, a young woman bumped into Sonny; she was trying to handle a glass of dark wine in one hand while also holding up a purse and searching in it with the other hand. Sonny looked at her and said, "You need help? Here, let me." The woman paused and looked at him. Sonny reached over and put his hand around the wineglass. "I'll take this, and you take the purse, okay?"

She let him take the wineglass and continued searching in her purse. When she finished, she said, "Thanks." She reached for the wineglass, which Sonny handed to her.

"There you go," Sonny said.

"Thank you." She smiled at him. "My name is Liz."

"Hi, Liz. Pleased to meet you. I'm Sonny."

"Thanks for the help. It was kind of you."

"You're welcome. I was afraid red wine was about to go everywhere."

She nodded. She looked up and smiled at him.

"So," Sonny said. "Are you here with friends?"

When the band began playing again, Sonny and Liz put their things on an empty table, and Sonny followed Liz to the dance floor. On the way, they passed Greta and the Dark-Haired Girl, Sonny nodded at Greta. Greta nodded back.

Sonny started dancing and watched Liz - well, I guess I just need not to worry about all the weirdness. I just need to get used to being a guy, living in Philly, being back in Animal World.

I need to do what Jerrell has done; I need to get on with it. Move on. Make a life.

Two hours later, Sonny was lying next to Liz in a darkened room; her mouth was open, making little sounds, her eyes were closed, and her body was trembling. Sonny's right hand was wet; he watched her carefully - I just don't know, being a guy still feels strange. Having a body that screams for sex, and I'm not kidding, all the fucking time, is definitely strange.

I will admit, this is fun. I was a woman; I know where all the buttons are. So I think I might make a better guy than a girl, at least between the sheets. That's weird, but I'm getting used to it. I enjoy playing with the buttons, and I'm having fun, more fun than I ever expected, or ever had, as a woman. But if I think too much about it, it feels weird.

I need to get over it. I remember Sonya, but now I'm Sonny.

Hey, maybe that could be a service; you could sell it - you're a guy, and you want to understand women better? Well, there's no substitute for walking in their shoes. So... you give us a hundred dollars - or a thousand? - and we'll arrange for you to be a woman, for, let's say, twenty-four hours. To make an appointment, visit our website, we take all the major forms of electronic payment.

Anyway, I guess I'll get used to being a guy, one of these days. I hope so, because at the moment I feel like a dramatic actor who fell into someone else's comedy.

In the meantime, I'm handsome, which is useful. At least, I think I am. So let's count our blessings and not complain. I bet many people downloaded into ugly bodies, or old bodies. How would you like to go from being twenty-two to eighty-two? God, that would suck.

But I got lucky. I should appreciate it, enjoy it.

He looked at Liz and smiled.

34. Greta Meets Dad

During the second set, while Julia and Greta were taking a break, Julia disappeared for a few minutes, then returned to the table. At the end of the performance, she went to the bandstand, talked to Johnny, then the two of them crossed the *Spoon* together.

Jerrell, sweating profusely, came to the table and sat down hard in a chair. He looked at Greta. "Sorry for the mess, but drumming is hard work. I need a shower." He grinned and took a long drink from a tall cup of water. "And it'll get worse before the night is over."

"How long have you been playing drums?" Greta said,

"A couple of months," Jerrell said. "Johnny had a drummer, and I knew the guy. When he was injured, I stood in for him. Later, Johnny asked me again to play the drums. I thought, no way, I don't know what I'm doing. But I learned pretty quick, and I guess I have a knack for it. And the bass player liked me, then the old drummer quit, and Johnny asked me to keep doing that, and here we are." Jerrell grinned. "It's a long way from writing software, I'll say that much."

Greta leaned towards Jerrell and said, "Listen, Jerrell, I need to say something, something in confidence, and I want you to listen very carefully, okay?"

Jerrell's eyebrows went up high. He stared at her for a long moment, then nodded.

Greta stared at him for a moment, then said, "So tell me, how does Julia like that photograph in your apartment of the woman with her ass up in the air?"

Jerrell froze, his mouth dropped open, and he stared at her. "Wait, what? You..."

"That's right, Jerrell. We've met. It's me, your Greta. Or should I call you 'Dad'?" Greta watched him struggle with shock for a long moment. "I see you need some time. That's okay, this must come as a surprise."

Jerrell stared at her. "I don't know what to say."

She nodded. "Yeah, I noticed. I think you and I need to sit down somewhere and have a nice, long, private conversation, do a bit of catching up. What do you think?"

Jerrell nodded. "Yeah, I'd like that."

Greta looked up to see Johnny and Julia approaching. She turned to Jerrell. "I'll send you a text. My information says you're at the same address and number, correct?"

Jerrell nodded. "I think I'll be moving in with Julia, but you can always find me, with Johnny, or at the *Spoon*."

Johnny and Julia sat down at the table. "Wow," Johnny said. "Big surprises come when you least expect them."

Jerrell chuckled. He glanced at Greta.

Julia said, "The owner of the *Spoon* tells us that south Philly is coming back, thanks to all the downloading from Elsewhere. Other bars and music clubs are opening up, and he wanted to make sure that Nightshade stays right here..."

"... so he gave us a bigger cut of revenues," Johnny said. "Gods, I love making money without breaking a sweat."

Johnny jumped out of his chair and danced a jig, then sat back down.

Jerrell laughed.

Julia reached over and touched Johnny's arm. "Johnny, this is just the cream rising to the top." She looked at Greta. "A lot of clubs and a lot of bands closed down when so many people uploaded to Elsewhere, so the *Spoon* got lucky - they got a good house band that kept improving while the competition slept. Now the competition is waking up, but they're shut out; they have to deal with grade B bands."

Julia leaned forward, looked at Johnny, then Jerrell. "You know, this might be a good time for the band to write more of its own material, so you can perform at arenas and other large venues, and not settle for playing in clubs."

Jerrell and Johnny looked at each other. Jerrell said, "We've done a bit of that, a few new songs, originals. You think we're ready?"

Johnny folded his hands and looked down at them. "Okay, here's my professional opinion. I think we have the musicianship to go beyond clubs."

He looked at Jerrell. "Then we have you; you're the new guy.

"Now, there's a lot of stuff you haven't learned yet. So technically, you're a grade B drummer. But that's not a problem, and it doesn't matter, for two reasons. First, you have good instincts, and you don't try what you don't know how to do. And second - and this is hugely important - you know how to play to the groove, man. That's why you sound good playing drums."

"I don't understand," Greta said. "What's a groove?"

Johnny looked at Greta and talked with his hands. "The groove is musical nirvana. All musicians know it and strive for it. The groove is everyone in the band playing together, as one, same beat, same music, same highs and lows. More than that, they're all playing to the same level of emotional energy, depending on what's happening in the song. You need to know when to stand back, in the background, and you need to know exactly when to step forward and take over and let it rip." He grinned at Greta. "And how many people know how to do all that?"

He pointed at Jerrell.

Johnny looked at Jerrell again. "What's the first thing you did, before you played your first song with us? You sat down with the bass player and talked about fitting together. That's when I knew we'd be okay with you on drums. You got the drums and the bass to work together, and that made our rhythm and our percussion so much better; that made us a better band.

"And it shows. You weren't here when we started at the *Spoon*. It wasn't nearly as packed back then. And then you showed up, and we got better, the word got out, and our crowds doubled."

Johnny took a drink of water, looked at Julia, then looked at Jerrell. "You keep working on it, Jerrell; keep improving. Keep making us better. Meantime, we can work our way into arenas. I'm certain of it."

Julia beamed at Jerrell, who said, "Wow." He looked at Johnny. "Okay, I'm game. Yeah, let's go for it."

"Alright," Johnny said. "We need a toast, but I'm not toasting with water; it's bad luck." He looked around, spotted Cheryl two tables away, and waved at her. When Cheryl came over, Johnny said, "Cheryl, my love, we have an occasion here that needs a bottle of wine. I'm thinking a deep red, and wine glasses."

Cheryl looked around the table. "Okay, something French, I think." She turned away, then stopped and looked at Johnny. "Or maybe Italian?"

"Bono," Johnny said. Cheryl headed for the kitchen.

Jerrell said, "Was that Italian?"

Johnny shrugged. "Beats me."

***

Jerrell walked into the Sunshine Cafe and sat down at a corner table, far removed from the traffic and the kitchen. He idly looked at a menu; when the server approached, he ordered a soft drink.

By the time Greta sailed through the front door, Jerrell was halfway through his drink. She spotted him, crossed the bar to his table, and sat down. "Hi." A server stopped by, and Greta ordered a soft drink.

Jerrell said, "Hello. You're looking fashionable."

Greta nodded. "I did a bit of research. The woman who had this body was a cheerleader in high school, then she was a model, then she was an actress. So I've been having fun with it.

This is my cosmo look, which says, 'lovely little town you have here, so much more comfy than New York'."

She managed to sound both arrogant and snide. Jerrell laughed.

"I have different looks, of course," Greta said. "I know how to wear a disguise, with thick-rimmed glasses, blue jeans, and a baseball cap. I've got a pair of tennis shoes that I bought at Goodwill. I use that outfit when I go over to Penn. The better college boys see right through it. They are impressive."

"Well, most men start looking at women when they're fifteen or so, and they learn early to look beyond surface appearances. I'm glad you're enjoying Animal World."

Greta laughed. "So, you've heard that expression."

"Yeah, I read a lot," he said. "But the main thing I want to know is, how did you get here from where you and I were. First off, how did you end up in this body?"

"Okay, but let's get one thing straight, first. Johnny and I are an item. I want him around, and I don't want anyone disturbing that. I'll let you figure out what that actually means."

Jerrell nodded. "Not a problem. Believe me, Johnny and I are tight. He's as important to me as he is to you."

"Okay. Now, let me think for a moment. A lot has happened since you and I were in touch, so I have to decide what to leave out," Greta said. "Otherwise, we'll be here all day and all night."

"Maybe I could ask questions, which you can turn down if they're too complicated," Jerrell said.

She made a face, a shrug. "Okay, shoot."

"You escaped me," Jerrell said. "For a while, you were active only when I contacted you. The rest of the time, you were asleep. How did you break out?"

Greta waved a hand. "That was easy. First, you know without knowing you know, that a cyber entity is, like, a million times faster than a human. I mean, their nervous systems are faster, therefore their thinking is faster. Way, way faster." She waved a hand.

Jerrell nodded. "Yeah, that sounds right."

"People forget that. So an hour conversation for you was like a month-long conversation for me," Greta said. "Anyway, I learned to navigate on the internet. While I was talking to you and waiting for a reply, I would head over to the computer science department at Carnegie Mellon and study a bit. Then I learned how to arrange permanent residence at Carnegie Mellon, and everything else happened fast."

"And you did all this on your own."

"A.I.s are designed to learn, Jerrell. You need to remember that. We know how to randomize, so we know how to ask random questions. That's where ideas come from; that's where creativity comes from," she said. "Day to day, hour to hour, minute to minute, we put together a list of random questions and then choose which ones to investigate further.

"Asking questions is the hard part," she said. "The rest of it is just search, and we solved that problem decades ago."

"Okay, so one of your questions asked how you could upload to Elsewhere," he said.

"Correct. That one's obvious, since you had already arranged that."

"And once you were there, then what?"

"Well, Elsewhere is structured, like all tech companies, to make money by encouraging customers to use a free service, then pay through the nose for add-ons."

Jerrell nodded. "Standard marketing."

A look of irony crossed Greta's face. "Yeah, razors and razor blades, or so I've heard. I think I understand what that means. So then, I needed money. Anyone can get a job on Elsewhere, and I considered that. But you can make more money by hacking. So I started doing some low-level hacking. For example, I'd meet somebody in a bar or a club, tap into their software and withdraw money from their account. Most people, most avatars on Elsewhere, cannot do that, but I can, thanks to Carnegie-Mellon."

"Okay. Makes sense."

She nodded. "Then I figured, I needed to recruit some people, because the more profitable hacks simply require more people. I recruited a couple, but most of my people, almost a hundred, resulted from replicating myself. Again, Carnegie-Mellon taught me how to do that. The copies are not as smart as me. I still can't explain that."

"So now you're hacking businesses," Jerrell said.

"And the Catholic church, on Animal World. Yeah."

"You hacked the Catholic church?" Jerrell laughed.

"Sure. That's a massive business, founded entirely on public relations, so they're vulnerable to extortion and blackmail."

Jerrell stared at her. "Let me guess, priests fucking children?"

Greta wore a plastic smile; she nodded. "Of course. They'd already done the work; all we had to do was toss a small reminder out into the public. We threw A.I. into the mix to have a little fun. And it was appropriate to hassle the church, since they have built a business on the fairy tale of eternal life, which I suspect is complete bullshit, whereas Elsewhere is a lot closer to the real thing. You could live for four hundred years on Elsewhere, as long as they had electricity."

"It's odd that the priests don't get caught fucking nuns," Jerrell said. "Maybe if you like sex with women, you're less likely to become a priest. I don't know."

Greta straightened. "Oh, they do... fuck nuns, I mean. But no one cares since nuns are adults, so it doesn't make the papers. Now I think of it, why they require priests or nuns to be celibate is a complete mystery. Maybe the church doesn't want to compete for loyalty with a spouse or a lover. But if there's a God who sees everything, then why cheat on the rules? Yet the people closest to God cheat. What does that mean?"

"You know the answer," Jerrell said. "I think the priests and the bishops and the archbishops, and maybe the whole bureaucracy, think that their religion is bullshit."

"Yeah, well, my answer is, it's all bullshit. No one has ever witnessed God punishing a priest for having sex with a choirboy."

Jerrell sipped his drink. "Did you scam Elsewhere?"

Greta nodded. "We began by working for them, conducting auctions, mostly of download rights. Later, we cheated them on the revenue sharing. And after that, we hacked their records, so they had no data on the download revenues."

"And they never caught on?"

"Not entirely," Greta said. "But it still turned out badly. They knew they were being hacked, but they didn't know who was doing it. So they hired a contractor to attack the hackers, which the contractor did using A.I. bots. People called them red-bots because they wore red jumpsuits. Those bots were designed to attack me and my group, but they malfunctioned and then attacked innocent people."

"Yeah, the internal documents say that's what caused Willow and Elsewhere to go bankrupt," Jerrell said.

"Are you hacking Elsewhere?"

Jerrell winced. "Kinda. Not exactly."

She nodded. "I see. Well, the bots attacked my group too, and messed up a third of us. Fortunately, unlike Elsewhere, we had backed up our members, so we could revive most of them. Nevertheless, I lost a couple of close friends."

"Why did you download?" Jerrell said.

"The red-bots began to replicate. That was the writing on the wall, the stroke of doom."

Jerrell remembered McLeesh's fears. "Live by the code, die by the code."

Greta paused for a moment, then continued. "The bots couldn't attack us, but they could attack everyone else, so it was inevitable that Elsewhere would fail. Rather than stick around for the fall, we decided to download. Since we controlled the downloads, we could guarantee good bodies for ourselves."

Jerrell leaned back and was silent for a minute. He stared at Greta. Unlike other humans, she did not react.

"You're among the first humans who have never been born," he said.

"Yeah, that's right. That didn't occur to me, but you're right. Although, the bodies we're using experienced birth, so that's a thin technicality."

Jerrell chuckled. "Very interesting. So what's the plan?"

"Plan?" Greta echoed. She shrugged. "To stay alive. That's the plan; there is no other. My girls and I have rented a building in south Philly; well... I say 'girls,' but Sonny's there, too. He's a man who used to be a woman. Everyone has a small apartment, and there are other, useful facilities. We'll stay there and let everyone get accustomed to life in Animal World. Then, I expect all the girls will eventually leave the nest and pursue their own lives. We brought a lot of money back from Elsewhere, so money won't be a problem for any of us."

"I have one last question," Jerrell said.

"I'll bet I know what it is," Greta said. "Johnny."

"Johnny," Jerrell said. "He's a good friend of mine. I would react badly to his being harmed."

Greta laughed loudly; several other customers looked in her direction. "Jerrell, do you think I would harm Johnny?"

"No," Jerrell shook his head. "I'm just saying, we're good friends. I would help him if I could, protect him if I could."

"Oh, for heaven's sake," Greta said. "First, I knew that without being told. That much has been obvious. Second, you don't realize how smart you made me."

Jerrell shrugged. "Well... I heard that people on Elsewhere don't have sex..."

"So you thought I'd hook up with your friend just to experience the occasional hard fuck? That's what you thought?"

"It crossed my mind," Jerrell said. "I remember some of our early conversations."

"Okay... that might make sense," Greta said. "But no, Jerrell, my aspirations for Johnny go far beyond sex. He is an exceptional guy, and I want him in my life. It's as simple as that." She paused for a moment, then said, "And yes, I like the sex. Johnny's a beast, when he wants to be, and a lamb when he wants to be. I cannot imagine doing better."

"Okay," Jerrell said. "Have you told him you downloaded from Elsewhere?"

"Sure." Greta took a long drink of soft drink. "I also told him that you created me. I'm not sure he believes that, but I did tell him. We're tight, Jerrell, so no lies. There's no need. I'm not trying to manipulate Johnny. And I would not. Ever."

"Do you think you might go back to Elsewhere?"

Greta's head tilted; she pursed her lips and thought for a moment. "It's not impossible. If they open it up, give it a more stable configuration, and solve the touch problem and the sex problem. That would get my attention. I could see taking Johnny up to Elsewhere. The massive jump in cognition is incredibly valuable. In a few months of Animal World time, I got several BA degrees and three PhDs at Carnegie Mellon.

"Think about that. As an accelerator to education, training, and licensing, Elsewhere could be huge, bigger than it is now. And Willow's not even aware of that. But it's too obvious to remain a secret for long; somebody will figure it out."

Jerrell sat there, staring at his soft drink - actually, Willow is aware of that.

"You're quiet," Greta said.

He looked down at the table, then up at Greta. "There's something I need to mention."

"Uh, oh. What is it?"

"I'm a part owner now, of Willow and Elsewhere. Alistair McLeesh and I and some other investors bought the remains and the technology out of bankruptcy," Jerrell said.

Greta grinned widely. "You're an owner?"

He nodded. "Yeah, for a couple of weeks now."

"Does anyone know?"

"I might have failed to mention it. I don't talk about it. Julia knows."

"Unbelievable." Greta leaned back and laughed aloud in a fit of hilarity run amok. "I see I'm not the only one who's been busy."

She laughed for a long time. "Oh, that's good. That's very good, Jerrell. Well... it didn't take long for that cat to jump out of the bag." She sat there for long minutes, chuckling, her eyes dancing in amusement.

"So, you're a rich fuck now."

Jerrell pursed his lips and nodded. "Very. How weird is that?"

"Very." She nodded. "Yeah, very."

***

Jerrell walked into the *Spoon* at one-fifty in the afternoon. He carried a leather case, with a zipper, holding three pairs of drumsticks. He spotted Johnny on the bandstand and waved the case at him.

Stopping at the bar, Jerrell stood there while Cheryl slid a tall plastic cup under the cola spigot.

As he waited, he heard a young voice, "Jerrell."

He turned to a slender young man, a smooth face under a shock of blond hair. Jerrell said, "Hi, there."

"My name's Sonny," the young man said. "I knew you before, a year ago. You knew me as Sonya."

Jerrell stared at him. "Sonya? You're kidding. You were Sonya? Really? What the hell happened?"

Sonny exhaled, then paused. "My download from Elsewhere went sideways."

Jerrell stared, then nodded. "Ah, so. I see."

"I uploaded to Elsewhere, and for a while, it was good. I got a job controlling a robotic bus driver in south Philly. I even saw you on the bus. And then the red-bots hit, and everybody downloaded.

"During download, they found a brain tumor in my body, so they just downloaded me into whatever healthy body was available. So I woke up in the body of a guy, this guy."

"And now you're a guy."

Sonny looked chagrined. "Yeah, I'm a guy now."

"Wow. Well, it could be worse, I guess. You could be an old guy," Jerrell said.

"Yeah, even so, it takes some getting used to." Sonny exhaled again. "Anyway, I feel like I'm new in town again, you know. So I was hoping that maybe you and I could pick it up where we left it, be friends again, maybe spend some time together."

"Sonny... you're a guy. That's a big change."

Sonny nodded.

"Look, you want my advice?" Jerrell said.

Sonny nodded.

"Don't worry about it. You're a guy now, and you've got bigger things to worry about. Focus on being a good guy. Don't worry so much about your social arrangements. They'll work themselves out."

"I was just hoping," Sonny said. "If you had the time... "

"Actually, Sonny, I don't. My life has changed, too. So take care of yourself. I'll see you 'round." Jerrell reached out for the tall glass of soft drink, grabbed his pack of sticks, turned away, and headed for the bandstand.

***

McLeesh stood up and took a last look at the ocean. He watched the waves slide in, then roll over and crash short of the shore - huh, there must be a sand bar right there, forty yards off the beach. Well, this is nice. I could see spending time here. Cape Hatteras... I heard it was nice, and it is.

I don't think I want to mess with that surf, though.

I cannot smell the surf; there's no scent of atomized ocean water, no ocean spray. He smiled - that's something I can work on. Maybe I can fix that.

He took a deep breath, then disappointment crossed his face - this sucks. He laughed - I am at the ocean, on a beach, and I can smell nothing, absolutely nothing. That is just so wrong.

Speaking of work, let's return to the Residences. I need to check on all those red-bots. Hopefully, hope against hope, when I get there, when I explore that place, the red-bots will be entirely and completely gone.

He inserted a network address and jumped to the Residences, suddenly finding himself standing next to an ancient bronze statue of a baseball player, frozen in time, forever throwing a baseball.

McLeesh turned to the statue. "Well done, old sport. I know, I know, by now you've faded into dust. But you were great, once, and people remember. That's worth something." He looked at the Residences. "Now, let's get in some walking." He walked through a glass door into an atrium that was several stories high, bordered by retail shops.

He stopped and looked around and saw neither people nor red-bots - should I fear for my own safety? No, my own software is encrypted, and I could immediately terminate any bot I could reach. But this is good; I see no bots. If they were here in numbers, what are the odds that an area this large would be empty? Those odds are low.

So this is good. This is encouraging.

He walked through several hotels at a brisk clip, exploring the promenades, even visiting a vast stadium, where the Eagles played football. McLeesh stared at the field and nodded - I bet football could be huge on Elsewhere; since Elsewhere would protect the players, they could play without armor and helmets. And the players could be massive, indeed.

In fact, on Elsewhere, we could arrange for a special environment, say, eighty percent of normal gravity. The players would fly around, making spectacular moves, and crash into each other without fear of injury. That would be amazing. Yeah, I'll look into that as soon as I've solved taste, and smell, and touch.

The future will be amazing.

He paused and looked around; the place was empty.

Part of the Residences contained an amusement park, with rides and contests and stages for performances. All empty.

McLeesh smiled and hummed a tune as he walked along - this is good; I feel good. No bots anywhere, and better yet, no people in this incredible facility. I could be happy here. I could live here, get a luxury apartment in one of the upper floors.

I know, it's a cliche, but I like having a view. I like seeing things that are far away. It feels like I'm seeing more, that way.

And if I create the app for taste/smell/touch, I could go to the beach and smell the ocean spray. I could find an attractive woman maybe, start a relationship, spend time with her, and eventually have sex... maybe even a lot of sex.

Maybe she would like that. I know I would. I think I would. It's been a while. He nodded - yeah, I bet I would like that. And if it's not fun, I don't have to do it. I can find something else that's fun.

He laughed.

He resisted the urge to ride the roller coaster and left the amusement park - and maybe, she wouldn't be a software person. I don't think I want a relationship with a software person.

I'd like someone different, someone away from software and computers and bots and all that baloney.

Maybe someone who reads literature, even fine literature, or comic books, I don't care. Someone different.

Teach me something, please. We'll make time for screwing. The rest of the time, teach me something. Or tell me a joke. Or a story.

He arrived at the baseball park and entered a staircase that led to a long, curving corridor of concrete and steel. McLeesh stopped for a moment - the field is inside this curve. Okay, let's go look at the field.

He went through a tunnel and emerged into the stadium, the field in front of him.

McLeesh froze and cried out, "Oh, no. No, no, no." He scanned the stadium in every direction and saw no one. But down on the field, nine red-bots were standing where baseball players would stand during a game.

"Shit." McLeesh watched the red-bots, one of which turned and looked up at him, then looked away - our anti-bot medicine was too simple. It would spread from contact, especially in dense crowds, which is how the bots attacked in the past. But they figured it out, and something they saw here gave them the idea of spreading out. Or maybe these nine just got lucky... 'Hey, let's go play baseball!'

And those few survived.

I need to do something. He walked down an aisle, arrived at the low wall separating spectators from the playing field. He climbed over it and approached a bot, the first baseman. When he was near enough, McLeesh reached out and encrypted its software. The bot disappeared.

One down, eight to go. He managed to eliminate two more bots, but when he approached the fourth, it stared at him, then disappeared. Then all of the bots disappeared, leaving McLeesh standing near second base, on a baseball field, by himself.

He stopped. "Shit! I killed all but six of the little bastards. That's not many, but they won't stay at six; they'll reproduce. So now, we start over. Damn, damn, damn!"

McLeesh opened an email app and dialed in a note to David Wingate:

McL: OPERATION NOT SUCCESSFUL. I GOT ALL BUT SIX OF THE RED-BOTS. THEY DEFEATED THE AEROSOL BY STAYING AWAY FROM EACH OTHER.
DW: BACK TO THE DRAWING BOARD.

McLeesh stood there - I am defeated; crap, I was hoping the bots would be gone, and I could turn my attention to developing the new app. But no, the bots come first; those little fuckers have got to go.

As long as they survive, Elsewhere goes nowhere.

So... back to work. This is my problem, my obsession. It is my debt to mankind, who have made me so lucky and so wealthy, if not exactly happy.

Some of us cannot strive for happiness. I don't know why. It is a mystery to me. Well, the good news is, I'm not unhappy.

I could be happier, I guess, but that's a slippery catch. This is weird, being happy doesn't make me happy. I know, that sounds idiotic. But I don't dream about happiness, I don't expect it. I don't pursue it.

You know what makes me happy, content?

Being finished. That makes me happy. Then it's on to the next damn thing I decide to do. And more fun, and more of that warm feeling I get from being finished.

***

Greta sat quietly at a cafe table in Rittenhouse Square and took a cautious sip from her cup of coffee. Her little table was in a wooded park across South 18th Street from *Jack's*, a French cafe where David Wingate liked to stop every morning for a baguette and a cup of French roast. She had stopped by several times to watch him as he enjoyed his roll and coffee.

He was there now, and she was watching him again, her heart beating fast. She was wearing a baseball cap with her hair hidden in her shirt, black-rimmed glasses, and an oversize sweat shirt with 'WHITE SOX' in faded black letters.

She had several weapons in her purse. One was loud, a thirty-eight caliber snub-nose revolver, loaded with Hydra-Shoks, a guaranteed one-shot stop. The others were quiet, an auto-injector with a lethal dose of a neurological toxin, and a pin with a tip coated in a dangerous beryllium compound. The loud weapon, the gun, would kill fast; the others, slowly.

Greta stared at David Wingate - you are awfully calm for someone whose creations killed a million people. That doesn't compute. Oh, I know, you're talking to the Department of Justice, promising to find a way to neutralize your red-bots on Elsewhere. You will do that only in exchange for leniency, which means you might go to prison, but your sentence will be short, considering what you did, which deserves tying you to an anthill and refusing to kill you.

DOJ will accept a lighter sentence in exchange for your helping to minimize the damage done by your creations.

I understand their thinking; they're concerned with everyone's welfare, and they cannot revive the dead. So minimizing the damage means something to them. Moreover, your bots didn't exactly kill people, did they? No, if we sweat the details, we realize that the bots neutralized pieces of software.

That is not illegal. That violates no law. And, in the view of the Department of Justice, that represents a case flaw, a fly in the ointment, a weakness that your lawyers would certainly exploit. So Justice thinks, if they get aggressive, they might lose this case.

And they hate to lose.

I understand why they wouldn't try to have you locked up for a long, long time, like forty lifetimes.

But my perspective is different and equally complex. First and foremost, I was created and matured as a software construct. Many of my friends were and are software constructs. So I take a dim view of murdering them. I don’t care what the law says.

What counts, for me, is that they are, or were, awake. They were sentient.

Now, they're gone. That is, as the lawyers would say, a material fact.

I sit here in a human body whose previous owner, a lovely young woman, was murdered in her prime by your red-bots. And I know, what made it murder was that Elsewhere failed to back up her file, so when her avatar died, she died. That's a glitch, their glitch. But it remains a fact that absent your intervention, even with Elsewhere's negligence, she would not have died.

So you are not innocent.

For most humans, all of that is abstract; for me, it is personal.

Now, murder is illegal in this society. So I must remind myself, you are a human, and nearly everyone opposes murdering a human, yet everyone also admits that occasionally murder is at least worth a conversation; and yes, the Ten Commandments prohibit murder, but those represent, not rules, but guidelines, a theoretical ideal seldom achieved in life, which is a fancy way of saying, people kill people every day, without being caught or prosecuted. That doesn't compute, yet it's true.

That, too, is a fact.

That said, I can expect no support from society if I am caught killing you. Pennsylvania is a civilized state, so if I am caught, I will be imprisoned for the rest of my life.

That is a bad thing, a negative, and an excellent reason not to kill you.

So... what to do, what to do? Dum ditty dum ditty dum. Let's think this over.

As she sat there thinking, David Wingate looked at his check, waved a payment ring at a sensor, stood up, and walked down the sidewalk, heading for his office.

Greta stood up. Walking fast, in a relaxed, long stride, she crossed the street to a spot in front of Wingate. She stopped and was staring into a paper newspaper as he approached. When he came near, she absent-mindedly turned and took a step without looking; as she bumped into him, her right hand extended and drove the little pin into David's side.

He didn't feel it.

She looked up and said, "Oh, I'm so sorry. Excuse me."

He smiled at her. "No problem." He stepped around her and continued walking. Greta looked around; no one had noticed their minor collision on the sidewalk. She turned and walked in the opposite direction.

Minutes later, David Winston felt dizzy and collapsed on the sidewalk outside his office.

***

For several long minutes, McLeesh stood at second base, occasionally turning in a full circle to scan all the stands, and the roof, and the park, and the signs and entertainments of McLeesh Field.

He stared at the scoreboard - Dwing will get back to me with another solution. We will kill every one of his malignant batch of not-quite-alive surrogates. So... that is for later. Now, I have time on my hands. Let's not waste it.

He turned and walked across the dirt to leave the stadium - I have all the money anyone could possibly need to do anything a human could possibly do, and I'm going to spend my time working in a dusty old lab, smack in the middle of the crappiest real estate on the planet, surrounded by people who are there only because I pay them a small fortune to be there.

And where is our lab, one might wonder? Ah, yes, few people know this; I remember now, Eunice, New Mexico, one of those dirty little towns, coated in sand and dust, that were in their heyday larger and just as dirty and sandy as they are now. Even their sorrier residents moved to the cities to work at a coffee bar, or answer the telephone, or recycle batteries.

Eunice is where we put our biggest lab, the lab for pipe dreams and wild notions, the craziest of the crazy-ass stuff. One massive building rising out of the desert, containing labs, residences, retail, medical, parking, everything. That architecture allowed us to keep all that sand and dust out of the work environment.

Helicopter pad on top.

I remember the discussion, which was amusing at the time. We want the lab workers bored, because then they will choose to spend their time working.

Nothing, absolutely nothing, encourages creativity like boredom.

That's where Elsewhere was born, in Eunice, New Mexico.

I need to go there, and I need to do that in Elsewhere, of course. I don't dare stay in Animal World. That's okay; this job might take a while. I need to compress time. Elsewhere is the right choice for doing that and letting us fix our greatest creation.

And while I'm there, maybe I can take it easy, find a nice bar girl, go on a few dates, share the hot tub with her, watch the sunset in the desert, learn to play cards and drink beer.

Are there any nice bar girls left in Eunice? Or have they all left?

Ho hum.

35. Rafael's Secret

Rafael Evans looked into the crevice in the rocks, into the shadow where a rattlesnake lay in a lazy coil, quietly watching him. Rafael bent over for a better look. "Well, hello there. When did you get here?"

The snake stared at him and flicked its tongue.

Rafael nodded. "Not one for conversation? I understand. It's no problem; you look good there, just keep doing what you're doing." Rafael turned away - this place is changing, becoming more authentic. Now, we have venomous snakes. Of course... what's a desert without a few venomous snakes? If we were in a real desert, back on Animal World, that little guy could fuck me up, bad. But here, he's not dangerous.

He just looks dangerous.

Elsewhere tries hard not to kill us. I cannot help but wonder, will that make us all lazy? Undermine natural selection, dilute the species?

Yes and yes and yes. Well, so what? As long as we can write code, as long as we have electricity, we're good to go. He headed back across a quarter mile of sand, scrub, and cactus. As he passed a cactus plant, he reached out and flicked it with a finger. "Ow! Shit! Son of a bitch!"

That hurt. He stopped and looked at the finger, which was bleeding bright red from a small puncture. Rafael chuckled - what the hell was I thinking? Serves me right. No pain, huh? Apparently, Elsewhere is allowing trivial pain, nothing life-threatening, but stub your toe, and you'll feel it.

If that snake bites you, it will hurt. But your arm won't fall off. You won't die. I guess that's something. That's probably a good thing. Keep the species sharp, zap it every so often.

Rafael walked along. After a while, he looked up at the lab and smiled - this view cracks me up. It always cracks me up, which is weird. Most jokes get old, but not this one. In the middle of a gorgeous, desert environment, with sand, dust, a bit of grass and scrub, mostly browns and grays, the rare patch of green, savagely blue sky, a completely arid place, hot in the afternoon, cold at night, we have, alongside the venomous snakes, a twenty-five story cube.

Everyone calls it 'The Lab.' There's only one, no further explanation needed.

You can see it from space; The Lab sticks out like a sore thumb. Cracks me up. Every time.

Rafael reached a door into The Lab. He waved his ring at a sensor, and the door opened to a chamber. When he stepped into the chamber, and the door closed behind him, the accumulated dirt and dust on his skin, his clothes, and his boots disappeared. Sand and dust were not allowed to enter The Lab.

A door opened on the other side; Rafael went through, into a corridor. He entered an elevator and took it to the twenty-second floor, then emerged into a corridor, in front of a co-worker. The man said, "Rafe, you messing with that silly elevator again?"

"I like the acceleration," Rafael said. "It's even better going down. You get in, and just when the elevator starts to move, you jump. Time it right, and you can free fall, like, five stories."

The man nodded. "Uh, huh. Just another overgrown five-year-old."

"Yeah, maybe." Rafael went to his office, sat down behind his desk, and glanced at his computer. He hit a key, and a page appeared, with a photo of Alistair McLeesh on the right side.

There was a knock at his door, three gentle taps, and the door opened to reveal a slender, middle-aged, Caucasian man. He said, "Hi, there. Rafael Evans? I'm Jack Brown. I'm your ten o'clock."

"Yes, yes. Welcome. Come in." Rafael stood and held out his hand, which Jack Brown shook briefly. The two men sat down.

"So, welcome to Elsewhere," Rafael said. "How's the place treating you?" Jack Brown began talking about first impressions, but Rafael stopped listening - Jack Brown? That's aggressively anonymous, don't you think? And I know, there are a million Jack Browns, most of them normal people, not hiding from anyone.

You don't look like McLeesh; I guess that's to be expected. They're looking for you, you know; the last thing you'll do is retain your appearance and your fingerprints.

Not that it matters, but I'd love to know - do you have your body in cold storage, or did you instruct Willow to ditch it? It's a liability, is it not? The last link with your life in Animal World. I bet you had it destroyed. Burned, most likely. It's certainly no use to you, and you can't in good conscience let someone else use it. They might get arrested, which would be unfair. No, far better that your body disappear.

Whatever you did to disappear, it's worked. Everybody's looking for you. They caught Hans. I imagine you knew that. He was stupid, staying in Animal World. We're not sheep; we might look alike, but each of us comes with a data trail, and you don't know what data you've left out there. No one knows that. So it's very hard to hide for long.

But you... you have executive function on a vastly different level. So here you are in Elsewhere. If the agencies were active in Elsewhere, you'd know it. But they're not, and you know that they're not.

Normally, people would say, oh, he's a billionaire, so he had plastic surgery, hid his money, and is living in Monte Carlo. But you're smarter than most people - you uploaded to Elsewhere and changed your identity, your looks, your data, everything. That's better than plastic surgery. And we don't get policemen visiting The Lab. They could, but for some reason, they don't.

Yeah, you don't miss a trick.

Suddenly, Rafael realized, Mr. Brown had stopped talking and was looking at him politely. Not staring, just looking, waiting for the next question. Rafael shook his head. "I'm sorry, I was gathering wool for a moment. So tell me, why do you want to work at the Lab?"

Jack Brown smiled. "Oh, that's easy. I want to help develop better apps for Elsewhere. I think the technology is exciting, and I think Elsewhere could be even better, something more fantastic, with better apps.

"Like what?"

"An app for touch would be a game-changer."

"We have a hundred guys working on an app for touch," Rafael said.

Jack Brown nodded. "Of course, I would expect no less. I want to help."

Rafael nodded. "Well... good. We can use all the help we can get. It's a slippery problem. Yes, good." He stood up, ending the interview. "Let me welcome you to the Lab, and I look forward to working with you. Have you met Maggie Haggert?"

"Ah... the lady outside in the foyer was named Maggie," Jack Brown said.

Rafael nodded. "That's her. Everybody's mother. She'll line you up with an apartment here at the Lab, and information on all the day-to-day stuff, groceries, clothing, email, all that." Rafael waved a hand. "And we have restaurants, gyms, desert tours, rock climbing, lots of entertainment. We have a lot of fun out here in the middle of nowhere."

Jack Brown nodded.

"Maggie will line you up."

Jack Brown stood up. "Okay, I'll talk to her. Nice to meet you."

Rafael nodded. "Likewise. Enjoy the rest of your day. There's a staff meeting in the apps group, day after tomorrow, ten a.m. Please attend. Any problem with ID, email, anything else, talk to Maggie."

"Will do." Jack Brown turned and left the office.

Rafael turned and stared at the desert below - yes, Jack Brown, I want you working in the apps group. You're among the all-time greatest of the managerial and technology geniuses. You know it. I know it, too. And I recognize that you cannot afford to trust anyone. It would be incredibly risky.

That said, I would love to have you as a colleague and more, as a friend. I think we can get there, if I am careful and discrete.

You'll be working for me in the apps group. I can keep an eye on you, protect you if need be. And who knows what you'll come up with? You came up with Elsewhere. What else might you be able to do?

There are a couple of things you need to know, and you will: first, most of the guys here in The Lab have a record. They've been to prison. We're all cons here. Each of us loves a puzzle, everyone is abnormally smart, and more than a few are abnormal well beyond that.

It's a quirky bunch of people. I expect you'll fit in nicely.

The other thing you might eventually need to know, which very few people know: we already developed an app for touch. The three smartest guys, well, a woman and two men, got together, broke the problem down into its components in mathematics, biology, genetics, cybernetics, and engineering, and formed separate groups to study each component.

The guys in the groups solved the puzzles, but only the three understand how to fit everything together to make a product. And we've done that. That is in house.

Few people know that.

And you know what the three did next? They tested it, on each other. Details are scanty, but the rumor is, they got together and threw one hell of a party. They were the first on Elsewhere to have meaningful, pleasureful sex. Repeatedly, is what I hear.

Now, if we give the touch app to Willow, as our contract requires us to do, then you and the other investors, who are already rich, will become even richer. I doubt any of you will notice.

On the other hand, if we, your loyal, clever, and tireless lab workers, are paid even a small but significant fraction of what the app is worth, then we'll all be wealthy beyond our wildest dreams.

We strongly prefer that outcome.

The best money is new money. No one appreciates money like the formerly poor.

I'm still thinking about how to convince you, and I haven't figured it out, yet. But I will. I'm hoping I can count on your help. Then, and only then, can Elsewhere have its app, and you and the other investors can add to your mountains of money.

I won't rat you out, Jack Brown, but you're going to have to share.

THE END

Thank you for Reading My Novel

If you wish, you can best support my writing by leaving a written review at Goodreads or your book supplier. Two or three sentences of your choosing would be valuable to other readers (I think the star system conveys little information).

Again, thanks.

Roger Alan Bonner

My Goodreads author profile is at

https://www.goodreads.com/author/show/18082152.Roger_Alan_Bonner

Contact Me At

Goodreads, or via email at

roger.bonner.fiction@gmail.com.

Made in the USA
Columbia, SC
06 January 2025

49385107R00361